Robert Burns, Robert F. (Robert Ferrier) Burns

The Life and Times of the Rev. Robert Burns, D.D. Toronto

Robert Burns, Robert F. (Robert Ferrier) Burns

The Life and Times of the Rev. Robert Burns, D.D. Toronto

ISBN/EAN: 9783337098933

Printed in Europe, USA, Canada, Australia, Japan

Cover: Foto ©Raphael Reischuk / pixelio.de

More available books at **www.hansebooks.com**

THE LIFE AND TIMES

OF THE

REV. ROBERT BURNS, D.D.

F.A.S., F.R.S.E.

TORONTO.

INCLUDING AN UNFINISHED AUTOBIOGRAPHY.

BY

The Rev. R. F. Burns, D.D.,

MONTREAL.

———————

TORONTO:

JAMES CAMPBELL & SON,

1872.

LIST OF ILLUSTRATIONS.

STEEL ENGRAVINGS.

WOOD ENGRAVINGS.

PREFACE.

The " Unfinished Autobiography," which forms so prominent a feature in the first part of this volume seems to have been written principally in 1867,—the year previous to its author's last visit to Fatherland. A few portions were penned during that visit.

The singular accuracy with which so many minute incidents are recalled, by one nearing fourscore, and the vividness and freshness with which they are related, make us regret the more that a work so successfully commenced should not have been carried to its contemplated completion.

It appears not to have been prepared consecutively, but in detached portions, on separate sheets, as he felt disposed. We have arranged them to the best of our ability, and have avoided intermingling editorial introductions or reflections, unless where it appeared necessary or desirable.

When the Autobiography failed us, we have drawn largely on his own letters and papers, and the willingly-rendered contributions of those with whom or for whom he laboured in his native and in his adopted country.

Hearty thanks are cordially tendered to the friends, too numerous to particularise, in the Province and beyond it, who have thus kindly substituted their many lights, radiating from different standpoints, and reflecting a variety of facts and phases, for the one which we could have but dimly supplied.

We would gratefully acknowledge, also, the services of the Rev. Professor Gregg, and Mr. John Young, of Toronto, who have largely remedied the difficulty connected with our distance from the place of publication, by the laboriousness and fidelity wherewith they have revised the manuscripts and proofs, and superintended their passage through the press.

We are fully sensible of the imperfections which must attach to a Work to whose preparation we could devote but fragments of time, amid the constant pressure of manifold duties. But if it serve, even in an inadequate measure, to embody and embalm the leading features of a remarkably forceful character, and the main facts of an earnest and eventful life, as well as, incidentally, to furnish a contribution towards the, as yet, unwritten history of Presbyterianism in Canada, our labour will not have been in vain.

MONTREAL, 1st August, 1872.

TABLE OF CONTENTS

CHAPTER IV.

PAISLEY MINISTRY.

CHAPTER V.

CHURCH COURTS AND SOCIETIES.

CHAPTER VI.

INTEREST IN FOREIGN MISSIONS AND HOME POOR.

CHAPTER VII.

VISITS TO OXFORD AND CAMBRIDGE.

CHAPTER VIII.

AUTHORSHIP.

CHAPTER IX.

CONTROVERSIES.

CHAPTER X.

THE TEN YEARS' CONFLICT.

CHAPTER XI.

GLASGOW COLONIAL SOCIETY.

CHAPTER XII.

VISIT TO THE UNITED STATES AND CANADA IN 1844.

CHAPTER XIII.

TRANSLATION FROM PAISLEY AND SETTLEMENT IN CANADA.

CHAPTER XVI.

MISSIONARY LABOURS.

CHAPTER XVII.

MISSIONARY SKETCHES.

CHAPTER XVIII.

PIONEERS OF PRESBYTERIANISM IN CANADA.

CHAPTER XIX.

MISCELLANEOUS.

CHAPTER XX.

VISIT TO SCOTLAND AND LAST DAYS.

CHAPTER XXI.

MEMORIAL TESTIMONIES.

APPENDIX.

LIFE AND TIMES

OF THE

REV. ROBERT BURNS, D.D.,

F.A.S., F.R.S.E.

CHAPTER I.

EARLY DAYS.

THE day of my birth is entered in the public record as on the 13th of February, 1789. My earliest distinct recollections reach no further back than the victory of Lord Howe, on the 1st of June, 1794. This was fresh on my mind when, in May, 1812, my first visit to London brought me into contact with that noble monument of a nation's gratitude to its brave defenders, the Naval Asylum of Greenwich Hospital. I was accompanied on that occasion by a kind friend, who had suffered the chopping away of the better half of the great toe of his right foot, the effect of which was a slight palpitation of limb, as he walked. On coming home from

B

sea, he became a manufacturer in Paisley, then at its
prime; made money, lived a useful and religious life,
and died in hope. This friend was my befitting companion in the visit to Greenwich; we chatted with the
old sailors; saw their neatly fitted up apartments; and
looked at their books. One of them was busily reading
a large folio, which, he said to me, was, in his opinion
"good for both worlds," a sentiment which I cordially
seconded, on finding it to be Matthew Henry's Commentary on the Holy Scriptures. My next visit to
Greenwich, was on June 1st, 1834, when William IV. and
Queen Adelaide kept the anniversary of the battle, and
when fourteen of the brave shipmates of Howe were still
alive, hobbling about with something like quarter-deck
authority, and hailing with patriotic cheers their unassuming and kind-hearted "Sailor King."

A grandsire by the father's side, and of my own name,
was in 1643 named by the authorities as one of the In-
spectors of the signing of the National Covenant at Falkirk, and a like relative by the mother's side, suffered in
persecuting times for conscience sake. "Hilderston and
his lady," the latter a daughter of Sir William Cunningham, of Cunningham Head, were both remarkable for
their attachment to the Presbyterian principles of the
Scottish Church, and their Mansion House at Hilderston
was often the hospitable resort of the persecuted Cove-
nantors. His son (afterwards Sir Walter Hamilton,* of
Westport) retained the same attachment to Protestant
and Presbyterian principles, which had characterized the
family from the days of their illustrious ancestor, Sir
James Sandilands, the personal friend of John Knox.†

My father, John Burns, belonged to a family of respectability and old standing in the town of Falkirk, Stirling-

* One of our early reminiscences is of father pointing out in a picture the figure of
his maternal uncle, Sir W. Hamilton, Bart., of Westport, standing on a jutting ledge of
rock at Quebec, and directing his brave men as they dragged the guns up the heights of
Abraham, in the grey of that memorable morning of July, 1759, when Wolfe fell in the
arms of victory, and Canada became a jewel in the crown of Britain. Major-General
Ferrier, once Governor of Dumbarton Castle, was also an uncle. The distinguished
metaphysician, Professor Ferrier, son-in-law of Christopher North, was nearly related.
The names of Hamilton and of Ferrier are enshrined in our domestic annals.—ED.

† New Statistical Account of Scotland, vol. II., p. 65.

shire, and till 1779 he was engaged in Scotland's "staple," the manufacture and sale of linen cloth. He was in that year appointed by Government to the office of Surveyor of Customs at the port of Borrowstounness. He held also for fifteen years the factorship on the oldest, and not the least valuable, of the estates of the Duke of Hamilton —that of Kinneil. He was present, though merely as a spectator, at the battle of Falkirk, in January, 1746, and often entertained us round the family hearth with anecdotes of that stirring period.

He was one of many in Scotland whose religious character was formed in connexion with the visits and preaching of the celebrated Whitefield, who occasionally resided under his father's roof. The pastor of the parish at that time was Mr. John Adams, a first-rate man every way, once (though not a D.D.) Moderator of the General Assembly, and whose name and memory are still revered by many in the locality. He encouraged the visits of the eminent Englishman, introduced him to Mr. Lindsay, of Bothkennar, and other genial brethren around, of the true evangelical stamp, and shared with them and "good old Bonar," of Torphichen, as Whitefield calls him, in the revival feasts of Kilsyth and Cambuslang.

My father managed the affairs of the estate of Kinneil so long as age and infirmities would allow him. Amid the gatherings of the numerous feu duties of the town of Borrowstounness, many of them small, and of somewhat doubtful ownership, while many thousands of pounds of land-rents passed through his hands, and were transmitted to the Ducal Commissioner at Edinburgh, and at a time when banks in the country districts were unknown, not one penny was ever lost.

In the beginning of 1817 my father died, after a short illness, full of years. He was born in 1730, and his whole course of life had been marked by simplicity and godly sincerity, piety to God, high-toned and warm, integrity and benevolence towards men, singularly disinterested. His sons, eight in number, were all present at his funeral, all settled in different places and positions in life, four of us ministers of the Established Church, and the other four occupying civil stations of respectability and usefulness.

The mortal remains of our nearest earthly relative sleep in the tomb of his forefathers in the ancient graveyard of Falkirk, famed as the resting place of Sir Robert Monro and his brother, both slain at the battle of Falkirk, June, 1746.*

His wife was a daughter of Mr. Ferrier, of Linlithgow, lawyer, who held appointments in the legal department of Her Majesty's Customs there, and married the daughter and heiress of Sir Walter Hamilton, Bart., of Westport. Their daughter Grizzell Ferrier, was my mother, who died at the age of 53.

It may not be uninteresting to the general reader, and cannot be to his now numerous descendants, to peruse one of the MS. letters of this " old disciple," whose hoary head was a crown of glory, and whose children rose up to call him blessed. The one before us is addressed to his eldest son, the Rev. James Burns, of Brechin, father of the Rev. J. C. Burns, of Kirkliston, and of the wife of the Rev. Dr. Guthrie, of Edinburgh.

"BONESS, 18th February, 1812.

" DEAR JAMES,—I duly received your good and precious letter of the 27th ult., and have great cause of thankfulness that I am still able to read it, and say somewhat in answer. Though with great weakness of intellectual powers, yet I bless the Lord I am not worse in that respect than for some years past. But as I am now arrived at the uttermost ordinary age of man upon earth, being 81, I cannot expect to hold out long, and am, therefore, endeavouring to improve time while some measure of health remains, and especially when I call to remembrance the wonderful preservations and long respite our Gracious God has been pleased to continue. It there-

---

* The epitaph on his tombstone, which is written in excellent LATIN, describes him as " distinguished for his holiness, benevolence and integrity. In life, he was favoured with the love of his family and friends, and in death his memory is blessed." His father, who was a writer, in Falkirk, is described on the tombstone (in Latin too) as an " upright and truly Christian man, who died on the 18th of July, 1774 in the 80th year of his age."

fore becomes me daily to watch, and so much the more as I see the day approaching.

"I am glad to hear of your and William's, as also of Robert's, zeal and diligence in discharging the duties of your high calling. For your encouragement I shall transcribe a note from the Rev. Basil Wood. His eleventh sermon, May, 1807 :—'The zealous missionary shall shine to eternity, enrolled in the ancestry of Heaven. Continue therefore steadfast,' &c.

"I rejoice to hear of the happy deaths you mention. May they be more and more increased !

"Robert was assisting here last week at the sacrament. He preached both on Sabbath night and Monday. He left us on Thursday, went to Cathlaw, all night, and next day took the stage from Bathgate. George passed examination before the Presbytery two weeks ago, and will soon follow you to the pulpit, an uncommon instance. May the Lord preserve me humble ! And I am, with best respects to your and William's good wives,

"Yours affectionately,

"JOHN BURNS."

The reference to Kinneil, with which early associations were linked, sets memory at work, and, after a fashion peculiarly his own, he groups diverse historical connexions. The thread of his narrative is dropped here (as elsewhere when it pleases him), that he may expatiate over congenial fields which the old Manor opens up.

Kinneil House, once the favourite residence of the Ducal family of Hamilton, has been associated almost within my own remembrance, with the progress of science and of mechanical art, for there dwelt Dr. Roebuck, the originator of the famed Carron iron works, and the patron of James Watt, in his first efforts in the improvement of the steam engine. Soon after my ordination, when on my way from Falkirk to Boness, I had the curiosity to do what I had not done when a boy ; I climbed up by a bye-path to one of the olden appendages of the Mansion, into which I succeeded in making my entrée, and there gazed upon the blackened and wasted *exuviæ* of the mechanical processes of the ingenious inventor, in this the humble

scene of his primary movements, which their speedy and
successful trial, within the circle of an adjoining coal pit,
changed into the sure and certain precursors of a magnificent scientific triumph.   But Kinneil House is associated
in my mind also with the name and the labours of my
revered instructor in the elements of mental and moral
science, the celebrated Dugald Stewart, who resided in it
from 1810 to 1828, receiving there the frequent visits of
the famed representatives of science and of literature, and
enjoying that *otium cum dignitate* which permitted
him to prepare maturely, Works which posterity, we
firmly believe, amid all the delusive witchery of later
forms of thought, will not suffer to die.   Of his ultimate
religious views I cannot speak positively, but I had
various opportunities of testifying to the reverence which
he cherished for the truths and ordinances of religion ; and
on a communion Sabbath, some years before his death,
there sat at the table, on my right hand, the venerable
patriarch—a representative of the philosophy of mind,
with all the seeming docility and complacence of a humble
disciple.

And who has not heard of "the incident," in Scotland's
eventful record, more than two centuries past ?   A peer,
heated with wine, had, in the hearing of royalty, declared
that there were " three kings in Scotland where one was
quite enough, and that he would take speedy measures to
rid the land of two of them."   Argyle and Hamilton
knew well the import of the threat, left the capital
secretly, and, by a short residence in the quiet halls of
Kinneil, saved themselves and their country from death
and from havoc.   My esteemed parish minister, Dr.
Rennie, in the first " statistical account" of the scene of
his labours, written but a few weeks after his ordination,
has said of this Mansion, with no less beauty than truth,
that there was a time when it was the residence of
nobles and the *retreat of Kings.*

But to the mind of a Christian this now somewhat dis-
mantled and yet stately mansion is associated with
circumstances of a more decidedly religious character.   In

the middle of the century before the last, the Ducal family of Hamilton could boast of a succession of representatives more or less sincerely religious. Kinneil was occasionally their favourite abode, and pious Presbyterian ministers frequently resided there as chaplains or as visitors. In the shady groves adjacent would Zachary Boyd carol his homely lays, when engaged in his celebrated "travails with the Pentateuch" and the Psalms; and in his "last Battle of the Soul" he seems to have happily anticipated what soon became blissful reality in the experiences of more than one of the male and female representatives of the noble house of Hamilton. May we not trace to this, in some sense, the fact that Kinneil and Borrowstounness had their confessors and martyrs in persecuting times. Robert Woodrow, first, and James Aikman, afterwards, himself a Borrowstounness man, have recorded the names of not a few who "loved not their lives unto the death"; and the story of the cruel and untimely deaths of Marian Harvey and Isabel Alison, at the Grass Market of Edinburgh, possess a painfully thrilling interest. Sir Robert Hamilton, of Preston, of Bothwell Bridge celebrity, lived at that place for years after his return from Holland, and died there in 1701; yea, even under the eye of the Muscovite Laird of Binns,* Donald Cargill was long sheltered here. Mr. Mackenzie, in his statistical account of the parish, has not only referred to these cases, but has in addition, given a comprehensive view of the names and positions of others, both ministers and laymen, who suffered in the various modes of imprisonment, fines, banishment and death; and thus my native parish, if it has not furnished a full "sacramental host" or "glorious army of martyrs," has presented to all ages a noble specimen of what has been suitably termed "the goodly fellowship" of holy confessors, that form the "cloud of witnesses" on high.

The Parish of Kinneil, though small, was important from its connexion with one of the mansions of the Ducal

---

* Sir. Thomas Dalyell, the noted persecutor, who had been for some years in the Muscovite service.

family, and from the Reformation downwards it seems to have enjoyed the pastoral services of a succession of pious ministers. About the middle of the seventeenth century, "the Ness," as it was called, had become the residence of not a few enterprising persons connected with the navigation and commerce of the Firth of Forth. For their accommodation a Church was built and endowed by the liberality of the inhabitants of the town, aided by the Lord of the Manor, and in a short time the two places were associated together as one pastoral charge. For half a century prior to the year 1793, the united parish was presided over by the Reverend Patrick Baillie, a pious and laborious evangelist, the very *beau ideal* of a truly consistent Scottish Presbyterian pastor of the olden times. He was succeeded by a well-meaning man, of weak parts, both mental and bodily, who retired from the charge within two years, and the people having had granted to them by the patron the privilege of election, Dr. Robert Rennie was chosen, who, till 1833, occupied the charge with credit and usefulness. His successor, Mr. Mackenzie, lately deceased, was also the choice of the congregation. At the disruption, in 1843, he remained with the Establishment. A portion of his flock united with a similar portion from the neighbouring Parish of Carriden, and formed the "Free Church" of the district, which has prospered under several faithful ministers in succession.*

From the under shelf of my library, a large, well-bound folio protrudes at this moment, its venerable head bearing the title, "Flavel's Works." In 1754, when this edition was printed, Glasgow enjoyed the able and faithful ministrations of a Maclaurin, a Gillies, a Findlay, a Corse, and others of high evangelical position, and real vital godliness flourished, for the motto of the city had not as yet been

---

* Like other mansions of Scotland, Kinneil House has been haunted for a century at least by the ghost of Lady Lilburn, wife of one of Cromwell's Generals, said to have been murdered here. In the interesting work of Mr. Smiles, on "Industrial Biography," we have the following curious statement :—

"Sir David Wilkie having been on a visit to Dugald Stewart, at Kinnell, the learned Professor told him one night, as he was going to bed, of the unearthly wailings which he himself had heard proceeding from the old apartments, but to him, at least, they had been explained by an old door opening out upon the roof being blown in on gusty nights, when a jarring and creaking noise was heard all over the house.

altered from its first edition, " Let Glasgow flourish by
the preaching of the word." A folio edition of the works
of the outed minister of Dartmouth, though rather high
priced, took well, and my father was one of the original
subscribers. Next to the Scriptures, it was his favourite
book, and as, at ten years of age, I could read pretty well,
and as my voice, to use my own expression, even then was
an "audible" one, he conferred on me the honour and the
privilege of now and then reading to him aloud, after the
labours of the day, one of Flavel's sermons. The style was
simple, the diction sweet and sappy, and the titles were
fascinating, " The Fountain of Life opened," " The Method
of Grace," " Navigation Spiritualized," Mount Pisgah," &c.
I got a fondness for the task, and often, while other
boys were at play, I was reading John Flavel. The idea
occurred to me of copying out in manuscript as many of
the sermons as I had time and paper for. Having provided myself with a *whole quire* of foolscap, I made a
commendable effort in my best hand. But I longed
heartily for the close of the first sermon, and proceeded no
further. An aged aunt who lived with us, and who belonged to the moderate school, said to me that to have
copied one of " Blair's" would have been " wiser like ;"
but Flavel was no favourite of hers. She accompanied her
suggestion with the broad hint that there seemed " something of the hypocrite" about the whole concern, and
perhaps she was not very far wrong. My religious belief
at this time was strictly orthodox, but it had a tincture
of antinomianism about it. I had clear ideas of the
"fountain of life," but as to the "method of grace."
I knew nothing about it. A lengthened period elapsed
between my clear apprehension of the foundation of hope,
and my cordial reliance on the grace of the Spirit to enlighten, to sanctify, and to guide. A still longer period
elapsed before I knew the defects of such a book as
"Law's Serious Call," and, although Whitefield's memoirs
were estimated in our circle above all price, the Calvinistic
system had as yet failed to " conquer me." This topic I
shall have occasion to notice again, and in the meantime

shall only say, in the words of Cowper, applicable equally to the Divine dealings with individual minds as with the larger economy of the universe,

"God moves in a mysterious way,
   His wonders to perform."

It is not easy always to account for the inclinations and tendencies that run in families, and determine the future of its several members. None of my forefathers, on either side, occupied the office of the ministry. And yet among the male members of our family there did appear at early periods, and in pretty regular succession, a somewhat uncommonly strong leaning towards the ministerial profession, showing itself in a singular love of pulpit occupancy, and somewhat premature pulpit oratory. My eldest brother, James, who was minister of the first charge in the parish of Brechin for nearly forty years, took a fancy, when about thirteen years of age, to devote all the little pocket money he had picked up, to the purchase of a wooden pulpit, in the ordinary sense of the word ; and my second brother, William, afterwards well-known as "the pastor of Kilsyth," a short time thereafter completed the ecclesiastical erection by the addition of a precentor's desk. A small room in the house was allotted to its reception, and it henceforth had affixed to it the name of "The Kirk." The domestic worship was pretty regularly performed, and occasionally more full religious services engaged in. At a somewhat later period, a summer-house in the garden was set apart for the same purpose, and in it the more juvenile attempts at preaching were carried on. These attempts were indeed juvenile, but they were always serious. We were not "playing at preacher." We were really in earnest, and much precious truth from the pages of approved authors was exhibited ; and it is interesting to state that sometimes the humblest efforts in the service of God, may be honoured with a measure of success.

I have just had put into my hands an interesting little memoir of a departed female member of his congregation, by the excellent minister of the Free Church at Craig, near Montrose.* The person who forms the subject of the narrative had in early life resided near our family residence in the town of Boness, and had occasionally attended the meetings referred to. " Many a solemn word," said she to her pastor, " many a warm prayer have I heard in that place, at times some words sunk deep into my soul, but going away to another town, and falling into different company, I fear I sinned these all away. You know the character of my life for years, but I can assure you I never was altogether without upbraidings of heart, and I knew in my conscience what was right and what was wrong. O! I wonder greatly how God did not give me up, and now, in my old age, those words and prayers of the young men come back upon me." The particulars of the case are to me very touching, and they present not an inapt illustration of the manner in which the sovereign mercy and grace of God may, by small and seemingly unlikely instruments, carry on to completion the great scheme of infinite wisdom and love in bringing many sons and daughters to him.

The pulpit first reared in 1787 found its last resting place at Kilsyth, where, in 1839–40, it stood as a silent witness of the great awakening.

---

* Sketch of the life of Mary P———, by the Rev. Hugh Mitchell, Ferryden, 1869. The woman was fifty years a confirmed drunkard, but became a wonderful instance of grace abounding to the chief of sinners. See last three pages of "Miscellaneous" chapter—pp. 399–401.

CHAPTER II.

HE parochial school which I attended was open six days in the week, with one exception of a half-day's play on Saturday. It was opened and closed daily with prayer, not read, but free, and suitable and short. Three hours on Saturday found us occupied with class readings in the Holy Scriptures; repetitions of the Shorter Catechism, miscellaneous historical questions and appropriate advices by the master, closed with devotional exercises somewhat enlarged. Six hours each day, Saturdays excepted, were devoted to the ordinary lessons belonging to the usual arrangements of such seminaries in Scotland—English reading, orthography and recitation, arithmetic as far as the cube root, book-keeping, navigation, Latin, Greek, and, to a limited extent and on occasions only, French. In the system of those days, the chief error lay in the department of classics, where the whole of the six hours were rigidly devoted to elementary branches, and to the simple translation and construing of the originals. An intermingling with this of historical and geographical information, and illustrations of antiquities, and biographical references and notes, would have been a valuable addition. Still, the seminary was well taught, and the annual examinations, by the Presbytery of the bounds, were duly attended to.

About this time, when running to school, he fell. A sharp stone pierced his forehead, and left a mark which he bore through life. He was carried home insensible. The kind school-boy who carried him home was Mr. Archibald Petrie (or "big Baldie Petrie," as he was called), who was for many years a respected citizen of Belleville, Canada, recently deceased. The two sons of Boness used often to meet and talk with amazing interest over the "old times." When my father died, it was with difficulty that his ancient friend, who outlived him, though weighed down with manifold infirmities, could be prevented making the long pilgrimage to his funeral.

From 1795 to 1799, I was under the Rev. John Duguid, afterwards minister of Eva and Rendal, in Orkney ; and from 1799 to 1801, under Mr. John Stevens, who continued in charge until twenty-five years ago, when he was succeeded by his son, the present efficient teacher. Both of my preceptors were superior men. With the second, my intercourse in after life was tolerably frequent ; but the first I never saw after April, 1799, when he sailed from Peterhead with his family for the (then) remote and scarcely known islands of the north. It is rather interesting to record that two generations after, his grand-daughter, the amiable spouse of a young banker in Toronto, became one of the members of my flock. Her father, Dr. Alexander Duguid, was a companion of mine at school for four years, at the close of the last century, and he has

been long an eminent medical practitioner in Kirkwall.
His son-in-law, Mr. Baikie, went back to his native island
in bad health, and a fatal affection of the lungs soon cut
him off; but he departed in peace, and his affectionate
widow and fatherless children have been spared and blest
by their common Father in Heaven.

In the end of October, 1801, I left the Grammar School
for Edinburgh College, being twelve years and a-half old,
certainly too young, and yet I was reading Juvenal and
Livy, and was able to read and construe through the Greek
New Testament, at least the Gospels.   Our Humanity
Professor was Dr. John Hill, author of the quarto volume
of " Synonymes of the Latin Language," and the life of
Dr. Hugh Blair.   He was a man of eccentric character,
and withal very narrow in his habits, but of great acuteness, ready wit, and admirable skill in clothing conceptions, often original, in English words, always pure and
racy.   To the young men of the second year, he gave
weekly lectures on three subjects—Roman Antiquities,
Universal Grammar, and the principles of Natural and
Commercial Policy.   Of these he put a scanty synopsis
into our hands, but what would I not give, even yet, for
the originals themselves, as they came from his lips!   Our
class-room in the old college was dark and glum, and he
had a slender and cheaply-constructed lamp to assist his
vision, even at broad day, and it was a great amusement
to the boys to see it occasionally blinking.

Our Greek Professor was Andrew Dalzel, A.M., who had
studied for the church, but who, being an apt and elegant
scholar, and having interest with the patrons of the Edinburgh chairs, turned aside—in the professional sense I
mean—from the pathways of Zion, to the heights of Parnassus and of Helicon.   He was a most amiable and
worthy man, and he kept his class always in good order,
which Dr. Hill never did nor could do.

But of all the Professors in the Arts Department in
those days, Dr. James Finlayson, the occupant of the chair
of Logic and Metaphysics, was by far the best.   He was
comparatively young when called to succeed John Bruce,

who was removed to a more lucrative post, which he was thought more competent to fill, namely, that of King's Printer for Scotland. I attended Dr. Finlayson two sessions, embracing the ordinary branches, Pneumatology in the first year, and Metaphysics, or the higher philosophy of mind, in the second. Our teacher aimed at being useful rather than at being brilliant. He did not perplex young minds with any such strange "conceits" as are now ordinarily submitted to them; but he gave us a plain and intelligible account of the powers and capabilities of the human mind, with most suitable rules and suggestions for their right improvement and guidance. He gave us quite enough, and perhaps more than enough, on syllogism, perhaps too little on Lord Bacon's method of induction, and next to nothing at all on Rhetoric and Belles Lettres. I look back on these lectures, however, with deep gratitude and interest. They were well fitted to form the mind to think, and they were read so slowly, and with so many repetitions (all for the sake of the pupils) as to render it easy for us to take down full notes. We had regular *viva voce* examinations, and six essays were prescribed during the course; and every student who wrote *three*, had the honour of reading one in the class at the close of the session.

The Teachers of Mathematics in the College of Edinburgh in my days were, Professors Playfair and Leslie, but they were both by far too scientific for boys; very few attended them, and we found a most excellent substitute in a private teacher, Mr. William Laidlaw, a Dumfrieshire man, of mild, gentlemanly manners, and competent abilities for his work. We were taught by him also the elements of Logarithms, of the use of which I now retain little more than the recollection that on a bright April morning, at five o'clock, we found ourselves along with our much respected teacher, posted on the soft sands of the Firth of Forth, at Portobello, and busily engaged with our varied apparatus, measuring the height of "Largo Law," and the most prominent of those "Hills in Fife," about the "prospects" from which I may tell, by and

by, a little legend. I had no taste for either Geometry
or Logarithms, but my friend, Andrew Irvine, was excellent at both ; and it commonly happened, yea seems
to have been understood in those days, that the skill
and attainments of one, became the "common good of
all."

Irvine and I were intimate, but he did not go with me
to the Divinity Hall. He went to the Church of England,
as did John Wightman, our Hall Librarian, and Thomas
Sword, one of our cleverest lads. Of all these I have
long lost sight. If they are still within the land of the
living, little doubt exists in my mind that they will be
found in the ranks of the "broad church" brigade. Nevertheless, I would give much for a sight of any one of them
now, and I can assure them that I would waive controversy for "the time being." Mr. Irvine has, I think
published a volume of sermons, which I am sure will be
able and logical. May I hope that the *sal evangelicum*.
is diffused through their pages as largely as it is in the
volume of my loved and lamented Episcopal friend Thomas
Bissland.

Saturday was always a play day in College, and we
enjoyed it in excursions to Arthur's Seat,.to Craig-Millar
Castle, or to the Hermitage of Braid ; but to those who
preferred scenes in the interior of the city, the Parliament House offered an agreeable lounge, for besides the
"living throng" of barristers and officials moving to and
fro in the "Outer House," we were privileged occasionally
with an ascent to the gallery of the "Inner," where the
whole "fifteen" were seated together in solemn conclave
on knotty points. The President, Sir Ilay Campbell,
of Succoth, was a profound but common sense lawyer,
always dignified, and universally respected ; but in those
days of Tory ascendancy, his associates were sometimes
men who owed their places more to political and family
interest than to legal talent. The Hon. Henry Erskine,
brother of the Earl of Buchan, and of the Lord Chancellor of England, was never elevated to the bench, but
he was a very successful pleader, and a wag of the high-

est class. His puns were endless, and often extremely happy. I shall give one as a specimen : on occasion of the first appearance in his robes of a newly appointed judge, a plain country gentleman of fair abilities, and of more than ordinary material bulk, Mr. Erskine took occasion " to congratulate their lordships on the large accession which had been recently made to the WEIGHT of the bench, without diminishing the respectability of the bar." "That's too bad in you, Harry," said the worthy neophyte; to which "Harry" replied, in one of his most aristocratic bows, and the pleadings went on. In common with most of the Lords of Session, the Doric-Scotch was the familiar vernacular of this good-natured senator; and he one day sought to check the vociferating energies of an over-excited advocate, and with most convulsive success, by an interlude perfectly irresistible. "*Mr. F——, dinna skriech sae heigh, mun ; you perfectly dumfounder me.*" I rather think that the amusing era of "Parliament House fun" ended at or soon after the multiplication of " Lords Ordinary," and the division of the chambers. Another "Harry" took away from the bar much of the " wit," when he mounted the bench as Lord Cockburn.

Dr. Davidson often warned the students who visited him, against frequenting auctions, buying useless books, and spending both time and money in something like useless play rather than pleasant recreation. There was need of such cautions, for we did often leave our lessons for the morrow, unfinished, and go down to "get fun," as we counted it, at one or more of the auctions of books, which were of nightly recurrence. On such occasions there was something like oratory of an inferior stamp indulged in by the main actors. I am not sure whether Mr. William Blackwood figured ever on this arena, before the days of Christopher North, but this I know, that his partner, Mr. Robert Ross, opposite the College, figured away from his elevated platform, and dealt out many encomiums on favourite authors, successively falling under his merciless hammer. By far the most popular of all

C

these humble orators on the literary platform was, beyond question, Mr. Peter Cairns, Bookseller, College Street, and·whose place of holding forth was more accessible than that of Mr. Ross. The comments and the blunders of this vulgar rhetorician afforded us often not a little amusement. To give one instance out of many. One evening Peter got into his hands an octavo volume or thick pamphlet, containing a collection of miscellaneous poetry, under a fanciful title. I had looked at the book before it was set up, and soon saw that the orator mistook its title. "Here," said he, "gentlemen, is a noble work, poems from the hill of life; human life a hill, valuable instruction for young persons; who says for the Hill of Life?" The offers began pretty fairly; but I whispered to Peter, that he had better look at the title again, for I thought he had not quoted it right. He took the hint, thanked me for it, and again began, "Gentlemen, it is the Hills of Life, not one, but many; a valuable work; who bids for the 'Prospects from the Hills of Life?'" It soon brought a good price; but what was his surprise, when the purchaser read the real title, "Prospects from Hills in *Fife!!*" and demanded back his money! Peter rubbed his eyes, and confessed his error, cancelling the sale, and was satisfied with half the price offered under the plausible misnomer, and a hearty laugh, in which we all joined; for our host never failed to exemplify before us young orators a well known rule in rhetoric, that if you wish to succeed in your pleading, be sure you keep your hearers in good humour. Indeed the interludes that went on in the way of dialogue, or otherwise, during the eventful period from the lifting of the volume to its being knocked down, were often vastly amusing. Many volumes we bought, good, bad and indifferent. Sometimes a book was valuable, and yet cheap; for instance, the lovely "Flores," of Erasmus cost me just *one half-penny!* and I made a present of it to our College Library, where its sweet savour remains. For that fine specimen of *multum in parvo*, the *Selectæ Historicæ*, I paid just *two pence!* but this is not all, for on the back of the cover stands the interesting autograph of the dearly loved young friend of the poet Cowper, William Cawthorn Unwin, 1756.

From the date of the foundation of Edinburgh College, by King James VI, in the end of the sixteenth century, due provision had been made for the religious superintendence and instruction of the students. It was part of the duties of the Principal to address to them on every Saturday, what was called the *sacra lectio*, and of these suitable appeals to the understandings and the hearts of young enquirers, the theological lectures of Leighton, when he held that office, are admirable specimens. Down to about the middle of the seventeenth century, accommodation on Sabbath was provided in the Easter High Church, and when Lady Yester's Church was erected, about that period, the main gallery in it was appropriated to the students. In 1801, when I entered College, the pastor of that church was the Rev. David Black, who had been for some years minister of the small Parish of St. Madoes, near Perth, and his valuable ministry I enjoyed for five years. Clergymen of greater talent, and of more comprehensive mental range, it might not be difficult to find, but you would search in vain for a man of higher pastoral eminence, and better adaptation in the pulpit to the capacities and affections of youth. Of his "Action Sermon" at the communion in November, 1801, on "This day shall be unto you for a memorial," taken in connection with the evening sermon on the same occasion by one of our most talented young ministers, the deeply lamented Mr. Bennet, of Duddingston—of the series of lectures on the "History of Joseph," and of a remarkably impressive discourse on the history of Naaman the Syrian—of these and other specimens of Mr. Black's pulpit powers I retain a vivid impression to the present day. A remarkable revival of religion had taken place at Moulin, in Perthshire, under the ministry of Mr. Stewart, afterwards of Dingwall, and the letter to Mr. Black by that gentleman contains a full and deeply interesting detail of the leading features in that revival, and its wide circulation did much,

with the blessing of God, in effecting and confirming a
genuine religious awakening. The mournful event of
the death of Mr. Black, in the spring of 1806, spread a
funeral pall over the land, and wide and earnest was the
question, "where shall a suitable successor to him be
found ?" All eyes were directed to Dr. Balfour, of Glasgow, then the most eloquent evangelical preacher in Scotland ; but the moral force of Scotland's commercial metropolis interposed an interdict that was irresistible, and
Dr. Balfour remained in Glasgow till 1818, when his
translation on high, by a remarkably sudden removal,
was hailed by the echo of a thousand voices, as was that
of the prophet of old, "My father, my father! the chariots
of Israel and the horsemen thereof." The mantle of Mr.
Black and Dr. Balfour fell on Dr. Thomas Fleming, an
admirable expositor, and an affectionate and judicious
pastor. Dr. F. was not so impressive in delivery as Mr.
Black, but in thought and in style he was more exact,
and his other substantial qualifications eminently fitted
him for occupying a college pulpit.

I had the privilege of attending Dugald Stewart one
full session, and partially a second ; but, alas! that second
was his last ! Dr. Thomas Brown had assisted him a good
deal during the session of 1804–5, and in 1805 he was
appointed as assistant and successor, Mr. Stewart remaining *emeritus.* On the interesting occasion of his taking
leave, the students drew up and presented to him an address,
to which the Professor made a short but not unsuitable
reply. The chairman of "the students' committee" was
the present Earl Russell, then Lord John, whose image is
now most distinctly before me, when, at the close of the
class meeting, he stept forward at the head of the members of committee, and read the paper in the hearing of
the Professor and the whole class, now more than sixty
years ago. I have no copy either of the address or of
the reply; indeed I don't think that either of them ever
reached the Press, for the newspapers in those days seldom
inserted articles purely literary. It was against the interests of the class, and even the fame of its illustrious

preceptor, that his "printed work," as he usually termed it, had been published so soon, and that it embraced so many of the usual topics of the class. No edition at a moderate price had as yet appeared, so that the students were inadequately supplied with it. Still there was very much in the lectures of Mr. Stewart that was captivating and instructive, and the fascinating charms of his style and delivery were felt, and richly enjoyed, by us all.

With regard to Professor Robison, I concur in all that Dr. Chalmers and others have said as to the bearing of his prelections, judging of them from the admirable articles which he contributed to the " Encyclopedia Britannica," particularly those on " Physics " and " Philosophy." The impression which their perusal made on my mind, at the distance of sixty years remains deep and fresh, but at the time (1804) when I attended his class he was weakened much by age and bodily infirmities. His countenance was remarkably striking, and he had all the impressiveness we associate with the idea of a truly Christian philosopher and sage. He died in the January following. During the vacancy his place was supplied by the services of the Rev. Dr. Thomas Macknight, one of the ministers of the city, and who soon after became a candidate for the chair of Mathematics, vacated by the elevation of Professor Playfair to the chair of Natural Philosophy. It was in connection with this matter that the famous controversy, regarding Mr. Leslie, (afterwards Sir John), arose, and shook Scotland to its centre. The contest brought out clearly the selfish character of the policy of the moderates, which had clothed itself with the garb of religion, and the defeat of Mr. Macknight and his party (for it was altogether a party strife) was the first blow that heralded the downfall of the clique that had so long held the Church in bonds. Candour at the same time leads me to say that, had Dr. Macknight pledged himself to resign his living in the church on his obtaining the chair, the best friends of religion would have given a preference to him above his successful rival.

It was in 1806, and in the first year of my theological

studies, that I joined the church as a member in full communion, by sitting down at the Lord's table. Frequency
of intercourse with the pastor of the congregation prior
to this, did, to a certain extent, perhaps, supersede minute
examination on his part, and I passed easily along; but
still I felt disappointed in the summary way in which the
matter was gone about; and I notice it as a caution to
brethren in the ministry, not to venture on the assump-
tion that academical attainments, however respectable,
necessarily presuppose accuracy of elementary religious
knowledge, far less personal experience in the things of
God. As to my own impressions, the "lights and shadows" of sixty years passing now over them cannot but
throw a bedimming influence around, and yet I have
always considered the period of one's first approach to
the table of the Lord as a most solemn era in one's spiritual life, the remembrance of it sweet, and the impress of
it savoury and profitable. The official relation of my
father to the tenantry on the Kinneil estate brought us
into close intimacy with all of them, and especially with
a few of the more pious and intelligent who had been
chosen office-bearers of the church. They were well
informed men, judicious and upright, with piety sincere,
if not very ardent. Spending a day about that time at
the house of one of them, Mr. Macvey, the conversation,
after dinner, turned upon books, and, among other things,
he asked me if I was acquainted with a remarkable work
just published by Mr. Wilberforce, Member of Parliament
for Yorkshire, "A view of the prevailing sentiments and
habits of the professing religious world" in England.
The work was quite new to me, not so to the worthy Scottish yeoman, and the hint I got from him was enough.
Our minister soon supplied me with the book, and I read
it with pleasure, not a little surprise, and possibly some
profit. The worthy man asked me, "Have you read the
Meditations and Soliloquies of Captain John Henderson?"
Of the man or of the book I had never heard; years
rolled away before I chanced to fall in with the volume.
I picked it up in Edinburgh, and it is now on my table

in Knox College, of whose library I have also made it an inmate. The author was a native of our little seaport town, and master of a trading vessel from Borrowstounness to the northern ports of Europe, and on shipboard, and among the rocks and shallows and *fiords* of the Norwegian coast, he mused and penned " soliloquies " on the profoundest themes of the " fatherhood of Jehovah," and " Trinity in unity," with a scriptural accuracy of thought and expression rarely to be met with. The " Traveller," and " Solitude sweetened," of James Meikle, and the " Memoirs " of Joseph Williams, are works of the same class, and our worthy " Scotch Elders " of the " olden time," were familiar with them all.

It is not at all unlikely that this worthy man belonged to that class of whom the celebrated author of " Robinson Crusoe " makes honourable mention in his " Tour through Britain," when he says that they (*i.e.* " the Borrowstounness men," as he calls them) are the best seamen in the Firth, and are very good pilots for the coast of Holland, the Baltic, and the coast of Norway. Defoe farther says that Borrowstounness " was a town of the greatest trade to Holland and France, except Leith." I have not ascertained whether there may have been any family relationship between the pious sea captain of whom I am speaking, and the late wealthy and philanthropic merchant of the same name, John Henderson, of Park. That gentleman was a native of the place, and I have a distinct remembrance of his father, Robert Henderson, shipowner, and the leading man in the old anti-burgher congregation. Mr. Henderson, who had been long a resident of Glasgow, died about a year ago (1867), and his ashes rest with those of his forefathers and other relatives, in the churchyard of the place.

[The reference in the foregoing to that devoted christian philanthropist, Mr. John Henderson, of Park, we cannot let pass without noting the life-long friendship which existed between the two sons of Boness, and the

prompt and generous responses given by Mr. Henderson
to the appeals made to him by his old fellow-townsman,
for various objects of benevolence.   The vicinity of Park
to Paisley made intercourse easy; nor, when the ocean subsequently intervened, was that intimacy suspended.   Frequent were such interchanges of friendship and of funds
as the following :—

"PARK, 14 Jan., 1864.

"I have been in receipt of your kind letter, and, agreeable to
what I promised, I send herewith a cheque enclosed for £50, to be
laid out to the best advantage, for the benefit of the library of your
College.   I notice what you mention about getting long credit from
the publishers, but my experience is that by far the cheaper way
is to send the money with the order, and, by doing so, you will
get them at about half the publishing price.   I am in the custom
of buying both from London and Edinburgh publishers, and this
is uniformly my experience.   We are glad to hear that the Gould
Street congregation is prospering.   I have seen the Rev. John Kerr
to-day, who was speaking with great pleasure of his visit to Canada.
I will always be glad to hear that matters go on well with you."

[Gould Street congregation, Toronto, seems at this time
to have shared also in Mr. Henderson's benefactions, for,
at the Annual Congregational Meeting, held in January,
1864, the following resolution was unanimously passed :—

"That this meeting would desire to record their heartfelt thanks to the Rev. Dr. Burns, for his many acts of
kindness towards this congregation in the past, particularly as the means of securing from John Henderson, Esq.,
of Park, so munificent a donation, and thereby aiding,
along with his own and Mrs. Burns' liberal subscriptions,
in very materially reducing une church debt."]

My last visit to the haunts of my youth was in June,
1868, ancient associations crowded around me, and Ark-
ley's nice crimped biscuits were still to be had, as in
1794, but, alas! Pennant's description of the "smoke" of

1776 was literally realized, for the "old pit" at the back of our school house, and which formed to us a somewhat dangerous playmate, had been made to "go again," and its murky accompaniments did not increase the amenity of the place. Extensive iron-works have added largely to the population, and a "Bank," unknown in my days, propitiously met my eye. The trees at Kinneil had lost nothing of their venerable, yet fresh and lofty aspects, and there stood still the spacious mansion as before, though somewhat scathed by the ravages of fire. The worthy Pastor of the Free Church, Mr. Wilson, introduced me to Mr. Cadell, the proprietor of Grange, in the garden of whose hospitable mansion I had an opportunity of examining the antique stone which had just been dug out of the grounds in the neighbourhood, whose distinct Latin inscriptions, round and round, go far to settle the disputed question of the termination of the celebrated wall of Antoninus Pius. The place of my birth stands about half a mile to the west, and on a splendid beech tree in the adjoining thicket, I read my name distinctly, inscribed with the date, "May, 1802." From the vista of two generations passed away what a crowd of profitable reflections rush forth, revealing at once the darker scenes of the past, and brightening with a higher tint the lights of the future.

CHAPTER III.

THEOLOGICAL EDUCATION.

HE date of my entrance at the Divinity Hall is November, 1805, which at that time, and for a long time after, embraced only three Professors. Dr. Andrew Hunter, the Professor of Theology proper, had long held the situation along with one of the city parishes, and, as a natural consequence, his attentions were divided betwixt a large class of from 150 to 200 young men, under training for the ministry, and a large and somewhat rugged metropolitan parish. Without any marked native talent, and with attainments in theological learning, respectable, but nothing more, he was, in respect of character and moral worth, truly one of the excellent of the earth. He commented on the Latin duodecimo volumes of "Pictet's Theology," and one day in the week was devoted to public examinations, but these were considered by us all as rather of the nature of ordinary catechisings of the people in the church, than as going into anything like the depths of systematic theology. But this was perhaps compensated for by scriptural and

practical expositions of the Epistle to the Romans. Dr.
Hugh Meiklejohn was the pastor of a considerable country
parish, fourteen miles distant from the city, and, after the
manner of those times, he held also the chair of Divinity
and Ecclesiastical History. He sometimes told us that
the Royal Charter which endowed the chair, entitled him
to lecture on these systematically or theologically, but
he limited himself to the second of these branches, together with lectures on the contents of the sacred books,
and a few miscellaneous but very valuable prelections on
preaching, lecturing, and the duties of the pastoral care.
His Church History lectures never reached beyond the time
of Julian the Apostate. Nevertheless, he was a man of
fair abilities, of extensive learning, and great kindness of
heart. Amid much that was heavy, and not very interesting, he brought before us much that was really valuable, and his written critiques on our discourses and
essays were always candid and discriminating. I don't
recollect of his ever examining the students on the lectures. Dr. William Moodie, the Professor of Oriental
Languages, was, at the same time, one of the ministers of
St. Andrew's Church, a man of competent learning, and
of most agreeable manners. With all our Professors we
held occasional private intercourse convivially, but Dr.
Moodie was the only one of the three who was gifted
with conversational powers, calculated to interest and
edify young minds. Biblical criticism and exegetics, with
Hebrew and Greek, did not then hold any distinct place
in the prelections of the hall.

Four lectures on the eloquence of the pulpit, by the
Professor of Rhetoric, we were invited to hear; and for
practical lessons on elocution we were indebted to the
classes of such private teachers in the city as Mr. John
Wilson, Mr. William Scott, and Mr. Jones, (formerly an
actor at the theatre,) the best reader by far of the three,
although they were all very competent instructors. I
attended three full courses at the Hall, and a partial one;
the average number of regular students was about 180,
but, alas! the number of those who were known by the

designation of "serious" students, or of pious young men, did not amount to above a tenth of that number. Nearly all were then looking for the smiles of a "worthy patron;" and patronage made "its appointments, and dispensed its good things," irrespective altogether of personal godliness.

In the memoirs of my brother, "the Pastor of Kilsyth," reference is made to the "old Theological Society," and the "broad church" influence which had been gathered around it. That society had ceased to exist prior to my entrance at the Hall, and the only field for debate and criticism then among the students, was "the Philo-theological." I was just 16 when I was admitted a member, having, however been connected with the Philalethic and other literary associations for two years before. In these latter, clubs as we may call them, there were some men of very high talent, and great powers of extemporary address, but the first by far, in my time, was Mr. Thomas Wright, afterwards minister of Borthwick, and author of the beautifully written "Statistical account" of that interesting parish, but who, unhappily, never seemed to be under the controling agency of devout and spiritual views. He was much given to theoretical and bold speculations, and often brought out original views. One night, when my scientific friend, David Landsborough, had spoken, and spoken well on the side of truth, in defence of the unity of "species," Wright perplexed us all, (for most of us were far his juniors,) by his ingenious rambles amid the "devious wilds," trodden since by a Darwin and a Gliddon, and many others, startling us by his facts, real or supposed, and at any rate, to us, quite new. John Smith, afterwards of Aberlady (a sweet "marine villa" it is), who hid in a napkin many rare talents and endowments, was the only one amongst us who could give him battle; but, ah! he himself was far away from the truth as it is in Jesus. His favourite principle, when a student of theology, was the whimsical idea of shaping "the extent of the remedy by the depth of the disease," and as his diagnosis of the latter was very slight and superficial, so were his estimates of the former; and this rule of proporₐion he thought might be applied to square everything, leaving the question as to abstract quantities in the proportion itself to be, as in modern parlance, matter of forbearance.

Mr. Wright, while at Borthwick, published "The Morning and the Evening Sacrifice," a book which took by its title, and by its splendid and somewhat gorgeous style. He afterwards came out with his "Living Temple," in which he evolved his pantheistic views, and thus exposed himself to righteous censure from the church, whose bread he was eating, while he aimed a blow at her vitals. Dr. Bannerman, now of the new College (Edinburgh), then a member of Dalkeith Presbytery, took him up, unveiled the hidings of the title page, and convicted him of grievous heresy. Dr. Candlish made his first appearance at the bar of the assembly in that case. I heard it all. The pleadings for truth were masterly; the cobwebs of plausible ·error were swept away, and the unhappily misled author was, in consequence, deposed from the ministry. He went to England, and, for anything I have heard, may be there still, climbing the heights of Parnassus rather than reclining in the peaceful vales of Mount Zion. And yet well do I remember the evening when, at the "Philalethic," William Hamilton, afterwards of Strathblane, was declared an honorary member; and when the ribbon with its medal were placed round his neck, and the congratulating speech made by this same Mr. Wright, the two men were perfect contrasts. Had Hamilton remained in the ranks, he would have been a befitting tilter in combat with Wright. But he left us for the work of God at Broughton, thereafter laboured at Dundee, then made the "land of the Blane, to flourish by the preaching of the Word," and from thence passed into glory.*

* Dr. William Hamilton, of Strathblane, was one of his dearest friends. Among father's most cherished Manuscripts is one dated 1835, by Dr. James Hamilton, containing full particulars of his father, which we reluctantly omit. In the deeply interesting Memoir of the son, is the following:—" Dr. Robert Burns, of Paisley, presided at the marriage ceremony, and survives in bodily health and mental vigour to the present day. Such was the fact when this sheet was sent to the printer, but ere it returned the race of the venerable Patriarch was run." Dr. Wm. Hamilton married a Paisley lady on the 19th January, 1813, and his distinguished son was born there, on the 27th November 1814.—*Editor's Note.*

In the Philo-theological Society I was much the youngest and the smallest member. Among the seniors we had Mr., afterwards Sir, Robert Sparkie, Sergeant-at-Law, and a judge in India; Dr. John Hodgson, afterwards of Blantyre, a man of genius and remarkable popular gifts, but with a mind somewhat bizarre; Dr. Patrick Macfarlane, of Glasgow, and thereafter of Greenock, eminent for talents and high principles; Mr. Archibald Campbell, from the Highlands, lecturer on Mathematics in Edinburgh, and author of a fine article on "Acoustics," in Brewster's "Encyclopedia," cut off, alas! in the bright morning of his fame; and many other "gems of purest ray serene," but of which "the deponent sayeth nothing."

At my entry as a member, I was asked to choose my subject for essay. Being sheepish and raw, I looked blank. A fellow-student, Peter Brotherston, afterwards of Alloa, helped me by saying, "I'll give you one," and he gave me one of the most difficult topics in theology, natural or revealed, "the permission of evil." I grappled with it, aided by Edwards, West, Hopkins, and others that came in my way. The production survives with all the vital energy it ever had, and that was not much. In criticism it was sadly mangled; but all acknowledged that, considering everything, it was a "successful nibble."

After two sessions the hollowness of the "Philo," in a theological light, broke on us, and, feeling that there was a sad lack of piety and of evangelical sentiment among the mass of the members, seventeen of us declared for a secession, and we constituted the "Adelphi-theological." If the terms of admission to the "Philo" were too lax, those of our new organization were too strict. We required a certificate, not only in the ordinary technical way, but, in addition, an expression of belief, that the applicant "was deeply impressed with a sense of divine truth." Moreover, the original members were too much of one mind, and the debates were deficient in zest. An element of feebleness thus entered into the composition of the society, and, although, I rather think it still remains in existence, its range of operations is limited to the peculiar business of a preaching society.

The "Adelphi" behoved all to be members of a "society for prayer and religious conference," and many delightful recollections I have of our meetings in the "Orphan Hospital," and in the private parlour of the "Master," the eminently pious and richly experienced William Peebles. This fellowship society is of venerated and holy descent. Its history allies itself with the days of Erskine and Walker and Macqueen, a century past, and its meetings were held at first, not literally *sub tegmine fagi*, but better still, under the spreading branches of a widely expanding oak tree in the Meadows. Thereafter this shady retreat was exchanged for the apartment in that benevolent institution where many young hopefuls have been trained for usefulness here and glory yonder, and whose extensive park had been the favourite scene of the out-door addresses of the "eloquent Englishman,"* on whose lips many thousands waited in breathless suspense, whom the nobles of the land delighted to honour, and on whom David Hume himself hung with amazement and seeming complacence. The funds of the Hospital benefited largely by such occasions as these, and far away, the "Orphan House" in Georgia shared also in the pecuniary results, while the friends of Christ on both sides of the Atlantic, by a species of spiritual telegraphic agency, then quite familiar to them all, re-echoed the whispering of the "one faith" and the "one hope." The spiritual and evangelistic history of Caledonia stands in close relationship to such rehearsals as these, and Scotland's Church and Scotland's religion owe not a little to the visits, first of Whitefield, and thereafter of Simeon, and of Rowland Hill, and of Fuller, by whose appeals not a few of Scotland's sons have been brought to sit under the "Plant of renown," and to eat the pleasant fruit.

Among fellow-students at the Hall with whom I had

---

* Rev. George Whitefield.

a close intimacy for two sessions, was Mr. John Codman,
of Boston, Massachusetts, afterwards the well known and
much respected Dr. Codman, of Dorchester, near that
city.   On his voyage to Scotland, in 1805, he had as his
fellow traveller the since world-renowned Professor Silliman, of Yale College, who, in the eager pursuit of professional knowledge and acquirements, visited various
parts of the continent, as well as England and Scotland,
and gave to the public those interesting volumes of
"travel," the perusal of which gave me so much pleasure,
many years ago.   It so happened that Dr. Miller's "Retrospect of the nineteenth century " had been lent to me
by our minister, and eagerly perused on its first publication in Britain, and thus I was rather "ripe" than otherwise on the colleges, churches and ministers of America.
My questionings about Dr. Ezra Stiles, Dr Eliphalet Nott,
and other worthies of the period, gratified my New
England friend.   He liked to meet with any one who took
an interest in the United States, and in the varied phases
of American theology.   All the "serious" students loved
Mr. Codman, and respected his abilities and attainments.
He had advantages over us, in having previously studied
in seminaries whose modes of tuition he was able profitably to compare with ours.   He was not a Presbyterian,
but was the next thing to it, and had he remained in
Scotland and joined the Established Church, he would
unquestionably have taken his place among the leaders
of the disruption of 1843.

The following little illustration of occurrences in our
early days may not be uninteresting as throwing light on
character.   Saturday, being a blank day as to college
studies, was selected as the day of our meeting to hear one
another preach, and to offer criticisms on the matter and
manner of the discourses.   One day it so happened that
the critical remarks which had been made partook of rather
an acrimonious character, and my American friend had felt
some of them rather keenly, and repelled them in the way
of sharp repartee.   It so happened that another student
and I had taken a walk after the meeting with Mr. Cod-

man, and he once and again, in the course of conversation, indicated considerable chagrin at the freedom of remark of one of the critics. It was a clear, though cold, afternoon in March, when our companion (Mr. Denoon, afterwards of Rothsay), turning round, pointed to the glorious orb of day just going down over the Corstorphine Hills, solemnly pronouncing the blessed Saviour's words, "Let not the sun go down upon your wrath." "I was not thinking of that," said Mr. Codman, as if roused from a reverie; "but do you think I could get to C——" (the student whom he felt he had repelled rather severely) "before the sun goes down?" "I think we may," said I, and, leaving our companion to make his way home, pleased, no doubt, that he had successfully made the suggestion, off we set for the house in Charlotte Square, where Mr. C—— resided, and, making good use of our locomotive energies, we found ourselves on the front steps of the house, just as the last rays of the setting sun were leaving the sky. We met the friend we sought. It was my lot to detail the circumstances of the suggestion thus promptly and liberally acted on, and with much good feeling, and some jocularity, the breach was healed, and the relationships of brotherly kindness at once restored. More than half a century has rolled away since the incident occurred, I am now the only survivor of the parties concerned, and no reason occurs to prevent me from naming the excellent brother most deeply interested. It was Mr. James Clason, afterwards the pious and now lamented minister of the parish of Dalziel, in Lanarkshire, and brother of the justly venerated Dr. Patrick Clason, principal clerk of the Free Church Assembly, and one of its former Moderators.

Dr. Codman, in corresponding with his friends in America, gave it as his opinion, that the general phase of opinion among the students at this period was Arminianism. This is perfectly correct, and the only way in which they expected to find themselves "at liberty" to sign a creed, whose utter hostility to the doctrine of the Leyden Professor they never denied, was by taking care never to

D

read the Confession of Faith prior to signing it. There were, in my day, very few symptoms of hard study either of Calvinism or Arminianism, and I have a strong impression that the real cause of the dislike to evangelical truth was a practical one, the want of a deep-toned sense of sin in the heart, and of high views of the majesty of a Holy God, and the spotless purity of His law. A decent mediocrity in sentiment and character, if even so much, was all that was thought needful to gain the favour of a "worthy patron," and to pass the ordeal of a Presbytery. My student days were brought forcibly to my mind on reading Dr. James Buchanan's admirable "Cunningham Lectures," in marking his quotation from the pious Robert Trail, of London, to the effect that "there is not a minister that dealeth seriously with the souls of men, but he finds an Arminian scheme of justification in every unrenewed heart."

A circumstance connected with the mental and spiritual history of Dr. Codman is worthy of record. While a student at Harvard College, then, as now, greatly under Unitarian influences, he had a small book put into his hands, with a request that he would write a reply to it: a matter, it was thought, of no difficult performance. It was a piece on the subject of "predestination," written by an evangelical minister of New England, of the name of Cooper. My friend undertook the task, and went manfully forward, his own mind not being at all fixed on the more recondite points in theology. Soon did he find that instead of his "mastering Calvanism," Calvanism fairly mastered him. His candid and serious spirit was open to the impressions of truth, and he finished the perusal of Cooper with a full persuasion of the scriptural correctness of his leading views. He brought the book over with him to Scotland, and, with the aid of Dr. Dickson, of the West Kirk, and other clerical friends, got a new and cheap edition published, and extensively circulated among the students then in the Edinburgh Hall, and with good success in the advancement of sound doctrine. My copy of this unpretending but able book, the gift of my friend, I can still look on with many pleasing re-membrances.

The clerical annals of my student days are bestudded with a number of bright stars. In the Establishment, and among the Dissenters, there were not a few able and successful ministers. Our College pastor was Mr. David Black, of St. Madoes, afterwards of Lady Yester's Church, Edinburgh, cut off, alas! prematurely *(sicut flos succisus aratro)* in 1806, but not before he had made full proof of a ministry of great power, much like that of Mc-Cheyne at a later period, though, like his, too limited in duration. There was his successor, Dr. Fleming, formerly of Kirkmichael, Perthshire, and latterly of Kirkaldy, a most correct and admirable lecturer, and a preacher ever in earnest, though he raised one of his hands only on an occasion, and ever appeared collected and calm, but certainly not cold. There was Sir Henry Moncrieff Wellwood, of fine baronial appearance, rather bold in prayer, perhaps, but in his preaching a perfectly heroic " exhibitioner " of solidity, of soundness and of good sense. There was Dr. Davidson, not profound perhaps, but savoury, scriptural, and, to a certainty, captivating and impressive. There was his colleague, Dr. Campbell, a prince among theologians, grandly solemn, the Owen and the Baxter in one. There was Jones, of Lady Glenorchy's, original, acute, richly experimental, and, while eternity was ever uppermost, never failing in "a word to the times." Among the Dissenters there was Peddie, the finest lecturer on the Old Testament I ever heard ; and Struthers, very passably orthodox, and splendidly eloquent.

Among the ministers of the time, who took special interest in the students, and did them much good, I note worthy Dr. Colquhoun, of Leith, the very Herman Witsius of his day, rich in his theology, and sweet and affectionate, and truly paternal in his addresses; the two Dicksons, father and son, models of excellent preaching, the latter with rather a husky voice, but clear-headed, and one of the first Hebrew scholars of his day Dr. Davidson, who kindly welcomed us in his study at an evening hour, and at once disarmed us with " Now lads ! tell me what you are doing; say away," and from whom we got many fine hints about books, and the way of using them, with anecdotes of his early days, when he studied at Leyden, and could tell of the Cocceians and the Wolfians of those times. Dr. Buchanan and his lady, of all our patrons and patronesses the chief, kindly affectionate, easy, and ever abounding in anecdotes of the pious Simeon of Cambridge, Newton of London, and the worthy missionaries at Serampore; and, though last, not least, John Macdonald, the "Apostle of the North," with whom we could use greater freedom than with any of the others, from his being nearer our own age and standing.

Dr. Macdonald was a ripe scholar, an adept in the exact sciences, and an acute, though by no means ill-natured, disputant. The sharp doctors of Aberdeen had been his instructors, and a Brown and a Kidd, a Gerard and a Beattie, he held in high esteem; not indeed as Calvinistic divines, for while the one had rather too much of what the wags of the new school termed " Cayenne pepper," the rest had by far too little of that exciting commodity. Dr. Macdonald's social qualities and accessible learning fitted him for being useful to students, and our occasional conversational evening parties, at his house, were at once agreeable and instructive. While he remained in Edinburgh he had occasionally a congregational student or two, from Hoxton or Homerton, boarding in his house. One of the most marked of these was a young man of apparently 18 or 19 years of age, of great acuteness, a most ready speaker, instinct with mental life, and not over-loaded with Dutch, or even German, theology. The young Englishman was well read, an acute and somewhat daring controversialist, not over fond either of the Highlands or of the Lowlands of Scotland, and we looked on him, taken as a whole, in the light of a " semi-Arminian brother." It was, I think, in September, 1833, I went to England to collect money for missions to Canada. Among other large towns and cities visited was Manchester, where a Presbyterian Church had been erected, in Mosely Street, by a wealthy and pious Scottish merchant, whom I once met at Dr. Buchanan's, of the Canongate, Mr. Robert Spear. The place had got into the hands of nonconformists of the congregational body (a thing not at all uncommon,) and was, at that time, filled by Dr. Robert S. McAll, perhaps the best preacher of his day among the English Independents. Not having an opportunity of hearing the eloquent preacher on the Sabbath, I went to his week-evening lecture. The evening was wet, but the attendance in the lecture-room below the the chapel might amount to 300. He preached off-hand, with pathos, clearness of doctrinal statement, and transparent perspicuity of style. The raw Arminianism of early days was all away; the smart and seemingly complacent critic of other times was absorbed in the "Apollos" of his day, the warm and lively preacher of that Gospel, which, when I first knew him, he certainly neither understood nor felt. After the blessing there was a pause, and deep feeling seemed to rest on many countenances. The preacher occupied a desk of no lofty elevation, so I came from the remote end of the apartment, where I had, on purpose, taken my seat, and stood before the preacher, who rose and bowed. "May I ask, sir, did you, when a student of theology, pass a winter in Edinburgh, and board with Mr. John Macdonald, of the Gaelic Chapel?" "I did, sir," was his immediate answer. "Then," said I, "let me claim you as an old companion and fellow-student." He looked at me, and I looked at him, but the shadows of a quarter of a century which separate a man of eighteen from the maturity of a man of forty, had stamped us both. On mentioning my name, however, he needed no more. Our memories of the past were "sweet and mournful to the soul." Circumstances rendered a prolonged interview impracticable, and, though I might cherish the hope of our meeting again, I saw him no more. Death did not very long withhold its seal from the matured attainments of one who seemed to ripen with a holy rapidity for the Heaven of the faithful. The interview, though short, was enlivening, sweet and richly suggestive, the remembrance of it is fresh as the morning; but, like the waves of the ocean, time rolls on, eternity is near, and the Macdonalds and the McAlls, the Spencers and the McCheynes, of kindred, though for the time separated, religious connections, are now blended together in one bright constellation.

The advantage of studying theology in a large city, rather than at such small places as Haddington or Selkirk, is the opportunity of marking the "varied gifts" of the ministry, and of thus, with the modesty ever, we shall presume, characteristic of young aspirants, "trying the spirits."

In the process of seeking out churches and ministers, I descried, one Sabbath morning, a spacious and lately erected place of worship in the Potter-row, where I had heard that a Mr. McCrie was the pastor. The congregation was pretty large, attentive, serious-looking, and, from the aspect with which they listened, by no means unintelligent. It was in 1806, and keen disputes were going on, as they had been for years, on points said to be important, but of which we, in the very midst of it all, knew as little as the inhabitants of the New Hebrides. But the minister of that church came forth on the day of the Lord, fresh, calm, well prepared, and apparently just from a region where the din of controversy had no place. From a passage in the first Epistle of John, he illustrated, in ten particulars, "the truth" to be sought, and the best means of finding it. I was more than surprised, but the surprise deepened into profit, and I entered all the particulars in my note book, where they still remain. I have no recollection of hearing the preacher again for years, and then, while the edification was heightened, the surprise was less, for the author of the "Life of Knox" was then bearing the stamped insignia of a Dugald Stewart and a Francis Jeffrey, and the star of his glory was shining with surpassing brightness.

In the spring of 1812, not long after my settlement in Paisley, my fellow-traveller, in what was then felt as a sort of pilgrimage, to Greenock, was the Rev. James Thomson, afterwards Professor of Theology to the Relief Synod, and for fifteen years my esteemed fellow-labourer in the secretaryship of the Paisley and East Renfrewshire Bible Society. During our ride in the mail coach, besides the ordinary topics of the day, and of the road, two themes of higher claim engaged our thoughts. One was Henry Bell's "Comet" on the Clyde, in her earliest and best days; " See how she ploughs !" " Well, Henry will succeed after all." The other was the recent publication of the " Life of Knox," by McCrie. My friend knew at that time, far more than I did about "those sort of things," and yet to him, as well as to me, the book was something quite new. He had read it, I had not. Soon, however, I procured it, and devoured it greedily ; a new mine had been opened, stereotyped errors were at once brushed away. David Hume himself, had he been alive, would no longer have dared to speak of the "rustic apostle ;" and the " apes of Epictetus," in the Church of Scotland, then began to fear, lest, on the shoulders of John Knox, the evangelical or "wild party," would gain a vantage ground, from which they would not easily be dislodged; and so it was. The labours of Dr. McCrie, from 1810 down to the period of his lamented death, in 1835, formed a lever, which, for a quarter of a century, kept moving ; and an agency derived from one of the smallest sections of the churches of the Reformation produced effects in regard to the revival of sound theology and true godliness in Scotland, second only to those of Luther and of Calvin and of Knox himself. Dr. McCrie was a real independent thinker, and withal a man of enlarged and liberal mind; and the careful study of the writings of such a man could not but form, even now, a most effective panacea against a host of evils, at present looming in Britain's horizon with ominous portent.

Second in the order of chronology (but only so) among the main revival agencies at this time in Scotland, is the accession of Thomas Chalmers to the great cause of evangelical truth. When Sir David Brewster arranged his subjects, and his contributors for his "Encyclopedia," he allotted the article "Christianity" to his talented friend Andrew Thomson, then at Sprouston, and soon after at Perth. On the prospect of his settling in Edinburgh, Dr. Thomson found that he could not overtake all his literary engagements, and recommended that the singular but noble genius of Chalmers should be called to grapple with the grand theme. Said the Pastor of Kilmany, yet far more alive to the claims of chemistry than to those of Christianity, "You ask me to write on a subject of which I know absolutely nothing." "Oh," said his correspondent, "You'll soon learn; we shall send you books, just begin." He did "begin," not so much to read as to think; for hitherto, as he said long afterwards on a retrospect of years, he had been "measuring all magnitudes, save only the mighty magnitude of eternity." Various influences were, in the course of the divine dealings with this distinguished man, brought to bear upon a mind of vast expansion and power, and on a heart warmed with strong impressions of benevolence and zeal, but hitherto alienated from the source of all that is excellent.

The rest is well known. The man was made over again; his noble mind was cast in a new mould, and, from 1812 to 1847, when he died, Chalmers may be said to have been ·the great centre pillar, around which all effective movements, in the way of reform and extension on the part of the church, were seen to move. At the great missionary May meetings, in London, in 1812, I heard, incessantly, of the wonders effected by his little tract, price one penny, "The two great instruments;" and the question was constantly put to every one from Scotland, "Who is this? Tell us about him." What with his pastorship at Glasgow, and its exemplified reforms in the style of the existing ministry; what with his sound and truly Christian teachings at St. Andrew's; what with his labours in the theological chair at Edinburgh, in the extension and non-intrusion cause, and in all fields of enlightened benevolence; there can be no doubt that the giant mind of Chalmers, associated as it was with a genial heart and a sound practical judgment, became under God one great means of producing and consolidating that propitious moral change in which Scotia's sons, of all shades of opinion and worship, have so cordially rejoiced.

Though last, not least, in this illustrious triumvirate, and, in some respects, taking precedence of the other two, Andrew Thomson comes full to view as a leading power in the forward movement. With less of the lustre of genius than the one, and far more limited in historical information than the other, he had a clearness of perception, a power of logical argument, and a native force of thought and expression that placed him in the first rank of debaters, while his sound judgment and his business talents gave him a mighty ascendancy among all his compeers. A series of letters generally ascribed to him, and with almost certainty, shook the Cronstadt of moderatism to its centre ; and the monthly issues of the "Christian Instructor," kept up for twenty years a running fire on the hosts of the foe. Beyond all question the power of Balfour and Macgill in the pulpit and in the Hall at Glasgow, the telling itinerancies of "the Apostle of the North," and the indirect but powerful contributing forces from various but friendly hands of the Secession, all blended together under the plastic influence of truth and grace in speeding the progress of Scotland's third Reformation. But in what I have now specially in my eye, assuredly Thomson stands full to view, the slayer of the hydra of stern moderatism, and the hero in the victory of evangelical truth, although, alas ! he was not spared to enjoy the victory he had won.

In close connection with the causes of spiritual revival already noticed, an important event took place in Glasgow in 1814, that powerfully affected the state of the Church, particularly in the west. I allude to the very unexpected issue of a keen contest for the Chair of Theology, vacated by the death of the learned and justly venerated Dr. Robert Findlay. That very accomplished divine had grasped the standard of scriptural orthodoxy with less vigour than might have been wished, owing partly to growing infirmities, and partly to constitutional tendencies. I once heard Dr. Balfour, of the Outer High Church, the most eloquent minister then in the Establishment, ascribe the election of Dr. Macgill to the chair, as a remarkable interposition of Providence in relation to the tide that had set in in favour of evangelical truth. It might perhaps have been possible to find a man of profounder attainments and bolder theology, but it would not be easy to name one who combined so many qualities essential to a successful leader in theology. Under his tuition, and enjoying the benefit of such preaching as that of Balfour and Chalmers, the students in the Glasgow Hall possessed high advantages both in learning and in spiritual character: while the successful efforts of Dr. Macgill, in the Church Courts, as the antagonist of pluralities and non-residence, place his name in the front rank of those who have been leaders in the revival of evangelical truth in Scotland during later years.*

On finishing my third session at the Hall, in 1808, I went to reside at the Manse of Cramond, five miles west from the city, and there remained for eighteen months. In taking the superintendence of the younger members of the family, and in holding district meetings for worship on Sabbath, I found myself very fully occupied, and my near residence to the city made it easy for me to get books from the libraries, both of the University and of the Divinity Hall. This was to me a very profitable and pleasing interlude betwixt the close of my student-life at College, and my entrance on the work of the ministry. Mr. Bonar, of Cramond, was justly esteemed one of the most valuable ministers of his day, the member of a family which has furnished, in our own and former days, a number of faithful messengers of the Cross. The great grandson of " good old Bonar," of Torphichen, so particularly mentioned by Whitefield in connection with the "Cambuslang awakening," in the middle of the last century, and

---

* In 1842 I published a Memoir of Professor Macgill in a duodecimo volume, embracing various references to public questions affecting the progress of the Church.

himself the uncle of three living ornaments of the ministry in the Free Church of Scotland, his name stands forth bright among "Scottish worthies." He was the father of Dr. John Bonar, late Convener of the "Colonial Committee," of the Free Church, cut off, alas! in the prime of his days. The associations of a commencing ministerial life in circumstances favourable to acquired experience, must retain an agreeable fragrance; and, in my case, the ties of friendship have been blended with attachments still more tender.*

I was licensed by the Presbytery of Edinburgh, on the last Wednesday of March, 1810, and I preached my first sermon on the following Sabbath, in the parish church of Cramond, my text being Romans i. 16. In the beginning of June thereafter I was requested to supply, for the summer, the pulpit of the East Church, in the city of Perth, then vacant by the translation of Dr. Andrew Thomson to New Grayfriars Church, Edinburgh. In that ancient ecclesiastical capital of Scotland I spent four months very happily, having got into intimate acquaintanceship with the clergymen of the place, and with not a few esteemed citizens. Among the ministers there were especially two of whom I cherish a fond remembrance. One of these was the Rev. James Scott, then the senior and *emeritus* clergyman in the city, whose intimate knowledge of the ecclesiastical antiquities of Scotland was made greatly available to me in the way of interesting conversation, and reference to ancient books and records. The other was the Rev. William Taylor, minister of the Old-Light Burgher Congregation, and Professor of Divinity to the body of which he was a member. From him I received much information regarding the controversy which had been going on for years, on the subject of the relations of the church and the civil magistracy. The matter was at that time under litigation in the highest courts, and it was not decided

---

* My first partner in life was the daughter of Mr. John Orr, first Provost of Paisley, and my second the daughter of Thomson Bonar, Esq., of the Grove, near Edinburgh, brother of Mr. Bonar, of Cramond. By my first wife I had seven children, of whom four died in childhood, the rest surviving, one in Scotland, one in Chicago, and the third in Toronto.

for several years thereafter. It did not, at that time, excite much interest amongst us of the Establishment, although, at a later period, and up to the present hour, covers questions of great practical value connected with the interests of social religion among men.*

---

* The Rev. Mr. Taylor, Free Church Minister at Flisk, in Fifeshire, has published a Memoir of his father, Professor Taylor, containing, within small bounds, the cream of a controversy which is, at this very time, affecting powerfully the union movements of the Presbyterian Churches.

CHAPTER IV.

PAISLEY MINISTRY.

SHOULD any one enquire the reason why it is that Mr. McNaughton, of Belfast, is a front rank man in theological polemics, civil, literary, theology, an enlightened landed proprietor, and a most skilful exponent of the crafty rules of the "man of sin;" and how it is that Dr. Begg, of Newington, is a tower of strength to any cause, indomitable in mental power, and inexhaustible in his resources; and why Professor Douglas, of the New College, Glasgow, though a very young man, was found worthy of a seat among the rabbis of eastern lore, my reply is short and easy, and of course eminently satisfactory to my own mind. They resided more or less in Paisley, defined by Rowland Hill in his "Journal," as " the paradise of Scotland, or at any rate, if they were not so signally privileged, they dwelt at one time so near it as to be within the range of its mystic influence.

Had not this enumeration been abruptly broken off here, he would have doubtless brought forth from his ntiquarian treasury, such names as Andrew Knox, a relation of the illustrious reformer, minister of Paisley, and afterwards Bishop of Raphoe, Patrick Adamson, afterwards Archbishop of St. Andrews, Thomas Smeton, afterwards Principal of Glasgow College, Robert Boyd, who had been successively Principal of the Universities of Edinburgh and Glasgow, and then promoted to be minister of Paisley, Alexander Dunlop, father of the Principal, Robert Millar, author of the "History of the Propagation of Christianity." John Witherspoon, afterwards President of the College of New Jersey, and Robert Findlay, Professor of Theology in Glasgow University, one of the best divines of the Scottish Church. He would not have omitted sons of Paisley so eminent in the literary world as John Herring, the modellist, Alexander Wilson, the ornithologist, Dr. Robert Watt, author of the "Bibliotheca Britannica," the poets Tannahill and Motherwell, John Wilson, the renowned Christopher North, and such recent ornaments of the pulpit as James Hamilton and James Buchanan.

The town in which so many men of mark were cradled, and where for thirty-four years my father's lines were to fall,* was distinguished for the morality and intelligence of its inhabitants, and their avowed attachment to the institutions of the gospel. The silver communion cups of his future charge, bearing date 1758, had engraven on them the old motto of the municipality—"Let Paisley flourish by the preaching of thy Word."

---

* For the "New Statistical Account of Scotland" he wrote (along with Dr. Macnair of the Abbey) the article on Paisley, filling 171 octavo pages, and containing a vast amount of important, in some instances of curious and rare, information.—Ed.

In the view of an election at Paisley, I was required to preach to the congregation on two Sabbaths, at the distance of three months from each other. Paisley wanted not its critics variously accomplished, and each of the candidates was favoured with remarks, partly written and partly oral. To the former of these classes belonged a letter of some length, addressed to me after my second appearance, and signed "*A Paisley Weaver*." Neither in thought nor in expression did it throw discredit on the class, its spirit and language were respectful, its argument very fair, and its theology sounder than mine. From the text in Romans iii., "There is no fear of God before their eyes," I had preached a carefully prepared sermon on "practical atheism." My correspondent, who was unknown to me, had no objection to anything that was said either in sentiment or illustration, but viewing the words as a quotation from the Old Testament, and as one of the links in a chain of reasoning, he suggested to me the idea of my exhibiting their connexion with the apostle's argument, and their bearing on the two cardinal points enlarged on by the apostle.

Of the result, "deponent saith not." From other sources we learn that, notwithstanding the objections of the worthy weaver, he who seemed as "the lad with the five barley loaves and the two small fishes," was, after all, the people's favourite. He had no mean rivals. Dr. James Carlisle, afterwards so useful in Ireland, was one of them. Carlisle's local influence was great, for his father was one of the baillies of the town. But the Boness youth carried it.

John Neilson, the philanthropic founder of the well-known institution on the old Bowling Green which bears his name, writing to a relative, absent on an annual tour to London, on the 4th May, 1811, says:—"There has been little domestic news since you left us, except the choice of a minister to the Low Church, and I am happy to say that Mr. Burns has got it by a great majority. The Town Council put four candidates in the list, viz., Messrs. Kay, Small, Burns and Carlisle. Mr. Burns had 121 votes, and the other three, put all together, came only to 109 votes." A nephew of this faithful chronicler*, who was ever a firm friend of the successful candidate, and who "remains unto this present" a veteran elder of the Free Church, was present at the ordination on the 19th July, 1811. At the customary "hand-shaking" which closed the solemn service, he was led up by his sainted mother to the youthful pastor, when Dr. Rennie, of Borrowstouness (the old family minister) who stood at the church door, by the young pastor's side, familiarly said, " Come awa', my wee manny, and shake han's wi' your minister."

Thus was he installed in the pulpit of the illustrious Witherspoon.

The Professor of Church History in Edinburgh was in the habit of giving a short series of lectures on pulpit duty, including the preparation and delivery of sermons, and other discourses of a like kind, and these were among his most useful prelections. He was anything but an eloquent preacher himself, and he was an accomplished moderate. But I often call to mind one of his favourite short sayings in connection with these discourses, " Gentlemen," he would say, "the lecture is the glory of the Church of Scotland." He held it as a matter of fact, (and so it was,) that above all other reformed Protestant Churches, Scotland's Church encouraged, and practised in her pulpits, the wholesome method of instruction by familiar and sound exposition of the Word of God, and he laid down rules both for preaching and lecturing profitably. These rules were not unlike those which Dr. Hill, in his

---

* Archibald Gardner, Esq., of Nether Common.

"Institutes," has so sagaciously drawn out, and it were to
be wished that they had been more attended to. For a
whole session I heard, every Sabbath morning, the lectures of Dr. Peddie, on the Old and New Testaments alternately, and I considered him an admirable model. My
resolution was taken, and immediately after I was ordained, I began a course of lectures in the morning service. First, on select portions of the Psalms, then on two
or three of the smaller Epistles of Paul, and then on the
harmony of the Gospels. This last should perhaps have
come first, but I was afraid to try it without some practice in lecturing, and after all I would not advise exposition in the way of a harmony, for it requires far more
piercing and critical adjustment than is consistent with
popular effect. In the course of my ministry of thirty-
four years in Paisley, I went over the whole New Testament, and the leading historical and prophetic parts of the
Old. My plan was to study the passage well, comparing
the parallel places and illustrating them by references and
suitable quotations, putting down on paper full notes to
the extent of six or eight octavo pages, and inserting distinctly the practical inferences or lessons to be drawn.
Many sermons have I read when the occasion was peculiar, and the subject difficult ; but never once did I read a
lecture. I defy you to do it with any effect ; only let a
preacher grasp his theme with point and nerve, throw himself into the trenches with all his capabilities about him,
and he need fear nothing.

In my early days, the main distinction of a moderate
man from a popular or evangelical one, was the habitual
use of paper or no paper. But the distinction carried
reality with it. The "paper man" was almost always stiff,
dry, scrimply orthodox, cold and formal. In our "book of
common order," the people were told that "a reader"
meant an inferior "kind of minister." That, indeed, is
not the meaning of the thing as defined, but it took well,
for the slavish readers of sermons were, in nine cases out
of ten, "inferior" preachers. The time no doubt came
round when a Moncreiff, a Chalmers and a Thomson read

E

their sermons, but these were felt to be rare men, who, in spite of their reading, were powerfully eloquent. Jonathan Edwards read, but Dr. Allen, his biographer, tells us that on the near view of death he declared his conviction that the parts of his sermons that were blest for the spiritual benefit of the hearers were the close and pointed applications, which were never read. Yea, moreover, he added, that if he had his ministry to begin again, he would throw aside his papers. The English (Established) Pulpit has at no time been a powerful one, inasmuch as the hierarchy has always encouraged the neat, and short, and "feckless" essay, "intoned" if you please; in preference to the *vivœ voces ab imo pectore* (living voices from the heart's depths). All the writers on the pastoral care, the Burnets, the Blairs, the Hills, the Gerards, and the Vinets and Spencers, of Europe and America, have been advocates of the unfettered style of delivery in the pulpit. Dr. Blair has wisely and correctly said that the dislike to papers in the pulpit, so strong among the people of Scotland, if a prejudice at all, is the most reasonable of all prejudices.

Three months after my ordination, I began to visit; the elder of the "Proportion," as it was called, always accompanied me. I could not have got on at all without him, and yet with him the work was by far the most difficult of all pastoral duties. The parish had seven thousand inhabitants, and of all denominations. Vast varieties of character behoved to be treated according to their phases. Men were shy of being familiarly and closely dealt with. I was young and inexperienced, often at a loss what to say or do, and withal, not over well furnished with the skill required in "rightly dividing the word of truth," and giving every one his portion of meat in due season, and hence I was tempted to become desultory in the work, a most fatal mistake. Visiting is the very life's blood of a successful ministry. If we don't go to the people they won't come to us. Difficulties in the work there undoubtedly will be, but they may be greatly modified or wholly removed by due discrimination, and by prudent and kindly measures. In a large town I have found the advantages of combining congregational with parochial visitation, and I never was charged with being a proselytizing intruder.

With regard to catechising, I generally attended to it in my pastoral visits, in so far as the young people and domestics were concerned, for I did not approve of exposing the ignorance of parents and seniors in the presence of juniors and children. I tried "public catechisings" on Sabbath evenings and they succeeded wonderfully; the discourses of the day were slightly reviewed, the "shorter catechism" explained in order, and occasionally a few of Whitecross's best anecdotes told. One of my elders, who generally attended on these occasions, once gave it as his opinion. " that one of those anecdotes was as good as a pinch of snuff." My " Bible classes " were always held weekly, and on week nights. They were well attended, and proved fine nurseries for the church. The Sabbath Schools in connection with our congregation, and under my immediate inspection, embraced upwards of a thousand young immortals, and when in Paisley, in 1857 and 1860, I witnessed the goodly gatherings of such under the faithful ministry which that much loved scene of my first labours still so largely enjoys.

A few extracts from Dr. Burns' letters of these years may be introduced. They touch on passing events, as well as reflect the " lights and shadows" of home life.

PAISLEY, Feb. 16, 1820.—We have our spring sacrament towards the end of April, immediately after which it will fall to me to open our own church, when my presence will be required for a few weeks at least, We have had a visit from Mr. Thomson, of St. George's, Edinburgh, last week, when he preached for me on Sabbath, and for the Sabbath Schools on Monday evening last. Collection £45 —very handsome, considering the state of our town, which, I regret to say, does not seem to be improving, either in a mercantile or moral view. His sermon was well fitted to rouse, and I trust it will have this effect. I have been attempting some improvements in the Sabbath

Schools of my own parish, somewhat on Dr. Chalmers' plan, and I anticipate good effects. We are also trying the plan of Female Bible Associations, with the immediate view of enabling the poor to supply themselves with the Word of God. More than this we cannot look for in present circumstances. We have been distributing largely to the wants of the poor, and still I fear we must do more. I am glad to hear that some efforts have been making with you for behoof of the ignorant and poor. When iniquity cometh in like a flood, then is the time for us to be lifting up a standard against it. We have too long neglected the mass of our people, who, in all our large towns, are not much removed from absolute heathenism. I am not certain if the late change with you will be very favourable to the cause of religion. Perhaps things have gone fully as well as could have been expected. The Dr. should try and keep his friend, the new Principal, right. I wish he may make as good a professor of divinity as of mathematics. I do not approve of the new plan adopted at Edinburgh, of ladies (especially young ladies) coming so prominently forward in the way of religious profession. As to the musical festivals, I am not a disinterested judge, as (in common with the strictest classes here) I attended on such occasions without even the suspicion of doing what was wrong. I do not know what they may be in Edinburgh; but the sacred oratorios we have had occasionally here, appeared to me to have a good tendency, and we were glad to find at least *one* species of relaxation or amusement which we could approve.

PAISLEY, JUNE 29, 1820.—I was at Irvine last Sabbath, introducing Mr. J. Wilson to his charge of that large and important station. Everything went on pleasantly, and he has been received with open arms. He is full of zeal and seriousness, and I trust he will have the wisdom which is necessary to direct in a place where anything prevails rather than true religion. It is a cold region, and their last two ministers were frigid. Mr. W. gave an excellent and suitable discourse on the angelic song, " Glory to God," &c., and my text in the forenoon was

Col. xxxi. 23, "Whatsoever ye do," &c., considered as the great principle of Christian and ministerial conduct. The church, which is large and elegant, was crowded with, it is thought, 2,500 people. It is pleasing to hear of the settlement of good men in important places.

It is a pity that political considerations should interfere in such matters. If James Brewster, who is truly a moderate man in politics, is to be objected to on this ground, I see not who could stand the test! I would object to G—n now on the ground of his low and satirical vein of writing, which does not recommend him, and must procure him many enemies.

There is likely to be a keen competition for the Moral Philosophy Chair in Edinburgh. Everyone who regards the interests of religion in the case, should support Mr. Esdaile, of Perth, who is well qualified, and very decided in his religious attachments. The other candidates are all hostile to religion, and not one of them at all equal to Mr. Esdaile in point of acquirements.

Our town is likely to be in a bustle for some time by the trials of the Radicals. The Lords arrive to-morrow, and the Grand Jury sit on Saturday. The place fixed on has been our *new church*. This, however, does not prevent our ordinary labours.

Our Sabbath Schools, we hope, are doing good, though not to the extent that might be expected. How are yours getting on? You ask me a question regarding female teachers. Lady Hope and her daughters regularly attend the Sabbath School at Carriden, and take part in the exercises, and here we have young ladies of high respect· ability who think it not beneath them. I never questioned the propriety of it, when conducted with prudence. As to the *place*, whether your own house or another, is of no great consequence. We were stirring up Anne and some other of the Boness ladies to it, and they are trying something. But my paper warns me to stop, and I must away to the examination of our public schools, which takes place to-day.

PAISLEY, March 17th, 1825.—Your Sabbath School Library is likely to do good. It is an agreeable exercise occasionally to catechise the children on what they have been reading, so as to see that they *do* read, and that they understand what they read. You say nothing about the settlement at Cupar. I fear it will not be popular, but I know nothing of the man. He is from a *cold* region, and recommended by those who will not put in a "wild man" if they can help it. They have got Campsie settled to their mind, and will get Greenock too. It is thought Row has also fallen into their hands. My only consolation under the idea of Mc. going to D—was the hope of a favourable change to the parish left. We are forming a society in Glasgow for sending good ministers to the North American colonies. Lord Dalhousie has embarked in it warmly, and has written me twice. Our general meeting is on the 31st, when he is to preside.

Miss A. recovered, to the surprise of all. Miss B. greatly worse, and no hope of her. She is in a most pleasing frame of mind, and her hopes are clearly built on the sure foundation. Mrs. P. rather better, but no prospect of recovery.

PAISLEY, April 22nd, 1825.—We are all, through divine kindness, in good health, and the fatiguing engagements of last week at Glasgow have not laid me up. What with the Sacramental season, the Synod, and half-a-dozen of public meetings, to say nothing of private calls, etc., my time was for eight days wholly occupied. One of my speeches (that on the Catholic claims) will probably reach your quarter soon in the shape of a small pamphlet. It was miserably reported in the *News*, and many friends applied to me to allow it to be published by itself, and to this I have consented; although it is no easy thing to recall an extemporaneous effusion, and that in the shape of a reply to what has been said by other speakers. The most agreeable of all our meetings were those of the different religious societies of Glasgow, which seem to be in a prosperous state. The spirit of zeal, and piety, and harmony which pervades the members, is one of the most pleasing symptoms of the state of religion at present, and the good done directly and indirectly is great. It gives us great pleasure to hear that Dr. Chalmers is exerting himself to promote a missionary spirit in St. Andrew's. My old friend, Dr. Codman, from Boston, U. S., told me that he had been at one of your monthly meetings, and was highly delighted. *These* are more pleasing scenes than the *college squabbles*, which I fear will do no good. The classes will be now nearly all up, and this will occasion an armistice or cessation of hostilities at least, but the elements are too uncongenial easily and readily to coalesce.

You may let Dr. C. know that his favourite overture on Theological education was carried by us—17 to 3—and the one on pluralities unanimously. Our Synod vote was 45 to 10—a most signal victory, considering the force that was brought in array against us. The party had corresponding members from Argyle, Lothian and Galloway to help them with speeches and notes, but they were sadly out-witted; indeed, some of their own packed men were so *cowed* they did not venture to vote at all. They are making *great efforts* to get a fierce moderate in St. Enoch's church, and I fear they will be too successful, as the people there like to have it so. Dr. C.'s successor at St. John's goes on nobly, and he and the agency are completely at one. By the way, one of his deacons, Mr. Wm. W. (of the house of Denniston, Buchanan & Co.), is to be married to our cousin, Susan A., on Tuesday first. I am engaged to officiate, and the young couple set off on a jaunt by St. Andrews. The Dr. has invited them to spend a day or two with him, and they expect to be there by Thursday. I mention this that you may have it in your power, at least, to call for them. The lad seems very pleasant, and the connection is every way agreeable to all parties. We had a visit of Islay lately, but his wife was unable to accompany him. He seems still to look towards the Fife-side, where some changes are contemplated.

A letter from George lately—Lord Dalhousie seems very friendly to him. I had a good deal of intercourse with his lordship when at the Canadian meeting last week, which was a very interesting one. He was in the chair, and gave a very good address, and seems very hearty in the cause. It will be of importance for G. to be in Scotland before Lord D. leaves it.

Anne's account of Mrs. Spence is still very dark. I mean to write Mrs. Coutts to-day or to-morrow. The Crossflat family have met with another shock in the death of a niece, Margaret Brown, aged 18, of consumption—a very promising girl. How affecting the changes!*

Though much in public life, my father was thoroughly domestic in his tastes. His heart was in his home. He was very fond of children, and, as a necessary consequence, they were very fond of him.

Our family circle was repeatedly broken in upon, and as one "who had seen affliction," he had to mourn "if I am bereaved of my children, I am bereaved." The last month of 1819 found him "in bitterness for a first-born," Agnes, an interesting girl of four; and within a month, on New Year's day of 1820, there was "another lily gathered." Soon after, another flower was "offered in the bud;" and in 1831, John, a most promising boy of ten was taken away.

He learned obedience by the things which he suffered and with the Master was able to succour, in that he himself

---

* His writing in most of the letters we have quoted, is remarkably good; though he had generally the reputation of being a very bad writer, he could, when he chose to take pains, write well. He wrote much and with exceeding haste. In a hurry one day he grasped a quill in its natural state, on which no knife had been exercised, and had scribbled off half a letter ere the mistake was discovered. Mr. David Wylie, of the Brockville *Recorder*, one of the fathers of the Canadian press, mentioned to me, that when a boy, serving his apprenticeship with Neilson & Hay, a well-known Paisley printing firm, he was sent to our house in St. George's Place, with the proof of one of my father's reports on Sabbath Schools, and one part of the MS. which the boy averred "nane o' them could mak' oot." Father was not at home. My mother (who blended with remarkable dignity a kindliness and homeliness which set every one at ease), meeting him with the pleasant smile which was her wont, and using the dialect he could best understand, replied: "Deed, laddie, I dinna wonner, for sometimes he canna' mak' it oot himsel'!"—ED.

had suffered. He was thus prepared, too, for our heaviest domestic trial, which was yet to come.

On Sabbath morning, the 14th December, 1841, after an illness of thirty hours, the desire of his eyes was taken away with a stroke. For twenty-eight years she had been his counsellor and comforter. She had always been in labours more abundant throughout the parish, and 1841 being one of Paisley's years of destitution, there came upon her daily the care of many poor women and children. She died on the field, almost a martyr to her self-sacrificing toil.

She was endowed with a comely and dignified personal presence, with rare good sense and admirable administrative ability, with the ornament of a meek and quiet spirit, with a piety sincere and unostentatious, but uncommonly practical in its outgoings, and a gently persuasive influence, which all who came within the circle of her acquaintance felt and acknowledged,—

> " She led me first to God ;
> Her prayers and tears were my young spirit's dew ;
> For when she used to leave the fireside every eve,
> I knew it was for prayer that she withdrew."

Many were the expressions of sympathy. Foremost and earliest of any beyond the circle of immediate relatives, was Dr. Chalmers, who two days after our sore sorrow, notwithstanding the pressure of professorial duty, just after the session had commenced, found time to write thus :—

"EDINBURGH, November 16th. 1841.

"MY DEAR SIR,—It is with real concern and heartfelt sympathy that I have been apprized of your heavy loss, and can enter into all that you must suffer under this affecting breach of the nearest

and dearest of all earthly relationships.   May the giver of all consolation bear you up under this sore bereavement, and grant that
on you may be fulfilled the saying of the Saviour (John xv. 2),
that if any branch bear fruit, the Father, our great Spiritual Husbandman, purgeth (pruneth) it, that it may bring forth more fruit.
It is truly marvellous, that with all the experimental demonstrations
we have of our mortality, a new death comes upon us with the
force and surprise of a new lesson, as if we had it yet to learn.
May we at length learn wisdom.   May we consider with effect our
latter end, and keep closer and more abidingly with Him, who alone
hath the gift of eternal life.   I take it very kind that you should
have sent an intimation, which makes me a partaker of the sorrows
of your heart.   It domesticates me with you and yours ; and it is
my earnest prayer in behalf of your afflicted family, that they may
all receive grace from on high, to become followers of them, who,
through faith and patience, are now inheriting the promises.

" Ever believe me, My Dear Sir,

" Yours with great regard,

THOMAS CHALMERS."

When that "elect lady," Mrs. Dr. Briggs, of St. Andrews, my father's sister, and the special friend, almost
biographer, of that mother in Israel, Mrs, Coutts, passed
to her rest and reward, there was found among her numerous papers, a lengthened correspondence of my sainted
mother, stretching over twenty years.   Because of the
light which they reflect on my father's private and domestic
character and history, and the love borne to her, whose
memory, as that of the just, is blessed, a few extracts
from these letters will not be unacceptable or inappropriate.

" INNERKIP, 24th July, 1817.

" Robert goes and comes as he finds it suits him.   He went up
last Saturday and will not be down again before Tuesday or Wednesday next, as the Lord's Supper is to be dispensed in his church
(and all the other churches in town) Sabbath first.   It was dispensed
in this place Sabbath last.   From the account you give of the communion in St. Andrew's, I suppose things went on much in the
same melancholy state here as with you.   The external decency
and order, great indeed ; but the heart appeared little engaged in
the service.

" Your brother preached all the fast day here, and I may say I never saw a more attentive congregation. They appeared afraid to lose one word. They are all enquiring when he is to preach again, for they never were better pleased with any minister. God willing, he is to preach here again Sabbath fortnight. Pray for the blessing of God on his labours, and Oh may there be a stirring among the dry bones."

" PAISLEY, April 17th, 1818.

" By this time you will have read Robert's letter to Dr. Chalmers. You must write me soon, and give me your candid opinion of it, and also that of the doctor, and the good folks at St. Andrews. In the west it has given general satisfaction. It is said the Dr. will soon be in the press again in answer to it. We have just been reading the life of Dr. Erskine, with which we are much pleased. It gives a great deal of information concerning the state of literature and religion in the time in which he lived."

" PAISLEY, 30th March, 1819.

" Mother is much comforted by Robert's prayers and conversation, as is my afflicted father. Robert is much with them. May the Lord send an answer of peace to his prayers.

" Robert and Agnes continue to enjoy great good health. The former has been kept very busy this winter with his book.* The second edition is going on fast, and will be out by the first of May. According to your order, he will s nd you four (4) copies of it. What think you of George in the press?—with both a volume of sermons and one of lectures? He seems well and happy, and I hope useful."

" PAISLEY, 13th December, 1820.

" It gave me great pleasure to hear the professorship was at an end. I hope there shall be no more of it. I would assuredly rather live on three hundred a year in this quarter than on three hundred and fifty at St. Andrews. Robert, also, has no great desire for such a change, and to give up preaching, and sit and hear such cold orthodoxy as you mention you have from your pulpits, is what he never could think it his duty to do, but he feels much obliged to your good Dr. and you for your interest in him. Robert and I are both in good health, which we desire to be thankful for. The return of this season we feel very painful, but our dear little ones, which were suffering so much this time last year, are now where suffering and sorrow cannot enter, for I am convinced they are in glory, therefore, if we felt aright, instead of wishing them back to this world of sin and sorrow, we would rejoice that they had gone to our Father in Heaven. Oh may we have the sanctified use of all our trials.

---

* His work on the Poor.

"We have just been reading Dr. Chalmers' volume of Commercial Sermons, and are truly delighted with them. All may derive benefit from them, but they are calculated to be very useful among a particular class. It is astonishing the knowledge of human nature he shows—he is surely raised up for some great purpose. May the blessing of God attend the reading of them to thousands, for it is only that which can bring them home to the consciences of men. We have not seen *No Fiction*—from what you say of it we are anxious to read it. We have been reading a life of Dr. Owen, by Mr. Orme, of Perth, which is really interesting, and introduces you to many great and good men before little known. But it is evident throughout that his great design is to exalt the Independents. It is a pity he shows himself so sectarian. Nevertheless, we were much pleased with the perusal of it. We shall be looking for William some day soon. I hope he will have pleasure in his visit to his intended flock."

"PAISLEY, March 13th, 1822.

" Our valuable friend, Miss Park, was seized with apoplexy about three weeks ago. She lived for eight days after the shock. She was often sensible during that time. Her faith was strong and lively whenever the stupor left her for a little. Robert saw her every day—he experienced much pleasure in his visits. Her affection to him was very sincere, for she always said that his preaching and conversation had been made very useful to her soul. Her conduct had been so consistent ever since she professed Christianity."

" 1st March, 1830.

" Robert left me on Friday for Kilsyth (yesterday being their Communion Sabbath). He was then in great health, and has been so since his return from Ireland. He has been lecturing for twelve months past in the Revelation. I am the voice of many when I say that his course of lectures on that interesting but difficult portion of the Word of God, has been particularly interesting and I hope profitable. He has reached the length of the 19th chapter. I am astonished how he gets on, for what with the business of the parish societies of various kinds, supplying and correcting the press, etc., etc., he is constantly busy, but he would not be happy otherwise.

"The Lord's Supper (God willing) is to be dispensed here on Sabbath eight-days. Let us have your *prayers* that there may be an outpouring of the Spirit, so that it may be a time of great refreshing from the presence of the Lord. Your brother's help are Mr. Smith, of St. George's; Mr. Welsh, of St. David's, on the Fast-day; Mr. Henderson, of Carmunnock, on Saturday; and Dr. Barr, of Port Glasgow, on Sabbath evening. They are all excellent preachers.

"5th February, 1835.

"Your brother has been absent since last Monday eight-days, on the North American Colonial Society's business. He was to preach at Perth last Sabbath. I do not know when at Dundee, whether he would have time to take a run your length; he was to be at Brechin on Tuesday, and in the course of this week he was to visit Montrose, Arbroath, and Aberdeen. I feel a little anxious about him after such a severe illness as that which he had so lately in Glasgow. I expect him home on Saturday. I have just received a letter this moment from him dated Brechin. He says he is in excellent health, and found Anne and the Manse folk all very well. Part of the letter is dated Montrose, where Mr. James and he had gone to dine yesterday, and to have a meeting in the evening. They were to return the same night to Brechin. He meets our friend Mr. McNaughton at Perth, where they are to have a public meeting this evening. You would observe by the newspapers that Mr. McN. is out on the same labour of love. Our dear boys are very well and busy with the schools."

"12th August, 1837.

"Your brother was called to London very unexpectedly, to plead the cause of our poor operatives. I hope they will be successful. Our worthy females are suffering very much, The Fund only extends to those who work at the deepening of the river, or breaking of stones, &c. I have distributed from £50 to £60 in a quiet way among our respectable females, who, I believe, would almost starve before they would apply for help."

Dr. Burns' sympathy with missionary enterprise was intense. His large parish furnished ample scope for schemes of moral excavation; such as of late years have become increasingly common in the cities and towns of Scotland. A faithful visitor himself, he had the faculty of systematizing the work, and of infecting others with somewhat of his own enthusiasm, so that when, in many a Black Sea of sin, as a fisher of men, he said, " I go a fishing," they were induced by his energetic will and active example to say, " We also go with thee."

The South Church was the fruit of earnest toil in a destitute section of the parish. From it again sprang the Free South, which, under the indefatigable pastorate of the Rev. A. Pollock, once one of his young men, a singularly efficient co-worker, has become one of the most thoroughly equipped churches in Paisley.   He maintained regularly the goodly practice of preaching to the young, and the mammoth gatherings of children in Old St. George's were seasons to be remembered.   The Sabbath afternoon diets of examination were also of signal benefit.

In the Sabbath School Unions of the town, both denominational and general, he took a prominent part.

Tract Societies received his countenance and aid.   The *Monitor* and *Visitor*, and other kindred tract serials, were as "leaven which a woman hid."   Not a few such women were furnished by him for the work.

For some twenty years he was Secretary of the Paisley and East Renfrewshire Bible Society, whose first meeting was held in the Old Low Church.

Within six months after the formation of the London Missionary Society, an auxiliary branch was formed in Paisley.   The movement started in March, 1796, the very year when the General Assembly of the Scottish Church threw the weight of its influence into the anti-missionary scale.

The original records of this fruitful Branch are before us, and reveal the pains and the prayers with which it was conducted.   Large sums were raised:—in one year, about £1,000 sterling.   Four months after his settlement, on the 4th November, 1811, Dr. Burns became Secretary of this Society, and continued so for many years.   He preached one of the annual sermons of the parent institution in London; and those missionary marvels, which have emblazoned its history, and re-produced in Asia and Africa, in the South Seas and Madagascar, the triumphs of Apostolic times, ever excited his gladness and gratitude. In the mission of Dr. Duff he felt a peculiar interest, and no heart beat more responsive than his to the thrill which ran through fatherland on the first return of that prince of missionaries from India. Subsequently in the new world, the intimacy of the old was revived.

When John Macdonald, the son of the Apostle of the North, having been loosed from his important charge in London, that he might go back with Dr. Duff, was designated to his distant field on the 8th May, 1837, the charge to the missionary, the full notes of which we have in our possession, was delivered by Dr. Burns. We have also a letter of twenty-four pages addressed to him by one of the most useful of the missionaries of the London Missionary Society in India, who was once a member of St. George's and married another, and who gratefully ascribes to his Paisley pastor much of the formation of his Christian character, and the first impulse he received to the missionary work. He was one of many whom my Father was instrumental in influencing in a kindred way.

With reference to the success of his Paisley ministry, many testimonies might be given. A thoroughly competent witness says :—

" He owed a deep debt of gratitude to his venerable friend, Dr. Burns, for his valuable instructions to him as a youth, and also in after life, and he regarded him as his spiritual father. He looked back with grateful remembrance to his attendance for a period of twelve years, at the Doctor's Thursday evening class, and to the great interest he felt, when a youth, in his minister's expositions of Scripture, in what was called his forenoon lectures. Dr. Burns, as a lecturer, stood unrivalled in the West of Scotland, his success arising, he believed, from his extensive reading, his wonderful memory, and his great readiness in recalling on all occasions whatever he had seen, read, or heard. The Doctor's language was clear, plain, pointed, vigorous, and terse, and pregnant with meaning. He never knew any man possessing such a wonderful memory, not for great matters only, but for the most trivial, as Dr. Burns. He remembered of taking supper in the house of Mrs. White, with him and the late Dr. Fletcher, of London—Mrs. White's brother—who had that evening, some thirty-six years ago, preached in the High Church. During supper they had a pleasant conversation (the doctor possessing at all times great conversational powers), and, looking around him, he (the doctor) said to Mrs. White, 'Did not the Rev. Mr. Smart live in this house ?' ' O yes,' was the answer, 'eighteen or twenty years ago.' 'Well,' said the doctor, 'I remember dining in this very room with Dr. Waugh, of London, and I remember it from the walls being painted green.'"

The following is from the *Free Church Record* for December, 1869 :—

" His ministry in Paisley, from the first, was extremely acceptable ; so much so, that a new church had soon to be provided of larger dimensions, and of a more modern style of architecture, for his over-crowded congregation, to which, accordingly, under the name of 'St. George's,' he and they, a few years afterwards, removed. His early popularity, doubtless, was due, in some measure, to his youth and youthful appearance, associated, as these were, with an almost premature ripeness and mellowness of theology—with an 'unction' which in those days was rare, and with a fluency which was never known to fail him ; but the position which he took as a preacher from the beginning he maintained ever after. There were solid qualities in his discourses which made them always instructive, often *telling* in a high degree. They were solid, without being heavy ; they were copious, and yet clear ; they were level to the humblest, yet such as to command the ear of the most cultivated among his hearers ; while, as a lecturer and expositor of Scripture, he had the reputation in the West of Scotland of being 'unrivalled.' One of his oldest surviving parishioners says of him : ' He was a model parish minister, visiting not only his own congregation (1,200 strong), but his parish, once a year, most regularly attending on the sick, and taking a special oversight of the godly upbringing of the young. He was a most valuable citizen, and there was not a religious, benevolent, or philanthropic movement in town, but he was to be found at the beginning, middle, or end of it. He was one of the original promoters of the scheme for supplying the town with water ; and by successive visits to London and otherwise, did great service in bringing in large sums of money during the periods of the depression of trade, when weaving was the staple branch of manufacture in town.' His capacity for work of all sorts was indeed something marvellous. A day in his life was like a week to any other man. We have heard of his composing two discourses, visiting a whole list of sick people, and having time for a constitutional walk, over and above, on a Saturday ; yet those discourses bearing no marks of haste or slovenliness when delivered, without the assistance of a note, on the Sabbath following. Nor less active was he with the pen than with his tongue, taking part more or less prominently in every question of interest which stirred the public mind."

Soon after his settlement in Paisley there came to him from the quiet manse, where he had spent a year and a half so happily, such cordial greetings as follow. Because of the light it sheds on his opening ministry, the freshness and fragrance of its heart-breathings, and the fine specimen it supplies of letter-writing from a father in Israel to his son in the faith, we think our readers will not grudge the space this communication from the "old disciple" at Cramond fills.

"26th November, 1811.

"MY VERY DEAR BROTHER,—I was much gratified and rejoiced at receiving some time ago, your affectionate and comfortable letter, and would have answered it before now, had not severe distress prevented me. But oh, my dear brother, I rejoice to inform you that my mind was most comfortable amidst all the gloomy prospect of leaving my flock and dear family and friends. The everlasting Gospel, the all fulness of Jesus and the hope of glory, were brought delightfully to view, and yielded both peace and joy in believing. I am truly happy that you like Paisley so much. I have all along thought it was a situation quite suited to your sentiments, talents, activity and Christian habits, and I trust you will be long spared to a people who prize the pure Gospel, at least as much as any town in Scotland. I really admire your plan of discourses on the leading parts of our glorious Lord's history ; you will find these discourses of great use to you afterwards, on many subjects ; you do not mention if you have yet begun a regular course of lecturing. It is difficult to determine where to begin ; worthy Dr. Gillies used to tell me that he was called to Glasgow when a young man and soon after being licensed, and he had very few lectures ; that very soon after his settlement he began to lecture through the New Testament, and when I knew him he had lectured over the whole Scriptures and was going a second time through the New Testament.

F

" You hint at being in this part of the country ere long ; all here will be rejoiced to see you, and I beg you will lay your account with spending a night or two with us—make this your home ; if you can so arrange matters, as to give us a Sabbath-day's supply, I need not tell you what a gratification it would be to us and to all our parish. Mr. Mackellar preached here last Sabbath, and was universally admired ; he will be a great acquisition to your country side, but I suspect he will remain a very short time at Carmunnock. We have not seen your brother, Mr. George, this very long time. Your old acquaintance, Mr. Glen, is doing exceedingly well ; had he not been previously engaged for Mr. McLean, of Dumfermline, I would have asked him here for a month or two. This is the first letter I have written since being laid up, and therefore must make it short. You have my earnest prayers for your success and happiness in the most honourable of all employments, that you may have many seals of your ministry, and may long continue a burning light in our Zion, full of holy zeal, and a shining light exemplary to all around. If you be a member of the General Assembly next year, and if I am still a sojourner in this weary wilderness, will you have the kindness 'to' allot a Sabbath-day's services to your old friends at Cramond. Nowhere can they be more prized. Dear brother, pray much for me, that I may not be doomed to be a useless cumberer in the vineyard. Grace, peace to you daily.

"ARCHIBALD BONAR."

CHAPTER V.

CHURCH COURTS AND SOCIETIES.

AS regards our Presbytery, a portly member of it gave me this precious information just before I joined it—" My elder and I hold the balance between the two parties." I dare say he was nearly right. At all events, we were in the habit of saying there were "three parties" in the Presbytery of Paisley. There was the "Moderate Party," and the "Popular Party," or "Wild Men," as they were called, and there was Mr. Fleming, a sort of unique character, whose bizarre movements could be kept under no rule. As a "party," *per se*, its dimensions were tolerably large, and its pretensions still larger. In the course of a few years we got amongst us another unique "party," in one of the ministers of the Abbey parish, a man of fine talents grievously misapplied; but he, most happily for the common peace around, went off from the old toryism, or conservatism as it is now politely called, and waged the "havocs of war" against the other son of Mars, who was "tory" to the bone. Many disreputable scenes of clerical antagonism would meet the eyes of "calm observers ;" and yet, after all, we had no *heretics*, in the ordinary sense, amongst us. All professed strict adherence to the standards, though some were suspected of being "broad churchmen;" thus proving the truth of an important matter of fact, that personal godliness may be at a low ebb when speculative orthodoxy shews no change. I think that during all my time we kept a majority of "right men," for the town of Paisley has, ever since its separation ecclesiastically from the Abbey, in 1720, been a stronghold of evangelical truth.

It may not be generally known that to our Paisley Presbytery the Free Church was indebted for its father, both in years and in ecclesiastical position. The Rev. George Logan, a native of Glasgow, and born in 1760, was a licentiate of our presbytery, and though ordained by the Presbytery of Perth to a Scotch church in Newcastle, where he also superintended a private classical academy, he was brought back to our bounds, in 1802, as minister of the Parish of Eastwood, where he laboured successfully for forty-one years. On the second Sabbath of July, 1843, he was gathered to his fathers, in the eighty-fourth year of his age, and the fifty-eighth of his ministry, the venerable patriarch of that church which he had so long adorned, and the achievement of whose freedom he had just lived to witness. A first-rate classical scholar, one of his favourite recreations was the perusal of the standard writers of Greece and Rome ; and, unlike the generality of parochial ministers, he not only preserved but augmented his literary stores. His mind was also characterized by a native quickness of perception, and he had always at command a fund of amusing anecdotes, with which he entertained the circles of his friends. On the settlement in Glasgow of that very eminent and distinguished minister, the late Dr. Balfour, of the Outer High Church, Mr. Logan was introduced to his favourable notice, and this introduction was always cited by him as one of the happiest events of his life. Dr. Balfour discerned his worth, encouraged him in his professional pursuits, and, till the period of his lamented death in 1818, acted to him the part of a faithful councillor and a most valuable friend. With other two venerable ministers of that city he was also associated in the bonds of affectionate endearment—the late Dr. Burns, of the Barony, and Dr. Love, of Anderston. These were all men of kindred minds, though marked by characteristic varieties. Mr. Logan knew the value of such acquaintanceship, and in the vale of years his heart was often cheered and refreshed by the recollections of other times; while his younger friends recognized in him one of the few remaining links which connect the present generation of pastors with those venerable men who have gone before. In a theological and literary society which was instituted by the evangelical ministers of the bounds, Mr. Logan was always at home on the Epistles to the Romans and the Hebrews, and his ready humour was always at command to lighten the sober gravity of lengthened argument. It need not excite any surprise that such a man joined heartily in the crusade against intrusion, and readily cast in his lot with the men who resolved to sacrifice their all for the sake of a conscience void of offence. In the beginning of April, 1843, and thereafter early in June, I paid him a visit when he lay on that bed of sickness which was soon to be the bed of death. On both occasions we touched considerably on the points in debate, and I found him on both occasions alike clear and decided. The only thing that vexed him on the second occasion was that the "Deed of Separation" had, by some oversight, not been sent to him, that on his couch, and within sight of glory, he might have affixed to it his signature. His removal so soon, was not anticipated by any one. But there was a marked grandeur in the scene which the chamber of the dying pastor did exhibit a very few weeks before his death. With perfect collectedness on his part, we joined in devotional exercises, surrounded by the family circle. Thereafter I witnessed the dying patriarch settling the time and the manner of his "leaving the manse," endeared by so many tender associations. I wish Sir James Graham and the other cabinet ministers of an earthly monarch had beheld the solemn scene. But the ministering angels of a heavenly King were hovering near, and sooner than any of us had anticipated did they receive their commission to translate his disembodied spirit to " an house not made with hands, eternal in the heavens."

The brother who went with me to the dying bed of our aged friend was the Rev. Duncan Macfarlane, D.D., of Renfrew, another of our co-presbyters, whose name deserves respectful record. We met by appointment of the lately constituted Free Presbytery of the bounds, with a special commission to convey the best wishes and sympathies of the brethren, long "one," but now joined in a still more emphatic oneness of principle and of trial. Of that noble-minded minister, who ministered where Mr. Patrick Simson in other days lived and laboured and died, a faithful record has been published by another co-presbyter, Dr. Robert Smith, of Lochwinnoch, at whose ordination I presided in 1815, and who lately finished his course after a ministry which stretched through the chequered scenes of upwards of half a century. Dr. Macfarlane was much younger than either Dr. Smith or I, but he was ripe in learning and in rich spiritual experience, a divine of the best school, and a Hebrew scholar whom Thomas Boston would have hailed with eagerness as a " fit and proper man" to help him in his perplexing warfare about the Hebrew " points and accents." Such men are blessings in their day, but they are "not suffered to remain by reason of death."

During my incumbency at Paisley, from 1811 to 1845, a considerable number of eminently excellent and success-ful ministers lived and died, and I cherish the clear remem-brance of them with fond respect. Dr. John Findlay, of the High Church of Paisley for nearly forty years, was characterized by perspicuity of thought and language; placid but earnest appeals to all shades of hearers; pointedness of preceptive announcement: faithfulness in the pastoral care ; and upright and unswerving sincerity of daily walk. Mr. Rankin, of the Middle Church, who succeeded in 1797, Dr. John Snodgrass, a man who ranks well with the "First Three" in the camp of Israel, laboured among his people with great meekness and unassuming faithfulness for upwards of forty years, leaving a character without reproach, and not a few, both old and young, ready to garnish his resting place with flowers. Dr. Andrew Stewart, of Erskine, allied to the peerage by marriage, was in every way a noble man in acuteness of mind and breadth of intellectual vision ; and Dr. Robert Stewart, of Leghorn, is the worthy son of such a father. Prior to the disjunction of Greenock from Paisley we had amongst us Dr. Scott, of the Mid Church there, "a master in Israel" for rare accomplishments, for an admirably furnished and arranged mind, and a practical zeal in the pastorship truly primitive and apostolic. And let us not forget the man who with noble Christian heroism dashed from his lips the fullest cup that Scotland's church could show, when the tasting of it would have involved a sacrifice of conscience more precious than all the gold of India. I mean Dr. P. Macfarlane, of the West Kirk, Greenock. I can only name Dr. Boog, of the Abbey; Dr. Monteith, of Houston; Mr. Douglas, of Kilbarchan; Mr. Telfer, of Johnstown; Dr. McNair, of the Abbey; and others of my earlier or later acquaintanceship whose memory is fragrant, and with whom, in times long gone by, I have had intercourse more or less close, but ever friendly and free. And can I forget in this connexion the pleasure I felt in committing the care of my flock in Paisley to the ability, the piety, and the pastoral diligence of my excellent successor, Mr. Thomson, whom, may the Great Shepherd long spare !

The first General Assembly where I was present as a member was in 1813, when the plurality question came on in the case of Kilconquhar and Dr. Ferrie, and I doubt not that had either Thomson or Chalmers been present on that occasion, in place of our losing it by the small majority of five, we would have decidedly carried the day. But still a blow was struck on that occasion which proved,

by anticipation, fatal to the claims of non-resident plural-
ism ever after. It was in 1817 that a cause from the
Synod of Merse came up to the Assembly, in which the
question of calls and of patronage was directly involved.
Thomson appeared at the bar on the popular side, in his
capacity of a corresponding member from the Synod of
Lothian and Tweeddale to that of Annan and Teviotdale.
Most fully did he enter into the history of patronage and
of the " call," and vindicated, by appeal to many prece-
dents, the inherent power of the church to refuse a settlement on the simple ground of " no call." Graphically did
he describe the miserable substitute which moderatism
had put in the room of the effective substantial " call" of
former days; and on referring to the mode of expression
used regarding it by Principal Hill, in his "View of the
Consolidation of the Church of Scotland"—"*a paper named
a Call*"—the Principal, who was present, rose with indignation, and called the speaker to account for putting such
language into his mouth. Dr. Thomson handed to him
his own volume; and on examining the passage and finding the speaker perfectly correct, acknowledged politely
his mistake, and with a very hearty laugh returned him the
volume. This incident, though in one sense trifling, spoke
volumes. It was one of the straws which, when thrown
up, indicate how the wind blows. Even in 1817 we lost
the cause only by a small majority; the tide, which had
set in in 1810, continued to roll in the right direction.

In 1824 and 1825 the plurality question was again discussed, and although the decisions went against the friends
of reform, the pleadings of Thomson and of others like-
minded told with tremendous effect on a cause that had
been sinking for years. Then also the independency of the
church was nobly vindicated, though by a small majority
of eight, in the question of Gaelic preaching as essential in
the Parish of Little Dunkeld.* In the meantime, movements were going on in various directions in favour of
popular rights in the election of parochial ministers. A

* Little Dunkeld (said Andrew Thomson) is the mouth of the Highlands, and ought
certainly to have a Gaelic tongue in it.—Ed.

"Society for improving the system of Church Patronage" had been formed, and both Dr. McCrie and Dr. Andrew Thomson had patronized it; but they both moved simultaneously in the way of a "further advance," and came out on many occasions, both in church courts and in private voluntary associations.

In the course of the year 1836 circumstances of a very painful nature occurred which had the effect of introducing elements of discord and disunion among leading members of the evangelical branch of the church, and the causes of these painful results were not finally removed for a period of four years.

The whole soul of Dr. Chalmers being set on the plan of church extension, it was not to be wondered at that any man of power and influence who took a side antagonistic to his could be looked on by him with any friendly feeling. Dr. Lee, from some cause or other, had placed himself in this position, and when the idea was mooted by the friends of the evangelical cause that he should be elected as Moderator of the Assembly, Dr. Chalmers firmly opposed it, and by a triumphant majority (for all the moderates joined in it) carried the day for Dr. Gardner rather than Dr. Lee. Had this formed the main element in the dispute, it would have been easily and speedily rectified and removed; but there had arisen nearly at the same time in the minds of certain ministers of the evangelical party in the church a fancy that some new plan for electing a moderator should be proposed, and it was seriously suggested that the junta of old moderators who had for a long time assumed the right of nomination should continue to act as they had done, only with the understanding that a candidate for the chair should be named by them from each of the parties in the church alternately. To this the more ardent and conscientious members could not agree. They held that "Moderatism" was, in fact, corruption in the church, that the system so called had for nearly a century been the grand supporter of patronage in its most rigid form, and with all its real or supposed abuses ; and that now, when the evangelical party had gained the ascendancy, it would be absolute folly in them to surrender their vantage ground and play into the hands of their deadly foe. A good deal of pretty smart controversy on this matter arose, partly in newspapers and partly in fugitive pamphlets. It so happened that, from some cause or other which has entirely escaped me, I became one of the combatants on the high side, as it was called, embracing mainly such as were the avowed and earnest advocates for the abolition of patronage. A lay friend of mine, to whom I ever felt a strong attachment, Mr. J. S. More, Professor of Scots Law in the University of Edinburgh, was my principal correspondent on the occasion, and a few sentences from one of his letters may shew the bearing of the controversy :—

"The question has now assumed a more serious aspect than it formerly did, and after the contemptuous and reproachful manner in which Dr. —— speaks of the 'Wild Men,' a very important interest has been attached to this question which it did not formerly possess. I am convinced that the prosperity and welfare of the church depend entirely on that vital Christianity which he stigmatized as 'wildness,' and that his plan of openly and avowedly recognizing no difference in our church courts between the conscientious men whom he calls 'wild,' and the thoughtless men whom he calls 'moderate,' is one of the greatest delusions, and would prove one of the sorest mischiefs which could be inflicted on our church."

Our opinion was in favour of the election of Dr. Lee to the chair, not at all on the notion that he was either an anti-patronage man or an earnest advocate of evangelical truth, but simply that he was a man of independent views, and one of the very few of any eminence that were so ; and we wanted effectually to break the chain of caste which had so long bound us all; and it did not appear to us that however we might regret the opinions of Dr. Lee on church extension, they were of such a kind as to preclude his being called to the chair. Dr. Hanna has given a full account of the painful *personalities* of the case in his "Life of Dr. Chalmers." With these, we, living at a distance from Edinburgh, had little to do, but we all grieved to read or hear of them ; and we rejoiced exceedingly when Mr. Charles Brown and other friends succeeded in applying a healing restorative.

The "Clerical Literary Society" of Glasgow was an association of clergymen of the Church of Scotland belonging to the city and to the country districts around, who met once a month during the greater part of the year, for the purpose of mutual improvement, particularly in the literature of theology. It owed its existence mainly to the efforts of Dr. MacGill, of the Tron Church; afterwards Professor of Divinity in the University. On his induction to the pastoral charge in the city, it occurred to him that amid the varied and laborious duties of the pastorship in a large community there was some danger of ministers losing their studious and classical habits; and the idea occurred to him that occasional meetings of the brethren for reading of essays, or for exercises of Biblical criticism, in the departments both of Greek and of Hebrew; friendly advice, literary conversation, and consultation on questions of mutual interest, might be useful in cherishing the academic spirit, and enabling clergymen to keep abreast of the age as regards the departments of literature and science. The idea was soon taken up by a respectable number of the brethren in the city and neighbourhood, and it was efficiently acted on for many years, and while subjects of a theological character were always kept prominent, each member was expected to give in turn some account of his topics of discussion in the pulpit during the intervals of meeting, and to submit questions of casuistry for consultation and advice. Nay, more, if any member had the daring courage to "put out" from the press a work of any magnitude, he was expected to lay some specimens of it before us for criticism and suggestion. In this way certain of the works of Dr. Chalmers, of Dr. MacGill, of Dr. Robertson of Cambuslang, of Dr. Hamilton of Strathblane, and of the writer of these memorials were inspected and judged of at their "first throwing up" by their appointed "Lords of the Articles."

As might have been expected, the labour of "tugging the oar," in this as in other departments, lay mainly with the popular or evangelical clergy; and yet we had always an agreeable minority of respectable moderates. At the time of my joining it, in the end of 1811, I found among the membership such men as Dr. Cooper, Professor of Astronomy in the University; Dr. Maclatchie, of Mearns, the early preceptor of John Wilson; and Dr. Gibb, then of St. Andrew's Church, afterwards Professor of Oriental Languages in the College. Party questions, if brought in at all, which was very seldom, were never discussed in an exclusive or sectarian spirit; and the meetings ever helped to cherish a friendly spirit among the members, and were cheered and crowned by a somewhat substantial, convivial repast at the close of each annual session. I was a member of a similar society in our own presbytery, the members of which met at each other's houses once a month; and the wives and families at the manse always regarded their meetings as pleasant interludes. Not a few of the "Essays and Dialogues" which figure in the annals of this friendly club adorn the pages of the *Edinburgh Christian Instructor*, from 1824 down to 1840, when that effective journal, associated as it was with the name of Dr. Andrew Thomson, closed its career.

The benefit of such self-constituted schools of literature and theology was largely felt by all who took a part in their healthful maintenance. My own case affords an apt enough illustration of this. In 1823 the chair of Moral Philosophy in the united College of St. Leonard's and St. Salvator at St. Andrew's fell vacant, and my friends in the locality of the college asked me to become a candidate for the chair. Nothing could be more preposterous than the proposal of taking a minister from the large manufacturing town of Paisley to be an active member of an academic corps. The habits and whole spirit of such a position as this, appeared to be altogether opposed to the duties and responsibilities of a college gownsman. There could be no question about it; bnt on the other hand, my *confrères*, in those humble haunts of literature which I have described, knew full well that I had been a most regular attendant on the exercises of those associations, and they had heard, and criticised too, my repeated lectures on such subjects as "the theory of morals," "the argument a priori," and such like. I had not yet reached my maturity, and such competent judges as Dr. Chalmers, Dr. MacGill, Dr. Gibb, Professor Jardine, and Dr. Scott, of Greenock, Dr. Andrew Stewart, of Erskine, and others certified me as amply qualified to occupy successfully an ethical chair. Other independent testimony was brought forward in my favour, and my own brother-in-law, Professor Briggs, was himself one of the electors. In one word, my chance of success was pretty fair, and the matter seemed to run betwixt my claims and those of an able and worthy man, lately deceased, Dr. Fleming, then the minister of old Kilpatrick, afterwards the successor of Professor Mylne in the Moral Philosophy chair at Glasgow. Of the very friendly feelings of Dr. Chalmers I had not the smallest doubt, and my intercourse with him on the subject of the approaching election was friendly and frequent. Some little circumstances conspired to produce on my mind the notion that overtures had been made to the great man himself, and that he indeed was in the eye of Principal Nicol, and certain of his colleagues, in the Senatus. On hinting my suspicions to a mutual friend, Mr. William Collins, the excellent Christian bookseller in Glasgow, he turned on me with vehemence, saying eagerly, " Do you mean to insult him, sir ?" So very unlikely did the thing seem of Dr. Chalmers leaving the high vantage-ground of Glasgow for the literary solitude of St. Andrew's, that the very idea was repelled with indignation. Did I feel disappointed in the unlooked-for issue of the contest? Assuredly I would, had some old worn-out moderate been chosen, or it may be some "broad" sceptical sciolist; but my highest, if not my exclusive, wish was—and all my best friends participated with me in it—that a larger measure of the "*sal evangelicum*" might be thrown into the academic waters, and that the heights of Parnassus and of Helicon might not be ever and only climbed by the haters of Carmel and of Zion. Circumstances in my position lent me a sort of " pull" for the place ; and there was no fear of Paisley being filled by a "right man." Still, I was aware that many of my most pious friends and fellow-labourers had very serious doubts as to the propriety of my leaving a spiritual charge so important, and offering myself a candidate for what seemed a purely secular office. It was not easy for me to vindicate my conduct in the case without seeming to indicate by doing so a somewhat conceited idea of perhaps thinking myself fitted to be of some service to the ineffably important cause of spiritual religion as deeply involved in right theological and college training. But in addition to the pleadings of some most competent judges, I was sometimes gratified by receiving encouragement from quarters where it was least expected. One evening, at a meeting of our Sabbath-school directors, on the subject being mooted, John Cairns, an elder of the West Relief congregation, and a fine specimen of a class that was fast passing away—the well-conditioned and respectable Paisley weaver —put in his word, to the effect that he was a native of St. Andrews, knew well the state of sentiment and of feeling among the teachers and students of that college, and that nothing was more to be desired than a change from the cold and withered sterility of moderatism to the genial influence of evangelical truth. He approved highly of the movement I had made, and recommended to my people a cheerful concurrence. Forty-five years have rolled away since the time referred to, and still I recollect well the feeling of satisfaction which the unlooked-for testimony of this plain unlettered tradesman, connected as he was with another communion, afforded me; and now, looking back through the vista of years, the contest referred to does not violently disquiet my conscience.

Political reform and the "popular party" were then rising into strength and form. But still the moderate ranks were strong, and the favourite haunts of the party were strongholds. I belonged to the "wild party," as it was called, and not the tamest of the "wild;" and St. Andrew's had long been the "lion's den" of moderatism. The case required caution, and some skill in tactics. Circumstances connected with the political aspect of the times brought to my side some "men in power," whose good opinion was not to be despised; and a few of the least "fierce" moderates befriended me. But "our men," i.e. those of the more marked and decided character, prudently lay by, and quietly watched their opportunity of service. Andrew Thomson, indeed, said that we had "tied up his hands too much," for he was ready to work if we had let him. "The use of terror" he had largely at command; but we were jealous of that, and preferred a quieter move: and he certainly proved himself a kind friend, for he not only gave advice which was invaluable, but he brought the matter under the notice of Sir Henry Moncrieff, whose favourable opinion of any one Principal Nicol well knew how to appreciate, and well did I know the value of the friendship of such a man as Sir Henry. He examined my credentials, weighed the case impartially, and gave his best advice. In ordinary circumstances I would, in all likelihood, have been the successful candidate. As things turned out, Glasgow and the west of Scotland were covered for a season with a saddening funeral pall; but the accession of Chalmers, first to St. Andrew's and thereafter to Edinburgh, were great turning points in the wheel of Providence.

The apparent crossing of his path by Dr. Chalmers caused no interruption of their friendly relations. These had commenced soon after the Doctor's settlement in Glasgow, and continued till his death. It was on the 21st of July, 1815, Dr. Chalmers was inducted into the Tron Church. Two months thereafter the following response came to an application from the Paisley pastor.

"GLASGOW, Sept. 26th, 1815.
" Rev. Mr. Burns,

" MY DEAR SIR,—I trust the time is coming when I shall be able to satisfy my friends with such assistance as they may demand, but that time has not yet arrived. I feel that ever since my arrival at Glasgow, I have been pressing so hard upon the limits of my strength, that I cannot go beyond the regular line of my exertions without doing a positive and serious injury to my constitution. In these circumstances, I have been under the necessity of refusing a number of home applications for sermons ; and, feeling as I do, that any spare strength I have should be directed in the first instance to the objects which are immediately around me, I am not at liberty to listen to any foreign applications but such as I consider a return for sacramental services. Do, therefore, indulge me in declining the request with which you have honoured me. I take your visits to me very kind, and trust I may soon return them. I hope we may see one another frequently on this side of time, but let us not destroy the health or comfort of each other by making a sacrifice of them to the itching ears and gaping curiosity of our people.

" It gives me great pleasure to perceive that you are much at one with me on the subject of Bible associations. Dr. Burns (Barony) has become a member of one of them, and the President of the S.E. district has just called upon me, and obtained my name also. I cordially agree in your sentiments that the true way of neutralizing all that is dangerous to the Establishment in the influence of dissenters, is to move cordially along with them in all that is good. With most cordial good will to yourself, and every sentiment of esteem for the zeal with which you carry on the all-important work of the ministry,

" Believe me to be, my dear Sir,
" Yours most truly,
"THOMAS CHALMERS."

CHAPTER VI

HAT the state of religion in Scotland during the last quarter of the eighteenth century was very dark and depressing is a matter of fact of which there can be no doubt. Dr. McCrie speaks of the "*lurid star*" of 1784; and Sir Henry Moncrieff, in his Life of Dr. Erskine, traces back the sad defection to the days of Hutcheson, Robertson, and other leaders in the downward march of sterile moderatism. Among the causes that led to a great revival may be mentioned the rise of the missionary movement in England in 1794, followed, as it instantly was, by similar symptoms and effects in Scotland. The sailing for the South Seas of a chartered vessel filled with warm-hearted candidates for missionary life and labours among savages and cannibals was a new thing in Britain, or perhaps in the world; and the question: "Any word from the *Duff?*" still lingers in my ears as associated

G

with the arrival of the weekly post or carrier from
the metropolis. Regularly on such occasions did I go
with or without my companions, to the humble sources
of information in our little town, with the significant
question "Any word?" When, on the second voyage
of the *Duff*, word came that she had been taken by the
French frigate *Buonaparte*, the announcement thrilled
through the awakening heart of Scotland as the signal of
a great national calamity. The General Assembly of
1796 did indeed by a majority (not very large, I am happy
to say) try to put down the rising spirit of missions. But
Paisley subscribed at the first call one thousand pounds
sterling as the primary offering. Edinburgh, and Glasgow,
and the North organized their missionary associations.
The *Evangelical Magazine* of 1793, and the *Edinburgh
Missionary Magazine* of 1796, helped wondrously the
" move ;" and four such men as Haldane, Bogue, Ewing,
and Innes (most distinctly do I picture the men now to
my mental eye, amid the shadows of the past) offered to
head a mission to Bengal, and four more like minded, and
like circumstanced, were ready to follow in their wake.
The visits of Simeon, and of Fuller to Scotland, at a rather
later period, told mightily ; and " the preaching tours" of
Rowland Hill, James Haldane, John Aikman, and Greville
Ewing contributed much to deepen impressions already
made 'for good in the hitherto stagnant national mind.
Those week-day services of "Strangers" amongst us did
immense good. When John Aikman, a native of our seaport, and a man every way remarkable for zeal and piety
and disinterestedness, preached in our school-house of an
evening, he gave out the 107th Psalm at the beginning,
and preached on "joy among the angels in heaven over
one sinner that repenteth ;" and the memories and impressions are still present with me. And I remember the
sermon of Mr. Slatten, of Chatham, in our town, the more
distinctly, perhaps, because we heard him under the impression that it was " *the Captain*" himself, meaning Mr.
James Haldane, who usually went under that name.
Great and salutary moreover was the era of the erection

of Sabbath schools, and the circulation of religious tracts
also did much good ; and the names of John Campbell,
John Ritchie, George Cowie, Alexander Pitcairn, and
many others like minded, are still fresh and fragrant in
Scotland. Independency, or Scottish Congregationalism,
indeed got then a strong pull ; but no matter of that.
The Established Church, whose deadness was the real
cause of this, shared largely in the happy issues ; for her
sleep was disturbed, she began to look through the curtains of her repose, and to rub her eyes with the feeling
of surprise. We that were boys, or little more, wondered,
and eagerly put questions, more or less to the point, and
moved on with the current. My father estimated the
Moulin revival at the close of the century (1796) as the
return of the days of Whitefield and the scenes of Cambuslang.

At an early period in his ministry Dr. Burns evinced
practically his interest in the missionary enterprise. Four
months after his settlement in Paisley we find him appointed secretary of the auxiliary to the time-honoured
London Missionary Society, which, fifteen years previously, had been established in Paisley.   The MS. minutes of
this fruitful branch during the first nineteen years and a
half of its history (from March, 1796, till November, 1815)
lie before us. We have also on our table the first missionary magazine ever published on this continent. The
two beautifully synchronize. The retrospect is suggestive. The movement in the New World was almost
simultaneous with that in the Old.

The magazine, which seems to have been occasional in
its publication, embraces in its 240 pages from 1796 till
1800. The purely missionary news being then but scanty,
its columns are largely filled with other matter suitable
to a religious journal. Special prominence is given to

the doings of the London Missionary Society, which had
been formed on a catholic basis on the 22nd of September,
1795, in presence of two hundred ministers of different
Protestant denominations, and an assembly which crowded
every corner of Spa-fields Chapel.   The designation of the
first missionaries, twenty-eight in number : their settlement amid the islet gems which stud the bosom of the
vast Pacific : the rise and progress of the work at Ota-
heite : the exploits of the good ship *Duff* and the devoted
Captain Wilson : the thanksgiving day on her return
after fifty-one thousand miles of voyaging, with Dr.
Haweis' discourse on the occasion, from Psalm cxxvi. 3 :
these and such-like form the staple of the thrilling story.

From the altar kindled by the " Spirit of Burning " in
the British, the friends of truth in the American metropolis received " a live coal."

McWhorter, and Livingston, and Mason caught inspiration from Bogue, and Wilks, and Waugh.

On the 1st of November, 1796, the New York Mission
ary Society was organized, with " John M. Mason, of the
Scots Presbyterian Church, Cedar Street," as secretary.

Six months before the movement in New York, and
after that in London, Paisley began to move in the same
direction.   In this, as in other religious and philanthropic
enterprises, she has proved a pioneer among the towns,
and made good her claim to Rowland Hill's eulogium—
" Paisley is the Paradise of Scotland, because there Christians love one another."

In the rise and progress of the Foreign Missionary enterprise in the Church of Scotland Dr. Burns felt a peculiar interest.   None mourned more deeply than he over

the sad defections of the past, when the church of his fathers had forgotten her first love; and none more ardently longed for her to remember whence she had fallen, and to repent and do the first works. He rejoiced greatly in the dawning of a brighter day, when the claims of the "great commission" received on the floor of her Supreme Court, where a generation before they had been contemned, a fitting recognition ; and when, shaking herself from the dust and loosing herself from the bands of her neck, she responded promptly to the appeal, "Awake ! awake ! put on thy strength !"

He gloried in the mission of Dr. Duff; and when that apostle of India first returned from the field of his trials and triumphs, and the electric shock which his marvellous oratory gave to the General Assembly—then unused to such visitations—vibrated to the extremities of the land, he felt in all the fulness of his ardent nature the thrill. While plodding on perseveringly at home work ; and his sympathies going forth to his expatriated fellow-countrymen in the remotest of Britain's colonial dependencies, he found time, with voice and pen, by labouring and travelling, to shew in many practical forms his interest in the perishing heathen.

Several ministers and missionaries were trained up under Dr. Burns' Paisley pastorate, and received their first impulses towards the work from him.

The Rev. Colin Campbell, for many years a faithful and successful missionary of the London Missionary Society, at Bangalore, in the Presidency of Madras, thus writes, in a letter full of interesting incident :—

"My ever-revered and much-loved Friend and Pastor:

"I have often had it in my mind to write to you. A very good likeness of you which hangs in my study, and which has been long in our possession, often gives occasion to speak of you, both among ourselves, and friends who may happen to be visiting us. But without this I know I should not be ready to forget you. I owe so much to your ministerial labours, to your kind advice, and to the interest you took in my welfare in my early days, and especially at the time I began to think of the missionary work, that I always think of you with the highest respect, affection, and gratitude. I am now stirred up to write to you by hearing from my sister-in-law that you have been paying a visit to Paisley, and that she has had the very great pleasure of hearing you again. I was agreeably surprised to hear that you looked so well, and that your preaching was still characterized by so much energy and power."

His labours in connection with the Bible Society and Sabbath schools we can only touch upon. It was in the Old Low Church the "Paisley and East Renfrewshire Bible Society" was organized on May 17th, 1813, at a meeting presided over by his father-in-law, Mr. John Orr, first Provost of the town. His speech on that occasion, which was one of great eloquence and power, is given in full in the August and September numbers of the *Christian Instructor* of that year. For many years he filled the post of secretary. With the Sabbath school Associations he was closely identified. The numbers of the *Instructor* for May and June, 1814, contain "the Paisley Sabbath School Report," which, though without signature, bears the impress of his hand, and of which the editor says, "the report is so creditable to the society whose proceedings it details, and so much calculated to be useful in the way of information and encouragement, that we shall give it without abridgment."

In behalf of Bible, missionary, and kindred societies he

made many tours, two of them in Ireland, which created a deep impression and won him many friends.

Not less in the temporal well-being of the poor, than in promoting the spiritual good of all, did Dr. Burns take a deep interest. With the poor of Paisley he naturally sympathised most deeply, and on their behalf exerted himself most actively. Here we recur to his autobiographical notes.

A very interesting enquiry has been lately instituted in England, and surely it may be extended to Scotland also, although it may be with greater limitation in the one case than in the other, I refer to the causes why the working classes in the community seem to be so indifferent to religion in its social character, so callous to the interests of eternity as compared with the keenness with which they struggle for secular rights. My settlement in Paisley and lengthened residence there necessarily led me to remark certain phenomena that did bear pointedly on such questions. Of course it was with the state of things within the pale of the Established Church that I had mainly to do, and I am perfectly satisfied that the facts to which I am about to refer were not realised at all to the same extent within the circles of secession or dissent as in the Establishment. I entered the church at a time when popular rights, whether civil or religious, were greatly in abeyance, when the notion of meddling with church patronage or anything of the kind was held to be purely absurd, and when even a recognition of dissenters at all, in our discussions in church courts, was repelled and put down as insulting. Toryism reigned in all its power in all the grades of society above or beyond that of the working classes, and to a limited extent in that immediately above it. By the established church courts the people were ignored ; and any allusion in our speeches to the popular mind or to the ordinary vehicles of popular sentiment were uniformly and contemptuously frowned down. The feeling, if not expressed, was nevertheless strong,—Who are the people ? We know them not; we are independent of them; we are the church, not of the people, but of the constitution. In perfect harmony with this, stood side by side with it a disinclination to do anything at all, ecclesiastically, for benefiting the temporal interests of the working classes. Often have I thought of the words of Paul in reference to an apostolic commission, "only they would that we should remember the poor," as in striking contrast with the apathy of so many modern churchmen. When I first published my volume on the poor in 1818, I had by no means got above the dominant prejudice. Circumstances connected with the depression of trade and with the civil disabilities that impeded the prosperity of Scotland gradually enlarged and liberalized my views, and during the second half of the period of my ministry in Scotland I not only felt and acted on the principle that the church ought to *do more* than she had done for relief of the humbler classes, but I pleaded occasionally from the platform and from the press in behalf of removal of iniquitous and oppressive laws, such as those which affected the importation of corn and provisions from foreign ports. With great difficulty did I obtain a scrimp majority of votes in our presbytery for a searching enquiry into the causes of prevailing distress among the working classes in our community.

I tried it in the Synod at Irvine, but signally failed. My experience led me strongly to the conclusion that ministers of the gospel, and especially those in the Establishment, ought to take a deeper interest in the temporal necessities of their people, by ever shewing suitable sympathy with them in their difficulties, and by bringing their influence to bear on the side of an increase of their comforts. Four times in the lapse of ten or twelve years was I sent to London, as one of a deputation to the " powers that be," on behalf of suffering operatives. The ministers and laymen who co-operated with me in these missions were fully satisfied as to the line of duty followed out, and never regarded the sacrifice of a few weeks' absence from our ordinary fields of labour as at variance with conscience, or as morally deleterious to the cause of religion—quite the reverse.

There can be no doubt that in large communities as Paisley, Dundee, Aberdeen, and such like, the prevalence of French infidelity, the introduction of Sunday drilling, and other causes of a like kind, tended greatly to eat out the piety of the people and to thin the churches. But I am not less persuaded that if, half a century ago, proper means had been used to remove the evils that beset the church, and to promote a kindlier feeling towards all classes of dissenters from her communion, Scotland would have presented a far more pleasing aspect than it has done. Old affection would have risen from its torpidity, and associations happy and healthful would have welded society sweetly in one. Had our General Assemblies dealt not in such "pastoral admonitions" as were levelled at Simeon, of Cambridge, and Fuller, of Kettering, the very best men of their age, but in such addresses as that of Mr. Bonar, of Cramond, entitled "Genuine Religion the Best Friend of the People," of which thousands of copies were showered among the people of the metropolis, what substantial good would have been the result!

Far am I from saying that Dr. Hill, of St. Andrew's, and Dr. Thomas Hardy, of Edinburgh, did no good by their printed appeal to the working classes in Scotland at the end of the last century; but this I know, that when Henry Dundas came down, at the request of Mr. Pitt's Government, to reconnoitre on behalf of trembling and panting patriotism, he found, and he acknowledged, that moderatism could do little to mellow the chafed spirits of a discontented people, and he made an affecting appeal to Sir Henry Moncrieff, as the representative of the Evangelical party, for help in the sad emergency. Kay, in one of the very best of his caricatures, giving utterance to a deeply-felt, wide-spread conviction, has shown how little the Carlyles and the Grieves of the moderate clergy could do to meet the swelling tide. The noble Baronet, with commendable highmindedness, said in reply, " Mr. Dundas, you have kept us always in the background, and lavished all your favours upon others."

One of his oldest Paisley friends thus expresses himself on his interest in the poor :—

" Dr. Burns was not only a popular preacher, but a model parish clergyman, visiting not only his congregation once a year, but all his parishioners. He was truly a valuable citizen ; for there was not a religious, benevolent, or philanthropic movement in town but he was to be found either at the beginning, middle, or end of it. The work which specially connects the Doctor with Paisley is his ' Historical Dissertations on the Law and Practice of Great Britain, and particularly of Scotland, with regard to the Poor : On the Modes of Charity, and on the Means of Promoting the Improvement of the People,' and known as ' Burns on the Poor Law.' This work is full of valuable local information, containing an epitome of the Ecclesiastical History of Paisley, from 1739 to 1818 ; the Census of the Population, from 1695 to 1811 ; the Ecclesiastical Provision for the Poor by the Established and Dissenting Churches ; a History of the various Charitable and Benevolent Institutions, Schools, &c., &c. ; and containing an account of the ' Town Guard' prior to the obtaining of the Police Act in 1806. The information is most varied and interesting."

This work met with general acceptance, and received the warmest commendations of the critics.* The first edition was rapidly exhausted, and a new edition was brought out. It was quoted as the great authority on the subject. Six years after its appearance, one just then rising into notice, but who was afterwards destined to occupy a front

---

* "A mass of evidence and information, of which the volume before us presents us with a distinct and valuable abstract."
" One cannot do better than quote the excellent and judicious observations of Mr. Burns in his own words."
" Our author's observations upon the management and application of the poor funds are equally just and practical."
" On this as on every other view and bearing of this subject, Mr. Burns writes with great information and good sense."
" The work itself, which is at once full and clear, and comprehensive in its statements and details, can alone speak for itself."
" Were we called upon to point out any single book which contained the greatest proportion of useful and accurate information ; of just, honest, and impartial reasoning upon the subject of the Poor Laws, in its broadest and most extended bearing, we would not hesitate an instant in fixing upon the volume before us."
In 1841 Dr. Burns published " An Enquiry into the State of the Poor, and a Plea for a Government Investigation " (which soon followed), being the substance of two lectures delivered before the Paisley Philosophical Institution.—ED.

rank in the coming struggle—Alexander Murray Dunlop, the future trusty counsellor of the church—thus wrote:—

> "EDINBURGH, Feb. 1825.
>
> "SIR,—May I beg of you to do me the favour to accept of the accompanying little volume, in testimony of the respect I entertain for the learned author of the admirable dissertations relative to the poor, to which I venture to hope my imperfect treatise may perhaps serve as a sort of supplement.
>
> "I have the honour to be, with much esteem,
> "Your very obedient servant,
> "ALEXR. DUNLOP, JR."

Though half a century has rolled away since its publication, this work is quoted as an authority still. The *Westminster Review* of October, 1870, has an able article "On the Scottish Poor Law," in which repeated quotations are made from it and references to it. In a foot-note at the beginning, the reviewer states "the principal works consulted in this part of our enquiry are 'The Scottish Poor Laws,' by Scotus, Edinburgh, 1870, and a work by the Rev. Robert Burns, 'Historical Dissertations on the Law and Practice of Great Britain, and particularly of Scotland, with regard to the Poor.' Glasgow, 1819. 8vo. pp. 397."

Dr. Burns' interest in the poor was no mere thing of theory. It was intensely practical. He was all the time in the streets and lanes of the town on missions of benevolence. He exhibited to the full, pure religion and undefiled, by "visiting the fatherless and widows in their affliction." All the local charitable institutions enjoyed his advocacy and felt his care. Connexion with their boards to him was no mere sinecure. He was chairman of emigration societies to facilitate the exodus of the deserving poor to those lands of promise which Britain's colonies supplied.

In those periodical seasons of commercial stagnation to which a town like Paisley, so long dependent on one great staple, was subject, he was prominent among his fellow-citizens in the proposing and carrying out of measures to meet the prevalent distress. Without making himself a fool in glorying, he might perhaps have said, " Howbeit I laboured more abundantly than they all ;" nor would the patient Uzzite's self-appropriated eulogium have been out of place—" When the ear heard me, then it blessed me ; and when the eye saw me it bore witness to me, because I delivered the poor that cried, and the fatherless, and him that had no helper; the blessing of him that was ready to perish came upon me, and I caused the widow's heart to sing for joy. I was eyes to the blind, and feet was I to the lame. I was a father to the poor ; and the cause which I knew not, I searched out."

The remembrance comes up to us of long rows of poverty-stricken people reaching from his study desk out into the street, eager to pour into his ready ear the story of their woes.

Four times he visited London and leading cities of England on missions for the poor. Frequently did he act as a member of deputations to confer with the Ministry of the day, and with prominent statesmen, with reference to the condition of the suffering operatives.

We remember how proud we were to handle and to read a letter he received from the Duke of Wellington on the subject, which has perished with a host of others which reached him, alike from the lofty and the lowly. He had a fashion of making periodical bonfires of letters and of sermons,—often when we were not aware of it. Thus, of the immense accumulations of nigh sixty years, not over a dozen of fully written out discourses have escaped the fury of the flames ; and in the general burnings, letters whose preservation we would have coveted, slipped in, sometimes by mistake, oftener intentionally.

Of these periods of commercial stagnation in Paisley, and of Dr. Burns' connexion with her public charities, one of her most public-spirited citizens, and closely identified with his Paisley life, testifies :*

" I shall not say much regarding him personally, but I must ask your indulgence while I state a few words regarding his labours during his residence in this place, which show that there is good reason for the esteem in which he is still held by us. To say that Dr. Burns was an eloquent preacher of the gospel—that he was the faithful and devoted pastor of a large congregation, and that he was an assiduous and hard working parish minister, is only to express the one half, and that probably the lesser half, of his labours. Dr. Burns was something more than an eminent clergyman—he was, in the truest and best sense of the word, a citizen of the town. He shrank from no labour, but threw himself with the whole force of his character into every good work. During his long residence among us there was no public question, no movement or organization having for its object the social and political amelioration of the people, or the material, moral, or spiritual wellbeing of the community, which did not command and receive his eloquent advocacy and indefatigable working. Although I am old enough to recollect Dr. Burns' settlement in Paisley, I was then too young to remember many of his earlier labours, but I had ample opportunities as I grew up, however, to witness his labours on behalf of all our educational and benevolent institutions. I was early associated with him in the management of Hutcheson's Charity School, and for many years he was the moving spirit of the direction. He was for many years chairman of the directors of our Infirmary, and devoted all his characteristic energy of character to the interests of that important institution. We also know the interest he manifested

* Provost Murray, father of Professor Murray, of Queen's College, Kingston, Canada, and uncle of Alexander Smith, the poet. Provost Murray's sister was married, and her distinguished son baptized, by Dr. Burns.—Ed.

on behalf of the Philosophical Society, by lecturing to the members and by acting as its president for many years.* There is one sphere of his labours on behalf of this community in connection with which I was perhaps more than any other brought into contact with him. Happily for our present magistracy and principal inhabitants, they know little of the care and anxiety and labour which devolved on former magistrates, when the town suffered so much from frequently recurring periods of depression of trade, which, by throwing our artizans idle, subjected them to the severest privations and distresses. I have no recollection of the first of these seasons, which occurred in 1812 ; but I recollect well that of 1825 and 1826. My first connection with efforts for the relief of unemployed operatives was in 1837, and I well recollect the active labours of Dr. Burns on that occasion ; and on a similar state of matters in 1841, 1842, it was my fortune to be associated with the Doctor as members of a deputation to London, to press the state of matters on the attention of Government, and to endeavour, by subscription, to raise money to relieve the starving population of this town, and I can never forget the herculean exertions which our friend put forth on that occasion."

As means of social improvement, Dr. Burns laid much stress on *pure water* and *savings banks.* He had much to do with the introduction of water into the town, though to the philanthropic Dr. Kerr (father of Dr. Wm. Kerr, of Galt, Canada) belongs the honour of founding the Water-works.

Those useful institutions for saving the earnings of the poor, with which the name of Dr. Henry Duncan, of Ruthwell (a special friend), is so intimately associated, he strongly advocated. To encourage the movement and teach his children habits of economy, he deposited in the first Savings bank a sum of money to the credit of each of them. We well remember how proud we were to re-

---

* For several years he acted as President of the Philosophical Institution, now connected, we believe, with the magnificent Free Library which Paisley owes, along with a beautiful Public Garden, to her two public-spirited sons, Sir Peter Coats and Thomas Coats, Esq. The question has been jocularly asked, " What could the 'Paisley bodies' do without their COATS?"

In Dr. Burns' Note Book, March 16, 1869 (during his last visit to Paisley), occurs the following:— Addressed Philosophical Institution. Retrospect. Institution began 1808. Addressed Dec. 1st :, 1813, 1815, and often afterwards, down to near the disruption in 1843. Subjects - Schemes for the Improvement of Society, History of Astronomy, Physical Science, Moral and Mental Philosophy, on Taste, Geology, &c., &c.—ED.

ceive the bank book with our name in it, of what an exhaustless fortune we regarded ourselves as possessed, and what an important part of our education it was for us thus early to learn the lesson of saving for useful purposes the money that else might have been squandered in selfishness and sin.

His repeated presidency of emigration societies, and unwearied efforts to further their objects, formed another phase of his interest in the poor. Many, now useful and honoured citizens in Canada, Australia, and New Zealand received from him their first inspiration to emigrate, and assistance in doing so. When, afterwards, he set the example himself, and was "roughing it in the bush," on many a weary pilgrimage, he would be saluted often with the grateful greetings and hearty hand-shakings of those he had befriended a score of years before. Often when passing along some lonely road, little expecting it, familiar forms, clad in comfortable home-spun, would issue from snug shanties, and voices, whose tones called up memories of the past, would ring cheerily out, "Hoo' are ye Doctor? we're sae glad to see ye!"

There are districts of Canada mainly settled from Paisley and neighbourhood, the hivings off at such seasons as we have referred to, with whose settlement he had not a little to do, and where his memory is embalmed.

His identification with the interests of the working classes, and the presentation to him, during so large a portion of his Paisley life, of what was a "present distress," pressing him on all sides, and constantly appealing to his sympathies, made him alive to all measures, social and political, calculated to ameliorate their condition. To this may be largely traced his earnest advocacy of franchise extension and of free trade, when it was the reverse of fashionable for clergymen of the Established Church to connect themselves with such movements.

He was ever a Liberal in politics, though many near and dear to him were on the other side. And, while he did not descend to the political arena, or mingle as a heated partisan in the exciting fray, he did not deem it inconsistent with the sacredness of his office, or calculated—as some of his High Church brethren thought—to "rub off the clerical enamel," to indicate distinctly his political preferences, and especially at imminent crises of his church and country to come out boldly, through the press and otherwise, in behalf of what he conceived to be the cause of truth and righteousness. He hesitated not, even in the presence of Royalty, to reveal honestly and plainly the condition of the masses, and to suggest how the " troubled sea" might be set at rest. In the course of a lengthened interview with William IV. (when it was said "the King appeared greatly taken with the conversational powers of the Scotch Presbyterian divine"), His Majesty asked about the state of trade in Paisley. The Doctor answered, " May it please your Majesty, the trade in that large manufacturing town is at present very bad." "Can you assign any cause, local or otherwise, for this?" enquired the King. "Yes, please your Majesty, it is generally ascribed to the great agitation caused by the Reform Bill, and we do not look for any improvement until it is passed." "My Ministers," said His Majesty, "must look to that"

Dr. Burns was always a strong advocate of *Free Trade*, and enemy of the *Corn Laws*. When the great conflict commenced which culminated in Sir Robert Peel's complete change of sentiment, a conversion which the magnanimous Premier frankly acknowledged, Dr. Burns took his position beneath the banner on which the names of Cobden and Bright were inscribed. He was a member of the Manchester League. He was the only minister (we believe) of the Church of Scotland present at the memorable banquet in honour of Richard Cobden at Glasgow.

In the winter of 1841 he delivered, in Glasgow, the seventh of the second series of lectures to Young Men : " On the Reciprocal Duties of Employers and Employed."

In 1842 he lectured under the auspices of the " Glasgow Young Men's Free Trade Association," in John Street Chapel, Glasgow, on " Restrictive Laws on Food and Trade tried by the test of Christianity."

" I honour much and know well," is the testimony of Principal Willis, " his labours in more than one department of philanthropy, beyond the range of direct pastoral work, though not alien from it. It was given to him beyond many to see the defects of the Scottish poor law, defects which were indeed recognised, so far, by Assemblies after Assemblies of the church ; the provision for the poor being acknowledged to be in a great measure illusory in numerous parishes of Scotland. But the real remedy was tardily applied. Our departed friend contended for the establishing of a legal provision more adapted to the changed circumstances of Scotland, and for a very considerable modification of what was tenaciously cherished by some as the Scottish system ; though perhaps rather to be called the misapplication to an altered state of society of an ancient scheme, which Knox and our early ecclesiastics acquiesced in, as a necessity of their times, rather than approved.

" The state has rightly, with the general consent of the Scottish mind, revolutionized its scheme of providing for the poor. No legislation in such an interest can meet every difficulty, and abuses must be watched against. But the principles of the new arrangement, I verily believe, are in far more harmony with a right juris-

H

prudence, and with the laws of the Bible, than what prevailed for a century before.   Dr. Burns in pressing his views on the public, —views which I cordially supported along with him,—had to oppose the specious pleadings of men of no small name, who set off with much eloquence views honourable enough to their warmth of heart, but neither resting on a solid philosophy, nor sustained by legitimate reasonings from the Word of God. . . . Hence, in what is now called the old system, the admitted and oft lamented inefficiency of the Scottish provision—necessitating, for eking it out, mendicancy with all its demoralizing effects ; and, more serious still, perhaps, the withdrawment from their proper spiritual vocation of religious functionaries—an evil, this latter, seen and regretted by none more than by the earnest opponents of the change which became necessary ; though they strangely failed to see that the cause of the evil was inherent in the very principle of the system they were so eager to uphold. . . . Besides the larger writings of Dr. Burns on this important question, a small synopsis of his argument, in a mere fly-leaf, came some time ago into my hands —I may have seen it before, but had forgotten it—of which I said to him, that no abler piece of reasoning ever came from his pen. . . . Besides other powerful argumentation, Dr. Burns never reasoned more conclusively than when he parried off the objection to a poor rate, viz :— that a regular statuted provision, more resembling that of England than what so long prevailed in Scotland, tends to shut up the sources of private beneficence."

CHAPTER VII.

VISITS TO OXFORD AND CAMBRIDGE.*

T was early in June, 1812, and on my way from London to Scotland, I paid a visit to the University of Oxford. The son of a much-respected clergyman of Glasgow was then studying at Baliol College, and as a "father's friend" I counted on a kind reception. In this I was not disappointed. Mr. John Gibson Lockhart, afterwards the editor of the *Quarterly Review* and the son-in-law of Sir Walter Scott, received me courteously and kindly in his academical apartments, and gave me the information which strangers commonly seek for, in regard to the varied halls of science and learning constituting the venerable "University of Oxford." Amongst other things demanding notice, I desired to stand on the spot where, in the days of "bloody Mary," stood the iron

---

* The autobiography here sketches two visits paid at different times to Oxford and Cambridge, and furnishes a specimen of a number of similar tours, made principally in connexion with public duty.—ED.

pillar to which Ridley and Hooper and Latimer were bound by iron chains, and, forgetting all their minor differences of sentiment, breathed out their souls together amid the flames of martyrdom. My friend placed me on the very spot. No martyr's monument had then been reared, but none was needed. The heart of England was then sound, and Oxford had not as yet taken any of those fatal steps in a retrograde direction which have since thrown around her an inglorious notoriety. Scotland at large, and Glasgow in particular, have an interest of substantial value in one at least of the literary halls of Oxford ; and, over and above this, the desire to have their young men "sunned in the south," has been greatly on the increase in the wealthy and aristocratic families of the north, and the effect has, almost in every instance, been fatal to Scottish patriotism and Scottish presbytery. Ritualistic Episcopacy has many charms for young minds not over-deeply imbued with sacred associations ; and my friend, with all his amiability, and all his ancient family attachments, had, imperceptibly perhaps to himself, got somewhat cold to "Old Scotia." "Have you anything in Scotland that can match Dr. Parr ?" was one of his early questions. I was somewhat nonplussed, probably from the feeling that as he was as much a Scotsman as I was, it might perhaps belong to him as much as to me to sketch a reply ; nor could I think of going back to invoke the venerable shades of an "admirable Crichton" or a witty "George Buchanan." I made the best retreat I could, with a few suggestive mutterings of such vocables of nomenclature as John Moore, of Glasgow, and George Campbell, of Aberdeen. If such men are not so profound in their scholarship as a Bentley, a Porson, or a Parr, their solid and lasting practical usefulness may give them a place in the same galaxy with these brilliant lights of the south. But our country is of small dimensions compared with England, and it has not anything that can compete with the rich literary endowments of England. Perhaps. my best reply might after all have been, " I will give you a Parr when you have given to me three such men in the department of intellectual philosophy as Reid and Stewart and Brown.

After a short but agreeable interlude I found myself in the house of a worthy dissenting minister, the Rev. W. Hinton, to whom I had been introduced by my venerable friend and father, Dr. Waugh, of Wells Street, London; and with him traversed the classic walks of Magdalen College. "Look here," said my *fidus achates*, pointing to half a dozen sprightly "scholars," or "fellows" perhaps, with something of the paraphernalia of college costume about them, and careering in company on the well-kept walk, "see the one on the right of the line, that is Daniel Wilson, of Edmund Hall, who has often taken a cup of coffee in my humble dwelling, but now he is among his college confrères, and he will not look our way." The learned platoon soon wheeled about, and came not again within our immediate horizon. But I learned that the man of whom I got only a glance, and who was afterwards the uncompromising advocate of a radical change, as the eminently pious and venerated Bishop of Calcutta, was of dissenting parentage, as not a few of the Butlers and the Tillotsons of the Anglican Church have been; and that promising in every way as he even then was, the very breath of Oxford bigotry and exclusiveness withers and benumbs the warm glow of an otherwise genial and generous spirit.

In 1834, and on my way to take part in the May meetings in London, I spent a Sabbath in Oxford, and contrived to press into it no fewer than four distinct services. In the morning I went to St. Mary's University Church, where five hundred of the *elite* of England's aristocratic youth were congregated to hear the learned Dr. Cramer, President of New Inn Hall. He gave us an able and orthodox vindication of the genuineness of the first two chapters of Matthew's Gospel against the Ebionites of the first or second century, and I was curious to see how he would apply the subject to the consciences and the hearts of the many young immortals clustering around him. The heaving mountain and the *ridiculus mus* of the Roman satirist came vividly to mind when the learned orator drew his weighty inference, and no other can I now remember,—" How wise the statutes of our venerable founders in excluding dissenters of all classes from the colleges of Oxford !" "Ebion," poor man ! belonged to that hated class, and down to 1834 his ghost seems to have hovered portentously between New Inn Hall and St. Mary's.

Having some curiosity to hear read or chanted the peculiar Oxford liturgy, I remained after the congregation was dismissed, and listened for an hour to the solemn and slow dronings of a grave clerk in the desk, and the quick responses, in purely Doric style, of a plain tradesman in his Sabbath attire, blue coat and shining yellow buttons, who acted as fugleman. The "turning to the east," and the bowing at the name of "Jesus," with other antics, the worthy man did, I doubt not, go through *"to rule;"* but as I never heard or saw such an exhibition before or since, I cannot compare him with any other actor, so that he must " stand alone in his glory." The most lengthened " piece" performed by the clerk or curate in the desk, and not repeated by the fugleman, was the weekly litany, or form of thanksgiving for the " benefits and blessings" conferred on the colleges of Oxford by the heads or chancellors in " apostolic succession," from William of Wykeham and St. Winifred, some six centuries ago, to the chancellor for the time being, " His Grace, Arthur, Duke of Wellington, whom may God long preserve !" There were no prayers " for" or " to" the souls departed, or still present in the body, but the tedious "invoice" of choice articles successively exhibited before us sounded to me very like something of the kind. My predominant feeling, however, was, that I was " not keeping the Sabbath holy," and I hastened away as fast as I could, that I might breathe in a more healthful atmosphere. I found it in the small but neat and commodious Congregational Chapel, where I knew there would be service at 3 p m. There I was so fortunate as to hear an excellent sermon, garnished with a few well-chosen anecdotes, from that prince in Israel, the now sainted Angell James, of Birmingham. O what a contrast betwixt the precious stones and gold and silver of the one place of worship, and the wood, hay and stubble of the other !

And now was my voracious appetite fully satiated ? Not quite ; for I learned that the son of my venerated old friend Mr. Hinton, now in glory, was to hold his usual evening service in his own chapel in the city, and as I had heard that "Young Hinton" had adopted some peculiar opinions, I had a wish to hear him. The expositions and the sermon were both evangelical and good. The Psalms of David in our version were sung to such tunes as "Coleshill" and "Martyrs," and the whole congregation joined in spiritual earnestness ; the only peculiarity in that service that struck me was the devotional part of it, and there my leading emotion was amazement. On the appeal for "intercessory prayer" being put forth to the audience, I should say that upwards of a dozen of written papers were given in, embracing a great variety of "cases," adapted to social sympathy, and calling for believing request to the great Father of all. They were all read in succession by the pastor as they came in, and he then arranged them before his eyes on the desk, according to a method of his own, and in the course of the prayer which immediately followed, not a "case" escaped the intelligent eye, and the appropriate clothing in suitable words, of the persistent "wrestler with the angel of the covenant," The "cases" seemed to me to be all more or less becoming, and one attached itself to my memory with peculiar tenacity, it may have been from something of personal and patronymical associations. It was the earnest request of a "young female member, on behalf of a beloved uncle, in the Highlands of Scotland, who had been long troubled with a constitutional temper at times unruly ;" and to my mind there was something truly picturesque in a venerable Celt, who had been cradled amid the storms of Ben Nevis, being thus remembered amid the classic halls of Oxford, and by friends far away.

Independently of all other considerations, a seminary

where two of the sons of John Knox were educated and
rose to academic honours, can never be uninteresting to a
Scottish Presbyterian. I had been repeatedly at Oxford,
but I did not find an opportunity of paying my respects
to the sister University till the spring of 1834. Being
acquainted with a student from Scotland then at Cambridge, and having been furnished with a letter from a
clerical friend in London to one of the tutors, I had no
difficulty in obtaining access to those halls of learning.
My first wish, as expressed to friends, was to hear as
many lectures or prelections as possible from such professors as might be found so occupied. What was my
surprise when I learned that such a gratification could
not be enjoyed, inasmuch as none of the ordinary professors were in the habit of lecturing at all; that all the real
work in the college was done by the tutors, and that the
only chance of hearing a professorial prelection was by
my going *beyond the walls*, and attending Professor Smyth,
at his lecture on " History," in the " Medical School."
Readily did I embrace the opportunity, and heard an excellent discourse on the " French Revolution," since published in the author's work on " Modern History." A
large attendance of gownsmen of all grades waited on the
learned orator, whose immediate successors in the chair
were the celebrated Dr. Arnold and Sir James Stephen.
The class was one of those that have been added in
very recent times to the original or primary stock; and
probably, like other additions of the same kind, had not
yet arrived at a full and legitimate recognition. Assuredly,
whatever be the history or the status of such additions,
they form a very valuable improvement on the venerable
though perhaps somewhat antiquated platform of the
original.

The difficulty of hearing a proper lecture from the lips
of a " real professor" was perhaps increased by certain
examinations that were going on in the different departments, and the information given me regarding these
certainly imparted to me a very high idea of the depth,
the accuracy and the fulness with which the several

branches of natural science, embracing the higher,—perhaps I should say the very highest,—branches of mathematics, and the "exact sciences" at large, were taught within the recesses of that venerable *alma mater*. In these, Cambridge is understood to take the precedence of Oxford, while the reverse may probably be held true as to classics. In regard to that department also, the son of a Scotch professor, whom I found among the students, told me that after going through all that was usually gone through in the classical curriculum at home, he found when he came to Cambridge that he was little beyond elementary principles. This was said thirty-four years ago, and great improvements have been introduced since that time in all our northern universities. One thing was very clear to me, that in the departments of logic, metaphysics, and moral philosophy, we, in Scotland, were far in advance.

The examination papers in these departments were presented to me, and 1 examined them with some care; and certainly the very surface character of these documents contrasted wonderfully with the character of depth, and elevation also, that marked other departments of human knowledge perhaps not so closely related to the practical business of life. The more I reflect on these things, the more am I satisfied that for all really useful purposes in the community of human beings, our northern colleges, *even then*, were better adapted for all the ends of general mental discipline and instruction than the colossal halls of the south; and this, be it remembered, at perhaps a *fourth-part* of the price.

Having been introduced to the Rev. Charles Simeon, at that time one of the Fellows in the University, I spent part of the evening in his room. From him I ascertained the matters of fact regarding the inadequate provision made within the University for the suitable training of young men for the church. Even after all the improvements and additions which later years had witnessed, the deficiency was still very palpable; and I felt gratitude to the Great Father of all, that such a man as the venerable

Fellow of King's College had been spared so long to watch
over the studies and the morals of entrants for the ministry. That excellent man has long since been called to his
rest on high, but his place has been well supplied by successors of the same spirit, who follow in the same path of
unostentatious and unpaid evangelistic labour. For this
a poor substitute would be found in the prayers read and
the fine pieces of music performed; and yet this " season
of prayer," or devotion, such as it is, I attended with a
feeling of awe and sublime elevation of thought; but alas!
I fear that the daily unvarying repetition of a religious
service, in the noblest " unpillared" chapel in England,
would have produced in me a ritualistic feeling of deadness and formality.

And now what have I got to say of the hospitalities of
Cambridge? My friend, the learned tutor of Trinity,
unencumbered of course with any domestic or social appendages, gave me early advice of what I had not been
aware of, that an old law was still in being which prohibited any stranger, of whatever class or creed, from
being admitted a guest at the dinner table; " but," said
he, " that does not at all interfere with our good cheer :"
and shewing me the " bill of fare," " we held a council"
together on the articles to be selected for us, from the as
yet untouched viands on the table of the great culinary
hall, to which was to be added a bottle of claret, burgun-
dy, or champagne, at our pleasure. Of course, as there
were only *two* votes to be given, mine was honoured with
the twofold character of a deliberative and a casting one.
My taste was very simple, and a veal cutlet with a
glass of sherry formed the *ne plus ultra* of my choice.
When the repast was about over, my friend said to me,
" Now, sir, though not permitted to sit down at any of
the tables, we may go in and be lookers on." As to the
fare, we were in advance of the general body, and I found
myself in the course of a few minutes mounted up to the
most prominent point of the gallery, from whence I had
a clear view of at least four hundred *literati* giving all
becoming heed to the wants of the outer man; and I rather

think not one Berkleyan among them. There appeared to be a regular hierarchy. The body of the large hall of Trinity, or the " pit," was crammed with gentlemen commoners ; on a sort of elevated platform or dais, of perhaps six feet above, sat the peers in solemn state ; and all around us in the gallery appeared the grim forms of the poor " sizers." The viands served out seemed to partake somewhat of the " pre-established harmony" of Leibnitz, with the distinctive class for which they were bound. The joints for the peers were magnificent, as was the dessert : the same, less so, for the gentlemen commoners : and as for our next-door neighbours, the poor " sizers," they had to exercise the virtue of patience, soothed in anticipation by the hope that by the kind forbearance of aristocratic gormandizers, the *exuviæ* which were handed up to them might be something more substantial than mere skin and bone. As for my friend and myself, ten minutes served for the interesting survey, and we made our retreat without waiting to see how the vinous beverage was adjusted. We made our retreat to the " grand kitchen," whose walls were largely adorned with shells of turtle, the remains of varied feasts. The whole scene I had witnessed filled me with ineffable disgust. I wondered how John Bull, with all his freaks, could tolerate such things But John, though a good sort of fellow, has got encrusted amid aristocratic distinctions of rank, and is not quite sure whether the highly-seasoned roast beef of Old England should be subjected to the acerating processes of vulgar jaws.

CHAPTER VIII.

AUTHORSHIP.

IT was in the autumn of 1825, my residence with my family for two months in the Parish of Stevenston, a well-known watering place on the Firth of Clyde, brought me into acquaintanceship with Miss Wodrow, the granddaughter of Mr. Robert Wodrow, of Eastwood, well known as the historian of "the sufferings of the Church of Scotland," and the indefatigable collector of many valuable books and manuscripts illustrative of the history of Scotland. A large proportion of the manuscripts collected by him had been purchased after his death by the Curator of the Advocates' Library, and by the Senate of Glasgow College; and from these stores many valuable articles of historical information have been from time to time obtained by different authors, and they still form a valuable repertory, as yet very partially explored. Miss Wodrow gave me ready access to what remained in her possession of the valuable memorials of

her venerable grandfather. Out of the dust and the cobwebs amid which these had been embedded for many years,
I succeeded in unkennelling about sixty volumes of letters
by and to Mr. Wodrow ; lectures and other papers by his
father, Mr. James Wodrow, the first Professor of Divinity
at Glasgow after the revolution; and many miscellaneous
pieces. After full examination of these interesting documents, with the assistance and advice of Dr. McCrie and
Dr. Andrew Thomson, I transferred forty of the volumes
to the shelves of the Advocates' Library, and for these a
valuable consideration was allowed to the proprietress. Of
these memorials much use was afterwards made by myself
in my edition of Wodrow's history, and in various articles
published in the *Edinburgh Christian Instructor;* and
by Dr. McCrie in his series of papers on " the Marrow
Controversy " in that periodical, and in his evidence before
the House of Commons, in 1834, on patronage. Some
years thereafter, the " Wodrow Society" was formed, and
by them three volumes of the " Wodrow Correspondence"
were published, besides other miscellaneous pieces ; and
by the " Maitland Club" were brought out, through the
liberality of the Earl of Glasgow, the three quarto volumes
of the well known " Analecta," embracing memorials of
daily occurrences in the life of Wodrow, both domestic
and public, with remarks, and extending over more than
thirty years of his life. By these curious relics much
light has been thrown on matters of national and ecclesiastical interest, and much of the valuable treasure remains unexhausted, yea, not explored !

The parish minister of Stevenston at the time now referred to was an old fellow-student, and thereafter a dear
fellow-labourer in the ministry, Mr. (afterwards Dr.)
Landsborough, a man of great skill in natural science, and
particularly in botany and conchology, a man of high
accomplishments, and a pastor of zeal and devotedness,
was removed from the church below to the church above,
and his name and memory are yet fragrant on the west
coast of Scotland.

The mansion house of Ardeer, the residence of the

ancient family of *Warner*, a name precious in the annals
of persecuting times, stands not far from the manse of
Stevenston, and one morning, when Mr. Landsborough
and I had breakfasted with the Laird, the conversation
happening to turn on ancient books, Mr. Warner told us
that in the under flat of his house were lying in solemn
repose not a few relics of the kind, which we might see if
we had a fancy for such things. The hint was enough.
We explored the Warner repositories, and found, among
other curiosities, a large collection of classics and works
on theology from Holland and Germany, which had been
brought over from the Continent by one of the Warners
who had been compelled to fly to Holland in troublous
times, and who brought over these works with him on
his return at the era of the Prince of Orange; but the
packages had never until now been taken down. The
books were in good preservation, and Mr. Warner allowed
my friend and myself to appropriate to ourselves as many
as we could carry in our arms, and my own library and
that of Knox College bear witness to the spoil thus legally acquired.

My labours in editing the new edition of " Wodrow's
History," undertaken by the enterprising bookselling establishment of Messrs. Blackie and Sons, Glasgow, were co-
temporary with the incidents now recorded. Had I had
more leisure, and better facilities for such a work, something more worthy of the name of Wodrow and of Scotland's church might have been produced. I contributed
the life of the author, the reply to an Episcopalian biographer of Archbishop Leighton, the illustrations, and the appendix, comprehending many valuable documents. As the
work was dedicated a century before to King George I.*

---

* A copy of the first edition had been presented to George I. by Dr. James Fraser, formerly of Aberdeen and afterwards of London, and one of Wodrow's regular correspondents. It was graciously received, and in a short time a gift of £105 sterling bestowed
on the author. Says Wodrow, in a letter to his wife dated at Edinburgh during the
sitting of the Assembly, 1725, " I find a letter in this post from Mr. James Fraser, with
an order for £100 from the Treasury, and what I own the hand of Providence in, and hope
He will help me to improve a providence we did not look for."—Wodrow Correspondence,
edited by Professor McCrie, Vol. 2, p. 557 ; of the new edition, 3, p. 191. The copy of
the order is given in the appendix to the fourth volume, and the original is among the
Wodrow manuscript letters.

it was deemed "right and proper" that William IV., the reigning monarch in 1834, should be asked for permission to dedicate the new edition to him.   A copy of the four volumes was got up in fine style, and presented by me personally to His Majesty, who accepted the gift readily, and at once granted the permission we craved.   Through the influence of our worthy member of parliament for Paisley, Mr. Archibald Hastie, and the kind offices of Sir James Mackintosh, I had no difficulty in obtaining access to Mr. Lushington, the Under Secretary of State for the Home Department, and through him to His Majesty, at the Pavilion at Brighton.   The dress, appearance, and manner of His Majesty were just those of a plain English gentleman.   He was "free and easy" in his conversation, which turned principally on two topics, very diverse from each other,—the history of his ancestors of the persecuting house of Stuart, and the reception of the Reform Bill among the then starving weavers of the "gude town" of Paisley.   The conference was comprised within less than half an hour.   I had no difficulty in getting in, but I felt some difficulty in getting out, for we must never turn our backs on royalty, and the eye of an inmate of the apartment was glaringly dazzled by the tapestry, and the mirrors, and the other ornaments that adorned the walls. The "Sailor King" understood it perfectly, bade me good morning, drew his arm chair, took hold of the poker, began to stir the fire (for it was the month of March); in the meantime, improving the opportunity, I made my escape.   The editor of a Glasgow newspaper having got possession of a private sketch of this somewhat unique incident, published it, to the great annoyance of myself and my friends.   But Colonel Fox sent me a message by my friend Thomas Pringle, the African traveller and the Teviotdale poet, to the effect that the King, worthy man, would probably never see it, and if he did it would only afford him a hearty laugh.*

---

* This "private sketch," which was characterized as "worthy of the Vicar of Wakefield or the Annals of the Parish," may be inserted now, without any breach of confidence or violation of the proprieties :—

In 1810, Dr. Andrew Thomson was translated from
Perth to Edinburgh. He soon became the chosen champion of the Evangelical party, and, till his premature and
lamented death, stirred the heart of his country to its
depths. The year following his translation, he started
the Periodical, into which he infused so much of his
own buoyant energy and burning enthusiasm, and which
played no inconspicuous part in securing for his party,
then in the weakness of comparative infancy, a power and

"His Majesty was sitting at a table, but rose and returned my obeisance
just in the way one gentleman is accustomed to do to another. I then
walked up to him with my volumes in my hand, and addressed him nearly
as follows :—'I have the honour of laying before your Majesty a work which
was published more than a century ago, and dedicated to George I. This is
the second edition, with a life of the author, notes, and other additions ; and
your Majesty has here a specimen of the progress made in typography in the
west of Scotland. The work is a national one, and has been highly approved
by Mr. Fox, Mr. Chalmers, and others, as a correct statement of facts,
illustrative of a very important period of our history. I have the honour of
requesting your Majesty's acceptance of this copy, and to return your Majesty the best thanks of the publishers, and myself, as editor, for the con,
descending manner in which your Majesty has been pleased to permit the
new edition of the work to be dedicated to your Majesty.' By this time his
Majesty got hold of the volumes, and was busily employed examining the
title-page, contents, plates, &c., with all which he expressed himself well
pleased. On turning up successively the engravings of Sharpe, Claverhouse,
Lauderdale, Carstairs, &c., remarks were made on each, and the King seemed
to be very well informed in their respective histories. 'The work,' he said-
'contains, I think, the history of the persecutions in Scotland in the days
of Charles the Second.'—'Yes, please your Majesty, it is the history of the
eventful period from the restoration in 1660 till the revolution in 1688.'—'A
very valuable record it must be,' he added. After speaking a little more upon
the subject of the book, the King asked, 'Pray, sir, what situation do you
hold in Scotland?' I told him, 'Please your Majesty, I am one of the parochial ministers of Paisley, so well known for its manufactures; and where,
I am sorry to inform your Majesty, there is at present very great distress
among the operatives, 2 or 3000 of whom are out of work.' His Majesty
asked the causes, when I adverted to several, such as the unsettled state of
the public mind, occasioned by the delay in the settlement of the reform
question—the prevalence of disease on the Continent, and the restraints on
trade by quarantine—the trade being overdone with us—and the periodical results of speculation, &c., &c.—'Have you many Irish in Paisley, and are they
mostly Roman Catholics?' I told him that we had a great many Irish families—that the greater part were Catholics, particularly those from the South
and West—that we had a good many Protestants and Presbyterians from the
North—that there are many poor amongst them—and that we felt the burden of supporting the poor of that country, which has no system of poor laws
for itself. His Majesty said, 'That is a great evil, and something must be
done by the Legislature ; but they must take time to deliberate on a matter

a prestige that issued in its final triumph. Through means of the *"Christian Instructor"* the thoughts and reasonings of his powerful mind were communicated to the public, like successive shocks of electricity, stirring the heart of the kingdom from its torpid lethargy, and spreading dismay among his discomfited antagonists.

Nothing could show more convincingly the influence of

of such consequence. The Ministry are determined to do nothing rashly, and they have had many things to occupy their thoughts of late.' I remarked that his Majesty's time must have been for some time past very painfully engaged with these matters; when he said, in reply, that he personally had not felt the burden so much, but that those who were his advisers had certainly done so. There was also a good deal said on the subject of the state of the poor in England, the objections to the theory and management of the poor laws, &c., and his Majesty shewed that he understood the subject well, and entered fully into the objections against the system of paying the price of labour out of the rates, and thus degrading the population of England into paupers, and representing those moneys as given to the support of the poor, which are, in fact, appropriated to far different objects. 'You manage these things better in Scotland.' 'Please your Majesty, our poor do not expect so much as the English poor. I observed a case in court, the other day, where the dispute lay between 5s. a head for each member of the family and 2s., and the judges decided as a medium 3s. 6d. In Scotland, in place of 12s. or 15s. for this family of poor applicants, the sum allowed for one member of it would have been held quite sufficient.' 'In Paisley, you are all, I presume, of the Church of Scotland?' 'Please your Majesty, we have many Presbyterians, Dissenters from us, yet our Dissenters differ from us almost wholly on one point—the law of lay patronage. Our standards and mode of worship are the same. We have also an Episcopal Chapel in Paisley, to the building of which, if I am not mistaken, your Majesty was pleased to contribute; and I have to inform your Majesty, that when I left Scotland, a few weeks ago, the erection was in progress, and it will be a very great ornament to the town.' 'Your people in Paisley, I think, are mostly engaged in weaving?' I told his Majesty that weaving was our great staple—that about a hundred years ago Paisley began its career as a manufacturing town —that successively linen, thread, silk, gauze, and cotton, in all its forms, had been prominent—that like Spitalfields we feel deeply the depression of trade—yet that, unlike Spitalfields, we had not so near us the wealth and resources of the metropolis. I noticed, however, the great kindness of the London committee in 1822 and 1826, in contributing to our fund to the amount of £16,000 or £18,000. The King spoke of there being no predisposition to riot either in Englishmen or Scotsmen, and this led us to notice the causes of excitement, such as poverty, evil advisers, bad publications, &c. After again thanking his Majesty for the honour done me, and expressing my fear of having obtruded too long on his time, his Majesty replied very graciously, and I retired." *

* My father was, on another occasion, the bearer of a magnificent Paisley shawl to our beloved Sovereign, and had an interview with her mother, the Duchess of Kent, in presenting it. It was while visiting London, on a mission for the poor. Of these visits, my

I

this powerful organ of the Evangelical party than the effort made at the Assembly of 1820 to secure its condemnation. Turn a torch on a frog-pond, and you will hear the croaking. It was thus when the lamp of truth flashed its light on the stagnant marsh of moderatism. When grossest instances of clerical delinquency were smoothed over as "alleged breaches of decorum," and ministers condemned by civil courts were covered by ecclesiastical manœuvring, it was not to be wondered at that a faithful and true witness, like Andrew Thomson, felt necessity laid upon him to cry aloud and spare not, and lift up his voice like a trumpet. The Moderates winced under the sharp lashings of his pen; and Dr. Bryce, whom in the Assembly of 1838 Dr. Burns jocularly claimed as a vetoist, became the mouth-piece of " Moderate" indignation. His resolutions condemnatory of the *Instructor* were carried by a majority of ONE, but no ulterior measures were taken. Dr. Bryce and his confrères found no reason to desire a repetition of such victories. Rising Evangelism, and roused public sentiment, could not be trifled with, and the great guns from St. George's, Edinburgh, kept booming as before.*

Four months after my father's settlement in Paisley, and when as yet personally a stranger to him, Dr. Thom-

---

esteemed cousin, the Rev. J. C. Burns, of Kirkliston (then of London Wall), has many racy reminiscences, *e.g.*—My father, entering the minister's seat with Dr. Baird, after the sermon had begun, whispered in the pastor's ear as he sat next him, " What *Moderate* is that, James, you have got to preach for you to-day?" It turned out to be a prominent ornament of " that order" from this side of the water.—ED.

* " In the year 1820, war was declared between the Moderates in the church and the *Christian Instructor*. The managers in the General Assembly, tortured by the trenchant periodical, passed a vote of censure upon it as ' highly injurious and calumnious.' The *Instructor* enjoyed the storm. If they wanted battle, they should have it.

" Month after month the *Instructor* lashed them. Assembly after assembly it kept them in fear. The Evangelical party gathered courage as their champion dealt his telling blows."—*Dr. Cunningham's Life*, page 30.

son opened up correspondence with him in the following terms :—

"EDINBURGH, Nov. 11th, 1811.

"DEAR SIR,—Though personally unacquainted with you, I know so much of your character as to encourage me to address a few lines to you on the subject of the *Christian Instructor*. This work, of the principles of which I hope you approve, has succeeded tolerably well, considering the circumstances of the country at the present time, and the opposition we have met with from the great bulk of our moderate brethren. But greater exertion and greater patronage are still necessary to render its circulation sufficiently extensive. I beg therefore to solicit your kind and active assistance. Ever since your establishment at Paisley, in which I sincerely congratulate you and your congregation, I have intended to write to you on this point, but my labours have been so abundant as to make the task of writing letters both difficult and irksome. The delay, I flatter myself, will not make you less willing to comply with my request. Your assistance may be given in two ways : first, by sending us occasionally contributions from your own pen, which I am confident would be such as to add to the value and respectability of our work ; and secondly, by procuring subscribers to the magazine. I know that in most manufacturing towns, and especially in such a town as Paisley, the present state of affairs is unfavourable to literary undertakings. But I know also that in Paisley there are many people who are both in easy if not opulent circumstances, and at the same time enlightened friends of true religion. Among them, I think, some might be found disposed to read and encourage such a publication as the *Christian Instructor*, were it recommended to them by a person in whose piety and judgment they placed confidence. May I beg that you will be kind enough to use your influence with your friends and acquaintances in Paisley and its neighbourhood, to promote the circulation of our magazine ? Perhaps it may be advisable to have a bookseller who will be inclined and have it in his power to forward these views. Be so obliging as let me know what bookseller or booksellers in Paisley may be considered as best for such a purpose,—as having most intercourse in the way of business with the religious world. With best wishes for your personal comfort and ministerial usefulness,

"I am, dear Sir, yours faithfully,
"ANDREW THOMSON.

"P.S. Might I trouble you to send me now and then an account of the ordinations, presentations, licences, &c., that occur in your presbytery."

The assistance thus frankly sought, was freely rendered. In acknowledgment, Dr. Thomson writes again :—

"EDINBURGH, Jan. 14th, 1812.

"MY DEAR SIR,—I return you many thanks for your kind exertions in behalf of the *Christian Instructor*. I am gratified by the favourable opinion which you entertain of the work in general; and not only take in good part, but feel grateful for, the remarks you have made on some parts of its execution. Nor must I forget to acknowledge the very acceptable communications which you have sent for insertion. This is the very way in which I wish to be treated by my friends. It is the way, however, in which I am treated by very few. One says, 'I like your publication very well, and shall recommend it,' but he never procures one subscriber. Another says: 'Your magazine does not come up to my ideas of such a work;' and that is just what he would say though the work were absolutely perfect. A third says: 'The *Instructor* is tolerably good, but then it has faults which must counteract its success;' and he very kindly leaves us to perish, without pointing out these faults, or telling us how they might be remedied. And a fourth exclaims most valiantly, 'Go and prosper, only get better communications and more of them;' but never lifts his pen to give me the least assistance in one way or another. It gives me real pleasure to find that you have avoided all these errors, and that you are a substantial, acute, and honest friend to the *Instructor*. What has been done in Paisley, through your patronage and that of Baillie Carswell, has far exceeded my most sanguine expectations. How much might we look for from Glasgow, were the same zeal to be employed in that populous and opulent city! I agree perfectly with you in thinking that our magazine should have more of a literary cast than it really has, and any papers that you may contribute for the purpose of supplying that defect shall be received with gratitude. Your critical remarks on Reid's works may perhaps do better to stand among the miscellaneous articles than among the reviews, as the book is not sufficiently modern. But if you will be so obliging as to send them by the first opportunity, I shall try to make the best use of them. Porteous' Life is in hand, and will appear soon. Let me know what particular subject you would like to discuss, and I shall endeavour to send you a book corresponding to it for review. The number of the *Instructor* for this month should have been published yesterday, but the printer has been so ill that it will not be out till to-morrow. The copies for Paisley shall be despatched immediately. I intend to write to Baillie Carswell, along with the parcel; but lest I should not find time so soon, tell him that I have received both his letters, and shall return an answer as soon as possible. You may be assured I shall not be in your neighbourhood without seeing you, &c., &c.

"ANDREW THOMSON."

Thus was commenced an intercourse which was con-

tinued with growing confidence and affection on both sides
till Dr. Thomson's death.

Frequently did they assist one another on sacramental
occasions. It was on one of these, and on the Thanksgiving
Monday, that Dr. Thomson, whose musical attainments
were well known, was closeted for several hours in our
house with R. A. Smith, the distinguished composer, then
precentor in the Paisley Abbey. At the dinner table, Dr.
Thomson produced, as the result of their joint commun-
ings, that grand tune adapted to the 24th Psalm, and
commonly known as St. George's, Edinburgh. Dr. Thomson, during his visits to Paisley, contracted a liking for the
Abbey precentor, and succeeded in securing him as leader
in the service of song in his own metropolitan cathedral.

For twenty years Dr. Thomson lent to the *Instructor*
the influence of his name and genius. He was succeeded
as editor by the Rev. Marcus Dods, of Belford, father of
the present accomplished bearer of that name; a man of
remarkable attainments, whose real worth was known
only to a comparatively limited circle, but of whose
" Eternal Word," and varied contributions to the literature
of theology, my father had the very highest opinion. The
Rev. Archibald Bennie, of Lady Yester's, who used to be
such a favourite amongst the Edinburgh students, discharged the editorial duties for two years.

Dr. Burns' contributions to the *Instructor* were very
numerous and highly prized. Of the benefit he derived
from articles penned twenty-one years previously, the
eminently godly and gifted Dr. James Grierson, of Errol,
thus writes on Feb. 1, 1835 (inviting him to come and
plead for the colonies) :—

" You say truly that we are not personally acquainted, and yet I feel that I ought to know you, as I used when at the logic class in Edinburgh often to step into the hall where you were finishing your curriculum, and often appeared as a *critic.* Moreover, I have never till now had an opportunity of telling you that, though I was *brought up* in *Calvinistic* principles, and was all along attached to them, yet, that two reviews written by you and published in the *Instructor*, in 1814, were, together with Horsley's Sermon on Providence, the means of SETTLING my mind in regard to the entire consistency between Calvinism and the Word of God. Do come, then, and see me, and give my people a Sabbath."

For three years (1838, 1839, 1840) my father acted as sole editor. This entailed on him a large amount of labour. If, when the month came round, there was any shortcoming of mental pabulum, he had to supply it. Often several articles in each number were contributed by him.

We well remember the delight we used to experience when the parcels of new books came in to be reviewed, and the work we used to have at the close of each year in the preparation of the index of contents.

The title during the period of his editorial incumbency evinced the leaning of his heart towards the colonies, for to the old original title he added that of *Colonial Religious Register.* This department, which was quite prominent in each number, furnished a channel for conveying a vast amount of useful and important information, with reference specially to Canada, but to all our colonial dependencies as well.

Many testimonials might be given as to the high position which the *Instructor* occupied under my father's editorial management. Its interest, which for some time previously had been on the wane, greatly revived, and it regained not a little of its ancient glory.

Besides his contributions to the *Instructor* and other

periodicals, which would fill several volumes, he had to do with the editorial supervision of several important works, and a great variety of other literary efforts, which were very favourably received. Had the pressure of parish and other public duty admitted of his devoting himself more to writing, he might have secured for himself a high place in the republic of letters.

The following fragment from the Autobiography, to which evidently additions were intended to be made, indicates my father's early mental bent, and describes his first attempt at authorship.

" A Short Essay on the Study of History" appeared in that grand national repository for a hundred years, the *Scot's Magazine.* It was written by me when little more than a boy, and a first appearance in print must be somewhat exhilarating to an opening mind. It shewed the bent of my inclinations thus early. The study of church history carried with it to me a peculiar charm, for the stones and the dust of our Scottish Zion I instinctively loved. The six octavo volumes of Stackhouse's "History of the Bible" soon after came into my hands, and their careful and continuous perusal directed my thinking. A good deal of " learned nonsense" perhaps there may be in it, but the work cannot be a trifling one that engaged the time and the labours of two learned editors and annotators from opposite points of the compass—a bishop of the Episcopal Church of Scotland, and the Presbyterian head of a northern Scottish university.*

The following is as complete a list of the works with which he had to do as I have been enabled to make out:—

1. An Essay on the Propagation of Christianity in the East, 1813.
2. Illustrations of Providence in Late Events ; a Sermon, 1814.

---

* Bishop Gleig and Principal Dewar.

3. A Letter to Dr. Chalmers, on the distinctive Characters of Protestantism and Popery, 1817.—Price 2s. 6d.
4. An Essay on the Eldership, 1818.—1s.
5. Historical Dissertations on the Poor, 8vo, 1819.—7s. 6d.
6. Trail's Guide to the Lord's Table, with Life, &c., 1820.—9d.
7. Bonar's Genuine Religion, the best Friend of the People, with Life, &c., 1821.—1s. 6d.
8. Active Goodness beautifully Exemplified in the Life and Labours of the Rev. T. Gouge, 1821.—1s. 6d.
9. Cecil's Visit to the House of Mourning, with Introductory Essay, 1823.—7s. 6d.
10. Cecil's Address to Servants, with Introductory Essay, 1823.—1s.
11. Henry's Address to Parents on Baptism, with Life and Preface.—6d.
12. Brown of Wamphray on Prayer, with Life of the Author.—2s.
13. Brown on the Life of Faith, with Preface, 1825.—5s.
14. Treatise on Pluralities, 1824.—3s. 6d.
15. Speech on the Roman Catholic Claims, 1825.—6d.
16. Three Letters to a Friend on the Moral Bearings of the Bible Society Controversy, 1827.—1s.
17. Sober Mindedness ; a Sermon to the Young, 1828.—6d.
18. A Voice from the Scaffold ; an Address on the Execution of Brown and Craig, 1829.—2d.
19. The Gareloch Heresy Tried, 1830.—1s. 6d. bds.
20. A Letter in Vindication of the above, 1830.—6d.
21. Wodrow's History of the Sufferings of the Church of Scotland; with Life, Notes, and Preliminary Dissertation, 4 vols., 1830.—£2 8s.
22. Jehovah the Guardian of His own Word ; a Sermon before the Society in Scotland for propagating Christian Knowledge, 1830.
23. Memoir of the Rev. Pliny Fisk, Missionary to Palestine, with Preface and Notes.—3s.
24. Bellamy's Letters, and Dialogues on the Nature of Love to God, Faith in Christ, and Assurance of Salvation ; with Introductory Essay.—2s. 6d.
25. Religious Endowments.
26. Establishments Vindicated, pp. 60.
27. Hints on Ecclesiastical Reform, 8vo. pp. 41.
28. Plea for State Churches.
29. Scotch Voluntaryism.
30. Plea for the Poor, 8vo. pp. 36.
31. Christian Patriotism, 1841.
32. Episcopal Liturgy.
33. Free Thoughts.
34. More Free Thoughts.
35. Life of Dr. Stevenson McGill, 1842, 12mo. pp. 358.
36. Edinburgh Christian Instructor (edited), 1838, pp. 642 : 1839, pp. 483 ; 1840, pp. 475.

37. Farewell Sermon, pp. 22, 1845.
38. Jewish Society, pp. 40, 1853.
39. The Eucharist, pp. 24, 1863.
40. Halyburton's Works.
41. Anti-Patronage Catechism.

A number of these works (written or edited by him) went through several editions.

In consideration of his literary and philanthropic labours he received from the University of Edinburgh, in 1828, the degree of Doctor of Divinity. He was also a Fellow of the Royal Society of Edinburgh and of the Antiquarian Society of Scotland, and had official connexion with several other literary institutions.

CHAPTER IX.

CONTROVERSIES.

D R. CHALMERS possessed much of the spirit of the pious and amiable Dr. Doddridge. They were both extremely candid and unsuspecting, endowed with the temper of large charity and liberality, and hence they were often in danger of being misled by imposing plausibility. It was in the spring of 1818 that Dr. Chalmers was asked to plead for the Hibernian Society, and he preached and published his sermon on that occasion under the title of "The Doctrine of Christian Charity applied to Religious Differences." The tendency of that discourse appeared to me to be dangerous to the best interests of the Protestant churches, and I was induced to pen and print a letter to the distinguished author on the distinctive features of Popery and Protestantism. Of this letter I sent a copy to the Doctor, and soon received from him the following reply:

" GLASGOW, March 21, 1818.

" DEAR SIR,—I have received from you a copy of your work and return you many thanks. I am at present very much engrossed with other matters, but hope when I am enabled to resume the subject that I shall have leisure for a full attention to your arguments. In the meantime I rest assured that your whole performance is characterized by that spirit of the Gospel which if infused (and why should it not ?) into our every difference, would disarm controversy of its sting, and reduce it to a calm and profitable contest of the understanding.

" I am, my dear Sir,
" Yours, with much regard,
" THOMAS CHALMERS."

The views of Dr. Chalmers were examined and controverted about the same time by Dr. Thomson, in the *Christian Instructor*, and in some instances with considerable asperity ; nevertheless, it does not appear that these controversial "passages at arms," ever interrupted the friendship which bound us all together ; so that here, for once at least, the calm philosophical thinker may rest assured that the *odium theologicum* had no place. Whether the Doctor ever found time to redeem his pledge to resume the discussion of the points at issue I never ascertained. I don't recollect that we ever touched on the subject in private conversation, and certain it is that the obnoxious piece that gave occasion to the skirmish, has appeared again and again among the printed works of the distinguished author, and so far as I can see without the slightest alteration. Mr. Wm. McGavin, of Glasgow, once told me that it was the attentive perusal of my letter which led him to commence his weekly periodical called *The Protestant*; a work which, perhaps, more than all others on the Romish controversy in later times, has contributed to enlighten the popular mind of Scotland on the errors and delusions of " the man of sin."

On one occasion after this the subject of Popery was fully discussed in the Synod of Glasgow and Ayr, in connection with the pending Emancipation Bill. On that occasion Dr. Chalmers took part in the discussion, and pleaded strongly for a full equalization of rights between Protestants and Papists in Ireland. But the voice of the whole west of Scotland was strong against all furthei concessions, and the advocates of the measure in the Synod were left in a small minority.

In the same year, nearly on the same occasion, it fell to me to plead at the bar of the Assembly in favour of an overture from our Synod for a day of "special thanksgiving," on account of the tri-centenary of the Protestant Reformation. Greatly to the surprise of my friends and myself, the best men in the Assembly, and the staunchest supporters of Evangelical truth, set themselves against us; not certainly from any disinclination to the thing, or any want of gratitude for the blessings of the Reformation, but from their dislike to the ecclesiastical appointment of working-days for special thanksgiving. They did not draw the distinction betwixt the fixing of a Good Friday to be permanently kept as a day of holy rest equally with the Sabbath, and the mere occasional proclamation of an observance of the kind on an occurrent Providential call.

As for the position assumed by the Moderate party in that instance, I recollect only one specimen of argument on their part against us " Whigs of the West," and it was received with calm thought and seeming acquiescence on all sides. If propounded eight years after, it would have been met with hisses, groans, and peals of laughter. Mr. John Wightman, of Kirkmahoe, a facetious and good-humoured man, but a keen devotee of the Moderate party, sagely clenched his reasonings with this unique finale:

" MODERATOR,—Reformation is a very good word, and perhaps it may denote a very good thing; but, sir, we live in evil times, and you have only to clip off the last two syllables of the word and it becomes *a term of fearful import.*" The thing took, the members of the court began to "*grue,*" and our overture was consigned to the "tomb of the Capulets," and yet, after all, Johnny Wightman was not generally thought to be the Solomon of the Assembly.

In the life of my brother of Kilsyth, the services of 1788, on the centenary of the "glorious Revolution," are particularly noted, and then it does not appear that Dr. Erskine and his friends opposed the appointment. I am inclined to think that evil is often done undesignedly by pushing sound principles to an extreme, or making of them an unsuitable application.

Dr. Burns delivered the annual discourse against Popery under the Hamiltonian foundation, for which he received an elegant copy of the Holy Scriptures.

In local courses of lectures on the same subject, he always bore his full share. He aided in giving direction to Charles Leckie's mind towards a field on which he was to win fresh laurels.

He had thoroughly mastered the genius of Popery, and subsequently made its rise and progress a specialty in his professorial lectures.

In the evening of his days he entered the arena of Papal controversy in opposition to Dr. Cahill. The latest of his literary contributions was on the Transubstantiation dogma. It reveals great accuracy in historical delineation, and keen critical acumen. There is also a frankness and fairness, an impartiality and charity about it, which won the admiration even of Romanists themselves. It is rare for any of the Papal dignitaries to come out in reply, but the tractate on the Eucharist was deemed of sufficient importance to draw forth a prominent Roman Catholic Archdeacon, who, while he tried ineffectually to meet the arguments, lauded the spirit and tone of his opponent's production.*

---

* Though known to live (as the noble Argyle said he died) "with a heart-hatred of Popery," my father was always on a friendly footing with Romanists. During his visits to Glengarry they were very kind to him. A recent number of the Montreal *Witness* (Feb. 8, 1872) contains the following anecdote, which it describes as a "perfectly true one." "When the late Vicar-General Hay, of Toronto, was on his death-bed, he succeeded in sending a message to the late Dr. Burns, who at the time lived opposite the

Grave consequences often result from trivial causes. Robert Haldane, the spiritual father of Merle D'Aubigné and the côterie of noble men who have formed the life's blood of the Reformed Church in France and Switzerland, happened to leave an umbrella at the headquarters of the British and Foreign Bible Society, Earl street, London. In that simple incident lay the germ of a controversy which raged fiercely for years, in which combatants of first-class mental calibre took part, and with which results momentous and wide-spread were wrapt up. Returning next day to claim his property, he got into conversation with parties in the office, who informed him that it was the custom of the Society to incorporate the Apocrypha with those copies of the Scriptures which were circulated in Continental and Eastern lands, so as to render them more palatable to the adherents of the Greek and Roman churches.

This admixture of the "words of the Lord which are pure words, as silver tried" with "reprobate silver" that had not the ring of the true metal and the image and superscription of the King, roused his honest soul. He withstood them to the face, because they were to be blamed.

Foremost amongst the opponents of this compromising policy was the minister of St. George's, Edinburgh.

"He drove home to the mind of the Protestant world

Roman Catholic Bishop's Palace, when he was dying, asking the latter to come and see him, 'as a neighbour, as a fellow-countryman, and as a dying man.' The Doctor was not at home when the message came, but as soon as he was informed of it he went over to the palace. He was, however, told there that Father Hay could not then see him, as he was labouring under a fit of coughing. The second time the Doctor called he was debarred from going into the presence of the dying man by the excuse that he was asleep. Soon after he had to go on a missionary tour, but before he returned Father Hay had passed into the eternal world." —ED.

the conviction that the Bible must be purified from this remaining taint. It ought to have been accomplished by Luther; its accomplishment will preserve for ever the name of Andrew Thomson." Much of human infirmity entered into the conflict on both sides. " The House of the Lord was filled with smoke." But there were both truth and beauty in the remark of Thomson to Haldane : —"All of human infirmity that now obscures this great work will pass away like smoke, but the flame will continue to burn and prove a beacon to distant posterity."

From his well understood principles, as well as his close intimacy with Dr. Thomson, it might be conjectured what side Dr. Burns would take, and that with him, on a question of this kind, neutrality would be impossible. In the 26th volume of the *Christian Instructor* (that for 1827) he has three letters (filling thirty-seven closely-printed pages) addressed to a " Friend," on the " moral bearings of the Bible Society controversy."

In introducing them Dr. Thomson says :—" We have much pleasure in laying before our readers the following letter from Mr. Burns to his friend. The discussion which it contains is very important and very seasonable, ably conducted, and deserving of serious consideration. Our excellent correspondent may be assured that we shall be most happy to insert his communications on the two remaining topics which he has yet to handle."

As he has himself noticed elsewhere, on the very first appearance of Dr. Burns as a Commissioner in the General Assembly, the *Plurality question* came up. It was in

1813, in connexion with the Ferrie case.* Dr. Ferrie, when Professor of Civil History at St. Andrews, had received a presentation to the parish of Kilconquhar, twelve miles distant. The Presbytery declined settling him unless he promised to resign his professorship. He refused —and the Assembly of 1813, by the small majority of five, supported him in this refusal, and reversed the Presbytery's decision.

In 1814, however, the General Assembly passed a Declaratory Act against plurality of offices, as inexpedient in itself, and inconsistent with the genius of the Church of Scotland. An issue was raised by the ultra-Moderates, who were vexed at this concession to rising Evangelism, to the effect that such legislation was unconstitutional, inasmuch as the Barrier Act had not been complied with, which required a reference to Presbyteries.

The Declaratory Act was not however rescinded by the Assembly of 1815. The Moderates continued to complain, and in 1816 a new Act similar to that of 1814 was introduced by Dr. Hill, which passed the ordeal of the Presbyteries, secured the approval of the Assembly of 1817, and became a permanent law of the Church. This rendered illegal any union of offices, involving non-residence in the parish.

In 1823, on the death of Principal Taylor, of Glasgow University, the Rev. Dr. Macfarlane, of Drymen, was presented to the vacant principalship, and soon after to the charge of St. Mungo's parish in Glasgow. The Presbytery, by a large majority, declared the presentee "un-

---

* Son-in-law to Principal McCormick of St. Andrews, and father of Mr. William Ferrie, formerly a Minister of the Canada Presbyterian Church.—ED.

qualified" to accept the latter appointment because of the incompatibility of the two offices. The Synod, by a much smaller majority, affirmed the decision of Presbytery, but the General Assembly of 1824, by a large majority reversed both decisions, and ordered Principal Macfarlane to be inducted into the parish.

It was this case which brought out Drs. Thomson and Chalmers in the fulness of their strength, and which occasioned the publication of Dr. Burns' work, entitled " Plurality of offices in the Church of Scotland examined. Glasgow : Chalmers and Collins, 1824."*

The composition of a work of three hundred pages, in little over a month was a marvellous feat. But he was anxious to have it out for the Assembly—and shut himself closely up for these weeks—and accomplished it.

A serious illness was the result of this undue strain on his powers, and the excitement of the Assembly which followed.

---

* Immediately on its appearance in April, 1824, Dr. Thomson, in the number of the *Instructor* for that month, said of it :—" This volume was put in our hands just as we were about to furnish the printer with copy of religious intelligence, and we immediately read it with the view of being able to give our opinion of its merits in the present number. Our perusal has satisfied us that it is a work of great excellence. It is full of important facts and able argumentation, and bears upon the subject of pluralities in general, and of Dr. McFarlane's plurality in particular, in such a manner as in our apprehension to set both questions completely at rest.

"We recommend it earnestly to all our readers, whether they are on the one side or on the other.

" Those who are hostile to union of offices will find their principles at once enlightened and confirmed by its discussion ; and those who are favourable to such a union will see reason, abundant reason, to adopt very different views on this topic from those which they have hitherto entertained.

"We really cannot express how much we feel indebted to Mr. Burns for his able, temperate and conclusive performance. It does much credit both to his understanding and his feelings, to his diligence in research, and to his power of applying his information to the cause for which he contends. And we are certain that it must prove highly useful to all who take an interest in the question of pluralities in our church, and whose minds are not totally blinded by selfishness or ambition."—*Christian Instructor, April,* 1824.

J

In that Assembly, the proceedings of which on the Plurality question were separately published,* his work was an oft-quoted authority. The review of the debate in the number of the *Instructor* for August, 1825, says : —" To this work many references were made by speakers on both sides, in the course of the debate. Of these, some have been omitted in the printed Report, but we give the following as a specimen. 'In investigating this subject I have followed a reverend gentleman (Mr. Burns), to whom the Church is much indebted for his researches, but I have chosen to verify his references for myself, and I have found them, in every instance, perfectly accurate."— Speech of Robert Thomson, Esq., Advocate, p. 44. " I bear testimony to its erudition and deep research, and the general accuracy of the Statutes and Acts of Assembly which have been brought forward."—Speech of the Rev. A. Fleming, of Neilston, p. 142. The Reviewer adds :— " That the praise bestowed on the work by *this* pleader should have been measured, was not to be wondered at, when we recollect that the professed object of his speech (as of Dr. Nichol's), was to attempt a refutation of the work."

To the author's speech in the Assembly frequent allusions are also made—as " See this fully illustrated in Mr. Burns' speech." " The cry of Infidelity has been most fully discussed in the speeches of Dr. Thomson and of Mr. Burns."

The book and the speech alike were regarded as masterly and exhaustive.

---

* Review of the Report of the Debate in the General Assembly of the Church of Scotland, on the overtures anent the Union of Offices, May, 1825, Edinburgh, 8vo. pp. vi. 189. Price, 3s. 6d.

In our College days, as on Sabbath morning we wended our way to St John's, Glasgow, to hear good Dr. Brown, or his acceptable assistant Mr. Grant (now of Ayr), we used to pass a plain but solid building, where ministered to a small audience John Macleod Campbell—formerly of Row, Dumbartonshire—an earnest, holy man, though mistaken. He had come under the spell of the noble but erratic Edward Irving, whose wild vagaries were for a lamentation, and whose weak-minded disciples, outrivalling the extravagances of their master, were playing fantastic tricks before high heaven! The faithful pastor of the sequestered parish on the lovely Gareloch did not go the length of the London enthusiasts—but he believed in universal pardon, and the revival of primitive miraculous powers, and became involved in other errors—which were borne with for three or four years—but which, at last, led to his trial before the Presbytery of Dumbarton, in June, 1830, and to his deposition by the General Assembly the following year.

When Dr. Andrew Thomson was told that Dr. William Cunningham was to be settled at Greenock, as assistant and successor to Dr. Scott of the Mid Parish, he exclaimed, "Good! he'll be a capital fellow for knocking the Row heresy on the head."

Similar was the estimate which he had formed of Dr Burns, as his eulogistic reviews of his writings on the same subject testify. Chief of these was the " Gareloch Heresy tried ;" an elaborate tractate of 88 pages, which rapidly passed through three editions.

It drew forth rejoinders from " Anglicanus" (123 pages)

and from a layman of the Church of Scotland, to the latter
of whom Dr. B. published a "Reply," of which the *Instructor* says :—"The 'Reply' is a work of extensive research, and, although consisting of no more than sixty
pages, and costing only a 'sixpence,' forms a *thesaurus* of
which every student of theology should be possessed."

Curiously enough the worthy minister of Gairloch in
Rosshire, who was orthodox to the back-bone, took it into
his head that the soundness of his theology was called in
question, and wrote to that effect. This led to the insertion in the "Reply" of the following postscript :—

"When I thought of levelling my piece among the wild fowl on
'the Gareloch,' it never once occurred to me that the reverbera-
tion of the report would be heard to such a distance as the hills and
the glens of Ross-shire, and yet 'true it is and of verity' that the
peaceful flock of the Parish of Gairloch, Ross-shire, have been
sadly annoyed with it ; and their worthy pastor has resolved on
this day (23rd February), to commence an action against the poach-
er on the principle of the game laws. Of the Rev. James Russel I
know nothing personally, but I have read many of his letters in the
Gaelic-School Reports, and I have always held him in esteem as a
worthy man ; and sorry am I that by a mere confusion of names I
should incidentally have given him one moment's uneasiness, or
rendered it necessary for him to draw out at great length the vindication of an orthodoxy which was never questioned by me. If any
thing shall be thought necessary to repair the damage done, I am
ready most willingly to make the following declaration when duly
called on in the proper court.

"Be it known to all men by these presents, that the arm of the
Clyde, called 'the Gareloch,' in Dumbartonshire, is not the same
thing with the parish called 'Gairloch, in Ross-shire ;' that 'the
Rev. John M. Campbell of Row,' is not the same person with the
Rev. James Russel, minister of Gairloch ; and that the terms
'Helensburgh' and 'Port Glasgow,' are not to be interpreted ac-
cording to the Linlathan code of criticism ; but mean, literally—
'Helensburgh' and 'Port Glasgow.'

"I apprehend that the whole mischief has been occasioned by a
misspelling of the name. The parish is uniformly spelled Gairloch. The lake is as uniformly spelt Gareloch. The proper orthography has been adopted on the title-page of the present pamphlet,
and the publisher will attend to the correction in future.

" The thing might perhaps have been designated as the ' Row Heresy,' but afraid that my old friend Mr. Story, of Roseneath, might feel himself overlooked, I thought it best to adopt a designation which might comprehend both sides of that beautiful arm of the Clyde, and therefore called it, very harmlessly at the moment —' The GARELOCH Heresy.' "

Dr. Marshall, of Kirkintilloch, sounded the tocsin of *Voluntaryism* in his sermon on " Ecclesiastical Establishments Considered," delivered before " the Glasgow Association for propagating the Gospel, in connexion with the United Secession Church." Mr. Ballantyne, of Stonehaven, had published " a Comparison of Dissenting and Established Churches," which supplied the more notable divine with some of his ammunition. Little notice was taken of these assaults by the Establishment till 1833, though, during the interval, the country was dotted with " Voluntary Church Associations," and echoed the sound of battle from afar. In that year the forces on each side mustered, and a general action commenced. For several years the conflict was keen. It developed some noble chivalry and splendid controversial ability, though marked and marred, as was inevitable, by not a little of that wrath of man which worketh not the righteousness of God, and of that envying and strife which are the parents of confusion and every evil work.

The pulpit, the platform, the press, were all enlisted. Sermons, lectures, addresses, debates were the order of the day. There was a snow-storm of pamphlets. On the Establishment side alone, it is said, that when the conflict was at its height, the Collins establishment sent forth monthly fifty thousand tracts. Seven magazines lent their aid on one side or the other.

It is not to be expected that Dr. Burns would be an uninterested spectator. He was one of the first to accept the challenge of the doughty knight of Kirkintilloch, who had rung forth the Philistine's cry, " Give me a man that we may fight together."

" The Religious Establishment of Scotland Vindicated" appeared in 1830—a sermon of 57 pages, preached on October 12th, before the Synod of Glasgow and Ayr, at Irvine, and "published at the request of the Synod," on motion of his old friend Dr. William Hamilton, of Strath-blane, seconded by Dr. Wightman, corresponding member from the Synod of Dumfries.

Subsequently appeared in succession a " Lecture on Religious Endowments," delivered in the High Church, and published " under the superintendence of the Church of Scotland Society" of Paisley. " A plea for State Churches, in reply to the Rev. Archibald Baird ;" " Scottish Voluntaryism, the Atheist's Ally," a " letter to the Rev. William Smart," etc., etc. These all attracted much attention at the time,[*] but, like the multifarious and prolific literature of this controversy in general, they have ceased to excite much interest among men, and have become the property of moths.

Dr. Burns was no intemperate partisan. He was no blind and bigoted defender of all that pertained to the

---

[*] "The Doctor, in a most spirited and powerful letter, demonstrates the truth of his assertion. He gives Mr. Smart a thorough and merited castigation. Dr. Burns' pamphlet is remarkably worthy of universal perusal. Like all the works of the same author, it gives proof of great acuteness and extensive reading. Mr. Smart will have the good sense not to attempt a reply." This estimate, by reviewers on his own side, of the last mentioned brochure, reflects that formed of the others.—ED.

" venerable Establishment." He was fully alive to her
errors and defects, and in the spirit of a true reformer,
bent all his energies to the setting in order the things that
were wanting. His " Essay on the Duties of the Eldership" and "Hints on Ecclesiastical Reform," furnish
ample evidence of this.

Nor were private friendships interfered with by the
keenness of public debate. Baird and Smart were " foe-
men worthy of his steel"—men of fine personal presence
and genial social qualities. When in the clash of intellectual gladiatorship, they ran tilt against each other, it
was " Greek meeting Greek"—but they were always fast
friends, and lived in love. In works of common interest,
such as Bible, Tract and other Evangelistic and Reform-
atory movements, they cordially co-operated.

Mutual tokens were interchanged. One of the most
valued treasures in my library is a ponderous volume of
" Mastricht's Theology,"—" presented to the Rev. Robert
Burns, D. D., as a small token of sincere friendship by
Archibald Baird."

The Voluntary Controversy gave rise to a number of
practised professional debaters who, not connected with
the regular army, did considerable execution. Prominent
amongst these was *Charles Leckie*, of Scoto-Irish parentage, a plain working-man in a Barrhead cotton-mill. Of
quick natural parts, sharp as a needle, lithe and supple in
his physical and mental build; amid the hum of the
factory, and the din and dust of the spindles, his had
been the " pursuit of knowledge under difficulties." Dr.
Burns was one of the first to discover and develop his

powers.   Leckie was a Reformed Presbyterian, brought
up at the feet of that noble theologian, Andrew Symington.   For six years, but a stone wall separated our house in
Oakshawhead from the Cameronian church and manse.
We often worshipped there.   Our families were on the
most intimate footing.   In that " School of the Prophets,"
a very plain upper room, the pastor of St. George's was
often found.   He counted Dr. Symington's six weeks
course better far than the six months of *his* day.   Leckie
thus was thrown in his way, and Barrhead being so near,
he often came in to see us.   My father aided him by
counsel and otherwise in the publication of his " Scripture References"—a larger and fuller work than Dr.
Chalmers' on the same theme—and encouraged his early
efforts.   With a voracious appetite for books and a most
retentive memory, accompanied with great coolness and
keenness, he proved a formidable debater, and with that
chivalrous hero, Macgill Crichton, scoured the country in
many an ecclesiastical foray.   We remember distinctly
his discussions with " citizen John" Kennedy, for nights
in succession, in the old High Church.

" His debating power was quite marvellous.   His ready wit and
brilliant repartee came, perhaps, from his Irish blood ; but he
drove home the rivets of his arguments like a Scot of the Scots.
He was a slightly made man, of middle height.   His features were
small and regular, his complexion dark, and his coal-black hair
stood straight up from his compact forehead.   A working man himself, he could deal with meetings of the working classes as no other
man in Scotland could do.   He encountered many a stormy scene,
battling with the fierce democracy, but his good humour was never
ruffled, and his cool self-possession never failed.   He was a gentle,
happy, humble-hearted Christian.   The Established Church found
one of its most effective defenders in this remarkable cotton-spin-
ner.   Some of his public debates lasted for three, and some of them

for ten, consecutive evenings.　Sometimes the eager crowd sat on till gray daylight streamed in upon them."*

The sixth great controversy in which Dr. Burns took part, was that which rent the Church in twain.

From its magnitude and importance, we must devote to it a distinct chapter, in which we shall again enjoy the aid of his own pen, which has failed us during most of this one.

* Life of William Cunningham, D. D., pp. 91-2.

CHAPTER X.

THE TEN YEARS' CONFLICT.

DR. SOMERVILLE, of Jedburgh, in his Auto-biography (p. 86) thus speaks: "So far from believing secession and schisms to be evils, I am inclined to think that they have been productive of beneficial effects with respect to the Ecclesiastical Establishment, as well as the more important interests of religion." He goes on to adduce the usual illustrations, in this relation, of the agency of Providence in over-ruling rivalships for ultimate good. We should be thankful that it is so, and especially that, during the darkest period of Scotland's Church History, the Secession Churches were the means of main-taining the steady light of evangelical truth in many parts of the land that would otherwise have been aban-doned to all the horrors of spiritual despotism and spiritual death.

I have not a doubt as to the truth of the averment that has been frequently made, and certainly it cannot be too

frequently remembered, that all the miseries which confirmed despotism on the one hand, and unbridled licentious-
ness on the other, have brought on nations may be traced
to the criminal neglect of those most deeply interested in
them to seize the proper opportunity of relief; to lay hold
of circumstances and events in the ordinary course of
things that might, had their voice been listened to in
proper time, have been the means of first alleviating and
then removing most grievous calamities. When the favourable moment is thus lost, it is seldom recovered. The
oppressing or offending party becomes stronger and stronger, the suffering party becomes weaker and weaker, for
impartial men are ever ready to ask the question : Why
did you not seize your favourable opportunity when you
had it ? The lengthened controversies in Scotland about
reform in the State, and the unpleasant position of things
at present (1867) in England on subjects and issues precisely similar, may suggest suitable illustrations of my
meaning. Precisely the same view may be taken of the
state of things in the Established Church of Scotland
when "the ten years' conflict" began. A finer opportunity never presented itself before of obtaining redress of
the grievance of Patronage,—either by actual removal, or
by a substantial bridling or muzzling (not by "muffling,"
as was done) the troublesome monster,—than was presented
in 1833 and 1834, when a movement was successfully
made in the House of Commons to have the subject fairly
canvassed. No doubt there were various motives ac-
tuating different parties in the matter; and after all,
an effective and final remedy might not have been secured.
But certainly the Church should have seized the opportunity, and lent all that influence to the "reform" movement
which she had been giving, and continued to give to the
plan of "extension." One great benefit incidentally
resulted from that movement. I mean the setting aside
by Mr. Colquhoun's, or rather Mr. Alexander Dunlop's bill,
of the claims of parochial patrons to the nominations of
ministers to all new churches, whether endowed or unen-
dowed, on assuming the rank of parochial charges. The

General Assembly had no difficulty in plying the civil authorities for aid, by public grants, for new churches; and why she should have hesitated to tell her mind on the far more vital question (certainly also the more popular one) of internal and constitutional reform, is one of those questions which I never could answer in any way that did not affect seriously her moral bearings, in regard to that political partizanship from which every church that has succumbed to it has invariably suffered.

Dr. McCrie, in his admirable and well-timed appeal in 1833, on the duty of the Church to petition the Legislature for the instant abolition of Patronage,—an appeal which wanted only his name to it to have given it all the weight which anything coming from such a quarter must have had—makes this remark : "Time was, and it has not long gone by, when such a proposal would not have been listened to in our supreme court, when it would have been difficult to find a person possessed of sufficient nerve even to move such a proposal." The remark is well founded. But to do justice to the memory of friends both clerical and lay, all of whom I rather think are now numbered with the dead, I must state a fact or two which came immediately under my own notice, a good many years before 1833. There was a fine lay movement in Glasgow for the removal of the grievance of patronage, headed by such excellent men as Mr. Henry Knox, Mr. John Robertson, Mr. John Wright, and others; and a pretty voluminously signed appeal was got up and presented to the General Assembly. The friends were certainly at a loss to find at once a clerical member of the house who would boldly, and in the face of frowns and hootings, present the deed in open house and advocate it when it came up in due order. At length they fixed on Dr. William Hamilton, of Strathblane, father of Dr. James Hamilton, of London, a name precious in literature and theology. One morning, on coming up to the Assembly, I met my friend carrying a pretty large roll under his arm, and I asked him what it was. "The root and branch petition," said he, "against patronage." Though all my days an

anti-patronage man, I was not quite "clear" as to whether
the time was come for a movement of the kind ; and not
being a member, of course I could not help him. But, oh!
how I often lamented that Thomson was gone, that McCrie
was not within the church, and that Chalmers, although
both wise and calm, struggled so long with the hydra before he saw, as at length (and alas! too late) he did, that
patronage was a power for evil not to be regulated, but
put down.

Since 1830 it has been my decided conviction, and the
longer I live is the conviction deepened, that in two instances of great magnitude as respects the future, our
Scottish Establishment failed egregiously in performing
her duty to her people. The one is, in that she overlooked
the great question of internal reform for the sake of simple
extension ; and the second is, that the Evangelical party,
after they gained the majority, did not sympathize with
the ascendancy of the advocates of political reform in the
State. Whatever may be said of the evil that arises from
clergymen taking part in politics, it is beyond all question,
that, whether they do so or not, a Church as established
by law is, of necessity, so linked with the Government of
the country, as to render it an object of very great moment
that harmony between them shall be carefully maintained.
But we all know full well that from time immemorial
there has been an irreconcilable difference betwixt the
two parties in the State, the friends of civil and religious
liberty on the one hand, and the conservators of things
as they are, on the other. And who can now doubt of
the fact that the Evangelical party in the Church of
Scotland were never privileged to bask in the smiles of
dominant Toryism ? The Church should have been more
alive to the mighty vantage ground she had acquired by
the passing of the Reform Bill—should have rallied round
the warm and honest-hearted friends of that measure—
should have moved with unbroken ranks in the direction
of vital reform ; and, when the first gleam of hope for a
century had dawned on her, should have demanded, if
not the literal abolition of patronage, at least a practical

relaxation of its iron grasp. Well do I recollect the communication made to the anti-patronage committee of Paisley by our member, Sir Daniel Sandford, that Government were favourably disposed to such a change of the statutes regarding patronage as would have placed the appointment of ministers on a largely popular basis. In March, 1834, I was a member of two deputations to Earl Grey, then Prime Minister—once on an appeal against an obnoxious clause in what has been usually called Mr. Colquhoun's Bill, for freeing all new erections from the grasp of the patrons of parishes—and again when our member, Sir Daniel Sandford, introduced us to his lordship as the bearers of various petitions from the west of Scotland for the abolition of patronage. On the first occasion we were handed over by Lord Grey to Lord Brougham, then Lord Chancellor, and we succeeded to the utmost extent of our wishes. In regard to the second, everything in his lordship's bearing to us was in harmony with our utmost aims, and all that appeared wanting was merely the *expressed view of the church herself.* Of the friends present on these occasions two besides myself survive—Mr. Dunlop, M.P. for Greenock, and Mr. Andrew Johnston, then M.P. for the Fife Burghs : the others were Mr. Thomson, Sir Andrew Agnew, Sir D. Sandford, Mr. James Ewing, M.P., for Glasgow, and Mr. A. Hastie, M.P. for Paisley.

The sudden and unexpected event of Dr. Thomson's death, on February the 9th, 1831, was a sad blow to the progress of enlightened reform, as the sequel soon shewed.

It was in the Assembly of 1832 that the question of popular rights in the election of ministers was first tried, on an overture for enquiry into the history and the practical working of the dominant system of Patronage, and " the paper named a Call," set side by side with each other. The overture was dismissed as unnecessary, but the ice was now broken, and the question came up in the following year. Though not a member of that Assembly, I was one of those who were invited to meet in the house of Lord Moncrieff, for private consultation on the subject, a

few days before the time fixed for the discussion. Having
learned from Dr. Cunningham that the law officers of the
Crown, though favourable to some change, were averse to
our touching the subjects either of patronage or of calls,
and had advised us to be satisfied with a negative or a
veto properly regulated, I declined attending the meeting.
and communicated respectfully to Lord Moncrieff my
reason for doing so.   I held, as I still do, that the method
of a direct and positive "call" from the people had many
advantages over that of a negative or a veto, and moreover that it had ancient constitutional usage, and not a
few legal decisions, in its favour.   Many were of the same
opinion; but as it was resolved by a large majority of the
friends of popular rights in the Assembly to go on with
the matter in the shape recommended, the greater part of
our friends voted on that side; a small majority of twelve
turned the scale against us, but we augured well for 1834,
when the same measure was triumphantly carried by a
majority of forty-seven.   In 1833 the question of direct
anti-patronage was also tried, and here, alas! we sustained a
blow, the more severe as being inflicted by ourselves.   The
regular Moderates sagaciously saw that we were at variance among ourselves.   They did not need to put forth
all their strength, and a milk-and-water motion made by
one of our own reforming friends was carried over a minority
of thirty-three, which was all that then openly rallied
around the anti-patronage standard.   It was not till 1842
that an anti-patronage measure was moved for, and carried by a large majority; but alas! it was too late.   The
favourable moment had been lost, and never could be regained.   Dr. McCrie was sadly grieved at the issue of
the overture of 1833, so different from what he had advised in his very able pamphlet on the subject, and so
different from what in all probability Dr. Andrew Thomson
would have advocated.

While these things were going on in the supreme court
of the Church, Sir George Sinclair, and the other friends
in the House of Commons favourable to popular rights,
moved for a committee of enquiry into the working of the

patronage system in Scotland since its re-enactment in
1712. There is no reason to question the sincerity of the
movers of this measure in their wish to aid and assist the
Scottish Church, at a time when the desire for social and
political reform was so strong, and especially in Scotland.
I do not say that all the friends of this measure were men
determined to put patronage down at all hazards. I think
the very reverse. But I see no reason to charge on the
measure the character of insincerity. The great error lay
in the friends of ecclesiastical reform in Scotland not
seconding it; and even the General Assembly itself ought
to have given it a public sanction, and recommended to
the ministers and members to give their evidence in the
committee, if called on to do so. There seemed to be a
truckling to Toryism—at all events a jealousy of the keener
or more radical Whigs. The scarecrow of an apprehended
overthrow of the Church Establishment, at the beck of
voluntaryism and of high church prelacy combined, was
held out to terrify the timid. Dr. Chalmers and many of
the best friends of ecclesiastical reform kept aloof; but
the Macfarlanes, the Cooks, and the Whighams* of shaking
moderatism saw the crisis as it was, and took their
measures accordingly, and with great practical wisdom.
There is good reason for thinking that Dr. Chalmers was
friendly to the proposal of a parliamentary committee to
enquire into the state of matters in Scotland with regard
to patronage. Yea! there is good evidence that he
strongly advised it, and was induced to change his opinion,
solely in deference to Lord Moncrieff. How it was that
a senator of such talents and knowledge of all the bearings of the case, became so afraid of any proposal to discuss
a question more closely connected with Scotland's best
wishes and interests than all the "bones and sinews" of
the reform question in civil polity, it is not easy to con-
jecture. I am inclined to think that his mind was still

* One of the most effective speeches delivered by my father in the General Assembly,
during the Church controversy, was in reply to Mr. Whigham, an eminent legal func-
tionary. It was published in pamphlet form, along with speeches of Dr. Candlish and
Earle Monteith, and forms a favourable specimen of a great variety of similar addresses
delivered by him in the various Church Courts and at public meetings on the absorbing
theme.—ED.

influenced more or less by the views thrown out by his illustrious father in the appendix to his Life of Dr. Erskine, regarding the reluctance of the Church to agitate a change in the patronage law. But surely times were wonderfully changed from 1814 to 1834.

If Sir Harry had lived to the latter of these dates the cast of his mind would have led him to long for a searching review of the whole subject; not indeed with a foregone conclusion as to a "root and branch" measure, but certainly with the hope of such vital changes in the law as would have made it work in harmony with the rights and interests of the people. Lord Moncrieff leaves us at no loss as to his views of this subject when he says, in his reply to question 1332 in the Report on Patronage, "In my opinion, if the law of patronage is put under proper check or control, it is, in the present state of society in Scotland, perfectly adequate and safe for the attainment of the great object of every such power of nomination, without ever being converted from its proper character of a sacred trust into the means of serving the interests of the patron himself."

I have never been able to see how the Church can retain her spiritual independence in any shape so long as the present patronage laws are in force. The patron is not within the Church or in any way responsible to her. He stands at the door of her every church and effectually defies her jurisdiction. It does not appear, indeed, that the Church did at the period of receiving her charter in 1592 consider the law as it then stood, or was ordinarily interpreted, as an invincible bar in the way of her accepting the benefits of a civil establishment; and yet, even so placed, she pressed for its removal. We adopt a "muffling" measure of our own to keep things as they are, in place of asking at once a legislative enactment for our people, and yet we resolve to stand by our spiritual independence. Where is the consistency here?

In connexion with the attendance of witnesses on the Commons' Committee on Patronage, I may note a little incident in which Dr. McCrie was the main party.

K

Going into the library of the House one day, I met the Doctor in the lobby, when he said to me, " Would you like to see the ' Booke of the Universal Kirke,' " which he had fully examined. Nothing could have given me more pleasure at the time than such a proposal. " Come this way," said the Doctor, and he led me to a desk where sat one of the clerks of the House, who had the sacred deposit under lock and key. That gentleman had no sympathy with us in our feelings at all, and while we were gazing on and ";gloating over" the venerable volumes, he broke out into this objurgatory soliloquy : " May a fire from heaven burn all you and your books and your Universal Kirks !" We laughed heartily at the ebullition of Puseyite venom on the part of this disciple of Laud, but little did we then think that the *quasi* prediction would be fulfilled in October following, by a conflagration which soon reduced the committee rooms and all their contents to ashes. Till 1860 I had a lingering hope that the venerable MS., so long kept back nefariously from its owners, and at length placed almost in their grasp, might in some way or other have escaped the flames. In 1860, a visit with my worthy friend Professor Lorimer, of the Presbyterian College of Theology, to the rooms of Zion College library, dispelled for ever all my hopes.

I have always looked back on the part I took in the Commons' Committee of 1834 on Patronage with perfect complacence. There were three points in particular on which I think that my labours in London at that time were of some service to the interests of truth. In the first place, I got access to the records of Parliament, and thoroughly verified the impression long prevalent that the proceedings of both houses of Parliament in regard to the Patronage Act of 1712 were originated in political discontent, and pushed on with reckless and indecent haste. In the second place, I was more minute and full than any other witness on the anti-patronage movements of the Church from 1712 to the period of the famous "Schism Bill" of 1767, which Principal Robertson, by a small majority, succeeded in consigning to a "committee of oblivion," in opposition to the motion of Dr. Wither-spoon that the overture should be sent down to presby-teries. In the third place, with the help of a clever young English barrister, incidentally brought in my way, and who was curious to know what I intended to say to their " high mightinesses," I discussed at great length the *pro* and the *con* as regards the famous *Veto Act*, which had not been passed, but which was carried triumphantly several weeks after in the General Assembly. Some lead-ing members of the anti-patronage committee felt that the successful issue of the motion of Lord Moncrieff on that occasion superseded farther action on their part, and the committee, which certainly deserved better treatment at our hands, forthwith dissolved. In addition, Principal Cunningham repeatedly told me that he felt himself per-fectly satisfied with the reason assigned by me for holding that the Act of 1690 was in no sense a patronage act, but rather a well-regulated method of popular election.

It was in the fall of 1839 that the non-intrusion commit-tee circulated an official account of the progress of the work on which they were engaged. The title of the piece is, "The State of the Case," and it has the authority of Dr. Chalmers and of all the members of the committee at-tached to it. Just about a year after, Mr. Bell, Procura-tor of the Church, made his famous speech in the Commis-sion of the Assembly, on the then position of the Church, and while defending ably the cause of non-intrusion, he shewed keen sensibility on the subject of anti-patronage, a fearful monster which had then begun to hold up its head, " hirsute and horrent," before the public; for Dr. Candlish, Dr. Cunningham, Mr. Maitland Makgill, and hundreds of other men of mark in the Church, had now come under a bond or engagement to see patronage torn up root and branch. In these varied movements great ability was shewn, and most satisfactory defences of the Church put forth. Such of us as had always been anti-patronage men did of course go readily along with the tide, now beginning to flow in the right direction ; but we could not but feel that it was rather too late. The auspicious moment was in 1834, when the Commons' Committee on Patronage was sitting, and when Dr. McCrie was yet spared. The Church had not then learned what she found out in 1842, that patronage was not a boon liable to abuse and requiring to be regulated, but an evil to be put down. Moreover, there had been too much crouching to the Tories, and too much scolding of the Whigs.

It was not until 1842 that the Church assumed her proper position on the anti-patronage principle. Prior to the assembly of that year a great meeting was held in the West Church of Edinburgh, when bold resolutions for the abolition of patronage were passed, and the anti-patronage standard was fairly unfurled. The meeting, of whose proceedings I have even at this distance of time (1867) a very clear remembrance, was a most harmonious and enthusiastic one. It paved the way for the great battle in the Assembly of 1842, where the late lamented Principal Cunningham took the lead, and when the combined army composed of the "Moderates" and the "middlemen" was overthrown. What I always lamented was that this was the *very first* occasion on which the Church had assumed her ancient protest against the fatally experienced evils of patronage. By this time also the Evangelical party, which had nobly gained and firmly maintained the ascendancy in the General Assembly, was broken in upon by a third party, known by the name of the "Forty," who in their first movement seemed to be sincere and honest, but whose ulterior proceedings were sadly prejudicial to the great cause at issue, by dividing our ranks, and giving to Sir James Graham and other wily politicians a plausible advantage, of which they failed not to avail themselves.

It becomes a fair and a very interesting question, what, in all probability, would have been the result had the Scottish Church joined issue with the friends of anti-patronage measures legitimately pursued? For my own part, I never had any doubt upon it in my own mind. I am far from thinking that the law of patronage would have been repealed root and branch, but am clear that most effective popular checks would have been laid on by law, and patronage would have lost entirely its character as a marketable commodity. Any approved measures for Scotland would in all probability have been followed up by similar measures on behalf of the now distracted Church of England, and the alliance between Church and State regulated on principles far more in harmony with the theory of internal jurisdiction and spiritual independence. Voluntaryism, as a system of national or of public procedure and action, would have gone down, and Moderatism would have "conclusively" obtained a mortal blow. Even the Veto, with all its cumbrous habiliments, wrought well for the ten years of its existence as a regulating law. During its continuance, many of the men who became afterwards leaders in the Disruption were brought into the Church. Much as I disliked the measure, because it stood in the way of something better, I never had anything in common with those professed advocates of the call and of anti-patronage who, in spite of neither of these having been got, and just because they have not been gained, remain within the Establishment.

Had there been no such body as the "Forty," as they styled themselves, and had the ministers of the Establishment, especially those who called themselves "Evangelical," stood firmly to their post, matters would in all probability have ended otherwise than they did. But after all, let us remember that "God's thoughts are not as our thoughts, nor His ways as our ways."

Looking back to 1843, may we not say, "What hath God wrought!" Looking at institutions worn out, it may be, partly by original defects in their construction, and partly by the abuses and sins of men, let us hope and pray for better times; and in the meantime let us adopt the language of the inspired apostle and say, "O the depth of the riches, both of the wisdom and knowledge of God! How unsearchable are His judgments, and His ways past finding out."

Never had he a busier summer than that which fol-

lowed the Disruption. Nor was he ever happier in his
work. The glorious liberty of the sons of God was in
an unusual measure enjoyed. Released from the crushing nightmare that had sat on them, and from the shackles
whose iron had begun to enter their souls, many felt
in these happy halcyon Disruption times, a lightsomeness,
a buoyancy, an enthusiasm, before unknown.

By a singular coincidence, during the interval of
nearly a year which elapsed before the handsome new
church was opened, those who followed him, and they
formed an overwhelming majority of his congregation,
worshipped in the " Old Laigh Kirk," in which thirty-
two years previously he had been ordained, and where he
had spent the first years of his ministry. It was a new
era, and he seemed (in common with many) to receive a
fresh baptism of the Spirit, so that his word was with
power.

Such cheering missives reached us every now and then
that memorable summer, at our " Hermitage" retreat, as
the following :—

"CAMPHILL, PAISLEY, August, 1843.

" MY DEAR ROBERT,—Our church is now contracted for, and
will go on immediately. It is to cost £1,200.   •
" We had noble work here on Sabbath last—3,000 people are
calculated to have heard a sermon at the tent, and the church was
also crowded. There were 1,500 communicants. All went on with
wonderful solemnity, and the crowds listened with apparent delight
—much precious seed sown. May the dew and rain of heaven
descend to refresh the thirsty ground! My action sermon was
Rev. vii. 13–end. Mr. MacNaughton's—'Awake O Sword!' My
evening sermon on John iv. 11. Uncle preached in the tent at the
South Church too, and in the 'Old Low' on Monday night, when
we had a *Thanksgiving* and a *thousand* auditors.
" Remember me affectionately to the ladies, and thank Miss Ann,
in name of Charles Leckie, for the valuable present."

The above seems to have been a United Communion Service—in which, at least, the Free High and Free St. George's participated. The "Tent" was brought into requisition; and seated on the green sod that roofed the sepulchres of loved ones long departed, with moss-covered monuments on every side, and the memories of other days crowding thick upon them, they sang the oft-repeated song of deliverance, and held communion with the God of their fathers, who seemed to come nearer to them than aforetime.

CHAPTER XI.

HE society originated with Dr. Burns. Several considerations contributed to form and to foster his interest in Colonial evangelization. His younger brother, George, had at an early period in his ministry, been settled at St. John, New Brunswick, where for fifteen years he wielded a powerful influence for good.

The dark days of 1816 and 1820 had sent forth many worthy weavers from Paisley. Dire necessity drove them from the mother-land to seek shelter and sustenance in the wilds of Canada. Roughing it in the bush, they

---

* Chronologically, the "Colonial Society" should have come in earlier; but as it is so intimately connected with my father's New World life, I think it preferrable that it should appear immediately before his first visit to America and his subsequent removal thither.—ED.

found ample provision for the life that now is, but as regards the higher provision for the life that is to come, they " began to be in want."

Appeals, coming time and again from parties closely connected with his own pastoral charge, wrought upon one whose ear was ever acutely sensitive to the cry of misery, and whose whole soul beat in sympathy with the wants and the woes of the poor. The emigrant's cry was to him like the beckoning Macedonian to the Apostle of the Gentiles in his Troas chamber.

Although he did not, as yet feel, that the " come over and help us" was addressed to him personally, he felt that necessity was laid upon him at least to do what in him lay to send others.

In 1824 he conferred with a few friends, but the Plurality Controversy came on for a season to monopolize his regards, and the severe and protracted illness which followed the publication of his Plurality volume—the result of the intense mental strain which its rapid preparation occasioned—delayed the immediate carrying out of his cherished project.

The Rev. James Marshall, then settled in Glasgow, afterwards of the Tolbooth, Edinburgh, son-in-law of Legh Richmond, subsequently a minister of the Episcopal Church, was one of the early friends of the Colonies with whom he conferred.

On the 15th April, 1825, the Society was formed at a large and influential meeting, held in the Trades' Hall, Glasgow. The chair was occupied by the Right Honourable George, Earl of Dalhousie, G. C. B., "Captain-General and Governor-in-Chief in and over the British Provinces and Dependencies in North America," who became Patron of the Society, and was always its faithful friend. At this meeting, Dr. Burns propounded his plan, which met with general acceptance. He was at once appointed principal Secretary—a post which he filled with universal approval during the fifteen years of the Society's active existence, till in 1840, it merged in the Colonial Scheme of the Church of Scotland. At different times he had associated with him such men as Drs. Scott, of Greenock, Beith, Stirling (then of Hope St. Gaelic Church, Glasgow), Welsh, Edinburgh (then of St. David's, Glasgow), Geddes, of St. Andrew's, Henderson, of St. Enoch's, Glasgow, and James Marshall. But though all of them rendered efficient aid, on him always lay the chief responsibility ; and the truth of the following kindly utterance of one of them, (Dr. Henderson) in proposing the grateful acknowledgments of the General Assembly of the Free Church of Scotland, in 1857, on occasion of Dr. Burns' first appearance there, after his settlement in Canada, was conceded by all :

" I want particularly to draw attention here, to the fact, which many know as well as myself, but which in the course of time some may not know, that we have had before us this evening, the father of the w hole Colonial Missionary enterprise.

" In 1825, before the Church had contemplated any operation of the kind, our venerable friend (Dr. Burns), borne on in the exuberance of his zeal and interest on behalf of our expatriated brethren, instituted what at that time was known by the name of the North American Colonial Society, and the labours of that Society lay upon his shoulders. I lent a little help to him, in a kind of secondary capacity for several years after I went to Glasgow, but had nothing else to do with it ; and this has made me fully aware of the great debt of obligation under which the colonies of Britain, east and west, have been laid by this venerable man. I cannot out think this Assembly will feel that he is entitled to a warm reception, when they see him coming here in his old age, with almost unabated vigour, and certainly unabated zeal, prosecuting the same good work."

It was not long till the Society secured the confidence of the churches, and across the mighty deep, many longing eyes were directed towards it. From all the North American colonies cases of destitution were pressed on its notice.

Many excellent ministers were, through means of the Society, settled in all the Provinces. In one year eight were settled over fixed charges and nine sent out as Missionaries. The seventh report, presented in April, 1833, mentioned "fourteen ministers sent forth in the course of as many months."

By this time, an interest was awakened throughout the Church, so that young men of more than ordinary promise "willingly offered themselves." Amongst "the rest, *Dr. Candlish*, who, at the time of his application to the Society, was acting as assistant to the Rev. Mr. Gregor, of Bonhill, Dumbartonshire." *

He was appointed to Ancaster, but circumstances prevented his going.

We may speculate as to what this eminent man might have been had his destiny been the quiet Canadian village, instead of the most prominent position in the Scottish metropolis.

But "all this cometh forth from the Lord of Hosts,"

---

* Some time previous to Dr. Candlish's application, Dr. Cunningham had been settled at Greenock, as assistant and successor to Dr. Scott of the Mid Parish. Old Kilpatrick had become vacant. Meeting a friend one day, Dr. Cunningham said :—"I mean to try for Kilpatrick to keep out a Moderate, of the name of Candlish, who is assistant to the minister of Bonhill."—*Dr. Cunningham's Life.*

" who appointeth the bounds of our habitation," and who is "wonderful in counsel and excellent in working."

We subjoin the main portions of the letters of Dr. Candlish :—

"BONHILL, 30th March, 1833.

" Rev. Dr. Burns,

" REV. SIR.—Knowing the interest which you take in the settlement of Christian churches in British North America, I take the liberty, though a stranger, of addressing you on the subject. I am disposed to regard that country as an interesting field of ministerial labour, and as I understand that at present there seems to be a call for additional labourers there, I beg to express my desire of serving the Great Head of the Church in any part of his vineyard where a fair opening may appear, and my willingness accordingly, to accept of any appointment which may hold out the reasonable prospect of professional usefulness and respectability. I have been a preacher of the Gospel now for about five years, during nearly four of which I have been regularly engaged in the discharge of pulpit duty, and latterly of parochial duty also, as an assistant in Glasgow, and in my present situation. I hope, therefore, that I may be in some measure warranted in my wish of forming a more intimate and permanent connection with a congregation of my own.

"Should you deem this application worthy of notice and encouragement, you will not, I am persuaded, find any difficulty in making the necessary inquiries, as to character and qualifications. Meantime it may be sufficient to mention the name of Dr. Smyth, of St. George's, Glasgow, as a person to whom I am well known. I shall be glad to receive any information which you may have to communicate, and to attend to any suggestions which you may nake.

"I have the honour to be, Rev. Sir,

"Yours, very respectfully,

"ROBERT S. CANDLISH,

"Assistant to the Minister of Bonhill."

"BONHILL, 13th April, 1833.

"REV. SIR,—Since I saw you yesterday I have been considering what you said, relative to the appointment to Ancaster, and I think it may be proper before anything more is done in the matter, to explain my views to you more fully than I was quite prepared to do at the time. The appointment seems in many respects a suitable one, more especially, as I understand it to hold out a reasonably distinct promise and prospect of being fixed and permanent. I confess, that at present, occupying a situation in the church at home, which, however humble, yet affords me the opportunity of regular professional employment in the duties of a parish, I should not feel myself either called upon or indeed at liberty to go to Canada in the character of a general missionary, and to wait when there, for a call from a particular congregation ; though knowing the want of ministers and the urgency of many congregations, I should scarcely hesitate, if not professionally engaged already, on the encouragement afforded by your Society to do so.   I think, however, it must be obvious, that being fully occupied in the care of a parish and congregation here, I should be unjustifiable, as well in point of duty as of prudence, were I to resign my present employment without some security of being immediately employed as a minister in the same way.

"This I contemplated in my former letter to you, when I expressed my willingness to accept of any appointment which held out the prospect of professional usefulness and respectability.   In so far, therefore, as the appointment in question is not of a vague nature, it better suits my views than any of those recently made. I will state to you, however, candidly, a probable difficulty which I see in the way of my accepting the appointment, should it be offered to me.   The willingness which I have expressed to serve the Church and the Head of the Church abroad, is not the result of a hastily formed resolution on my part, (for I have previously and deliberately looked on Canada as a very important and promising field of ministerial labour, and one having peculiar claims on the attention of our church,) but the announcement of it will be sudden as respects my friends.   Now I am not disposed to take so important a step in life, in a hurried or seemingly precipitate manner ; and I very much fear it will not be possible for me now to make the necessary arrangements for leaving this country before the season is too far advanced, or in sufficient time for occupying the situation in view.   Besides that, circumstances of a private nature would make an abrupt departure very inconvenient, some regard is plainly due to my engagement and situation as assistant here.   Though not bound to remain for any definite period, I am unwilling suddenly to desert my post ; and there are considerations which make me feel, that by leaving this place immediately and without some little preparation, I should not only put the minister to very serious inconvenience, but materially incommode and perhaps injure the congregation.   I have received great kindness from Mr. Gregor and it would ill become me to do any thing in this affair without consulting as far as possible his feelings.   I know that he will be averse to part with me, and I should wish that he had such previous notice of my intention as might enable him better to dispense with my services.   I may mention too, that within these few months I have, with Mr. Gregor's concurrence, begun to adopt measures for the more effectual discharge than hitherto of parochial duty here, and I feel myself in some degree bound to see these measures carried into effect, at least so far as to prevent them falling to the ground in the event of my going away. The works and plans which I have begun I should like to leave in such a state that any one coming in my place may, without difficulty, take them up. These reasons may require my continuing here for some time longer, and may render it impossible for me, with propriety, to leave my present charge, before the summer is pretty well over. At least, I think it fair to state they will weigh with me considerably in deliberating upon my call to go abroad sooner.

"I wished to make known my disposition to forward by my personal exertions the aim of your excellent Society. That disposition I still retain, and I am prepared accordingly to give all serious attention to any proposal that may be made to me. If, therefore, after the explanation I have given, you should be disposed to recommend me as a fit person for the situation in question, I will fairly estimate its advantages and recommendations, and will not, without some sufficient reason of duty or necessity, hastily decline it. But at the same time, it is for you to judge from the circumstances which I have stated, how far it may not be expedient to suggest, for the present appointment, some other individual more disengaged than I am, and better prepared for an immediate departure. Only I trust you will believe that my purpose, though, from necessity, it may be deferred for a while, is not on that account abandoned, and that I am not the less inclined on any subsequent occasion, if I shall be at liberty to look abroad for employment, to consider the claims of our countrymen in the colonies.

"In the meantime, I have thought it right to send you this full statement, in justice to you and to myself, as well as to the gentleman with whom the appointment rests, that he may not lose time and opportunity by relying upon aid from a quarter where, perhaps, he might be unavoidably disappointed.

"I have to request your excuse for the trouble which I give you, and your candid interpretation of what I have said and written. You will give me credit I hope, for sincerity at least, and for an honest desire not to be misunderstood.

"With gratitude to you for the kind and cordial reception which you gave me.

"I remain, Rev. Sir,
"Very respectfully yours,
"ROBERT S. CANDLISH."

The Rev. Henry Gordon, of Gananoque, narrates a visit to Paisley "on occasion of his application to the Society." "Having, along with Wm. Turnbull Leach (now a minister of the Episcopal Church in Canada), been designated by

the 'Glasgow Colonial Society' as missionaries in Upper
Canada, and on the 15th July, 1833, been ordained by the
Presbytery of Haddington, we visited Dr. Burns at his
house in Paisley, and in his official capacity as Secretary
enjoyed close intercourse with him. I was impressed by
the affability of his manner, the vigour, vivacity and
freshness of his mental powers ; the graceful ease of his
conversation. But that which most deserved admiration
and which was most congenial to the objects of the visit,
was the devotedness with which he had given himself to
the interest of the Redeemer's Kingdom in the British
Colonies. The one thing into which your father threw
his remarkably active mind, was to have an active part
in the diffusing Christ's name, and His truths in their
purity, over Britain's Colonial territory. Even now that
I am writing, methinks I see the joy on his face, when,
from the large map of Canada, fixed on the walls of his
study, he pointed out to Mr. Leach and myself the topo-
graphy of Canada with such painstaking particularity
of description, as that we almost believed that we were
actually there, choosing our location. That Canada had
even then, *i. e.*, in 1833, a large space and no mere corner
in his heart, was too manifest to admit of concealment.
But little did I then know to what this interest in Canada's truest well-being would grow."

The Rev. Thomas Alexander has furnished me with a
copy of the commission he received from the Colonial
Society, on the 2nd June, 1834. It guarantees him £100 a
year—and closes with " and so, may his labours be blessed, and his health preserved by the Head of the Church."

Mr. Alexander gives a graphic account of his journey, in which the suffering of shipwreck at the mouth of the Moira, near Belleville, comes in as a prominent incident. He hastened forward to Cobourg to succeed the Rev. Matthew Miller, a remarkable man sent out by the Society in July, 1833, who was drowned in the Bay of Quinté, in February, 1834.

The Eighth Report of the Society, submitted by Dr. Burns, on the 10th March, 1835, speaks of the "Directors having designated the Rev. Messrs. Bayne and Anderson as missionaries to the Upper Province, and these gentlemen they cannot but consider as a valuable accession to the roll of colonial labourers."

Had the Society done no more than donated to Canada two such men as John Bayne and Matthew Miller, its labours would not have been in vain. But others besides those named—such as Rintoul, Roger, Reid, Stark, McGill, and many like minded, hold honorable place on its roll.

The secretaryship was no sinecure. The selection and sending of missionaries; the correspondence with them; the attendance at the meetings of committee; the advocacy of the Society's claims in pulpit and on platform; the collecting tours in England, Scotland and Ireland— and a multiplicity of nameless duties, devolved on Dr. Burns a vast amount of labour. The following letters to Dr. Welsh,* will give a glimpse of the kind of work he had to do, and a specimen of many kindred communications :—

---

* Dr. David Welsh, then of St. David's, Glasgow, afterwards Professor of Ecclesiasti ca History in the University of Edinburgh, who, as retiring Moderator tabled the Protest on the memorable 18th May, 1843. He was one of the earlier colleagues of Dr. Burns in the secretaryship.—ED.

"ABERDEEN, Sept. 3, 1830.

"MY DEAR SIR,—Your patience will be nearly exhausted by my silence, if it has not given place to a sympathising concern, lest your colleague Secretary should have been swallowed up in the Caledonian Canal, or mayhap, in the more terrific whirlpools of Corrievrekin. No! I have been preserved amid my journeyings and voyagings —minus only my voice—which left me in consequence of a bad cold caught in or about Loch Lochy, by sleeping all night on the sofa of the cabin, and without any covering.

"It prevented me from preaching at Inverness, on the forenoon of Sabbath, as designed. Our cause was ably and powerfully pleaded by my friend, Mr. Clark, who is much respected in Inverness, and from whom we received much attention. I tried to preach, or something like it, in the evening, and collected well. We had also a public meeting in the church on Monday evening, when I entered more at large into details, and collected again. This will issue in the appointment of a permanent committee of correspondence, and I have not the smallest doubt that, from the interest excited, and the spirit which I saw at work in our favour, Inverness will be a most important auxiliary to us. I could have spent a month at least, preaching every day, and if you had been with me we could have done much more than we did, but a fair commencement has been made, and nearly £40 realized.

"I went on to Tain, and although I did not preach, I got from Dr. McIntosh, £40, as a donation from the Northern Missionary Society, and the promise of permanent aid. A good deal of information also from him, regarding candidates. He is a warm friend to our Society, and a most judicious and valuable adviser. I saw also Messrs. Carment, of Rosskeen, and Flyter, of Alness, who are very friendly; visited the garrison at Fort George, and arranged for a sermon in the chapel, by Mr. Clark, when it is expected the officers and men will give a day's pay. Many of them have been in America, and almost all of them have friends there. We had a sermon and collection at Forres, by Mr. Clark, as I had to come on to Elgin, in the splendid church of which I preached on Wednesday, and collected £5—small—but large for that cold place. The clergy very languid. The only person whom I found at all anxious to serve us, was the editor of the Elgin *Courier*, who promised to advocate our cause by the insertion of intelligence at any time. This may be of use. Here I hope to do some good, as also at Peterhead and Fraserburgh.

"Dundee and Perth will also be visited."

The notices in the foregoing letter of his trip to the North of Scotland, suggests another at a subsequent date to the South. It was one of the pleasantest of all his

L

journeys, and rendered memorable by his association, during it, with Dr. Chalmers.

In June, 1838, he received from Sir Andrew Agnew, the following :—

"LOCHNAW CASTLE,
"STRANRAER, 7th June, 1838.

"REV. DR. BURNS.   DEAR SIR,—Your avowed attachment to the best interests of the Colonies, prompts me to make a request of you at this time.   Doctor Chalmers has kindly promised to visit us here immediately on his return from, France (God willing).   It is an old engagement of many months standing, and which he has repeatedly ratified.   His object is to awaken from sleep our torpid country, by giving repeated addresses on Church Extension and the other schemes of the General Assembly.

"In order to make as lively an impression as possible on the minds of our people, I am very desirous of seeing at the same time, all the several schemes *personated* by the living eminent divines of the national church—and I would pray you to personate the Colonies !   It would give Lady Agnew and me much pleasure if you would honour us with a visit here.

"A steamboat, (the *Lochryan*) arriving every Friday, (in 12 hours from Glasgow,) at Stranraer, would land you within six miles, and there a carriage would be in readiness to bring you up. Dr. C. expects to be here the end of July—but of this more particularly I shall make it my business to let you know when I hear from him again.   Only let me beg you, in the meantime, to have the goodness to give a general assent to my scheme, and let me hope that you will yourself take a part therein.   The necessity which exists amongst us, for some such enlivening proceeding, I will not attempt to describe.   You are yourself, I doubt not, well aware of the state of the case ; and I confidently look to your helping hand for benevolent aid.

"Trusting that you will pardon the liberty which I have taken,

"I have the honour to be,

"My dear Sir,

"Yours very faithfully,

"ANDREW AGNEW."

This kind invitation Dr. Burns accepted, though he had some hesitation about the "Combination" scheme. Whereupon Sir Andrew wrote again :—

"LOCHNAW CASTLE,

"STRANRAER, 16th July, 1838.

"MY DEAR SIR,—You are very kind in so cordially expressing your willingness to give us the pleasure of seeing you here.

"There is much force in what you say regarding the difficulty of pleading more than one of the four great schemes of the church at the same time. But on the other hand, it has been found that where an interest in any one scheme has been awakened, attention is the more easily called to all the others. A general awakening is what we desire. How that is to be done can be best told, when we have felt our way a little more. The Church Extension cause is, as yet, but partially understood, and would need all the aid which it can receive from its Rev'd. champion and his friends.

"As to the Colonies, we have largely contributed towards the augmentation of their population, and there are few families amongst us where a chord would not vibrate, if touched by the Master's hand. Nor must this be your only visit ; having found out your way, and discovered that steam-power has brought us to your very door, you will admit the responsibility which now lies upon you to make our latent energies marketable, by making Stranraer a suburb of Paisley. Let us have a spiritual as well as a temporal benefit from the new facilities of intercourse.

"Hoping to be enabled very soon to have the pleasure of writing more distinctly as to the day of Dr. Chalmers' coming,

"I have the honour to be,
"My dear Sir,
"Yours very faithfully,

"ANDREW AGNEW."

On the 31st July, Sir Andrew writes a third time, intimating that the week from the 19th to the 26th August had been agreed upon, and urging Dr. Burns to take part with Dr. Chalmers "in this awakening." Dr. Chalmers' journal testifies what a week of unalloyed enjoyment it was. Dr. Burns was accompanied by one of the members of his family. He had a peculiar pleasure in meeting with the Presbytery of Stranraer. In 1799, that Presbytery had licensed his brother William, "the Pastor of Kilsyth," who had been tutor to Sir James Hay, of Park, Glenluce.

In 1835, this presbytery published an address to the congregations within its bounds, warmly eulogising the efforts of the Colonial Society and commending it to their confidence and support. The very name too of the pious and patriotic Baronet, whose munificent hospitality he was enjoying, was of itself a passport to their hearts and homes.*

I am not aware that any represented the other schemes of the church, but Sir Andrew accompanied the representatives of Church Extension and the Colonies in a pilgrimage stretching over two weeks, with a loving interest and hearty enthusiasm, which riveted them to him in the bonds of a deathless friendship.

It was at this time also Dr. Burns formed the acquaintance of General McDowell, of Stranraer, who became a fast friend of the Colonies, and from whose library the shelves of more than one Canadian college were richly replenished. The correspondence of the old veteran with Dr. Burns, was terminated only by his death.

Dr. Macintosh McKay, who subsequently evinced his sympathy by devoting the maturity of his powers to Colonial service, lent early to the Society the benefit of his efficient advocacy. He writes to Dr. Burns from

---

* The founder of the Agnew family came over with William the Conqueror. The Parliamentary Act of 1661, which confirms the family in the possession of its rights and privileges, quaintly describes them as having been enjoyed " past all memorie of man." But though, as descended from the Agnews of Normandy and the de Courcys of Kingsale, (Premier Baron of Ireland,) there flowed in his veins the blood of two of the most ancient and honourable families in the Kingdom, no heart beat more truly than that of the chivalrous Champion of the Sabbath, in sympathy with the sentiment :—

> " Howe'er it be, it seems to me
> 'Tis only noble to be good :
> Kind hearts are more than coronets,
> And simple faith, than Norman blood."—ED.

Dunoon, February, 1836, complaining of the indifference
of a leading town, which was destined, afterwards, to
witness special divine manifestations, and whose response
to the fine sermons of himself and colleague, reached the
magnificent aggregate of £13 5s. 5½d.

" I am inclined to say : ' I'll gang nae mair to yon toon.'

" The Ladies' Society of Perth extends over the entire county.
Would it not be a grand matter if the ladies of every Highland
county would be stirred up to form a similar association.

" I trust some plan will be formed to draw together an Association of Ladies in Glasgow, similar to Mrs. McKay's in Edinburgh.

" The church must put on a bolder attitude, and arouse itself to
energy in the missionary cause at home and abroad. Some united,
concentrated, powerful movement must be made all over the church.
The Colonies must not be neglected. I am quite certain that if ministers will do their duty, the people will do theirs. Some plan must
be matured at next General Assembly for the forming of every
parish into an Auxiliary and Missionary Society for Home and
Foreign purposes.

" At all events I am quite clear about one thing—that you ought
to get charge as convener of that committee of the Assembly on
Colonial Churches, at the head of which the venerable Principal has slept for some years back. I trust, my dear sir,
you will continue having your heart encouraged and your hands
strengthened of God, to plead and speed forward the cause of precious, perishing souls. Many, I doubt not, are the blessings on
your head already, from hundreds and thousands of our brethren
in America, for what you have already done. All our friends in
the East country are loud in their commendations of your labours
of love, and may these be increased and favoured abundantly."

The first published suggestion of a Presbyterian College for Canada that we can discover, is in the Third
Annual Report of the Glasgow Colonial Society, drawn
up by Dr. Burns, and presented by him at the Anniversary, held on the 22d April, 1829, twelve years prior to
the passage of the Royal Charter which formally ushered
it into existence, and three years prior to the first movement of the Canadian Church. In his Report of the fol-

lowing year, (27th April, 1830,) Dr. Burns returns to the
subject thus :—"The Colonies seem particularly to stand
in need of institutions sacred to the great business of the
general and theological education of young men, natives
of the Colonies themselves, who might thus be trained up
from time to time for the service of the sanctuary."

The first Synod of Canada, held in 1831, seems to have
passed without any allusion to the matter.*

At the second Synod, held in Kingston, commencing on
the 2nd and closing on the 4th August, 1832, the subject
of Theological Education was introduced by Mr. Rintoul.
This Synod was presided over by Dr. Mathieson, of Montreal, and attended by twelve ministers and three elders.

In 1839, a Bill was obtained from the Local Legislature
to establish a college in connexion with the Church of
Scotland, under the title "St. Andrew's College of Canada." It vested in the Rev.. Messrs. W.Rintoul, A. Gale,
W. T. Leach, R. McGill, J. Cruickshank, H. Urquhart,
and twelve lay members of the church, the right of
holding "Lot No. 32, in the 3rd Concession S. of Dundas
street, in the Township of Trafalgar," purchased with
£500 stg., placed at the disposal of the Presbytery of
Toronto, for the establishment of a college, by Sir Wm.
Seton, of Pitmeden, Bart.; and 200 acres of land, being Lot
No. 4, in the 5th Concession of the Township of Nissouri,"
donated for the same purpose by the Hon. William
Morris. The name was changed tó "The University at
Kingston," altered still further to "Queen's College at

---

* The Abstract Minutes of 1831, covering four small pages, contrast strikingly with
the 184 well filled pages of our "Acts and Proceedings" in 1871. These minutes are a
mirror reflecting the relative progress of the church these forty years.

Kingston," when on the 16th October, 1841, a Royal Charter took the place of the Provincial Act.

With the establishment of this institution, Dr. Burns had much to do, and to the formation of its library he gave very freely from his own.

He had copious correspondence on the subject with the Hon. William Morris, Alexander Gillespie, Esq., and Rev. Messrs. Rintoul, McGill, Machar and others.

When in 1840, the Rev. Dr. Cook and Mr. Rintoul went home as a deputation in its behalf, he rendered them most efficient aid.

Dr. Burns took special interest also in " Dalhousie College," Halifax.   In 1828, he was in search of a President for it, and applied to the Rev. Marcus Dods, of Belford, father of the Rev. Marcus Dods, of Glasgow, whom the Presbyterian Church of the Lower Provinces recently endeavoured to secure as their Professor of Theology.

The following is one of the letters in a correspondence which seems to have terminated unfavourably :—

"BELFORD, 17th March, 1828.

"You seem to me to be in pursuit of the philosopher's stone. Where in these degenerate days do you hope to find a man possessed of all the qualifications that you require ? In some of the things you mention I am much rusted. The rust, however, might by a little scouring rub off. But of one of them, Chemistry, I have just sufficient knowledge to enable me to put a proper quantum of salt in my kale. If this *hiatus valde deflendus* in my mental furniture should not form an insuperable bar to any further negotiation, I certainly am not disposed to put the proposal lightly away. But in the meanwhile, if the above defect be not fatal, I should like to have some more particular information with regard to the College, of the existence of which I had not previously heard. I do not feel much disposed to leave this place for a distant land.

"Yet my reluctance would readily yield to aught that I might consider a call of Providence, or to the prospect of greater usefulness. With thanks for your offer of recommendation and best wishes."

We had copied out eighty pages of Colonial correspondence which we are compelled to omit.

These were culled from seven large quarto MS. volumes
into which my father collected the greater part of his
Colonial letters.

In three thoroughly characteristic epistles, Dr. Mathieson finds vent for the Scottish exile's longings, and his
strong attachments for the "Kirk." He ridicules the
Episcopalian proclivities of a certain class. He deplores
the deadening influence of ministerial secularities, sighs at
times for a quiet country parish in his loved native isle,
and gives expression to breathings after the higher Christian life.

Dr. McGill relates his settlement in Niagara, is severe
on High Church grasping, and handles as it deserved, the
notorious ecclesiastical census of a certain deceased prelate.
He propounds a scheme for raising $120,000 for Queen's
College, and pleads for two professors, " the best in *braid
Scotland.*"

The letters of the Rev. William Rintoul are very
numerous, dating from his leaving Maryport onwards, and
reflect his earnest spirit. As pastor in Toronto and Streets-
ville, and for a time Superintendent of Missions, he pleads
most meltingly for increased supplies to meet the prevalent spiritual destitution. As one of the first Colonial
ministers who moved in the matter of the college, he gives
special prominence to it, specifying Dr. Cooke, of Belfast,
and Dr. Burns as suitable men to fill the post of first
Principal.

The Rev. John Clugston, of Quebec, long acted as the

faithful agent of the Colonial Society for Eastern Canada, and was a most valuable and voluminous correspondent. His letters are full of matter respecting his department of the field, noticing the arrival of many missionaries who always found counsel and comfort under his hospitable roof. He has graphic touches on the doings of Dr. Harkness; the Canadian Rebellion; the obnoxious rectories; Lord Durham, &c., with an occasional burst of honest indignation at high-handed Episcopal assumptions.

The Rev. George Romanes, afterwards Professor in Queen's College, gives many interesting details of his missionary experience, places the East before the West, and speaks in favour of an order of circuit preachers.

The Rev. P. C. Campbell, M. A., now Principal of Aberdeen University, in a beautifully distinct hand, furnishes a very minute and instructive account of his travels, and of the position and prospects of the church, lit up here and there by fiery flashes at the insult offered by the then Solicitor General (Hagerman) to Scotland and Scotland's Church.

Dr. Machar, whose name is yet fragrant in Kingston, returns thanks for files of *The Witness* and " Chests of Books ;" commends Dr. Cook and Mr. Rintoul, the College Delegates, to home sympathy and support, and expresses a decided preference for a Principal and Professors from the old country, in opposition to my father's not less decidedly expressed conviction that the selection should be made from Canada.

The Hon. William Morris,* is the most voluminous

* Brother of the Hon. James, and father of the Hon. Alexander Morris. In one of his many letters he remarks, "Our family left Paisley in 1801." He possessed many most estimable qualities, and proved ever a true friend of the Presbyterian Church.

of the lay correspondents.   His letters abound in interest
—bearing principally on Queen's College; the efforts to
pass the Local Acts, and to obtain the Royal Charter, the
importance of the preparatory education, and of securing
first-class men, his published letter to Principal Macfarlane and Dr. Burns, with occasional references to the
vexed questions of the Clergy Reserves and the Rectories.

Mr. Alexander Gillespie, of Gillespie, Moffatt & Co.,
indicates by his letters a peculiar interest in Colonial
Presbyterianism.   He encloses correspondence with Lord
John Russell, about securing a Government grant to the
college, recommends application to Governor General
Thompson;* is delighted with the union with the United
Synod, and counsels maintaining friendly relations with
the Synod of Ulster.

On this last subject there is a fine letter from Dr. Kirk-
patrick, of Dublin, who pleasantly recalls Dr. Burns' presence at his Ordination in St. Mary's Abbey,† in 1829,
along with Dr. Heugh, of Glasgow, as Delegates from the
Scottish Missionary Society.   He speaks of the healthy
spirit of the Irish Church since the cutting out of the
Unitarian cancer, her interest in missions, her looking to
Canada as a field, and the desire of a cordial understanding, which was fully reciprocated, with the Glasgow Colonial Society. .

Among old country correspondents may be named the
Rev. James Marshall, who speaks of the Glasgow brethren
as waiting for my father's recovery from the severe illness

---

* Afterwards Lord Sydenham.
† Dr. Kilpatrick's colleague in Dublin for many years was the late Dr. James Carlile,
the former competitor of my father for the Low Church, Paisley, who was succeeded by
Dr. John Hall, now of New York.

of 1824, that he might make the first move in connexion with the formation of the Society.

The venerable Dr. Scott, of Greenock, eulogised so warmly by Dr. Cunningham, who acted for some time as his colleague, was one of the early Secretaries of the Society. He encloses letters from John Galt, the celebrated author,* respecting preachers from Scotland—dwells on the kind of men required—the difficulty in getting them, and the importance of exceeding prudence in the selection.

Dr. Welsh, the leader on the Disruption day, when Minister of St. David's, Glasgow, acted as a Secretary of the Society for some time, and these volumes contain a number of his letters, as also of Principal Lee, of Edinburgh, Principal Macfarlane, of Glasgow, Dr. Patrick Macfarlane, of Greenock, Dr. Macdonald, of Ferintosh, Fraser, of Kirkhill, Kennedy, of Killearnan and Redcastle, and a host of others. Elect ladies also, who felt a deep interest in the Colonies, such as the Lady Mary Murray, and Mrs. Mackay, of Rockfield.

The estimate formed of the gratuitous services rendered by Dr. Burns to the Colonies in connexion with this Society, may be judged from two, out of many, testimonies.

In a letter received from Dr. Henderson (of date, Glasgow, 28th September, 1871,) Dr. Burns' quondam associate in the Secretaryship, that accomplished veteran in the service, says :—

"I was never gifted as Dr. Burns was, with a strongly retentive memory, and now in my age much of what was committed to it has

---

* Father of Sir A. T. and of Judge Galt.

faded from it ; I am glad however to have the opportunity to express my distinct conviction, strongly held and often expressed, that among Scotsmen, Dr. Burns is entitled to be regarded as the greatest benefactor (spiritually) to the Presbyterian people of Canada, and the founder of her Presbyterian Church.

"Before the institution of the Colonial scheme by the Church at home, or about 1833 or '34, there were 50 ministers or thereby in Nova Scotia, and about 30 in Canada (of the Church of Scotland). These were mainly the fruits of the operations of the North American Colonial Society, of which Dr. Burns was the life and soul. At that time the missionary spirit had hardly began to awake in the Established Church.

"The time and pains taken in this work by Dr. Burns cannot be told. Besides his labours in this Glasgow Society, on behalf of the American Colonies, he stirred up an interest in the good cause in the church courts—moving overtures in the Synod of Glasgow and Ayr, which, being carried there, Principal McFarlane introduced to the Assembly ; and on his motion, the Colonial scheme was adopted, and thereupon the Glasgow Colonial Society superseded.

"Most of us felt that on the ground of ability, zeal, and preparation of every kind for the office, Dr. Burns was entitled to the honour of the convenership of the committee. Some of the best friends of the Society looked upon the appointment of Principal McFarlane to this office instead, as alike ungenerous and unwise. Dr. Burns himself took no affront, but continued as a member of the Assembly's Committee to take the same interest and to spend the same energy in the service of the Assembly's scheme, as he had done in the Glasgow Society.

"I have stated this, being aware that some time ago, the claim was put forth by a minister of the Established Church, to the origination of the Colonial as also of the Foreign Mission scheme.

"The truth is precisely as I have here stated it. In regard to both schemes, the case is precisely similar. Dr. Inglis moved the Assembly to the institution of the Indian Mission. Principal McFarlane moved there, as I have said, the adoption of the Colonial scheme, but a "Scottish Missionary Society" and a "Glasgow Colonial Society," stood outside the General Assembly, the results of private Christian faith and zeal ; and if they did not knock for admission, year after year, did not do so because they had often been neglected or refused, and had been shown no sign of willingness to open to them. This, I believe, is the simple truth."

The Rev. Dr. Beith, of Stirling, who, like Dr. Henderson, was one of the most honoured Moderators of the Free Church of Scotland, and the immediate predecessor of Dr. Cunningham in the office, was also for two years (1825-7,)

associated with my father as Colonial Secretary of
the Society.

In a very interesting letter from Dr. Beith, (dated
Stirling, November 20th, 1871,) he says :—

"Your father was the very life and soul of the enterprise. I
acted very much as his *sub.* If he did not himself write all the
letters (and they were very many,) which our work required, he
always indicated to me by jottings on letters, what required to be
answered, or by various hints, when any correspondence was not in
answer, the nature of the communications which, on such occasions,
were to be made to friends abroad and at home. The late Mr.
Richard Kidston was the practical man on our committee.
His intimate acquaintance with our American Colonies, and especially with those parts of the country which engaged our attention
and called forth our energies, eminently qualified him to be our
guide and adviser. He was at the time immersed in the cares and
the toils of an extensive business, but he never was absent from
our Council board when the business of the Society was to be done.
Your father's confidence in Mr. Kidston was unbounded. I am
not aware that we ever had reason to think, that we, on any occasion erred, when we yielded our convictions to the views of Mr.
Kidston.

"The wonderful facility with which your father wrote often
amazed me. So did the quantity of matter which flowed from his
pen. I have no record of the amount of the correspondence which
occurred during the years I acted with him, but I know it was very
great.

"Dr. Welsh became my successor on my leaving Glasgow for a
parish in the Highlands. He used to compare notes with me.
His impressions of the incessant, irrepressible and productive activity of Dr. Burns, were quite in accordance with mine.

"A few years ago your father paid me at Stirling a most gratifying visit of two or three days. Among other subjects on which we
conversed, was our intercourse with each other in the Colonial
Society.

"All the world knows and has heard of the wonders of his memory—a memory, as Dr. Guthrie once said to me, approaching the
divine - but the experience I had of its power on this occasion far
surpassed all my previous conceptions. Numerous, almost innumerable as the letters had been which he wrote, or which I wrote
by his instructions, during the years of our colleagueship, he
seemed to remember them all ; the dates on which they were
written—the persons to whom they were addressed—the subjects
they discussed—and the results which followed in the case of every
one of them. As for me, I could recall no more than simply that I

had been engaged with him, as I have narrated; that generally, but none of the details.

"A poor widow woman of my congregation had a son who, about twenty years before this visit of your father to me, had emigrated to Canada with his wife and one or two children. She had heard from him once or twice after his arrival in Toronto or Montreal—but he had ceased to write to her, and though she had repeatedly addressed letters to him, she had had no reply. She heard of your father's being with me. She came modestly to entreat me to speak to Dr. Burns; perhaps he knew something of her son and of his family. I introduced her to him after asking his consent. He received her with the greatest kindness and affability. She told her story. He put some questions referring to the communications she had had from her son—his personal appearance, handicraft, &c. After a pause of a few minutes, he came out with a flood of information to the poor woman. He knew her son for he had been of his congregation for a time. He knew his wife, all their children, their names. He told all about their present condition, and the occupations of those who had gone out from their father's house—everything. The poor woman's heart overflowed with thankfulness. She often afterwards spoke to me of the 'comfort Dr. Burns had given her.'

"I saw less of Dr. Burns on the occasion of his last visit to this country than on the occasion of his previous visit. On one of the Sabbaths during the Assembly, 1857 (I think), we preached as colleagues for Dr. Clason. We afterwards dined together at his house. They were both my seniors by several years. Their conversation led them back to the scenes and exploits of the days of other times. Dr. Clason's memory was good, but it was not to be compared with that of Dr. Burns. For him—he remembered every text of every sermon he had preached in his earliest days—and all the way down. He remembered, moreover, all that he had ever heard from our host, who seemed not a little gratified, and not a little inclined to draw largely on the stores of your father's marvellous recollections of the past. It was to me a pleasant and a profitable evening.

"Of course you know how much your father was the friend of Dr. Andrew Thomson, and how much he was his coadjutor in public matters—how much he aided in the great Evangelical movement which distinguished the beginning of this century. That matter does not belong to me here.

"With much desire for your success in the work with which you are engaged, and with expressions of profound respect and regard for the memory of your father.

"I am, very faithfully yours,

"ALEX'R BEITH."

CHAPTER XII.

VISIT TO THE UNITED STATES AND CANADA IN 1844.

THE Churches in America were not slow in sending fraternal greetings to their new-born sister in Scotland,.and kind offers of substantial aid. It was therefore deemed advisable, at an early day, to send a deputation to the New World. Dr. Burns was asked to join Dr. Cunningham, of Edinburgh, who had preceded him, on this mission. His devoted nephew, on being asked *when* he could start for China, significantly pointed to his portmanteau, and said, "To-morrow." He, too, was "ready to depart on the morrow." The first insertions in his "Journal of my Visit to America" run thus:

"Thursday, Jan. 2, 1844.—Went from Kilsyth to Edinburgh, to see friends, and to hear Dr. Chalmers lecture. Heard him twice.

Visited the College.   Dr. C. carried the resolution of the committee
of that morning.   Dr. C. had hinted it before.

"3rd.—Settled matters ; came west ; attended congregational
soiree in the evening, and made it known.

"4th.—Arranged supplies ; made necessary calls ; to Glasgow ;
ticket in mail to Liverpool.

"5th.—Set off."

On the eve of his sailing we received the following :

"LIVERPOOL, Monday, 8th Jan., 1844.

"About to embark at 12, with good hopes.   Sabbath spent agreeably here, preaching twice, &c.   Let us often meet at the throne
of our gracious Father.   I am well, thank God."

The voyage was long, but not unpleasant.   Two old
residents of Montreal were his fellow-passengers ; and
through one of them we have learned how useful and
pleasant he was on shipboard.   She has shewn me a copy
of his Life of Dr. McGill with which he presented her as
they parted, bearing a kindly address.

Now, again, the autobiography comes to our aid.

Dr. Cunningham was appointed a deputy to the American Churches on behalf of the building fund of the Free
Church of Scotland in the end of 1843, the year of the
memorable "disruption."   On my reaching New York on
the 7th of February, 1844, I found that he had spent two
weeks in that city, had preached in various churches, had
addressed different public meetings, and had organised an
effective committee for obtaining subscriptions from the
friends of the Free Church.   With that committee I had
a most agreeable conference on the day after my arrival,
and advocated the cause in two of the largest churches on
the Sabbath following.   In the meantime I received a
letter from Dr. Cunningham, then at Philadelphia, urging
me to come on immediately, so as to aid him at a great
public meeting in that city, fixed for the Tuesday following.   Leaving New York on Monday morning by train, I
spent the greater part of that day and the following at
Princeton, with our excellent friends Drs. Alexander, Mil-

ler, and Hodge. As I was the guest of the first of these eminent men, we had much conversation together on the subject of our visit to America. Dr. Cunningham had been with the Princeton friends for several days, and they had assisted him in his arrangements. My venerable host told me that, in addition to the plan drawn out, he thought that Dr. Cunningham had limited himself rather too much in his range of visits, and named a variety of large and wealthy cities *in the South* which ought not to be overlooked. It did not appear that Dr. Cunningham had specially noted the slave element as a hindrance in the case. Neither did I ; for besides trying to obtain contributions to our cause, I felt a great desire to bear a testimony in our own way against a great national sin, and it seemed to me very necessary that we should see something of the character of the system to which we were opposed ; indeed my " testifying processes" began that very afternoon, for in my note book of that date there stands the question put by me to my venerable host, " What is the reason, Dr. A., why the Old School Presbyterian Church has relinquished its former testimony against slavery ?" And the answer follows : " Sir, slavery is a political institution, with which the Church has nothing to do." My very decided answer on the opposite side led to a keen but friendly discussion on several points at issue ; but in was never hinted, either by my kind friends or myself, that our views on slavery would interpose a bar in the way of our paying a visit to the wealthy cities of the South, that we might preach the gospel in the various pulpits that might be put at our service, and let the hearers throw their dollars into the plate without any questions being asked by us or by any one else. The question of casuistry involved in this view of the matter did not present itself either to Dr. Cunningham or myself till about ten days after, when a good part of our collecting work was over in the cities of Philadelphia and Baltimore, and the idea of a " raid" upon the South was again mooted. Dr. Cunningham was much set against it, but I was supported in my views of the case by our friend the Rev. Geo.

M

Lewis, another deputy who had just arrived, and whose admirable volume of "Impressions" ought to be carefully studied by every one who takes an interest in these matters. The doctor uniformly held that we had just one thing to aim at, and that was to obtain aid to our building fund. He was moreover of opinion that our zeal in "testifying" would not be valued highly by our kind cousins ; and moreover there was something hazardous in the thing. I dare say he was right; but my way of reasoning, be it right or wrong, lay here—that the advocacy of the slave system was by no means confined to the South; that in the cities of New York and Philadelphia I had found more keenness on the wrong side than we were likely to meet with in the South ; that the links of connexion between the middle states and the South on this *questio vexata* were very strong; that we were not entitled to advance indiscriminate charges against the very mixed population of a whole country ; and that our friendly remonstrances and suggestions might be of some service in strengthening and cheering many of the citizens both in the North and in the South who sighed for a better system. From jottings in my note-book I see that on my return to New York two excellent anti-slavery men— Messrs. Tappan and Jocelyn—called on me, and asked of me an explanation of our proceedings in the premises; and that such was the substance of my reply to them. After all, we did not penetrate far into the South, and our receipts from that quarter did not exceed a fifth of the gross amount ; and much kindness did we experience there. With many excellent men, both clerical and lay, did we meet; and our "Naphtalis," or "feats of quiet witness bearing," did not at all interfere with a scathless retreat.

Dr. Cunningham and I were together as deputies from the beginning of February till the beginning of April. Our proceedings were of course marked by considerable uniformity, but great was the variety of character, both national and Christian, that met our eyes. Dr. Cunningham has furnished a fine *vidimus* of the results of his visit to the States in the admirable article from his pen in the

January number of the *North British Review* for 1845.
I may just add, that in all our arrangements for public
meetings and addresses, we always placed the Principal
in the foreground as the vigorous and successful ex-
pounder of "Acts of Parliament" and "claims of right."
But he generally unbended when he paid a tribute to
worthy "Janet Frazer," and the "Crook in the Wa'". On
such occasion the starched features of our dear American
friends were pleasantly relaxed into something not unlike
a laugh by the exciting contrast betwixt the outgoings of
a massive intellect and the playings of fancy around the
circle of a "good story."

Dr. Rainy touches thus on these "testifying processes,"
in the deeply interesting Life of Principal Cunningham :

"Dr. Burns was associated with Dr. Cunningham during a large
part of their operations.
"Any one who knew the Doctor, so full of knowledge, so pro-
nounced in judgment, so instantaneous, copious, and unintermit-
tent in utterance, so prompt to give voice to the precise reactions
which the impressions of the moment caused. Any one who knew
how little he dreamt of giving offence, and how much he enjoyed a
tilt with any apparently objectionable person or idea, may conceive
the situation. Such a man—his mind full of the animation of those
days and of the excitement of travel—coming into the midst of a
society new to him, where many things were unexpected, and all
more or less strange, was sure to have plenty of thoughts. As at
home, so in America, he was always ready, in public and private,
to tell his auditors all he thought of their ways and their institutions, great and small ; and this in a flow of rounded sentences so
finished, plentiful, and epigrammatic, that his hearers must have
thought he had spent his whole voyage across the Atlantic in con-
cocting them. I have seen a letter from Dr. Burns, in which he
notes that his 'testifying processes' began on the very day he arrived at Princeton. He reports also that Dr. Cunningham did not
consider 'testifying' to be any part of their appointed work, nor
likely to be highly valued by our American cousins. It turned out,
however, as he intimates, that his efforts in this line did *not* prove
to have any tendency to produce serious embarrassment.
"The source of this was simply that immense constitutional
eagerness which was closely connected with some of Dr. Burns' best
gifts and aptitudes for service. As age tamed it down, not quench-
ing what it chastened, it left that venerable old man, whose appearances in extreme old age in recent General Assemblies were

surpassed only by his appearances in the pulpit : the zeal for his Master's cause and gospel absorbing and ennobling all the man, and the wonderful stream of utterance coming more manifestly than ever from a pure heart, and a good conscience, and faith unfeigned."*

One of Dr. Burns' pastoral letters will serve to show how faithfully, during his absence, he kept his attached flock apprised of his doings.

"PHILADELPHIA, 14th Feby., 1844.

"DEAR CHRISTIAN FRIENDS,—It becomes me to acknowledge the mercy of our God in my preservation, both on the wide ocean and on the banks of the Delaware. We had gales of strong wind and what is called squally weather for a week, when hovering on the Banks of Newfoundland ; and the snow and frost, and intense cold, since I began my journeyings in these parts, are somewhat different from what I had been used to at home ; but the weather on the whole has been dry and healthy, and I never felt more vigorous. Since I reached New York on Thursday last I have enjoyed the privilege of joining in and assisting at the communion of the Supper of our Blessed Lord, in one of the principal Presbyterian churches of that city, and of addressing in the evening a very large congregation in another of the churches, belonging to the Dutch Reformed Church ; and of preaching the same truths which my predecessor Witherspoon proclaimed on the spot, at Princeton College, where that eminent man so long edified and instructed those under his care. In the course of an hour or two, on Monday afternoon, a large congregation of ministers, and professors, and students, and of the people at large, were brought together. It was easy to gather them on the shortest notice, for there had been there for some time past a deep religious impression, a revival of the best kind, and on the most approved principles ; and I preached, not on the church question (for they had already got that from my friend Dr. Cunningham, and collected 500 dollars), but on Romans xv. 29 : "When I come to you, I will come in the fulness of the blessing of the gospel of Christ."

"The College is a noble institution, and so is the Seminary for theology adjoining. I heard my friend and correspondent, Dr. Charles Hodge, Professor of Divinity there, author of the *Exposition of the Epistle to the Romans*, examine one of the finest classes of students I ever saw, on the all-important doctrine of justification ; and my intercourse with the President and Drs. Millar, Alexander, &c., was most agreeable. "Are they not a noble class of men ?" said Dr. Cunningham. And yesterday, when we met for the first time on this side the great waters, my impression was, and is, that they were so ; and that the educational institutions of Princeton, with

* Dr. Cunningham's Life, pp. 210-12.

their seventeen professors and tutors, most of them eminent in literature and theology, form one of the finest nurseries for the American churches. I stood by the grave of Witherspoon, and read the Latin inscription on his tomb. I was in his manse and in his study, and occupied a chair which he took with him from his house at the head of Lady Lane, Paisley. I saw the original drawing of his picture, which is quite different from the engraving I have in Paisley; and old Dr. Green, his venerable pupil, and his successor in the presidency, tells me that the one I saw here is the true likeness. With his grandchildren, and great-great-grandchildren, three generations, I have had a great deal of intercourse. Many questions about Paisley did they put to me, and I promised to see them again, if at all in my power. I came to this great city yesterday (Tuesday), and we have had a full meeting yesterday, and a sermon to-night, in the large and beautiful church of which Dr. Bethune, the grandson of Mrs. Graham, formerly of Paisley, and whose life you all know, is pastor. It is midnight. To-morrow we go to Baltimore, where two Sabbaths must be spent; and then we go to Washington, where Congress is sitting, and before whom we are expected to preach.

"This is a noble country, and the public institutions of this large city are unrivalled in the world. I have seen most of them to-day, and in one of the best of them (the Penitentiary) I found, as under-superintendents, two Paisley men, one of whom I had assisted as an emigrant about two years ago. Another of these emigrants came to hear me last night, a weaver, who is getting on remarkably well. There is much true godliness here, and in New York; but I rather think that the work of God prospers more in the smaller places, like Princeton, than in these large cities. I preach here again on Friday three times, at New York one Sabbath, and then on Monday again.

"It will delight me to hear that you are regularly supplied with gospel ordinances, and that the collections for the missionary schemes of the church are regularly made. Bear with me if I be not home before May, for Canada I must visit, and it is at present not so easily got at.

"May the Lord bless you and keep you, and all the families of the congregation. May He cause His face to shine on you and on your friends.

" From your affectionate Pastor,

"ROBT. BURNS.

"P.S. Please read this to the congregation, and to any of the parishioners, and to Mr. Crichton." *

---

* Mr. Thomas Crichton, born in 1761, died in November, 1844; father of the General Kirk Session in Paisley, and friend of Dr. Witherspoon, whose life he wrote in the *Christian Instructor*. He was a remarkable man. He aided Dr. Burns in several literary enterprises. A long letter of his, dated 14th of December, 1824, with which his excellent

He found many warm friends in America.   The friendships even of college days were revived.

He wrote thus from the elegant home of his comrade
in the race of love and forgiveness forty years previously
in Edinburgh,—the same kind, conscientious John Codman whom he helped to exemplify the precept, "let not
the sun go down upon your wrath."

" DORCHESTER, NEAR BOSTON,
" 30th March, 1844.

" MY DEAR ROBERT,—You are not forgotten by me.   From day
to day we meet, I trust, in the presence of the Hearer of Prayer,
and at that gracious mercy-seat which is equally accessible from all
points and from all distances.   I have heard repeatedly of you and
William, and I write you both by this mail.   It will cost you the
postage, for I cannot pay it here,—all the postage taken on this side
is a *cent*; in other words, a halfpenny !

" I trust your studies have been going on prosperously.   Before
I can be home with you, the 1*st of May* will be over, and all prize
matters will be over too ; but whether you be successful or not, the
benefit of the exercise is of itself a reward.

" Yesterday Dr. Codman took me to Cambridge, three miles from
the city, to visit the University of Harvard, a noble institution,
where I saw a very fine library, and some interesting MSS., with a
copy of the Bible in the Indian language, translated by John
Eliot, the celebrated apostle of the American Indians, whose place
of labour was within three miles of Dorchester, where I now am.

" We visited also the Cemetery of Mount Auburn, a very interesting place, like the Necropolis of Glasgow, but ten times as
large.

" I have yet other *lions* in the city to see, but yesterday we met
at the house of Governor Armstrong (at dinner) no less than the
real living lion of this country, the celebrated *Daniel Webster*, undoubtedly the first man of the States, a very pleasant and intelligent man.   We had also the whole of the Supreme Judges, and a
number of the clergy, &c.—a most sumptuous and splendid entertainment.

" I am staying with my old class-fellow at Edinburgh College,
Dr. Codman, who lives in great style here, for he is a wealthy man
and much respected.   I preach for him to-morrow, and twice in
the city."

---

son in Paisley favoured us, aided the Colonial Society at its start.   With another son,
John, who settled in Canada in 1820, my father used often to sojourn when " roughing it
in the bush."

Referring to this visit to Boston, the Rev. George Lewis says :

"I was much amused with Dr. Codman's account of the examination to which my colleague, Dr. Burns, subjected one of the Indian teachers paid by the Scottish Society for the propagating Christian Knowledge. Desirous of beginning at the beginning, and ascertaining the Indian teacher's elementary knowledge, the doctor asked gravely, 'Who was Nicodemus ?' The Indian, thinking he was in jest, answered, with Indian gravity, 'A great warrior !' Yet, to the no small surprise of the doctor, he seemed afterwards perfectly to understand the distinction of President Edwards between moral and physical inability." *

In August, 1868, I visited Harvard University. The venerable custodian of the hundred thousand volumes of its noble library asked me to insert my name in the visitors' book. He looked at it, then at me, and asked if I was related to Dr. Burns, of Toronto. I told him who I was. He then said, " Over twenty years since, that gentleman visited this place, and donated to us some valuable contributions. I wish I had more of them."

Meeting at the same time with Dr. Blagden, the patriarchal senior pastor of the " Old South," of revolutionary fame, I found his recollection equally distinct. He spoke most warmly of my father's appearances in his church and the other leading city churches, and of the deep impression produced.

The celebrated Dr. Bethune, of the Reformed Dutch Church, then in Philadelphia, when he preached for me at St. Catharines, shortly before his much lamented death, spoke similarly of his visit to the City of Brotherly Love. Dr. Henry Boardman, also of that city, when we met him two years ago at Chicago, and others whom we have met

* Impressions of America, p. 383.

during our residence in the United States, gave kindred testimony.

In his *Familiar Letters*, Dr. J. W. Alexander (then Professor at Princeton, afterwards of the Fifth Avenue Church, New York), thus writes of Dr. Burns' visit :

"PRINCETON, February 20th, 1844.

" The Scotch delegates thicken upon us : we have had Rev. Dr. Burns, and Elder Ferguson, and are daily expecting Lewis, who has arrived at New York.   Burns, you know, is in Witherspoon's pulpit at Paisley ; he has been settled there thirty-three years.   He is one of the most learned men in Scotland : has edited Halyburton's works, Wodrow's History, and is author of Memoirs of Professor McGill.   Burns' manner in the pulpit (gesture excepted) is more *outré* than Cunningham's.   But his sermon was noble, rich, original, scriptural, and evangelical ; and in diction, elegant ; and his closing prayer was seraphic."

"PRINCETON, March 22nd, 1844.

" Dr. Burns has been here, and in spite of my prejudices I must say he preached on Wednesday evening one of the very noblest discourses I ever heard.   The text was from Zec. xiii. 7, " Awake, O sword," &c.   It was teeming with scripture, but even the most familiar texts were made brilliant by their setting and connexion." —Vol. i., 388–391.

Three years afterwards we find this notice of a subsequent visit :

" May 8th, 1847.

" Dr. Burns, of Toronto, left town this evening, after a sojourn of two or three days.   He goes to Halifax, about a new theological school there,   I think he has more exactness and extent of knowledge, and a greater outpouring of it in vehement and often affectionate discourse, than any man I ever met, unless I except Chancellor Kent, whom he resembles in his contempt for all conventionalities."—Vol. ii. 68.

Very large sums were collected by the deputies from many parts of the United States for the treasury of the Free Church.

The Rev. Dr. McCosh, President of the College of New Jersey, writing from Princeton (6th Jan., 1872), adverts to the impression produced by his visit there, of the traditions respecting it, of " how he preached an admirable sermon," &c. Then, reverting to their first and last interviews, he says : " I met him first at Dr. Guthrie's, where I was amazed at his activity. He was up long before me, and at two or three meetings before breakfast. I saw him at Brechin in the autumn of 1868, when he was so deeply interested in the sketches he was preparing of men and events in the Church of Scotland."

The Deputies of the Free Church of Scotland were urged to include Canada in their programme. Among the documents that have come into our hands are lengthened communications signed by Mr. John Redpath, as chairman, and Mr. D. Fraser (now Rev. D. Fraser, D.D., London), as secretary of a committee in Montreal, as well as by a number of well-known office-bearers and members of the Presbyterian churches there. A sketch of the projected tour is appended. Circumstances prevented Dr. Cunningham from complying with this earnest invitation. Dr. Burns accepted, and gave two months of unremitting toil to the provinces.

Dr. Burns entered Canada by Niagara, where he was met by Messrs. McGill and Gale. His first meeting was at Toronto, on the evening of the 10th of April; his last was at Halifax on the 3rd of June. The interval was crowded with a ceaseless succession of sermons, speeches, conferences, and receptions. He visited the leading cities and towns in the provinces, and everywhere, from all the Protestant denominations, met with the most cordial reception. By the representatives of several of them, and

by deputies from different Presbyterian congregations, he
was waited on and presented with addresses, most fraternal towards himself personally, and the cause he advocated.
'Among others, a body of Indians was in attendance, who
greeted him heartily, and whose "talk," couched in the
true Indian style, wound up thus eloquently :—"May
your sky be always clear ! May your council fire never
be extinguished ! May the smoke of it ascend till rolling
ages cease to move."

Of this visit the venerable Mr. Smart writes :

" Dr. Burns' visit as a deputation from the Free Church of Scotland was of singular benefit to the Province.   Delegates from the
greater part of the churches in these parts met Dr. Burns at Brockville and Prescott to confer with him as to the future proceedings
of the Church in Canada.   His reception was most enthusiastic.
He was escorted from Brockville to Prescott by a long train of men
on horseback, and men, women, and children in all kinds of waggons and carriages, so that when the procession was joined by that
from Prescott, it extended, it was said, for upwards of half a mile.
In fact his reception in this part of Canada was like a military
triumph.

" At Brockville and Prescott public breakfasts were given, and
the doctor gave interesting sketches of the history of the Church
of Scotland, and a good many anecdotes of the disruption in Scotland.

" Dr. Burns had a wonderful memory.   At a dinner of ministers
and friends at Mr. Smart's the docter surprised us by his mentioning the date of my own ordination, and remarked both of our
ordinations were inserted in the same month of the *Evangelical
Magazine*.

" The doctor related, among other things, his first visit to London, where he met at Mr. Hardcastle's with the board of directors
of the Missionary Society of London."

The Rev. Thomas Alexander, then of Cobourg, speaks
thus of the visit :

" When your father came out as a deputy to this country I rejoiced
at it, as I knew that Canada did not bulk very largely in the eyes
of Presbyterians at home, for I had been home in 1841, and could
not induce a single preacher to come out.   I was with your father

a good deal, and had much pleasant intercourse with him. When
the Synod met at Kingston, before our disruption, I remember
going with him to the Governor, to ascertain his mind in regard to
the Government grant, should our Church carry out our resolution
to follow the example of the Free Church at home. He told us
that if we were unanimous all our privileges would be confirmed :
but if any remained they could claim them. We told this to the
Synod, but some of them were afraid of losing the loaves and fishes.
Now there was no need of disruption in this country. All we had
to do was to drop the words '*in connexion with the Church of Scotland*,' for we were independent in our actions of the mother church,
and besides, we had passed resolutions approving of the step the
Free Church had taken. But the majority would not venture, and
so about twenty-three of us broke off, and organized the Canada
Presbyterian Church. God has certainly prospered His own cause,
and the services of your father and other deputies helped it on.
These were glorious times."

Mr. Gordon, of Gananoque, gives similar testimony,
and adds :

" I may here introduce a pleasant little episode illustrative of the
happy effects of the social and genial nature of a pastor on his flock,
among many proofs of the affectionate impressions left on the minds
of settlers in Canada who had been connected with your father's
congregation at Paisley, which travelling much gives occasion to
discover. One of those warm-hearted women, whom I happened to
know, came to him, when he was in Kingston, with the gift of a
huge piece of maple sugar, that was sufficient to sweeten the tea of
a log-house family for a month perhaps. The doctor was too well
acquainted with the effects of refusal on a simple, loving heart not
to accept the kindness. But after the donor had gone, a grave consultation was held by us respecting the disposal of the sugar. Your
father's desire was to take it with him to Scotland, as a large and
fine specimen of Canadian life in the woods. But a difficult prob-
lem started up, which was this—how to convey the specimen.
'Where there's a will there's a way,' as goes the old proverb. The
doctor's travelling trunk was pretty large, but then it was already
so stuffed that it almost baffled ingenuity itself to get room for it.
Then if the warm weather should come on before the great Atlantic
was crossed, was there not a danger of its melting, and injuring
much, expensive clothes ? Upon a careful calculation of the time
that had to run in the voyage, that fear was silenced. But when the
actual work of *stowing* this ponderous, rebellious, unmanageable piece
of sugar came we were all but to our wit's end. But here again the
all-precious adage, ' where there's a will there's a way,' came to our
help. Not having much, if any, of a Hogarth's pictorial genius to

make life-like photographs of scenes strange as is the actor man
himself, but just gravely to impress the importance and value
of perseverance in a good cause, I may just, in simple unadorned
narrative of truth, state that by your father's getting in, with all the
weight of his solid body, pressing on the contents of the trunk, and
then tramping with all his might, and, poor as I am in bulk, by my
also sitting on the parts of the clothes most unmanageably projecting
and hindering the locking of the trunk, as the only make-weight he
could get the use of, this most troublesome lump of sugar was got
into some safe hiding-place, and conveyed across the seas ; and the
consolation for all the toil and vexation is in the hope that it
sweetened some cups of tea, enlivened innocently some of the social
gatherings at Paisley, brought God's kind bounties to Canada before
the eye, and your father's kind, loving consideration in bringing it
so far to give pleasure."

Mr. Lewis says, with reference to this visit to Canada :

" I had many opportunities of witnessing the good effects of the
visit of Dr. Burns. The doctor was prepared, by his former connexion with the Glasgow Colonial Society, for coming hither, and
his visit was hailed by the Scottish settlers with unfeigned pleasure.
" In reply to the appeal of Dr. Burns, the Canadas contributed
above £2,000 to the Free Church,—plain indication that the heart
of the people is toward us."*

A few extracts from the "Journal" my father kept of
his visit to America (especially to the South and the
Provinces) may here be introduced :

" 1844. Feb. 21st.—At Baltimore ; good progress ; meeting in
the evening, collection $400 ; kindness.
" 22nd.—Arranged for the South. George Lewis arrived ; sent
for. Dr. Breckinridge, bold man, funny. Washington's birthday
this ; went up to top of the monument—of solid marble, beautiful,
tasteful, simple ; statue of Washington on the top like Knox's ;
resignation of his command ; the paper in his hand was shot away
by a young fellow who, in a frolic, said to his companions that he
thought he could fire through it ; he did so. Splendid view of the
city ; at least three places where slaves are or were kept for sale.
Medical school or college. Healthy town ; police poor, as in all
the towns ; bad streets ; well supplied with water. Labourers a
dollar and quarter per day ; live well ; no squalid poverty.
" 24th.—Methodist churches, 13,000 communicants, 4,000 of
these blacks, 20 black preachers. At tea at Mr. Kelso's (the gentleman who gave us $1000) ; had a delightful meeting—represen-
tatives of Presbyterians of America, Methodists, German Lutherans,

---

* "Impressions," pp. 366-7.

German Reformed, and of the Free Church, very interesting men. Bishop Waugh, Kurtz, &c. Had exposition of chapter, and prayer. This the plan among the Methodists.

26th.—Met in the morning with twenty Methodist preachers and ministers, Dr. Cunningham present; questions put; arranged to hear a black preacher; prejudice among the Methodists against them. Mr. Cullman, the leader of the blacks; 4,000 blacks in communion in Baltimore alone; 9,000 whites. 20,000 blacks in all in this city; 3,000 of them slaves. Gen. Ross slain at East Point; his body sent to Halifax, and interred in St. Paul's Churchyard.

"27th.—At Bishop W.'s large party, heard of the arrival of the venerable Bishop Soule, after a journey of 7,000 miles, attending eleven conferences, and appointing to stations 1,300 preachers.

"March 2nd.—Went to Petersburgh. Mr. Foote, agent for the Foreign Missions. Crossed the James river, saw the seat, or part of it, of old Powhatan, the father of Pocahontas, whose blood flows in the veins of many of the best families in Virginia. John Randolph, of Roanoke. Most of the old Glasgow and English families before the Revolution gone. "Our old kingdom of Virginia" most Tory. Barren land; lumberers; swamp. Chatted with one who told me that he was a member of the Legislature of North Carolina; like a dog-breaker, or a second to Pratt in Dickens' Chuzzlewitt; dirty shirt, red necktie, poor drover; conversed; 'You represent the district or county?' 'Yes, I expect so.' 'Are there divisions?' 'Great; two parties, but Whigs carry. Governor is Hon. T. W. Morehead. Poor land, poor settlers; rear a little wheat or corn, but chiefly slaves; slaveholder myself, and have just been at P., with five men and two women, my own; put them in the waggon, with goods, eighty-five miles from Halifax, on the R. Roanoke; highest, a boy of 20, for £130; lowest, an old negro, for £40. In all, made £720; pretty fair: bought them for two-thirds six months ago; labour and tolerably fed—good trade! In the market early this morning, no food, fifteen minutes' job; twenty-eight present, but one of them goes to the corporation of the city. Every day, from 10 till 4, at the Bell Tavern, two places open to anyone to look at. Separate man and wife and children; but he does not do this.' Favourite argument.

"March 3rd.—Saw the process of tobacco manufacture in all its stages, from the field, &c. About 100, young and adults, men, women, boys, and girls, all busily employed; most of the women free, and a number of the men (slaves) are married to free women; in that case the children are free. These workers (free) make from 1s. to 2s. a day. The slaves, if married, go to their wives and families at night. Work from sunrise to sunset in summer, and till eight o'clock in the winter; easy work; many of the slaves happy, and the masters kind; not allowed to be taught to read, nor to meet in any place after eight at night, and no black man allowed to preach or address, except by special license, and then constables

attend, to hear whether he agitates or not. A black man marrying
or having intercourse with a white woman is liable to death ! Lately, a man for killing his negro by 1000 lashes was sentenced to two
years' imprisonment ! 39 lashes allowed ; cowhide very severe.
A Methodist leader is one of the chief auctioneers ! A Baptist
preacher, who had denounced slavery from the pulpit, was stripped,
whipped, tarred and feathered. Lynch law strictly, this ; also in
the South, but prohibited in Virginia. Whipping only legal on the
upper part of the body, but this often evaded. Men and their
wives and children often separated ; much distress. The country
slaves worse treated and most numerous ; domestic slaves generally
well treated. Demoralizing effects of slavery very manifest on the
very manners of the people : style of preaching affected by it.

" March 5th.—Came to Richmond. Met Mr. Hoge, who accompanied me to the Church Hill, at Castle Hill, where the old
Indian chief Powhatan, the father of Pocahontas, was supposed
to have dwelt. Splendid view of the James River ; thought of
former days ; scenes on the spot where Richmond now stands. Met
Bishops Jones and Mead ; good men. Saw Governor Macdonell ;
intelligent man ; conversed on civil and religious polity, traced the
conduct of the Dukes* to the system of England ; entails ; establishment ; England subjugated religion to the ends of civil government,
and made religion (or the church) a mere political machine. We
(Americans) seek to infuse the spirit of Christianity into all our institutions, and thus make it leaven the mass. An Establishment
here bad, no need of it ; but it does not follow that the rulers of
the earth, in their public capacity, can do nothing for God and His
cause, or that they ought to do nothing. Such men a blessing. He
came to Mrs. Forbes' next night, and took some of the ladies with
him in his carriage to hear the lecture. The theatre burnt, 1811.
A church on its site. 60 burnt. A monument. Saw the sale room,
Belle Tavern ; the auctioneer and two or three more walked about ;
twelve or so slaves, men, women, and children, all looking stout,
well dressed, waiting for company ; man, respectable appearance,
very dull, came that day from Brownsville county, forced by his
master to repudiate his wife, that he might be sold without encum-
brance ! A woman, too, member of Baptist church in the place,
husband in the country, separated from her, and he to be sold, shedding tears, but very intelligent and manly ; suspicion. Came away ;
saw the cashier. Dined at Mr. Styles'. Camp meeting ; anxious,
seats defended : Presbyterians seldom try them ; the Methodists do ;
gave them an account of ' Speaking to the question ; ' greatly interested. Saw Mr. W., an English clergyman, not a Puseyite, real
minister, but irregular. Dr. P. a slave defender ; lady denied the
cowhide ; five slaves in Dr. P.'s, all white. ' God bless you, sir,'

---

* Probably the Dukes of Buccleuch, Sutherland, and others, who, at the time, were
refusing sites for Free Churches.—Ed.

lamented the want of opportunity of instruction. Old Mammy fine old creature. Curse of Ham, the favourite argumeut ; mystery of Providence ; cut our throats ; Paul's ' Let every servant ;' all politics ; Dr. P. a democrat or locofoco. Many of the clergy of the Presbytery. Visit to Scotland. Rage at the abolitionists as the cause of retarding their progress.

"March 6th —Came to Fredericksburg, spent two days. Same arguments for slavery ; violent ; ignorance ; African apprentices ; East Indies ; Popery ; shake off the dust ; religion did not prosper for long ; now, revivals. Saw Captain Howe and Mr. Pollock, farmer ; bad land ; slavery against it ; tobacco scourge ; fine land on the Rappahannock, near Dalhousie. Reid and Matheson not liked by any of the clergy ; L. and M. declared they would not speak to them.

"March 9th.—To Washington ; Alexandria ; battle of Whitehouse ; saw the spot where Ross was and his companion ; Washington Capitol.

"March 10th. Preached, Zech. xiii. 7 ; Mr. Knox's in the afternoon, Rom. iv. 17 ; evening, Rom. xv. 30. Delightful singing in the forenoon and evening.

"Washington, March 10.—Two ministers in Congress. J. Q. Adams. Mr. and Mrs. Graham. Mr. P——; sensible man ; Col. Stone's reply on education ; enquire at New York about Maryland not making any effort for paying their debts. Two parties ; levelling democracy ; Mr.—— saw fifty negroes chained together on their march to Virginia ; not five who would vote for abolition ; bad influence on ministers and the young ; shut their eyes ; infidelity on the throne ; little effect of preaching in the Congress Hall ; ministers study too much, and do too little ; too wide a gap between religion and civil matters ; death of Bertrand, who was here lately. La Fayette, a great friend ; Harrison ; Clay, the greatest ; wonderful affection for titles ; hereditary honours ; singular combination of pride and hatred of all British distinctions. Oregon question ; dined with Mr. and Mrs. S——; near relations of Mrs. Graham, of New York.

"March 11th. Introduced to the President (Tyler)*; tall gentleman ; talked familiarly for some little time on the church question ; Establishments ; went to the Capitol again ; yesterday had heard J. Q. Adams, and to day the Senate on Oregon ; heard Mr. Buchanan, Senator of Penn., and Mr. Crittenden, of Kentucky ; talented speakers ; great dignity. Went to the House of Representatives, but great confusion ; question on Oregon, not very honourably brought in ; negociation is going on, yet they defend it, because it is not exactly the same question ; national immorality ; repudiation palliated by the religious people ; slavery

---

* President John Tyler, formerly Vice-President, who succeeded General Harrison on the 4th of April, 1841 ; one month after Gen. H.'s entering upon office. He continued in the presidential chair till 4th of March, 1845.—ED.

in same way. G. and his books not only tolerate, but defend it. On your principles it would be sinful to do it away. Colonization Societies, not an Emancipation scheme, but the reverse. The great argument is the good treatment, only comparative ; same with horses ; no education ; no regular attendance at worship. In Brazil the laws are good, but they are not executed in favour of slavery, and the slaves in a most debased condition. The state is bad ; the negroes are of a cheerful and happy temperament. So in Brazil, and there they are more severely treated—see Dr. Walsh's account of Brazil. Saw John Watson, the Attorney-General and his lady ; heard also the pleadings in the Supreme Court ; saw four Judges, Judge ——, &c. ; loud pleader ; water ; tedious. Evening meeting in Dr. L.'s.

" 13th.—At Alexandria ; saw Mount Vernon ; poor house ; cemetery not worthy ; met C ——; present from the Government offices ; addressed the Methodist Episcopal Conference ; three bishops present ; very friendly ; collected ; bad roads ; preached in the evening in Dr. A.'s, Isa. lxii, 11, Standard.

" 15th.—Disappointed in the morning ; to Baltimore ; left this fine family ; came to Baltimore in the evening ; saw Mr. Morris and Mr. Smith, and family.

" 16th.—Came on to Philadelphia, and preached next day ; 1st, for Mr. Machlin, on Acts viii., 26, to the end ; 2nd, for Mr. Boardman, on Rom. xiv., 17 ; 3rd, for Dr. Cuyler, on Rev. i., 17, 18. Gilbert Tennant's Church, inscription on him ; see Dr. Cuyler's letter ; labours of G. Tennant and his brother William, whose scene of labour was New Jersey (Dr. A.'s account) ; pass near it on the way to Princeton ; also Crossweeksung ; scene of David Brainerd's labours. Anecdote of William Tennant.

" Philadelphia, 18th.—Saw the almshouse. 1700 souls, nine-tenths Irish, Germans too, very barbarous and uncivilized ; very far below the poor blacks ; bad affair ; accounts not well kept ; not a proper thing to encourage dependence on alms. Sheds at Montreal better. No religion. Roman Catholics. Girard College, sad throwing away of money ; each pillar $15,000 ; fine masonry. Anti-christian. The Mayor : 'My party tells me I must either accept of a place, such as this, or be laid on the shelf. May be cast off, but lay our account with this. My son carries on my business.' Agrees with me as to the almshouse. Too far from the city, ladies cannot visit. Went to Wilmington in the evening, preached and collected.

" 19th.—Evening at Princeton ; preached to students on Zech. xiii., 7th.

" 20.—Heard Dr. Miller. Pulpit eloquence, three students read ; allowed to criticize each other ; asked if the people of Scotland sat at prayer ! long prayers ; Dr. M —— valuable man, easy and interesting. Condemned the slow and drawling and feckless manner of speech in clergy. Dr. Alexander on new school, able view of the atonement. Dr. Wardlaw he had not seen, spoke to him on conditions; fund of information.

"21.—Came on to Elizabethtown and Newark.

"March 22.—Neat and elegant town of Newark. Last year sad speculation on the extension of the city, everything neglected for this, returning now, after great loss. Rash spirit of adventure; 'never mind, begin at once, quick.' Elizabethtown, favoured spot, 700 members; revivals often. Dr. Magee, anecdote, he deserved it, for his book is good! Dr. Nesbit; remarks apply. Dr. Witherspoon; land speculation, great good to America.

"New York, 24th.—Preached in Dr. Stark's, Dr. McLeod's, Dr. Dewitt's, Lafayette Place. Questioned by Mr. Tappan and Mr. Jocelyn about asking money from the Southern States; price of blood; cuts too deep; cotton; the produce of slave labour and sugar, too! American character: 1.—Eager pursuit of wealth; keen, shrewd people; calculating, inventing schemes of wealth; matter-of-fact men; grave; not a smile. 2nd—Political parties: two parties, democracy rules all; popular opinion, worst part of the people; all public offices have been and are controlled by these parties; public good neglected for party ends. 3rd—Conceit. 4th—Constant rage after novelty, want of accuracy.

"25th.—Went to New Haven, Drs. Duncan and Reid; beautiful views of the sound. Blackwall, rampart and battery. Orphanhouse and farm schools. Beautiful bay of New Haven, lovely city. State house, churches, Yale College, new library, minerals. Dr. Silliman not at home. *Journal of Science* to be discontinued, Dr. Day, Dr. Taylor Goodwin. Trumbull's pictures, caves of the Regicides; Quarterly Review.

"27th.—Set off for Boston, arrived next day. Dr. Codman, his case. Dorchester, old times renewed. Best library, history of Harvard by President Quincy. Massachusetts, historical collections regarding the work of God among the Indians. Samuel Willard, pastor of the South in Boston, and Vice-President of Harvard, died 1707. History of D—— published by L—— and Prince, 1726, in Boston, one of the first folios printed. Pemberton preached his funeral sermon, the doctrine of justification. Limited atonement seems to have been making ground in his day; clear views of election, page 282. The covenant of redemption, as to the articles with those of the Gospel covenant, as to its eternal dispensation.

"March 31st.—Sabbath forenoon, Dorchester, Rom. xiv., 17. Afternoon, Dr. Edward Beecher's, Rom. xv., 30. Evening, Mr. Phelps, Rev. i., 17, 18. Dr. Beecher, of Cincinnati, father of Dr. B——. Dr. B——, senr., did much good in Boston, went to the west to elevate it; refused all offers of removal.

"April 1st.—Spent some hours at Harvard College. See notes separate.*

---

* These we have not discovered.—ED.

N

"April 2nd.—Went to Lowell, the Paisley of America ; 9,000 factory girls, 200,000 dollars of theirs in the Pr. Bank. The Magazine. Improvement circles, good appearance, healthy, daughters of farmers, three to five years, wash three times a day. Each has her looking glass ; not five cases of immorality in a year. Most respectably married, decidedly moral ; not the wish of the Superintendent to train up a manufacturing population. Saw the splendid carpet-weaving machine, invented by Bigelow, of Boston, very clean. The Merrimack a noble stream. 30 or 40,000 : spoke in Mechanics' Hall. All publications ; noble schools, three large Universalist churches. Saw Dr. Woods at Andover. Fine library, 14,000 volumes, One manuscript of the Greek Testament, 13th century. Noble piece of ground, endowment very moderate. Saw Messrs. Smith from Brechin, excellent people. Mr. Dow, great advantage of emancipation. Saw many Paisley folks of the name of Wilson or Millar, or Halden.

"3rd.—To Salem. Preached from Rom. xv., 28. Witches 1692. See the pious ! Records of moral justice, 1639-40. First church set up here ; Unitarians.

"Boston, 4th.—*Heard Daniel Webster.*

"5th.—Fast-day by Governor Briggs. Sadly abused. See newspapers. Poor attendance. Preached twice, Dr. Sharp's, Dr. Blagdon, John iv., 13. Meeting in the evening, all spoke, crowded.

"Monday, 8th.—Schenectady, Amsterdam, Utica, Rome, Syracuse, Rochester, Batavia, Buffalo. No conveyance to Niagara. From elevation on inn saw Canada, both lakes. Preached for Mr. Lord. Saw kind friends, also enquired for the woman, whose house was spared by General Rial, by a cup of tea. Stands still. Woman alive, keeps an inn, but also had daughters who sewed.

"April 10th.—Steamer down to Niagara town and Toronto. Disappointed last night at N——— ; met Messrs. McGill and Gale.

"April 10.—On to TORONTO. Met many friends ; conveyed to inn, afterwards to church ; pretty large meeting, addressed, arranged for Friday.

"11th.—Went to Hamilton. Indians with John Jones, brother of Peter. Met at Credit River ; address ; man of intelligence. Saw afterwards Kerr, the Chief of the Five Nations, a half-breed, but married the daughter of the younger Brant (Life), an elegant woman. Interesting meetings at Hamilton at three and seven. Many addresses from various bodies of Christians. Not so many Presbyterian congregations as should have been. Mr. and Mrs. Campbell, Mr. Crooks, Ferguson, Kerr, who took me round the height, Dundas, Ancaster. Noble facilities of trade to the West. All the towns on the Ontario well settled. Good prospects.

"12th.—Returned to Toronto. Meeting successful. St. Andrew's church. Badly off; noble station. College; an awful job, letters on it (see book).

"13th.—Went to York Mills. Saw Mr. S——; poor man, promised aid, but failed. Impressed with sense of importance of Toronto. Met in Canadian Institute at twelve. Respectable meeting; Messrs. Roaf, Lillie, &c., good men. Mr. Rintoul left, dined in Judge McLean's.

"14th.—Preached in St. Andrew's, Independent and Methodists; large audiences, much room for an efficient ministry.

"15th.—Breakfast. Fine opportunity; much interest excited; left for Cobourg by steamer, accompanied by friends from steamer; free passage. Captain friendly and intelligent. A fine assembly at Cobourg. Went to church, and preached; introduced subject.

"16th.—Met at eleven, full meeting, many addresses, £190 collected. Afternoon, at five, at College, £5 additional. The students; Dr. Ryerson. Sabbath school at three, £3; seventy scholars.

"17th.—At Grafton. £8 Fast day; evening at Cobourg; large assembly.

"18th.—Breakfast, Lambert's Inn; went on to Kingston, noble sail. Bay of Quinte; death of poor Millar, monument in church, inscription. Mr. McDowall's place; approach to St. Lawrence river.

"19th.—Landed in the morning. Active committee met me; waited on the Governor, kind, intelligent; had been tampered with; no right to stop the salaries of Boyd and Smart. Responsible Government. Hopkirk, Assistant Secretary. Evening meeting, good. Saw in the forenoon Messrs. Liddell, Machar, &c., here.

"20th.—Breakfast; dined at Mr. Hopkirk's; spoke in the evening, at Meth.

"21st.—Forenoon, afternoon, and evening, in so many churches, Richie, Lillie, &c. Much kindness, went out to the country fatigued.

"22nd.—Set sail for Brockville; H. Gordon left me at Gananoque; the lake of Thousand Islands, 1,300 of them; met at Brockville; large meeting, the Sheriff in the chair.

"23rd.—On to Prescott; cavalcade met; address, Crane, M.P., presided. Seven churches, not shanties; Messrs. Boyd and Smart vindicated themselves; went over to Ogdensburg; small audience, £7; nice church; a Judge who spoke of going home; liberal views.

"24th.—Breakfast at Prescott; went on to Cornwall, from Osnabruck to C—— bad roads; sail delightful; good meeting, £17 17s; met here the French and Protestant minister, Lapelleterie (see his journals, &c.).

"25th.—Mr. H. accompanied me by land to Lancaster, Glengarry House; in last Mc D—— died lately; part of the property

entailed, but the family extinct, in a manner ; painful event,
death of a young woman ; meeting at L—— ; 300 acres, church
on it, four miles off another ; no collection ; Glengarry an important post ; visited a Scotch farmer on the way ; very comfortable ;
Indian lands, 100 acres, good ; one dollar and half bushel of
wheat ; Scotch farmers needed ; noble land.

" 26th.—Went on with Mr. McL——, Coteau du Lac, five or
six miles of good road ; a swamp ; passed the boundary of Upper
and Lower Canada ; soon see the difference ; Canadians, a simple
class ; 200 years ago, more priests ; excellent farmers ; no spur to
excel ; cascades by coach ; bad roads ; timber used ; steam to
Lachine, Indian settlement, Caughnawaga ; saw a squaw, bad
weather ; Scotch church at Lachine ; got to Montreal ; Mr. E.'s
child gone ; went to Mr. Redpath's ; zealous friends ; required to
preach at seven ; American church filled ; addressed, Wilkes,
Girdwood, &c., with many laymen of piety ; evening meeting in
Mr. Dougall's ; addresses on Temperance, £250 subscribed.

" 27th.—Funeral, Dr. Mathieson addressed.

" 28th.—Meeting in Mr. Esson's, Mr. Strong's, and the Methodists, all crowded.

" 29th.—Saw Mrs. Kerr, the cathedral ; Mr. Osgood's school.

" 30th.—Ride round the mountain ; meeting at Mr. Ferrier's,
address by Canadian missionary.

" May 1st.—At Mr. Esson's ; marriage, Mr. R—— to Miss
C——.

" 2nd.—Breakfast ; went down to Quebec ; scenery, parish
churches, Belœil, Bishop of Nancy's cross, Jesuits.

" 4th.—Visit to Montmorenci and Lorette, Indians, Popery.
Preached in the evening in the Methodists' ; met many excellent
people.

" 5th.—Preached in Mr. Clugston's, Mr. Atkinson's, Dr.
Cook's ; not crowded. Saw Messrs. Gibb and Munn, —— frank
for Mr. Guthrie or Mr. Begg ; another for Dr. Chalmers, from R.
Carter, New York. Visited Mr. Hale's Sabbath school ; taught
class ; five sects ; Miss Gore.

" 6th.—Breakfast. Much interest ; set off at five ; Bishop on
board

"7th.—Could not go to the Grande Ligne from weather ; met
friends at breakfast in Mr. Orr's. Saw Mr. Davidson ; must have
a Theological School ; conference with C—— about Academy ;
each denomination has one, why not we ?

" May 13th.—Newburyport by railway. Saw Mr. Whitefield's
skull, handled it ; inscription ; see Reid ; flat skull, but broad ;
noble high forehead ; not in order ; the church just as when the
great man occupied it, large but plain ; a neat chapel adjoining ;
lecture room. Employed all day in getting my articles on board
the steamer, and seeing friends at Dorchester, Dr. C—— and his
family ; much pleasure in the visit.

" 15th.—Came back to Boston.

" 16th.—Set sail with letters on board to Dr. C——, Dr. Lord, and Mr. A. Ferrier, at Uniontown.

" 17th.—At sea ; employed in reading and writing various articles.

" 18th.—Came to Halifax at six a.m.   Saw Mr. Robb and other friends, who prevailed on me to remain till next steamer ; agreed to do so, and wrote a letter to my congregation ; met friends at breakfast and after.   Appeal to the trustees and others, who agreed.

" 19th.—Preached in the morning in St. Matthew's ; afternoon, in the New Methodist ; and evening, in St. John's, crowded houses, except the morning.

" 20th.—Preached at Dartmouth at eleven in the forenoon, and in the evening in St. John's ; public meeting.

" 21st.—Address in the evening to the Young Men's Association. Rode out.

" 22nd.—Preached in the Baptist from Rom. xv., 30.

"23rd.—Set off for Pictou with Mr. and Mrs. Robb ; dreary road, one hundred miles ; one beautiful spot, Truro ; Dr. Macgregor.

" 24th.—Saw various triends ; went over to New Glasgow ; held a meeting in the afternoon ; Mr. Macrae.

" 25th.—Returned to Pictou ; addressed in the evening in St. Andrew's.

" 26th.—Preached in the forenoon in St. Andrew's, from Acts viii., 26, and afternoon at New Glasgow ; evening, in Mr. Macauley's.

" 27th.—Went on to Prince Edward Island ; friends there had sent the steamer ; beautiful island ; Charlottetown ; preached in Methodist, and Mr. Robb addressed.

" 28th.—Visited the country ; fertile, no large trees, nor marks of fire, as on the road from Halifax to Pictou ; held a meeting in the evening ; Mr. Stewart and Mr. Farquharson preached in different places in Gaelic.

" 29th.—Made calls ; preached again ; meeting of congregation, no doubt of their all joining the Free Church, but great difficulty about dispensing with Gaelic.

" 30th.—Returned to Pictou, and held a meeting in the evening.

" 31st.—Returned to Halifax by coach.

" June 1st, Saturday.—Engaged variously; dined with the Speaker.

" 2nd.—Sabbath, preached in forenoon in Baptist, Dan. xi., 10 ; afternoon, at Dartmouth ; evening, in St. John's.

" 3rd.—Public breakfast at hotel ; set sail at twelve, in the ' Britannia' ; eighty passengers ; many friends ; one Catholic priest."

On the 3rd of June he left Halifax in the steamship *Britannia,* and, after a favourable voyage, reached home, having been absent over five months. His attached flock received him joyfully.

Free St. George's Church, an elegant edifice, had been erected while he was gone, and been opened for divine worship by Dr. Thomas Guthrie.

The Colonial Committee, to whom he furnished an elaborate report, specially bearing on his visit to the Provinces, expressed in the heartiest manner their acknowledgments for his services ; and the illustrious Chalmers wrote thus :

" EDINBURGH, July 16, 1844.

" MY DEAR SIR,—I regret much that I did not meet you. I was in the country (Burntisland) at the time you were in Edinburgh.

" I have had repeated testimonies from America of your great acceptance, and the deep impression that you made there. I have said to many that we could not have sent out a more efficient representative than yourself. I feel very grateful for your important services, and for the full acquittal you have made of your generous undertaking.

" Ever believe me,
" My dear Sir,
" Yours very truly,
"THOMAS CHALMERS."

On his return, he was besieged for addresses on America and the colonies. To his power, yea and beyond his power, he complied. Much important information was communicated and interest awakened. Among other places, he was invited to Taymouth Castle, and for a week received much munificent hospitality from the Marquis and Marchioness of Breadalbane.

It was in connexion with this visit we received the following :

"TAYMOUTH CASTLE, Saturday,   Oct., 1844.

" MY DEAR ROBERT,—I wrote you from Perth rather hurriedly, and I am happy now to let you and Willie know of the progress I have been making since leaving the ' fair city.' I came to Dunkeld by the mail coach from Perth, and then got the mail gig up to Kenmore, which is a distance of twenty-four miles. On my arrival at Kenmore I found a card, in the handwriting of the Marchioness of Breadalbane, inviting me to dinner at seven o'clock, and to stay at the Castle.

" I have been here since Thursday afternoon, and have enjoyed much kindness.

" The ceremony of laying the foundation stone took place yesterday, and it went off very successfully. The *roof* of the church is on, and yet the *foundation* was not laid till yesterday at twelve o'clock. A small hole had been left in the east corner wall, and within that hole the box containing the documents was placed, and the whole closed up again. The ladies of the congregation had subscribed for a silver trowel, which was presented to the Marchioness, along with a mallet and rule, and with these instruments her ladyship most methodically and scientifically went to work, putting in the lime with the trowel, measuring the stone and proportions of the whole with the rule, and hammering the whole down with the mallet. All these articles are now lying in the library, beside where I am now writing. The members of presbytery were present. The Moderator presided. The Marquis read the reply by the Marchioness, and her address, which were excellent, and both will be published in the *Witness*. It fell to me to give the prayer, and afterwards we adjourned to the Timber Church, where I preached a short sermon (Rom. xiv. 17) and gave an American-Highland address on the state of the Gael in those lands, and the general state of the Colonies and the Republic of America. There was a large assembly, and the Marquis remained from *twelve to four o'clock*, his lady retiring at the end of the foundation service. We had several persons of consideration present with us, particularly a Captain Mackenzie, who had been the fellow-prisoner with Lady Sale in the dungeon at Caboul, and whom the Affghan chief (Dost Mohammed) ordered more than once to be ' shot away' from the mouth of a cannon ; when, as the captain remarked, ' there was not the slightest occasion for anything of the kind.' He and his lady are religious people, and took a great interest in what went on. The cause of the Free Church prospers here under the powerful patronage of these distinguished persons the Marquis and Marchioness. We have daily worship, when the whole servants, &c., are assembled. I am to preach all day to-morrow at Kenmore, and in the evening at Aberfeldy. On Monday I go to Killin to address a meeting, and the Marquis accommodates me with carriages to all these places. I am busy most of this day rummaging through his extensive library ; and ranging, when the day allowed, in the splendid domain."

The generous host and hostess at Taymouth Castle treated Dr. Burns with the greatest kindness and consideration, and hearing incidentally of an important change contemplated in his domestic relations, bestowed on him in parting an elegant and substantial token of their regard.*

He attended, as corresponding member, the Synod of Dumfries, enjoying delightful intercourse with Dr. Henry Duncan and other old friends.   He became the bearer, at the same time, of gold spectacles and sundry other keepsakes, which our kindhearted American cousins had sent to worthy *Janet Fraser*, whose "not fearing the wrath" of the "bold Buccleuch" set her name almost alongside that of the redoubtable Jenny Geddes, the heroine of the cutty-stool.   The remainder of the year was filled up to the utmost, and it closed most auspiciously with his marriage, on the 12th of December, to Miss Elizabeth Bell Bonar, daughter of Thomson Bonar, Esq., of the Grove, near Edinburgh, and niece of his early friend and counsellor at Cramond.

* In her beautifully natural "Journal of Life in the Highlands," our beloved Sovereign thus touchingly refers to a visit paid two years earlier to Taymouth :

"I revisited Taymouth last autumn, on the 3rd of October, from Dunkeld (incognita), with Louise, the Dowager Duchess of Athole, and Miss Macgregor. As we could not have driven through the grounds without asking permission, and as we did not wish to be known, we decided upon not attempting to do so, and contented ourselves with getting out at a gate close to a small fort, into which we were led by a woman from the gardener's house near to which we had stopped, and who had no idea who we were.

"We got out, and looked from this height down upon the house below, the mist having cleared away sufficiently to show us everything, and then unknown, quite in private I gazed—not without deep emotion—on the scene of our reception twenty-four years ago by dear Lord Breadalbane in a princely style, not to be equalled in grandeur and poetic effect. Albert and I were then only twenty-three, young and happy. How many are gone that were with us then ! I was very thankful to have seen it again.

"It seemed unaltered.—1866."

CHAPTER XIII.

TRANSLATION FROM PAISLEY AND SETTLEMENT IN CANADA.

D R. BURNS had scarcely got home from his American tour when overtures were made to him from Canada. Montreal and Toronto vied with each other in the effort to secure his services. In the former city he had many warm friends. The friendship of that "Israelite indeed," Mr. James Court, he had gained several years previously. He, with Mr. James R. Orr—that seraphic spirit,—and Mr. John Redpath, a man of many sterling, noble qualities, and others like minded, pleaded with him to return. A few extracts may be given from two of the letters of Mr. Redpath, who conducted the correspondence:

"MONTREAL, 28th May, 1844.

" We have been busily employed during the last few days in pre-paring a memorial to the Convener of the Colonial Committee for a minister and an evangelist. The names we mention are the es-teemed deputy who has just visited us, Mr. Tweedie, and Mr. McDonald. Any one of them form the types thereof ; and W. C. Burns for the Evangelist, to make the tour of Canada, from which we expect the greatest benefit. We have not named any other person for this trust, as he is the man to whom all eyes are directed, as being peculiarly qualified for such a great and important mission. I got a portrait of you out of the *Scottish Pulpit* (a capital likeness), got it framed, and took it home, to the great gratification of Mrs. R. and all my family, the youngest of whom knew it immediately, and said : ' That is Dr. Burns.' I mention this little anecdote to remind you that you are kept in warm remembrance at Terrace Bank."

" TERRACE BANK, 27th July, 1844.

" It gave me, as well as the rest of your friends in this place, very great pleasure to hear of your safe arrival on your native shore, as an answer to our earnest prayers. Mr. Fraser wrote you by last mail, with the account of the Disruption which has taken place in the Synod of Canada, and you will get by this mail a more particular account of it in the *Banner*. They have gone through the sifting process. I will not say that those who have come through are all ' wheat' and the others all ' chaff.'

" The committee here are doubting, hoping, fearing, the result of their application, but they have still a hope that if all fails, and if there is no man of fitting gifts to be had, that our own dearly beloved doctor will say, ' Here am I, send me.' Great things are expected from Montreal, but nothing need be expected till God sends us a man acording to his own mind ; for what can we do without a preacher ?

" I think a good University might be formed here, in which the other evangelical bodies might take part, each one having their own theological chair. I think the Congregationalists and Baptists would readily join, and the Secession body will no doubt now join the adherents of the Free Church principles at once. The com-mittee have had a special prayer-meeting since your departure, for the purpose of supplicating the great Head of the Church that He would look favourably on our application, and send us a man suitable to His mind and will. Some of them are consoling themselves that you will really come in case of necessity ; but I can scarcely dare to hope, from what you intimated to me about your own people : but I may safely say that none would be more welcome, for wherever you have been you have gained golden opinions, and nowhere more so than in this city."

Toronto also put forth its claims. During his visit he had been greatly impressed with its central and commanding position. Soon after his visit, an influential body of people left St. Andrew's Church (Church of Scotland) and formed a union with the congregation of the Rev. James Harris, who had faithfully laboured in Toronto since 1820. Mr. Harris retired, and the new organization—under the title, "Knox's Church, Toronto,"—joined in a united and urgent call to Dr. Burns to become their pastor. They sent home their strong reasons, and these were accompanied by the following reasons from the Colonial Committee of the Free Church of Scotland:

"I. The vast extent and resources of Canada, the amazing rapidity with which its population is increasing, and generally its rising importance, point out the propriety of its being supplied with the services of ministers of zeal, ability, and piety.

"II. The peculiar circumstances in which the brethren of the Presbyterian Church of Canada have been placed in consequence of the disruption, render it exceedingly desirable that they should enjoy the presence of a minister of experience from Scotland—more especially one who is fully acquainted with the systems which have been pursued in this country for organizing congregations and for the sustentation of the ministry.

"III. While the call to Toronto attests the strength of the Presbyterian interest in that city, both as regards numbers and wealth, this call must be viewed as connected with the nomination which Dr. Burns has received to the Chair of Theology at Toronto; and while the duties of both offices must be discharged, for a time at least, by the same individual, the learning, ability, readiness, and untiring energy of Dr. Burns point him out as possessing, in an eminent degree, the rare qualifications which are necessary for so arduous a service.

"IV. The reception which Dr. Burns has already met with in Canada, indicates the cordiality with which he will be welcomed, and affords the most pleasing prospects of the success which would attend him in that great and rising country.

"For the Colonial Committee,

"J. A. BALFOUR, Jun.,

"Secretary.

"Edinburgh, 13th January, 1845."

The chairman of the congregational meeting of Knox's
Church, which sent him the call, was Mr. Isaac Buchanan,
now of Hamilton, and a tried friend of the church in
many ways. In one of his letters, of date 24th July,
1844, the following passage occurs :

> " It is impossible for me to express the deep feeling of anxiety
> entertained by every member of the congregation, that you may
> come among us, having in view not only their own edification and
> eternal interests, but looking to it as vitally important to the inte-
> rests of the infant church, that we secure the advantage of the great
> knowledge and experience which you possess, especially at her out-
> set."

Others thus earnestly wrote :

> " What are we to do ? The Lord can raise up labourers in his
> vineyard, and relieve us from our sad difficulty and distress. But
> is his hand not pointed to the Free Church in Scotland, and does
> his voice not say, ' Help your brethren in Canada, and help them
> immediately.' Dear Doctor, by your love to the glorious cause in
> which you are engaged, by your regard for the souls of men perish-
> ing for lack of knowledge, although professedly hearing Presbyte-
> rian ministers, send us help. *Come* yourself ; you know our wants ;
> you know our localities. Our infant church must take up high and
> holy ground. It is only from that eminence that we can fight the
> Lord's battles.
> " We earnestly hope that you will come to open Knox's Church,
> and not be later than the twelvemonth. *None* will do but you ;
> for the people have all made up their minds about it."

To these earnest appeals, after mature and prayerful
consideration, Dr. Burns felt it to be his duty to lend a
favourable ear. So soon as his mind was made up he
broke it at once to his attached people—endeavoured to
get them to see the matter in the light he did himself, and to aid them all in his power in securing a suitable
successor. It was a great trial. His handsome new church
had been opened. It was fast filling up. He had resumed
work after several months' absence with great enthu-

siasm. His home, over which the dark shadow had rested, was graced and gladdened by the presence of one who, for the remainder of his days, was to prove in every sense a help meet for him. The congregation in its new relation seemed dearer to him than ever. But while cords of love so tender bound him to home, the claims of Canada were so borne in upon him that his heart was fixed, and he felt that he must not be disobedient to the heavenly vision. When once his resolution was formed, he never hesitated.

It was about this time we received from him such notes as the following :

"PAISLEY, Nov., 1844.

"I saw Dr. Cunningham at Dr. Abercrombie's funeral. I would advise, as he does, attendance at Dr. Chalmers' lectures. I would not wish you to hurt your health, and we must not tempt Providence by overtasking ourselves. May all your studies, whether secular or sacred, be conducted in the spirit of humility and the fear of God."

"Dec., 1844.

"If I go to Canada, which is very likely, Mr. Macnaughtan* advises you to take another year of the home advantages before crossing—a very good idea, perhaps. I am anxious that you should confer your services as a preacher of the glorious gospel on the virgin soil of Canada, where every footmark tells, and where a new empire and a flourishing church will yet be reared. I leave it, however, to yourself, requesting only that you may not allow your mind to be pre-occupied by the well-meant but injurious remonstrances of friends who know nothing of Canada, and whose views are narrowed by circumstances."

"PAISLEY, December, 1844.
"Saturday evening.

"I am favoured with your letter, and return you many thanks for its contents. You are very busily engaged, and in the noblest of all pursuits. May strength be given you for the successful prosecution of your studies, and may the blessing of the God of truth go with you. Your Professors are all able men, and the church is blest in having such instructors to guide her rising hopes. I *must* be in for a week or so, to hear the lectures and to confer with professors on the best means of teaching theology. My nomination as Professor of Divinity in Canada will require me to enter immediately on

---

* The Rev. John McN., of Belfast, then of High Church, Paisley.

its duties, and an address to the students at Toronto may probably be the first thing that it may necessary for me to print. They are under the charge of Mr. King at present; and, though few in number, are very promising. I must set about a *Library* for them.

" Your certificates from the Duke have come back this day only.

" I must have some days hard work with you when you come out, on the themes and exercises of all the classes."

On the "Presbytery" day, his devoted brother, the " pastor of Kilsyth," thus wrote :

" KILSYTH, Feby. 5th, 1845.

" DEAR ROBERT,—This, I believe, is a day of importance in your history and that of the Church. We consider the event, however, as already certain, as far as human things can be, and that you leave your native shores and engage, if the Lord will, in important labours in another hemisphere. May all be well with you, your beloved partner and your family, and flock *left* and *to be*. We shall often be remembering you at the throne of grace. May all be eminently promotive of His glory whose we are, and I trust whom we desire to serve."

The formal loosing, which his own unalterable decision rendered inevitable, was effected in the most kind and considerate way. The regards and regrets of his ministerial brethren were expressed in the most fitting terms, and embodied in a suitable deliverance. Seven weeks intervened till the embarkation. These were crowded with multifarious work—the needed preparations, the gathering of books for the college, the consulting with the Edinburgh professors, the farewells to friends, the aiding his attached flock in obtaining a faithful pastor, and the dealing out to them, by private visitations and in his public ministrations, such counsels as their peculiar circumstances required. He had previously despatched a fervent, fatherly letter to the students at Toronto. As the ties were being loosed which bound him to his old, his heart went out toward his new home.

The College was a special care. With prodigious energy he set about collecting for the library; and, mainly from his own shelves and those of brethren and friends, he collected between two and three thousand volumes; to which from time to time, in after years, he made many additions.*

The farewell meeting was an overpowering demonstration. Brother ministers and friends from Glasgow and other places were present, and were lavish in their expressions of esteem. All sections of the congregation and community joined heartily in their generous testimonies. The substantial tokens were numerous, and (one of them especially) of great pecuniary value.

The "farewell sermon" was preached in St. George's Free Church, on the afternoon of Sabbath, the 23rd of March, from 2 Cor. xiii. 11 : "Finally, brethren, farewell. Be perfect, be of good comfort, be of one mind, live in peace, and the God of love and peace shall be with you." The crowd so compact as to form a living pavement, over which one could have walked; the sea of up-turned faces, now sparkling under the sun-blinks of the past, then surging under the swell of deep emotion; the memories recalled, the associations clustering round, the thirty-three years looking down on them, the "cloud of witnesses,"

* In addition to the many volumes given from his own shelves, near relatives contributed 500 volumes. Dr. Chalmers, Sir David Brewster, Dr. Keith, Dr. Hetherington, Dr. Wm. Brown, and others, presented complete sets of their works. Messrs. Collins, and Blackie & Son, Glasgow, and A. Gardiner, Paisley, contributed donations of books more or less numerous and valuable. Dr. Black, formerly of Aberdeen, presented the splendid Paris Polyglot. General Macdowal, of Stranraer (whose acquaintance Dr. Burns had formed during his visit with Dr. Chalmers to Sir Andrew Agnew), presented from his fine theological collection 230 volumes. The Free Church Colonial Committee furnished Dr. Burns with £150, with which he made many valuable purchases.

Associated with Mr. Black, now of Manitoba, we made the first catalogue of Knox's College Library, which then embraced over 3,000 volumes, the most of which were the result of this special effort made by my father when on the eve of starting for his new home.

combined to render it a season much to be remembered.
One extract, from the closing portion of this discourse, is
all that we can give :

"The period of my ministry embraces a generation of human
beings. Of those who were office-bearers and members in full
communion at the time of my settlement, a fraction only survives.
Of those whose names stand on the 'lists' appended to the 'call'
then addressed to me, two only remain. Many who were then
the children and youth of families committed to my charge, have
since grown up and occupy important stations in society. The
number admitted by me to communion at one hundred and thirty-
four sacramental occasions falls little short of thirteen hundred
individuals, being nearly the ordinary number of communicants
twice told. Of these several hundreds had been catechumens at
the weekly classes for religious instruction, and over many of these
I have had cause to rejoice. In the course of my ministry God has
permitted me to go through the whole of the New Testament in the
form of expository lectures, together with the evangelical types
and prophecies, and the larger part of the history, of the Old. My
aim has ever been to unfold to you the mind of the Spirit, and to
commend to every sinner the grace of the Divine Redeemer. We
have walked together amid the rich pastures of Zion, and my
humble aim has been to direct you to the Chief Shepherd."

Our passage was taken in the ship *Erromanga*, a new
vessel just built for the firm of James R. Orr & Co. Captain James Kelso, an excellent Christian man, brother-in-
law of the proprietors, and himself a member of the firm,
commanded for the last time before retiring from the sea.
On Saturday, March 29th, we set sail, many friends having
"accompanied us to the ship." The previous night was
spent in a precious prayer-meeting, in the Rev. J. J.
Bonar's church. Dr. Keith, the celebrated writer on
prophecy, took part, and his weighty words lent a peculiar
charm to that Greenock gathering. The six weeks'
voyage had the usual "lights and shadows" which chequer
life on the ocean, but was, on the whole, a season of much
enjoyment. We had some severe storms, but only once

were we in serious danger. Sweeping merrily along before a favouring breeze, one dark night, we ran into a great field of ice. The crashing, grating sound started us from our hammocks. For thirty hours we were girdled with floating masses, and were afterwards told that, but for the good ship having been constructed of the strongest material, the consequences might have been fatal. Many books of interest were read; Pictet's Theology, in French, was studied; a good deal of writing was got through with. Amongst other things, the farewell sermon,* which had been delivered from notes, was fully written out on board ship, and afterwards printed at Toronto.

On Friday, the 9th of May, we reached Quebec. The first to welcome us, as we stepped on shore, was our now sainted relative, W. C. Burns, who had complied with the earnest wishes of his uncle and the Montreal friends, by coming out on an evangelistic tour a little ahead of us.†

---

* "Circumstances having put it out of my power to comply with the wishes of friends at Paisley, that I should print my Farewell Sermon before leaving Scotland, I have endeavoured to follow out that wish by devoting part of my leisure time on the voyage to the preparation of the manuscript for the press at Toronto. My design is to send it to my much-loved brethren and friends, as a small token of remembrance endeared by distance. The wide Atlantic now separates me from those to whom, for more than thirty years, I stood in the relation of pastor, and whose best interests are still near my heart. While I write these lines, the waves of the mighty deep are rolling around us. We are entering the great Gulf of St. Lawrence. A few days are expected to bring us within sight of some of the most magnificent displays of the majesty of God. Already have we witnessed his wonders in the great deep. Hitherto He hath held us in the hollow of His hand. Amid the howling of the storm, and the crashing of icebergs, we have been mercifully preserved. The prayers of our ship's company have regularly ascended with united voice before the throne, morning and evening; and in these we have remembered our friends at home, as they, we believe, have remembered us. May He who sitteth on the floods reign in their hearts and in ours. May His testimonies, which excel in faithfulness, be our united inheritance in this the house of our pilgrimage ; and may His omnipotent grace establish in each heart and perfect that 'holiness which becometh His house for ever.'"—Gulf of St. Lawrence, May 1st, 1845.—*Prefatory Note to Sermon.*

† One of Dr. Burns' last literary employments was to write the record of that visit, which forms Chapter X. of the deeply interesting memoir of that apostolic missionary, by the gifted and honoured brother who has so soon followed him to glory. His sojourn in Canada extended over two years. Wherever he went he left "footprints." In many parts of the backwoods eyes will yet fill, and hearts heave, and voices become solemn and tender, when his name is spoken.—ED.

o

It was the Friday of the Communion season when we reached Quebec. His old correspondent, the Rev. John Clugston, of St. John's Church, asked him to aid in the service; so he was into work at once, foreshadowing thus at the start, his New World life, which from its commencement to its close was " in labours more abundant."

My brother and I kept by the ship. Father and mother followed us on Monday by steamboat, reaching Montreal about the same time with us.

The few days of our sojourn in Montreal were spent with kind friends, " some of whom remain unto this present, while others have fallen asleep." The Rev. John Bonar, then of Larbert, had come out to supply for a season the faithful band who, for years prior to their enjoying a stated ministry, were favoured with the temporary ministrations of some of the choicest spirits of the Free Church. These were the days of the wooden structure which preceded the present Coté Street Church, and which was a Bethel and a Peniel to many. Dr. Burns was associated with Mr. Bonar in the inauguration of this tabernacle. Some of the students happening to be in Montreal, conferences were had with them. The following Sabbath was spent at Kingston, where a full tale of work awaited him, and an enjoyable intercourse was resumed, which our subsequent eight years' settlement there, extended.

We reached Toronto in the *City of Toronto*, under the kind care of Captain Thomas Dick (who has ever since proved a faithful friend), full of gratitude to that loving Hand which held the ocean in its hollow, and us on its bosom, and which brought us safely through perils of waters to our desired haven.

The induction into the charge of Knox Church took place on the 23rd of May.

On the afternoon of that day the Presbytery was entertained at dinner in the Eagle Hotel, Wellington Street, on which occasion Dr. Burns publicly and formally identified himself with the temperance movement. Though strictly temperate in his habits, he had hitherto been what is known as a "moderate drinker." But becoming increasingly convinced of the enormous evils of intemperance, especially in a young country whose character was in process of formation, as well as of the power of ministerial example, he determined to identify himself with a cause then decried by many, and to make the memorial entertainment connected with his settlement the occasion of announcing his change.

On Sabbath, the 25th, he commenced his pulpit labours.

The news of his safe arrival gave great joy to his old flock. Their feelings found expression thus :*

"PAISLEY, 18th June, 1845.

"Your highly esteemed and much valued favours of 10th and 12th of May came duly to hand. The members of the congregation were exceedingly delighted to hear of your safe arrival, together with Mrs. Burns and your family, and all that were with you in the ship. Your letters were read at the deacons' court ; and the one to the congregation was read at the prayer-meeting and afterwards from the pulpit. At the meeting, prayer was offered up, and special thanks given to Almighty God for the protection afforded you, and for carrying you through all the dangers of the deep, and landing you in safety at your desired haven. It must have been a season of rejoicing to you all that you were so soon permitted, after landing, to enjoy a communion Sabbath, enhanced by the striking coincidence of its being the same Sabbath of our commu-

* From Clerk of Session.

nion, and that we were engaged in the same sacred ordinance. It is a matter of great thankfulness to your people here that you were strengthened and enabled to engage in your Master's service, and to proclaim the good tidings of salvation to so many thirsty souls in that land whither you have been called in the providence of God. You will now be settled as pastor of another congregation, and the union formed in obedience to the command of the great Head of the Church cannot fail to be abundantly blessed. Our prayer to Him is that He will hallow the sacred union thus formed, and that you will be long spared to be, as you have hitherto been, a faithful ambassador of Christ, an honoured instrument in the hand of God in training young men for the ministry, in promoting the spiritual well-being of many souls, and bringing many 'to the knowledge of the truth as it is Christ Jesus our Lord.'

"After you left this a sadness came over us ; we felt we had experienced a loss which our Saviour only could supply. The important day of the induction of your successor arrived. After all the various steps had been gone through, and the call unanimously given to the Rev. Mr. Thomson, the Presbytery appointed Friday, 13th of June, for his settlement as our pastor. The Rev. Mr. Hutcheson preached, Mr. Salmon addressed the congregation in defence of the principles of the Free Church ; Mr. Forester presided, and laid the injunctions on pastor and people. The proceedings were all of the most interesting and solemn kind : and your valuable labours, as pastor of this congregation for the long period of thirty-four years, were prominently brought to view. We were all much pleased with your brother, Mr. Burns, of Kilsyth, being present. At the dinner on Friday Mr. Thomson made beautiful allusions to your pastoral labours ; and in his discourse on Sabbath he dwelt much on his own weakness, and that he came amongst us with fear and much trembling, when he thought of the responsibility of the charge, on succeeding one of such powerful talents, energy, and activity.

"We had also invited Mr. King, of St. Stephen's, Glasgow, to be present at the dinner and soirée. He interested us all very much when he detailed the particulars of the state of Toronto, and the cordial welcome you would there receive from an immense number of warm friends. The audience were perfectly overjoyed when your name was mentioned, and the prospect of comfort to yourself and family in your new sphere of usefulness, in the magnificent country in which you are now dwelling."

This affectionate remembrance of him was shared in by many besides his own people. The old family physician. Dr. McKechnie, who to great skill in his profession added a warm and generous heart, and who had not seen it to be his duty to follow his old pastor into the Free Church, sends him a valuable token of regard, designating it as " from a friend who has long esteemed him for his worth, who has always admired him for his talents, and who now venerates him as a faithful and devout pastor."

Sheriff Campbell,* too, who, like the worthy "old doctor," remained behind in the Establishment, and whom we were wont to look up to in our boyhood as the very *beau ideal* of a judge and a gentleman, thus writes on the 30th of December, 1845 :

"You mention that you do not regret the step you have taken in going to Canada, and I am very glad of it, and trust that you never will. In that large field your active benevolence will find much to do, and will take delight in doing it ; and I shall receive with much satisfaction any accounts that tell of your welfare."

This strong attachment of his dear old Paisley friends continued to the last. In 1864 one of them (Mr. A. R. Pollok), writing to him, says :

"In Paisley, yours is quite a household name, and fondly do many speak of their past experience with you. Dr. A. S. Patterson was telling me that he is nowhere so popular as in Free St. George's here, for he recals you to so many still in the congregation, and that thus he shines in that pulpit with a borrowed, but not unwelcome, lustre."

This chapter may fittingly close with the first communication received by Dr. Burns from the then Convener of the Colonial Committee of the Free Church, Dr. James Buchanan, who, as a native of Paisley, had once enjoyed Dr. Burns' ministry, and whose model pastorates at North Leith and Edinburgh, and well-known writings, have made his name so familiar :

* Father-in-law of Dr. Begg, of Edinburgh, who, as minister of the Middle Parish, Paisley, was one of my father's colleagues, with whom soon after his arrival in Canada the pleasant intercourse of bygone days was resumed.

"EDINBURGH, 30th June, 1845.

"MY DEAR DR. BURNS,—It gives me very great pleasure to find that the first letter which I am required to write as Convener of the Colonial Committee must be one of congratulation to you on your induction into the charge of Toronto, which, important as it is in itself, is doubly so when viewed as a central and commanding position whence an evangelical influence may emanate over the whole of Canada. We look forward with much interest and sanguine hopes to your future labours in that interesting field, and it will be our fervent prayer that both in your pastoral charge and your academic chair you may enjoy, as heretofore, a rich blessing from on high, and that you may have many precious souls given to you as your crown of joy. It is impossible, I think, to over-estimate the importance of your present position, whether considered with reference to the existing state of Canada, or the future prospects of the church in that country : and it is a source of heart-felt satisfaction to us all that one so eminently qualified in point of talent, and learning, and piety, has been found willing to devote himself to the work of training up, by precept and example, a band of native ministers for the supply of its spiritual wants."

CHAPTER XIV.

PASTORATE IN TORONTO.

R. BURNS was pastor of Knox's Church, Toronto, from May, 1845, till June, 1856. These eleven years embraced a vast amount of varied work.

During part of the time he combined professorial with pastoral duty. The students were on his heart from the outset, and he never ceased to feel the warmest interest in their welfare. To Pluralities, however, he was always decidedly opposed, and the junction in his case he counted "good" only "for the present distress."

Whenever the college staff was sufficiently reinforced to admit of it, he laid his account with a separation.

To the pulpit of his new charge he brought substantially the same qualities which gave him so commanding a position in his old. His discourses, even those most hastily prepared, ever bore marks of clearness of thought, correctness of diction, and cogency of reasoning. They were delivered with the earnestness and unction which always characterized him. The Scottish "Lecture" retained its own place. His sermons were often *in course.*

He was faithful and systematic in his visiting as he had ever been.

The Sabbath School was very dear to him. The peculiar liking which children always had for him, showed the warm seat which they held in his own heart.

To his *Bible Class* he brought the weight of his matured experience and the wealth of his extensive knowledge.

He loved to have young men visit him—and was ingenious in devices for their benefit. The minutes of the earlier Young Men's Associations of the church, which have come under our notice, give evidence of this.

He established "Mutual Improvement Circles," which were not confined to his own congregation.

Dr. Burns was unanimously appointed Moderator at the first meeting of Synod, after his arrival in the Province, which was held in Cobourg, in June.

He opened the meeting in Hamilton the following year, with a discourse on the "Headship of Christ."*

During the summer succeeding his arrival, he was much engaged as Convener of the committee appointed by the Synod to visit all the congregations of the church. He took a large share of the work himself. The results

---

* At the time of the Union in 1861, the Moderatorship was gracefully conferred on a venerable and revered representative of the body which, numerically, was the smaller—but, the year following, the honour was with exceeding cordiality tendered to Dr. Burns, who, however, felt it to be his duty to decline.—ED.

are recorded in some fifty or sixty MS. books, which are deposited in the library of Knox College. An abstract embodying these, with important recommendations, was subsequently submitted by him, and ordered to be published.

Immediately on his arrival in Canada, Dr. Burns began those periodical visits to the churches, which formed such a prominent feature of his New-World life. His missionary spirit found full scope both in the "bush" and in the "clearings" of his adopted land.

Let a few out of many testimonies to the beneficial effects of these visits suffice.

The Rev. John W. Smith, of Grafton, formerly a faithful missionary in Ireland, writes:—

" He was often at Grafton, generally in company with his loving partner. He was present on at least four communion seasons during my ministry, besides other visits.

" His presence was hailed with joy, and our communion seasons were times of refreshing and comfort. There was something in his hallowed and comforting intercourse in the household peculiar to himself. He was pleased with everything—the slightest attention from the humblest was noticed in the kindest manner—the youngest in the house loved him—delighted to serve him, and remember with delight something Dr. Burns said or did, that has left a favourable impression. He knew all the aged, must see them every time he came, and when any of his aged friends were removed, between his visits, he soon missed their presence. He entertained a strong affection and great respect for the elders, and had always some word of encouragement for them. He was the Christian, and Christian minister, wherever he went, and the most indifferent soon felt they were in the presence of a man of God. We loved him tenderly here, and just when removed we had the prospect of another visit.

" He did for the Presbyterian Church in the British Provinces what no other man could do. We owe much to him under God. He loved his church—he knew every corner of the church, and his life was bound up in the success of the cause of God in the Dominion."

The Rev. Thomas Wardrope, formerly of Ottawa, now

of Guelph, the first student licensed, and ordained after the disruption in Canada, describes the part which Dr. Burns took at his settlement, and a portion of the tour with the programme of which it was connected :—

"Dr. Burns' first visit to Ottawa, (then Bytown,) was in August, 1845. That visit was embraced in a plan which he forwarded to me at Kingston, in the neighbourhood of which I had been doing some mission work for a week or two at that time. A synopsis of his plan may be interesting, as showing the extraordinary amount of work that he was in the habit of undertaking—and I may safely add, of accomplishing.

"'Leave Toronto, Wednesday 6th, by steamer; make direct for Brockville; preach there on the arrival of the boat on Thursday, and at Prescott on the evening of that day. Friday, preach at Edwardsburg, and any other place that may be near enough to be overtaken on the same day. Set out for Kingston on Saturday, stopping at Gananoque to preach there. Then make for Kingston, where three appointments may be made for the Sabbath; two in in the city, and one wherever required in the neighbourhood. Leave on Monday by canal, for your ordination at Bytown, on Wednesday, the 13th. Then proceed to Perth; am sorry that I cannot go to Osgoode also; but could I not take Belleville on my way home? I must be in *Toronto for Sabbath, the 17th.* Try and make the best of the above. Improve on the plan any way you please; but keep the leading features in view, securing a meeting for Perth, where I have promised to preach.'

"We met at Kingston, on Monday, the 11th August, and set out for Bytown by steamer. Of necessity, the Monday and Tuesday were days of rest. But the doctor enjoyed the rest—I was almost about to say—as much as he enjoyed his work. The islands, the bays, the curious nooks, the beautiful scenery, the strange mean-derings of the route; all arrested his attention and excited his admiration. My wife has often remarked that she can never for-get the family worship, the intercourse, all the varied enjoyments of these delightful days. The other passengers seemed to appreci-ate them as highly as we did; for he had a word of kindness and of instruction for all. And the words were so appropriate to—in fact suggested—by the scenes through which we were passing, that they could hardly fail to be remembered. For instance, at a par-ticular spot in one of the little lakes, where a stranger, looking ahead, could see no outlet for the boat, he said : 'There we have an illustration of faith. We can see no way through among the rocks and the overhanging foliage; but we have faith in the pilot; we believe that he knows the way, and can bring us through.' From this text he took occasion to preach a short open-air sermon on the blessedness of trust in Him who guides His people amid all the perplexities of life, and at last brings them in ' through the gates into the city.' As to myself, in view of my ordination which had been appointed for Wednesday, I had addressed to me in the same colloquial style, at intervals and in more quiet corners, a brief course of lectures on ' Pastoral Theology.'

" We reached Bytown on Tuesday evening, and I remember, as if it was but yesterday, our conversation which was just brought to a close as we steamed down the ' deep cut.' He was speaking of various texts ; and with that openness which so characterized his intercourse with young ministers, was asking me from which of them he should preach on the following morning. Several had been set aside ; and the choice was at last narrowed down to these two : Rom. xv. 29, ' When I come to you, I shall come in the fulness of the blessings of the Gospel of Christ ;' and Isa. lxii. 10, ' Go through, go through the gates ; prepare ye the way of the people ; Cast up, cast up the highway ; gather out the stones ; Lift up a standard for the people.'

" The latter of these was finally chosen ; and both text and sermon are spoken of by many of the people in Ottawa unto this day. The services connected with the ordination on Wednesday, were conducted in the stone building on Sparks street, then the Wesleyan, and now St. Andrew's Roman Catholic Chapel. On Wednesday evening, the doctor preached again in the same place, from Song of Solomon, ii. 10, 13. All the passages that have been referred to, will be recognized by many as having occupied prominent places among his favourite texts. It is needless to say how highly his preaching was appreciated at Bytown and elsewhere ; but, it is much to be able to add, that he gained the affection and esteem of those with whom he was brought into immediate contact, not less by his whole spirit and deportment than by his preaching."

The following from himself foreshadows similar work :—

"TORONTO, 25th May, 1846.

" On the 14th June, I open the church at Binbrook and then go down to Belleville and Kingston, to look after both places. My Owen Sound visit I delay till August or so. Mr. McTavish* will do much good alone just now, and his visit will pave the way for one from me after.

" You are expected to begin at Niagara, on the 21st. Mr. Nisbet goes down the way on the 7th, and labours six weeks. Mr. Esson, also, about the middle of June, and my day at Fredericksburg, &c., will be the 21st. The *Islands* will also come under my notice. A trip to Amherst and Wolfe Islands may do for *The Record*, or for the first number of our new paper if it goes on."

---

* Now of Woodstock.

Though the ocean rolled between, he forgot not his old-world friends. To his college companion, the Rev. James Clason, of Dalzell, between whom and Codman, the young American, he had acted forty years before the part of "peacemaker," he thus writes :—

"TORONTO, C. W., 24th January, 1846.

"MY DEAR SIR,—You are one of the oldest friends I have in the world, perhaps the very oldest—and I must not even seem to forget you ; but our intercourse has not depended on me altogether, otherways you might have had reason to tax me with forgetfulness.

"I have one near me who is a good amanuensis, and she has been my secretary on many occasions. I do not wish, however, to devolve on her the whole business of correspondence, and more especially in the case of such old *confreres* as you and I. Many considerations of an interesting kind rise to view, when we look back on bygone years—and another year has been seen by us both, while the goodness and mercy of our Heavenly Father have followed us all our days. A good many months have passed away since our arrival in this far land, and I can now form some idea of what a residence in Canada is. I do not repent my voyage across the great ocean, nor do I feel that I did wrong in breaking asunder so many tender and endeared ties.

"A wide field of usefulness spreads before me here, both as a pastor and as a teacher. I have just finished (Saturday,) one of my most interesting weekly exercises, with 22 students—two hours of prayerful searching of the Scriptures on cases of conscience and visitation of the sick—for we take up Pastoral Theology on Saturday ; while two hours each other day is devoted to Systematic Theology and Church History.

"Three months have been employed by me in this way ; and whatever may be the style of the execution, assuredly the work itself is most important and valuable ; more so than anything that ever before engaged my mind.

"The regular lecturing and preaching on Sabbath go on also, and here I find the labours and preparations of former years of great use to me.

"A large Bible Class also takes up two hours of Sabbath, and Mrs. Burns has upwards of 30 young women regularly at her's.

"The missionary work is over and above, and a large part of my time during summer was occupied in that way. When Dr. Willis returns from the Lower Province to take my class and pulpit for three or four weeks, I expect to get away on a tour beyond Lake Simcoe—the latest settled townships, and almost all Scottish ; as usual, entirely neglected. It is to my mind revolting in the extreme to witness such palpable proofs as I have seen, of the heartlessness of the churches at home. It is wonderful that there should be so much Christianity in Canada as there is, considering the treatment our countrymen have received and are receiving at this moment ; for, alas ! not one minister has been sent out as yet by the Free Church to this Province, and every mail has carried to the committee most earnest appeals. If such a man as your neighbour, Mr. Buchan,* would come to this land (and he is just the man), he would do incalculable service ; but men very inferior to him every way, if they are persons of real piety and liveliness, would do great good.

"Some hopeful lads are at the Hall, but years ought to elapse before they go forth, and what is the church to do in the meantime? Vacancies must be filled up, with such as we can get. The patience of the people is exhausted, and *Scotsmen* you know *will* have ministers. We have above thirty stations in this one Presbytery of Toronto to supply, and Mr. Rintoul and I are the only ministers ; our young men are therefore sent forth as catechists, and this interrupts their studies. I feel myself sinking under the burden, more however, from discouragement and disappointment, than want of strength.

" The conduct of the home churches is what I complain of ; here every encouragement is given.

" Not one of us has had any sickness—not an hour's illness—it is the finest climate in the world.

" Young Robert is fairly launched as a preacher, nor are we without tokens for good.

" In new songs, we are called to bless and magnify His name who is all in all.

" Please remember us to all enquiring friends.

" Most affectionately yours,

" ROBERT BURNS."

After labouring two years successfully in Toronto, he had a season of discouragement. He thus writes :—

" My discouragement preyed so much upon me, that when, in March, 1847, I thought of a visit to Nova Scotia, to help the churches there and in New Brunswick, in their sad destitution, it occurred to me that possibly my services might be transferred to another colonial field. In May following, my son was licensed, and with the not unnatural feelings of a parent, I entrusted my pulpit and my charge to him for two months.

" On this occasion, besides an affectionate address and present of books to Mrs. Burns, from her senior Bible class, the following

---

* The late Rev. Wm. Buchan, of Hamilton, Scotland.

document, signed by some hundreds of sitters and members in the church, was put into my hands :—

"MAY, 1847.

"The memorial of the undersigned members and adherents of Knox's congregation, respectfully sheweth—

"That we have with the deepest regret heard mooted the question of your leaving the congregation for some other sphere of usefulness.

"Under the strong conviction that that event, were it now to take place, would seriously impair the present prosperous condition of the congregation, if not, indeed, as it is to be apprehended, wholly endanger its existence, we are most anxious to avail ourselves of every means within our power, to induce you to relinquish, if you should have formed any intention of leaving us. So much of what is favourable in our present position, both in the congregation and in the Church to which we belong, is attributable to your ability and untiring energy, that the apprehension of losing the advantage of these qualities at the present time is alarming. We cannot doubt that, to an unbiassed judgment fairly considering the whole case, it will manifestly appear that your translation from among us would be attended with consequences disastrous to our ecclesiastical and congregational interests.

"We therefore desire to express our earnest hope that a serious consideration of the welfare of the congregation will impress upon your mind the conviction that it is your highest duty to continue to devote your eminent talents to the labours of your present charge ; and we fervently pray that, by the blessing of the Almighty, you may be long spared to spend a happy life among us as our most highly esteemed pastor."

This earnest appeal weighed with him to remain in Toronto. He goes on to say :—

"In the course of my three months' absence from Toronto, I visited the States, and collected and purchased a thousand volumes for the College Library of Halifax ; supplied Halifax, Pictou, Prince Edward's Island, and the city of St. John, New Brunswick, with preaching on Sabbaths and week-days, to a greater or less extent ; visited nearly all the families of the Free Church in the two cities of both Provinces ; obtained a subscription of £1000 for the erection of Chalmers' Church in Halifax ; opened the Mechanics' Institute as a temporary place of worship in St. John, N. B., and organized the nucleus of the Free Church congregation there. All this, with kindred labours of a similar kind before and since, I looked on and still look on as a donation, if not in money, at least in work (which is the same thing) from the Christian members of Knox's Church, Toronto, to their more destitute fellow-members of the body of Christ. Two years after, I made a shorter visit to Nova Scotia, and opened the new church in Halifax, then under the ministry of my esteemed co-pastor once in Paisley, Mr. Forrester, now the Chief Superintendent of Education for Nova Scotia.

"While I was in Halifax, in 1847, the temporary erection called Knox's Church, in this city, was burnt to the ground."

We well remember the "burning." Having been appointed supply during father's absence, our's was the last voice heard in the old edifice. The last sermon preached in it was on Sabbath evening. the 31st May, 1847.

The Sabbath following we met in St. Andrew's Church, which was kindly placed at the disposal of the congregation, who subsequently engaged the Temperance Hall.

Dr. Burns returned with as great rapidity as his engagements in the Lower Provinces would permit.

Within six weeks after his return, the foundation was laid of the present stately structure.

A sentence of his comprehensive address on this occasion contained the germ of what was known as the *Mare Magnum* controversy, in which some of his United Presbyterian brethren took friendly issue with him. It was conducted with spirit and ability on both sides.*

He kept closely by his post while the work went on. Nothing occurred to mar it. We were soon receiving such notes as these :—

"Toronto, 26th May, 1848.

"We are getting on successfully, the vane on our spire having been put up on Wednesday last, and towering aloft over all other erections of the kind in the city. We are in great danger of getting vain of it. These are externals, but they are of importance in their relative connexions. Our church is now nearly ready for

---

* To one of the leading champions on the U. P. side, he once said (when this old controversy was recalled), "I did not agree with your letters at all, but you treated me like a gentleman." For such intellectual gladiatorship he had a strong liking. In a keen argument on some great principle he was in his element ; and though in the warmth of debate he would not unfrequently say or write severe things, he was ever quick to make the *amende*, and slow to resent any fancied or real wrong.

being opened. We have fixed the height of the pulpit, and in a few weeks all will be completed. Mr. Bonar's letter will show you how things are as to the deputies.

"I am thinking of writing Dr. McGillivray, and Mr. Bayne, of Galt, who may both preach on the first Sabbath of July, and the evening diet would fall to myself.

" The only subjects on which a difference of opinion is likely to prevail at Synod, will be the sustentation fund and the college. Both are well worthy of serious consideration. It is rather curious both subjects seem to be agitating our friends of the Free Church at home also.

" A rival college at Aberdeen would not be a bad thing; the evils of monopoly are great.

" I have just completed my visits to all the Common Schools of the city, and the report is in to-day's *Banner*. There will be controversy about it of course."

"TORONTO, 11th July, 1848.

" Our opening is just at hand. We are already *in*, *i. e.*, below, having commenced in the basement floor, Sabbath before last. Thus, we are gathering. Our "Laigh Kirk" is crammed. We now take in 200 or 300 more than before, and our collections show it. I am kept busy just now by the Academy examinations, and as Mr. Gale is laid up by sickness, so much devolves on me."

"TORONTO, 15th August, 1848.

" Our opening is fixed now for the 3rd of September. Mr. Patterson (of Tranent), the deputy, is to be up to preach, and possibly another (one of our own men).

" I would have preferred a week-day for the opening, but this could hardly be, from secular considerations and engagements.

" We had a large congregational meeting last night for arranging the plan of an extraordinary collection on the 3rd. The plan we have adopted is :—

" ' The distribution of blank tickets to each family of the congregation, on which the name of each member (parents, children, domestics, &c.,) is inscribed. These family gatherings to be laid up for the 3rd, and put into the plate on that day.'

" Of course, although you are not now an inmate with us here, we still look upon you as a member, and I would like to have inscribed on *my* card the names of all our members."

The new church was opened at the time fixed, Sept. 3rd. The Rev. J. Patterson, of Tranent, deputy from the Free Church of Scotland, preaching in the forenoon and evening; Dr. Burns in the afternoon.

A few extracts from the many letters to his devoted partner, when we visited Scotland together in 1850, may suffice to give some idea of the work of these years :—

"I trust that all goes well with you—a kind Providence watching around you—friends happy to see you, and the light of our Father's countenance shining on your soul.

"I rather think you will not return to Church street again. I have taken another house in York street. The accommodation will not be much greater than at present, but there are many more conveniences—the house more elegant every way—near the College, not farther from church, and only ten dollars more of rent. We' get possession to-morrow, but the rent dates from October 1st. I have been at home the last four Sabbaths, and am keeping up the classes as well as I can. Your young folks meet only occasionally. We had a pretty good meeting on Monday eight-days, but the night was very wet ; we got nearly five pounds, which I will set down to account.

"Mr. Lyal* leaves us for Nova Scotia in a few weeks ; he preaches for me this evening (Thursday). You will think I am getting rich on marriages ; for three, I got 17 dollars. You see what you are losing by being away. I fear these dollars will have fled before you come home. They will cover the flitting, and this belongs to your department you see.

"Say to Robert, the supplies will be duly attended to. The opening is fixed for the first Sabbath of November, and by me ; this only conditional. I will take charge four Sabbaths. May the presence of the Good Lord be with you. I am wearying for next mail.

"My visit to Hamilton and the West, occupied me nearly three weeks. The voyage up and down Lake Erie, (nearly 300 miles,) from Buffalo to Detroit, by the splendid steamer *Mayflower,* was very delightful and healthful. I did not find the state of matters at Amherstburgh just as I would have wished, but we have done our duty, and truth must triumph in the end. It was on Saturday morning I got home, and preached all last Sabbath. I endeavoured to improve the solemn events which had taken place on both sides of the great Atlantic—the death of President Taylor and Sir R. Peel.

"I am busy in the work of visitation, taking the afternoon and evening, which makes it more pleasant than the warm forenoon.

"A pleasing event is the probable accession of Mr. McLachlan, the Cameronian minister, to our body. He has made his formal application to the Presbytery, and unquestionably will be received.

"We have had pleasant, and I think profitable prayer-meetings, and good attendance on the Lord's Day. Let us hope good is doing."

---

* Professor Lyal, then of Knox College, now of Nova Scotia.

P

In the extensive Saugeen District which was just beginning to be settled in 1851, he thus indicates his interest :—

'5th August, 1851.

"You will not be altogether pleased with my depriving you of
Mr. Duncan, at your late solemn season of fellowship. The truth
is, there seemed a loud call on us to send a missionary to those
Huron lands, whose spiritual state was so affecting; and the nephew
of the Crown Commissioner, (McNab,) just setting out to explore
and organize the settlements, and a religious man, anxious to help
on our cause, presented an opening not to be rejected by us."

In 1851 he secured for over 300 of the 71st Highland
Light Infantry the right to worship God according to their
consciences. That right had not been conceded before.
It was claimed that the Established Churches of the
Empire had the exclusive privilege of ministering to the
soldiers. Dr. Burns disputed that claim. The authorities
were at first disposed to insist. Red tape seemed likely to
carry the day. But, after a persistent effort, he succeeded.

The men were marched to the church of their attachment. The unflinching advocate of their rights ministered to them for over a year without fee or reward. In
addition to the Sabbath services he regularly held a
prayer-meeting amongst them. Many a lonely toilsome
walk he had to the distant barracks, and without the remotest expectation of salary, which went in another
direction. We had the same regiment under our care the
following year, and a noble body of men they were—but
we were more kindly treated by the powers that be.

When they left Toronto they presented their friend
with a splendid gold watch and chain, and a warm hearted
address.

To anything bearing on the *eldership* he was specially

partial. He had himself written and published much on the subject, and counted an efficient body of elders the sheet-anchor of the church.

> "Toronto, 5th February, 1853.
>
> "Your papers on the eldership are valuable and well timed. I wish we could get a supply of really good elders. They are invaluable.
>
> "Death is making ravages at home among my old friends, and the loss of such men as McLaggan, Sievewright, &c., must be deeply felt."

Two months afterwards he had to part, in circumstances peculiarly sad, with one of his best elders and dearest friends:

> "Toronto, April, 1853.
>
> "Our excellent friend, Mr. John Burns, took his departure yesterday to a better world. Our grief is deep; the loss is great; the widow and family much to be sympathized with."*

Within a single year John Burns, of Toronto, John Fraser, of London, and James R. Orr, of Montreal, three of the noblest elders in our church, to whom he was specially attached, were not suffered to continue, by reason of death.

Eighteen hundred and fifty-four was to him an *annus mirabilis*—a wonderful year, in consequence of the visit of the Apostle of India—a blessed *avatar* to this entire continent.

The provincial arrangements devolved on him, and he went about them with his whole heart.

> "Toronto, 10th April, 1854.
>
> "It is my intention to go down with Dr. Duff to Cobourg and to Kingston, but I cannot stay over the Sabbath; at least I would like to return by Saturday morning, my single object being to pay respect to a distinguished man and esteemed friend. The doctor accepts your invitation of course. He has been with us

---

* As agent of the church and editor of the *Record* Mr. Burns was singularly useful. When cut off in mid-time of his days, linked with such noble compeers, many cried, " Help, Lord, for the godly man ceaseth, for the faithful fail from among the children of men."

since the afternoon of Saturday, and our house is still an inn. Yesterday, we had noble work of it, and such an audience I fancy, as was never seen here or in Canada before. Many went away.

"This day he addresses the students of the three halls, at 4, and *we* have a social meeting in the evening. To-morrow tho great meeting takes place in the Wesleyan Chapel, and on Wednesday, we have the breakfast in the St. Lawrence Hall. The doctor is greatly overwrought, and yet he spoke yesterday with great vigour till near 6 o'clock, and many solemnly interesting truths he brought before us. W. Lyon Mackenzie and Charles Lindsay stood at his right hand on the pulpit stairs all the time. We made collections for the missions as you should do, but the crowd was against our success. We mean to spend two hours at Cobourg, on Wednesday, Captain Colcleugh having kindly agreed to pause ; thus we may not be with you, till breakfast time."

The satisfaction of the distinguished visitor was expressed in many ways, and when about to leave on the 20th April, of that year, he writes from Montreal :—

"And now I cannot leave Canada without saying how thankful I feel to God for even this short visit. Above all, my dear old friend, and father beloved in the Lord, allow me to express to yourself and dear Mrs. Burns, the joy of heart which I experienced in meeting and conversing with you, and the gratitude of heart I shall ever cherish for all your uncommon kindnesses towards myself. The Lord recompense you both a hundred-fold ! Excuse haste, and believe me ever,

"Affectionately yours,

"ALEXANDER DUFF."

Six years afterwards, during which the country of his love and labour had passed through a reign of terror— writhing in throes, which ushered her into a new and nobler life—Dr. Duff, acting as the mouthpiece of the missionaries, who from the ends of the earth sounded out to Christendom the summons to prayer, thus wrote :—

"CALCUTTA, 8th August, 1860.

"MY DEAR DR. BURNS,—Often, often, do I think of my visit to Canada, and of the warm hearts I met with, from London on the West, to Montreal on the East.

"Since then great events have transpired in many lands. But

in a Christian point of view, the most memorable are the great revivals of religion in America, Ireland and other lands.

" How intensely we have been longing for a shower in this dry and parched land, the Lord knows ! That, to a greater extent than heretofore, the spirit of prayer has been stirred up, is undoubted. But, oh ! how feeble are our prayers and all our efforts ! Remembering, however, that we ought always to pray and not to faint, we wish to persevere and to 'give the Lord no rest' till He arise in His glory and in His majesty, and shine before all nations.

" The enclosed invitation will explain itself. Copies of it have been sent to all the ends of the earth, and should the object commend itself to you and your friends, you will kindly give it currency through the religious papers and magazines of the Canadas. Oh ! that the Lord would rend His heavens and come down ! Let that be our unceasing prayer !

" Things here, to all outward appearance, have settled down, but not so in reality.

" There is an under-ground rumbling which betokens men's minds to be ill at ease. But the Lord God omnipotent reigns. That is our happy assurance. And, whatever be the trials in store for His church and people, the *issue* will be glorious, for the mouth of the Lord hath spoken it. To Mrs. Burns and all friends in Toronto and elsewhere, my warmest remembrances, and believe me ever,

" Yours very affectionately,

" ALEXANDER DUFF."

On my father also devolved, several years afterwards, the making of the arrangements for Dr. Guthrie's expected visit to Canada—arrangements, which, to the regret of all, had to be abandoned on receipt of the following :—

" COPLEY HOUSE, THORNTON HOUGH,

" CHESHIRE, 15th April, 1867.

" MY DEAR DR. BURNS,—You will probably have heard before this reaches you, that I left the *Scotia* at Queenstown, *hors de combat*, not through sea sickness, but suffering from my old heart malady. It is impossible for me to describe my feelings, but they were not new to me. I had endured the same horrible sensations on a night voyage aboard a steamer, two years ago, when passing from Geneva to Leghorn. On that occasion, I resolved I would never pass another night at sea, so long as there was a carrier's cart rumbling along the road. I was so anxious to undertake and go through the American enterprise, in the hope that I might do something to draw the churches and countries nearer to each other, that I cast all warnings behind me. We had a capital passage to Queenstown, so far as the ship was concerned. The *Scotia* never seemed to feel herself out of the dock. I would have endured other two or three such nights, but I could not bear the prospect of 12 or 14 of them, and unless I got away at Queenstown, I knew there was no other escape ; and I embraced it, almost as glad as the Israelites when the Red Sea opened them a means of escape, and the way to the other shore. However, at the suggestion of some kind Americans, I let Charles go on—very much delighted he was that he also was not doomed to disappointment.

"He will, I hope, be turning up in Toronto, and I am sure he will find no lack of kindness so long as he is with you and Mrs. Burns. This is a sore disappointment to Ann as well as to me— but it just affords another illustration of the adage 'man pro- poseth and God disposeth.'

"So we must just hope to see you and Mrs. Burns among ourselves again. We would welcome you both with much joy. May the Lord richly bless your and her abundant labours.

"Ever yours affectionately,

"THOMAS GUTHRIE."

These were Tabor visions and visits. He had other experiences as well. Thus :

"February 14th, 1856. Confined by severe inflammation of side till Sabbath, 24th February, when I preached all day. Phil. ii. 12–19 ; Isaiah vi. 27.

"Feb. 27th. Lists made up of communicants, 25. Pleasing prayer-meeting.

"The Communion was dispensed on the first Sabbath in March, Mr. Inglis, of Hamilton, aiding.

"Action Sermon, Rev. xix. 7, 8.

"From that day, for five weeks, I was laid up by a severe bilious complaint, but through much mercy was restored, and after being on five Sabbaths in succession, absent from my pulpit, was enabled on the third Sabbath of April, to take part in the public service, and on April 27th, I preached forenoon on Judges, vi. 13, 'O my Lord, &c.' Since May 4th, have been able for all duties, including Bible Class. Up to this day, May 24th, I have been engaged in calls on members of the church and on others, in health and in sickness."

The preceding brief extract from his day-book records the severest sickness he ever had, "for indeed he was sick nigh unto death, but God had mercy on him."

It followed one of the most trying periods in his personal and public history, when his mind was on a constant strain and his heart knew its own bitterness.

He notes but the simple facts, without a word of comment. His vindication came from an unexpected quarter.

One of the two parties who formed the immediate occasion of the trouble, wrote on November 17, 1856, to a friend, during what proved to be his last illness :

> " Dr. B. and I were good friends at last. He came to see me frequently. If I had seen matters then as I do now, I should have often said : ' Get thee behind me Satan.' I was under a most powerful influence, with much malice, backbiting and lying, which I could not perceive in the mist around me. I hope the Lord will pardon all connected with that matter."

To the widows of ministers his sympathies flowed out very warmly. A minister once filling posts of honour and usefulness in the Free Church of Scotland, had " erred through wine, and through strong drink was out of the way."

Fleeing his native country he took refuge in Canada. We found him one day in the Toronto House of Industry —a haggard, woe-begone looking object.

He left soon after, no one knew where, but there was strong reason to believe him dead. In the interests of the poor widow in Scotland he took up the case. He advertised freely in the papers ; corresponded for long with Insurance Companies in which the party had life policies, and with the managers of the Free Church Widows' Fund. At last he got evidence which was deemed satisfactory, that the unhappy man had been found on the doorstep of a tavern, speechless through intemperance, was taken to the Hospital, and soon after died. At different times it seemed as if he would fail in his benevolent design ; but he kept persistently at it, till he had collected each missing link, and formed a chain of evidence which was irresistible.

The Insurance Companies paid the amounts, and Professor Macdougall, professor of Moral Philosophy in the Edinburgh University, and convener of the Free Church Widows' Fund, wrote thus :—

"EDINBURGH, 6 CLARENDON CRESCENT,

" 12th May.

" I received your obliging reply yesterday, just as I was starting for our annual meeting. It will gratify you to learn that the Trustees have unanimously voted to Mrs. ——, the full annuities for the current year.

Before the *Widows' Fund* of our church was established he took up individual cases as they occurred. In connection with one of these we received this reminder :—

" TORONTO, 31st Dec. 1850.

" I rather think you had moved long ago in favour of the H. Fund. We are anxious to get the whole collected and put into one sum, for the purpose of investment for behoof of the family.

" A new-year's-gift thus bestowed will not be lost. A boon to the widow and fatherless will receive a blessing. Try and gather a little, and send it up to me as soon as possible, that the sum may be completed and invested at interest."

Often did he thus cause the widow's heart to .sing for joy.

The repetition of such instances impressed on him the need of a general provision. He was familiar with the working of Life Insurance Companies. With the " Scottish Amicable" he was long connected, and for many years was chairman of its Paisley board. In the working of the funds, both in the Established and Free Churches, for the widows and orphans of deceased ministers, he was thoroughly versed. When the matter was mooted in Canada, he took it heartily up. Those who initiated the movement found him a willing worker.

On one of several tours in its behalf, he writes to Kingston to us :—

"MONTREAL, August 1851.

" We are coming on very successfully with our collections on behalf of the Widow's Fund. St. Gabriel street, already £153 ; Coté street, £192 10s. I think we shall make out £450 or £500 from both. I expect to go down to Quebec on Friday, and Mr. Walker, of Newton-Stuart has come up to assist Mr. Fraser on Sabbath. This day (Fast Day,) falls to me. I am counting on being with you on the 12th, and you will circulate the address when you please, notifying also on Sabbath first my intention of submitting it to the practical regards of the congregation. I am counting also on Amherst Island, on the 14th, and Picton and Belleville as proposed. You will send circulars and a note. All this if the Lord will."

Rev. Henry Gordon, of Gananoque, accompanied him during part of one of these tours, and was with him also on his first visit to Ottawa. Linking the two, with a glance at his last visit to Gananoque, he says:—

" The next intercourse with your father which I enjoyed, was in the summer of 1845, I think, when he came to Canada as pastor of Knox's Church, Toronto, with the determination to devote the remainder of his life to the interests of the Church of Canada, and in Canada, the land of his adoption, to leave his bones ; which he did—but not before the good Lord had given him about a quarter of a century, and not much less than the period assigned for a generation, to do his Canadian work, which was carried on with little or no interruption, in continuously sustained vigour and elasticity of mind, almost to the last hour.

" When he came to spend a considerable portion of the Christmas holidays of 1867 with me, the limbs indeed gave tokens that the outward house was tending to decay, but declension in mental vigour in the pulpit was very little visible, and on the occasion of collecting at my house some of his old Paisley acquaintances, and a good many others, giving a pretty fair representation of the Gananoque community, the American part inclusive, there was so little lack of that vivacity so characteristic of Dr. Burns, that at the close of this social gathering, I was thanked, as one by one they

wished good night, for having given them the opportunity of meeting so pleasing a specimen of a cheerful, entertaining, instructive
old age.

"But to take up the thread of my narrative. It was on the
occasion of Dr. Burns' coming to Ottawa, then called Bytown, to
preside at the ordination of my much valued friend, the Rev.
Thomas Wardrope, that on coming to the spot where travellers
land, the face so well and so long known, and which seemed to
say, 'I love the work on which I have come,' was recognized by
me, and the well-known voice thus greeted me :—'Mr. Gordon, I
am glad to see you ; I have seen your missionary pony and Mr.
Hepworth on it, and I am glad he is using it for missionary work ;'
alluding to my friend, Mr. Hepworth, a gratuitous labourer in the
Lord's vineyard, nearly if not altogether, and who surpasses the
fame of Goldsmith's Country Parson, 'passing rich with forty pounds
a year ;' for I can attest that my friend has been engaged in voluntary evangelical labours, in a circuit of perhaps 30 miles in circum-
ference, since 1845, and 30 dollars a year would be a fair average
estimate of his income, perhaps less. He has acquired an art, not
known in our days, of living without money.

" Your father preached a good many discourses at Ottawa, and
many belonging to different denominations were hearers. The
comments of a person with whom I was not acquainted, but who
entered frankly into conversation with me, (I do not think that he
belonged to the Presbyterian Church,) comes to my mind, and were
to this effect :—'That's the preacher fitted to do much good—
sound, lively, but no *wild*-fire about him.' His visit to Ottawa left
these impressions on the brethren and congregations of our church,
that the Lord had sent a man of preaching qualifications, of those
active and, in a good sense, flexible social habits, suited to a young
rising country of mixed races.

" I had a good deal of intercourse with your father, in his jour-
neying labours in behalf of the schemes of the church ; in particular, at the time of founding 'The Widow's Fund.' I went round
with him in my own locality and somewhat in Brockville, and was
struck with the zealousness, cheerfulness and knowledge of human
nature with which he went about it. I remember that, in visiting
a widow lady, whose son, a farmer, happened to be absent, we
came into the house after a journey from Kingston, on one of these
cold sharp days, not a little tending to the sharpening of physical
powers—it being about 4 o'clock, p. m., and not having dined.
The Canadians' serve-all tea, butter such as we find at farmers'
houses, and cakes, that kind we never saw in Scotland, *crullers* I
think they call them, were among them ; but, as far as I can remember, the common help at all times, ham, was awanting—well, abundance of all this was soon seen spread out on the table—and another
strong proof was added to the innumerable proofs before, that
alcohol is not needed for raising the spirits.

"For altho' your father in his constitutional temperament was generally lively, I think that I never saw a more generous, copious outflow, than when partaking of that kind woman's repast, and praise of the cakes (not so dangerous as praises to our poor imperfect fellow creatures,) was not spared. Your father's kindly way with the people had won this woman's heart, and her remark to me was 'dear me, I was in trouble that I had sae unco puir a table for the Doctor, but his fine homely way made me soon forget,'—a lesson for the stiff and stately ones. This stiffness is often an excrescence which needeth the knife."

My beloved old friend recalls a marriage feast fresh in my recollection, when my father (as was not unusual), did the honours of the table. Reverting next day to the display by him of the very feature which came out in the Gananoque cottage, the mother of the bride, in the exuberance of her feelings, exclaimed, putting a strong accent on the second syllable of "comfortable," and giving a little variation to the first :—"Oh, but the doctor was the _confôrtable_ man that nicht."

To lend a helping hand to ingenuous youth commencing life, was a real pleasure to him. Many applications he made to men in business, and sometimes to those high in power, in their behalf. Thus, for a young man in no way related to him, he applied to the War Department when the present Earl of Dalhousie (then Mr. Fox Maule), was in office, and received from his lordship a reply, an extract from which will be found interesting :

"WAR OFFICE,
"11th January, 1849.

"I received your letter some few days since, and am rejoiced to hear that it has pleased God to prosper you in the land where you are placed. The prosperity of His Church is at all times a source of delight, but that of the portion of it with which we are connected, is peculiarly so. Your college beats that of the Presbyterian Church in England in its numbers, and I trust will be sufficient to supply preachers of the Gospel to our North American Colonies, without drawing away from the old country such men as yourself. I read with great interest the account of Knox's Church, and I am happy to see that you agree with me in opinion, that beauty of structure of the House of God, is not inconsistent with purity of devotion to God himself. I have been in Toronto many years since, but my visit was hurried, and the condition of the place at that time, left no great impression of its advantages in my mind. It must be greatly altered since then, and it would gratify me more than I can say, were I able to revisit that loved haunt of my youth, from Quebec to Niagara.

"To come, however, to the marrow of your note, I fear that M's. son can receive little help from me.

"People are apt to think that because a man is in power, he can get anything. It is exactly the reverse. Unless you have it in your own department, you have less chance than the humblest supporter of Government. Moreover, every step, at present, is towards reduction, and so my difficulty is insurmountable.

"I regret to return so ungracious an answer to your request, which, however, I am glad you have been induced to make, as it has given me the pleasure of hearing of your doings and yourself."

He was often the "*afflicted man's companion*." In the chamber of sickness his visits were peculiarly prized. He knew how to speak a word in season to those who were weary. In the morning of his ministry he had learned obedience by the things which he suffered, and thus obtained an aptness to teach those occupying forms in the same school, its severe though salutary lessons.

"31st Dec. 1850.

"We have been in painful anxiety these days past, regarding our beloved Rebecca. Every hour we are expecting a telegraphic announcement. If the dear sufferer is still present in the body, let her know from us that we constantly remember her at the heavenly throne—that we desire her spiritual advancement and joy—that we commend her in faith to Him in whom she trusts, and that we sympathize most tenderly with the afflicted, and we fear, by this time, bereaved husband. My dear partner would write at length, were it not that the last intelligence seemed to be the prelude of an hourly-expected fatal announcement. Assure the Messrs. G. that all the wishes and hints in their letters will be most punctually attended to, and that our house, whether by day or by night, is at their service. May the God of all grace be with the interesting sufferer, and at even-time—may there be light!"

To his life-long friend, Mr. Clason, he wrote thus sympathisingly, when "the desire of his eyes was taken away with a stroke" :—

"TORONTO, 5th May, 1848,

"MY DEAR OLD FRIEND,—Your late painful trial in the loss of your beloved partner, demands a token of sympathy from me, and I willingly offer it. We had heard through various channels of dear Mrs. C.'s illness, but had not anticipated a fatal result. We have since learned the particulars from mutual friends in Edinburgh, and yet a detail of them from yourself or Rebecca, (when you can bring your mind to it,) will be to us most agreeable, more especially as regards interests more sacred and solemn than those of the body and the termination of a life temporal. What we have heard in this respect is so pleasing, as just to excite a desire to hear more. In the meantime, we offer our united condolence. We have met with you often at the heavenly throne, and commended all your concerns into the hands of our common Father, praying that divine support may be imparted in this your time of need, and that all things may be made to work together for your good. We sympathize with you in the removal of one, so many years your companion in this vale of tears, and the sharer of your joys and sorrows ; and we sympathize with each and all the members of your family on the breaking of a tie betwixt them and her, so tender and so endearing. You and I have often been called to minister consolation to others ; now you are called to test the value of that consolation in your own experience ; and I can say from personal knowledge in circumstances similar, that never does the Gospel which we preach commend itself more to the understanding and to the heart, than when, amid bereavements, it lays open its blessed fountains of comfort and of joy. Many lessons also will spring out of the retrospect of the past, while the hope of a re-union in a better land is sweetly soothing.

"Amid your growing infirmities—for both you and I must think of these while we feel them—the new tie to heaven thus formed in your case, will be at once comforting and strengthening, and your closing days may be among your brightest. It is now upwards of forty years since you and I used to exchange letters, and our period of sacramental intercourse has been not greatly short of this, and without interruption from any cause of an unpleasant nature.

"It was just this week, twelve months ago, when enjoying for the *first* and *last* time, fellowship in communion with our old friend at Dorchester, near Boston, we had *you* and *yours* before us, and many recollections of other times. He is gone, and you and I must be getting our houses in order, for the knell is striking for us both. Oh, my dear friend, there is indeed a reality in the things of God, and in the solemnities of a coming world ; a reality, which such events as the present presses more strongly upon us. May we grow in experimental acquaintance with the truths we have so long been honoured to preach, and may we exemplify their spirit more than we have hitherto been enabled to do. My partner will accompany this with a few lines to R. My son is with us at present, (from Kingston,) and I go down to take his pulpit on Sabbath. I have had many causes of gratitude in Robert, who has early been called into the vineyard, and whose field is large and inviting."

Travelling four years ago in a distant part of the State of Wisconsin, we chanced to be entertained by one who had served during the late American war as a brave Commodore.

After dinner, his wife mentioned that for a season they had sojourned in Toronto, under the ministry of Dr. Burns. A very promising daughter left behind at school had fallen sick and died. She spoke with a beating heart and swimming eyes of his assiduous attentions, and showed me a long letter written by him to her (dated August, 1850,) directed to her Western home, in which he tenderly broke to her the sad intelligence, and conveyed words of counsel and comfort.

Nor did he lose in Toronto his Paisley character of the "*friend of the poor.*" He was ready to distribute, willing to communicate. No one can enumerate his benefactions, for "not letting the left hand know what the right hand doeth" was fully acted out by him.

"His warm friend, Alexander McGlashan (says one who knew him well),* occasionally blamed the good doctor for being more generous than his means could afford, and as they often went about together, Dr. Burns sometimes adopted measures to prevent his friend knowing the extent of his liberality. On one occasion they visited a widow with whom the doctor sympathised in her need, and when leaving the house he left a glove, saying to Mr. McGlashan when about to enter the carriage, that he had left it. Then,

* Rev. R. Wallace, West Church, Toronto.

returning alone, he placed an envelope in the hand of the widow containing twenty dollars."

"I have met him on his missionary tours (continues the same kind friend), which were frequent, preaching daily, or almost every day, and presenting to the people where he stayed the 'Memoirs of McCheyne,' volumes of sermons, such as 'Burder's Village Sermons,' and other works that he thought would advance the interests of godliness among the people. In order to this he spared no expense and grudged no outlay. He truly despised the unrighteous mammon, and followed his Master's admonition, 'make friends to yourselves of the mammon of unrighteousness.' He was noted for the generous liberality with which he aided new and weak congregations and mission stations ; in several instances encouraging them to purchase pulpit Bibles by contributing freely to that object, as well as to the erection of new churches. On one occasion, after he had preached at a missionary station, the treasurer offering him five dollars to pay his expenses from Toronto, he asked, 'What is this ?' Being told that it was to meet his expenses, he took out a five-dollar bill, and, putting it on the other, said to the treasurer, ' add this to it, and get a pulpit Bible.'"

Be it remembered too, that he was quite dependent on his salary. But he would stint himself for other's good. *He gave to feel.*

In the *public questions* which agitated his adopted country he felt a deep interest. His extensive correspondence as Secretary of the Colonial Society made him intimately acquainted with these. The vexed subjects of the Clergy Reserves and Rectories had not to be studied by him for the first time on his arrival. With their nature and bearings he was perfectly familiar, and he entered at once the lists as an accomplished athlete, in a contest which was ere long to eventuate in triumph. He participated in the feelings which the "liberal spirits" of the day cherished towards the "Star Chamber," under whose crushing despotism the country had groaned.

By speeches and letters, by joining in deputations and otherwise, he aided those faithful men, who had been so long fighting the hydra of bigotry and exclusiveness.

which had been feeding on the fat of the land, and to whose voracious maw, truckling politicians were ready to sacrifice the dearest interests of their country.

A few years saw it in its death-throes, and none rejoiced more than he in its dissolution.

In 1847-8 he published in the *Banner* a series of letters to the Earl of Elgin, the Governor General, on the liberalizing of the University at Toronto, the non-partition of the University Fund, and the introduction of important improvements into the course of study.

In September, 1849, he printed in the Montreal *Witness*, in a similar way, some suggestions of a practical nature, which met the approval of members of the Government. The bill of the Hon. Robert Baldwin covered the whole ground which he had sketched. The main points for which he and others had contended were secured with an unanimity that failed not to excite surprise.

With the political leaders on both sides he was intimate, as also with the then Governor, (Lord Elgin,) whose cause he warmly espoused at a period when he considered him unjustly treated.

Dr. Burns had a remarkable *insight into human character.* On various occasions during his Canadian life, he was under the painful necessity of exposing the base and baseless pretensions of parties who professed to be the agents of certain religious and benevolent societies. On two of these occasions he was subjected to much trouble and annoyance, and knew what it was to be " persecuted for righteousness sake."

He was ever a warm friend of Israel, and every well-

designed and well-directed effort for Jewish Evangeliza
tion met his cordial approval. But, convinced of the un-
reliability of some of the accredited agents of a certain
Jewish Society in New York, he "withstood them to the
face because they were to be blamed." They made repeated visits to Canada between 1850 and 1853, and
carried away from an over-credulous public considerable
sums of money.

The revenue of the society in a single year rose occasionally to fourteen thousand dollars. Some of the best men
about New York allowed their names to be put forward
among the office bearers, with an easy trustfulness, which,
however amiable and kindly, Dr. Burns felt not to be
right.

He wrote and spoke, and put himself to great labour
and expense, to convince them of their error. He travelled
to New York to make enquiry on the spot; and published
in a pamphlet of forty pages, a scathing exposure.

The result was, that those who formed the elegant
frontispiece to the society, convinced of its hollowness,
withdrew, and the whole institution soon after went down.
"unwept, unhonoured and unsung."

No sooner had one Hebrew bubble exploded than
another rose on the surface.

One Lublin, who professed to be a Hungarian Jew,
sought to palm his pretensions upon the religious public
of Toronto, in April, 1853—and too successfully for a season. Dr. Burns stood all but alone amongst his brethren
in the belief that the man to whom they were opening
their arms and their pulpits was an arrant impostor. He
had successfully practised on the gullibility of many,

Q

when Dr. Burns handed him over to the police, but the legal evidence not being deemed sufficient, he was let go.

So soon as he got out of the clutches of the law, he immediately disappeared, and was afterwards discovered to be a scoundrel of the worst class.

This was a dark epoch in Dr. Burns' history—but "my God will stand by me and the cause of rectitude will triumph"—was his resolute language, and soon he found that "unto the upright there ariseth light in the darkness." The triumph in both instances was so signal, that his fellow citizens of all shades of sentiment gave expression to their respect and gratitude, and a magnificent gold medal, and a handsome sum of money, presented by a large and influential deputation, headed by Dr. Ormiston, were the substantial expressions of it.*

Many other illustrations of his skill in "trying the spirits" might be adduced. As for example—the case of the Roman Catholic Priest L——, a pretended convert—who had excited considerable interest and sympathy in the city. A public meeting was to be held in Toronto to hear this celebrity. In the forenoon of the day of the meeting, he called to get Dr. Burns' name on the list of friends, and after some conversation, presented a very formidable-looking diploma, or something of the kind, as his credentials.

* The inscription on the Gold Medal was this :

"VERITAS VINCIT (Family motto),

"Presented to the Rev. Robert Burns, D.D., of Knox's Church, Toronto, by a large body of citizens and others, as a token of respectful esteem, and in testimony of his faithfulness and zeal in the cause of *Truth*, in having on various occasions detected impostures practised on the public; and more especially of his exalted moral courage under peculiarly embarrassing circumstances, in having, notwithstanding the most unscrupulous conduct of volunteered abettors, successfully frustrated and exposed the audacious career of the accomplished *impostor and swindler*, Lublin, a pretended Hungarian nobleman, Moravian Bishop and convert from Judaism, and an agent of the 'New York American Society for meliorating the condition of the Jews.' Toronto January, 1854."

Dr. Burns read a little of it, and then, turning to his visitor, said : " Sir, there are many bad things at Rome, but there is *good Latin ! That* never came from the Vatican as you say." The fellow, wincing under the startling rebuke, withdrew, and left the city as fast as he could.

Referring on one occasion to eight kindred instances, some of them applications for admission to the ministry, when his keenness of discernment did good service to the interests of religion and morality, he said : " In every one of these cases I happened to know just a little more than my brethren knew, and while they complained of me at first for my ' rashness,' our church (but for this) would have been far more corrupt than it is, by reason of foreign admixtures."

As to the results of his pastorate in Toronto, a brief statement of his own may be given :—

" Of the progress of the congregation, since the commencement of my ministry, the following table of admissions of members may give some idea.

A Communion List of Knox's Church, extracted from the Session Record, this 10th December, 1855.

Roll as it stood on 23rd May, 1845, the day when Dr. Burns was inducted...		215
Admitted in Sept. 1845, First Communion		80
" " Feb. 1846—48.	Sept. 1846—23.	71
" " Feb. 1847—38.	Sept. 1847—34.	72
" " Feb. 1848—33.	Sept. 1848—18.	51
" " Feb. 1849—40.	Sept. 1849—51.	91
" " Feb. 1850—74.	Sept. 1850—21.	95
" " Feb. 1851—55.	Sept. 1851—25.	80
" " Feb. 1852—25.	Sept. 1852—34.	59
" " Feb. 1853—39.	Sept. 1853—30.	69
" " Feb. 1854—37.	Sept. 1854—70.	107
" " Feb. 1855—35.	Sept. 1855—39.	74
		1064

Being an average of about 80 per annum.

CHAPTER XV.

PROFESSORSHIP.

D R. BURNS visited Kingston as delegate from the Free Church of Scotland on Friday and Saturday, the 19th and 20th of April, 1844. On the 7th of March, 1842, Queen's College, had been opened, with Thomas Liddell, D.D. of Lady Glenorchy's, Edinburgh, as Principal, and the Rev. P. C. Campbell, M.A., as Professor of Classical Literature and Belles Lettres (now the Very Rev. Principal Campbell, of Aberdeen). Seven theological students were in attendance at the time of Dr. Burns' visit. Six of these waited upon him, intimating their intention of separating from the Established Church of Scotland and of connecting themselves with the Free Church.*

---

* The names of these six students were, we believe, Angus McColl, John McKinnon, Robert Wallace, Lachlan McPherson, Thomas Wardrope, and Patrick Gray.

In July, 1844, the disruption in Canada occurred. The new body took the old name, " The Presbyterian Church of Canada," dropping simply the words " in connexion with the Church of Scotland." In the Fall following, Knox College was established. The Rev. Andrew King, M.A., of Glasgow, afterwards of the Theological Seminary at Halifax, who had come out as a delegate, was induced to remain over the winter, and to act as interim Professor of Theology and Hebrew. With him was associated the Rev. Henry Esson, M.A., as "Professor of Mental and Moral Philosophy, Classics, and General Literature." The college was opened on the 8th of November, 1844, with fourteen students. For a time it dwelt " in tents," shifting from James street to Adelaide street, in small unadorned edifices ; then to something better, in what forms part of the present Queen's Hotel; thence to its present quarters, which it is hoped will give place by and by to a building more in accordance with the advancing spirit of the age and the increased wants and resources of our church.

We have already noticed that Dr. Burns for a time combined the professorship with the pastorate. His first communication, after deciding for Canada, was to the students. So soon as he arrived he commenced arrangements for their benefit. He prevailed on the Rev. Alexander Gale to devote a month to the preparation for winter work of those who had remained in the city. He laid great stress on the preliminary training,—on what he denominated " grinding,"—and that gentleman kindly undertook this duty.

"HAMILTON, Tuesday, Sept., 1845.

"Mr. Gale, at my request, agrees to take charge of the students for one month, and to reside at our house, where the students will meet with him for at least three hours a day, for exercises in languages and philosophy. Mr. Gale is well qualified in every way for this work, and I hope that the young men will profit much under his tuition. He will also preach for me on the 10th. I need scarcely say that we rely on your paying all attention to Mr. Gale's comfort."

We were privileged to enjoy the teachings of that amiable and accomplished man, with the little band that had gathered some weeks before the commencement of the session in the humble tenement in James street, which formed the cradle of Knox College. His fatherly counsels, and the exercises upon "Watts on the Improvement of the Mind," and kindred text-books, were of lasting benefit.

In those days, when Upper Canada College was largely under High Church influence, and our public school system was but in its infancy, feeling the importance of a preparatory school as a feeder to the college, Dr. Burns urged strongly the establishment of such an institution. Toronto Academy was the result. He drew up the circular regarding it, and acted as chairman of the board. Mr. Gale was made Principal of the Academy, and Professor of Classical Literature in Knox College. Associated with him were the late Rev. Thomas Wightman and Mr. Thomas Henning. Both boarding and day schools were conducted with distinguished ability, and proved a great blessing. When the public educational institutions were placed on a footing in accordance with the views of our church, the Toronto Academy, which had satisfactorily served its end, was discontinued.

In the higher female education, Dr. Burns also felt a

deep interest.   He prevailed on Christian ladies of sound
principles to open seminaries, which might be an offset
against those well-known establishments to which parents
of lax notions are too prone to send their daughters at an
age when the character is most susceptible of impressions,
and the mind receives a set.

" TORONTO, Aug. 26, 1853.

" The S—— are now fairly embarked.   Perhaps Kingston may
bring a few boarders.   We have embraced the range of the evangelical churches, and they seem hearty.   These Popish and Puseyite
seminaries are eating out our vitals.   Female seminaries, if properly
conducted, and on sound evangelical principles, will exercise a
commanding influence on the churches and on the community—a
subject of far greater importance than many suppose.

" I send you a letter from Dr. Guthrie, that you may let Mr. O.
and others see the light in which the thing is regarded in Scotland."

Dr. Burns served in the college till the arrival of the
Rev. Dr. Willis as permanent professor and Principal.   His
prelections embraced Church History and the Evidences of
Christianity, with occasional lectures in cognate departments.   He had a good deal of " grinding" in the elementary branches, and was ready to set his mind in any direction where he felt there was a want.

On the matter of " preparatory training" he laid great
stress, and published, in 1848, a lengthened document ex-
planatory of his views.   These did not meet at the time
with that measure of favour which he desired, but they
were subsequently carried out, substantially, in the tutorial
arrangements.   Such supplementary provision for ground-
ing in the elements was needed, at the period of his persistent advocacy, to a degree which, with our present
improved educational advantages, we cannot fully appreciate.

After Dr. Willis had entered on the duties from which he has recently retired with a record of over twenty years' honorable service, Dr. Burns at intervals rendered efficient aid as occasional professor.

On the 17th of June, 1856, he was appointed to the chair of Church History and Apologetics, and loosed from the pastorate. A few extracts from his diary thereafter may be given :

"June 24th.—Over to St. Catharines; drew the address on college buildings.

"27th.—Examined books on church history.

"July 29th.—Have now got six lectures on the Evidences ready.

"Aug. 8th.—At Guelph ; collected £22 for College.

"10th.—Hamilton, forenoon, Judges vi. 13, Gideon ; evening, 6.30, Dundas.

"11th.—Making calls with Mr. Walker, collecting.

"12th.—Went down to Wellington Square, preached on 2 Cor. v. 21 ; at Waterdown at 7, on Rom. xv. 39.

"13th.—At Cummingsville, on Luke xxiii. 46.

"14th.—Collected of money, £90 ; but the amount of subscription is £175.

"15th.—Dundas ; subscription £20 ; arrangements made for collecting.

"16th.—At Galt ; preached forenoon and evening, 2 Cor. iii. 18.

"19th.—Set off for Doon ; sermon at 7. New Hope omitted—a pity.

"21st.—At Berlin and Woolwich.

"24th.—Preached at Fergus, 2 Cor. v. 21 ; and Elora, 1 Peter iv. 18, 'Scarcely saved.'

"26th.—Preached at Mount Forest, forenoon and evening ; rising place ; conversed about the site ; agreed to enquire about it.

"27th.—At Durham, church roofed ; shall they sell? examined the ten acres ; preached, Rom. vii. 9 ; addressed on College ; keen contest about M. P.

"28th.—Dangerous ride up to the Sound.

"29th.—To Collingwood ; church matters there going on well."

In September we find him preaching and addressing at Grimsby, Clinton, Niagara Falls, St. Catharines, Port Dalhousie, Niagara, Woodstock, Innerkip, Ingersoll, London Lobo, Williams, Komoka, Westminster, &c.

"October 1st.—Delivered (opening) lecture on the Literature of the Christian Ministry—large attendance ; good many students coming."

To the discharge of his duties in the seminary he brought an enthusiasm which never flagged. Looking out for students, gathering books for the library or curiosities for the museum, influencing friends to establish bursaries and scholarships, collecting subscriptions for the college buildings, securing works of standard theology for students at reduced rates, and commending the institution in every way he could to the sympathies, the prayers, and the liberality of the church.

In its behalf he undertook a journey to Great Britain in the summer of 1857, in company with the Rev. Donald Fraser, then of Montreal, afterwards of Inverness, and now of London, himself a graduate of the institution. It was his first visit since leaving his native shores, and his appearance and advocacy on the floor of the Free Church General Assembly awakened much interest. A considerable amount of money was collected, and much advantage in various ways accrued to the institution. Latterly he made a specialty of the bursary fund, establishing a bursary himself, Mrs. Burns founding another, and several relatives and friends following their example.*

---

* My father always set a high value on bursaries or scholarships as aids to deserving students. The obtaining of these he made a specialty in his efforts for the college. On one occasion, in Scotland, he made an effort in this direction in behalf of a member of his own family ; for with his limited income and open-handed charity it was not easy to make the "ends meet." An omitted portion of his autobiography refers to this. "Forty years had rolled away, and three peers in succession had occupied the ducal chair of the palace at Hamilton, when it came into my mind to make a slight experiment on the memory and the heart of a Scottish nobleman to whom of course I was totally unknown. My son Robert, formerly of St. Catharines, now of Chicago, Illinois, U.S., was in 1842 commencing his studies in theology at Glasgow College. The Hamilton bursaries are 'golden' ones ; and a gift worth the taking is surely worthy of being asked. I amused myself penning a letter to the duke, when at the palace, stated the facts of the case, my father's claims, and my son's standing at college ; sending at the same time my friend Professor Buchanan's high certificate. Ten days brought me an answer from the duke's

The circulation, at half price, of Dr. Cunningham's works which he accomplished on a large scale among the students, was a great boon. This he was enabled to do through the generosity of several gentlemen, specially of Mr. Joseph McKay, of Montreal, who had previously done so much to defray the expenses of preachers coming to Canada.

Through a similar arrangement "Mosheim's Church History" and other works were secured for a trifle. Many young men on their settlement in charges received donations of books from him.

He was frank, generous, and kindly in his intercourse with his students. To the stiffness and starchedness of magisterial authority he was ever a stranger. The punctilious etiquette which stands on its dignity, and insists on ceremonious deference to its exacting behests, he could not away with.

To empty-headed conceit when accompanied by flippant impertinence he would show no mercy. A shallow youth, desiring to annoy him by unearthing a buried controversy, asked him if he could let him have a copy of a long-forgotten pamphlet, which he had issued during the heat of it—he replied " No ! but I once published a discourse on 'Young men exhort to be *soberminded*,' and if you come across a copy, I would advise you to study it."

A student being examined before Presbytery, who

confidential adviser, that his grace had considered and respected my claim, and that my presence at Hamilton was immediately called for. With a light and joyous heart I obeyed the summons. An offer of three years at thirty guineas or two years at fifty were in my choice, and the deliberations were pleasantly going on, when the trying event of the disruption of the church took place ; and I and my son, with every expression of gratitude to our noble patron, respectfully declined the proffered boon."

was not distinguished for his profundity, was asked by him : " Where was the *Westminster* Confession of Faith compiled ?" He received, in a hesitating tone, the reply— " I suppose at *Edinburgh*, Doctor !" He would not smile on such occasions, though the scenes were sometimes ludicrous in the extreme. Tired with the inaccurate answers of another who aspired to a student's position in Knox College, he pointed to a folio copy of "Brown's Self-Interpreting Bible" on the table, and asked " What does self-interpreting mean ?" " It means, sir" (was the sage response), " John Brown's Bible, interpreted *by himself*— meaning, sir, that it was himself that done it !"

Another who had launched out into a prayer of prodigious dimensions, had to be stopped by the associate of the Doctor, though at his suggestion, to prevent their losing the conveyance which was to carry them to another appointment.

One of the Synod bores, no longer in this country (and there were a very few such), had taken the floor, and was descanting in grandiloquent style on the Headship of Christ over the nations—reaching the climax of his oratory in the scene of the Gadarene "Pork Sellers." Thoroughly tired out by his windy wordy vapouring, the Doctor rose, and said—" Moderator, I am amazed that this venerable Court can listen to such *balderdash.*" The orator was confounded. Floundering about, he exclaimed—" Moderator, I don't know where I was last." " You were among the SWINE," replied the Doctor. The caustic response took amazingly, and did the delinquent good.

But these cases of seeming severity were exceptional.

His general bearing was genial and kind. He loved story-telling. His fund of anecdotes was inexhaustible. An overflowing treasury of incidents and illustrations, with first-rate conversational powers, made him the best of company. The puckering of the lips, the sparkling of the eyes, and the wreathing of his countenance with smiles, would be the precursors of some happy hit, which would convulse the company, or "bring down the house." He never deemed it a sin to laugh, or considered that there was the remotest connexion between godliness and gloom. He generally looked on the "sunny side," and found the joy of the Lord to be his strength.

He was ever ready to tender advice, when asked, to students, in the prosecution of their studies, or to young ministers, amid the struggles and difficulties of their early ministry.

"I cannot look round my study (writes one of them, who speaks for many), without my eye falling upon some book, or manuscript, or manual, that is closely identified with his personal and fatherly counsel and advice. So accessible, so frank, and so painstaking, that every moment found him engaged with some one or other of the students, in private, helping them out of either personal or educational difficulties."

A few extracts may be given from his correspondence, illustrative of this. They exhibit his views on Pastoral Theology—a department to which he was specially partial—and into which, occasionally, he loved to turn aside, though it came not directly within the range of his professorial duties :

"TORONTO, 15th Nov., 1847.

"With regard to *pastoral visits* they are not easily m•naged so as to be edifying, and nothing has given me more concern than the conviction that I have not succeeded in making them so useful as I would have wished. My second visitation of all the families in Knox's Church is just closed; upwards of two hundred—and far greater pleasure has attended it than on the first round. This has arisen, partly from my getting better acquainted with the people, and partly from an impression on my mind that *things are advancing with us* as to personal and family religion. The impression also, on the part of the *persons visited*, has been, I learn, more pleasing and salutary. Our church is *crammed*.

"One plan will not suit for all cases. Where there are a number of young persons and domestics I mingle a good deal of *catechizing*, with direct address to the parents, and prayer. Where there are mostly *adults* I try to converse with *each* on the state of religion in their own minds, &c., basing this, however, generally, on a suitable passage of Scripture, read and spoken from, the exposition going first, and occupying, perhaps, ten minutes. It is very difficult to get persons to open, or to converse freely at all on religion. In that case I do not urge very much, but address earnestly and affectionately.

"The *different classes* I always speak to *separately;* not in different rooms, indeed, but insulating them, as it were, and pointing out the duties and snares and responsibilities of each.

"Half an hour to each family. Notice sent before. Twelve visits a day. I generally enquire after the family library—Bibles, Testaments, Catechisms, Confessions of Faith—and recommend a *Commentary*, such as the Tract Society one, and pay particular attention to the question as to FAMILY WORSHIP. *Here* there is much to distress. Some have it on Sabbaths; some once a day; many, *never*. My greatest difficulties have arisen from this quarter, and you will find it so, too. The duty, however, is far more attended to *with us* than *formerly*. Recommend the District Prayer-Meetings. These are better, and distribution of good tracts is useful, along with the visits, although I have not done much in this way. The education of the children and the religious state of the servants always noticed : domestics of whatever denomination always present and conversed with. In the case of Roman Catholics, NO CONTROVERSY, but warm appeals in regard to the Word, the work of Christ, the danger of looking anywhere for salvation except to Christ, the solemn prospects of Death and Judgment, and the folly and madness of dependence on man.

"*Gathering pupils* for male and female Bible classes and Sabbath schools *always* attended to. Thus there is a mutual *feeding*, as it were. Great carelessness I find, however, in these things. Your Sabbath school, by being re-modelled under your own eye, will be improved. Our Bible classes please me much. Keep regular books of visits; parents' name; profession; each child; communicant or not; servants; denomination; remarks, &c. These hints may be of some use, but they are *hurried*."

TORONTO, March 13, 1848.

"I sympathize with you on the difficulties you must have felt on the subject of admission to sealing ordinances. I have felt them all my days, and they are increasing every day with me. My opinion is, that time and forbearance, and painstaking, with much prayer, are the only means of conquering them. Both you and I have sort of safety valves; and yet, I am always sorry when persons, tired of my efforts for their good, go away. Our standard has been greatly raised, and is rising. The whole system of our Free Church, if properly *acted out*, will issue in this. The style of preaching, too, will affect it, and above all, private communing and earnest appeals."

"TORONTO, 19th July, 1848.

"There is no peculiar difficulty in the case of discipline which you bring before me. After communing on your part with the parties, they must both appear before the Session, and make confession of their guilt. They are then rebuked, and appointed to converse with two members of Session, who are understood to satisfy themselves, not only of their apparent penitence, but of the regularity and consistency of their walk and conversation. On a favourable report to the Session, the parties are admonished, and prayed with, and suitably exhorted as to their future conduct. They are thus held to be absolved from the scandal, and re-admitted (if members before) into fellowship. If not previously members, they may then, one or both, be received (after due examination), and enjoy the privileges of the church. This was *our* uniform practice in Scotland. No case has come under my notice in Canada. Much depends on the *symptoms* of penitence and *steadiness* of walk since marriage. I have seen us *keep back* parties for months and longer, because they exhibited no other symptom than merely a fixed determination to have baptism at all hazards. From your account of the case, there seems to be no danger in this instance, and I hope and pray that the blessing of the Great Head may rest on this, apparently your first call to a faithful and godly discipline."

"TORONTO, 7th Jan., 1850.

"I am so much occupied with my Church History and Normal School attendance, in addition to all my other duties, that I have scarcely a moment for extra work. We have heard that you have taken possession of your basement floor as a temporary place of worship. In our basement I had two months public labour in preaching, prior to the opening of the church, and these two months were to me very sweet; large crowds of hearers, all near me, and the impression on the whole, more in unison with my feelings than since our entry into the greater place.

"May souls be converted to God by your ministry! May your

humble place of assembling be a birthplace for precious immortal spirits !

"I feel no discouragement from anything, *except myself*, and I believe that causes in OURSELVES are specially the obstacles in our way.

"I should be sorry if anything like depression should affect you in your private or public labours.   Any tendencies this way must be guarded against, and we have much in our own power.   Let us simply rely on strength beyond our own, while we are diligent in the use of all means.

"In quickness of utterance I was considered, when a young minister, to be faulty, and after my first visit to London I began to imitate the solemn pace of the Evangelical clergy of England, when a letter was sent me, complaining of my "teasing slowness," and entreating me to go back to my former rapidity.   "*In medio tutissimus ibis.*"

"Simplicity of manner is of great importance also.   But these are the externals.   Still, they are of value.   Oh ! to be able to choose acceptable words ! and to carry Divine truth to the minds of our hearers in a way somewhat suitable to its Divine character, and the awful responsibilities it involves !"

"KNOX COLLEGE,

Friday, April, 1861.

"We have now got the labours of the Session brought to a close. Our final examinations were very full, and on the whole successful. But the charm of the close was Professor Young's exposé of the Oxford Essays, a very able and eloquent piece, which I regret to say, he refuses to publish.   I lent him the book, and recommended the theme to his attention ; and his compliance with my urgent request was to me very gratifying, and the style of its accomplishment still more so.   The subject had necessarily engaged much of my own attention in my evidence class.   That class I would like Professor Young to take charge of, as the state of my eyesight renders it very difficult for me to peruse fully all I would need to examine on the new phases of Infidelity.

Dr. Burns had lectures fully written out, but his general practice was to prelect from elaborate notes.   He emphasized the passages which he intended the students to take down, repeating them slowly and distinctly, so that no one need mistake the meaning.   He was a good catechiser.   His questions at the close of each Session. to which written replies were required, were very clear and exhaustive.

His Church History course embraced the Old Testament in condensed form, with a *vidimus* of Church History proper, selecting certain epochs for fuller elaboration, with occasional dissertations on cognate topics. He did not believe it was his province to be a mere chronicler of dates and' facts, or a delineator of ecclesiastical battles. With the prominent controversies he made the students sufficiently familiar, often enunciating the principle: "If you wish to refute an error trace it to its source." He would indicate without illustrating, directing to the sources of information instead of going into all the minute details, erecting finger posts or mile stones for the travellers along the pathway of knowledge, rather than being by their side at every step. He supplied seeds of thought and spurs to mental effort.

His lectures on Apologetics partook also of this character. With the tactics of the old opponents of the truth he was thoroughly versed. Having been from his youth a devourer of books, and retaining the habit to the last, he was intimately· acquainted also with the modern modes of attack. He was abreast of what is called "the advanced thought" of the times—though often sorry that his increasing defect of vision precluded his reading more of the teeming productions of the press. He was well aware, however, that many of the present instruments of assault on the citadel of our faith were but the spent shot of former battles—the ancient cannon re-moulded and re-mounted that have been spiked times without number, and even turned on the retreating foe. He was generous in his treatment of honest and sincere doubters, but with the sophistical lucubrations of pretentious sciolists he had no patience.

His interest in Knox College remained unabated. All through his last visit to the old country it was on his heart. He spoke for it in the General Assembly, and in private circles. He also published a circular on those departments in which aid was specially required.

The last letters he wrote were to its Principal and to Dr. MacVicar of the sister institution. Between the two Colleges he always endeavoured to maintain the most friendly relations. He strongly advocated the claims of the Montreal College, and did what he could for its benefit.

In the report, submitted by him on July 9, 1844, to the Colonial Committee of the Free Church, of his visit to the Provinces of British North America, he thus writes :

" Were a Theological Institution set up there (Montreal) under the charge of the ministers of our church in the chief cities of that province, it would not only receive nearly all the young men at present under the charge of Queen's College, Kingston, but large accessions from the districts around. A circumstance of which I was not previously aware demonstrates the facility with which Theological Seminaries may be instituted, and even kept in efficient operation. At Toronto, at Cobourg, and at Montreal, I found institutions of this kind belonging to Methodists, Independents, and Baptists maintained ; not on the plan of expensive and imposing buildings, to meet the eye and nothing more, but on the plan of an able, a learned, and a truly humble and pious agency, adapted to the wants of a young country, and kept up at a moderate cost. One thing is certain, that the want of regularly organized plans of Theological training, adopted at an early period of the settlements in North America, was an evil whose consequences are developing themselves even to the present day."

The last article he penned was with reference to Knox
R

College, and it was a striking coincidence, which was noticed by many, that the Institution within whose walls so much of his time was spent, and for whose interests he laboured and prayed so earnestly, became the scene of his last illness and death.

The testimony of one of the earliest students of the College, may fittingly terminate this chapter:

" There is no department of our work in which Dr. Burns took a deeper interest than the training of young men for the ministry. He soon made himself thoroughly acquainted with the wants of our Canadian church, and his sagacious mind clearly perceived that the main hope of our church was in raising up a native ministry, men brought up in the country, feeling at home here, and both understanding and sympathizing with the peculiar circumstances of the people. Hence, he devoted himself with characteristic zeal and energy to the establishment of Knox College for the theological training of our students for the holy ministry. Besides doing so much to collect a library for that institution, and devoting himself with untiring industry, at a very advanced period of life, to the instructon of young men in his own department, he also took the deepest interest in the personal welfare of all the young men attending the classes, enquiring after their circumstances, providing help for the needy, and conversing with them on the state of their hearts, endeavouring to impress on their minds the greatness and grandeur of the work to which they were looking forward, and especially the necessity of being entirely consecrated to the service of Christ. Deeply convinced himself that an " earnest ministry" was the want of our times, he did much, both by his own example, and by his instruction, conversations and prayers, to give to our church the priceless boon of such a ministry."

CHAPTER XVI.

R. BURNS rejoiced in being a missionary at large. His labours in the mission field were distributed, at intervals, throughout the entire year.

In the matured glories of "the Fall" he took great delight. The mild and mellow "Indian summer," with its gauze-like haze overhanging the landscape, the genial air, the varying tints of the trees, the gorgeous tapestry of nature, presented a fairy scene on which he loved to gaze. To the winter sleigh tour he was specially partial. It became a standing institution with him. He loved to visit the churches, to see how they did, especially in the new townships where men are "famous according as they lift up their sharp axes upon the tall trees." In many a forest cathedral the stump of a tree served for a pulpit, the canopy of heaven for a sounding-board, while his clear, sonorous voice carried the notes of salvation to the utmost limit of the thronging multitude, and amid throbbing hearts and trembling voices and tearful eyes, there ascended the sacrifice of praise. That familiar verse found a new meaning :

> " Lo, at the place of Ephratah,
>   Of it we understood ;
>   And we did find it in the fields
>   And city of the wood."

Without regard to chronological order or geographical position, some extracts may be given from a mass of correspondence devoted to these missionary tours :

KNOX COLLEGE, TORONTO, Dec., 1859.

" We are just out from our joint devotional and hortatory meeting with all the students, the Doctor and I dividing the work with Professor Young.

" *We* go off for Osprey, Artemesia, and three other northern townships, to-morrow morning by the Northern Railway, and two Sabbaths, with the intervening week-days, will be devoted to mission work. I say *we*, for my dear partner goes with me for the first time on a sleigh excursion to any distance, and I trust that no evil will befall us, and that by preaching, visiting, and distributing books and tracts, some good may, by the blessing of God, be done.

" Quebec, Aug., 1863.—Arrived at this ancient historic capital. I have had one Sabbath-day's labours in Chalmers' church, and warm as the weather is, I have stood my work well. To-morrow evening I preach at the " Cove," and on Thursday in the church, the ordinary week-day service, and I am arranging with Mr. Clark for our united missionary labour in the neighbourhood. The communion is fixed for the second Sabbath in September, and after that I expect to come direct home, as the Sabbath I mean to give to Montreal will be before that, and after Mr. Redpath's return from England. I find I will have a good deal of time on my hand here, for my preparations for winter. Mr. C—— has a great collection of old and valuable books, and there are also public libraries that are accessible. Thus, I will be at no loss for useful employment in my own direct line of study. There is also a reading-room at my command for papers and reviews and magazines. Miss B—— has picked up a Scotch gowan among the bushes, at the back of the house, and I send it.

" I am getting on very comfortably with my work, only rather little to do. Last Sabbath was spent at a small Scottish settlement, fourteen miles to the north, and among the hills. The place reminded me much of the hills of Perthshire, and the scenery around is nearly Dunkeld over again."

The Rev. W. B. Clark, of Quebec, thus interestingly writes of his labours in that region :

" QUEBEC, 28th Nov., 1871.

" It was in the summer of 1863 that your father visited me at Quebec, and assisted me efficiently both in my own pulpit, and by missionary operations in the neighbourhood. He remained for about six weeks altogether, but during that period had to make a journey to Ontario, and was absent from us one Sabbath. His visit was a source of great enjoyment to myself and family, and I am sure we all profited, both intellectually and spiritually, from his company.

" During this period Dr. Burns visited Stoneham, where we have still a small station among the mountains, about seventeen miles north of Quebec. He visited Lorette also, an Indian village, where a small remnant of the Huron tribe still reside, and preached to a few Scotch people who are occupied at the paper-mill there. He also visited Portneuf, and spent one of the Sabbaths among the Scotch settlers there.

" It was his earnest desire to visit the stations on the Kennebec road ; but as there was no public conveyance of any kind to that remote district, and the difficulty of travelling a distance of nearly ninety miles very considerable, I opposed his going, a good deal to his annoyance, and arranged that Mr. Crombie, then of Inverness, should spend two Sabbaths in the Kennebec district, while I occupied his pulpit in Inverness ; the Doctor officiating for me on one of these Sabbaths, and somewhere in the neighbourhood of Quebec on the other.

" On the 13th of September it was our communion in Quebec, when the Doctor preached the action sermon, with great power and effect, from Revelation i., 18. I do not think his pulpit power was in any degree diminished, even at the advanced period of life which he had reached then. He was feeble on his legs, and was glad to get hold of my arm when walking, but when he ascended the pulpit all the vigour of youth seemed to return.

" He was a laborious man even then ; and I admired the industry with which he collected information for his college lectures and some literary work with which he was then engaged. With a view to this he availed himself of the rich stores of material in the Laval University, a Roman Catholic institution, where he was kindly received, and afforded all facilities of reference, by the respected librarian of that institution."

At this time he spent two Sabbaths in Montreal, which he often visited, and of which he writes :

" A visit to the commercial capital of our Province (as Montreal unquestionably is) is always interesting, and peculiarly so in a moral and religious view. The city is rapidly on the increase in population and wealth. Its near vicinity to the States, its valuable railway communication with Portland, its ocean intercourse with Britain, and its many mercantile and commercial advantages give it, with almost moral certainty, the prestige of the " New York of the North." Alas ! it is the stronghold of Popery ; and yet Protestantism is nominally, let us hope really, on the increase.

" The Protestant Church is, generally speaking, in a healthy state ; and the friends of Christ, though sectionally divided, love one another.   There are able ministers in all the churches, and there have been of late pleasing revivals ; and the noble Institution of McGill College, under the superintendence of an accomplished, liberal-minded, and pious Principal, aided by a thoroughly qualified staff of Professors, is a prominently pleasing feature· in the moral picture.   The Grande Ligne Mission, and the Institute at Pointe aux Trembles, are refreshing exceptions to the general apathy of Protestants in Canada to the claims of the numerous victims of a degrading superstition.

" The British commercial mind in this city is highly enlightened, and intelligence on all subjects of mercantile and international interest is steadily diffusing itself among all classes in the community."

"LONDON, ONTARIO, Monday, April, 1864.—Not quite so lazy this morning ; up at seven, and feel refreshed with sound sleep. What thanks do we owe to the Great Keeper of Israel, who never slumbers nor sleeps. I preached twice yesterday from Rom. v. 7, and 2nd Thes. i. 10 ; attended also the Bible class and Sabbath school, and addressed both ; well attended they all are. In my last I quite forgot to refer to what you say about a call from Mr. H——.   In reply, I say this : On the subject of the Immaculate and Supernatural Conception of the blessed Redeemer, there never was any difference of opinion in the Roman, Greek, or Protestant Churches ; but as the worship of Saints, and particularly of the Virgin Mary, advanced in the Church of Rome, from the fifth century downwards, there appeared a great wish to secure for Mary the same prerogative as belonged to her blessed and divine Son, namely, perfect freedom from the taint of original sin. By many Popes and by many Councils, attempts were made to have this declared an article of faith in the Church, but without success. No agreement could be come to, and the Council of Trent itself was compelled to abandon the attempt. At length, about nine or ten years ago, the present Pope, Pio Nono, with his Cardinals, who are his sworn advisers or privy councillors, solemnly enacted it as a dogma of the Holy Roman Catholic Church, and so it remains.

"I think if you will look in the library for Edgar's Variations of Popery, you may find something about it."

Then follows an extemporized picture of his book-case, and the whereabouts of "Edgar" marked:

"I paid a visit on Saturday to Huron College, and spent an hour very agreeably with Archdeacon Hellmuth, who is also Principal and Professor of Divinity. It is a very promising Institution, and the building superior to ours.

"ORILLIA, July 4th, 1866.—How I wished to have had you all with us on the voyage and at the sermon! We had a company of thirteen in all from the Manse, and from Mr. Paterson's, and we were two hours on the Couchiching Lake, in a small pinnace belonging to Mrs. P——. The place, Rama, is seven miles to the northeast, and there the minister (Mr. Brooking, W. Meth.) met us. We took our pic-nic with us, and enjoyed it on the green grass near the church, which, with its beautiful spire, stands on the loftiest part of the ground. At two p.m. we met in church for public worship, and had a large congregation, fifty being Indians. I preached by an interpreter, who happened to be the Indian schoolmaster, and who seemed to be really in earnest. It is not easy to preach by an interpreter, and yet I learn that nearly all the Indian missionaries do so, Dr. O'Meara being an exception. The prayers are all in English, and *not* interpreted, most of the natives having as much English as lets them enter somewhat into the solemnity of a devotional service. We collected seven dollars to help them to get a bell. We returned by eight p.m. in safety, after as pleasant a day as I have ever spent. It was an interesting sequel to the holy communion on Sabbath, a season of joy, and let us hope, of profit. To-day we go on to Medonte, and there, and at Oro, the same interesting service will be gone through as here and at Beaverton.

"I forgot to say that on Monday evening was the anniversary of the Orillia Bible Society, when we had grand speechifying and a fine band, Mr. Dallas in the chair. I am in perfect health; my limbs strong, and fourteen public appearances, with twelve different subjects of address, have not at all disabled me."

"KINCARDINE, July, 1867.—Constant engagements, both in preaching and hearing, have rendered it impossible for me to find the time or even the place for penning letters. Now, the morning dawns upon me between four and five, bright and lovely, after rather a sleepless night, for I had the whole English work yesterday morning, noon, and night, to carry out, and by the rich mercy of our Heavenly Father, have found the promise amply fulfilled as on many occasions before: "As thy days, so shall thy strength be." What a delightful communion season we have had! How you would have enjoyed a really Highland Sacrament! The church crammed as full as it could hold, and 1,500 in the Grove, about a mile distant. *There* the Gaelic preaching went on, and there the tables were spread under the canopy of Heaven, nicely covered with fine white linen, and a nice tent erected for the minister, &c.

"All was deeply solemn, and conducted with beautiful order and quietness. Mr. Fraser tells me that it was, in every part, an exact specimen of a Ross or Inverness-shire communion, for in the Highlands no church could hold the multitudes that assemble from all quarters—sometimes to the number of 10,000 or 12,000. Friday was devoted as usual to what is called "speaking to the question," and Professor Caven and I enjoyed wonderfully *four* hours hearing in an unknown tongue, amazed that we could so easily enter into the sentiments and feelings, without understanding the language of the people.

"It was a genuine specimen of the thing, and Mr. Fraser presided with great propriety, and I am told, by those who knew the language, that not an unsuitable idea or word was introduced—for eight experienced "men" spoke at greater or lesser length, and much to the purpose, the text being John iii. 3, and the signs and evidences of regeneration distinctly brought out. We both spoke also in English, after being told of the leading topics that had come under review. *To-day* I rest, Mr. Caven taking my place in English, and Mr. Grant, of Ashfield, in Gaelic.

"To-morrow I go north to Tiverton and North Bruce, and every day has its meetings—one or more—sermons, pic-nics, and my visit will also be helpful to five sacramental occasions.

"Jan. 1868.—The Artemesia falls, seventy feet in height, are beautiful, and our station at the mills there, is in fact, our best. I had ninety hearers on Tuesday evening, and the miller, Mr. Hislop, is earnest and active in our behalf. The 'City of Eugenia,' indeed, is only on paper as yet, but there are a good many settlers in and around, mostly Presbyterians of the 'old kirk,' who are flocking to join us; a number of them from Paisley. 'Inkerman-street' is about a mile long, and graced by two small cottages; one of them is inhabited by an old emigrant from Paisley, of the name of Macbraine. Mr. and Mrs. Beattie are within six miles, and our meeting again in one of the most romantic spots in Canada is very pleasing.

"The numerous memorabilia of former visits in 1859, 1861, 1862, and 1863, and especially of the one when you accompanied me, are very numerous and very pleasing, such as the books to the Kinners, the Psalm-book to the Winters, &c. William and Elizabeth Kinner are both in full communion, and Adam promises well.

"Yesterday I preached in the house of Mr. P—— to about forty, including children, and the old woman is still as blind as she was in 1841, and as keen as ever to come down to Toronto to 'get her eyes pulled out and put in again,' but still averse to any experiment in the way of operation.

To these extracts, which are principally from letters to Mrs. Burns, may be added the reminiscences of several esteemed brethren in whose districts he itinerated. With reference to his last visit to Ottawa, the same kind friend (Mr. Wardrope), who detailed an earlier visit, adds :

"So far as I know, he was then about seventy-five years of age ; yet, as in days that had long gone by his much loved *three* services on the Sabbath were undertaken.

"He preached in Knox Church, Ottawa (which name had then superseded the name of Bytown), from 1st Cor. iii. 21-23. 'All things are yours, &c.' In the afternoon he preached in Nepean, whither I accompanied him. The place of meeting was the building occupied by the Presbyterian church under the pastoral care of the Rev. I. L. Gourlay ; and his subject was 'Family Worship,' a theme on which he loved to dwell. When the service was concluded, it was within little more than an hour of the time appointed for the evening meeting in Ottawa, and we had six miles to drive He was a little tired, but could not forego the anticipated pleasure of preaching, and so he requested me to drive on before and open the meeting, in the hope that, by a more leisurely drive to the city, he would be quite recruited. I did so, and in his hope he was not disappointed. For, when he had got into the pulpit at the close of the second singing, he was able to preach with all his wonted vigour. His subject was "Christ appearing in the presence of God for us ;" and the discourse was listened to with attention, corresponding in some good degree to the earnestness with which it was delivered. When he had concluded, there were, in many hearts, thoughts too deep to be lightly uttered— thoughts of Jesus, the glory of whose mediatorial work the preacher had sought to set forth. But yet about the preacher himself, some who had heard and known him a quarter of a century before could not withhold the remark 'When he's ance in the poopit he's as gude as ever.'

"I was present," writes the Rev. Daniel Clarke (formerly of Indian Lands), in the Free Church of Lochiel, in 1848, "when he preached. The church was without doors and windows. The text was 'If our Gospel be hid, it is hid to them that are lost.' The discourse was indeed very, very impressive, and listened to with very marked attention. I believe it did much good. It produced good effects in many, some of whom still remain, and their goodness does not appear to be like the morning cloud or the early dew that passes away. I invited him to Indian Lands. The expectation of seeing and hearing him drew together an immense crowd. I believe the like had not been in the Indian Lands before that time or since.

" After this, the worthy, greatly beloved and venerable Doctor paid visits to Glengarry, when I had not the pleasure and privilege to meet him."

There was no spot in the province my father loved so much to visit as Glengarry. The Rev. D. Gordon, who for so many years laboured most faithfully in that region, writes thus regarding these visits :

" Among the most distinct and pleasant of the pictures furnished from an experience of twenty years as a minister are those of ' sacrament weeks' in Glengarry ; and of these weeks, some of the most delightful reminiscences are those of your sainted father.

"I think I may safely say that the respect and esteem with which he was regarded by all the Free Church Presbyterians of Glengarry amounted to a kind of enthusiasm. He knew it was so in Indian Lands with both minister and people. His first visit during my residence there was in the summer of 1854, on the occasion of our communion. I remember on one of the days, the Gaelic and English portions of the congregation were thrown together at his request, and he preached in the tent in the woods to about 2000 people.

" He was in one of his very happiest moods, and preached with great freshness and power ; and I believe there are not a few of his hearers that day who could now, after the lapse of seventeen years, give you, not the ' text' alone, but some precious ' notes' of the sermon, and perhaps name the Psalms that were sung on the occasion.

" That communion week was an Elim in the wilderness journey of some of the Lord's people among us ; and to lengthen out the enjoyment of it, many of them followed him to Lochiel the next week, where he was to assist at the same solemn service.

" Speaking of this visit, in a letter dated 21st of August, Dr. Burns says, ' I look back on my visit to Glengarry with peculiar relish ; much have I enjoyed it, and my warmest wishes and most ardent prayers are with you and your fellow-labourers in that interesting field.'

" His next visit was in 1858, and in replying to my letter asking his assistance, his only stipulations were, that he should have plenty of work to do—that after the five days' service in Indian Lands he might go to Lochiel sacrament, and thence to Vankleek Hill. He says : ' You are at liberty to arrange for me up to Aug. 4th, when I must wend my way homewards, or, it may be, farther east.' On the Sabbath referred to (the third Sabbath of July) he preached one of the most powerful sermons I ever heard, from John xix. 30.

The people seemed much impressed. On the Wednesday following we accompanied him to Lancaster, where, by previous arrangement, he was to assist the Rev. J. Anderson at the communion. Many of our people came to join in the service, a distance of twenty-four miles ; and some of them felt themselves well repaid for the journey in hearing one sermon, from the 2nd chapter of the Song, 10-13 verses.

"On May 24th, 1865, Dr. Burns again writes : 'I have a great desire to pay a visit to Glengarry this summer, but I fear that your arrangements for the communion may not comport with my previous engagements. It so happens that the third and fourth Sabbaths of June are already taken up with sacramental duties in the west ; yea, also Sabbath, July 2nd. Thus it is that the first day I can offer to be with you is Sabbath, the 9th of July. Will this do ? Could you make such an arrangement as would allow me to asssist at two, or even three, sacramental occasions ? say, at Lochiel, or Lancaster, or any other place where the communion may not have been. I don't mean to be at the Synod, but will reserve my strength for Glengarry. I have certainly a wish to see something of the good work that has been going on among you.'

"In tracing the pleasant impressions of these communion-weeks to their source, however, I find that they are due quite as much to the social Christian intercourse with your revered father as to his pulpit services.

"I remember as distinctly as if it were yesterday, being greatly struck with his appearance and manner as, coming out of his room, he gave or responded to the salutations of the morning. That air of genial content and devout cheerfulness spoke of a serenity and a joy in the deep places of the heart, with which the world might not intermeddle.

"His conversation in the family, at the table, and in the other intervals of public duties was a great treat to us all ; and more than once the time at the breakfast table was lengthened out, quite unconsciously, to more than two hours.

"We will ever entertain a vivid remembrance of one of these occasions, when the old man seemed to grow young again, as he gave us a graphic and minutely detailed account of the beginning of the Kilsyth revival. I think I can hear yet the ring in his voice as he repeated the message brought to him in the manse by his sister, 'Robert, Robert, come to the church—the days of Cambuslang are back again !'

"We often sought to turn the conversation to this or that passage of the Word, that we might have the benefit of his opinion in regard to them, and, indeed, I have met with few from whose familiar conversation so much might be learned."

The Rev James Cameron, of Chatsworth, writes thus of his visits to the Owen Sound region, vividly narrating a thrilling incident which nearly cost him his life :

" He visited these parts many times, in summer and in winter, when the country was almost a wilderness, and after it became settled and covered with Presbyterian churches. With perhaps one exception, nothing can be said of these visits to us but what may be said of his ministrations in scores of cases, somewhat similar, from the Atlantic to Lake Huron. He came brimful of happiness and kindness, of zeal and of sermons. His progress through the country had in it something of the nature of a triumphal march or an episcopal visitation. Crowds of all countries and religions came to hear him preach, and after the service he held a kind of a levee, at which there appeared to present their respects people whom he had married nearly half a century ago in Scotland ; others whom he had baptized ; others whom he had admitted to membership or office in his former city congregations ; with lots of newer and younger Canadian friends who had seen him or heard him or heard about him in out-of-the-way places, and felt therefore that he had a right to know them. And the good old man knew them all in a fashion of his own, not by sight, but by their voices and his wonderful memory, and the quickness and perception that is generally given to those whose vision is defective. But I sketch here a picture of no unusual occurrence.

" A remarkable incident, however, occurred on one occasion ; and this constitutes the exception to which I have referred. Your father had fulfilled his engagements in Owen Sound, where the Rev. Mr. McKinnon, who has gone to his rest, was then pastor, and had set out for Durham. When within six or seven miles of Durham, the waggon in which he was travelling drew up in front of a little wayside inn, that the horses might be watered. That the animals might drink more freely, the driver had removed their bridle. The day was hot, and to shield himself from the sun Dr. Burns raised his umbrella, when the animals, now destitute of blinkers, took fright, and with their bits hanging before their collars, and their reins draggling in the dust, they ran away over what the editor of our *Record*, in a notice of the event, calls ' the roughest road we ever travelled.' The road is now as fine a road as there is in the Province, and over it Dr. and Mrs. Burns travelled afterwards in a covered carriage and pair, when he pointed out to Mr. Cameron, of Priceville, and myself the spot where the horses came to bay ; but at that time it was a horrid piece of road. There were on it an abundance of stumps and stones, ruts and mud-holes, and, worse than all, a ' piece of corduroy,' notorious among the ' corduroys' of the Garafraxa for its badness. For nearly two miles the maddened brutes ran without slackening speed. The old man made a feeble attempt to check the horses ; his seat flew from under him, and he sank down and lay prostrate in the bottom of the waggon. He was perhaps unaware that straight in front of him, and in dangerous nearness, lay the Rocky Saugeen River, with its steep banks and ricketty bridge, and abrupt curve, which always required steady and cautious driving. Had the horses taken the river, he could not have escaped ; but when within half a mile of the dangerous spot, they suddenly, and with none to check or guide them, turned to the right, and walked into a fence corner beside two hemlock logs, which were pointed out to me as still existing, last week, by Mr. MacKechnie, into whose house Dr. Burns was taken after the runaway. In the bottom of the waggon were found his gold watch and communion tokens scattered about, but with the exception of a few bruises, he himself was unhurt; and after a little repose he went forward to Durham and preached that very evening to an audience that listened to him as one that had almost come from the dead."

On another occasion, at the Rouge Hill, the stage in which he was travelling upset. He fell undermost; passengers and luggage came down on him. Had it not been for the great "strength of his chest, and God's kind interposition," he remarked, he might have been killed. Sometimes his experiences of travel partook of the ludicrous. He was nearly shot on one occasion for a bear! He was driving with a friend through a snowstorm, when something went wrong with the harness. They were passing a farm-house "in the bush," and while his companion went for a bit of rope, my father, dressed in his huge bearskin coat and cap, and with immense hairy gloves on his hands, stepped forward in the snow, and began feeling the harness. The woman of the house, coming to the door and looking out through the falling snow, discerned the strange object, and cried out that a bear had attacked the horse. The man came running out with his gun, and was taking a sight, when he burst out with a loud guffaw, and cried, " Tuts wumman, that's Dr. Burns."

Dr. Ormiston, now of New York, mentioned to me his being associated with him once at a country church opening. On a bitter winter morning, entering his chamber to see if he was up, he found the window blown open, the snow drifting on the coverlet, and the water in the basin frozen hard. My father was shivering in the blankets, but bearing the inconvenience, which would have disturbed beyond endurance many younger brethren, with philosophic patienceand Christian resignation. With the thermometer sometimes far below zero, amid the pelting storms that assailed him in his Christmas sleigh journeys, he had often to " endure hardness," and to put to practical proof the question " Who can stand before His cold ?"

Once going along the Northern Railway, the snow and ice so impeded his course that he had to spend the whole night in the cars, some respected Wesleyan Methodist brethren being his fellow-travellers. One or two of the cars rolled down a steep embankment, but he mercifully escaped. In the grey of early dawn his faithful friend and former precentor, Mr. John Ross, came several miles along the track on a hand-car, and took him to his destination, where his appointments were fulfilled as if nothing had happened.

In February, 1858, when travelling along the Garafraxa road we visited a shanty on the road-side where he had repeatedly stopped. It consisted of a single apartment of the very plainest description, and in somewhat dilapidated condition, within which were huddled, in addition to the family, pigs and poultry, bags and barrels, and all sorts of farming implements and provisions. But beneath the coarse home-spun in these lowly shielings, there beat hearts of loyalty to Christ, and love to his

servant ; and he was never happier than in front of the
blazing log-fire, or when partaking of the homely fare
which such true-hearted hospitality supplied. Mr. John
Gunn, of Beaverton, one of our most devoted elders, who
was with him in many of his earlier tours, bears frequent testimony to this. He tells of how cheerfully he
endured annoyances, and never wearied working. He
speaks of his great frankness and affability with the people.
Coming into the house after preaching, he would generally say—" Well, Mr. Gunn, any remarks ?"

Having alluded, in one of his discourses, to mercy as
God's "darling" attribute (a favourite expression with
him), Mr. G. asked him one day if there was any " PET
attribute in the character of God." He then poured forth
in earnest affectionate discourse, an explanation of the
expression.

Mr. Gunn (in a recent conversation we had with him),
dilated with delight on the prominence which my father
gave in his preaching to the pure simple Gospel, and how
it melted the hearts and opened the hands of the people.
He spoke of regions where the liberality of the people
would flow out at the stroke of his rod in fourfold larger
measure than when the rock was struck by many others.
" The Doctor," exclaimed he, " could get a couple of dollars from people who would give half a dollar to others.
He came to one place in the country where the people
were so pressed that I thought they would give little or
nothing, and they gave him a hundred and twenty dollars
for Home Missions." He mentions how bent my father
was on carrying out his engagements. If he made an

appointment he must fulfil it at all hazards. On one
occasion he had arranged to go from Beaverton to Orillia.
Mr. G. told him he could not go. My father suspected
that it was a scheme of the worthy elder to detain him.
Mr. G. pointed to the sky and to the lake. The storm
was such, as the day advanced, that it would have been
tempting of Providence to attempt the journey. Most
reluctantly he was compelled to abandon it. He would
call the family together for exhortation and prayer before leaving; then, in parting with them, he would often
add to kind expressions of interest in their welfare—" I
hope to see some of these lads at the College."

" He watched the walls of our Zion," was one of Mr.
Gunn's quaint expressions regarding him. " Three or four,
I remember, he succeeded in keeping out from the ministry of our church, who would have disgraced it." He
mentioned certain instances where the parties turned out
drunkards. One of them was on the eve of settlement
at a country place not far from the city, and the people
were not a little disconcerted at the obstacles thrown in
his way. To make up for their disappointment Mr. G.
assures me that my father offered to give them supply
every Sabbath afternoon for a whole year for nothing.

When engaged in his customary sleighing tour during
the Christmas holidays of 1867-8, he was suddenly
summoned home by what proved the fatal illness of my
beloved brother William, a rising barrister in Toronto,
and office-bearer in Knox Church, whose sun " went down
at noon" on the 4th January, 1868.

My father being beyond reach of railway or telegraph,

in the back townships, the Rev. Wm. Burns, now of
Perth, kindly consented to go after him. He made up to
him far in the interior, when just starting for more distant settlements. That esteemed friend, whose kindness
at this sad domestic epoch we can never forget, writes regarding it :

"His first question, quite unsuspicious of the cause of our meeting, was : 'Have you been preaching in this neighbourhood?' Being
told that the illness of his son William was the reason, he immediately prepared for a return to Toronto. And now was seen the influence of what appeared conflicting duties and his high regard for
his promise. It had been arranged that he should visit the charge of
Mr. Milligan, of Douglas, on his way to Fergus, where he was to
preach for Mr. Smellie ; and while on his way to Orangeville he
was in great trouble about the disappointment of these brethren.
More than once he felt inclined to fulfil his engagements with them,
and return to Toronto on the Monday following. When, however,
it was urged upon him that the dangerous condition of his son demanded his immediate return, his whole fatherly feeling seemed
aroused, and after a few searching questions he turned full round
and said : 'Have you told me the worst? Is Willie still living?'
And these questions he frequently repeated on the journey home.

"Arriving at Orangeville, the time taken up in changing horses
was spent in taking a little refreshment, and in sending word to
those who were expecting him, feeling himself bound in honour to
do all in his power to prevent disappointment.

"On the way from Orangeville to Brampton his mind seemed to
be constantly occupied, now minutely relating the circumstances connected with his own sickness some years previous, and noting points
of resemblance between his own case and that of his son, he would
become hopeful that a vigorous frame might be able to throw off
the disease ; and again, after a lapse of silence, during which he
was evidently thinking of the deeper things of the soul, he would
speak feelingly of the spiritual well-being of his son, more than
once committing him to the care and love of a covenant-keeping God.

"Arriving at Brampton in the evening, after all the regular trains
had passed, we were, by the kindly interest of the station-master,
to whom the case was presented by the Rev. Mr. Pringle, taken on
a freight-train to Toronto, where we were landed at the west end of
the freight-yard, narrowly escaping an accident from a locomotive
on another track. After, with some difficulty, making our way to
the street, we proceeded slowly (for the Doctor was much fatigued)
towards William street, and as we drew near the house he became
violently agitated. In a whisper he asked me, while clinging to

S

me very closely, 'Do you see a light in Willie's room? Do you think he is alive? Is there any sign at the door?' While standing at the door, when the servant intimated that he still lived, his whole feelings, roused to the utmost, burst forth in the cry, ' Praise the Lord !' when, being led into the parlour, he sank into a chair, thoroughly exhausted, having sustained a day's travel and anxiety under which many a younger man would have sunk."

There were certain missionary enterprises of our church with which Dr. Burns had specially to do.

As convener of the " Red River" committee, he had the principal share in planting Presbyterianism in that interesting settlement. First formed by the Earl of Selkirk, in 1812, it has had a history than which romance can furnish nothing more thrillingly eventful. These hardy and heroic settlers passed through many martyrdoms. The fire, the famine and the sword did their worst against them. But these they felt not, so much as the long continued deprivation of ordinances administered according to the time-honoured usages of their fathers. As they went out, scarce knowing whither they went, it was fully expected that a faithful Highland pastor would accompany them, but this arrangement failed. For many years, weary, wistful eyes were directed athwart the mighty ocean, and ever and anon they hoped " their eyes would see their teacher," but " the vision tarried."

Some, disheartened by delay, left the " old paths," but many held fast the profession of their faith without wavering, "mid perils of waters, mid perils of the wilderness, mid perils of robbers, mid perils among false brethren, mid weariness and painfulness and watchings often, and hunger and thirst, and cold and nakedness."

His whole soul went out lovingly towards them, and

when in 1850 the clamant case was transferred from
the Home Church to the Canadian, he determined not to
let it drop till the melting prayer of these worthy settlers
was granted. In this he was nobly seconded, especially
by Mr. Rintoul and Mr. John Burns. Dr. Bonar also,
the indefatigable convener of the Colonial Committee of
the Free Church, gave him every encouragement.

Mr. Ballenden, a leading officer of the Hudson's Bay
Company, offered free transit for a minister.

After many disappointments, which made some faint-
hearted ones ready to abandon the enterprise, my father
had the satisfaction of writing Mr. Ballenden on the 8th
May, 1851 :—

" I beg, in name of our committee, to say that we have every
reason to rely on a missionary of approved character being prepared to embark by the caravans from St. Anthony's Falls, about
the beginning of July next ; and in this confident hope, we request
of you to make for our missionary the arrangements to which you
referred in conversation with Mr. Rintoul, at Montreal. In the name
of the members of our Synod, who have been consulted with on
the present occasion, I feel myself authorized to give this pledge,
and to return you our hearty thanks for the deep interest you have
taken in this important matter."

In this hope he was again on the eve of being disappointed. With fields white at home, our means of
supply limited, and our missionary spirit only beginning
to flow out towards the regions beyond, it was difficult to
get any suitable person to look at this distant and destitute region.

It was in such circumstances I received from him the
following :—

" TORONTO, 2nd July, 1851.

" We are perplexed somewhat about the Red River case. Mr.
McK. wishes to go, but his people oppose. I rather think, how-

ever, that we will send him. I have got from a traveller here, (Paul Kane,) who was guide to Sir J. Richardson over the Rocky Mountains, the fullest information as to the case. There are 2,000 Highlanders still, and many Indians and half-breeds besides, among whom a missionary would labour.

"*We asked J. Black, but he refuses.*"

A month after the penning of this note, he had the great satisfaction of securing the Rev. John Black's consent. After a solemn designation, he went forth to the field where for over twenty years he has laboured so successfully.

On the 7th August, he wrote my father from Galena, which he reached after a break-neck journey of over three days from Chicago—missing the deputation that had come a thousand miles to meet him.

On the 29th, Mr. Alexander Ross, the father of the Presbyterian cause in the settlement writes :—

"Your letter had no sooner got here with the news of a minister's coming, than the Presbyterian party held a meeting. At this meeting steps were taken and immediately executed to secure a large lot, and commence the erection of a church and manse, and the opening of a school.

"These were the steps taken previous to the return of the party from St. Peter's, yesterday, as already stated, with the account of 'no minister.' You can easily imagine the state of our feelings at the disappointment. Relying, however, on the confidence we place in your letter, we see no just reason yet to despair. We therefore mean to sustain the move that has already been made, and follow it up with all the energy and means in our power."

Hope deferred made their hearts sick ; but though the vision tarry, they wait for it, hoping against hope.

Mr. Black very providentially overtook Governor Ramsay, of Minnesota, who was going with an escort to Pembina, and under his pilotage and protection, enjoying the utmost kindness and courtesy, he entered the settlement, and writes on the 21st September, of his hearty reception.

For many years he was our solitary sentinel at this distant outpost, till we had the pleasure of commissioning Mr. Nisbet, another early alumnus of Knox College, to join him ; and all who have entered the field since have been from the same fruitful Institution.

My father at one time entertained the idea of visiting the " Red River" country. With reference to this, Mr. Black wrote :—

"KILDONAN MANSE, April 10th, 1858.

"REV. AND VERY DEAR SIR,—It is truly gratifying to myself and to many others here to be informed of your still robust health, and seemingly undiminished activity in body and mind. May you be long preserved to serve the Lord in helping to lay, broad and deep, the foundations of a truly Scriptural church in our young and interesting country ! We, last year, expected some one to visit us, and I gave five pounds to a man to take a horse to bring him— but no one came. James Ross mentions that *you* sometimes speak of it. Now, we would be most delighted to see you and to hear your voice in our church, but I fear, at your advanced age, you would find the journey too severe. As far as Crow Wing, you could come easily and comfortably, but after that, the road leads through a perfect wilderness—woods and swamps, creeks, rivers, &c., requiring much toil and exposing to some dangers, besides the discomforts of sleeping in a tent and living in a way to which you are not accustomed. Still there is no man whom I should like so well to see here, and none whose visit, I am persuaded, would be of such advantage to the church."

Though he had all the heart for it, he yielded to the advice of friends who regarded such a perilous and protracted journey as unadvisable at his time of life.

After Mr. Black had been two years at Red River, and when there was fear of his withdrawal, Sir George Simpson, Governor of the Hudson Bay Company, who, all along took a warm interest in the mission, wrote to Dr Burns, urging his continuance :—

"HUDSON'S BAY HOUSE,
"LACHINE, 5th Sept. 1853.

"During his short residence at Red River, Mr. Black proved himself eminently qualified for the peculiar duties of that remote station, as, while he was an able and zealous minister and upholder of the Presbyterian Church, he avoided, himself, and checked in his congregation, that spirit of sectarian rivalry which is apt to prevail, and to be productive of so much evil in small communities, and in other respects, apart from his sacred duties, his conduct was always judicious, and he was admitted on all hands to be a very useful member of society. Under these circumstances I am very anxious, if possible, to make sure of his return, and as an inducement to that end, and at the same time, as an evidence of personal esteem for Mr. Black, I am willing, on behalf of the Hudson's Bay Company, to add to the stipend he may receive from the Presbyterian congregation, the sum of £50 (fifty pounds,) sterling per annum. As the season is rapidly advancing, and travelling on the plains after the present month will be very difficult, you will excuse me if I urge this matter on the immediate consideration of the Synod and yourself."

Mr. Black continued at Red River, and continues still —the father of the Presbyterian church there. A second missionary went forth to join him, and another, and another. The mission to the Cree Indians of the Saskatchewan, 400 miles from Red River, grew out of it; a mission in which Dr. Burns felt a peculiar interest, and with which Mr. Nisbet, brother of the devoted Samoan missionary and Mr. Black's "true yoke-fellow," is so honourably associated. And now, Red River has come, as the Province of Manitoba, into the great British North American family of colonies, with a bright future in store for it; and our church has a flourishing Presbytery there, with Synodical powers, and a rising college, and all the requisite machinery for doing its part in "going up to possess the land;" promising thus to bring to pass what is written,—"though thy beginning be small, thy latter end shall greatly increase."

My father had an unquenchable hatred of slavery. It was intensified by his intimate relations with Dr. Andrew Thomson, who was the chief champion of the Scottish emancipationists. He loved to dilate on the memorable meeting in Edinburgh, when that noble man rose in a distant part of the hall, and in a speech of thrilling power, turned the tide against the "gradual" party. "Give me the hurricane, rather than the pestilence," the winged words which formed its climax, shot like a lightning flash through the land, and rung as by a thunder peal, the knell of British slavery. He wrote and spoke much on the subject. With the friends of the Negro in Europe and America he had a close intimacy. Thomas Pringle, the African explorer, poet and philanthropist, was very dear to him ; and some leading members of the Society of Friends he highly esteemed. Hence his re-peated references to the question in connexion with his visit to America. To the apologists of the system he found it hard to give any quarter.

It was to be expected therefore, that when an "Anti-Slavery Society" was organized in Canada, he would be active among its officers, and that when a movement was inaugurated to establish an asylum for the fugitives from slavery, and to ameliorate their social and spiritual condition, it would receive his warmest sympathy and support.

In 1848-9, a large tract of land was purchased in the township of Raleigh, near Chatham, which secured at a low rate comfortable and happy homes for several hundreds of these children of sorrow. The Rev. William King, M.A., the "Clayton" of Mrs. Stowe's "Dred," has favoured

us with the following narrative of this benevolent enterprise, whose projector he was honoured to be, and of my
father's connexion with it.

"I first became acquainted with the late Dr. Burns in November,
1846, when I landed in Toronto as a missionary from the Free
Church of Scotland. The Doctor called on me at the Wellington hotel, to inform me that the boxes containing my books
and clothing had arrived safe from New York, from which place I
had forwarded them to Toronto to the Doctor's care. He then
kindly invited me to go to his house, and remain until I should get
my appointments from the Toronto Presbytery, but as I had only
a few days to remain in the city I wished to get myself brushed up
after my long voyage and journey (having visited Louisiana, after
landing in New York, before I went to Canada); I thus preferred
remaining at the hotel, and declined his kind offer. During the
winter of 1846 and the spring of 1847 we often met on missionary
duty. In April, 1847, I received a letter from the South, requesting me to go there as executor, for the purpose of settling the
estate of my late father-in-law. It became necessary for me then
to divulge a secret which I had kept in my own breast up to that
time, namely, that I was a slave-owner, and that I must go South to
give them their freedom, as the legal difficulty that formerly stood
in the way was then removed. This statement fell like a bomb-shell
in the midst of the Presbytery, and made quite an explosion. Mr
E—— was furious, Mr. R—— otherwise calm, was quite excited.
The Doctor and Mr. Gale saw the difficulty of my position at once,
and asked me how long I had been a slave-owner. I said 'since
1842.' 'Did the Free Church know that you were a slave-owner,'
enquired the Doctor! I said 'no, I did not think it necessary to
inform the Presbytery of Edinburgh who licensed me, as the views
of the Free Church announced in the General Assembly of 1845,
by Doctors Candlish and Cunningham, were the same as I held,
that slavery *per se* was not a sin : that the relation of master and
slave was not necessarily sinful ; but the burden of proof rested
with the master, to show that the power which he possessed was
not abused, but was used for the best interests of the slave. This
was my position ; I owned a number of slaves, but could not set
them free. There were legal difficulties in the way, and when
these were removed I could not manumit them in Louisiana.
No planter at that time could manumit his slaves and leave
them in the State. He was bound to remove them beyond the
jurisdiction of the Southern States. This I was then prepared to
do, and I informed the Presbytery that I intended bringing them
to Canada. But as I was about to leave the Province for a time,
I would resign the commission which I held from the Free Church
into the hands of the Presbytery, with the understanding that

when I returned again to Canada with my slaves, I would resume the connection, and labour as their missionary.

" I left in May, 1847, for Louisiana, and returned in May following with the slaves that I had set free. The Doctor was the first to meet me on my arrival in Toronto, and from that time till his death, he took a warm interest in the coloured population of Canada. In June, 1848, I brought the spiritual destitution of the coloured people in Canada before the Synod, then met in Toronto. A committee was appointed by the Synod to mature a plan for a mission ; the Doctor was on that committee, took an active part, and in the following year the Buxton mission was established. At the same time the Fugitive Slave Bill was passed by the Congress of the United States, which, in the fall of 1849, sent 5,000 fugitive slaves into Canada, stripped of everything but life, without a friend and without a home, and for whose soul no man cared. In the spring of 1850, the report had reached the friends of the slave in the United States, of what the Free Church in Canada was doing for their social and moral improvement. A committee in Pittsburg invited the Doctor and me over in November, 1850, to tell them what we were doing in Canada for the fugitives. It was in November we visited Pittsburg, and as there were few railroads in those days, travelling was not so pleasant at that season of the year, especially as part of the journey had to be made across Lake Erie ; and about 200 miles of it through rugged mountain scenery, in the old fashioned stage-coach, with leather straps for springs. On that journey, and the labours that followed it, the Doctor gave full proof of his power of endurance, and of his missionary zeal, which never abated till the close of his life. We left Buffalo on Wednesday evening, in a steamer for Erie, where we arrived at three o'clock on Thursday morning. The night was stormy, and we slept but little, most of the passengers being sea-sick. On our arrival at Erie, the stage was waiting to take the passengers going to Pittsburg. We had barely time to take a hasty breakfast, and twelve of us were packed inside the stage, where we were to remain for two days and two nights, the time generally required to cross the mountains and reach Pittsburg. During the first day we got along tolerably well, but as night came on, cold and wet, the rain falling during the night in torrents, the Doctor and I tried to sleep some, as we had got but little the night before, but the jolting of the conveyance over the rough roads was such that we found it impossible. Early on Friday morning we reached the summit of the mountain range, and breakfasted at the mountain house, a place that was as cold and cheerless as the mountain itself. The passengers were not in a very good humour, and expressed their dissatisfaction in terms not very agreeable to the landlord. The house was cold, the victuals were cold, and there was nothing comfortable about the place. The Doctor alone was cheerful, praised the beef-steak and tea, of both of which we had an abundance. The passengers became

more reconciled, and by the time we were ready to start all appeared
in better humour.   The remaining part of our journey lay among
the hills that form the western slope of the Alleghany mountains.
The valleys were studded with villages and well cultivated ; a
Presbyterian population having settled at that part of Pennsylvania
at an early period, and made to themselves comfortable homes.
The village church, with its spire rising in the midst of a cluster of
trees, could be seen as we passed along.   The rain had ceased, the
sun began to shine, and the Doctor kept the passengers in good
humour with his remarks on the scenery, and pleasant conversation.
The day passed pleasantly, and at night we were informed that we
would reach Pittsburg by three o'clock in the morning.   This was
glad news to the passengers, and especially to the Doctor and myself, who had scarcely got any sleep since we left Toronto on Wednesday morning, unless what we could get in the stage going over
rough mountain-roads.   We arrived at Pittsburg a little after
three o'clock on Saturday morning ; went to bed four hours ; were
up and breakfasted at seven.   Visited during the day all the ministers in Pittsburg, and made arrangements each to preach three
times on Sabbath.   Everywhere we went, the ministers of all denominations gave us a warm reception, with but one exception,
and that was Dr. R——, of the New School Presbyterians.   He
declined to have anything to do with us.   He had been Moderator
of the General Assembly at its last meeting, and had taken his
stand against any discussion of the question of slavery.   The
Doctor argued the question with him, and said that we were not
going to lecture on slavery, although we held strong views on that
subject, but it was not to discuss these that we had come to Pittsburg.   ' We come,' said the Doctor, ' to tell you what we are doing
to improve the social and moral condition of those coloured persons who have found an asylum in Canada.   We have nothing to do
with the law in the United States that drives them to Canada ; our
object is to give them homes, give them the Bible and the capacity
to read it.'   Dr. R—— refused his pulpit even on that ground, and
as we rose to leave he expressed the hope that we would not think
hard of him for refusing his pulpit.   The Doctor simply remarked
that we could not form a favourable opinion of a minister of the
Presbyterian Church who would refuse his pulpit to advocate the
cause of giving the Bible to those who have, by the laws of the
United States, been deprived of the privilege of learning to read
it.   On Sabbath the Doctor preached three times to crowded
houses ; on Monday we held a public meeting in one of the largest
churches in the city, which was well filled.   The Doctor preached
every night during the week, and three times on the following
Sabbath.   All the Professors of the three Theological Institutes
generally attended ; the Doctor was in high spirits, and spoke with
power and eloquence.   One of the Professors remarked, on coming
out one evening from hearing one of the Doctor's eloquent ser-

mons, ' Well,' said he, ' we have had delegations here from Ireland and Scotland, but none of them ever preached and spoke on the platform with the power and eloquence of Dr. Burns.' The result of the visit was a handsome subscription for the mission, and a fine-toned bell, sent expressly for Buxton, and paid for by the coloured people.

"In the summer following our visit to Pittsburg, the Doctor spent a week with me at Buxton, where he preached on Sabbath, and during the week he visited Chatham, Tilbury, and most of the mission-stations in the west. From that time till 1857 the Doctor frequently visited me at Buxton. On one of these visits, in 1853, he dispensed the Lord's Supper, and received a number of communicants for the first time. One of these was a woman named Lydia, with three of her children, who had escaped from North Carolina. She had never been baptized, and the Doctor, after the manner of the Apostle, baptized Lydia and her household ; the first household that he had ever baptized during his public ministry. In April, 1860, the Doctor and I visited Scotland and England in behalf of the Buxton Mission, where we collected most of the money that built the mission-church. The Doctor was to attend the Tercentenary of the Reformation, and was frequently separated from me ; and as we had only three months to remain, and most of the time were in Scotland, we only visited London, Manchester and Liverpool, in England. We agreed, on visiting Scotland, that I was to make all arrangements, and the Doctor was to speak when I called on him. The interval between my meetings the Doctor filled by preaching and visiting his friends. It was a season of great enjoyment both to him and me."

When home with Mr. King, in 1860, in the interest of the Buxton Mission, in addition to addressing the Free Church Assembly and other public bodies in Scotland and England, he appeared before the General Assembly of the Presbyterian Church of Ireland, and met with a very warm reception. Following so closely the "year of grace," he had the opportunity of marking the influence of the mighty revival-wave that had swept over the land.

When in London, he had an interview with Lord Brougham. He conferred also with the Portuguese Ambassador, on the slave trade. The pecuniary result of this visit was over four thousand dollars for the mission.

With many other home-mission enterprises Dr. Burns had to do—occasionally too, with the stated supply of congregations during important eras in their history. He supplied, during a large part of two years, Georgetown and Limehouse, some 30 miles distant from Toronto. Such services were always freely rendered, to his power, yea, and beyond his power.

His connexion, for a similar period, with one of the Toronto churches, may be briefly dwelt on, as illustrating this side of his character.

For several years Dr. John Taylor, (formerly of Auchtermuchty), had ably and faithfully served the United Presbyterian Church in Canada, as her Professor of Theology. Conjoined with the professorship was the pastorate of the Gould Street Church in Toronto. A few months previous to the auspicious union of the churches, Dr. Taylor felt it to be his duty to return to his native land.

The congregation (which had erected an elegant structure on an eligible site), was in comparative infancy and burdened with a heavy debt. Its very existence was imperilled.

Dr. Burns was asked to aid in the emergency. He at once consented, and by two years of unsalaried and unceasing service, he tided the struggling cause through its difficulties. The remuneration which he would else have earned he insisted on going to the reduction of the debt. Under his energetic leadership, the wavering band of faithful ones was rallied, their flagging spirits were roused; re-inforcements came, the debt was diminished; and the way prepared for the settlement of the faithful and devoted

pastor, under whose earnest ministry the congregation
has grown to be one of the best in the body. In many
ways the Gould-street people showed their appreciation
of his disinterested labours ; and when they insisted on
his acceptance of a very handsome sum of money, he
took it, to gratify them, but only to invest most of it in
the form of a bursary for Knox College.

He often visited the Lower Provinces.

In Nova Scotia he had to do with the founding of the
College, and of Chalmers' Church, Halifax.

The long and honourable connexion of his younger
brother George with New Brunswick, drew him specially
towards *it*. Thence he received his first strong impulse
to Colonial life and labour.

To Prince Edward Island, that "garden enclosed,"
which will be ever linked with the name of the father of
our beloved Queen, he was specially attached.

Mrs. Mackay, of Rockfield, a noble woman, was the
foundress of Presbyterianism in Cape Breton. She consulted with Dr. Burns all the time, and was guided by
his advice.

The seven large volumes of Colonial correspondence
which he gathered have far more of her letters than of
those of any other single correspondent. The glimpses
which they give of the inner life of the Island thirty or
forty years ago, enhance our estimate of the importance of
that great religious awakening, of which it has recently
been the scene.

This interesting region, whose spiritual welfare he had
so long consulted, he had peculiar pleasure in visiting.

He visited Newfoundland in 1858. The intercourse
he had with the Rev. M. Harvey, who is securing
for himself a prominent place among Colonial literati,
and with Lady Bannerman, the excellent wife of Sir
Alexander Bannerman, then Governor of the Island, was
specially refreshing.

Lady Bannerman, writing Mrs. Burns in 1860, records
her impressions :—

"St. John's, Newfoundland, 1860.

" It is a pleasure to find that you and Dr. B. have so affectionate
a recollection of the short visit you paid to Newfoundland. All
who had the happiness of meeting or of listening to the earnest
and talented instructions of the Doctor, have reason to remember
the refreshment of such an arrival amongst us, and will gladly hail
your return."

In another letter Lady B. writes :

" I was much instructed by the last sermon Dr. B preached here,
(All things are yours, &c.,) few days pass without my remembering
some part of it. Had I been as well acquainted with the force and
fulness with which he is enabled to teach Gospel truth, as I ought
to have been, this would not have been the only sermon I would
have listened to from him ; but now I can only mourn over the lost
opportunity, and hope I may some day have the privilege, I unwit-
tingly failed to secure, brought again within my reach.

" I shall not forget, if we are spared, the kind hint Dr. Burns
gave me to show our catholicity of spirit, by occasionally attending
other branches of the Protestant Church. I have thought that
when our appointed minister had prepared a portion for each one
of his flock, it would be unkind and discouraging to seek for spiritual food from another; but there are times when he may be absent,
when I may follow the friendly advice."

Amongst other regions outside his own province, which
he visited, we must not lose sight of Chicago and the
great West.

Between March, 1867 and April, 1870, I was first pastor of the First Scotch Presbyterian Church in Chicago.

connected with the Canada Presbyterian Church. My father's visit lasted a month, in August, 1867. He enjoyed amazingly the stir and enterprise of Chicago. He was bent on seeing every object of interest—nothing seemed to escape him. None would have joined more sincerely in the general lamentations over the colossal catastrophe which has overtaken this marvel of the West. Many Scotchmen, and Americans too, richly enjoyed the services he conducted at the Metropolitan Hall, the Memorial Methodist Church, and in other places.

Always enthusiastic in his admiration of the Gael—he determined to visit the little colony of faithful Highlanders, 140 miles from Chicago—where we have enjoyed many precious seasons of fellowship. He took charge of the communion there, and it recalled many kindred scenes in Canada, in which he had taken part.

At this time we visited Monmouth College, and enjoyed the hospitality of its worthy president, Dr. Wallace.

When he returned from this tour, he visited my former flock at St. Catharines, and for over an hour he talked to them about it, recounting with amazing accuracy of statement and minuteness of detail every incident. As one of my old friends said : "he shut his eyes and gave us a perfect photograph."

In bringing the church of his attachment to its present advanced position, Dr. Burns bore his full share.

"It was his happiness to break ground in many a district which has since borne abundant fruit, and in others to revive what was weak and ready to die—his exuberant energy and resolute will serving, in not a few cases, to rally the friends of Presbyterian order in districts where he found them weak and disheartened. The country was ripe for such a labourer when he came to it, and he saw and seized the opportunity, preaching far and near, undeterred by distances and severities of weather, which many persons of much younger years would have hesitated to encounter. In this way he contributed, we are safe in saying, more than any other individual, to give to the Presbyterian Church in this Province, the wide influence for good which it holds to-day." *

* Sermon preached in Gould Street Church, Toronto, on the 23rd of August, 1869, by Rev. John M. King, M. A.

CHAPTER XVII.

MISSIONARY SKETCHES.

R. BURNS kept copious "jottings by the way," in his day-books.

The following brief notice of a Canadian "Paisley" is a specimen: this "city of the woods" has made rapid progress since:

"1864.—August 6th, 7th, 8th. Paisley. Preached four times; two stations, eight miles distant; 180 communicants; ten years since settlement, not less than 500 in the village, sixteen miles from Southampton; thirty-four from Owen Sound; sixteen from Walkerton. Communion twice a year in the village; five prayer-meetings connected with the congregation; five Sabbath schools, and a Bible-class; pupils, 150 in all; one common school, 100; a first-class teacher; $2,000 for a building; one Episcopal; one Kirk; one Free; two Methodist; a Temperance Lodge, improved as to Temperance; progressive advancement, fourfold in four years; Muir, an old Paisley weaver of 71, was at my ordination in 1811."

T

After his missionary excursions, my father was in the habit generally of writing out fuller notices. From a mass of material of this description we make several selections:

"TORONTO, 29th Aug., 1845.

"On my way to London I preached or addressed meetings at three places—Dundas, St. George (Dumfries), and Galt. Owing to the wetness of the night the attendance at the first of these was smaller than it would have been; but judging from what I saw, I would say that the congregation of our friend Mr. Stark seem to be decided in their principles, and united as one man. At St. George I occupied the pulpit of Mr. Roy, a worthy minister of the United Secession Church, who preaches here and at Brantford every Sabbath. At Galt the meeting was a very crowded one, and it was manifest that the interest felt in the debate a few weeks before, between Dr. Liddell and Mr Bayne, had whetted the appetite of the people to hear a little more about the principles of the Free Church. The town of Galt is the chief place in the township of Dumfries; beautifully situated in a valley on the Grand River, and possessing great capabilities of increase. The township is fourteen miles square, and the land nearly all arable; a large proportion of it being cleared, and of the finest quality. The position occupied by a minister so talented as Mr. Bayne is a very important one, and his congregation is one of the largest and most influential in Canada.

"On my way to the west, I had also an opportunity of paying a visit to the Rev. Thomas Christie, at Flamborough, a venerable minister of the United Secession Synod of Canada, whose strength has, for fourteen years past, been spent in the work of evangelistic effort, and who has been the instrument of planting a number of congregations. On his arrival in the district, without a friend to direct him, Providence led him into conversation with a plain man who was breaking stones by the way-side, and whose judgment and piety were of considerable avail to him. Of the knoll or rising ground which then caught his eye, Mr. C—— said, "there is the proper spot for a house of worship." On that spot his church was soon thereafter reared, and his then unknown acquaintance has been for years an elder in the congregation. With the brother of this worthy minister, formerly of Edinburgh, now a very extensive proprietor of some of the finest land in the township of Dumfries, we spent a few days. It was the throng of harvest. Many reapers we found at work, all men of suitable strength and skill in the exercise; among the rest an Indian chief and several of his tribe, with intelligence and activity in all respects equal to the rest: and here I saw what I had it not in my power to witness for many years—the master, the family, the domestics, and the reapers all congregated in one large company at evening worship, while the early hour of five in the morning witnessed the same assembly similarly engaged, prior to the commencement of the work of the day. With Mr. Christie and his labourers, prompt payment, healthful and abundant provision, and entire abstinence from spirituous liquors, are the standing rules, and the blessed effects are palpable to every eye.

"Whenever I have been called to address a congregation on these visits, I have made it a rule first to preach the Gospel of the grace of God to sinful and dying men ; and thereafter, if it is deemed proper in the circumstances, to address the hearers on their duties as a congregation connected with the Presbyterian Church.

"Among the respectable Scottish proprietors whom I had the pleasure of meeting in the vicinity of Hamilton, I must be allowed to particularise the Honourable Adam Fergusson, of Woodhill, who settled with his family in Canada West twelve years ago, and whose patriotic efforts for the improvement of the colony are exactly what might have been expected from the enlightened public spirit he ever manifested in his native land. His communications to the Highland Society of Scotland (afterwards embodied in a volume for the public) are very valuable. He has presented me with a copy of the second edition of this work, inscribed to the library of our Free Church College here, and in his letter to me he modestly speaks of the work as ' belonging to a day that has past, and if looked into now' says he. ' it can only claim notice as affording a pleasing and a cheering record of the advances we have made in the last ten or twelve years.' Well may he add, from his own experienced observation : ' I see no reason to shrink from the sentiment of ' *Spero meliora.*'

" My visit to London soon convinced me that the pious habits of the Christians of Ross and Sutherland had accompanied the emigrants from these counties, who are settled in large numbers in and around that place. A day had been set apart during the previous week for solemn humiliation, and its public and private services had been waited on by large and attentive audiences. On Friday there had been held an experience meeting for 'speaking to the question' as it is called, and several aged and pious Highlanders had entered into subjects of spiritual and practical theology with the depth and unction of a Baxter or a Bates. Saturday was ushered in with early prayer-meetings ; at eleven we had public service in English and in Gaelic, the evening also being devoted to prayer-meetings. On Sabbath the spacious Scots Church was packed with English hearers, while one of the Methodist Chapels accommodated the Gaelic part of the congregation till three o'clock, when they got possession of the church, and the communion service in Gaelic went on. The singularly affecting strains of the music of the Gael, their slow and cautious approach to the table, and the whole solemnity of the scene brought forcibly to my mind what I had often heard of but never saw, the sacramental scenes of Ferintosh and Kirkhill. The evening service was in English ; but on Monday we had both English and Gaelic. Our excellent friend, Mr. McKenzie, of Zorra, took the entire charge of the Gaelic department, and a large number of his people came in to join in the service. His services in this district, along with those of Mr. McMillan, of Williams, and Mr. Allan, of Stratford, have been eminently blest. Nor must I omit to notice the debt of gratitude we owe to Mr. John Fraser, of the Bank*, who by his own almost unaided efforts has kept together the congregation in London— conducting public worship both in English and Gaelic, with faithful and judicious exposition of Scripture, and, in every way that sound judgment can dictate, building up the Church. O, that our brethren of the Free Church at home had just seen for once what I have seen of these interesting assemblages of an industrious, well-conditioned and pious peasantry from the hills and dales of Caledonia ! They would need no pleading further to send us over a few of their Macdonalds, and Frasers, and Stewarts to occupy such a noble field. Nor let it be supposed that the English part of the population here is less interesting than the Gaelic. There is great need of the ministrations of the gospel to all classes. Indeed for the town of London an able and acceptable English minister is perhaps of more importance at present than a Gaelic one ; but St. Thomas, Eckfrid, Mosa, and other settlements in the district are almost wholly Gaelic, and these warm-hearted Highlanders are really hungering and thirsting after the bread and water of life. Would the Free Church only send us just now were it only one Gaelic minister, of power and popular gifts, we might, with the aid of Mr. Fraser, and the occasional visits of the Gaelic ministers from other townships, ' get along' pretty well, as the men of the United States say. But if these townships are left much longer without help in either language, one of the finest openings of a missionary character in the world is closed perhaps for ever.

" Prior arrangements required my leaving London on my return on Monday evening. My regret is that I had not another Sabbath for the visit. London may be considered as the centre of a noble country, equal in extent to the whole lowlands of Scotland, and in agricultural resources, far superior. I felt a great desire to go along through the whole of the districts of Lake Erie round to Goderich, knowing as I did, that there are masses of our countrymen there who would have given me a hearty welcome. The round Presbyterianism of our Free Church is the very thing that these districts require, along with good schools, to form a great country. Deeply also do I lament that our Deputies from Scot-

---

* Father of the Rev. Dr. Fraser, of London. He died within a few years after, universally regretted.—ED.

land have kept so far to the east. The finest parts of Canada have not been reached by them as yet. May the great Head of the Church speedily send forth standard bearers, to display the banner of his cross and crown in those goodly lands!"

"TORONTO, Sept. 17, 1845.

"The second Sabbath of August I spent in Kingston, preached three times on the Lord's day, besides giving a discourse on Saturday evening, specially addressed to the members of the congregation. At that period there was every reason to hope that Mr. King would have been among his affectionate friends in that place, and that matters would, under his faithful ministry, go on prosperously. The disappointment in this respect must be injurious to the religious state of that congregation, and every effort must be made both by the Presbytery and Synod and Home Mission Committee, to carry on the supplies vigorously in that important station, in hope that the Free Church may yet be induced to send forth one of her sons duly qualified for occupying a place so influential. I left Kingston on Monday morning by the Rideau Canal. The scenery was new to me. At first the mud and the marsh were not particularly attractive, but that part of the scene was soon succeeded by something more picturesque and inviting. All at once we seemed to be transported to the far west regions of the States, where deep waters and leafless trees of varied size and height growing up out of the wide waste of waters, seemed so many masts of ships under the sea; and the only sound heard being that of our steamer, as she made her turnings and windings in a narrow but deep stream through the dense forest, reminded us of the first invasion of an unknown land. But the broad expanse of the Rideau Lake, with its clusters of islands, was peculiarly gratifying to the eye; and the massive works at ' Jones' Falls' gave us a very high idea of the skill and enterprise which had been embarked in this mighty national undertaking—the Rideau Canal. Our excellent Free Church chairman at Montreal, Mr. Redpath, who superintended the execution of these vast works, was present to my mind; and I felt grateful to that gracious Disposer who had given to such a man the great elements of doing good—ample means and an enlarged heart.

Bytown is a most important station for our Church to occupy, The Free congregation here is not at present very large, but it is composed of the very best materials. They have got their neat place of worship well advanced, and with every prospect of a vigorous eldership, the interests of the congregation will be successfully consulted, while our excellent young friend, their pastor, will have his hands strengthened by an attached people. The meetings which were held in connexion with this settlement were very pleasing, and the affectionate greeting he received from Christian fellow-labourers of different denominations was a feature in the case not to be overlooked.   May the Chief Shepherd bless his own cause in this rising locality.   The magnificence of nature, combined with great beauty, mark the splendid falls in its vicinity, and filled me with admiration.   May the wonders of grace be seen here also with an impressiveness still more captivating !

"At Beckwith and Ramsay I had the pleasure of addressing large congregations, united and prosperous.   At the former, a call, signed by 240 members and adherents, had been drawn out in favour of the Rev. Mr. McMillan, of Cardross.   This call was committed to my charge, and is now, I trust, in the hands of my excellent friend, Dr. James Buchanan, of the Free Church College, Edinburgh, to be by him, and the Committee of which he is chairman, put into the hands of Mr. McM.   At the latter of these places, a call was in the course of signature in favour of the Rev. W. G. Johnston, late of Pittsburg.   Thus both congregations are in a matured and settled state—perfectly able to support the Gospel creditably, and presenting most promising situations for laborious and effective ministers.   The rising village of Carleton Place, too, was not overlooked.   An hour's notice brought out a respectable, though not a large, audience ; among whom I was privileged to meet with a few very pious Presbyterian.

"The township of Ramsay is almost wholly Presbyterian.   Of six hundred families in it, I am informed that five-sixths are either Scotch or Irish, and decidedly Presbyterian and Free.   A large proportion of Beckwith is Gaelic ; many of the settlers are from the Marquis of Breadalbane's country ; and all of them more or less flourishing.   The kindness I met with in both of these townships disposes me, irrespective of all higher considerations, to repeat my visit.

"Lanark had not been put into my list at all.   This, however, was no reason why I should not pay my respects to my old friends, whom I had known of old in that place ; and, short as was the notice, we had a tolerable audience.   An adjoining settlement, called Middleton, I visited also, and preached to about two hundred in the open air.   Here I met with such warm-hearted men as Messrs. P—— and R——, and others, whose intelligence and piety cheered me.

"Perth demands all that we can do for it.   The congregation here have built a Free Church, most advantageously situated.   Here I spent the Sabbath—preached three times to crowded audiences, and on Monday held a church meeting, at which the Member of Parliament for the County of Lanark, Mr. Cameron, a member of the Free Church at Port Sarnia, presided ; and where the very best spirit prevailed.   There are here a number of sensible and active elders and others, who take a lead in the congregation, and the cause would prosper exceedingly could a young evangelist, of talent and piety, be obtained as pastor.   A central situation like this will diffuse a healthful influence all around.

"The Dalhousie District was to me personally very interesting. There I met with not a few whom I had seen and known twenty-five years before in Renfrewshire, and whose circumstances now contrasted most favourably with their situation then. It is wonderful what may be effected by industry, sobriety, and contentment, even when physical disadvantages are very great. The land here is far from being the best, and the distance from markets great, while the roads are bad. And yet, it was refreshing to find, that our industrious and well-behaved people of the west of Scotland had come on amazingly well. A fine spirit prevails among them. Sobriety is prevalent, and they are what may be called a religiously disposed class. The library of St. Andrew's Hall, I had the opportunity of examining, and I have no doubt that the reading habits which that Institution has cherished, have proved salutary in promoting intelligence and sound morals. The number of volumes is nearly 1,000, but they are mostly old and worn out, a good sign of the proper use which has been made of them. I preached in that hall, and at another station in Dalhousie proper. The Free Church decidedly predominates, and a staff of *nine* Elders is a very good commencement. There are *three* stations which will form together one charge. The site for a Manse on the beautiful lake of Mississippi, was pointed out to me, and the people are both able and willing to support a minister. A more promising station for an active pious labourer, cannot be. I undertook to have the Sacrament of the Lord's Supper dispensed among them in the course of the season.

"Of Brockville, Prescott, and Gananoque, I need not particularly speak. I visited and preached at each, and held conferences with the sessions at each, the results of which are on record. To the kind friends in these places I owe many thanks ; may they and theirs prosper in the best sense ! I regretted I could not visit South Gower, one of the largest of our congregations ; neither could I visit Edwardsburgh and the adjoining settlements ; but it gave me pleasure to learn that there was a good prospect of the ordination of pastors over these congregations soon. Mr. Boyd, of Prescott, has long laboured among them in the way of occasional visits, and he will feel gratified in seeing them comfortably settled under pastors of their own.

"In the Bathurst District, I found a peculiar attention had been paid to the cultivation of sacred music. The singing delighted me, and my associations led me back to the earnest and ' grave sweet melody' of the Kilsyth audience, inspired by the revival of religion in that place. The practice of sacred music I found to be one of the relaxations in which the people took much delight. Long may such be the relaxation which pleases ! St. Andrew's Hall was expressly built for what is technically called a *spree* on St. Andrew's day. That is now past. The Temperance Society has gained its laurels here, as everywhere in Canada, and the voice of psalms is the music that now fills the place."

"TORONTO, 22nd Nov., 1849.

" Immediately after the celebration of the holy ordinance of our Lord's Supper in Knox's Church, in the beginning of September, I resolved, in humble dependence on God, to carry out my intention of a missionary tour to Canada East, Nova Scotia, and New Brunswick. In much mercy I have been enabled to do so, and eight Sabbaths, embracing nine weeks, were devoted to the work. Every colonial minister must be, to a greater or less extent, a missionary; and the time devoted to the mission field is by no means lost, even to the congregation more immediately his own. A missionary spirit is favourable to active effort in every way; and an affectionate flock will lose nothing by extra evangelistic labours on the part of their pastor.

" The Free Church congregation of Côté Street, Montreal, has always had a peculiar claim on our church. Its members were the first who raised the standard of the protesting Church of Scotland in the colonies, and they have continued to grasp it with an unflinching hand. They erected, at great expense, years ago, an excellent and commodious place of worship, with lecture-room, Bible class-rooms, and accommodation for week-day schools. The Free Church at home has supplied them, from time to time, with faithful ministers, in the character of deputies, who have remained for periods of from three to six months each. With all the inconveniences inseparable from frequent change of ministers, the congregation has never lost a member by desertion; and it is at present in as flourishing a state as at any time since its first opening in May, 1845. Its staff of elders and deacons comprises a band of faithful men, characterized by sound judgment, elevated piety, and active habits. The number of members exceeds 200. An addition of twelve was made at the communion on the 24th September last; and I have not the least doubt that were a talented and laborious pastor settled permanently amongst them, the increase would be rapid. It is not, however, to *mere numbers* that the office-bearers look. They prize a godly discipline; and, in carrying out this principle, they have set an example which all churches would do well to imitate. I found not the smallest difficulty with them on this head. Our views accorded well; and I was not conscious of any difference in the practical carrying out of these views in the congregation of Knox's Church, Toronto, or of Côté Street, Montreal.

" The deputy who had laboured last among them was the Rev. James Lewis, of Leith, one of the most talented and eloquent ministers of the Free Church. The effects of his preaching and of his visits were very visible in the state of the congregation. My prayer has long been that God would put it into the heart of some such godly minister to come over and help us, not in the way of occasional and limited residence, but as a fixed pastor, ' to take part with us in this ministry.' It is to my mind one of the most perplexing mysteries in human character, and in the movements of churches, that the finest of all fields for evangelistic and mission effort on the face of the earth, should have so long escaped the notice of men and of churches who stand first unquestionably in apostolic zeal.   In the city of Montreal, Satan has pre-eminently his seat.   The whole province is unquestionably one of the finest of the *preserves* of the man of sin.   Everything in the political department is working into his hands, and the churches of the Reformation seem respectfully quiescent.

"Four out of eight Sabbaths were devoted to Montreal—one of these the communion Sabbath.   On these seasons I look back with singular pleasure—they were refreshing and gladdening.   In the meetings of the Sabbath school and of the Bible-classes, I saw the germ of growing prosperity to the congregation.   In the services at the wharf too, and on board the *Erromanga* and *Montreal ;* in the visit to ' Pointe aux Trembles ;' in the weekly prayer-meetings and lecture, and in other occasional exercises, a deputy to this place sees at once the freshening field of his labours, and the extent of influence which they command.

"In the operations of the ' French Canadian Missionary Society' the members of Côté Street take a deep interest.   The society is catholic, and liberal in its basis ; and since its commencement in 1839 its operations have been characterized by energetic harmony. A day devoted to the institution for boarding and educating young *habitants* of both sexes, was, to my friends and me, very delightful. The place is about eight miles below the city—beautifully situated on the banks of the river—a large brick erection, capable of accommo- dating upwards of one hundred pupils ; and a hundred acres of the finest land attached.   With Mr. and Mrs. Tanner, with the teachers of the different departments, and our excellent friend, Mr. John Black, who occupies a most important department in the society, we had much agreeable intercourse.   The examinations were con- ducted both in English and French ; and we left the Institute with a deep impression of its value, and of the paramount duty of Pro- testant ministers and members looking specially after it.   The superintendent of the farm, Mr. Symington, from Johnston, near Paisley, soon hailed me as an old acquaintance.   He has already introduced Scotch improvements in the system of agriculture.   A well-written appeal which he drew up, soon brought from Mr. Playfair, of Glasgow, and other friends, an ample supply of imple- ments of the best kind.   The stouter boys, with one or two of their teachers, were busy making a drain round the premises, and we felt as if translated to the Lane Manual-labour College at Cincin- nati.

"While at Montreal, it was proposed that a missionary visit should be paid to Vankleek Hill, and Lochiel, in Glengarry.   Four days of the first part of a week were devoted to this ; and our valued friend, Mr. James R. Orr, lately returned from Jamaica with renovated health, accompanied me.   We sailed up the Ottawa in the regular steamer, sixty or seventy miles—and a magnificent scene it is—as far as St. Andrew's, where we landed, and travelled by car to Lachute (or *Jerusalem*, as the new Popish nomenclature calls it), where our worthy brother, the Rev. Thomas Henry, is settled. It is quite a rural district, Scottish in its aspect, and most of its inhabitants Scottish. On the evening of the day on which we left the city, we had sermon and address in Mr. Henry's church, and to a respectable congregation of his people. On all such occasions, it is the best plan to declare to the people, first, the simple truths of the glorious gospel, and, having done so, to exhort them in a separate address on their special duties as church members, with appeals to our distinctive principles. This last is not in every case necessary, but in no case should the direct preaching of the gospel to perishing sinners be neglected. Visits of this nature tend to strengthen the hands of the minister, while they cheer and encourage his people.

"At St. Andrew's, we observed, rising near the Roman Catholic Chapel, a large building, which we learned was intended as a Popish College or seminary—one of many such erections all over Lower Canada. They are all more or less under the influence of the Jesuits, and exert a power, of no slight kind, in strengthening the hold which the Papacy has over the minds of the people.

Next day we crossed the Ottawa, and after a journey of some thirty or forty miles in all, reached Vankleek Hill, a place which brings many pleasing associations with it. It is a village in the west of the township of West Hawkesbury, eight miles south from the Ottawa river, containing about three hundred inhabitants, many of them originally of German or Dutch extraction. In the village there is a steam grist-mill, several factories, and not a few symptoms of progressive advancement. The Presbyterians here and in the neighbourhood generally adhere to us, and we had a good attendance at church in the afternoon, of persons not only from the village, but from the country round. We went in the evening to see the manse which had been built for Dr. Macgillivray, when he resided here as deputy from the Free Church, and the people cherished the hope of his becoming their pastor. Although that able minister did not see it to be his duty to remain with the congregation here or at Lochiel permanently, his residence and his labours among them were eminently useful, and of both a most grateful remembrance will long be cherished. It is proper also to state that in Canada and the United States Dr. Macgillivray, by his energetic appeals, collected £200, of which £80 have been appropriated to the erection of the church at Lochiel, £20 granted to Lancaster and Dalhousie Mills congregations, the rest devoted to Vankleek Hill, and applied in part to the purchase of a glebe and the finishing of the manse; the residue being reserved for building a new church, which may become necessary. It is but justice to notice these valuable efforts of my worthy friend, at whose manse (to be) we called, surveying its comfortable but tenantless apartments ; admiring the deep grove within which it is embedded ; marking out the precise spot for the ' manse garden ;' and thinking of Dr. Paterson, and the fascinating pages of his enchanting book.

" Lochiel is eight miles south-west of Vankleek Hill, and at twelve o'clock next day we found ourselves there, surrounded by seven hundred brawny Highlanders, assembled within the rising stone walls of their large and handsome erection, and listening for three hours to the message of salvation, in the delivery of which I was most thankfully aided by the valuable assistance in Celtic of our faithful catechist and missionary, Mr. Alexander Cameron, and the Rev. Daniel Clark, of Indian Lands, a godly man, of primitive simplicity, who, with piety and prudence, combined with some good measure of Highland tact, has for years held up single-handed the banner of truth, and borne the brunt of many a residuary onset.   He had come to meet us upwards of twenty miles.

" It was a very small part of Glengarry I had it in my power to visit.   There are in all four large and populous townships, besides the Indian reserve on which Mr. Clark is located.   The district teems with Highlanders, the descendants of those worthy men who, seventy years ago, fought the battles of loyalty on the American soil.   It was here that my young relation, Mr. W. C. Burns, now in China, had many of his most delightful tokens of success.   A considerable number of Gaelic ministers, from the Free Church of Scotland, also visited this district, and their labours, with those of Dr. Macgillivray, have left the best effects.   This last summer, Mr. Alexander Cameron, student in theology, has laboured successfully as a Gaelic missionary in Vankleek Hill and Lochiel, and on his return to college a few weeks ago, Mr. John Ross, lately licensed by the Presbytery of Toronto, has agreed to give his valuable services during the winter.   My visit to these places brought me into acquaintance with many of our friends of whom I had often heard, such as Mr. Cattanach, Mr. Neil Stewart, Mr. Buchanan, and others, for whom I pray that the blessing of the Most High may rest in rich abundance on them and on their families.

" On our return next day we again crossed the Ottawa, at St. Andrew's, and after a very weary journey of many miles, reached St. Eustache, a place well known in the annals of the late rebellion in Lower Canada.   The marks of the balls on the doors and window-shutters of some of the houses, were pointed out to us as melancholy memorials of fearful events.   The Popish ch irch, which had been burnt to the ground with many miserable beings who had taken refuge within its walls, has been rebuilt, and its double towers or spires, with their tin roofs, catch the eye at a considerable distance.   Here, and at Ste. Therese, we were in the midst of the settlements of the old *habitans*, and we could not but mark the contrast betwixt the husbandry to which we had been accustomed, and that of these poor people, whose situation seems to be very

little changed from that of their ancestors two centuries ago. The
state of the roads and the agriculture, indicated that we were not
in the midst of British settlers. The influence of Popery, even on
the external circumstances of men, was seen in palpable contrast
with that of Protestantism. I felt somewhat as I did when travelling in Virginia, where the withering effects of the system of
slavery are seen in the very blasting of the fields, as well as in the
degradation of man, ' the growth that dwindles there.' Near Ste.
Therese we saw a large stone-building of four stories in height,
which we were told was a college and boarding-house, under the
control of the Jesuits. Here, education, after the fashion of
Popery, is given to upwards of eighty young men, with board, at
a remarkably cheap rate. The driver of our car told us that his
three sons, lads somewhat advanced, were kept and educated there,
in a style which he considered the best, at fifteen dollars per
month, for the whole. The education given, I have reason to believe, is superficial, at least, in so far as the communication of real
knowledge is concerned ; but I doubt not that attention is paid to
the comfort of the inmates. It is the interest of the concern not
to be wanting in this respect ; and the college has good endowments from those lands which, to a prodigious extent in this Province, belong to the Romish church. The temptations offered to
lax Protestants are thus very numerous, and we fear that from this
cause, and from the frequent intermarriages betwixt Protestants
and Roman Catholics, the career of pernicious error is much advanced.

" In both St. Eustache and Ste. Therese, there are congregations
and churches belonging to our Church. In Ste. Therese, the Rev.
David Black, son of the eminently pious Mr. Black, formerly of
Lady Yester's, Edinburgh, has been settled for a number of
years ; and in St. Eustache, we have, since the disruption, had
from time to time, a missionary and catechist settled. Mr.
Swinton, formerly, and Mr. William Maclaren, this last summer, both students of Knox's College, have been very acceptable. Our friends rent the church for a nominal sum,
and it may, perhaps, be looked on now as substantially their
own : at least, they are not likely to be disturbed in the
possession of it. How important such a station as this ! The
Scottish settlers may not indeed be very numerous in the district,
but they are very influential, and rapidly on the increase. If our
Church had it in its power to plant here and there, in these Lower
Provinces, faithful men, and were these faithful men also qualified
to go among the French settlers, and talk to them in their own
tongue, and distribute suitable tracts among them, much good
would unquestionably be done. Several of the agents of the
French Canadian Society are settled at stations in this neighbourhood. One of them has lately been asked to officiate in the parish
church, in place of the curé whom the bishop had sent, but who

was unacceptable to the people. An aged priest has also been lately brought to the knowledge of the truth, and is labouring amid much discouragement. Thus we see, that were faithful and consistent men here and there among the *habitants*, they would have a wide sphere of usefulness, not only among their own countrymen, but among the natives also, whose prejudices would dissolve away amid the genial influences of kind treatment and disinterested pastoral faithfulness.

" On our return to Montreal we crossed the ' Isle Jesu,' and saw its four parish churches. When within eight miles of the city, we passed a village in which we noticed a specimen of the completeness to which the ecclesiastical establishment of the Popish Church in these lands is carried. In one clump, we saw an elegant parish church, a parsonage or rectory, male and female seminaries, with a nunnery and *maison de Dieu*. No place in the Lower Province is more than four miles from a parish church. So carefully has Popery watched over its interests ! Indeed, the wealth of the Papacy in this Province is immense. The annual rates levied from property in the Island of Montreal, alone, exceed £30,000 ! Great efforts have been made during last session of Parliament, to grant incorporating charters to the Jesuits, who hold property in land ; and it is thought that soon one-half of the real property of the country will be theirs. This is a fearful prospect as regards the civil and religious liberties of Canada.

" TORONTO, Jan. 1850.

" My journey from Montreal to Boston was rendered doubly pleasing by my having as my travelling companion Mr. James Court, of Montreal, Treasurer to the French Canadian Mission, who was on his way to the States, to plead with the friends of evangelical truth in behalf of that important institution. We left Montreal at twelve (noon) on Monday, September 24, and reached Boston next day at eight o'clock p.m., having rested on Wednesday in Burlington. The sail along Lake Champlain has many attractions, and not a few interesting associations to recommend it ; and the journey from Burlington to Montpelier (by coach) opened up to us many beautiful scenes of hill and dale, reminding us forcibly of Perthshire and some part of the Inverness Highlands. Vermont, New Hampshire, and Massachusetts, were the three States through which we passed by railway ; and the agricultural and pastoral character of the first two of these, with the rapidly rising manufacturing prospects of the third, were in different ways abundantly interesting. The Merrimack is a noble stream. For public works, Manchester already rivals Lowell, and the town of Lawrence—so named after the ' Lord of the Manor,' the Hon. Abbot Lawrence, Ambassador from the States to Great Britain—already numbers seven thousand souls ; while all the three present clear evidence of the prodigiously rapid rate with which towns and cities grow in these States, and form indications of the future ascendancy of the American Union as a manufacturing country. In Boston we stayed at the Marlborough Hotel, where we had the pleasure of witnessing, what I regret to say is too rare in such cases, the assembling of the household, morning and evening, for family worship. This is the law of the house, as it is at the Delavan Hotel, in Albany; and these two establishments are, especially on this account, entitled to the friendly countenance of religious men, while in accommodations of a more ordinary kind they are fully equal to the most respectable establishments in both cities.

"I was accompanied on board the British steamer *Canada*, next day, by my friend Mr. Court, who soon after left for Montreal. The interest of the scene usual on these occasions was increased by the circumstance of the embarkation of Mr. Lawrence, the American Ambassador to Great Britain. He is a descendant of the pilgrim fathers—a man of high honour and respectability—who has raised himself by his own talent and perseverance to the possession of five million of dollars, and has lately given *seventy thousand* of these to the endowment of a chair of engineering and mechanics in Harvard University. I was introduced to him by an old Paisley parishioner, Mr. Lawson, now at the head of a large carpet-manufactory in Lowell. We had much agreeable conversation during the sail from Boston to Halifax, and in the accuracy of the information furnished by the American Ambassador, on all subjects, I had every reason to place the most implicit confidence.

"On my arrival at Halifax, on the evening of the day after leaving Boston, the hearty welcomes of many well-known friends were blended with the pleasing associations of former visits, and I soon found myself at home with my excellent friends, Mr. and Mrs. Forrester, whose house was my comfortable abode during my stay in the city. The next day, Friday, was employed in visiting some of the active friends of the church in and near the city, and in making arrangements for the opening of Chalmers' Church on the 14th current. A commodious building presented itself to my view in the very centre of the city, among whose prominent ornaments the handsome spire most legitimately counts. The interior presents a compact and well-arranged provision made for the comfortable accommodation of seven hundred sitters; and the proofs of judgment, liberality, and good taste in the *tout ensemble*, reflected much credit on the members of the congregation. We held a devotional meeting in one of the rooms of the Academy, in the evening, when various matters were adjusted in the view of the important services we had in prospect.

Arrangements having been duly made for a missionary tour in the eastern settlements and in Prince Edward's Island, Mr. Forrester and I left Halifax on Saturday morning, by coach, for Truro, a beautiful settlement of old standing, about sixty miles eastward.

Here we made arrangements for sermon on my return, and passed on to Londonderry, where we found the Rev. John Munro, ordained missionary of the district, waiting for us, accompanied by Mr. Maclean, a lay friend, whose services on this and other occasions were to us very valuable. Mr. Forrester went on to Pugwash or Waterford, and I remained at Wallace. We had travelled this day nearly one hundred miles, and the mercy of a faithful God preserved us. Next day our services were divided amongst the settlements at Wallace, Gulfshore, and Waterford ; and the attendance at all these places was very encouraging.

"On Monday and Tuesday we held meetings at all these places, and also at New Annan and Earlton, and the town of Pictou, where the principles, proceedings, and prospects of the Free Church of Scotland were, more or less fully, illustrated in connexion with the preaching of the gospel to perishing sinners. The whole land was spread out before us as a wide field of missionary labour, and we felt deeply the want of suitable labourers. Mr. Munro has been engaged very usefully in part of this field, for nearly a year, as a Gaelic missionary. The Rev. Messrs. Stewart, Sutherland, and Campbell occupy large districts in the range of Pictou, and are deservedly esteemed by the people to whom they minister. My old friend, Mr. Stewart, 1 found waiting my arrival at Pictou, and on Wednesday I accompanied him to New Glasgow, where a portion of his congregation assembled. After sermon and address on their appropriate duties, we re-crossed the harbour, and preached in the evening to an excellent congregation in the town of Pictou. The Free church there occupies a commanding position, and will be, when completed, a commodious building. Of it, and of the church at West River, and perhaps one or two more in course of erection, I may remark that some help from the friends of colonial churches would be highly desirable, as the great body of adherents to our cause, in these places, are in humble circumstances, and a succession of unfortunate harvests has crippled sadly their resources. In the district of Pictou, the great body of the people are our warm friends, and they cannot be fewer than from twelve to fifteen thousand souls. Six Gaelic ministers would be required here in addition to those already settled, and there are numerous Highland settlements to the east and west of Pictou entirely destitute. A finer missionary field there cannot be. Ministers of the Presbyterian Synod and others have indeed done much to supply the spiritual destitution, but still the harvest is very plenteous. May the great Lord send forth faithful men, who may be able to teach the people in their own tongue the wonderful things of God.

"It was arranged that Mr. Munro and I should go to Prince Edward Island ; Mr. Forrester, who had accompanied us thus far, returning to Halifax. On Thursday, we went by steamer to Charlottetown, a distance of seventy miles. Unfortunately, the letters giving notice of our intended visit had not reached, and thus no

arrangement for missionary work had been made. In the circumstances, we made the best of it ; Mr. Munro setting off to visit his
countrymen in different settlements, from ten to thirty miles distant
from Charlottetown, while I remained in the capital of the Island,
and in its neighbourhood, till Monday. I had two opportunities of
preaching in Charlottetown on the Lord's Day, by the kindness
of the Methodists and the Baptists ; and at three o'clock in a chapel
about seven miles out of town, which seems to be common to different evangelical bodies, we had a crowded audience. At this place
also I had the pleasure of meeting with my excellent friend, the
Hon. Charles Young, who, five years ago, welcomed Mr. Robb and
me as deputies from the Free Church, and rendered us most valuable services. It has often been to me a matter of deep regret that
the suggestions of that gentleman, at that period, had not been
promptly acted on. The whole island was then ready to welcome
us, and an effective minister located at Charlottetown would have
been the centre of Free Church influence, and of sound evangelical
truth through the colony. As matters have been, and are, our interest in the island, except among the Gaelic people, is not extensive ; and those friends of the Redeemer who, five years ago, or
since, were thirsting for the water of life, have gone away from us
in different directions. As to the Scottish Establishment in the
island, however, it is in religious feeling and character below zero.
One young man, from Ireland, had hovered among the residuaries
here for a whole year, keeping up something like a Sabbath-day's
meeting in St. James's Church, but doing nothing effective in the
way of ministerial duty ; and a Gaelic minister of some talent, who
had been with them for a year and a half after, did not appear to
have altogether repaired the injury that had been done. A missionary from the Free Church (Mr. McIntyre) had laboured faithfully among his Highland countrymen, but Charlottetown had not
been supplied.

Monday and Tuesday having proved very wet, serious obstacles
were interposed in the way of the projected missionary visits to
Belfast and Murray Harbour ; but Mr. Munro's perseverance and
zeal overcame many difficulties, and at my request he agreed to remain
a month in the island, the Presbytery sanctioning this arrangement,
and Mr. Sutherland, of Earlton, agreed to succeed him for the
same length of time. Both of these gentleman had, by former
visits, done most effective service to the cause in the island, as had
Mr. Forrester, Mr. Stewart, and Professors King and Mackenzie,
of Halifax Free College. Indeed the brethren of the presbyteries
of Pictou and Halifax, could not have done more for the island
than they have done, consistently with other calls. The great
error has been in the want of a resident minister of our church
at Charlottetown, as the centre. That place has at least five
thousand inhabitants, and many of these are Presbyterians of
Scotland and of Ireland, who would have combined with us readily.

Of the Gaelic population in the island, amounting to many thousands, we have a very strong hold, and their attachment to our principles is based on something better than mere expediency. Mr. McIntyre, the Free Church Gaelic missionary in the island, has proved himself a faithful and successful labourer; but he had left some time before, for Cape Breton, and from the state of his health, it is feared that he may not be able to resume his labours in Prince Edward. It was to me matter of regret that want of time put it beyond my power to follow him to Cape Breton ; but I rejoice in the favourable aspect of the cause there, and in the good effected by a late visit of our active and energetic brother, Mr. Forrester. Let us hope that the call addressed to Mr. McLeod, of Logie, will be favourably responded to by that esteemed minister. The accession of such a man is just what is needed to cheer the hearts of the worthy pastors who have been labouring long, amid many difficulties, and who are earnestly desirous of the presence and countenance of one so well fitted to be at once their fellow-labourer and their guide. The enlightened efforts of Mrs. Mackay, of Edinburgh, have told most successfully on this interesting field. Reflection on what this Christian lady has been honoured to accomplish for churches and schools in Cape Breton, must be to her own mind matter of lively gratitude, as assuredly it is subject matter of thankfulness to not a few who will prove her joy and crown in the great day.

"While in Prince Edward, I had an opportunity of hearing from Captain Nelmes, of Bermuda, the particulars of the death of Mr. Morrison, and the present position of the Free Church in that island. Mr. Morrison, and Mr. Struthers, of Cornwallis, were the first ministers whom the Glasgow Society designated to the Colonies, in 1826. Mr. Struthers is still spared, after years of useful labour both in Demerara and Nova Scotia. Mr. Morrison laboured first at Dartmouth, and in the Acadian School of Halifax, but latterly he was for a series of years minister of the Scotch Church in Bermuda, and the notices I received of his pastoral faithfulness, were very satisfactory. With the advice and aid of the Free Church Colonial Committee, at Edinburgh, he lately went to Trinidad, partly for the recovering of his health, and partly to assist in the settlement of a Free Church minister in that island. In much feebleness he was enabled to discharge that duty, and he returned to his post in safety, but not with any perceptible benefit of health. He lingered for a short time under complicated sufferings. and died in hope, amid the prayers and regrets of an attached people, who were cheered by his dying testimony, as they had been edified by his pastoral labours. Application has been made to the Free Colonial Committee for a successor to Mr. Morrison, and let us hope that a station so very important will not be left long destitute of a settled minister.

"On my way from Prince Edward Island I had an agreeable

U

meeting with the Presbytery at Pictou, when various matters regarding supplies for different stations were settled. Along with
Mr. Sutherland I went on to Rogers Hill, Earlton, and Truro.
Unfortunately, circumstances prevented me from fulfilling my engagement at the first of these places, where a large congregation
had assembled at the hour which had been fixed. At the church
of Earlton, embedded in the centre of a grove without any dwelling near, we had a large meeting ; and it was very gratifying to me
to meet personally with some venerable Highlanders who had been
amongst my earliest correspondents as Secretary of the Glasgow
Society, and whom in this sense, I had long known. These patriarchs of the bush presented to me fine specimens of the ' men' of
the parishes of Sutherland and Ross. Thirty years ago they had
been ' cleared off' from their patrimonial domains, and had wept
as they beheld for the last time the sepulchres of their fathers.
Many severe difficulties had they to overcome in their first settlement in the wilderness ; but God has befriended them when men
were unkind, and they now present gratifying spectacles of successful colonization. Mr. Sutherland, the son of one of these
hoary veteran Christians, studied at Edinburgh College, and is
now the spiritual pastor of his kinsmen and his countrymen in the
pilgrimage to Zion. Earlton was like many other places left long
unoccupied by a regular minister, but the good men of the old
land were the ' holy seed' here, and by their powerful efforts here
religion was kept not only alive, but in a healthful and thriving
state, while not a few fields that had been occupied by licentiates
of churches were withered.

"At Truro—long highly favoured by a succession of excellent
ministers of the Presbyterian Church, and still enjoying many privileges—we had a successful meeting in the Baptist chapel in the
evening. It was the time of the sitting of the Assizes, and the
respected Judge, with Crown Counsel and other official gentlemen,
closed the labours of their circuit, by attendance on the preaching of the gospel in the unassuming but comfortable meetinghouse.

"It was on Sabbath the 14th, according to appointment, ' Chalmers' Church,' as the new edifice has been designated, was opened
for public worship. At all the three meetings we had large and
respectable audiences. The part of the services allotted to me
embraced the morning and evening meetings ; and Mr. Forrester,
pastor of the church, officiated in the afternoon, delivering a most
appropriate discourse on the character of the good Centurion, who
had shewn his love to the nation of Israel by ' building a Synagogue.' The collections this day exceeded £100. Much praise is
due to the members of this congregation for the liberality they
have shewn in carrying on and completing the building. The Free
Church has now taken up its right position in the centre of the
populous city. St. John's Church, at Dutchtown, will, however,

be still kept up as a place of worship, and may the blessing of the Great Head rest on both.

" It was interesting to find in Halifax a well appointed literary and theological seminary for the training of young men for the ministry. As the classes had not met, I had not an opportunity of meeting with the students as a body, but with five or six I had intercourse, and my impression of their abilities and piety was exceedingly favourable. I have learned since returning home that eighteen have enrolled in the preparatory and theological departments, and the able prelections of Professor King and his coad· jutors will, by the blessing of God, tell favourably upon them. In Halifax as in Toronto, the same impediments will be found to arise from the defective state of elementary education in the province. Canada is decidedly in advance of Nova Scotia, both in normal schools and in common ones ; and I rather think in district grammar seminaries also. The friends of education in that province are perfectly aware of this, and the question of academies and schools will be a vital one in the Legislature. But whatever issues may be arrived at, assuredly the members of the Free Church at Halifax must keep their institution in vigorous operation. Perhaps there, as here, there may be some danger of aiming all at once at too perfect an organization. In the infancy of all churches, one or two really effective instruments have been compelled to do the work which may, in a more matured state of a church, be spread over a number. Assuredly the very existence of Free Presbyterianism both in Canada and the other provinces, hangs upon rightly constituted and successfully conducted seminaries in Toronto and in Halifax.

" On Monday and Tuesday we had public services in Halifax, and at Dartmouth on the opposite side of the bay ; and on Wednesday evening a crowded audience assembled in Chalmers' Church to listen to an exposition of the distinctive principles of the Free Church. On this occasion, Professor King acquitted himself with all his well known talent and tact ; and the effect of the meeting on both friends and foes were unquestionably good.

" After enjoying much agreeable fellowship with kind friends, I bade adieu to them and to Halifax on Thursday for Windsor, on my way to St. John, N. B. Whom should I find in the coach as my fellow-traveller but my respected friend the Rev. Henry Wilkes, of Montreal, on his way from England, having left Liverpool by the steam-packet on Saturday se'nnight. The details of his visits to England, Scotland, Switzerland, and France, were to me exceedingly interesting. We stopped together a night at Windsor, and next day set sail for St. John by the steam vessel that plies on the Bay of Fundy. We reached the city by the morning of Saturday, very early—betwixt two and three a.m.—and found Mr. Thompson, Dr. Miller, and other friends waiting for my arrival.

From Saturday to Tuesday I had the gratification of enjoying in St. John much agreeable intercourse with our friends of the Free Church, and others also like-minded in the essential matters of Christ's kingdom. On Sabbath we had three services: in the old Methodist church, Germain street; in the temporary Free Church, St. Stephen's Hall; and in the Centenary Church of the Wesleyan Methodists. To that body we are under great obligations for their readiness in accommodating us with the use of their places of worship. On Monday evening there was held what was announced as a meeting of the 'Evangelical Alliance,' in St. Stephen's Hall, when brethren of at least four different denominations met in fellowship, and when Mr. Wilkes favoured the meeting with refreshing details of his visits to Britain and the Continent. Malan, Merle D'Aubigné, Gaussen, and other eminent men of the Evangelical school of the Continent were brought visibly before us. Sketches of evangelistic effort were given, and many practical lessons inculcated. Nor did the St. John friends listen with any appearance of indifference to the details which were given them regarding the progress of the Gospel among the churches of Canada.

"To my mind, St. John possesses a peculiar interest. In 1817, my brother, now at Corstorphine, was settled as the first minister of St. Andrew's Scots Church in that city, then with a population of ten thousand—not one-third of its present magnitude. Those whom he baptized are the men and women of the present generation. A few of the more aged settlers, then on the active and busy scene, remain; and their reminiscences of other days were to them and to me very affecting. The Scots Church has had many occupants since the departure of its first pastor, and now it is presided over by a minister lately sent out by the Establishment. The Free Church, after overcoming many obstacles, has now for its pastor the Rev. John Thomson, formerly of Alnwick, Northumberland,* a faithful, talented, and acceptable minister of Christ. The foundation of the new church had been laid about six weeks before my visit, and it has already been roofed. Its position is commanding, and when the elegant fabric is completed, it will accommodate at least a thousand hearers. The Sabbath schools and classes are in a flourishing state. On the whole the prospects of our brethren in St. John are exceedingly encouraging. It is proper to add that in the city there has been for five years past, another Presbyterian congregation in connection with us, under the ministry of an active and energetic clergyman, the Rev. Robert Irvine.† My earnest prayer is, that both congregations may have entire fellowship with each other while they seek the glory of the common Lord.

---

* Now the Rev. Dr. John Thomson, of New York.
† Now Rev. Dr. Irvine, of Augusta, Georgia.

" It was on Tuesday, October 22nd, I left the commercial capital of New Brunswick, and came by steamer to Portland. The sail through the Bay of Fundy and the islands that lie between the British and American possessions, is exceedingly fine. Portland is a large and prosperous city of the State of Maine, and when the railway from Montreal to Portland is completed (probably in two years) this will become the great line of communication with Canada and the United States. I had spent some hours at Portland on my visit two years ago to New Brunswick, and part of that time I passed within the walls and in the pulpit of the church which was for years honoured in the ministry of Dr. Payson. I remembered Dr. Andrew Reed, and the expression of the worthy elder to him, when pointing to the pulpit he said, emphatically, ' That is the place, sir, where Payson prayed !' 'I was struck,' says Dr. R. ' with this remark. It gave me Payson's peculiarity in an instant. I had thought that whatever might have been his power as a preacher, it was greatest in prayer. I was now sure of it.' Our countryman, Dr. Carruthers, is now the successor of Dr. Payson, but as he was from home, I had not an opportunity of seeing him.

" Boston is about one hundred miles from Portland, but the railway car brought me up in the course of four hours. After stopping a night again at the Marlborough, I left the city next day by the Fitchburg line, and reached Burlington (partly by coach), at eleven p.m. As we were too late for the steamer for St. John's, I was detained a day at Burlington, and did not reach Montreal till Saturday morning. Having supplied the pulpit of Côté Street on Sabbath, and visited and addressed the Sabbath schools, an opportunity was given me of examining the male and female Bible classes on Monday, and of meeting with the Home Mission Committee of the Presbytery. Tuesday and Wednesday were nearly taken up in the sail from Lachine to Kingston, and after spending a day among our kind friends in the quondam capital of Canada, we reached Toronto safe and sound on the morning of Friday. In a journey of three thousand miles or upwards, one is exposed to many casualties, and our gratitude cannot be too ardent to Him who holdeth our goings."

" TORONTO, Dec. 1852.

" The history of our church in Quebec is connected with interesting associations. In 1802, the religion of Quebec, nominally considered, was divided into two parts. The genius of Popery brooded over the one, and that of rationalism or Unitarianism over the other. A few friends of the Redeemer felt a longing for something more in harmony with evangelical truth, and a small Congregational church was formed. The London Missionary Society sent

out a minister to this *pagan* city, and serious religion flourished for
a season.   The prudence of the missionary, however, was not equal
to his zeal, and he got into difficulties.   The cause of civil and religious liberty was well nigh crushed by the overwhelming influence
of the high church bigotry of the Anglican hierarchy.   David Dale,
and a few like-minded men in the city of Glasgow, interposed ;
and the services of these noble men will never be forgotten in the
annals of the Protestant Church in Quebec.

"The first missionary was followed by a succession of good men,
and one of these, Mr. Francis Dick, a native of Monifeith, Forfar-
shire, Scotland, and at one time settled in Montrose, deserves
special notice.   A plain Scotchman, and with few attractions of
eloquence, Mr. Dick grasped the standard of Zion with a firm hand,
and kept it flying on the citadel for years.   Many rallied around
it, and the recollections of those days are fresh and fragrant still.
In the course of providence, Mr. Dick was called to leave America,
to minister to the Scotch inhabitants of Hamburg, where he occupied the same pulpit with Dr. Merle D'Aubigné, then a young and
promising evangelist, and since that day the world-renowned historian of the Reformed Churches.—One church was allotted for the
Scotch, the Germans, and the French ; and these two pious ministers divided the services betwixt them.   Mr. Dick returned, after
many years, to his native land, and died not long ago, at Cavers,
where that noble-minded and truly catholic gentleman, James
Douglas, had been for years his patron in everything that was
good in missionary effort.

"About twenty-five years ago, the plan of connecting the Congregational church with the Presbyterian Establishment of Scotland was devised ; the Rev. John Clugston became, in this new
ecclesiastical position, its first pastor, and St. John's became a
stronghold of evangelical truth.   The pious and pains-taking ministry of Mr. Clugston is an era of no ordinary interest, in the religious annals of Quebec.

"I spent nearly seven weeks in the city and in the Lower Province.   The congregation I found to be considerably dispirited,
by a succession of painful disappointments in their attempts to get
a minister.   The circumstances of the last of these had been really
disastrous.   Still, the members and adherents are cherishing hope
that the Church at home will yet take pity upon them, and commission an able minister of the New Testament, to occupy this
first-rate station in the visible church of the Redeemer.   It is needless to disguise it.   An ordinary man will not do for Quebec.   If
the thing is properly managed, the new Free church of that city
will become a noble rallying point, otherways it will be a monument
of folly.   It is, indeed, a lovely gem ; but a congregation of eight
hundred is not easily raised in Quebec.   It is right that our friends,
both in Canada and Scotland, should know this.   The obstacles in

the way of success are great, and nothing short of commanding talent and untiring zeal will conquer them.

But this is only one view of the case. The Free church of Quebec ought to take the lead of the evangelical community ; and what a field of usefulness is opened to its future ministers. In a population of nearly 50,000, the number of nominal Protestants is a small fraction of the whole, and yet, under an able and pious pastor, the influence of such a ministry must tell over the city and Province to an incalculable extent. The near presence of a cunning, skilful, and all but overwhelming foe consolidates the Protestant mind, harmonizes jarring elements, and secures evangelistic union.

" The lateness of the season put it quite out of my power to visit Metis, the remotest of our settlements to the east. But it so happened that Mr. and Mrs. Pasche, the teacher and his wife, lately appointed by Knox's College Missionary Association to occupy the station, reached Quebec, on their way down, exactly at the same time with me, and thus, on the Wednesday after my first Sabbath in the city, we held a meeting specially on their account. The weather was very unfavourable, and thus the attendance was not so good as it would have been. But the meeting was an interesting one. Mr. Pasche gave an address in French, which was interpreted by Mr. Hadden, one of the elders. Special prayer for the mission was offered up, and an appeal in its favour made to the audience. Next day we had pleasant intercourse in private with Mr. and Mrs. Pasche, and my impression is, that they are admirably qualified for the situation they are called to fill. It is partly educational and partly of a missionary character ; and amid many difficulties, and the great opposition which may be looked for from the priests, there can be no doubt that a good beginning has been made. The acquisition of the whole seigniory, upwards of 30,000 acres, by our friends the Messrs. Ferguson, of Montreal, is highly favourable to the progress and success of any measure having in view the advancement of the cause of Christ. In connection with this station, I could not but think with melancholy interest on the fact, that it was on his way to visit Metis, in August, 1851, our excellent friend Mr. Rintoul was called home to his Father's house on high.

" While in Quebec, a visit to the friends of the French Canadian Mission of Montreal was paid by their newly appointed agent, the Rev. Mr. Clark. It was a refreshing season. The public meeting held in the Methodist church was admirably attended ; many heart-stirring appeals on the subject of Popery and missions made ; and a handsome collection of nearly £60 realised. Quebec ought to be a stronghold of that Mission. A French Protestant minister of ability and zealous piety ought to be located here. The idea of such a a man as Merle D'Aubigné, the great historian of the Reformation, being settled as pastor of the Free church in Quebec, and President of a Protestant Seminary for training young men for the ministry, in the Lower Province, caught my fancy; and most will say it was a dream of the night. I do not think so. That distinguished man preaches well in all the three languages, English, French and German; and if he desired to add a volume to his valuable history, I know not a finer topic than the history of reli- gion in Lower Canada. That Province was the scene of reforming and evangelistic efforts in other days, though crushed by the overwhelming influence of Popery. 'The influence of the Vatican;' it is remarked by a late historian of the Province, and a Roman Catho- lic, 'was opposed to the prosperity of a colony whose real interests Italy did not understand.'

"One of the out-stations which were visited, from Quebec, was Port Neuf, on the shore of the St. Lawrence, about thirty miles up from the city. There are here about twenty families, chiefly Scotch, and connected with an extensive paper mill, belonging to Messrs. Macdonald & Co., Quebec. Mr. Macdonald has also lately acquir- ed the entire seigniory. He is a warm friend of our church, and his ready and liberal kindness, with that of his partner in the con- cern, and Mr. Miller, and others, has been the means of keeping up an interest in this locality, for years past, highly favourable both to education and religion. Mr. Young,* one of the students at Knox's College, is at present engaged as teacher of the school in the place, and he conducts worship on Sabbaths and at other times; the same place serving both as school-house and chapel.—His labours are justly appreciated. The accommodation is excellent. The day school is well attended, and the Sabbath classes are in a prosperous state. I received much kindness from Mr. Miller, with whom I stayed four days. We had two meetings for worship, and the at- tendance was good. Although the number of Scotch families, in the immediate vicinity, is not very great, there are scattered here and there in the district round, a considerable number of Presby- terians, partly Scotch and partly from the north of Ireland. A faithful missionary or catechist settled here, might be the means of getting together a considerable congregation, and the moral and religious influence of a spiritual community, amid the darkness which broods around, cannot fail to prove highly beneficial. The acquisition of a seigniory by an enlightend Protestant, is an event of no inconsiderable moment in the prospective history of Lower Canada.—The proximity of this settlement to Quebec, and its easy access from that city, would render the superintendence of it, by an able minister settled there, a matter of no difficult accomplish- ment. A snow-storm detained me a day longer than I intended at Port Neuf, but I did not regret it, as it gave me an opportunity of visiting the most of the families, and of holding agreeable inter- course with Mr. Young on his literary studies."

---

* Now Rev. Alex. Young, of Montreal.

"January 25th, 1853.

" It was on Wednesday, November 17, I went by steamer to St. Nicholas, a port on the south side of the St. Lawrence, and about ten miles above Quebec. It was in the afternoon we embarked, and a few miles only of the land journey could be overtaken that night. My guide was a worthy son of Erin, who, with his sleigh, had been sent down some fifty miles expressly for me, and without any notice of the wishes or expectation of the people, farther than just an order to 'bring me up.' This is always to me the best proof of a *desire* to obtain the services of a missionary ; and when at all practicable I make it a rule always to comply with *hints* so broad and so intelligible, and I never yet had cause to repent doing so. We stayed all night at a house of refreshment, nine miles up the country, where the privilege of evening and morning domestic worship was enjoyed. In the surrounding district, however, only three Presbyterian families are to be found, and these are at considerable distances from each other. Passing on next day southward, we soon got beyond the range of French Popery, and in the Township of St. Sylvester came into contact with about twenty families, mostly from the north of Ireland. In the house of one of these families (Mr. Woodside's) we made our arrangements for preaching ; my guide going on before me to give the due notices as fully and effectively as in the circumstances was practicable. After partaking of the kind hospitality of the worthy family, I was conveyed two miles further to the church of St. Sylvester, adjoining to which is the house of Mr. and Mrs. Heddle, and their family, originally from Shapinshay in Shetland, but for many years resident partly in Quebec and partly in St. Sylvester.

" With this worthy Christian family I stopped for the night, and in the afternoon notices were sent round for sermon next day (Friday,) at 12. A congregation of about fifty assembled—as large a number as, in the circumstances, could have been expected. The usual services were gone through—a sermon preached, and a congregational meeting for conference thereafter. On Saturday, a similar meeting was held at Mr. Ross's, seven or eight miles further on, and in the township of Leeds, and here the number of hearers was about the same. (Of the probable amount of the regular congregation in such places, however, it would be wrong to judge from an occasional and transient visit, not duly announced. There is no doubt whatever, that were an acceptable pastor settled in Leeds and St. Sylvester, these two stations would produce good congregations on the Lord's Day, while the pastor could, with perfect ease, supply both. Mr. Ross is father-in-law to our excellent friend Mr. Swinton, now at St. Louis de Gonzague, but formerly the catechist and missionary in Leeds, where his labours are remembered with much affection.)

" My Sabbath services were divided betwixt the two stations in

Leeds, one at Lambie's mills, and the other seven miles distant, and in a school-house at Mr. Reid's. The substantial place of worship at the former was well filled by an attentive and serious looking congregation, of probably more than two hundred; and from eighty to one hundred were assembled in the other place. These four stations of Leeds and St. Sylvester would form together one manageable charge, and they are fully ready to receive a minister. —The past services of such faithful young men as Messrs. Swinton, Alexander, McLaren and Murray,* have been duly appreciated. The earnestness and the skilful propriety with which the praises of God were sung in these localities, as well as in those of Inverness, formed a pleasing feature as an index of pious feeling, and a proof of congregational organization. Sabbath schools and Bible classes also appear to have been successfully conducted.

" In St. Sylvester and Leeds the number of families adhering to us cannot be fewer than one hundred and twenty. But there are out-fields which must not be overlooked.

"There are Frampton, Broughton, and Kennebec road, in all five stations at least, and upwards of one hundred avowedly Presbyterian families, but scattered at varied distances over a large extent of country. In connexion with a fixed pastor at Leeds and St. Sylvester, a lay missionary or catechist for these appendages, would be of great value. On the Kennebec road, the Rev. Simon Fraser, now of McNab, laboured for some years ; and our friend, Mr. Angus Macintosh, now in Scotland, in one of his zealous mission tours, first brought to light the existence of settlements of Presbyterian families at the other places, who had been many years without the knowledge or the spiritual aid of the Church whose children they were. In regard to temporal support for a gospel ministry, there will be, as there has been, some difficulty ; but there can be no question as to the call of duty addressed to us, to look after those children of our people and of our Church, now scattered abroad.

"On Monday, 22nd, I went on to Inverness, where I preached that day and the next day in the same place, and at the same hour, to congregations of betwixt eighty and a hundred. On both occasions a conference was held after sermon, and every encouragement held out to the people to keep together, and to wait for more regular supply. The number of families in Inverness belonging to us, professedly, cannot much exceed fifty, and they are for the most part Gaelic. To show their real desire to obtain a minister, they have built a nice manse in a convenient situation. My two days' intercourse with these excellent people, was

---

* Messrs. Swinton, now in United States :
McLaren, of Ottawa ;
Alexander, of Baptist Church, Brantford ;
Murray, of Grimsby.

of the most pleasing kind. Much intelligence and warm-hearted piety met my observation. I was greeted with real Christian affection, and left them with the full impression, that a pious young minister, having the Gaelic language, would find in this township a most promising field of useful labour. In looking into the *libraries* of the families with whom I stay, I am often delighted to find in their proper places of influence, some of the standard works of our most venerated authors ; and here, I found that several pious colporteurs from the United States had given extensive circulation to new and cheap editions of the works of the Flavels, and the Charnocks, and the Baxters, and the Howes, of the justly venerated Christian authorship of other days ; and, moreover, that these visits of young men, most of them aspirants to the ministry in the Presbyterian churches of America, had been in other respects pleasing and salutary. Here also I found some promising specimens of attainment both in family and congregational singing. Need I add, that both in Leeds and Inverness, there is much physical beauty to meet the traveller's eye ; while the 'falls of Inverness' remind me of similar scenery in other lands.—Disappointed was I to be told, that the river on which these 'falls' were, was not called the *Ness* (as I anticipated,) but the 'Thames.' This, however, did not take from the beauty of the scene.

"Richmond and Melbourne are seventy miles from Montreal—nearly half way to Quebec—on the line of the great railway now in progress from Montreal to Portland in Maine, U. S. They are on the river St. Francis, a beautiful stream, of considerable flow, and admirably adapted for public works.

"I spent one Sabbath in this interesting locality, and preached four times on the Lord's day and Monday. To the friends in Danville, Richmond and Melbourne, I am under obligations for their great kindness. Their pleadings for a resident evangelical ministry shall not soon fade from my memory. God grant that such an invaluable blessing may soon be enjoyed ; and then shall the spiritual graces of the lovely district more than vie with its physical beauties and commercial capabilities.

"Had it been in my power to have devoted at least *one month* to missionary labours in the eastern townships, I might have obtained some idea of the extent of the field and the religious condition of its inhabitants. A whole season would be needed to do anything like justice to such a work ; and yet I know not a missionary tour which, if properly prosecuted by a minister of Christ of due experience and energy, would be of more avail to the cause of Christ and the interests of his Church in this western world. The superiors of these townships are, properly speaking, the shareholders of the American Land Company of London, and there are among them, and occupying stations of influence, those who have felt the power of the truth in their own minds, and know the value of religion to the well-being of a community, even in a temporal point of view. Will no apostolic man be sent out from the capital of the British empire, who, with the weight of influence which that Company could command, and the far loftier influence of zealous and enlightened Christianity in his heart, in his sermons, and in his whole career, would devote six months to an enterprise which would almost to a certainty issue in the permanent 'lifting up of a standard' for the people inhabiting one of the finest portions of the habitable globe? O that the Presbyterian Church in England would think of this, and, making common cause with us in Canada, send us, for a season, one of their ablest champions of the faith, accompanied by one of their pious lay members—say a Nisbet, or a Barbour, or a Gillespie. 'The thing would pay'—ah, that it would —not, it may be, in the sordid dross of this world, although there is gold in that land too—but in the durable riches of the kingdom that cannot be moved."

"KNOX COLLEGE,

"TORONTO, Oct. 15, 1858.

"It had been for years my wish to visit Cape Breton and New-foundland, that I might thus complete my survey of the religious state of the British provinces of North America. In the course of events, the summer recess from College duties put it in my power to carry my plan into execution. The first two months of the recess of 1858, April and May, were devoted to the supply of the pulpit of Knox's Church, Toronto, now filled up by the accession to the list of Colonial ministers of a tried and faithful pastor. June and July were occupied by Synod duties ; by visits to Durham and the West ; and by sacramental engagements in Glengarry. These last formed a repetition of what it had been my privilege to enjoy four years before ; and I look back on both occasions with singular relish. While the associations with the settlement of Glengarry, or the Eastern District of Canada West, are invested with a historical prestige peculiarly interesting, these older branches of our Colonial Empire present to the members of our Free Church a scene at once captivating and encouraging. They form a stronghold for evangeli-cal truth. Our congregations there have been gathered together and organized on the best principles. The standard set up is a high one ; and the thousands who rally round it seem to be actu-ated by the best spirit. In more than one instance has their sin-cerity been severely tested. They now enjoy the ministrations of six or seven faithful men whom they love, and their fields and dense forests bear testimony to the vitality of that power, which can con-gregate hundreds, and even thousands, to listen to the Gospel sound.

"It was on the 2nd of August we sailed from Portland, U. S., for New Brunswick and Nova Scotia ; and it was on October 2nd, exactly two months after, we left Portland for Toronto, on our return. In addition to my special objects, I had hoped to spend some time in the east and south districts of Nova Scotia, and in the city of St. John's, N. B. It has been matter of deep regret to me that the engagements prospectively made behoved to be broken up, and intercourse with these interesting fields suspended for the present. In the old Acadian settlements the aspect of our sister church is exceedingly promising ; and the city of St. John's, N. B., can never cease to live in my memory, as the scene of fifteen years' labour of a very near relative of my own, whose name is yet fresh and fragrant there, although the majority of those who enjoyed his ministry in earlier or in later life have not been suffered to remain by reason of death. In 1817, when he first settled in St. Andrew's Church, as in some sense the pioneer of the Colonial staff, the city had its ten thousand inhabitants ; now its citizens fall not much short of four times that number. The history of Presbyterianism in that city has been somewhat chequered ; but the Free Church now numbers, in and around, four congregations ; and the prospect is at present more cheering than it has ever been. The brethren have lately been visited by the deputies of the Presbyterian Church of Ireland, and we in the Colonies, always prize such visits as refreshing and edifying.

" Passing by steam through the Bay of Fundy, we reached Windsor, N. S , by six in the morning of August 3rd, and arrived at Halifax, by railway 45 miles, early in the forenoon. Our arrival was hailed with much cordial kindness by the worthy family whose hospitality we enjoyed during our stay in the city ; and a whole host of old and much attached friends clustered around us, all vying with one another in their offers of friendship. The congregation of Chalmers' Church I found in a healthy state under the pastoral charge of the Rev. John Hunter, who succeeded Dr. Forrester, on the appointment of that gentleman to the superintendentship of Education in the Province. We had much agreeable intercourse with Mr. Hunter, as also with Professors King and Lyall, of the Free College, and Mr. MacKnight, the Hebrew tutor, who has also the pastoral charge of Dartmouth. My earnest wish and prayer are, that the health of all these gentlemen may be preserved in vigour, and that their important labours, in the several departments allotted to them, may be crowned with goodly success. Great hopes are entertained of an union being consummated between the two branches of the Presbyterian body which seem to approximate nearest to each other in sentiment ; but whatever may be the issue of this matter, there is much in the condition of the Free Church of Nova Scotia to fan the zeal and concentrate the energies of its members. The college has been eminently successful in sending forth promising young men into the field ; and one pleasing feature in my late tour has been the opportunity given me of holding intercourse with a considerable number of the ministers who have been the first fruits of an Institution so valuable.

"One Sabbath I spent at Halifax, on my way to Newfoundland, and another on my return. I had also an opportunity of visiting and addressing the Sabbath School of Chalmers' Church ; and on the Tuesday after the first of these Sabbaths, we enjoyed, in common with many friends, a pleasant social meeting of the teachers and pupils of all the schools in connection with the Free Church ; embracing those of Chalmers' Church, Dutchtown and Dartmouth. Between two hundred and three hundred pupils attended. Addresses suitable to the occasion were delivered by ministers and lay friends. A corresponding member from Cornwallis, 70 miles distant, attended, taking a lively interest in the meeting ; and the occasion was gratifying to the elastic minds of the young, as well as to the more matured feelings of their seniors. This rural fete took place in a grove, not many minutes distant from the city.

"On Friday morning, August 13th, we sailed for Newfoundland in the steamer *Osprey*, one of the vessels connected with the Cunard line, and which pays a fortnightly visit to that Island from Halifax, calling at Sydney, C. B., on her way to and from. Our voyage of 600 miles was prosperous ; Captain Sampson being attentive to his passengers, and all on board anxious to promote each other's comfort. We spent Sabbath, 15th, at sea, and had public worship on board, when all the Protestant portion of the inmates of the vessel gave devout attendance. On Monday, we were sailing along the strong iron-bound coast of Newfoundland, and at four o'clock of the afternoon of that day, we landed at St. John's, the capital of the island ; passing through the picturesque 'narrows,' as the entrance is called, and announcing by the successive booming of our ship's brass cannon the arrival of Her Majesty's mail at this the most venerable of her Colonial possessions. The Bay of St. John's is just one of perhaps sixty, round the coast of the island, characterized by the like features of security from storms and invasions. The choice of it for the capital was made three centuries ago, and nothing has occurred to render the wisdom of the selection questionable. It is at once safe and commodious, its waters deep, and its position relatively to the island as a whole, and its bearing on the home connections with the East, just what might be desired. The wharf was covered by hundreds, serenading the entrance of the *Osprey*, and welcoming friends and visitors. Among the rest we soon saw the face of our excellent friend, the Rev. Mr. Harvey, who with several members of his congregation including the kind-hearted editor of a ' Tri-weekly,' gave us a right hearty welcome. Not many minutes elapsed ere we realized from our own experience, what we knew from report before, that Newfoundland and St. John's were proverbial for kindness and hospitality.

"Newfoundland was discovered by Cabot, in 1497, and its history is associated with such eminent names as those of Gilbert, Raleigh, and Lord Bacon ; and this last sage, on being asked his opinion of the mineral resources of the island, gave it as his impression that the best of all its minerals were the cod and the seals. The company of which his Lordship was a director, did nothing to explore the internal resources of the island ; but an American Association has within these few years done something, and promises to do more for developing that valuable treasure.   Mr. Cormack, in 1822, traversed, in company with a single Indian, the central parts of the island, and from his statements, which I have just perused, there can be no doubt that the resources in agriculture, in minerals, in fisheries, and in woods abounding with deer, have been as yet scarcely touched. Mr. Page has also favoured me with the ' Geological Report' by Mr. Jukes, the sketches in which form a rich repast to those who are conversant with such researches. I do not dwell on those topics, but I venture an inference—Let the island remain in our exclusive possession, and let our rulers at home settle with France and America as best they may, only let us keep what we have.

"It is more than thirty years ago since a church in connection with the Scotch Establishment was set up in St. John's.   The number of resident settlers of the Presbyterian denomination had considerably increased, and the congregation was organized under the Rev. Donald Frazer, whom they called from Lunenburg, N. S: At the time of the disruption, great efforts were made to retain the whole in connection with the Church of Scotland ; but a series of circumstances in the providence of God, led to the formation of the present Free Church.   The attention of the Home Colonial Committee and of the Presbytery of Halifax was early called to the help of the struggling society, and by the correspondence and personal visits of ministers, and of the Home Colonial Committee, matters were brought into a promising state.   Dr. McLeod, now of Cape Breton, was, on his return voyage as a deputy of the church at home, shipwrecked on the coast, and this event was over-ruled for good.   He remained for six weeks in St. John's, and was eminently useful in giving information and advice, while the congregation was consolidated and cheered by his preaching and his visits. Two-thirds of the people adhered to our principles, and they brought along with them the piety, and the sound views, and the strict discipline which constituted the main elements of a flourishing Christian society.   The congregation had to struggle with difficulties, arising from the loss of property and other causes ; but they have stood firm to the cause of the Redeemer—having reared a very neat and commodious place of worship, admirably located, and filled by a united body of sincere and affectionate fellow-worshippers.   For six years they have flourished under the pastoral care of the Rev. Moses Harvey, formerly of Maryport,* in Cumberland,—a gentleman who seems highly qualified for the situation he occupies, by

* This English seaport gave also to Canada the Rev. William Rintoul, one of her most useful ministers.

talents and acquirements which command respect, by a piety at once unaffected and warm, and by a measure of prudence, good sense, and sound judgment rarely exemplified. Besides his pulpit labours, and pastoral visits, and Sabbath schools and classes, Mr. H. has been in the habit of delivering, during the winter season, short courses of lectures on subjects of a general nature, but bearing on religion, such as—the connection of science with revelation ; the discoveries of Layard and others ; the poetry of the heathens ; and on these subjects he has edified and instructed his own people and many others, by publishing as well as delivering these valuable prelections.

" Of the two Sabbaths spent in Newfoundland, one was given to St. John's and the other to Harbor Grace ; and these are the only Free churches as yet in the island. In addition, I preached in St. John's on two week-evenings, and addressed the classes both on a Sabbath and on a week-day evening, after a very pleasant 'gathering of the clans,' on the grounds adjoining the residence of the minister. With the leading families of the congregation our intercourse was frequent and of the most friendly character. We cannot look back on the days we spent among these intelligent and liberal-hearted people, without the most grateful recollections. Indeed, it is to the spontaneous and hearty liberality of the friends in Halifax, in St. John's, and Harbor Grace, I am indebted for all the expenditure incurred within the Lower Provinces. The experiment which has been made satisfies me that, whether a 'federal union' among the British Provinces is realized or not, such an union among the churches is highly desirable ; and the occasional interchanges of visits which would ensue, could not fail to advance the cause which is common to them all.

" St. John's is the seat of a Roman Catholic Bishop, and Harbor Grace is the seat of another. Newfoundland is one of the favourite preserves of Popery. Of 120,000 inhabitants, nearly one-half are Popish ; and of 25,000 in St. John's, 18,000 are votaries of Romanism. This gives a vast ascendency to Popery in the Colony, and its influence moulds the Legislative and Executive, as well as the Province generally. The present Governor, Sir Alexander Bannerman, holds the reins, however, with a firm and independent grasp ; and had the Episcopacy of the island acted with the spirit of the Sumner, the Tait and the Bickersteth school, we might have good hopes for evangelical Protestantism. A monkish mediævalism is a poor set off against the sternness of an iron Romanism. It is well that for thirty years the Methodist Church has been commendably zealous in Newfoundland, and at present the number of its adherents is 36,000. I know no field where an union of Protestants against the common foe would be more commendable ; and for this end the prayers of all good men should ascend to the heavenly throne, that evangelical truth may be maintained in purity, and that scriptural godliness may give the tone to the community at large. In connection with these views, I cannot allow the opportunity to pass without paying a slight tribute to the character of Lady Bannerman, whose moral excellence and consistent religious character throw a lustre around the influential station she has been called to occupy. Her sentiments are decidedly evangelical and liberal, in the best sense of these terms. She is exemplary in her attendance on religious ordinances, she takes the chief superintendence of the Sabbath school, in connection, *not with the Cathedral*, but with the less imposing fabric which owns an evangelical ministry. She visits the sick and afflicted. She distributes funds, books and tracts ; and is the patroness of everything patriotic and Christian. Her religious influence and example have already, here and in other places, been owned of God for great good."

"KNOX COLLEGE,
"TORONTO, Nov. 4, 1858.

" Tyre has a name in history, both sacred and civil, and the ruins of Old Tyre are most graphically and characteristically described in prophetic record as places on which ' fishermen would spread their nets.' What the ruins of Tyre are in the East, those of the once famed town and fortress of Louisbourg are in the West. Macgregor, indeed, in his excellent history of the British Colonies, imputes to 'fanaticism' the capture of this city and fortress in 1745, because it was the preaching of Whitefield that formed the proximate cause of that bold undertaking on the part of a few merchants and farmers of New England, which humbled the pride of France, and led to the extinction of her empire in North America. The Colonial historian perhaps had forgotten his own acknowledgment elsewhere, that the Jesuits and the '*freres*' and the St. Sulpice ' Sisters' of Cape Breton, were the great ' hounders on' of the poor Micmacs, in their scalping experiments on defenceless Englishmen.

" It has been said that the destruction of its capital threw the island beyond the limits of vision. It may be so, for assuredly Britain has up to this moment shut her eyes on a colonial gem, compared with which Ceylon or Jamaica are baubles. Its agriculture and its woods are most valuable, its minerals and fisheries are boundless, and its local situation, relatively to Europe and America, makes it the very Thermopylæ of the West. Its population is sixty thousand, but its capabilities will suffice easily for ten times that number. Down to the close of the American war, when a few loyalists settled in it, the island was absolutely ignored by the mother country. It was not till the beginning of the present century that Cape Breton was thought of as a field for emigration. The first settlers were Scotch Roman Catholics from Barra, South Uist, Harris, and the Lewis ; and being the first, they very naturally and laudably chose the best of the land. The eastern half of

v

the island is still theirs, but fishing has occupied their attention more than agriculture, and the best of their farms are mortgaged. About 1810 the 'clearings' of the North drove away many valuable Protestant families from their loved native abodes, and for twenty years successive colonies of these reached Cape Breton, and settled principally in the south-eastern, western and northern parts. At first they were poor and dispirited ; nevertheless they have done, on the whole, well, and are now in a fair thriving state. One fact is sufficient to show the progress of the Island. In 1832, when Macgregor published his history, 'one school' at Sydney is mentioned : now (1858) there are about *one hundred* schools.

" It was in 1827 my acquaintanceship with the late Mrs. Mackay of Rockfield, Sutherlandshire, began. At that time her attention was directed to the state of the emigrants from her own county to Merigomish, Earlton, New Lairg, and the district around Pictou, Nova Scotia. Her first efforts were directed to the sending out well-selected libraries of religious books for the use of the settlers. The libraries thus formed were conducted on the circulating plan, and, from some letters of thanks to Mrs. Mackay, which I have just been perusing, it is plain that the gifts were justly appreciated and profitably improved. In the view of obtaining the services of a few pious Gaelic missionaries, Mrs. Mackay felt a desire to concentrate her efforts and those of her friends on some one point ; and, as many of the northern emigrants had settled in Cape Breton, that island was fixed on as a suitable field. So early as 1827 the Glasgow Society had received very affecting details of the spiritual wants of the Island, and different individuals were fixed on as pioneers in the enterprise. In all such cases it is well known that the disappointments in the experience of all Missionary Societies, in the outset, are numerous, and it was matter of great satisfaction when Mrs. Mackay resolved to take 'her little island,' as she called it, under her care. This 'little island,' nevertheless, contains 3000 square miles. Its number of settlers had been increasing year after year, and no evangelical association had as yet given it any place in their benevolent regards. The mission of the Rev. Alexander Farquharson, in 1833, was on this account an important event in the religious history of the Island. That excellent man had to encounter a host of difficulties, particularly at the outset of his labours, but by divine grace he was enabled to conquer them all, and after twenty-five years' active and laborious missionary toil, he was gathered to his fathers in peace. He was a single-hearted devoted minister of the cross, and the blessings of his attached flock will rest on his widow and family.

" Mrs. Mackay was spared to see a very considerable number of the leading Gaelic settlements in the Island taken up by missionaries whom she was mainly instrumental in sending out ; and their labours were aided and encouraged by catechists on the itinerating plan, as in Scotland ; by teachers ; and by supplying pious books gratuitously to them. The number of leading stations now is about a dozen, and if these are multiplied by four, the result may give us an idea of the number of spheres of labour. The extent of each charge is great, as the settlers are scattered ; and the demand for additional churches and ministers is at present very clamant. Three of the more remote charges I had it not in my power to visit, but the two Sabbaths I spent in the Island, and the meetings held successively at Sydney, Myra, Sydney Mines, Bras d'Or, Boularderie, Bedeque, Cape St. Ann, Wycokoma, and Plaster Cove, will dwell in my remembrance to my latest days.

" The arrival of Dr. Macleod, of Logie Easter, first as a deputy from the Free Church, and afterwards as minister of Sydney, is one of the leading events in the religious history of the Island. A man of ability and experience was earnestly longed for by the pastors already settled, and such a one they have had in Dr. Macleod. By his personal exertions in Cape Breton, in Nova Scotia, in Canada, and in the United States, he has succeeded in obtaining the necessary funds for raising churches in several parts of the Island. These neat and commodious places of worship raise their white spires in all directions. Among these, at Myra, not far from Louisbourg, is a large and handsome, but plain structure, capable of holding two thousand hearers ; and stormy as the Sabbath was when Dr. Macleod and I preached there, a dense collection of people, to the number of fifteen hundred, met us, gathered, some of them, from the distance of twenty miles. Dr. Macleod has six churches under his own immediate care, and assuredly the church at home would do well to strengthen his hands by sending out additional labourers. In the meantime I rejoice that he has in his immediate locality two such associate fellow-laborers as the Rev. Matthew Wilson, the esteemed pastor of Sydney Mines and Bras d'Or, and the Rev. James Frazer, of Boularderie, now the oldest resident minister in the Island. Boularderie is an island *within the Island*, eighteen or twenty miles long by four or five broad ; a spot characterized no less by fertility of soil, in many parts, than by its being a stronghold of evangelical truth and experimental religion. The number of inhabitants exceeds sixteen hundred. With a few exceptions they may be said to be all of the Free Church. Mr. Frazer is the only resident minister of any denomination on the island, and the number of intelligent ' men' who strengthen his hands is large. I preached to five hundred persons on the afternoon of a week-day in harvest, and in a lovely hollow encompassed with trees, where the communion had been dispensed some weeks before. The scene was deeply interesting, and the grasp of the hand, and the tear in the eye, were unmistakeable marks of a hearty spiritual welcome.

" The three churches at Wycokoma, Bedeque, and St. Ann's Bay forming one extensive and beautiful vale, are supplied by three excellent ministers, Messrs. Mackenzie, Macintosh, and Ross, who had all been students at the Halifax Free College, and are now fellow-labourers in localities bordering on one another. We had week-day services in each, and the number of hearers in two of these exceeded four hundred, while in the third, St. Ann's Bay, it reached nearly nine hundred. The settlements at Middle River, North Cove, and St. Peters, the want of time prevented me from visiting, and the sail in an open boat from Boularderie to West Bay, sixty miles, was so retarded by want of wind, that the hour fixed for service was long passed before we arrived at the place; and the painful intelligence met us, on our reaching the house of the intelligent and pious minister, the Rev. Murdoch Stewart, that two days before, his barn, his horse, and his hay had been burned to ashes by the hand of a deranged young man in the vicinity. We passed the night under the hospitable roof of the excellent minister, and next morning he accompanied us twenty-five miles, to Plaster Cove, where the Rev. Mr. Forbes labours, and where I gave my last discourse in the Island. After enjoying the hospitality of kind friends, I crossed the Strait of Canso, which is here narrow but extremely picturesque, and went on next day, sixty miles, to the house of my worthy old friend, the Rev. John Stewart, of New Glasgow. With him and his excellent family I stayed two days, preaching to a good audience on Friday evening. The Sabbath following was spent at Pictou, where we had two crowded audiences and a well attended Sabbath school. On Monday I went on to Roger's Hill and Salt Springs, on my way to Truro, preaching in both places. Wherever I have been the people have come out well, even on week-days, although on these later occasions the pressing labours of harvest did sensibly, as was reasonable, affect the audiences.

"At Truro we had the pleasure of spending a few days under the hospitable roof of our esteemed friends Dr. and Mrs. Forrester. The Educational College and Provincial Training Establishment, over which Dr. F. was three years ago called to preside, is an honour and a blessing to Nova Scotia. We attended, on two successive days, the various examination and lecture meetings, previous to the closing of the session. The eminently lucid, practical and pointed addresses and expositions of the Principal; the aptness to teach, as well as the science, exhibited in their varied departments, by the teachers, in English literature and history, mathematics, algebra, and the kindred sciences, as well as in the subsidiary sections of physiology, botany, geology, and agricultural chemistry, to say nothing of æsthetics, belles lettres, and music; and the warm, enlightened, and liberal religious spirit which pervaded all, accompanied, as the whole was, with encouraging and eloquent appeals by Messrs. Archibald and Creelman, members of the Legislature and Commissioners of Education; all these furnished to my mind a treat, intellectual and moral, of very rare enjoyment. Truro is one of the oldest and wealthiest of the settlements in Nova Scotia, and its prevailing type is Presbyterianism of the Scottish Secession Church. That religious body has lately erected a commodious Theological College in the village. Its session had just been opened, and the venerable Principal, Dr. Keir, who had given the inaugural address, was suddenly called away by death, amid the deep regrets of that section of the Christian community which had so long enjoyed his valued labours.

" On a retrospect of my visit to Cape Breton, my impressions as to its religious state are very favourable. Under the labours of the present faithful ministers, those of Mr Farquharson, lately removed by death, and those of the Rev. Mr. Maclean, of Lewis, Scotland, who ministered four years in the Island, revisiting it afterwards, preaching daily once or more for three months, and realizing ' fruit unto life eternal'—the cause of Christ has remarkably prospered.

" In reviewing the history of the Free Church in Nova Scotia generally, a careful observer of Providence must be struck with the large number of witnesses for the truth whom her annals have presented to us, as glorifying God in their lives and by their deaths. It is also interesting to notice the representatives of varied classes of witnesses as standing out in bold relief to the eyes of the careful observer. Do you desire a specimen of befitting qualification for duty, zeal in its discharge, and success in the preliminary training of young men for the ministry ? The lamented Professor Mackenzie, cut off in the very dawn of his usefulness, may be honourably named. Do you wish to see the picture of a pious labourer who, for a quarter of a century or more, toiled in a very unpromising field, but who lived down his difficulties, and saw very clearly the fruit of his earlier and later toils ? We point you to the Rev. Alexander Farquharson, the pioneer in Mrs. Mackay's band of pious heralds to Cape Breton, and the father of its infant but promising church. Do you desiderate a second specimen of the same class more recently ? You have it in the late Rev. Murdoch Sutherland, of Pictou, over whose early grave the residents and visitors at Rothsay, Scotland, will long shed a tear of respectful sympathy. Do you look round for one among the rising hopes of the College of Halifax, ripening fast in attainment and already an active and successful missionary, but gathered prematurely ripe, as we would say, into the garner ? The image of the late Mr. John Macdonald rises before us, while, as one of the great cloud of witnesses on high, he seems to beckon his surviving fellow-students to catch his mantle as he ascends. Do you desiderate one example out of many on the roll of departed Christian citizens who, amid diligence, and toil, and humble integrity in secular life, have never lost sight of the paramount claims of the cross of Jesus ? I would name the late Mr. John McIntosh, of Halifax, associated under the ministry of the lamented Mr. Robb as one of the early leaders in the Free Church movement in that city, and whom all its members lamentingly revere as the very *beau ideal* of a devoted and judicious lay brother in Christ. In

fine, do you look for a pattern of Christian humility, decided principle, and active usefulness in a female member of the church, and
a mother in Israel ?   You may see it in the late Mrs. Mackenzie,
of Pictou, who has so lately finished her course of rare godliness
with triumphant joy.   With most of these I was more or less acquainted.   Memorials of each have been laid before the public, and
I would deliberately give it as my opinion, that a church within
whose orbit such a bright galaxy has been seen, cannot fail to be
honoured by her Head with many additional evidences of his approving smile."

"TORONTO, 18th October, 1859.

"The third Sabbath in July having having been fixed on for the
celebration of the ordinance of the Supper at Nottawasaga, the
Gaelic portion of duty was allotted to Mr. Stewart, of Oro,
and the English to me.   In view of the ordinance, there were services at Sunnidale on Thursday, and at the Scotch Corners on Friday and Saturday, when there was also an ordination of elders.
The Lord's Day witnessed an assemblage of at least seven hundred
hearers, the majority being Gaelic-speaking persons, and they assembled for worship in a small grove of trees near at hand ; the
rest meeting in the newly-erected but not yet finished church.   On
Monday there was service in both languages ; and thereafter, the
congregation, having elected Mr. Russell to the chair, passed a cordial vote of thanks to the Presbytery and to the ministers who had
dispensed among them the bread of life.

"There can be no doubt that the cause of religion and of our
church in Nottawasaga is greatly indebted to Mr. James Mair, who
has for fifteen years discharged the duties of a lay missionary in
the district.   His public addresses in English and Gaelic, his visits
to the sick and aged, his judicious management of private fellowship meetings, and his consistent walk and conversation, have
contributed greatly to the maintenance of true godliness in the
locality.   But his health has been often infirm, and he has felt the
burden to be too much for him.   The church ought to have interfered long ago in the way of regular systematic organization.   A
faithful pastor, having both languages, ought to have been there
settled.   How this is to be remedied now, is a grave question.   The
field is still very wide, but the number of our adherents is comparatively small.   My impression is, that an union would require to be
formed betwixt this district and the adjoining stations in Sunnidale.

"In the township of Osprey, two different stations which had
been visited by Mr. Nisbet,* of Oakville, in March last, were re-
visited on the present occasion, and congregations varying from
fifty to four hundred assembled to hear the word.   On the last of
these occasions, the ordinance of the Lord's Supper was dispensed

* Now of the Saskatchewan mission.

to about sixty persons, the number of members in the district in all being eighty, of whom seventeen were admitted on the present occasion for the first time. The day was delightful. Ample accommodation was provided in a large barn, the use of which Mr. Hunter, the proprietor, though not of our communion, granted us. The occasion was every way most solemn and impressive. During the summer, first Mr. Eadie, and then Mr. McLennan, Gaelic student, were employed as missionaries here, and their labours have been most acceptable and useful. Indeed, no mission tour has impressed me more deeply than this one with a conviction of the value of a pious missionary's residence and labours. And this was only one illustration out of many. My two months' mission brought me into contact with at least a dozen of our promising students, in different localities, whose faithful labours were deservedly prized. I am satisfied that these labours interfere less with the peculiar avocations of the student in theology than any other work that could be assigned him.

"Osprey, though part of it was surveyed and settled eight years ago, may be considered as a new settlement, the greater portion having been occupied during the last four or five years. The opening of the Northern Railway made access to it comparatively easy, and the soil, generally speaking, is good. A considerable number of settlers from King, and other localities near, have purchased bush farms, and thus Osprey is profiting by toils already gone through, and experience already acquired. The settlers vied with each other in their tokens of kindness ; and my earnest desire is, that a faithful pastor or itinerating missionary may soon be resident among them. Two villages, Singhampton and Feversham, begin to rise in the midst of the forest, and the fact of each having already its post office, and the additional fact of a fine road having been opened up from this locality directly west towards Durham and Lake Huron, mark the prospective importance of a range of country which had been. till very recently, shut out from observation. The roads in many of the localities are still very rough. The cross-paths from settlement to settlement seldom admit of waggons of the ordinary kind ; and this obstacle in my way did, in one instance, occasion a most serious disappointment, for which, however, I afterwards made up by availing myself of the kind services of a quiet and sure-footed quadruped of the horse species, unencumbered with any appendage in the shape of buggy, or cart, or waggon of any kind.

"Artemesia lies between Osprey and the Garafaxa road, and contains much good land but recently occupied. It is crossed diagonally by what is called the Toronto road, from our city to Owen Sound, by Mono and Orangeville, in length about 120 miles. On the northern part of that road, towards Owen Sound, there are many settlements of Scotch and Irish Presbyterians. I spent some days amongst them, and preached to attentive audiences in five crowded school-houses. The number of persons in this township who claim membership with us, or were ready to give in their names as applicants, was about forty, and there seemed to be among those several pious and intelligent men who might be set apart as elders over them. On submitting this matter to the Presbytery they were so much satisfied in regard to it as to authorize an application to Messrs. Cameron and Grant, of Sullivan and Owen Sound, though within the bounds of the Presbytery of Hamilton, to give their assistance in organizing a congregation, electing elders, and dispensing the ordinance of the Lord's Supper amongst them. All this has been done, and Artemesia now holds the rank of a recognized congregation. By a union with some of the adjoining districts a pastoral charge might be formed, but it must remain at present as a missionary station. It is a considerably older settlement than Osprey, but both the one and the other afford painful specimens of what meets a Canadian missionary wherever he goes—the evil that inevitably arises from the neglect of the Presbyterian Church to look after her scattered members early, and to throw over them the shield of a kind guardianship.

"Our excellent young missionary, Mr. Eadie,* by his information and tact, aided me much in my visit to Artemesia, and it has been the result of my experience in this as in former instances, that our Presbyterian 'succession,' in the way of guides and friendly helps knows no interruption—no gaps—for just when about to part with Mr. Eadie and other friends here, Mr. Andrew Elliot, an intelligent and pious elder in the neighbouring township of Sullivan arrived with his substantial two-horse waggon, to conduct me to his own newly-erected mansion in Sullivan, which his family had taken possession of the day before, and of which I happened thus to be the first visitor *ab extra*. This intelligent gentleman had come lately from Perth, C.W., whither his excellent father-in-law, Mr. Halliday, and other friends had come in 1815, when Government chartered vessels and sent out the *first settlers* to 'this Canada.' These worthy representatives of the first disturbers of the wolves and bears of the forest, I had the pleasure of meeting with a few weeks after, when Mrs. Burns and I paid a visit to Mr. Duncan at Perth, on occasion of the dispensation of the sacrament of the Lord's Supper. It is exceedingly interesting to converse with fresh and hale *octogenarians* in Canada ; to hear the story of their chequered scenes in the bush, the obstacles they had to overcome, and the success with which Jehovah has blessed them. Of their earlier movements we, youngsters, know nothing ; we listen with profound awe to the rehearsals of the men of those days, the 'jocund' heroes of the bush, who could not for a season boast of a 'team' to drive 'a field,' but who, from the very first, made the tall pine to bend 'beneath their sturdy stroke.' What a

---

* Now Rev. John Eadie, of Milton.

fine contrast the noble roads at the 'Scotch Settlement' of Perth
present to the unbroken forest of 1815 !

"Our ride to Sullivan led us through a wild part of Holland
township, and some melancholy instances of lawlessness were
brought to my ears, impressing me with a deeper conviction, that
the churches of Christ have not done, and are not even now doing
their duty to Canada. There has been too long a sad disruption
of colonization from Christianity ; and William Howitt has done
good service to the cause of both, by his church-reproving book on
that great subject. The settlement of such men as Mr. Elliott and
his enterprizing sons in such regions is a public blessing ; and they
know full well the vast importance of a faithful ministry to a rising colony. On Thursday, July 28th, the large and substantial
church recently erected for the Rev. James Cameron, the lately
ordained pastor, was nearly filled by noon—and short as my
intercourse with the congregation necessarily was, very satisfactory
proofs on this occasion were blended with those of my former
visit a twelve month past, to satisfy me that a fine vantage ground
had been gained ; and later information satisfies me that the Owen
Sound road *shall* not be given up to spiritual neglect ; that the
wilderness shall yet blossom like the rose ; that here and there
through a stretch of seventy miles, a standard shall be lifted up for
the people.

"The last Sabbath in July had been fixed on as the communion
day at Euphrasia and St. Vincent. My former visit to these places
two years and a half ago was marked by unbroken sleigh rides ;
this one exposed me to the broiling sun of a Canadian summer. It
is wonderful how the human constitution adapts itself to the oppo-
sites. All elements are under the ceaseless control of Him who
makes second causes bend to his pleasure. My worthy friend, Mr.
John Crichton, junr., was at my service with his sleigh in the one
case, and now he was alike ready with his light waggon in the
other. And what are twenty miles whether in the summer heat,
or in the winter's cold ? We provide for both ; and the God of
the seasons protects us in our going out and in our coming in, up-
holding our goings. On the present occasion we passed through a
rich country, marked here and there by massy ridges of limestone,
and the sweet flavour of the hay.gathering and the waving of the
golden corn-harvests ready for the sickle, blended pleasantly together. I did not expect a large attendance at 'the Saturday service', and therefore was not disappointed. But on Sabbath we had
the newly-reared frame fabric of the church thoroughly packed by
a respectable audience of probably four hundred. The communion
roll presented a list of ninety-one persons, and the number who
convened at the table on the present occasion exceeded sixty. I
preached four times in connection with the holy ordinance, and on
the evening of Monday a well-attended prayer-meeting was held in
the house of Mr. Walter Story, where also the ordinance of baptism was dispensed.

"On August 2nd, a pleasant steam sail of thirty miles from Port Meaford, brought me to the town of Collingwood, where, and at the neighbouring village of Nottawa, Mr. James Robertson* has been labouring as missionary for a few months. The station was in rather a depressed state when he began his labours, but his able and indefatigable ministrations have very considerably revived it. There was a good congregation in the evening, and my impression is that ours is the best attended place of worship in the town. It would be matter of deep regret were the station relinquished. The prospects of Collingwood commercially are fair; the means of intercourse with Toronto by railway are easy; and the adjacent stations on different sides of it, give to Collingwood somewhat of the character of a connecting nucleus.

"After meeting with the Presbytery and giving in my report of stations visited, I remained a week at home, and then, August 13th, entered on my allotted duties as interim supply for two or three weeks at Thorah, Eldon, and Mariposa, during the absence of Mr. MacTavish at the Red River colony. Two Sabbaths' supply was given, and a third by exchange with Mr. Gray of Orillia. The intermediate week-days were more or less occupied by preaching visits to the different stations. The attendance on all these occasions was good, and my impressions of the extent and value of the field occupied by Mr. MacTavish were so deepened by actual observation, that I almost longed for his speedy return, that he might address his own people in their much loved native tongue; for although I was ably aided by interpreters, the great deficiency could not but be painful. Many evidences I had that the good work of God was progressing within that wide district. The men of intelligence and of gifts for prayer and exposition of scripture are numerous : they are ready on all occasions to give valuable help, and the numerous prayer-meetings kept up by them are opportunities and means of much spiritual good. On its ordinary day the weekly prayer-meeting was held in the church at Mariposa at eleven o'clock, in the midst of the very throng of harvest. It was amazing to find more than two hundred present, and of these *one-half* at least were men.

"The energetic and pious pastor has since returned, after enduring a good many hardships and paying a truly acceptable visit to a colony long isolated from the rest of the world, and now about to become the primary element of a scheme of extended and successful colonization.

"A limited notice of my visit to the east is all that now remains of my two months' mission record. Allusion has already been made to Perth, and that town has certainly increased a third since my last visit in 1848, and the erection of a handsome new church and tower very recently, is one proof among others of the progress of

---

* Now Rev. J. Robertson, of Paris.

our church under Mr. Duncan's ministry. The communion season [Sept. 11th], was a very delightful one ; and we were profitably prepared for it by our Christian intercourse with Mr. and Mrs. Mackinnon, formerly of Owen Sound, now of Beckwith. The week-day congregation there exceeded three hundred. Opportunities were also given me of preaching at Ramsay, at Dalhousie, at St. Andrew's, at Lanark, and in Mr. Aitkin's church at Smith's Falls. Remembrances of our visit last year to Nova Scotia were also brought fresh to our minds by agreeable intercourse with Professor King and Mrs. King, of Halifax, whom we met on a visit to friends at Ramsay. Such unexpected occasions of friendly Christian intercourse on the highway of life, are pleasing and edifying,

"On our way to Ottawa by Brockville and Prescott, we met with much kindness from Mr. Sherwood, the Sheriff of the district, and had agreeable intercourse with Mr. and Mrs. Smith, of Brockville. After spending a night and part of two days with our worthy friend, the Rev. Mr. Melville, at Spencerville, we reached the ' city of Ottawa,' at two o'clock on Friday, Sept. 16th, where we were met by Mr. Wardrope, and conducted in safety to the ' Manse.' In the absence of Mrs. W., who happened to be on a visit to her relations in Kingston, we met with every attention from Mr. W., while Mr. Durie and other friends shewed us much kindness. The evening of the day of our arrival happened to be the time fixed for a public meeting of the friends of the London Religious Tract Society, and thus we had an opportunity of listening to the eloquent appeals of Dr. Davis, the secretary, and of meeting with ministers of different denominations, and hearing some of them address the meeting. Saturday was in part devoted to a seeing of the falls, and other prominent features of this anticipated capital of the British empire in Canada. The locality presents the complete prestige of a noble city, and if ' Rupert's Land,' in whole or in part, is added to the Canadas, the position of the capital will be at once central and safe.

"On Sabbath the 18th, I preached twice at Ottawa, to fine congregations, in Mr. W.'s church, and once at Nepean, nine miles distant, a branch of Mr. Gourlay's charge. The other branch, Aylmer, I visited on Monday, and in Mr. G.'s absence, Mrs. G. had made such judicious arrangements that an audience of more than one hundred assembled in the Town Hall, and listened attentively to the preaching of the word. After passing a night under the pastor's hospitable roof, we set sail next morning on the Ottawa, and enjoyed a pleasant voyage of fifty miles, interrupted only by three miles of portage by a primitive sort of horse railway. Next day the Presbytery of Ottawa met for the ordination of Mr. Wm. Lochead, to the ministry of Renfrew ; and assuredly it was something new to find here an assemblage of ten ministers of the Presbyterian Church to conduct for the first time the solemn rites of ordination according to the forms of the Presbyterian Church. It was laid on me, as the senior minister, to preach and give the ordination prayer, and Messrs. Mackinnon and Simon Fraser, of McNab, presided ably in the other departments. All was conducted with due solemnity. Indeed, all my experience, whether in the old country or the new, fails to produce an instance of ordination to the ministry conducted with greater external order, and more marked spiritual savour."

"KNOX COLLEGE, 17th Dec., 1863.

"1 spent three Sabbaths in Quebec, and as one of these was the communion season, a pleasing opportunity was presented of holding Christian fellowship with the pastor, office-bearers, and members of Chalmers' Church. Mr. Clark, formerly of Maxwelltown, near Dumfries, Scotland, has been minister of the congregation which meets in this handsome edifice, for more than ten years. The field of labour is an interesting one ; but ministers of Christ placed in the very centre of the stronghold of Popery, have multiplied difficulties to struggle with. The moral atmosphere all around is chilled, while it is surcharged with clouds, heavy and depressing. The love of professing Protestants waxes cold amid the overwhelming obtrusions of an imposing anti-Christian Hierarchy. Our excellent friend feels this, and assuredly he and his people are richly entitled to all the co-operative assistance which the brethren can render them. God forbid that they should sink in despondence ! They grasp the standard of Zion, and they are honoured to display from the Diamond rock a banner, because of the Truth.

"The mission-fields in the neighbourhood of Quebec, are on a limited scale in regard to numbers of Scottish or Presbyterian settlers. The want of a French-speaking Evangelical ministry is felt by all denominations, and the efforts of the Protestant Church are thus necessarily circumscribed almost within the narrow range of its own adherents. With regard to Presbyterian settlements, the following is a list of those I visited, lying at distances from the city varying from nine to thirty miles :—Stoneham—a beautiful pastoral district or valley ; Beauport Lake—a favourite resort of the citizens for sport on the lake, or for a summer residence ; the village of Lorette, where there is a well-known Indian settlement ; and the seigniory of Port Neuf. From our countrymen in all the settlements I received a hearty welcome, and the attendance at the services was, perhaps, as good as from the limited and scattered population, might be expected. In two of these places small churches have lately been erected through the zealous efforts of a pious and single-hearted friend of religion, who, as agent of the Bible Society, has much in his power in the way of facilitating intercourse with these out-posts. At Port Neuf there had been for years a Scottish congregation under a regular pastorship, but circumstances of an adverse nature, in regard to the staple trade of the place, have greatly diminished the resident population.

"On the different occasions of our holding meetings in these places, the audiences respectively numbered from twenty to above a hundred. Small and limited as these localities are, they are important points in the map of Protestantism. There are difficulties in getting them suitably superintended, and visited with sufficient frequency; but they offer ample encouragement to Christian ministers and friends who kindly take an interest in them. With 'the Mother Church,' at Quebec, as the church there may be called, there are connected a goodly number of pious men, office-bearers and others, who are indefatigable in their evangelistic efforts; and while they are led on by the pastor of Chalmers' Church, their labours are countenanced by the occasional visits of Christians of other denominations. A zealous missionary, resident in Quebec, might be the 'episcopal' visitor of each alternately. In winter, no doubt, the state of the roads and the intense cold may interpose serious obstacles, but zeal and a robust constitution, with the blessing of God, will overcome them all. The missionary experience of two years in such a field as this would be a noble preparation for a permanent pastoral charge. Its labours would break a man into all the habits of easy and judicious spiritual toil; and the presence of the Spirit of God would assuredly not be wanting either to him, or to the subjects of his anxious and loving care. This plan has been adopted in years past, and, in all the settlements, there have been found, and will be found, persons in full communion with our Church who may be expected from time to time to embrace the opportunity of joining in fellowship with the church in the city on communion seasons. A spiritual visit paid to one of the settlements by the pastor, during my residence in the city, led to some promising additions to the roll of membership, and was felt in other respects to be a season of refreshing from the presence of the Lord.

"In the programme of arrangements, drawn up for my guidance, two important stations of an outlying description were allotted to me; but the distance and the heat of the weather rendered a plan of interchange absolutely necessary. Application was made to Mr. Crombie, the excellent minister of Inverness, fifty miles distant, to share with me in the duties of the Mission; and, he having readily complied, Mr. Clark cheerfully devoted two Sabbaths and the intervening week to supply for Mr. Crombie at Inverness; devolving on me the charge at Quebec for the same period.

"The worthy people, among whom Mr. Crombie labours, had been visited by me more than ten years ago, when they had not as yet realized the benefits of a regularly settled pastorship. Recollections of that visit led me to desire its repetition; and, on my way from Montreal to Quebec, I had an opportunity of spending two days at the Manse, and of preaching on two several week-days to very encouraging audiences. It was in the very throng of harvest, and yet the people flocked willingly both at noon and in the evening to hear the Gospel. Mr. Clark and I cordially concurred in our estimate of the religious condition of that interesting people. He found the work of God prospering among them. They have lately reared for themselves a handsome brick church, ornamented with a tower, and filled from Sabbath to Sabbath with a large and affectionate congregation.

"In a spacious school-house at 'Wolfe's Cove,' belonging to Mr. Gilmour, the great Quebec merchant, I had an opportunity of preaching on two week-evenings, to small but attentive audiences. The occasional local preaching here is kept up by brethren of different denominations. At St. Foye, two miles from the city, but almost a suburb of it, I had an opportunity of addressing a crowded meeting in the district school-house.

"My visit to the city brought me in contact with a considerable number of Christian friends, office-bearers of the church, and others, many of whom I had known of old, and with whom renewed intercourse was at once sweet and profitable. In a city where formality and will-worship predominate it is the duty of all pious Protestants to love one another, and to strive together for the faith of the Gospel. It is now thirty years since my correspondence with Christian friends in that city commenced, and on the subject, ever dear to them, of colonial evangelization. Twenty years have well nigh elapsed since I paid my first visit to the 'historic capital.'"

"TORONTO, September, 1867.

"In the Autumn of 1864 I had spent three weeks and as many Sabbaths in the parts of our Province which lie on the great Huron Lake, and although it was but a limited portion of that territory I could visit, I saw enough to fill me with astonishment at the great physical and moral changes in the district, from 1847 when I first saw it as one unbroken forest, to the time when the same district rose to my view with its millions of acres 'all taken up ;' Lowlanders and Celts in hundreds, yea thousands, settled peaceably and comfortably along road-lines judiciously marked out ; and schools and churches provided to an extent that augured well. My visits to my brethren and friends three years ago were fresh in my memory, and the names St. Helen's, Kinloss, Kincardine, Tiverton, Greenock, Paisley, Southampton, Elgin and North Bruce, had taken familiar and firm hold of me, and gathered around them a multitude of sincere good wishes ; when in the course of events a second opportunity of a visit opened to me. It was readily embraced ; and with the exception of Paisley and Southampton and St. Helen's, the localities already named were re-visited, and successful progress marked. In particular, I found that Kincardine had obtained the services of an able minister in both tongues, Mr. Fraser, formerly of Thamesford ; and that a number of excellent

men, principally from our own college, have been added to the list
of pious pastors. The celebration of communion at Kincardine, and
North Bruce, with the to me, a Lowlander, somewhat rare accompaniment of ' the speaking to the question,' on Friday, brought
to mind what I had seen years ago in Glengarry, and what I had
often heard of at home but never witnessed. At Kincardine the
church, which has been greatly enlarged since 1864, and the 'grove'
adjacent, were both occupied on the week-days and on the Sabbath of
the solemn occasion. The number of attendants in all could not be
much below 2,000. The tables spread, with their pure white coverings, under the canopy of heaven ; the powerful appeals of men in
real earnest, and which were conveyed to listening multitudes in a
language which distance of removal from its native haunts rendered even more touching ; mingling too with the vocal strains of the
wild but sweet Gaelic melodies ; these all blended together could not
but produce a deep and hallowed impression. It was a matter of
deep regret to me that want of time and other causes put it out
of my power to visit, as I wished, my friends at Paisley, Southampton, and Egmondville. My previously-fixed visit to Illinois was
pressing upon me ; and the arrangements for it admitted of no
change.

" It was on Thursday, August 1st, we set out for Chicago, by the
Great Western Railway. We stopped that night at London, in the
hospitable mansion of Mr. and Mrs. Chisholm, whose kind attentions now as before will never fade from our remembrance. From
Detroit to Chicago the distance is 280 miles, and the ' Michigan
Central' with its comfortable 'Pullman' dormitories, brought us in
safety to that large and rapidly growing city. The surface of the
prairies is peculiarly favourable to railway travelling, and all my
journeys through Michigan and Illinois, to and from Chicago, have
been accomplished, through the kind providence of God, without
any untoward incident.

" Till 1830, Chicago was known only as a depot for Indian furs,
and as a military post for two companies of the American army.
For fifteen years after it began its rapid rise, its position on the
prairies of Illinois and at the southern end of Lake Michigan was
anything but inviting. Nevertheless, during twenty years past, it
has grown with amazing rapidity till its inhabitants are estimated
at 230,000. It is now the acknowledged metropolis of the vast
North-West. It is the great thoroughfare of produce from all the
seven Prairie States, and particularly of corn and cattle of all kinds.
Its streets are wide, well built and paved. Its 'Wabash' and
'Michigan' avenues, the former four miles in length, are superior
to anything in the older cities of the Eastern States. Its manufactories in machinery of all kinds, clocks and watches, and in musical
instruments of different names, are on a great scale. Its ingenious
contrivance for obtaining an ample supply of pure water from the
lake, has been executed within three years, and at the expense

of one million dollars. Its system of ordinary and grammar-school education is most complete ; and its colleges for the higher branches of education are established on the best principles. I had the pleasure of being present at the opening of the Presbyterian Seminary of Theology, on the 5th of September, when an excellent lecture was delivered by the Professor of Exegetics, Dr. Halsey. The other Professors, Drs. Lord and Elliot are well associated with Dr. H. as men of learning, ability and worth. This seminary is the fourth institution of the kind belonging to the Old School Presbyterian body ; but the other branches of the Protestant Church, whether Presbyterian, Congregational, Methodist or Baptist, are all provided with admirably appointed seminaries ; and it was to my mind peculiarly refreshing to find all the larger distributors of knowledge, whether literary or religious, under a decidedly Christian influence.

" The population of the city, as already stated, is estimated at 230,(00, and constantly increasing. The number of churches, including all the places that are set apart for the worship of God,and also four Jewish synagogues, amount to about 120. Of the Christian denominations, the Methodists and Baptists, under varied modifying designations, are perhaps the largest in point of numbers ; but Episcopalians, Presbyterians, and Congregationalists, have each a fair proportion of the inhabitants. Presbyterianism, embracing the Old and New Schools, the United Presbyterians, the Dutch Reformed, the Scotch and the Welsh churches, with a few European sects of the same type, claims twenty-four congregations of greater or less extent. All this looks favourably ; but when we come to the question of actual attendance on the public worship of God, the report to be given is any thing but pleasing. I have heard the number of church attendants estimated at an average of seventeen thousand ; and well-informed persons assured me that this was an estimate too high. There are large masses of citizens to whom the habit of regular church-going is a stranger. The German population exceeds sixty thousand, and among the professed adherents of both the Roman Catholic and Lutheran communions, the evidence is too marked and palpable that the day of the Lord is fearfully profaned. That sacred season seems to be given up by large multitudes to the varied forms of sinful indulgence and pleasurable amusement. The friends of the Sabbath, in and around the city, have lifted up a noble protest against prevalent abuses of this nature ; but alas ! the enemies of the Sabbath have congregated in larger assemblies on the other side, and secular interests of a local and political character stand greatly in the way of a faithful execution of the statutes of public law on this vitally important matter. It is, however, a favourable symptom that the friends of evangelical truth are becoming more and more united among themselves, and more generally alive to the necessity and duty of combined and prayerful effort on the side of truth and of godliness.

" Amidst much that is flagrantly immoral and wicked in this great city, I believe that in regard to active, energetic, and united zeal and Christian effort, Chicago will bear a favourable comparison with the other large cities of the Union.   The formation of moral and religious character in a rapidly increasing community, becomes a subject of befitting thought to all good men ; and in this city the measure of the forms of Christian energy is truly gratifying to the moral observer.   A large and united branch of godly ministers ; a well conducted religious press, though as yet on a limited scale ; a compact and well-arranged system of Sabbath schools ; young men's associations for the mental and spiritual benefit of that vital portion of the community ; daily meetings for prayer and religious conference ; these and similar agencies are all at work in a humble but determined spirit, and under judicious superintendence. Among leaders in such goodly undertakings, the name of Mr. Moody deserves honourable and grateful notice ; and he is surrounded by a goodly band of faithful coadjutors, both clerical and lay.

" There are understood to be in Chicago at least ten thousand Scotchmen and Canadians, and so far as religion has any concern in the matter, they are more or less attached to the forms and usages of Presbyterianism.   Earnest and untrammelled Calvinistic preaching ; the regular habit of pastoral household visitation ; the simple celebration of the ordinance of the Supper with accompanying week-day services ; standing in public prayer ; vocal and congregational singing of the praises of God ; and the regular though not exclusive use of the authorized metrical version of the Psalms ; these are the understood features of Scottish Presbyterianism ; and many pious persons in Chicago felt the want of such a thing ; while they also longed for a faithful ministerial superintendence that might gather in wanderers, and seek after those other Scotch and Irish Protestants for whose spiritual interests no one seemed to care.   Hence originated ' the first Scotch Church' in Chicago.   On application to the Canada Presbyterian Church a supply of ministers has for some years past been regularly sent them, chiefly through the kind offices of the Presbytery of London ; and in March last, my son, formerly of Kingston and St. Catharines, was inducted into the charge.   In July last a suitable piece of ground in a central part of the city was purchased ; and within less than two months a goodly fabric has been reared, the first flat of which, raised six feet above the ground was so constructed as to make a commodious place of meeting for 500 persons.   It was opened on the first Sabbath of September ; when three public services were engaged in and all largely attended.   It fell to me to take the larger portion of the work on the auspicious occasion ; but the Rev. Mr. Bradford, of the United Presbyterian Church, and the pastor himself, took part in the services ; on the Tuesday following a social religious meeting was held, when ministers of various denomina-

W

tions, and several distinguished citizens, made suitable addresses ; the collections altogether, on occasion of the opening, being to the amount of one thousand dollars. It is expected that from the commendable liberality of the members and other friends, the church, when finished, will not labour under the burden of a heavy debt.

"At the distance of 140 miles from Chicago, and at about seven from Kewanee, a rising business village on the Burlington railway, a scattered, but beautiful prairie settlement, meets the eye. That is Elmira, where from twenty-five to thirty Scotch families reside ; mostly from the Highlands and islands of Scotland from fifteen to twenty years ago ; and the greater part understanding their native tongue far better than the acquired Saxon, which only few have arrived at. For the sake of their children, however, and the neighbouring settlers, English is as necessary as Gaelic in the minister who may be sent to them. They have asked and received acceptable supplies from the Canada Presbyterian Church, and mainly by the kind offices of the Presbytery of London. I spent nearly a week among these worthy settlers, having public worship for four days in succession largely attended ; and on the intervening Lord's day the holy communion was dispensed to forty communicants. The people are all in comfortable circumstances, and well able to support a fixed ministry, but determined to have none but from the Canada Presbyterian Church. I found here Mr. John Macnab, the worthy representative of a 'regular apostolic succession' of pious Celtic brethren from our church ; and by this time he will be succeeded by Mr. Alexander Mackay, of Tiverton, one of my esteemed Huron brethren. Of no other 'living branch' of the original Celtic Church in the States could I hear ; but several Gaelic families at a distance expressed to me their desire to choose Elmira as the place of their future abode, provided only they could there enjoy the glorious Gospel in the language which no distance of time or place renders less dear to their hearts. The good folks of Elmira have already built a nice church and manse, and the future occupant of these, presuming on his being a man of the 'right kind,' will soon find himself placed in a most desirable sphere of growing usefulness.

"About sixty miles south of Elmira, and within thirty of the great Mississippi, I had the pleasure of spending two days with Dr. Wallace, the President of Monmouth College, a literary institution recently established in connexion with the United Presbyterian Church of the States, or at least under their superintendence, and attended by upwards of three hundred students ; and, what is rather uncommon, both sexes are admitted to the benefits of the prelections under very judicious rules. There is also a theological seminary in the same place, and in the same connexion. From all I saw and heard of these institutions, and of the men who have the charge of them, I am led to entertain a very high opinion of their literary and theological character. It is seventeen years since I became acquainted with Dr. Pressly, the venerable head of the older school of theology at Pittsburg, in the same ecclesiastical connexion.   Some things have recently occurred in their synodical proceedings and otherways, which lead me to hope, that by some modifications that involve no sacrifice of principle, the way may be opened for a closer fellowship between us, and that elder branch of the once undivided Presbyterian Church of Scotland and of Ireland.

"On my way back from Monmouth and Elmira, I stopped two nights on a visit of sympathy to the Rev. Mr. Ebbs, formerly of Paris, now of Aurora, a beautiful rising town of 12,000 inhabitants.   Mr. Ebbs is a faithful and acceptable minister of the Congregational Church, and it has pleased God to visit him lately with a very distressing domestic trial in the loss of his only son who was drowned while bathing ; a most promising young man. I also, when in the city, paid two visits to our worthy friend Mr. Duncan, formerly of Perth, now at Evanston, a peculiarly attractive sphere of pastoral usefulness, twelve miles from Chicago, on the banks of the lake.   In other instances, my visit to Chicago, and to the lovely prairies of Illinois, revived the acquaintanceships of other years, leaving on my mind impressions salutary and sweet."

CHAPTER XVIII.

T is not ours to assume the part of the Historian, yet it seems a suitable sequel to the record of Dr. Burns' labours, to say something respecting the earlier History of Presbyterianism in the region which formed their more immediate scene.

The Rev. George Henry is the first Presbyterian minister of whose ministry in Canada we can find any record. Retiring from the post of military chaplain, he settled in Quebec six years after the transference of the Province to British rule, and from 1765 till 1784 he discharged the duties of his office in full. He died on the 6th July, 1795, at the advanced age of eighty-six. For several years previously he had been assisted by the Rev. Alexander Spark, an alumnus of Aberdeen University, who came to Quebec in 1780, in the capacity of tutor, was ordained in 1784, received from his *Alma Mater* the degree of D.D. in 1804, and died in 1809.

Dr. James Harkness, from Sanquhar, having been ordained by the Presbytery of Ayr in March, 1820, ministered in Quebec for fifteen years—a man of peculiar idiosyncracies, whose successor was the present distinguished incumbent of St. Andrew's Church, the Rev. John Cook, D.D.

The Rev. John Bethune having retired from the chaplaincy of the 84th Regiment, held the first Presbyterian service, in Montreal, on the 12th March, 1780. He removed to Williamstown, Glengarry, in May, 1787, where, after eighteen years of faithful service, he died on the 23rd September, 1815. The present Episcopal Dean of Montreal, and Bishop of Toronto, were among his sons. He was succeeded in Montreal by the Rev. John Young, from Perth, Scotland, who laboured from 1791 till his removal to Niagara (then Newark) in 1802. The Lord's Supper was first administered by him in Montreal, according to the Presbyterian form, on the 18th September, 1791—within the *Recollet Roman Catholic Church.* The Recollet Fathers refused any pecuniary compensation from the "Society of Presbyterians" for the use of their building. Two hogsheads of Spanish wine, containing sixty odd gallons each, and a box of candles, amounting in all to £14 2s. 4d., were subsequently donated, and gratefully received. The first Presbyterian church, the venerable St. Gabriel, which still stands, was opened on the 7th October, 1792. On the 18th September, 1803, the Rev. James Somerville, of the Scotch Relief Church, succeeded Mr. Young in the pastorate of this church. On the day preceding, the first Presbytery of which any record remains, was convened.

"Montreal, 17th September, 1803, the former Presbytery of Montreal having been, by unfortunate circumstances, dissolved, the Rev. Mr. John Bethune, minister of the Gospel at Glengarry, Upper Canada, formerly a member of said Presbytery, and the Rev. Alexander Spark, minister of the Gospel at Quebec, conceiving that it would be for the good of religion to form a connection and constitute themselves into a Presbytery, did accordingly meet at Montreal this Seventeenth of September, in the Year of our Lord, One Thousand Eight Hundred and Three, and, after prayer, the said ministers, together with Mr. Duncan Fisher, Elder, took their seats. The Rev. Mr. John Bethune was chosen Moderator, the Rev. Mr. Alex. Spark, Clerk. Absent, the Elder from Glengarry and the Elder from Quebec. The Presbytery agreed that they shall be known and addressed by the name and style of the Presbytery of Montreal."

The "former Presbytery," whose records were lost, must have been composed of Messrs. Bethune, Spark, and Young, together with their Elders. Nor are there any records of this second Presbytery save the one quoted.

Certain parties seceded from St. Gabriel Street church in 1803, under the Rev. Robert Forrest, the germ of the present St. Andrew's church. Mr. Forrest left for New York the same year, and was succeeded in 1804 by the Rev. Robert Easton, from Roxburghshire, who was suddenly cut off in 1824. In 1817 the Rev. Henry Esson, afterwards the accomplished Professor in Knox College, became assistant and successor to Mr. Somerville, who died in 1837, leaving £1,000 for a Manse to St. Gabriel Street church, and the same amount to the Natural History Society of Montreal.

Dr. Edward Black, who arrived in Montreal in 1822, was associated with Mr. Esson till 1831, when St. Paul's congregation was formed under his pastoral oversight.

In 1798, the Classis, of Albany, of the Dutch Reformed Church, sent the Rev. Robert McDowall to labour in Canada. He proved a zealous and devoted missionary for over forty years, dying in 1841, at Fredericksburg. His widow I distinctly remember. One of his sons belonged to my church, in Kingston. Mr. Gordon, of Gananoque, writes thus of him—

"I was very intimate with Mr. McDowall, of Fredericksburg, who was sent to Canada by the Dutch Reformed Church, U. S., in compliance with an application from Canada for Christian labourers, at a time that there were so few of such as the applicants wanted, (they, as I understand, being Presbyterians,) or indeed of ministers of other bodies ; and in our confidential conversations he told me that his missionary labours stretched from Quebec, and below it, I think, eastward, and Toronto, then 'Little York,' and a small insignificant place, and beyond westward. He told me that he had much acquaintance and personal intercourse with Governor Hunter, I think he said the first Governor sent to Canada, whom he spoke of very favourably, and that if he, Mr. M., had changed his church and become Episcopalian, the Governor's influence was all in his favour. But Mr. M. was of that single-eyed, single-hearted character that no temptations of a worldly nature could weigh with him against higher and more sacred considerations. Mr. M.'s heart was always set upon Presbyterian Union on a right basis.

"I had much enjoyment in a preaching tour with this devoted servant of Christ in autumn, nearing to winter, 1837, the year that our Canadian Rebellion broke out. We preached in the evenings either in the same school-house or near to each other, and lodged with some of this venerable, loveable man's old friends for the night, and I remember a laughable incident that one night occurred. A man who kept a tavern, about eight miles west of Kingston (Tictch, I think, was his name), and whose loyalty to Queen Victoria had been brought into suspicion, tried some shifts to redeem it. Instructions had just at that time gone out from Government to have a keen eye upon travellers passing through the country, as it was thought that spies of the pseudo patriots, who soon after this made an incursion into Canada, were out on their mischievous errands. Well, I was riding on a light, beautiful and spirited horse, lent me by my much esteemed friend, Colin Macdonald,

brother to the Hon. John S. Macdonald, whom you knew so well, as
a suitable servant for moving about with Mr. McDowall. I had
stopped at this man's inn to bait the horse, and as I wished to look
over my notes for the evening's sermon, I said very little to the
host beyond what business required, and retired during the feeding to a room.   But this zealous loyalist had on my departure
straightway gone to Mr. Fraser, Mr. M.'s particular friend, and a
Magistrate, to give him a description of all about the visible outward personality, of such minuteness as could identify, and make it
safe to get a warrant to lodge the suspected spy in any of Her
Majesty's jails.   Size, the peculiar fitness of the horse, the valise
strapped behind it, the light-weight rider on it, all so peculiarly
adapted for flight and escape, if required.   Above all, the dark
treasonous taciturnity that could not look honest men in the face.
So well had this informant—so to the life—described the suspected
person's outward personality, with a view to unmistakeable identification, that when Mr. M. at night introduced me to Mr. Fraser, the
real so exactly answered to the person previously described, that
Mr. Fraser had enough to do to refrain from a good loud laugh as
the salutation."

The Session Records of Niagara, which date from 1st
October, 1794, tell of the Rev. John Dunn, a licentiate of
the Presbytery of Glasgow, coming over from Albany,
where he had ministered for some time.   For two years
he laboured in Stamford and Niagara, then left the ministry and became a merchant in the latter place.   In 1803,
he perished with all on board the *Speedy*, a vessel carrying ten guns, which foundered in Lake Ontario.   Mr.
Dunn was succeeded by the Rev. John Young, who came
to Niagara from Montreal, where he had briefly laboured.
He remained from 1802 till 1804, when the Rev. John
Burns, a Scotch Secession minister, father of Judge Burns,
arrived from the State of New York.   He preached every
third Sabbath in Niagara till 1812, when the second
American War broke out, and the town was reduced to
ashes.   He resumed in 1815, combining with the Pastorate the charge of the District School, till his death, in

1844. Mr. Thomas Creen, from the North of Ireland, succeeded him, who soon after became Episcopal Rector of the place. In 1827, the Rev. Thomas Fraser, of the Relief Church, Dalkeith, Scotland, now residing in Móntreal (a vigorous preacher still), fulfilled a brief ministry in the old town, followed in 1829 by the Rev. Robert McGill, from Ayrshire, who remained sixteen years. In the old Niagara district laboured long and faithfully "Father Eastman," as he was generally called. He came into the Province from the United States in 1799 or 1800, and planted "seven churches," most of which remain until this present. We remember him well—his erect gait, and springy step, and ringing voice, and warm hand-clasp— though when we knew him he was totally blind. We joined with some of his spiritual children in laying him in one of the quiet churchyards he had marked out, when, "an old man and full of years, he was gathered to his Fathers."

In 1808 or 1809, Mr. William Smart was under training for missionary service in the West Indies, at Gosport, within whose useful institute many hopeful youth were being brought up at the feet of the venerable Bogue. A petition came from the people of Brockville for a minister, addressed to the London Missionary Society. Mr. Smart, feeling that his own countrymen had claims, at least equal to the heathen, gave a favourable answer. He was ordained in London, " to the work of the ministry, in Elizabethtown, U. C.," and commenced labouring in Brockville in 1811. He planted the first Sabbath School in Canada. He formed the first Bible Society in the Province in 1817 —the first Missionary Society in 1818, and the first Reli-

gious Tract Society in 1820. Mr. Smart's field of labour
stretched from Gananoque to Osnabruck, from ninety to
one hundred miles in length—to Bastard (twenty-five
miles) and South Gower (thirty-five miles) in rear of the
St. Lawrence. In all Upper Canada there were but two
Presbyterian ministers when he came—Mr. Bethune and
Mr. McDowall. In concert with Dr. Boyd, who arrived
subsequently, he had to do with the planting of Presbyterianism in fourteen different places, all of which have
now buildings of stone. He preached the first sermon in
Perth, with an unfinished store for his church, and a flour
barrel for his desk. Returning from a missionary tour in
1812, after the breaking out of the second American War,
a stray, spent twelve-pounder passed over the neck of Mr.
Smart's horse, fell near the fence, sank in and ploughed
up the ground. Mr. Smart can look back over sixty years
of honourable service; nor yet is his eye dim, or his
natural force materially abated. Dr. Boyd, from Ireland,
ordained in 1821, has recently died on a field signal-
ized by the indefatigable labours of half a century. The
Rev. William Bell, in 1817, followed the emigrants from
Lanark and Renfrewshires, who had settled in the Perth
district the year before. He sailed on the 5th April, and,
" after fifty-seven days of horrors," reached Quebec. He
took twenty-four days to travel between that city and Perth.
Eight days were spent between Montreal and Prescott, with
batteaux, oxen, and horses. From Brockville he walked
most of the way. His first house consisted of log walls,
a roof, and a floor of loose split basswood logs over a pool of
stagnant water. The closeness of the floor may be under-

ʌtood from the fact that one day one of the children fell through, and was, with some difficulty, rescued from drowning. There were no partitions. No furniture could possibly be had. Dr. Thom gave him two boards, from which he made a table. His pastoral visitation lay through stumps and swamps, over fences and fords, mid broiling suns and swarming mosquitoes—fourteen miles at a time along blazed tracks, with the occasional howl of the wolf and hiss of the serpent; lodging in wretched hovels, sometimes upset from canoes to the danger of drowning, and, when escaping, having no opportunity of getting wet clothes changed.

Over a shocking road he has to travel on foot forty-two miles to Brockville, to get leave to perform marriage, but, opposed on technical grounds by High Church officials, he has to trudge back, and return on foot three months after to the Quarter Sessions, accompanied by seven members of his church. He collects money for a school-house, which he occupies as a church. An Episcopal clergyman comes to the settlement. He is unceremoniously ordered to give up the school to him. He resists for a time, but at last gives it up, observing in his Journal: *" It is not safe living in Rome and falling out with the Pope."* He is brought into court and fined heavily for trying to put down Sabbath desecration. The proxies of drunken parents demand " christening " for a child. On being refused, they go off in high dudgeon to a Roman Catholic priest, who goes through the ceremony, for half a dollar, in French, of which they were entirely ignorant. The enraged father complains to a magistrate, and next morning, after a dreadful night of cold, is found stretched on the snow a stiffened corpse.

Mr. Bell's MS. Journals, which are very copious and numerous, contain many similar incidents, with records of journeys to Presbytery meetings, requiring from four to six days to reach the place of meeting, perhaps two days being spent in travelling on foot, and the remainder by means of horseback, riding waggon, small boat, or sleigh, as the case may be.*

About the same time the Rev. Joseph Johnston, from Ireland, laboured in Cornwall, teaching also the district school, and was succeeded, in 1822, by the Rev. Harry Leith, who held the same plurality till translated, in December, 1826, to Rothiemay, Aberdeenshire, when Dr. Hugh Urquhart, who had arrived in the country in 1822, came into the post, from which death has just removed him.

In 1818, the Rev. Hugh Kirkland, and in 1820, the Rev. William Brunton, laboured at Lachine, and, for five years, from 1821 till 1826, when he was cut off in his prime, Kingston enjoyed a ministry of much promise under the Rev. John Barclay. The Rev. James Harris, from Ireland, was the first planter of Presbyterianism in Toronto.†

The name of Jenkins must be joined with the honoured names of Bethune, Bell, McDowall, Eastman, and Smart, and others who, in the early period of our country's history, served as Presbyterian pioneers.

"Father" Jenkins, when labouring as a missionary among the Oneida Indians, in New York State, was in-

* See in Appendix II. some interesting extracts from the journals of this venerable man, kindly furnished me by his excellent son, the Rev. Dr. George Bell, of Clifton.
† See valuable memorabilia of Mr. Harris in Appendix I.

duced to visit Scarboro', in 1820, a township which began
to be settled by emigrants from the south of Scotland in
1799. His field embraced the Townships of York, Mark-
ham, Vaughan and Scarboro'. The Rev. James Harris,
whose fatherly address as Moderator of the Presbytery of
Toronto, on my receiving license, I will never forget,
thus writes me with reference to Mr. Jenkins:—

" With respect to Father Jenkins, I became acquainted with him
in the fall of 1820, a short time after my arrival in the town of
York, and for many years maintained uninterrupted ministerial
communion with him. He was a zealous and indefatigable labourer
in the Master's cause. Not unfrequently I accompanied him to
some of the recently-formed townships north of Toronto, conversing with, and preaching the Gospel of Christ to many poor and
destitute settlers, organizing congregations, and occasionally dispensing the Lord's Supper. Such visits were always cordially welcomed."*

The Rev. Arch. Henderson, who was ordained in 1810,
came out to Canada in July, 1818. He belonged to the Associate Synod in Scotland. An excellent preacher, and a
faithful labourer he has proved, to whom I am indebted
for some interesting facts in connection with the early
history of our church in the East. Father of our church,
moderator of our presbytery, and now over eighty-six, he
brings forth fruit in old age.

He describes the rise of our church in Montreal and
Quebec, the ministers who came over with Dr. Mason, of
New York, and the planting of Presbyterianism at Lachute, where some dissentients from the original congregation applied to the Kirk.

The Rev. John McKenzie, in 1818, succeeded the

---

* A certain dignitary who, ecclesiastically, had forgotten his first love, meeting Father
Jenkins, remarked the threadbareness of his coat. Caustically, yet courteously, the old
gentleman replied, " At any rate, I thank God it isn't a *turncoat!*"

venerable Mr. Bethune, at Williamstown, and was the Moderator of the first Canadian Synod. It was held in St. Andrew's Church, Kingston, in 1831, from June 8th to 13th inclusive, and was attended by fifteen ministers, four elders, and five commissioners. The Synod agreed to a division of the church into four presbyteries, viz., the Presbytery of Quebec, six ministers; Glengarry, four ministers; Bathurst, four ministers; and York five ministers.*

Besides the Rev. Wm. Rintoul, M.A., who had a few days previously arrived at Toronto (then York), we find west of that city, belonging to the Church of Scotland, but these four names, Alexander Gale, M. A., Amherstburg; George Shedd, M. A., Ancaster; Alexander Ross, Aldborough; Robert McGill, Niagara.

A few extracts from letters of an early Paisley emigrant, addressed to his father, who used regularly to show them to Dr. Burns, and to copy off portions, may supply glimpses of the early religious condition of Canada, and of the influences which drew out his sympathetic nature towards these distant and destitute settlements :

"BROCKVILLE, UPPER CANADA,
"18th June, 1820.

"When we landed at Montreal the first thing that struck our attention, being the Sabbath, was the whole shore covered with people fishing, and the market place covered with stands of different kinds of goods, just the same as it had been a fair day, and in the neighbourhood of the town numerous parties going about with guns, or amusing themselves with playing at the ball."

---

* After lengthened and mature deliberation, it was unanimously resolved—
"That this Convention of Ministers and Elders, in connection with the Church of Scotland, representing their respective congregations, do form themselves into a Synod, to be called the Synod of the Presbyterian Church of Canada, leaving it to the venerable the General Assembly to determine the particular nature of that connection which shall subsist between this Synod and the General Assembly of the Church of Scotland."
The Rev. John McKenzie was chosen Moderator of the Synod, and the Rev. Robert McGill, Clerk.

"York, 18th Sept., 1820.

" I think that religion is at a low ebb in this country. There are very few churches in it, and the inhabitants in general are very depraved. It is not unusual to see them working in their fields on the Sabbath day, or going out a shooting. The law does not appear to interfere with them, and therefore they do what they please on that day."

"Caledon, 10th Sept., 1823.

" You wish to know how we spend the Sabbath in Caledon. I have therefore to inform you that I and a number of the emigrants assemble at eleven o'clock, forenoon, in the house of J. M. The service in which we then engage commences with prayer and praise ; a chapter of the Bible is read, then one of Burder's village sermons, which you gave me when I came away, is next read. After this the children are catechised, and the service concludes as it began, with prayer and praise. I am much obliged to you for the tracts and other useful pamphlets you have sent me, for they are agreeable company to me here in the woods."

"Caledon, 27th June, 1826.

" You mentioned in a letter lately sent, that a society has been established amongst you for sending out ministers and teachers to the British Colonies. I heard a sermon preached about seven weeks ago, and with the exception of that opportunity, I have not heard a sermon for the last seventeen months.

" When the news of the establishment first reached us, Mr. S. came to Caledon and called a few of the settlers together, to see what means could be adopted to get a pastor, through means of the society, when it was resolved that Mr. S. should write to the Rev. Mr. Burns, Secretary of the Society, and to inform him of our situation, and I should write to you, so far to corroborate his statement, which I accordingly did. Among other things, I mentioned that the minister would have to preach to three townships, viz. : Esquesing, Erin and Caledon. I also mentioned that the population of Caledon consisted of eighty families, chiefly Presbyterians, and that the population in Erin was nearly the same, and the number of families in Esquesing to several hundreds, and you were requested to converse with Mr. Burns on the subject."

"Caledon, 1st March, 1827.

" We are as yet deprived of the privilege of hearing the gospel regularly preached. We have, however, been lately favoured with a sermon, once a month, by a Methodist missionary, who preaches to us every fourth Sabbath, in the house of John McDonald, jun.

We are now deprived of the labours of Mr. Redpath,* of whom I gave some account in a letter I wrote to you last January. He was a man of small stature, and of a delicate constitution, while to have undergone the fatigue which he underwent in spreading the glad tidings of salvation, would have required a strong and robust frame, and indeed one of the best of constitutions. So wide was the circuit in which he itinerated, that he could only give us a sermon once in three months. All his journeys he performed on foot, and though the roads were at some seasons of the year nearly impassable, yet a word of murmuring or complaint he never uttered, but endured all his privations and hardships with manly fortitude. He was always cheerful, and when once asked, 'How it was possible he could get along, the roads being so bad?' He smiled, and replied 'that they were broad enough, and when a place impassable came in his way, he could go round a little space in the woods. After having itinerated in this manner for a number of years, he at last sunk under his labours and extreme fatigue, and died in Yonge Street; and, from all accounts I have heard, of extreme exhaustion. When on his last circuit he did not intimate his appointments as he used to do, and when last here, when urged to do so, he replied, 'Some time after harvest,' and we were therefore daily expecting him, when we heard of his death. You will not, therefore, be surprised when I inform you that the tidings affected us greatly, as we were deprived of the labours of the only minister, who for a long time had come amongst us. The last sermon he preached was from a passage in the 21st chapter of Revelation, on the beauties of the New Jerusalem, which I was informed was on the day immediately preceding his death."

"CALEDON, 10th Oct., 1828.

" We are still as badly off as ever with regard to the preaching of the Gospel. I have only heard five or six sermons since I last wrote you. All of these, excepting one, were by Methodists, and that one was by a Baptist.

" Several new sects have arisen in the province of late, spreading erroneous doctrines among the ignorant. One of these sects call themselves *Christians*, and their religion is a compound of the tenets of several others. Amongst their other errors they deny the divinity of Jesus Christ, and they are said to be gaining ground in the country. Another sect, calling themselves Dunkards, wear long beards. A person of the name of Wilson has started in Yonge Street, as a leader of a new sect, consisting chiefly of females. Their doctrine and mode of worship I am ignorant of; but I understand that their progress has caused separation to take place in several instances betwixt husbands and wives."

Mr. Redpath was (we believe) a devoted Congregational minister.

The following extract is written by a friend of Mr. C., dated

"ANCASTER, 19th Nov., 1829.

"I saw at York the other day a minister sent out by a Glasgow Association to Niagara. He has given great satisfaction since he came to this country. We much want such men as Mr. McGill. Our Sabbath day is not generally spent as it should be. The religious and moral condition of this people is lamentable; but our wants begin to be known, and we may hope that things will not remain long as they are in this particular."

Mr. C.'s letters continue:

"CALEDON, 5th July, 1830.

"I received a letter lately from a Mr. Carruthers, informing me that he had written to Dr. Burns, Secretary of the North American Colonial Society, proposing an extended scheme of Sabbath school usefulness under their patronage, and that he had offered himself as a travelling catechist for planting, organizing, and strengthening Sabbath school instruction, and I consider him a person well qualified for that office. If the proposed measure should obtain the sanction of that society, I think it might be productive of much good, as it might be the means of establishing Sabbath schools in many places, where there are at present none, and of stirring up those that have already been established to more diligence; and it is probable that they might supply the schools with religious tracts, of which we stand in great need. Will you be so good as recommend this to Dr. Burns, or any of the members of the society with whom you may be acquainted."

"CALEDON, June 11th, 1831.

"In the latter end of April last we gave the Rev. Duncan McMillan a call, which was accepted of, and he was ordained on the 26th of last month. The Rev. Mr. Harris, of York, made the introductory prayer; the Rev. Mr. Ferguson, of West Gwillimbury, preached the ordination sermon from 2 Cor. iv. 7: 'But we have this treasure in earthen vessels,' &c. The Rev. Mr. King, of Nelson, put the questions to Mr. McM. in the usual form; the Rev. Mr. Jenkins, of Yonge street, offered the consecrationary prayer; the Rev. Mr. Eastman, from the head of the lake, delivered the charge; and the Rev. A. Bell, of Toronto, addressed the congregation in a very impressive manner. The place of ordination was about thirteen miles from Caledon. It was a fine day, and a good many went from this neighbourhood, as well as from the neighbouring townships. It was indeed a very interesting scene. There were a great many wet eyes in the congregation, and some of the clergymen were also observed shedding tears. That prophecy was then fulfilled in its most important sense, 'The wilderness shall blossom as the rose,' &c. In this place, where lately nothing was

X

heard but the howling of wolves and the raging of the elements, is now heard the joyful sound of salvation ; and where the Indians lately bowed to their imaginary gods, the ambassadors of Jesus Christ proclaim the triumphs of His cross."

It was amid such antecedents and surroundings that the Glasgow Colonial Society was formed. How it fulfilled its mission we have already seen. In 1826, soon after its formation, Dr. Mathieson, of St. Andrew's Church, Montreal, thus eloquently pleads for the land to which he had recently come, in a characteristic epistle :

"The settlers in Canada are chiefly Scotchmen ; and, do not think that the rigour of our winters chills the warm feelings which characterise our countrymen '*at home.*' Distance from 'our dear own native land' but fans our native ardour, and makes to cling to us more tenaciously all the sturdy but honest prejudices of Scotchmen.

"The language of. the captive Jews by the rivers of Babylon is the language of many of your countrymen by the rivers of Canada, when they think on the religious services in which they were accustomed to join with their fathers : ' If I forget thee, O Jerusalem, let my right hand forget her cunning. If I do not remember thee, let my tongue cleave to the roof of my mouth.' Often does '*their home*,' with all its associations rush upon their recollection. The cottage where they first received a father's blessing and shared in a mother's care ; the fireside group, where

'The sire turns o'er, wi' patriarchal grace,
The big ha' bible ;'

the country church, half hid among the trees, whither they were early taught by pious care to turn their steps ; and the simple and the sublime worship in which there they joined—all recur, and place at the disposal of a skilful minister of our church a power which he might wield to the noblest purposes.

" But let this generation pass away, and nothing be done to keep alive religious feeling and preserve religious knowledge, and it is clear this advantage must be lost. The rising generation will grow up in comparative ignorance, and devoid of those impressions that public ordinances are calculated to make on the mind, and will present an untractable material both to the philanthropist and the teaching of religion. May God and the General Assembly and our gracious King avert the evils which are likely to flow from such a state of society. Many of these are Highlanders, whose sentiments may be expressed generally in the words of one of their number that I met with lately at the Sacrament in Glengarry : ' I came into these woods, where the foot of a minister of the gospel had never been. I prayed that I might see *one* minister of this persuasion, in which I was brought up, settled amongst us. I saw that. I prayed for another ; thought another would do much good ; the labour was too much for one. I saw another,—but so happy a day as this I never expected to see in Canada,—five ministers of the Kirk of Scotland in Glengarry !'

" It is said of us that we are all very apt to become Episcopalians when we come to this side of the Atlantic. This may be true with respect to some of our *big folk* who wish to be fashionable, and our little folk who wish to be big ; and among the latter is your friend McL——, who has renounced his church, and has applied for Episcopalian ordination, as I am informed, ' from a conscientious preference to that church ! !' But with respect to the great body of the people, nothing can be more false than such a statement. Many of them, it is true, laudably attend the services of the English church, because there is no other within their reach. They (the Church of England) have been certainly much more zealous in attempting to plant themselves in Canada than our good Kirk has been hitherto ; but the time is not yet gone by, I hope, when what is lost cannot be retrieved, but now or never, I think, is the time both for the Assembly and for individuals to exert themselves, and if they do, I do not despair but very soon, and precisely from the same causes, there will be exhibited on the bosom of the boundless forests of Canada many as lovely moral pictures as Scotland now presents from the bosom of the ocean."

At an after date, Dr. Mathieson closes another letter thus. Our readers will not grudge the space occupied by these two selections from the manuscript volumes of colonial correspondence :

" I would call upon the people of Scotland generally, and the clergy in particular, to bestir themselves in our behalf. We still retain an ardent love for our national church. We look upon our connection with it as a link, and a powerful one, in the mighty chain of affections which unites us to the beloved land we have left. Her ordinances are viewed by many in Canada with a regard which, I am afraid, those who constantly enjoy them do not always feel. The God of their fathers is more impressively felt to be their God when they sing to his praise the same Psalms in which in their infancy they joined with their parents. The English liturgy may be an excellent composition, and every page of it may be full of pure devotion ; but it does not, and it cannot, awaken in our hearts the feelings which our Scottish worship calls up. It has no share in our previous associations. It calls up no recollections of the solemn stillness of the Scottish Sabbath, or the more delightful and hallowed sounds that, amid the glens and hollows of our native country, rise through the morning and evening stillness. The plant may be fine, but it is an exotic ; its fragrance may be fault-less, but it is strange. It stands alone, unconnected with a single recollection, unless, indeed, it be this, that our forefathers were persecuted for rejecting it."*

The Rev. George Cheyne, who arrived in the Province on the 5th of September, 1831, subsequently to the meeting of the first synod, has given me some interesting jot-tings of the era immediately succeeding the organization of the society. He was designated to "Amherstburg or any other part of North America." He went there, as his predecessor, Mr. Gale, had done, without any induc-tion service. In 1832, travelling to synod at Kingston, he took three days to reach Hamilton, most of the way in open lumber-waggons with wooden side-springs, and the roads " corduroy,"—little better than an Indian track in some places. Hamilton was an insignificant town, and he had to stage it to Niagara, then a place of great importance, the starting-point of stages for the West and steamboats down the lake.

In the summer of 1834 he visited Sarnia, which was just commencing—the surrounding country an unbroken forest. After a bitter cold night in one of these primitive houses, the worthy host called out, "Are you frozen, Mr. Cheyne ? Are you frozen ?" But Mr. C. was none the worse. On his way through Tilbury to Chatham, then a wilderness, he stayed in a shanty twelve feet square, two men, two women, and some children occupying the single apartment. All through that western region, now dotted with flourishing churches, he faithfully proclaimed to the

---

* An interesting memoir of Dr. Mathieson has been published, from the vigorous pen of Mr. James Croll, who, in so many ways, has rendered signal service to the church of his attachment.

scattered settlers, amid many privations, the unsearchable riches of Christ.

Other branches of the Presbyterian family laboured actively and successfully in Canada, with whose doings then Dr. Burns had not directly to do, but always fully sympathised.

A few faithful brethren, chiefly of the Associate Church in Scotland and the North of Ireland, formed themselves into the Presbytery of the Canadas in 1818, which, in 1820, became the "United Presbytery," and subsequently the "United Synod of Upper Canada," numbering eighteen in 1840, when it merged into the Church of Scotland.

In September, 1831, a foreign mission was determined upon by the United Associate Synod of Scotland, and Canada selected as the field. To the Church's call for volunteers, responses came from three faithful and devoted ministers,—Mr. Robertson, of Cupar; Mr. Proudfoot, of Pitrodie; and Mr. Christie, of Holm in Orkney. Their sympathies went forth towards their expatriated fellow-countrymen, and to live and labour for their benefit they left posts of comfort and usefulness, in compliance with the call of God and His Church. Bearing commissions from their respective presbyteries, and from Dr. John Brown, chairman, William Peddie, secretary, James Peddie and John Ritchie, members of the Foreign Missions Committee, they set sail about the beginning of August, 1832. There was an understanding amongst them that Mr. Robertson should labour in Eastern, Mr. Proudfoot in Western, and Mr. Christie in Central Canada. Within a month after arriving, the first member of the little band was cut off by cholera. Mr. Proudfoot settled in London, where he was counted worthy of double honour, discharging for many years, till removed by death, the duties of an earnest pastorate as well as of First Theological Professor to the body with whose settlement in the country he had so much to do.

Mr. Christie, for thirty-eight years, laboured faithfully at Flamborough. On the 8th of September, 1870, at the ripe age of 86, having served his generation, by the will of God, he fell asleep.

Such were the heroic pioneers who founded what became the "United Presbyterian Church" in Canada, which has done a noble work in the land, and with which, at Montreal, in June, 1861, the Presbyterian Church of Canada formed so auspicious a union.*

This glance at the past is well fitted to make us " from this time say, What hath God wrought ?"

The oft experienced and expressed feeling of him whose life and labours we have been attempting to delineate, in looking "before and after," was, " The Lord hath done great things for us, whereof we are glad."

The Canada Presbyterian Church of to-day has 308 ministers (an increase of 20 in a year), 30,000 families, 50,000 communicants, over 8,000 office-bearers (including Sabbath-school teachers), and church accommodation for 128,210. During the past year 21 churches have been erected, and 11 manses, the latter now numbering 161, an increase of 47 in three years. She has two theological colleges, with 150 hopeful young men, either directly en-

---

* We had hoped to have received from a respected minister of the former United Presbyterian Church a fitting record of its most useful history, but have not succeeded, and must content ourselves, for the present, with this meagre notice.

rolled as theological students, or in preparatory departments, having the ministry in view. There is a flourishing widows' fund, and a fund for aged and infirm ministers. Her Home Mission embraces 122 distinct fields (90
last year), these including some 700 stations. Our Foreign
Missions are in China and among the Cree Indians of the
Saskatchewan, and it is a hopeful symptom that the collection doubled during the past year. The total contributed for congregational purposes during the year was
$403,014; for the schemes of the church, $47.990; for all
purposes reported, nigh half a million dollars.

With a territory touching two oceans, fitted to sustain
a population twenty times larger than the four millions
now peopling it, and containing within it all the elements
of material prosperity, our Church in the Confederated
Provinces has amplest scope for the exertion of her utmost
energies.

Taking the Presbyterian Church as a whole throughout
the Dominion, it has been stated, on reliable authority,
that, numerically, she ranks first of all the Protestant
bodies; and taking the world-wide view, recent statistics,
collected with care and published authoritatively, give
her the same front rank. Surely then it behoves her to
do her part, along with the other sections of evangelical
Protestantism, in coming up to the help of the Lord against,
the mighty, and to listen to the voice of her glorious Head
as in His providence He says, "Enlarge the place of thy
tent, and let them stretch forth the curtains of thine habi-
tations; spare not, lengthen thy cords and strengthen thy
stakes, for thou shalt break forth on the right hand and
on the left."

CHAPTER XIX.

MISCELLANEOUS.

OUR readers will remember the shadow on his hearth in the morning of his ministry. Deep called unto deep, wave rolled in on the back of wave, yet though to his feeble sense and fallible reason, it seemed as if "all these things were against him," he found them among the "all things that worked together for his good," and that there was a blessed "afterward," when, being "exercised thereby," the affliction for the present, not joyous but grievous, yielded "the peaceable fruits of righteousness."

During these nights of weeping he found himself often as

" An infant crying in the night,
And with no language but a cry."

Yet had he full sympathy with the sentiment—

> " I hold it true, whate'er befall,
> I feel it when I sorrow most,
> 'Twere better to have loved and lost,
> Than never to have loved at all."

By the empty crib, in the darkened chamber, he thus writes to his sister, Mrs. Briggs, amid the wreck of his hopes and the eclipse of his happiness, when those little lights which gladdened his home, and in which he was willing for a season to rejoice, went out :

" PAISLEY, January 1, 1820.

" MY DEAR JANE,—It has become my painful duty to inform you that our dear girl Agnes died this morning at nine o'clock, after a severe illness of seven weeks' continuance. She suffered much acute pain, but her last moments were peaceful and serene ; and she was sensible till within a very short time of her removal. It is matter of gratitude that the transition was so placid, as, from the nature of the complaint, we had reason to fear much greater suffering immediately before death. For some weeks past we have been kept in a state of the most painful suspense between hope and fear, each alternately predominating. The shock, in the end, was sudden, and felt to be such. The dispensation is a painful one to her mother and me, but it is mingled with much mercy. We are thankful that we enjoyed her so long, and that her whole life was one uninterrupted career of health and enjoyment, and that her latter end was peace. We are especially thankful for the amiable disposition she displayed, and for the interest she took in what was good. She had arrived at that time of life when the mind begins to open and take an interest in what passes around it. She had begun to be our companion in private and in public devotion, and so late as yesterday, or rather this morning early, she referred to the worship of the family, which she took pleasure in attending. Her affections were ardent, and nothing seemed to give her greater pleasure than to be allowed to go to church, and to put her pence in the plate for the poor. She was beloved by all who knew her, and many have been the kind enquiries that have been made respecting her. *Our* loss is *her* gain. She is now infinitely happier than our most ardent wishes could make her. Her departure loosens one tie which bound us to the earth and adds to the interest with which we contemplate heaven. Ever since her trouble began we had reason to apprehend a fatal termination ; although, from the circumstance of the complaint not being fully understood, and from its having assumed frequently a favourable appearance, we naturally cherished some degree of hope. The complaint, whatever it was, had its seat in the head, and appears to have been some affection of the brain. She was reduced to a skeleton, and appeared at last to sink more from the exhaustion of the frame than from the violence of disease. I was supporting her when she expired, but so gentle was the transition that I could not ascertain the precise moment when the pulse ceased to beat. Her mother has been wonderfully sustained throughout. Her bodily health has been uncommonly good, and her mind has been brought to a resigned and tranquil state. She feels much gratified by your letters, and requests me to return her best thanks for them. She feels at not having been able to answer them, but I know that you will find too ample an apology in the circumstances in which we have been placed. Your first letter reached us about the time when Agnes began to complain, and since that time our time and thoughts have been completely occupied. I intended to have written you, but you can easily conceive what it is to be agitated between hope and fear ; and domestic sorrow like that we have experienced must tend to indispose as well as unfit for even the ordinary occupations of life. I do not know how I am to get through with the labours of to-morrow. I am prepared for the whole day, and must bring my feelings and my mind to it. Being the first Sabbath of the year, and having an extraordinary collection for the poor, makes me more desirous to appear personally.

Before the month expired, the Lord caused "breach upon breach." Agnes, their "firstborn," for whom in this letter they are "in bitterness," was a lovely girl of four years. The "other lily gathered," of whom the next letter speaks, was but opening its blossoms in this inclement clime, when translated to the region of unsetting suns and unending summer. "A flower offered in the bud" they found to be "no vain sacrifice."

"PAISLEY, January 29, 1820.

"MY DEAR JANE,—Little did we think that we would so soon require the renewed sympathy of our friends. The wound lately opened has been made to bleed afresh, and attended with painful circumstances. Our only son, John, has been taken from us this morning, after an illness of seven weeks. He had got a bad cold about two months ago, which fastened on his throat and lungs, and gave him great uneasiness, reducing his frame to a shadow. For some time past he was alternately better and worse, and our hopes and fears prevailed accordingly. Yesterday he seemed to be considerably better, and we entertained hopes that the crisis of the disorder was past. During the night he became rapidly worse, and about four in the morning it was evident that the painful change was fast approaching. He died without a struggle at a quarter past eight. We are thus left *childless*, for God hath taken away the desire of our eyes with a stroke. This day four weeks, at nearly the same hour, our dear Agnes was translated from us. We felt her loss deeply ; but we were supported and comforted, among other consolations, by the thought that we had still remaining one dear object of our affections. That is now taken from us, and the double loss is peculiarly painful. Nature must feel, and grace does not eradicate feeling, although it is designed to chasten and sanctify it. We desire to adore the hand of a Father in the stroke, however painful : but experience has taught me that it is an easy thing to describe and recommend patient resignation and fortitude under trials ; it is not so easy to put them in practice. We have been comforted during our sufferings by the precious word of the living God, and we now begin to enter more deeply into the spiritual meaning of those promises with which it is stored. It is, no doubt, one wise and gracious design of God in the trials, to fit me for the duty of sympathizing with and comforting others who may be in affliction. Speculation and theory will not do ; it is the actual participation in suffering which gives the requisite qualifications. ' Tribulation worketh patience, and patience experience, and experience hope.' I am happy to say that my dear partner has been wonderfully supported throughout the whole of the fiery trial. She is composed, but at times overcome. Our boy was just six months old ; he had begun to shew signs of intelligence, and there seemed to be something peculiarly gentle and amiable in his disposition. He was indeed the object of our hopes and anticipations, and now he appears lovely even in death. I began this letter on Saturday, but did not finish it. It is now Monday morning, and we have had cause to renew our vows, and sing of mercy and of judgment. Yesterday my pulpit was supplied by Messrs. Ranken and Geddes (Dr. Findlay's assistant), and I expect a friend from Glasgow for next Sabbath. Friday is the day fixed for the funeral. It will be some little time before my mind can be brought to its ordinary state, and before I can enter fully into my public duties. A change of scene, as you observe, would no doubt be desirable, but at this season we cannot think of that ; and besides, our sacramental solemnity comes on, and the preparatory duties will occupy my time and thoughts. We were much gratified by your kind and edifying letter, and when Janet or I are able shall endeavour to answer it. In the meantime, I will take it kind if you will write a few lines of sympathy and comfort to Janet. A father feels the loss of children, but a mother's feelings must be much more tender and

acute. We have been much edified by the perusal of some tracts
suited to our case, particularly 'Cecil's Visit,' and 'Flavel's Token
for Mourners,' and Mr. Thomson's 'Address on the Loss of Friends.'
Yesterday fortnight I endeavoured to improve the dispensation by
two sermons, on Jonah iv. 9 : 'Dost thou well to be angry for the
gourd?' shewing, first, when men may be said to imitate the spirit
and language of the prophet. When they murmur, refuse consolation, allow passion to triumph over reason and truth, neglect to
mark the great ends of all trials, and fail to improve by them. 2nd.
Reasons why we should not be angry. It is the Lord ; afflictions
are the effects of sin, they are the chastisements of a Father, they
render the gospel and its privileges doubly interesting, and they
recall our thoughts from this world to another and a better,—ad-
verting particularly to the precious consolations which God has provided for those in trial, &c. Yesterday we were all in mourning
for the Duke of Kent. Death assails all ranks. The nation has
sustained a loss,—may it be sanctified to all concerned.

"I had almost forgot to notice that, in compliance with the wish
of the physicians, our dear girl's head was examined, and a large
quantity of water was found lodged in the cavities of the brain, as
also a part of the substance of the brain in a state resembling the
cartilage of the ear. We are thus satisfied that the disease was
beyond the power of human skill, and every suitable means had
been used. We desire your sympathy and your prayers, and with
every kind wish for the Doctor and you, in which Janet cordially
joins,

"I remain, my dear Jane,

" Your affectionate brother,

" ROBERT BURNS."

Enough reference has perhaps not been made to the
domestic side of his character. It is not always that those
moving on the public arena as much as he, have those
dispositions formed and fostered which make a truly
happy home. Naturally of a warm, loving temperament,
the members of the home circle were especially dear to
him ; and when anything occurred to annoy him outside,
the sweets of domestic retirement yielded additional solace.
As he advanced in life he found increasing pleasure in the
joys of his own fireside.

The many young persons who latterly sojourned, for a

longer or shorter period, under his roof, love to speak of his unfailing cheerfulness, his entire freedom from all exactingness, his ceaseless flow of spirits, his almost juvenile playfulness, his ready dealing out from an inexhaustible store, of apt reference and happy anecdote, blended with a constant regard for the interests of the higher life.

His table talk had always a charm. Many of his racy stories and ready repartees will be recalled, by those who were his familiar friends.

His interest in his family entered into the minutest details of daily life. The contents of their wardrobes, the books they needed in study, the state of their health, were ever a care to him. When at College, such notes would come in on us as :

"Peggy has been looking for your bag with the clothes to wash, and I think you should send them out immediately. I would like to see a catalogue or inventory of all your articles, that I may know how you are provided with these things."

When in our summer retreat, at Helensburgh, preparing a prize essay, we sent to him for a needed volume. The request is at once complied with, though costing him, amid manifold labours, a journey to Glasgow :

"CAMPHILL, Wednesday, Aug. 1843.

"I went into Glasgow *once errand* to-day, in pursuit of ' Verres, and I was so successful as to find him.

"Dr. Willis last week shewed me in his library the whole works of Cicero, in 16 volumes, and, although he was not at home to-day, I got access to his room, and brought away the two volumes which I now send—leaving a note, and knowing that you would take care of them and restore them safe in good time, along with some other books of the Doctor's which I have."

A year prior to our settlement in Kingston, when temporarily labouring there, we were laid aside for a brief period, from duty.

It reached his ear on his return from a missionary tour, when he had been mapping out work for us and others, and drew from him characteristic expressions of parental solicitude.

"TORONTO, May, 1846.

"It grieves me to hear on my return from the West that you have been so poorly. My first impression was, that I must get off in 'the captain's' steamer, and see how matters are with you, and give our Kingston friends a day—leaving Mr. McTavish to do my work here. This, however, is not in my power, having engaged for too many places on Sabbath first, in other directions. I am rather anxious about your preaching in the large church on Sabbath first. My impression is that you should rest at least one-half."

To the peculiar difficulties of a pastorate entered on without any experience, and when very young he was fully alive. His advice was always readily rendered.

"I sympathize with you in the difficulties you must have felt on the subject of admission to sealing ordinances.

"I have felt them all my days, and they are increasing every day with me. My opinion is, that time and *forbearance* and *painstaking*, with much prayer, are the real and only means of conquering them.

"I am always sorry when persons tired of my efforts for their good, go away. Our standard has been greatly raised, and is rising."

We never consulted him without getting a prompt and decided answer.

The correctness of his calculations on many difficult and delicate points, was often proved by the result.

In his estimate of the suitableness of individuals for particular posts, we found his advice ever reliable.

In connexion with the contemplated mission to the American Indians, when Convener of our church's foreign mission, we asked his opinion, and at once got this, which entirely harmonized with our own :—

" Dr. W. and I have conferred on the subject of a missionary to the Indians.

" He spoke of a young man of the name of R——, a promising young man, but, in my view, too young and raw for such work. Really, I would feel a great difficulty in venturing to name any one for such a charge. Mr. Nisbet, is the man (I rather think), and then, a successor in the mission (at Red River) might easily be got."

Writing to him on the desirableness of making more popular and public the meetings at the commencement and close of the College, he replied :

" I am writing on the Pope's Encyclical and other points. Could hardly venture a free address in a college, and before a learned audience. But I agree with you entirely, and have always advocated such views."

Every movement that was fitted to widen the range of our acquaintance, and to increase the sum of our knowledge ; every measure that seemed likely to benefit us intellectually or spiritually, and to make us more useful in the Lord's work, he was sure to encourage. Learning that we purposed (in company with our esteemed relative the Rev. William Gregg,) to attend the Missionary Anniversaries at New York—he sent us the following :—

"TORONTO, April, 1854.

" I am happy to hear that you mean to go to New York, on occasion of the Missionary and Conference meetings. You will not only see Dr. Duff again, but meet with many ministers and others of whom you may have heard, and whom you may never have the opportunity of seeing again. You may remember me very affectionately to Dr. McLeod, Dr. Alexander, Dr. Phillips, Dr. Krebs, and indeed, all the good men whom Dr. Cunningham and I had the pleasure of meeting when out on the deputation. Kirwan, (Dr. Murray,) in particular, I would like you to see. You may ask him his opinion now of the McG.'s and the American society for ameliorating the condition of the Jews.

"At the mission rooms, Nassau street, you will meet with Mr. Lowrie, secretary, and the father of the young missionary who was murdered by the Lascars some years ago. He is a good man. He may be able to tell you some things that may be useful to you. Try and stop a day at Princeton, to whose president (Dr. McLean,) I am writing, at any rate, to-day and will name you."

When most unexpectedly to him and ourselves, an honorary degree came to us, from one of the oldest and most honoured of American colleges, he expressed his gratification thus :—

TORONTO, August 28th, 1866.

"I have been hard worked by missionary labour since the Synod, and the trifling labour even of letter writing, is beyond my strength, still I have no difficulty in preaching when I can get into the pulpit, which is sometimes a work of difficulty from my enfeebled strength. I hope to fulfil my engagements with you for 9th and 16th of September.

"The announcement of the honour conferred on you by the Hamilton college was gratifying, and I sincerely congratulate you on it. It is forty years and more since I read 'Dwight's Travels in New York State, as far West as HAMILTON COLLEGE,' of which he gives a full description. See the book if you can."

Seldom in his correspondence with us, did he allude to incidents in his own personal history. To relations of experience he was averse. Even on memorable epochs in his public life, he was reticent, yet, an occasional allusion occurs, as when his year of jubilee came round—though he shrank from its going farther.

" TORONTO, June, 1861.

"I wrote you on Saturday regarding the day of my jubilee. It is rather singular that, after noticing an erratum on your part, I should have fallen into one myself. Having the curiosity to look at my opening sermon on the 'Word of God not bound;' the following announcement at the top met my eye. 'Preached in Low church, Paisley, on Sabbath, 21st July, 1811.' I know full well that the *ordination* took place on the Friday before, and, thus, on clear evidence the day in question, turns out to be, not the 8th—

but the 19th of the month, thus bringing round, by the cycle, the jubilee day to the same day of the week as well as of the month—an interesting fact. The lapse of half a century suggests many solemn, and let us hope, salutary lessons."

More than many suppose, who knew him only as the missionary at large, did he love the regular routine of parish work.

He was fond of "walking the Hospitals," and ministering counsel and comfort by the bed of sickness and death.

During the ship fever of 1847, and the cholera of 1848-9 and '54, his hands were full. Yet, amid the ravages of the "pestilence walking in darkness," he can think of promising portions of the home field, that were white already to harvest, and use hospitality without grudging to God's faithful and persecuted servants.

"TORONTO, 1st August, 1854.

" I got home safe and sound. I am glad I came home, as many duties have devolved upon me, in connexion with the prevailing epidemic which still rages around us. I preached all day last Sabbath, and endeavoured to improve the solemn calls of Providence.

" Dr. and Mrs. Kalley, from Madeira and Illinois, are with us just now. The St. Catharines people have made a move our way. I am not prepared to say that it would be a duty to refuse, if called to occupy what will become one of our most important stations and specially a missionary one, and a field on which the cause of right Sabbath observance may be beneficially fought for."

When absent on his missionary tours, he kept up constant communication with home. As he went forth " Mizpah" embodied his heart's desire and prayer for those who, though "absent," were "ever dear." " The Lord watch between me and thee when we are separated the one from the other."

A covenant-keeping God wonderfully " preserved his going out and his coming in.'

Y

However crowded with work and pressed for time, missives fragrant with a love with which a "stranger intermeddleth not," were sure, with clock-like regularity, to reach those whose hearts went out, often anxiously, after him. If other days had sometimes to be missed, Monday morning would be sure to tell of the "high days" preceding, when he "mounted his throne," and was enabled to "triumph in Christ and manifest the savour of his knowledge in every place." These letters were often undated.

"LINDSAY, Monday morning.

"MY VERY DEAR ELIZABETH,—The weather has changed from the loveliness of sunshine to the dreariness of a bleaching rain. But Jehovah changes not, and by his graciously preserving care I am sustained in health and strength ; and yesterday was able to preach both forenoon and evening, though the audiences were small. My visit to Cobourg was a very agreeable one, and besides sojourning with the Frasers and at the manse, I had the opportunity of spending an hour twice with the daughter of Mr. Milne, who is to all appearance near her last. The case is a very interesting one. Under great bodily suffering, her mind is kept in perfect peace, hoping in the Lord.

"On Friday, Mr. Laing took me down to Grafton, where we took tea with our esteemed friends, Mr. and Mrs. Smith, who are both remarkably well and quite delighted to see me, and many were the enquiries they made about you and your praiseworthy labours. . . .

"On Saturday, I came by the Port Hope Railway to Lindsay, forty miles, arriving at 7 p.m. Mr. and Mrs. Hudspeth are very kind, and they send you their best remembrances. This evening I give a lecture in the Town Hall, on Canada, and to-morrow I go to Cambray, seven miles out, where Mr. Douglas, the missionary, preaches every Sabbath afternoon."

"OIL SPRINGS, Monday, 10 a. m.

"MY EVER DEAREST,—After the labours of yesterday I feel quite well this morning ; having gone to bed early and got five or six hours' sleep, and up however at half-past six. In the forenoon at eleven, I preached at seven miles' distance, in the Township Hall, which is a very comfortable place for worship, and there we had a full and respectable attendance, not of bush people at all, but of respectably dressed settlers. The singing was admirable, and the audience had all the appearance of intelligence and seriousness. There I saw Mr. Patrick Barclay, who lives three miles off, whose place I am to visit to-morrow at three.   I preached here in the Methodist Episcopal church, of which the Presbyterians have the use at certain hours, having helped to build it.   It is seated for about 300, and was well filled.   There are in the village one Episcopal place of meeting, and two Methodist ones ; and great harmony seems to prevail among the people.   The Sabbath seems to be well kept, and I attended and addressed a large union Sabbath school at nine in the morning.

The chief proprietor here is Colonel Elliott, formerly mayor of Cornwall, whom I had known of old, and who came to both of our meetings.   He is a religious man, and, though a Congregationalist, is very friendly to us.   He is the proprietor of the plank road between here and Wyoming, (15 miles) and makes the staves for the oil barrels, many of which passed us on the road on Friday ; a good deal of the 'crude' oil is refined here and around,. but the largest part is sent for distillation and refining at a distance.   Any unpleasant smell is from the refineries, and as none of them are going to-day there is no smell at all.   There is here published a weekly newspaper, called the Oil Springs *Chronicle*, of which I must send you a specimen, very well printed it is.

" I am to conduct meetings on Wednesday and Thursday.   As yesterday, we expect two meetings for worship on Sabbath, and a sermon in the evening of Monday.   My present intention is, (God willing,) to be home by *Tuesday evening*, the 26th, at half-past seven or about eight.

" Remember me kindly to Miss McCaskell, Miss White, and all the young ladies, not overlooking Minnie and the *infan*try brigade.

> " My ever dearest love,
>> " Your ever affectionate husband,
>>> " ROBT. BURNS.

In the course of his missionary travels, reaching Paisley, he bethought him of the old world town.

The " City of the Woods" made memory busy.   Of his old friends, he could say with the Apostle, " I have you in my heart."

Getting plans of the Canadian Paisley, he sent them across the water as a present to the Town Council of his early home.

He received from the authorities the acknowledgment :

"TOWN CLERK'S OFFICE,

"PAISLEY, 12th Dec. 1866.

"REV. AND DEAR DOCTOR,—I received from our mutual friend, Mr. Russell Pollock, your letter, dated September last, addressed to the Town Council, and relative to plans of the town of Paisley in your adopted country.

"These I laid before the Town Council, at a meeting held upon the 6th inst., and I have the pleasure to inform you that they expressed themselves highly gratified at receipt thereof, and in acknowledging receipt, I was directed to convey to you the thanks of the Council, for your obliging gift, and to state that the same has been directed to be put up and preserved with the town records.

"To me individually, it is pleasant to find you taking so warm an interest in this town, and in all that relates to its welfare, where you spent so many of your best years. You will be glad to learn that this town is improving, though slowly—that there are many new trades introduced since you left, adding greatly to the comfort of the people.

"Yours faithfully,

"WM. HODGE."

He had a very high sense of the responsibility of the office of a Professor of Theology. On the dignity and solemnity of the Christian ministry he loved to dilate. He felt a holy jealousy for the motives of aspirants to the sacred office. Amongst requisite qualifications, whilst rating at their proper worth the intellectual, he attached the highest value to the spiritual. Especially did he insist on being "mighty in the Scriptures." The expertest employment of the sharpest weapons which the armoury of science and literature supplied, could never, in his esteem compensate for the lack of the ability dexterously to wield the Sword of the Spirit. How aptly he could quote Scripture; how deftly interweave it with the texture of his preaching and his prayers, many will remember. On these and kindred themes which formed the frequent subject of subsequent prelections he dwells in the very first letter he penned to the students after his call to Canada, which pressure for space kept out of its appropriate chapter, but which may be introduced here. It suits the candidates for the ministry of to-day as well :

"PAISLEY, December 28th, 1844.

"MY DEAR YOUNG FRIENDS,—The Synod of your Church has called me to take the inspection of your studies. The divine Head of the Church, will, we trust, speedily raise up some one, who, to the full vigour of mental power, adds that, for the want of which, neither talent, nor learning, nor eloquence can atone—the living energy of a spirit quickened from on high ; the holy activity of the men of other times, who counted not their lives dear to them, provided only they could spend and be spent in the service of Him whom they loved. I feel my utter incompetence to take the charge of those on whom shall be devolved the mighty responsibility of conveying the message of Heaven to degraded and ruined man ; and I feel it the more, inasmuch as it has all along been my clear conviction, that the pastoral office is of itself quite sufficient, and more than sufficient, to engage all the time and all the energies of one man. In accepting this charge, therefore, I feel as if guilty of a glaring inconsistency ; and such an impression cannot but add indefinitely to the weight and responsibility of the charge. In the infancy of the church, such an union of offices is tolerated, because it is unavoidable. The fathers of the reformed churches of Europe found it necessary to act on the same principle ; and the men who have been instrumental in promoting the religious improvement of the American settlements, in former and in later times, have done the same. Such considerations, however, do not diminish, but enhance the responsibility incurred, while they demonstrate the duty of every church, in seeking to embark the service of ministers untrammeled, in the more laborious department.

"If I have had the temerity of closing with a proposal, from which my sense of inability would have led me to shrink, it was not till after all my efforts to obtain the service of one or more of the ablest men in the church at home, had ended in painful disappointment. I rejoice that my esteemed friend and brother, the Rev. Andrew King, of Glasgow, has engaged for a season, to superintend your studies. The thought has more than once struck me, that possibly this excellent servant of Christ may, in the holy providence of Almighty God, have been sent to Canada, that he may remain with you, and the churches there, for their and your furtherance and joy of faith. If it is permitted to me again to cross the great ocean, and to settle in the west, I shall rejoice not a little in finding such a fellow-labourer in the field, and that field we know, is sufficiently wide.   In the meantime the labours of Mr. King among you will be by you duly appreciated, and when the season of his charge of you shall terminate, the pious ministers of the districts to which you may remove, will, I doubt not, exercise over you a kind and edifying superintendence.   My earnest prayer for you from day to day shall be, that your studies may all be conducted in the spirit of humble diligence, and entire dependence on God ; and that each and all of you may ever be constrained by the love of Christ as your animating principle ; and that the commanding view you shall take of the Christian ministry, may be that of a divinely appointed means of converting men to God, and saving souls from death.   Oh ! how miserably low and degraded are those views of the Christian ministry which elevate it no higher than a species of moral police ; a kind of decent instrumentality for keeping the people in order, and smoothing the rugged surface of society !   Let *your* views rise far above this drivelling level ; for let me assure you, that just in proportion to the magnitude of your aims, will be the measure of your spiritual activity in the prosecution of your studies.   An activity which is merely secular, I would not desiderate in candidates for the sacred office ; but a vitality that is spiritual, and an activity that is heaven-directed, God the Spirit will assuredly bless.

"In common with your able preceptor, you must at present feel the great want of properly selected books in theology, for reference and perusal.   Whether I may ever be permitted to see you in the flesh or not, one thing I pledge myself to do for you, and that is, to endeavour to collect for your use, a Library of Literature and Theology ; and the church at home will, unquestionably, help me in this.   They have already promised to do so ; and private friends in the mother country, and perhaps on the continent of Europe, may make presents to you of suitable publications.   But I am strongly inclined to give thanks that you are at present almost entirely shut up to the Bible !   The divine author of that Holy Book, is taking each of you by the hand, and is leading you directly to the fountain that is pure, and healthful, and life-giving.   And do you think the blessing will be withheld if you are found day after day drinking at the sacred springs which are exclusively his own ? "Bonus textuarius est bonus Theologus," said Martin Luther ; and if the historian of that remarkable man, and of his times, has succeeded in throwing one charm around his work more pleasing, more fascinating than another, it is that derived from the scriptural allusions with which it abounds, and the Biblical "Theopneustic" spirit which it breathes.   Merle D'Aubigné is not only a learned man, whose researches into the archives of other times have been profound, but above all other things he is mighty in the Scriptures, and he has drunk deep of the river that makes glad the city of our God.   I might say the same of *our* great historian, Dr. McCrie ;

for every one who has read his sermons and lectures, must have been struck with the extent and accuracy of his scriptural attainments, as well as with the vigour and independence of mind, which his profound and hallowed study of the oracles of God has imparted to all his writings.

"Dear young friends, let me give you an advice. If your adoption of theology as a study, is merely professional,—if you have no reason to think that you have been renewed in the spirit of your minds,—if faith in Christ, the gracious Redeemer, does not occupy the place of a commanding principle within you,—if, in a word, you are not really "living members of Christ," and partakers of that faith which unites to the Saviour,—and is the animating principle of all obedience; pause before you go one step farther. It is not *Licentiates* that Canada needs. It is not in the want of a professional Christianity, that your country withers and is blasted. She needs a larger supply of men of power—men of unction—men of spiritual life and holy energy. My prayer is, that such may be raised up from among *you*, and that the "Free" Presbyterian Church of Canada, may prove an instrument of mighty efficacy for advancing the interests of evangelical truth. With my best wishes and earnest prayers for your progress and success in all your studies.

"I remain, affectionately, and sincerely, Yours,

"ROBERT BURNS."

We have had occasion to notice the importance which Dr. Burns attached to the *mental discipline* of the students. The inadequate provision made at the time by the Grammar Schools and the Provincial University, with the limited early advantages of the young men, rendered it the more necessary that our church set in order in this matter the things that were wanting. Esteemed brethren differed from him in this, and he had to encounter a good deal of opposition. But the church came round in the end, substantially to his way of thinking, and granted most amply the provision he sought. He submitted his views in 1848 to the College Committee, and, to aid in carrying them out, offered his gratuitous services.

The face of things has greatly changed since then. Our Grammar and Common Schools are on a higher platform. Our Provincial Universities are on a liberal footing, and with their course of instruction re-arranged, and their staff of instructors re-equipped, are being rapidly placed abreast of the times. Our young men are feeling increasingly the importance of pursuing a regular curriculum of preparatory study, and taking their degree as University graduates. With exhibitions and scholarships multiplied, and their worldly circumstances improved, they are the better enabled to do so.

But those who can look back over even a quarter of a century of our country's history, and remember our college in its infancy, will acknowledge that there was much of truth in Dr. Burns' communication, the main portions of which we subjoin :

"Toronto, C.W., 23rd March, 1848.

" To the Members of the College Committee.

"Dear Brethren,—In the prospect of a meeting of the General Committee, in the month of April, there are some matters to which I wish to call your attention. It is desirable that your minds should be directed to these prior to the meeting, in order that any measure which may be proposed may not be absolutely new to you. Of course, any proposal that may meet your views, will still require the sanction of the Synod ; but such sanction may be counted on, provided only the committee are unanimous, or pretty generally agreed. No other motive can be supposed to influence me beyond a wish to see an institution, on which so much depends, properly organized and successfully conducted.

" I. Too great facility in the admission of students appears to me to be an evil which ought to be strenuously guarded against. Our Institution is peculiarly a Theological Seminary. Those young men who are admitted to its benefits, enter not on a general course of study which may ultimately bear on any professional object ; they are received expressly as candidates for the ministry ; and the Church, in receiving them as such, throws over each the shield of her patronage and encouragement. Hence the necessity of peculiar care in this matter. Not only ought we to be satisfied with regard to moral conduct, right motive, and apparent piety ; there ought to be, in addition, some good evidence of a decided change of heart in the applicant. If this is not attended to, we need not expect to realize the true object of our union as a Church in these lands, the rearing up of a spiritual ministry, with a special view to the conversion of men to God. And then in regard to mental qualification and attainments in applicants, I am clearly of opinion that greater strictness than hitherto is absolutely necessary ; and that in this matter, as in the one just referred to, unanimity in the examining committee ought to be held as indispensable. A mere examination before a Presbytery does not appear to me to be sufficient. A special committee of Synod might be named for this purpose, or a sub-committee of the College Committee, who might act under strict regulations, and with power to treat with applicants in the way of conscientious advice, rather than judicially and on probative evidence. A certain measure of previous literary attainment ought to be required in every one who is to be received into the seminary. It does not appear to me that Knox College ought to be considered as designed to furnish merely elementary instruction in the classics ; and one design of the setting up of an academy certainly was to supersede this, so as to retain on behalf of the College its peculiar character as a training seminary for the direct work of the ministry.

" II. While I hold these views advisedly, and attach great importance to them, I am, nevertheless, of opinion that even the students at College, *as distinct from those of the Academy*, stand in need of much more *preparatory training* than they have been in the habit of receiving. Here I use the term, preparatory training, not in reference to further *literary* pursuits, but rather in reference to studies *peculiarly theological ;* and therefore, high as may be my hope of the indirect good to be derived from the institution of a preparatory school or academy, I am very clearly of opinion that an additional professor in the department of mental training, or philosophical education, is essential to the success of our Seminary ; and that under such an institution our young men will be far more likely to realize the desired advantage in point of intellectual progress, than if mixed up with the pupils of a mere academy, or subjected to the ordinary routine of a grammar school.

" In the *first* place : the department of English literature, with a · special view to the principles of composition, associated also with the rules of correct and graceful reading and elocution, ought not to be overlooked. A special exercise of this kind two or three times a week, would be highly advantageous ; but to mix it up with any school-boy exercise, would defeat its end. It must be greatly mental. The young men of the College, and they only, should be its subjects ; and they ought to view it as a part of philosophical training, far more closely connected than may appear at first sight with the more immediate objects of the Seminary. The disadvantages under which settlers in the provinces, in a literary view, labour, demonstrate the necessity of such exercises ; while the age of the young men, and their general status as to mental development, place them beyond the ordinary range of scholastic forms, and render a training specially for themselves absolutely essential.

"In the *second* place : Interesting and important as may be the prelections of a professor of mental and moral philosophy, it has always appeared to me very desirable that something of a character more directly practical and elementary—I mean in a philosophical sense—should be provided for the young men.   For example (1), a plain common-sense view of the powers and capacities of the human mind, with rules for their improvement.   This has little in common with the speculations of metaphysics, or the more recondite parts of intellectual philosophy ; but it may be highly advantageous as a preparation for such departments of human thought.   (2).   An exhibition of the nature of evidence, and the laws of its regulation. This is of very great importance in all pursuits ; but its importance is mightily increased, when we take into view its bearings on the evidences of natural and revealed religion.   (3).   The laws of reasoning, or logic proper—including, of course, correct but condensed views of the methods of syllogism and induction, with analysis and synthesis, and the rules of correct *definition*.   I know not a better mental exercise than an occasional examination on the ' ambiguous words' in Archbishop Whateley's Logic, or on the ' definitions' in Taylor's Elements of Thought.   (4).   The nature and sources of prejudice ; the causes of error ; the idola of Bacon, and the large tribe of *fallacies* in argument, present a wide, but most inviting, field for young enquirers ; and here the dangerous errors afloat among philosophers, as to the nature of *causation*, demand careful searching.   Some of the most plausible and pernicious forms of modern scepticism may be traced to these errors.   (5).   The *ideal theory* ought to be explained to our students, not only in its older forms, as held by the ancients, and by such earlier moderns as Descartes, Malebranche, and Locke, but as recently revived by Dr. Thomas Brown and his admirers.   The theory is, that the mind sees only images of its own creation or the representations of things without it, and not things themselves.   This is the famous hypothesis out of which Bishop Berkeley formed his theory of the non-existence of a material world ; and following out whose principles Hume succeeded in satisfying himself that neither mind nor matter had any existence.   The world is under infinite obligations to such men as Reid, Stewart, Campbell, Beattie, and others, who exposed the baselessness of the theory, and appealed successfully to primary principles of human belief, as ultimate facts in the arrangements of God.   I tremble when I think of the readiness with which the exploded theory has been received ; because I look upon it as not only destructive of all the evidences from final causes, in proof of the existence of God, but as directly subversive of all belief in the existence of any beings in the universe except ourselves. (6). Modern discoveries and speculations in Geology render it essential that our young men should be informed on such subjects so as to detect and expose the fallacies of such writers as the authors of the ' Constitution of Man,' and the ' Vestiges of Creation ;' and such information may be easily communicated, irrespective altogether of any peculiar fondness for the exact sciences. The theory of ' world building,' as well as the theory of ' ideas,' will soon fall before the lessons and the inductive processes of an exact logic.

" I wish it to be distinctly understood, that, according to my conceptions of preparatory training, Knox College is, in regard to the above matters, essentially defective ; and my complaints on this account, for two years past, I do not feel ashamed to acknowledge. My brethren may deem them groundless, but all I ask is enquiry, and a fair tribunal for final judgment.

" III. The remarks hitherto made respect the Institution in its primary bearings only, but I attach to them great importance in any circumstances, and more especially in the present position of our young country, as contrasted with the advancing intellect of the age. It must not, however, be inferred that my objections are limited to the elementary or preliminary departments of study. In the higher walks of metaphysical and moral science, I would desiderate for our students a pretty full view of the leading questions in morals, and the various *theories* of morals which have been put forth, with such philosophical parade by ingenious men. An acquaintance with these is necessary, together with a knowledge of their comparative merits, and above all, an exposure of their errors, when tried by the test of revelation. Along with this, I would recommend a concise system of Christian ethics.

" When, in October, 1844, I received the appointment from the Synod, ' to be the Professor of Theology, and to have the charge of training the young men for the holy ministry,' I undertook the office under the impression that it comprehended the right and the obligation to see that the preliminary training, as distinct from what is properly theological, was adapted to the end in view. The young men I was led to consider as *all students in theology*, that is, ' under training for the holy ministry ;' and this is the plain explanation of the fact, that so soon as I saw, or thought I saw, a deficiency in the ' training' department—a deficiency which neither the learning nor the assiduity of the Professor of ' Science and Literature' appeared to me likely to supply—I set myself, in some temporary way, to make up the deficiency. With this view, besides personal examinations, I prepared and .delivered to the students, in November and December, 1845, about twenty lectures on the philosophy of mind, and the nature of mental discipline ; the Baconian method of induction, with its relations to theological study ; the theories of morals ; and the errors of Brown's moral system, in reference to the scripture doctrine of rewards. I also sought to

obtain the assistance of several intelligent ministers of our own
body, who might devote a month or two to such studies for the
benefit of the young men, the church supplying their pulpits in the
mean time.　Although disappointed in this expectation, I still resolved to make another attempt, and in September, 1846, I applied
for the second time, personally, to Mr. Bayne, of Galt, to undertake the department of Logic, with a special reference to the *philosophy of evidence.* He entertained the proposal favourably, and
took with him a copy of Hedge's 'Elements of Logic,' for examination as to its fitness to be used as a text book.　Circumstances prevented this plan from being realized ; and at the commencement of
the session of 1846–7, I found for the first time that I had been
labouring under a misapprehension as to the extent of the powers
entrusted to me, and that, in reality, the preliminary department
of study was wholly independent of that allotted to theology, and
that *with this last* only had I to do.

"On the arrival of Mr. McCorkle, however, in November, 1846,
I made known to him my difficulties in regard to the preparatory
classes ; and on finding that he had been engaged for several years
in giving lessons to young men at Glasgow College, in Logic and
Rhetoric (prior to their entrance on the more direct departments of
philosophy), I drew up and read to the College Committee a scheme
for the winter studies, which would have put under that gentleman
all the students who had not been instructed in these branches.　I
succeeded so far as to obtain the consent of the College Committee
to his undertaking a class for *Rhetoric ;* but Logic was not included ;
and even the time allotted for the other, only *two hours in the week,*
was far too short.　Still, good was done by this arrangement ; and
looking back upon it as an experiment on a small scale, it seems
to me to have been a successful one, and amply to bear out my
suggestions and views in the matter.

"From all that I can hear, it does not seem to me that the deficiency has been at all supplied during the winter session now
drawing to its close.　I made offer privately to the students, that
if any number, not fewer than six, wished an hour a day for logic
and practical dialectics, my time and my labour were at their command.　The time of the young men, however, was so fully taken
up by other pursuits, that this number could not be obtained, and
nothing was done till about a month ago, when my much esteemed
friend, Dr. Willis, resolved to devote two hours weekly to the work.
His class for Logic, however, embraced *none of the junior students ;*
and its application to the *senior* classes rather confirmed than dis-
proved the soundness of my impressions.

"I am aware of the objection on the ground of expense ; but I
am not inclined to infer from this that no effort should be made to
supplement an existing defect by the means which are in our power.
There are members of Synod who, if asked, would cheerfully give
their services gratuitously, for periods more or less extensive.　Dr.

Willis, also, might with ease appropriate one hour daily to this department; taking in connection with it, perhaps, the Evidences of Christianity, as affording the very best specimens of the application of that part of logic which has to do with the rules of evidence. With regard to myself, it would give me great pleasure to assist the young men in any way that may be thought best, to the extent of an hour a day. During the absence of Dr. Willis this summer, nothing would to me be more pleasant than to make myself in any measure useful in the department of mental training to the students who may remain in the city or near it."

While thus anxious to have our own institution set upon a solid and satisfactory basis, he was not the less interested in the welfare of our public educational institutions. Finding that the University (then King's College), with its liberal endowment made over by royal largess to all the Protestant denominations alike, had become a close corporation to whose doors ecclesiastical exclusiveness had affixed its padlock (as we have already seen), he joined, immediately on his arrival in the Province, the band of Reformers, who sought to throw it open, and so to restore it to its original foundation. In the meeting which formally started the agitation, he seems to have taken a prominent part, reading the letters of absentees, which were addressed to himself, moving one of the leading resolutions, and at the close, the vote of thanks to the Chairman.

In the *Banner Extra*, published for the occasion, it is headed "Great King's College Meeting." It was held in the Congregational Chapel, Adelaide Street, on Tuesday, the 3rd Feb., 1846. The chair was occupied by the Hon. Adam Ferguson, of Woodhill, who aided so materially in his day the interests of scientific agriculture and liberal reform—and typified so well the fine old SCOTTISH

Gentleman, all of the olden time. The first resolution
was moved by the Rev. R. A. Fyfe, seconded by the Rev.
Adam Lillie, and supported by Mr. R. H. Brett. The
second was proposed by the Rev. John Roaf, and seconded
by the Rev. John Jennings. The third resolution was
proposed by the Rev. Dr. Burns, seconded by Mr. Wm.
A. Baldwin, and supported by Mr. Tyner. The fourth
resolution was moved by Mr. John Wetenhall, and seconded by Mr. Peter Brown. Mr. James Hodgson proposed the fifth resolution, in which he briefly expressed
his concurrence in the opinions which Dr. Burns had
brought forward. The mover and seconder of the sixth
resolution were the Rev. James Richardson and Mr.
James Leslie. Then "the Rev. Dr. Burns, with a few
brief remarks, moved the thanks of the meeting to the
Hon. Adam Ferguson, for his able conduct in the
chair."

These familiar names embrace the leading men that
had to do with this great provincial movement, over
whose triumphal issue we have had long reason to rejoice.

The motion with which my father had specially to
do was to this effect :—

"That in order to these objects being effectually realized, and
the educational interests of the Province secured, it is indispensable that the patronage of the chairs and the whole management
of the estate should be vested in a colonial body (distinct from the
members of the faculty, or others holding paid offices within the
College), who shall report annually to the Colonial Legislature."

The substance of his remarks is reported thus:

"Mr. CHAIRMAN,—I have been entrusted with a motion on
patronage and management. The importance of such a motion

cannot be overstated. On the supposition of a right management in this College, nearly all the abuses of which we complain in its establishment and constitution would have been prevented or neutralized. On the supposition of the trust remaining as it is, all your movements will be useless, and all the essential evils of the system will remain. What shall we say of a management under which the benefits of a great provincial institution for the colony have been intercepted and turned into a narrow and sectarian channel? Sixty thousand acres of the finest land belonging to the College sold or given away by the illegal authority of trustees! One hundred and twenty thousand pounds of money raised from sales or otherwise, and appropriated to any purpose rather than the education of the people; transactions gone into and carried out, of which Lord Sydenham said that a Court of Equity behoved to make inquiry! Charges of a most grave character have been brought against the managers of this Institution, and these, though circulated in every possible shape, remain uncontradicted. My impression is, that in all cases of trust, the management ought not to be committed to those who have a personal and selfish interest distinct from and at variance with that of the Institution itself, and to the neglect of this salutary rule may the evils complained of be mainly ascribed. The motion in my hand says it is 'indispensable' that this state of things be no longer allowed. Whether or not the right of nomination to chairs and other offices should be vested in the same persons who have the charge of the funds, may admit of doubt; but there can be no doubt at all that in the present case there must be a radical change in both. I do not see any good reason why the patronage and management may not, under an improved system, be vested in the same body. The question is, what may that body be? Home nomination might do very well in the infancy of the colony, when teachers as well as ministers must necessarily be brought from the mother country; nor even in an advanced state of the colony would I be understood as shutting up that source of supply. But you can easily see that a Downing Street or Whitehall nomination is liable to many objections, partly on the ground of politics, and partly on the ground of private influence; and, moreover, that the native talent of the colony ought as far as possible to be cherished. If you transfer the nomination from Great Britain to the representative of the Sovereign in the Colony, apart from his Council, you recognize a vicious principle of internal discord, which almost necessarily involves civil dissention; while you leave what we call sinister or back-stairs influence its full sway. There is and has been, and no where more than in Upper Canada, a malignant influence which has worked unseen, a deleterious miasma, like that which rises out of the chinks in an Italian soil; a dark and hidden agency, which, like the simoom or samiel of the desert, carries death and desolation every where, and is, indeed, the 'pestilence which walketh in darkness,' such an agency we must try and trace out, and even where we merely suspect it to exist, seek its destruction. In whom shall we repose the patronage and management of the College, is, indeed, a grave question, and there will be difficulties in every view of it; but we may surely avoid the crying evils of the present system, and especially those which arise out of a scheme of self-election and self-control. Let the trust be essentially colonial, and let it be controled by regular review of the Legislature. Let there be adopted a plan by which there shall be presented the fewest possible temptations to make the concerns of the University subservient to private and family interest. Let various colonial bodies or departments be recognized, and the trust partitioned among them. Let there be no nominations for life; and even let the elective system be strictly guarded. The great and rising interests of agriculture, I would especially wish to see represented in the government of the College, not only by the establishment of a chair for Agriculture, but by giving a seat in the Board to the chairman or head of a provincial association, on the plan of the Highland and Agricultural Society of Scotland. The department of Law, as represented by the Benchers in the Law Society of Toronto, might also have a place, in the person of their President or head for the time being. Medicine, too, whose interests have been so shamefully neglected in the present constitution of the College, would have a claim to a seat; as might have the Board of Trade. It is highly politic that the cities, as the great masses of the population, should be represented either by their mayors or otherwise. The Principal of the College, too, might be one of thirteen or fourteen managers; the Rector chosen as in Scotland, by the votes of all matriculated students, and the head of Upper Canada College, when reduced to, or rather elevated into, the rank of a High Grammar School, a feeder of the University, as originally meant by Sir John Colborne. You will ask, do I allot no place to the Government of the land? I do; three seats may be reserved for three nominations by the Governor in Council; one of these to be Vice-Chancellor, to represent the Governor, who may be *ex-officio* Chancellor, but without a seat at the Board. An University court constituted in something this way, would be saved from many of the evils of the present system, and particularly from the dangers of personal, private, sectarian, and political influence.

"The cry about 'vested rights' I dismiss. The munificent boon was clearly meant for the general benefit. Private patrimonial interests, and trusts for the public benefit, are clearly different things; and this belongs to the last of these; and can we doubt the readiness of the Queen and Council to give up even a 'vested right' for the sake of such a Province as Canada. I would not reject a bill otherwise good, even though the patronage were vested in the Governor in Council, provided they were bound regularly to report their minutes. But remember, the Governor and Council are now at Montreal, not in Toronto, and the distance, together with the multiplicity of their affairs, might occasion a neglect in the trust ; and the management might be committed absolutely to a factor, something on the present plan, and who would undertake to give his present employers as little trouble as possible, provided only his salary were liberal and well paid. Keep, my friends, by the words ' colonial ' and ' indispensable,' and let the responsibility be complete. We seek the interest of literature and science and art ; and these will be secured by such a reform as we propose. Theology we set aside ; knowing that it will be well attended to by the different denominations. Tests also we dispense with, not because a man's religious principles are of little moment, but because in point of fact, the plan of tests has not succeeded well. We think that the great object which we seek will be best attained by a proper patronage of the chairs. Is religion all comprehended within the chair of theology ? Is it not secured otherwise than by religious tests ? Is there no Christianity in the Province ? And are not the men who may be called in to the patronage and management of the College bound to act as religious men, and expected to do so ?   I give up tests, but not as some of the brethren of different denominations seem to say, because electors to chairs have nothing to do with the religious opinions of candidates. Does it make no difference whether a candidate be an atheist, or a socialist, or an adherent to demoralizing systems, or a sound and godly man ? Would you care not whether the man were a devout observer of the Lord's day, or whether he were seen careering in folly on the holy day through the grounds of the College ? Would my friends who have spoken in the terms to which I allude, administer no oath at all *de fideli,* to the holders of the sacred trust of the College investment ?   But is an oath worth anything without the fear of God ? And is not the fear of God and his oath a religious act ?

" All education ought to be based on religion ; and a main element in the election of teachers, ought to be their religion. I do not know on what grounds the last speaker has said that a ' blustering infidel ' is not in the least likely to be chosen to any chair. I am not sure of that. I look at France in the days of atheistical ascendancy ; and I look at some of the German Universities, too ; and I see a bustling and a blustering infidelity getting along, alas ! too well. But I hope to see such men kept out, by the rising Christianity of the country ; by the force of public opinion ; by views of duty and expediency both. Men are bound to be religious when acting as guardians of a public trust like that of a College : they are bound to carry their religion with them everywhere ; and nations, as such, are bound to honour God and support His cause. We differ much on many things ; but there are common principles in which we agree. My friends, I call myself now a colonist and a Canadian, and my wish and aim is, that your College may be redeemed from its gross abuses, and raised to what it should always have been, an

z

enlightened, liberal, well-managed, and successful school of instruction to all classes in our large and growing community."

My father was fond of characteristic sketches. Many of these (such as of Dr. Balfour, Sir Harry Moncrieff, " the Apostle of the North") he drew up for the *Christian Instructor*, the *Record*, &c. He had an ample treasury of incident from which to draw. In such literary labours of love he wrote out of the abundance of his heart. When in an ordinarily happy vein, these rapidly-executed productions of his prolific pen were vivid and graphic, and eminently readable. The following, on his Brother, the Pastor of Kilsyth, may give some idea of these. We select it, not because superior to many others, but because it sheds light on his own history, and reveals the happy relations which obtained between the older and younger brothers:

" Dr. William Hamilton Burns, late of Kilsyth, was born at the town of Falkirk, Stirlingshire, on the 5th of February, 1779. His father, John Burns, was at that time a merchant in the town, but was soon afterwards appointed to the office of Surveyor of Customs at the port of Borrowstowness, and he held also, for fifteen years, the factorship on the Duke of Hamilton's estate of Kinneil. He died in 1817, at the venerable age of eighty-eight. He was present, though merely as a spectator, at the battle of Falkirk in 1746, and often entertained the members of his family with anecdotes of that remarkable time. He was one of many in Scotland whose religious character was formed under the ministry of the celebrated Whitfield, who occasionally resided under his father's roof.

" Dr. Burns began his studies for the ministry in the College of Edinburgh, in 1791, and with the exception of one session which he spent at St. Andrew's, the whole of his curriculum was passed at the metropolitan university. In all the departments of study he stood high, particularly in languages and theology. As he was my senior by ten years, he had become a parish minister two years before I entered college, and the summer vacations of 1803, 1804, and 1805 were spent by me at the beautiful manse of Dun, a small parish of six hundred souls, which enjoyed his ministry for more than twenty years; and there we read together more Greek and Latin, from the classic authors, than it has been my lot to encounter, with equal success, ever since. At St. Andrew's he was intimate with Dr. Chalmers, and often battled with him on deep points, in regard to which that eminent man, as he afterwards acknowledged, was in grievous error. I do not think that my brother ever met with Chalmers from the time of their residence together at St. Andrew's till 1804, when that eminent man was in my elder brother's manse at Brechin, on his way to the ordination of David Harris, another fellow-student, over the parish of Fearn, a small country charge, which would have been unknown to fame had it not been that its family biography could boast of the classic ancestry of a Gillies and a Tytler. In those days Chalmers was heard of in the 'Kingdom of Fife' as a 'genius,' or sort of 'warlock,' and as I was then sojourning in "the bishop's palace," in Brechin, well do I recollect the awe, not unmingled with terror, with which I gazed on his large head, bushy raven locks, and penetrating eye. I did not hear him utter a word, and this confirmed me in the truth of the information that had been previously given me, that he was 'a dungeon of knowledge.'

" At Edinburgh my brother had as his confrères, both in the Hall and in the 'Old Theological Society,' such men as John Leyden, Dr. Robert Watt, author of the 'Bibliotheca Britannica;' Sir Robert Spankie, afterwards one of the Supreme Judges of India; Dr. Corkindale, of Glasgow; and Sir Andrew Halliday. With two of these, Dr. Watt and Sir Robert Spankie, he contested the honours of prizemanship, coming off senior to the one and second to the other. The subjects of essay were 'Regeneration'

and 'Prayer.' With both subjects my brother was even
then practically and experimentally familiar; not so the
others, for their views were latitudinarian, and after
gazing for a period on the depths of Calvinistic theology,
they, with a high-toned honesty which did them credit,
bade adieu 'to the Divinity Hall, studied medicine and
law, and rose to distinguished honour in both departments.

"From 1797 to 1799 my brother resided at Park Place,
in Galloway, as tutor to the present Sir James Dalrymple
Hay, whose son, Captain Hay, of the *Indus*, has written
so ably on the improvement of the British navy.   His
predecessor in the family was the warm-hearted, witty,
and facetious John Wightman, of Kirkmahoe; and his
successor was Dr. Thomas Gillespie, a scholar and a poet,
afterwards Professor of Humanity at St. Andrew's, and
brother-in-law of Lord Campbell, the present Lord Chancellor of England.   At a distance of years, the same place
was held by my much esteemed friend, Dr. Forrest, a ripe
scholar too, and now Chief Superintendent of Education
in Nova Scotia.   It was while preceptor in this family
my brother had an opportunity of spending a winter in
the City of York, where he got acquainted with a number
of pious and learned divines of the English Church, who
esteemed him not the less that he 'took license' for himself and not from the bishop, and 'opened his mouth' on
one or two occasions in an Independent or Congregational
assembly.   In those days such uncanonical doings were
held as allowable only *south* of the Tweed.

"It was in the summer of 1799, my brother received his
real license from the Presbytery of Stranraer, and preached his first sermon in the pulpit of Dr. Coulter, the venerable incumbent of that town and parish.   He then bade
farewell to Galloway, but he carried with him, and ever
afterwards retained, a warm attachment to the land which
had been watered with the blood of martyrs, and where,
amid the freezing soil of moderatism, he saw, or thought
he saw, oozing out some of the living drops or streams of
an undisguised covenanterism.   Many years rolled away

ere he paid another visit to these haunts of his earlier days; but he kept up a constant intercourse with some of the branches of the respected family of Dunragget, and when Dr. William Symington, then of Stranraer, now of Glasgow, and a man of no mean name, introduced me in September, 1838, to the inmates of that mansion, how delighted they were to tell me little stories of the venerated preceptor and his pupils.

"My brother never enjoyed the ambiguous delectabilities of a 'preachership at large.' We in Canada call that sort of thing now a 'mission;' but it was not so dignified in our early days, and be its joys many or few, my brother never had them, for in autumn of 1799 he became regular assistant to the worthy old minister of Dun, the Rev. James Lauder. On the 4th of December, 1800, my brother was ordained assistant and successor to this venerable minister of 'the olden time,' and for two or three years, during which the colleagueship continued, the harmony was perfect. It was not from the identical pulpit of the great 'superintendent of Angus,' the Baron of Dun, that my brother gave forth the same message that thrilled on the lips of the evangelistic Brownlow North of his day, but it was in the same parish church, now unroofed indeed, and converted into a family necropolis; but still exactly what Samuel Rutherford's church at Anworth is, a simple but impressive memorial of Knox and his days. I have a lithograph of it and a history now before me, and I shall present both to the museum of our college. Need I say that the publication of the 'Life of Knox' in 1810, was soon followed by a visit of the distinguished McCrie to the manse of Dun, to examine the 'Dun papers,' and to gaze on the interesting localities. The superintendent died in March, 1590, at the advanced age of eighty years.

"From 1800 to 1821, my brother discharged the duties of the pastorship in this lovely but small parish, with a painstaking piety, and earnestness rarely equalled, never excelled. During the same period he acted as clerk to the Presbytery of Brechin, and never did official enjoy more thoroughly the confidence and the warm affections of all his brethren.

"In 1820, the large and influential parish of Kilsyth, in Stirlingshire, became vacant by the death of Dr. Rennie, a minister of learning and of piety who, though a native of the parish, was much respected. Our family had interest with Sir Charles Edmonstone, of Duntreath, the principal heritor, and a crown presentation was issued in favour of my brother, who, with the free and hearty approval of all parties, was inducted to the charge in 1821. What a change! From a pastorship of six hundred to one of nearly four thousand! But the minister was in the full vigour of his manhood, his graces developing with mental progress and application, with a large experience, and a well prepared stock of lectures and sermons. To quote the words of Dr. Smyth, of St. George's, Glasgow, the endeared friend and fellow-labourer who preached one of the sermons on his death : ' Of the value of his ministerial services it is hardly possible to give an exaggerated estimate. With talents of a decidedly superior order; literary and theological acquirements alike accurate and varied ; depth and tenderness of spirit in addressing all classes of hearers ; and pre-eminently distinguished by the spirit of grace and supplication, our beloved and lamented father was truly a master in Israel.' His speech and his preaching were not with enticing words of man's wisdom, but in demonstration of the spirit and in power. His theology was that of the good olden school of the Scottish professors, the Erskines, Fishers and Bostons of the last century ; these men 'mighty in the Scripture,' whose names are identified with all that is sound in doctrine, and powerful in appeal to the conscience and the heart.

"It was in July, 1839, the first symptoms of an awakened concern in regard to religion and eternity showed themselves among the people of Kilsyth. Just about a century before in 1742-3, Cambuslang, Kilsyth, and the West of Scotland generally had been scenes of great awakening; and there cannot be a doubt, but amid a good deal that was discouraging, as may be ever expected in all such cases, many hundreds ascribed their first religious impressions to such seasons of revival, and passed through the pilgrimage of life thereafter in the full habit and with all the usual features of genuine discipleship. And so it was in regard to the awakening of 1839. In the ' New Statistical Account of Scotland," my brother has given a condensed account of the awakening, and after two years had elapsed, his impressions of the good done in that season of divine visitation are thus summed up: 'There are, we have reason to hope, not a few who have been savingly turned from sin unto God, while in other respects, the religion and morals of the people at large are much improved. The places of worship are better attended, and there is more general seriousness during divine service than formerly. Many family altars have been erected. There is a greater degree of zeal among us for missionary objects ; and there are about thirty weekly prayer meetings of a private kind among our people, not including those which are connected with dissenting bodies.'

"During the whole period of the 'ten years' conflict,' my brother's mind never wavered. He had taken up his position, from long tried conviction, and he kept it without shrinking. And yet, few of the brethren in the ministry made a more costly sacrifice. His living in the Established Church, taken all in all, could not be less than from £350 to £400. This he surrendered without a grudge, and for fourteen years thereafter considerably less than one-half of this income became his portion. His was indeed the lot of many ante-disruption ministers, who had thus largely a trial of 'the spoiling of their goods.'

" From the commencement of his ministry my brother kept a diary of occurrences both domestic and public, with sketches of character often very graphic. Such memorials are interesting, and they form the very best sources of authentic narratives and of historic delineations. When in Scotland in 1857 I had an opportunity of perusing many of these sketches. The substance of those which refer to the ' revivals' is already before the public in various shapes; and it may admit of a doubt whether it would be advisable to print the other memorials during the present generation.

" Till within the last three years Dr. B. had no regular help in the performance of pastoral duties. Up to the 78th year of his age he was enabled by the help of God to discharge both the public and the private duties of the pastoral office, but he felt it then his duty to apply to the Church for a colleague and successor. This was granted, and the Rev. Mr. Black was called to this office. On that gentleman have now devolved all the responsibilities of the charge, and great are the advantages connected . with an entrance on fields of labour already successfully cultivated by predecessors who have made full proof of their ministry.

" The minister of Kilsyth was one of the earliest movers in Scotland in behalf of the interests of temperance. The field of his pastoral labours, and the scenes presented in the neighbouring city, furnished most impressive practical arguments in support of the cause; and he continued a steady and active advocate of abstinence principles to the close of his life.

" The death-bed scene of this tried servant of God was not prolonged beyond a few weeks, but he suffered severely towards the close of that period. A calm serenity marked the complacency of his soul in God, and in those great and precious promises which it had been his delight to expound, and still more experimentally to realise. His life had been one undivided course of fidelity, uprightness, and deep-toned spirituality; and the evidence of such a life is self-testifying. His dying bed was surrounded by his nearest relatives, by his affectionate and pious surviving partner, and by his children and his children's children. The words which issued from his lips were sweet and edifying, and he glorified God in dying, as he had done in living. Happy in his family—all of nine members he had seen comfortably settled in spheres of usefulness— and literally without on enemy on earth, his soul winged its flight gladly on high, and his mortal remains repose with the ashes of not a few of his spiritual children, with whom he shall again appear in the day of the retribution of all things; for 'he was a good man and full of the Holy Ghost and of faith, and much people was added unto the Lord.'—Acts xi. 24.

"Toronto, July 8, 1859."

Among his many admirable qualities, " Uncle William." was a capital letter writer. Distinctly do we recall his full, venerable form ; his pleased, placid countenance ; his staid gait, " the measured step and slow ;" his deep bass voice, with its almost oracular utterances of heavenly wisdom,—terse, sententious, at times quaint and curious ; and that atmosphere of holiness and happiness encompassing him, which revealed ever the "conversation in heaven."

Between the brothers a regular correspondence was kept up. One of his last letters to my father was the following :—

"KILSYTH, Nov. 29th, 1858.

"Andrew Moody is a pupil of Hetherington, and of Douglas. He has obtained the first prize for an essay which is highly creditable to him. If health be given him, he promises to be a distinguished éleve of the new college. Your son William, made a very favourable impression on us all. We have good news of our William's kind reception in a new place, five miles from Swatow, where he preached to a large assembly in the open air, and was hospitably received, and his assistants, by a wealthy Chinaman, who seems to be embracing the truth. D. Sandeman's death was truly an afflictive event—most unlooked for ; he was so stout and vigorous—to our view.

"The excellent mother writes to me in reply to my letter of condolence—in a truly gracious spirit. 'As days so shall strength be,' to them that know HIS NAME and trust in Him. Husband and three sons have been removed within a very short period. Old brother John, wonderfully well at his age—lately in Edinburgh. I'm glad to see William's gift to your college library acknowledged. George will, no doubt, be corresponding direct with you. He preached here two months ago, with fully more than average vigour. Mr Bain, (C. Angus,) and J. C. B., of Kirkliston, were with us at our communion on the 7th, and also Johnston, lately from China. Your Elizabeth has really done her part wonderfully, as your companion in travel. Our Elizabeth is also a great help to me, and my good Lady Edmonstone puts entire confidence in her as her almoner. We both are in our usual health, and with strength more than common at our time of life. But what do you think of Mr. Anderson, senr., (United Presbyterian minister, Kilsyth, and father of Dr. William Anderson, Glasgow,) preaching the other day an hour and ten minutes, in his ninetieth year? But this is a rare exception indeed, and not to be made too much of. 'YET A LITTLE WHILE, AND HE THAT SHALL COME WILL COME.' This was often in our revered father's prayers."

Within six months, and the lively hope of this "old disciple" became fruition. On the 6th May, of the following year, the chariot was at the door, for whose coming he waited patiently all the days of his appointed time. It was but "a little while."

"I die in peace. I will see His face, and I will behold His glory—GLORY, GLORY, GLORY."

"I hear His voice, let me go. Thanks, thanks, be to God, who giveth us the victory." With these words of triumph on his lips, as the first faint streaks of a May Sabbath morn stole in at the casement of the quiet manse, this good and faithful servant entered into the joy of His Lord, and passed up to the songs and services of the never-ending Sabbath.

Between him and the brother to whom he thus pleasantly wrote, exactly ten years intervened in life—and in death, they were divided within a month or two of the same time. They both more than rounded their four score, and for fifty-nine years served their generation in the ministry of the Gospel.

My father aided Dr. Sprague, of Albany, in the preparation of his sketch of Dr. Codman, for the " Annals of the American Pulpit."

He also prepared for him a sketch of his predecessor Dr Witherspoon—which was too late for the first edition. In connexion with these sketches he received the following:

"ALBANY, 10th December, 1860.

"MY DEAR DR. BURNS,—I thank you sincerely for your kind letter, and the accompanying corrections of the typographical errors in your admirable letter, concerning Dr. Codman. I shall see that the list is placed in the hands of the printer, before the next edition is issued, so that I hope you will find hereafter that the types have done you full justice.

"In regard to publishing an appendix to my work, I cannot now speak with much confidence, as it will be at least two years before the last volume comes from the press. But, however, this may be, I think it of great importance that your hereditary reminiscences of Dr. Witherspoon, should in some way become the property of our Presbyterian church, and I venture earnestly to request that you will write them out at your leisure, and let me secure their publication—if not immediately in my own work, yet in the *Presbyterian*, or some one of our monthlies or quarterlies. I am sure that by doing this, you will place our church under great obligation to you ; for if there is any one among the fathers, whom we all delight to honour, and whose history, even in its minutest details, we cannot permit to let perish, it is Dr. Witherspoon. Thank you, for your very kind opinion of the several volumes of my work already published.

"In regard to the Methodist denomination, I have not found it so unproductive or difficult a field as you might suppose. In regard to intellectual culture, I do not think that, as a denomination, they fall behind the Baptists ; and there is no doubt, that among their comparatively uneducated men, they have had some of the first pulpit orators this country has ever produced. It is equally certain that, with all their extravagances, both of doctrine and of practice, many of them have evinced the most heroic self-denial in penetrating into the wilderness, and anticipating every other denomination in planting the Gospel in the very darkest parts of it.

"I record many things in my volume, both as matters of fact and as characteristics, which I should be far from endorsing, and some which are exceedingly distasteful to me ; but notwithstanding all this, I am satisfied that living Christianity owes them a debt in this country, which has hitherto been but very imperfectly acknowledged.

"You *had* told me in a previous letter, of your finally recovering the box of books, though I regret exceedingly that you were subjected to so much trouble about it. I remember at the time that I thought it difficult to account for it, without supposing foul play among some of the railroad officials.

"Our country, as the newspapers tell you, has reached a fearful crisis. Unless God interposes in some marvellous way, the days of our union as a nation, will soon be numbered. I thank God there is one government in the universe that the caprice and folly of man cannot overturn.

"Ever, my dear Dr. Burns,

"Sincerely and affectionately yours,

"W. B. SPRAGUE."

Dr. Sprague's antiquarian likings suited him exactly, and they had much pleasant and profitable intercourse. He made some valuable Scottish additions to Dr. Sprague's extraordinary collection of autographs, and received from him in return, some valuable American ones, and several of his works kindly addressed.

A sketch in the *Instructor*, of Hog, of Carnock, drew from the distinguished historian of the church of the Netherlands, the Rev. Dr. Steven, this friendly criticism:

"ROTTERDAM, 20th Nov. 1838.

"REV. AND DEAR SIR,—I trust to your forgiveness for the liberty I take, though personally unknown, in thus addressing you. Indeed, I have been so long acquainted with your public character as an author, and a valued leader in our national church courts, that I feel convinced you will not regard as obtrusive the communication of a brother clergyman, however humble that correspondent may be. If I am not mistaken, you have some connection with the Edinburgh *Christian Instructor*, a periodical which appears to me vastly improved, having all the freshness of its best days—and freed from that heaviness which, at times disfigured it.

"In the October number of the *Instructor*, I find an excellent paper on the Rev. James Hog, of Carnock. The writer of that memoir, which I have perused with great pleasure, does not appear to have been aware, that Hog was the son of the minister of Larbert, and that he was nephew to Mr. Thomas Hog, of Kiltearn. I am anxious that the respected author of the life in the *Instructor* for last month, should, through your kindness, be put in possession of the accompanying copy of a letter from James to Thomas Hog. I had transcribed it, some time ago for my own use, but conceiving that it may be of service to the biographer, I transmit it to you. I have the original letter now before me, and several other old letters from Craighead, of Londonderry, Wodrow, &c., addressed to my predecessor, Mr. Thomas Hog or Hoog. These interesting relics belonging to the venerable Burgomaster Hoog, of this city, have been discovered among the family papers, since I published my account of the British churches in the Netherlands.

"Should you, or any of your friends be engaged with memoirs of ministers once resident in Holland, it will afford me great pleasure to facilitate such researches—as far as lies in my power. I have a third edition of my pamphlet on 'Constitution of the Dutch Reformed Church,' in the press at Edinburgh.

"I shall be delighted to hear from you."

The knowledge of his skill in the line of historical reminiscence and graphic biographical delineation, led the late Rev. James Mackenzie, of Dunfermline, to whom had been entrusted the preparation of the Life of Dr. Cunningham, to invite his assistance.

A life-like sketch of Dr. Macdonald, of Ferintosh, had attracted special notice, and he writes as follows :—

"DUNFERMLINE, July 12th, 1866.

"REV. SIR,—The family of the late Dr. Cunningham, have put his papers into my hands, requesting me to prepare a memoir, in which work I am now engaged. I would not be in my duty if I did not apply to you, for any materials or recollections that you may have.

"Your knowledge of Dr. Cunningham extended over a long time, and your letter on the 'Apostle of the North,' in the June *Record* of the Canada Presbyterian Church, encourages me to hope that you may favour me with something similar, in regard to Principal Cunningham. Your connection in the Presbytery of Paisley, and in the American journey, must have left reminiscences, which, if you will kindly impart, will be a very great obligation.

"Hoping that you will grant this great favour,

"I am, Rev'd Sir,

"Your most ob't servant,

"JAMES MACKENZIE,

"Minister of Free Abbey Church."

It does not appear that this request was complied with
The death of the lamented writer, in the midst of his
work may have interfered. Of this we feel assured, that
none would have been more willing than my father to do
honour to the name of Cunningham, his old co-Presbyter and co-delegate, for whom he entertained an enthusiastic regard, and to whom, in certain features of his
character, he bore a strong resemblance. In reading some
of the delineations of the one, we have felt as if the other
had almost sat for the picture.

Thus—for example :—

"The kindliness which struck every one who met him in private,
was joined with a transparency that never left you in doubt for a
moment, that you saw the whole man. What you thus saw, was
full of nobleness morally, and power intellectually. Then his
faults or infirmities, which were perhaps the most unconcealed parts
of him, were so allied to his force, clearness, and scorn of baseness
—were indeed such delightful exaggerative illustrations of these—
that they merely printed him larger on the mind ; while the touch
of exaggeration or over-vehemence, soothed you with the sense of
an imperfection to be tender to, and warmed the whole mode of
feeling with which he was regarded. Indeed, it must have often
crossed the mind of those who knew him, that what no doubt were
his faults and weak points, and were so regarded by himself, were
somehow the points in his character that nobody would have liked
to dispense with ; and if he had been enabled, totally and absolutely to eradicate them, as there is no doubt he often and sorrowfully
strove to do, I am much afraid his friends would never have forgiven
him for his success ; so near of kin were they to that in him which
we admired and trusted. Nor was this feeling confined to friends.
In all his successive controversies, the same feeling existed among
opponents—if only they had chanced to get near enough to know
the real man." *

A case with which, as a party, he had to do, in almost
boyhood's days, may here be recalled—the case referred
to at page 11. It is a very singular one, and deserves a

_____

* Life of Dr. Cunningham, pp. 382-3.

fuller notice, which would have caused too lengthened a digression there, but which in this "sketch" department of our miscellaneous chapter may be not inappropriately introduced. Our readers may remember the juvenile efforts of the boy preachers, and the "wooden pulpit." In this extraordinary instance, at the expiry of fifty years, they had their reward.

Mary P——, for half a century was a noted drunkard. In the delirium of a drunken debauch she fell into the fire, and was all but consumed. In 1849, when cholera struck down her two manly sons, she crept, in the half-unconscious stage of drunkenness, amid the infected clothes and blankets of the bed from which the corpses of her boys had been taken. Yet—she escaped—only to cry " When shall I awake ; I will seek it yet again ?" She returned for years succeeding, " as a dog to his vomit, or as a sow that has been washed, to her wallowing in the mire." The demon of drink dealt with his hapless victim, like the Devil with the youth in the Gospel story —and it was not until she seemed likely to represent the " sinner dying a hundred years old, accursed"—that the Angel of the Covenant interposed to snatch her, saying :—" The Lord rebuke thee, O Satan, is not this a brand plucked out of the fire."

In 1859, one dark night found her at the pastor's study, an applicant for communion, for the first time. Her hard life had whitened her locks and furrowed her cheeks. Into the wondering pastor's ear she poured this confession :—" You well know that my besetting sin was the love of drink. It has been a sore fight, but through the

blood of the Lamb, I have got the victory. I saw it was
necessary for me not only to pray, but, to use other means,
so that, with the help of God, I would not be carried
away. I knew Jesus was able to keep me from falling,
but I must watch for my soul. The desire was strong in
me, for for fifty years I had been a drunkard. I could
not pass a public house without the wish to taste. It had
been my first work in the morning and my last work in
the evening, to take a glass. How was I to keep myself
from the tempter and the temptation? I knew no way
but this. I lay in bed for days—for weeks, in prayer, in
thought, until God should take away from me the very
wish to taste. I felt that I must fight the devil out, and
that I must fight him out now and there. In his great
mercy, God gave me such peace of mind, and such comfort
in Jesus, that I began to think that I might rise and walk
safely, and from that day till now, I have not tasted
drink, and I think the desire of it has gone from me for
ever."

Subsequently, when conversing with her more particularly on the causes of her change, he got from her the following :—

"When a girl, I was sent to live with an uncle far away
from this place, at a seaport in the Firth of Forth. My
uncle was in the Customs, and I was a servant in the
house. Beside us there lived another family—the father
in the same service with my uncle, and he had a numerous family—six sons, I think, and three daughters. I remember four of their names yet, James, William, Robert,
George.

" In their garden there was a large summer house, and it was fitted up as a place of meeting. I distinctly remember when the young men came home from school or college, they used to assemble all the neighbours to speak to them about religion. Many a solemn word—many a warm prayer have I heard in that place, &c."

" Well Mary, (replied the pastor,) I know to whom you refer. The names of those young men have become household words in the church of Christ, and are connected with all that is living, and earnest, and devoted in religion. Two of them have already entered on their eternal rest, leaving fragrant memories, and the other two have reached an extreme old age in their Master's service. Their children too, have inherited the blessing.

" So—Mary, in your case also, it seems, the bread cast upon the waters, has been found after many days."

She lived a wonderfully earnest and consistent Christian ; and her end was peace. On her death-bed—to alleviate her acute pain, gin was offered her—but with the Master when " wine mingled with myrrh" was offered to him—"she would not drink." " I know not yet, (said she,) but what I might fall under the old lust, and I will rather suffer than sin."

A A

CHAPTER XX.

VISIT TO SCOTLAND AND LAST DAYS.

N April, 1868, he revisited Scotland, together with his faithful partner.*   The Rev. J. M. King, M.A., their much esteemed pastor and friend, accompanied them.   He originally purposed returning in time for the College Session, but was prevailed on to spend the winter at home.

He appeared at the Free Church General Assembly in May, along with Mr. King, and met with a cordial reception.   He spoke with his usual vigour and animation.

---

* He sojourned for a short time in Montreal on his way, among his kind friends at Terrace-bank. Mr. John Dougall, the founder and senior editor of that remarkably useful Journal, the *Montreal Witness*, who remembered his Paisley ministry in his youth, records thus pleasingly his impressions at the time:

"This venerable patriarch of the Presbyterian Church, bears the weight of fourscore years with that vigour which has characterized all his previous history, and appears, in fact, fresher and stronger than he did ten years ago. His intellectual powers, including

The Moderator, the Rev. Wm. Nixon, of Montrose, thus addressed him :

" With the deepest sentiments of respect, esteem, and thankfulness to the God of all grace, to the God of our life and the length of our days, we welcome this renewed visit of such a veteran of our church, and of one whom we have been familiar with from our youth, as one of the ablest, most accomplished, and most active and laborious of our ministers, and the most devoted and effective of all loving friends of Presbyterianism and true religion in the Dominion of Canada. It is pleasant to think of the recompense of all your unwearied exertions in the present comparatively advanced condition of the church in Canada. We rejoice to see that in the highest sense your eye has not yet become dim, nor your natural force abated. And we pray and hope that you may yet be spared for years to do yet more and more for the kingdom of your Lord, and to see His goodness in the land of the living, and that in due time you will rest from your labours, by having an abundant entrance ministered unto you into the kingdom of your Lord."

His diary reveals how crowded with varied duties were these months of sojourn—sabbath and sacramental engagements—attendance at Dr. Wylie's lectures before the Protestant Institute, those of the Rev. J. H. Wilson, on the Pilgrim's Progress, and those of the Professors at the College;—ransacking treasures in the Advocates' and Free College Libraries, favourite places of resort; poring over books in private libraries; collecting books for Montreal and Knox Colleges, at Clarke's and elsewhere; conversing with friends about bursaries and scholarships,* or with likely men, about Canada as a

memory, are in no way impaired,—the latter being, indeed, extraordinary. He remembers, with the utmost precision, the persons and incidents and occurrences of the time of his settlement in Paisley, in 1811, or the radical time of 1818, or, in fact, any year of his long and useful career ; and, consequently, his conversation is a rare treat to those who take an interest in the past. His knowledge of Canada is also very extensive, on account of his frequent preaching tours through various parts of it. Dr. Burns belongs to a family remarkable for the number of ministers it has furnished to the church, as does Mrs. Burns, *née* Bonar. They leave to-day to take the steamer at Portland, and many prayers will be offered for their prosperous journey and safe return."

* Through his application the "Scottish Reformation Society" made offer to the three Colonial Colleges, of one-half of the sum required for two prizes in each, of £10 and £5 sterling for the successful competitors in examination on the "leading principles of the Romish Controversy." "I have just received," he writes from Edinburgh, April

field of labour; visiting missions, and re-visiting the old familiar churches; speaking to companies of students on congenial themes; travelling in the Highlands to help ministerial brethren, and to visit friends; addressing conferences on the state of religion; writing letters—sometimes ten a day; preparing the Canada chapter of W. C. Burns' life, with occasional autobiographical jottings.—These were among the duties which occupied him.

A few extracts from letters of this period will give some idea of how he was employed:

"EDINBURGH, April, 1869.

"I had a noble congregation yesterday at Mr. Morgan's, Foun tainbridge. The thought of the deep interest your dear brother* took in the erection of that church, was much with me, and pressed favourably on my mind.

"We are going down to a grand meeting at Queen Street Hall, at two o'clock, where we expect to hear a number of great men (see list in *Daily Review* of this morning).

"My 'chapter work' gets on (chap. x., W. C. B's memoir), about half done, and many letters to write. I cannot do much more to the MSS. without your help. My eyes are sadly worn by gazing on the MSS., and trying to decipher and condense. Don't make haste on this account, however.

"The conference at Glasgow has asked me to take part in it, and Mr. Wilson urges me. Independently of this I feel inclined to go.

"Monday, 19th April, 1869.—Attended seventy-first meeting of Sabbath schools. Death of Mrs. Briggs.†"

Dr. Burns was at Paisley at the time, after having

14th, 1869, "from Professor MacVicar, Montreal, the following notice of the reception of the Society's offer:" 'May I ask you to be so kind as to inform the Reformation Society that the conditions of their minutes have been complied with, and to convey to them our best thanks, and our deep appreciation of the kind interest they have thus shown in our work. The Society have singularly anticipated our desire to offer our students special inducements to study the Popish question, which is daily growing in practical importance in this province and on the whole continent. We intend, hereafter, to require students to study the French language, so as to enable them to operate upon the dense spiritual ignorance of this province. I hope to be able next Session to superintend theological studies in that language.'"

* Late Thomson Bonar, Esq.

† His sister Jane, widow of Professor Briggs, of St. Andrew's, special friend of Mrs. Coutts.

spent some days with her.   "Dear Robert," she said, "you have come from Toronto just to see me die.   I like to see you praying, though I cannot always hear."   On receiving the notice he writes:

"Yes! the event has taken place sooner than I anticipated. Her end was peace.   The testimony of the life is of far more value than any utterances on a death-bed."

A truth, this last, to be exemplified subsequently in his own case.

"ST. ANDREWS, April, 1869.—The solemn scene of the inter-ment has passed with all becoming seriousness and decorum.   A large concourse of mourners, as might have been expected, and a number of apologies from Edin. and elsewhere.   These were all addressed to me, as my name was at the invitation circular."

His appearance before the General Assembly of 1869 was one of peculiar interest.   He was accompanied by the Rev. W. Cochrane, of Brantford.   His address is very fully reported, and was received with great enthu-siasm.   It contains a condensed view of the progress of the church in all the British North American colonies. The Union Question, so prominent then, was touched on with great delicacy and skill, as it had been by him the previous year, in a way to elicit enthusiastic demonstra-tions from both sides of the house.

The greetings tendered to Dr. Burns are thus re-. ported.   They were embodied in a resolution moved by Dr. Candlish and seconded by Dr. Begg:

"Dr. Candlish could not abstain from expressing the warmest delight with which he had again listened in that assembly to their revered and beloved father, Dr. Burns.   He was sure they would all join in thanking God that his visit to this country had contri-buted to the re-establishment of his health, and in praying that it might please Almighty God to continue to the last that health and strength which he had manifested amidst the infirmities of old age, though still so vigorous, still so lively, still so much "the old man

eloquent," that he was before he left this country. He did trust
that to the end of his days he would be able to take the same loving,
lively, spiritual, and godly interest in all that pertains to the
advancement of God's work and call to his church."

The Moderator (Sir Henry Moncrieff, Bart.), said—

"In addressing you, Dr. Burns, I feel myself utterly incapable
of expressing either my own feelings or those which are evidently
filling the hearts of the members of this Assembly. When I remember my first intercourse with you, about the commencement of
my own ministry, more than thirty years ago—when, as Dr. Burns,
of Paisley, you attracted the notice of younger members of the
Synod of Glasgow and Ayr as one of our most earnest and eloquent seniors in the ministry—to hear you now is to hear the same
man, but the same man with a still richer eloquence than before—
an eloquence flowing out into a stream of profitable light for guid-
ing us in our thoughts concerning the matters which are stirring
the breasts of yourself and your brethren in the land of your
adoption—the same man bringing all the matured wisdom of your
venerable age to increase the spiritual force and fervour which we
always attached to your character. We have listened with intense
interest to your impressive statements regarding the settlement
near the Red River, the objects to be aimed at in connection with
British Columbia, and the calls addressed both to you and us by
the colonies of Highlanders whom you have so forcibly described
to us. We have great delight in seeing you. We congratulate you
on your vigour both of body and mind. It is an intense gratification to hear you. You raise the tone of our minds by your strikingly clear and full representations, as well as by your fervid and
scriptural appeals. The affections of our heart go strongly toward
you. We pray for your preservation in the service of our Lord,
and we bid you God speed in the prosecution of your intention to
return to the chosen sphere of your labours. We shall not forget
you or your prayers. Our own prayers will follow you. May the
blessing of the Great Head of the Church be upon you abundantly for the peace of your old age and your everlasting joy !"

The last letter he had from Dr. Guthrie speaks of the
joy it gave him to hear of "your ovation at the General
Assembly." This remarkable recognition by the supreme
court of the church of his fathers was a fine rounding off
of his life.

He had paid many visits to Paisley, and preached in

most of the churches.   In anticipation of his leaving, a
gathering of singular interest was held in his old church
on Tuesday evening, the 29th June.   Representatives of
all the churches were present, and sentiments, the most
kind and cordial, were expressed.   His old friend, Provost Murray, presided, and indulged in many pleasing
reminiscences.   *There* was the Rev. William France, the
able and accomplished delegate in 1871 of the United
Presbyterian Church to the American churches—the only
remaining member of the ministerial fraternity in Paisley at the time he left.   *There* was Mr. Pollok, once
one of his most active young men, now just retiring from
a most laborious and honourable pastorate.   *There*, was
one of his Sabbath-school boys, now a rising member in
the British Parliament.   *There* were many on whose
brows he had sprinkled the waters of holy baptism, whom
he had united in the bonds of wedlock, and whose loved
ones he had followed to their long home ; many to whom
he had sustained the relation of pastor and friend, and
whose " children rose up to call him blessed."   A purse
with two hundred and twenty-five sovereigns was presented to him by friends of all denominations, with a
warm-hearted address from Mr. Gardiner, of Nether Common, the little boy now grown venerable, who had been
led up to him by his mother at the church door on the
day of his ordination.   A portion of his reply may be
given :

" My feelings are overpowered by the very unexpected honour
that has been paid me.   I had counted on being permitted quietly
to slip away, loaded, however, with the best wishes, ' understood '
rather than ' expressed,' of many friends.   You have not allowed
it so to be, and words are wanting wherewith to indicate my sense

of obligation.   Nearly threescore years—two generations—have rolled away since my introduction to the ministry in this place. Prior to 1811, when I came to Paisley, the trade had been for years very prosperous, and the wages of the operative weavers averaged weekly from one guinea to three times that sum.   But a time of darkness came, and in 1812 there was a crash, from causes connected with the war then raging.   In the spring of that year I was in London, my companion in travel being a respectable Paisley manufacturer, the late Mr. William Burns, of Gateside.   We attended a public meeting for relief of the suffering manufacturers of England.   Three of the princes of the realm attended the meeting— the Dukes of York, Kent, and Cambridge ; all spoke, and all spoke well.   Mr. Wilberforce and other philanthropists pleaded the cause of suffering humanity, and a fund was then created which continues to this day, and out of which we have drawn from time to time to an extent somewhat commensurate with our necessities.   More than twenty years passed before I had an opportunity of enquiring after the healthy state of this hopeful fund, and the worthy treasurer, whose ominously pleasing or euphonious name was Mr. Help, told us, without the least hesitation, that he was burdened with the load of twenty-five thousand pounds.   It is characteristic of ' a Paisley man,' I fancy, that he never fails to benefit by a good hint ; and yourself, Mr. Chairman, and Dr. Baird and I, failed not to draw plenteously from the mine so propitiously opened to us. The fund was originally devised for English manufactures, but we had influence at the very commencement of it, as above alluded to, to get the word ' British' substituted in place of ' English,' and this made all the difference possible in the matter ; while ' a King's letter,' in 1826, circulating through the cities and counties of the south, replenished the fund when it began to diminish.   With our pilgrimages in and around the metropolis, you, Mr. Chairman, are well acquainted, and for years after I had left Paisley and settled in Canada, you continued to ' walk the course,' knocking at the doors of Whitehall officials and west-end *noblesse;* having acquired, I presume, a kind of liking to such sort of things, and cherishing the thought that you were at once feeding the hungry and establishing great and liberal principles for the public good.   My entrance on the ministry was at a period rather early ; the field vast and difficult, and my experience small.   ' Who is sufficient for these things ?' might I well enquire ; and satisfied have I long been that a smaller preparatory scene of labour would have been more desirable.   Nor did I then thoroughly know the peculiarities of the 'Paisley character.   The Presbyterian clergy, both of the Establishment and the Secession, were all substantially Conservative, and any who breathed more liberal things were afraid to utter them. Still we were all at one in our views of doctrine and duty.   By reason of the love of all the brethren to one another, Rowland Hill called Paisley ' the Philadelphia of Scotland.'   A change of sentiment on some important points no doubt arose, but unity of doctrine and similarity in worship, kept us amicably together, and ' the word of the Lord had free course amongst us and was glorified.' To later changes I shall not advert, but may I not still say, ' one faith, one hope, one God, one Redeemer, one Sanctifier, one home.' "

It seemed providential that Prof. Murray, of Queen's College, Kingston, son of the Chairman, and the Rev. W. Cochrane, M.A., of Brantford, were present, and gave their estimate of the services which Dr. Burns had rendered to his adopted country. In addition to bearing generous testimony as to the extent and influence of Dr. Burns' labours in Canada, Professor Murray said :

"I was brought up, in my earlier years, under the ministry of Dr. Burns. It was under his ministry, and by himself, that I was introduced to the Church of Christ in the ordinance of baptism, of which important ceremony I have no doubt Dr. Burns has about as distinct a recollection as I have myself. It would now be impossible for me to recall to remembrance the sermons which I was privileged to hear from the lips of Dr. Burns ; but I know that a minister often unconsciously moulds the tenor of our whole lives, even although we may not be able to distinctly recall the particular instances where the truths which he proclaimed began to have an influence upon us. Therefore I do not think that I am wrong in saying that even in these earlier days of my life, I may have received from Dr. Burns' ministrations, under which I sat, some of the most valuable influences that have acted upon my subsequent life."

In a like spirit, Mr. Cochrane remarked :

"I cannot help going back twenty-four years ago, when our venerated father, Dr. Burns, preached his farewell sermon in this church. He had then arrived at an age that most professional men regard as entitling them to comparative rest and leisure for the remaining portion of their lives, and had accomplished a work in the West of Scotland second to none of his contemporaries. But at the call of duty, he severed the fondest ties of flesh and blood, bade farewell to his brethren in the ministry, left behind him a numerous, influential, and devoted congregation, and went forth to Canada to help other self-denying men who had preceded him, in laying the foundations of Scottish Presbyterianism in that rising colony. I shall not attempt on the present occasion the most meagre epitome of Dr. Burns' labours in Western Canada during the past twenty-five years. As minister, as professor, and as a sort of universal bishop, he has had the care of all the churches, and the results of his abundant labours are now manifested in many parts of the land.   Why, Mr. Chairman, there is scarcely a spot in Canada where the voice of Dr. Burns has not been heard.   Travelling in summer and in winter enormous distances, and often at great personal inconvenience, with the thermometer varying from blood heat to 20 degrees below zero, and over roads that would shake to pieces a much younger man, the Doctor has accomplished a work that no other minister of our church has ever attempted.   We in Canada feel truly thankful to the Great Head of the Church for having spared him so long, and strengthened him so fully for his abundant labours ; and our prayer is, that for years to come he may adorn the ministry of the Canada Presbyterian Church."

Mr. Cochrane has kindly supplied me with the following very interesting statement, which furnishes vivid glimpses of these closing months, and groups the principal occasions of their meeting in Fatherland :

" It was my good fortune to spend the summer of 1869, in Britain, when Dr. Burns was making his last visit to his native land.   The friendship which existed between us, and official business connected with the church in Canada, brought us frequently together.   On my arrival in Edinburgh, to attend the United Presbyterian Synod, I found him absent on a preaching tour, and assisting at a sacramental season, somewhere in the neighbourhood of Brechin. When I returned a week afterwards, for the Free Church Assembly, the Doctor was in the city, and in almost daily attendance at the Assembly hall.   He had procured tickets of admission to the students' gallery, for several Canadian students then on a visit to the old world, being anxious that they should hear the famous union debates and the various reports on home and foreign missionary operations.   Dr. Burns' love for, and unwearied interest in the welfare of the students of Knox's College, is too well known in Canada to call for remark.

" This attention to their wants, and his willingness to be useful to them, in circumstances where trivial acts of kindness were of special value, were most marked in Scotland.   No labour was deemed irksome that in the smallest contributed to their enjoyment or afforded them opportunities of hearing and coming into contact with men of note in the ecclesiastical world.   As was to be expected, he did not forget, both in public and in private to press the claims of the colonial field, and especially those of Canada, upon the attention of those more immediately interested in that branch of the church's operations.   Several applications in person and by letter had been made to the Doctor, by preachers and students who were turning their thoughts to Canada as their future field of labour. These applications, and the suitability of certain candidates, were a frequent topic of conversation when we met. Eager though he was for additional ministers to fill our vacant pulpits, and occupy the far off regions now opening to emigration, he was exceedingly cautious in selecting.

"No man in Canada had such opportunities of exploring the field and understanding its demands, and no one could so quickly and accurately decide as to the likelihood of success in given cases.

"The evening came when we were to address the Assembly. On many former occasions, the deputies from the Presbyterian churches in the United States, had precedence of the Canadian commissioners. This arrangement the Doctor considered unfair, considering the close relations of the Home to the Colonial churches. In private conversation some days before, he told me what steps he had taken to change the order, although he was by no means sanguine of accomplishing his object. Having succeeded, however, in obtaining for the Canadian deputies *a first hearing*, his next concern was that we should maintain the good name and standing of the church in Canada. Dr. Burns had often in former days, both as deputy and as member of court, addressed that Assembly. To him it was indeed no labour, even at the age of 'four score years' to secure the ear and rivet the attention of any audience. As Dr. Candlish well said, in moving the vote of thanks—he was 'still the old man eloquent,' whose well known voice in former years had thrilled the hearts of thousands and given forth wise counsels in times of threatened danger. On this occasion, however, he seemed more than usually anxious, not only as to how the younger member of the deputation should comport himself, but also in regard to the subjects of his own address. The almost certainty that this would be his last address, before the great Assembly of his much loved mother church—the memory of scenes and associations, and fellowships of other days, and with other leaders long departed, and probably premonitions of the coming end, unperceived by friends, may have tended to increase his solicitude. I need hardly refer to his address before the Assembly, suffice it to say, that it was a noble ending, to a long and arduous life of toil and self-denial, on the platform—in the ministry, and in every department of Christian enterprise that engaged his energies. To say in the somewhat stereotyped language of the press, that he was 'received with applause,' would give but a faint idea of the enthusiasm that prevailed in the vast congregation. It was a simple and spontaneous, but sincere recognition of the services he had rendered to the Scottish church in pre-disruption times, and the sacrifices he had made in sundering tender ties and going far hence to spread the principles of a church he dearly loved.

"After the meeting of the Assembly and previous to his return to Canada, we met frequently, both on public occasions and at the table of mutual friends. I took part with him in assisting the Rev. Alexander Pollok, of the Free South Church, Paisley, at a sacramental season, and was present on the following Tuesday evening at the farewell gathering in Free St. George's. The magnificent testimonial presented him by his fellow townsmen, among whom he had laboured for thirty-four years, brought together representatives from all the different churches in the town and neighbourhood, and was to him an occasion of great joy and heartfelt gratitude. After this he preached a special sermon in behalf of the Paisley Tract Society, and breakfasted on the Monday morning at the house of Dr. Richmond—all the ministers of the town and office-bearers of the society being present. He seemed in the best of health and spirits, and not in the least fatigued by the repeated services of the preceding Sabbath. I never heard him talk more vigorously than on this, the last occasion on which we met. He called up the numerous incidents connected with the formation of the Tract Society—mentioned the names one by one of its early presidents and office-bearers—the sermons he had preached in its behalf during his ministry in Saint George's, and the tracts he had written for circulation under its auspices. The conversation then turned to the various seasons of commercial distress, through which the town had passed, and the frequency of his visits to London to seek government aid for the destitute poor. Then followed the various political contests in which he had occasionally taken a somewhat active part, and finally the great voluntary controversy prior to disruption times, in which the Doctor was an honest and un flinching defender of Establishments. His pen was busy as his tongue during these years—so busy that he had all but forgotten certain pamphlets he had published, until their names were mentioned. It was on this occasion, that the incident which I mentioned in the Toronto Assembly of 1870, occurred. His friend, Dr. Richmond, in referring to ecclesiastical movements and startling events of bygone days, alluded to the little asperities which the voluntary controversy engendered, and the unseemly breaches that were made among Christian brethren of the same faith ; and added ' but I need hardly say that all this was a strange work to our father Dr. Burns—he had no taste for such work, and no love for such a controversy.' ' Stop, stop,' said the Doctor, interrupting his friend, the chairman, ' that is hardly so—I rather think I liked it.' The downright honesty and candour of Dr. Burns were never perhaps more conspicuously seen than in this simple incident. Not that he loved controversy for the sake of controversy or the display of intellectual acuteness, but believing that his opinions were scriptural and right, he threw himself into the arena of debate, and was so thoroughly absorbed in it, that it became congenial and not distasteful work.

" In our occasional meetings, the Doctor talked freely about Can-

ada and his future plans in the land of his adoption. He spoke
hopefully of his return to professorial and ministerial duty, and
coming years of occasional service in the church. The new house
then building for him—but which he never entered—'which would
be so conveniently situated to the college,' was matter of repeated
remark.

"Those of his friends who imagined he would remain in Scotland,
little understood the intense love which he bore to the Canada Presbyterian Church, and all that appertained to her history. In a
modified sense, the closing stanza of Augustine's hymn expresses
the feelings of his soul towards his beloved Zion :—

> "Jerusalem my happy home !
> My soul still pants for thee ;
> Then shall my labours have an end,
> When I thy joys shall see."

For notices of his last weeks in Scotland, and his last
days after his return, we gladly avail ourselves of the
deeply interesting journal of her who, for a quarter of a
century, had been truly "a help meet for him;" to whose
thoughtful solicitude for his personal comfort, and practical sympathy in his public work, he owed so much.

"On the 7th January, 1869, Dr. Burns and I accompanied Rev.
Mr. Thomson to a district missionary meeting, in Gray's Close, Canongate. The Doctor was deeply interested in his audience, such a
crowd of hitherto poor uncared for outcasts.

"He spoke to them on the 'faith of Abraham' and at the close,
was surrounded by many to shake hands and express their gratitude. We then walked up High street, along Grassmarket, to
Vennel United Presbyterian Church, where there was a similar
meeting, and there he also spoke, not getting home till a late
hour.

"January 18th.—Dr. Burns attended a missionary meeting of Rose
street United Presbyterian congregation, in Queen Street Hall.
Very fine meeting. Rev. Dr. Finlayson presided, and Dr. Burns
was most enthusiastically welcomed.

"In the early part of the Spring of 1869, he had a great desire
to visit the Continent and supply one of the churches there for a
few weeks. He made application, but the arrangements having
been made, his wish was not gratified.

"He was satisfied afterwards, for he would have been absent
during the last illness of his sister, Mrs. Briggs.

"Many homes were open to him in Paisley, but our principal

headquarters were at Mr. Morgan's, Greenlaw, where unbounded kindness and hospitality were enjoyed. Mrs. M. had formerly been one of the children of his flock ; and it was her joy now to see her venerable pastor take her baby in his arms, and for the elder ones to gather around his knee and get his smile and blessing. One sweet little lamb was soon after our visit, gathered to the fold above."

" Thursday, 17th February, 1869.

" Dr. Burns and I spent an hour or two in the Parliament House with Mr. Nicolson. Visited the Advocates' Library; 200,000 volumes; first Bible published ; saw the original MS. of Waverly ; copy of every piece of music published. Dr. Burns made enquiry about the Wodrow MSS. The librarian, who had not been long there, did not know where they were, Dr. Burns pointed to the corner where they used to lie, and there they were. In a small room, there is preserved above the door, the flag or banner taken at the Battle of Flodden ; the motto is the most entire part of the relic, and to us was very interesting, it is *Veritas Vincit*. It was the Keith motto —(Burns' family motto, as well).

"It was on the 16th of this month that Mrs. L. wife of the Rev. Mr. L, (librarian Free college,) died. Dr. Burns had visited her frequently during her long severe illness. She said 'you have come from Toronto to be a blessing and comfort to me.' She was an excellent Christian woman.

" It was during this month he was occupied with the manuscripts of W. C. B., and had a good deal of correspondence, regretting much that *Canada* had to be compressed into one chapter, when there was material for much more."

" Saturday, 19th February.

" Mrs. McNider called upon the Doctor to consult with him about the annual meeting of the French Canadian Missionary Society. She had been much discouraged by the failure of previous meetings. The Doctor promised to attend and do what he could to excite some interest. So he wrote to some ministers, waited personally on others. The meeting was held on the 25th, and was the most successful that had been for many years. Mrs. McNider was greatly cheered. Mr. Haldane was in the chair, and there were interesting addresses by young Mr. Monod, Dr. Wylie, Dr. McCrie, Dr. Cullen, Dr. Burns, Rev. Mr. Marshall, United States.

"Mr. McDonald read the report, and the Doctor had some conversation with him afterwards. When we came home, he said to me ' I am disappointed with Mr. M. ; I don't think his heart is in his work.' The result proved so.*

* My father always felt much interest in this excellent Society. At the time of its formation, in 1839, when Dr. Taylor and Mr. Court, of Montreal, visited Scotland in ad-

" On the 21st of this month, Dr. Burns attended the annual meeting of the Gaelic schools, having been present at its first meeting in 1810.

" When we were arranging about our visit in 1868, I said, 'now I hope you will not undertake any collecting this time, for you are not able for it ?' He said that he did not intend that, 'but if I can put in a word for a book or a bursary, you won't object to that !'

" At a private meeting of friends at Mr. Crichton's, in Paisley, some reference was made to some inconveniences and difficulties the Doctor had encountered in the back woods. He seemed quite annoyed about the report, and took the opportunity of enlarging on the kindness and hospitality he had always experienced. 'I am always well taken care of.' "

" 18th July.

"The last Sabbath Dr. Burns spent in Scotland, was at Portobello. He officiated all day for the Rev. Dr. Ireland. We drove down with him on the Saturday, and returned for him on Monday, being accommodated with Dr. Guthrie's carriage. His last public meeting in Edin. was on Monday evening, (the 19th July,) in the Free High church, on the occasion of designating two missionaries to India (Rev. Messrs. Stephens and Whitten). Dr. Burns was going in as one of the audience, and near the door, Dr. Duff observed and took hold of him. ' You are the very man ; we must make a change in our programme.' Dr. Duff presided ; read portions from Ephesians, and then spoke of Dr. Burns being so happily present as their veteran missionary about to return to the far West, while the two younger were going to the East. Before asking Dr. Burns to pray, Dr. D. said ' I never see Dr. Burns but I think of the last verses of the 92nd Psalm. I cannot do better than repeat them,' which he did with peculiar impressiveness."

" Thursday, 22nd July, 1869.

" Thursday, the last day we spent in Edinburgh. In the forenoon, called about books for Professor Young. . . . . .

" We called at Johnstone and Hunter's to leave some letters of introduction for young Mr. Thornton,* who was on his way to Edin. —then to Ogle, bookseller, and picked up one or two old works. The Doctor said he could not leave Edin. without visiting the Industrial Museum, so we spent an hour or two there, and he looked at as many objects as time and strength admitted of. We called on Dr. C. Brown and Dr. H. Bonar, who, within three months, had a second family bereavement The evening was spent at home.

---

vocacy of its claims, he rendered efficient assistance. He attended and spoke at the first meeting held in Glasgow, which was the first occasion on which a minister of the Establishment fraternized with his dissenting brethren after the excitement and asperities of the voluntary controversy.
    * Rev. R. M. Thornton, M.A., of Montreal.

" On Friday, 23rd, after early breakfast, we all joined in family prayer, and parted with dear relatives at Lauriston Park, a little after 9 a. m. A number of friends were at the Caledonian station, among others, Dr. Guthrie, who had some minutes conversation with the Doctor after we were seated in the carriage, principally on the subject of a visit to America. He and others cheered us off, and we had a very pleasant journey to Liverpool, where we arrived at 6 p. m. ; remained at the Waterloo hotel till next morning ; at 10, went on board the Cunard steamship *Russia*, and sailed at noon. The Doctor stood the voyage as well as usual, but I thought he was not so lively—was disappointed that there could be no arrangement for worship in the evening.

" He was cheered when Captain Lott intimated to him on Saturday, 31st, that he would have an opportunity of preaching next morning, and introduced him to Rev. Mr. Goodwin, an Episcopal clergyman. On Sabbath, August 1st, he arose before 7, arranged for service, which was held in the saloon at half-past 10. The English service was read solemnly, and then Dr. Burns preached a short sermon from 2 Cor. v. 21 : ' He made Him to be sin for us who knew no sin.' He dwelt on the doctrine and blessed results. Most of the passengers were present, also the captain and about thirty sailors. The audience listened very earnestly, and seemed amazed at the force and readiness of the speaker, as some of them said after, they expected to have listened to a read discourse.

" There was no other service, so after lunch, we spent the sacred day in our berth.

" On Monday he felt rather languid, but in the afternoon he went on deck and revived, having a good deal of conversation with an American lady and gentleman. Mr. and Mrs. Lawrence, and a number came round to enquire for him, and speak of yesterday's service. Our pleasant intercourse seemed then to begin.

" We had not as much reading as usual, we were inclined to rest after past excitement, and there was considerable rolling of the vessel. The season being early it was rather cold to sit long on deck. We read the life of Robert Brown—some reviews, and the Synod's discussion on the Galt revivals.

" Tuesday, 3rd August, land in sight. As we approached Staten Island (unknown to any but the officers,) detectives came on board, as among the passengers were a party of forgers, hailing from London—apprehended as soon as they landed.

" We were nearly two hours getting to Jersey City, where our nephew J. J. B., met us and helped us through all our Custom House difficulties, &c. We rested at the Everett house, enjoyed dinner and night's rest, but with much reluctance the Doctor gave up the idea of a visit to Princeton, which he promised to Dr. McCosh. He proposed to go and return next morning, and then leave by train for Toronto.

" The heat was great—besides an addition of 140 miles journey,

and the uncertainty of Dr. McCosh being at home. 'Very well,'
then he said, 'I suppose I must give it up, as you are all opposed to
it.' He took breakfast in bed next morning, seemed quite refreshed, and enjoyed a drive which our nephew gave us round the grand
Central Park (1,800 acres, twenty-five miles of walk). He allowed
then, that it was better than going to Princeton. In order to avoid
the heat, we thought it best to travel during night, so we left at
half-past six, a beautiful evening, came on comfortably, though
tired, to the Suspension Bridge, then by Hamilton to Toronto.

"Not getting access to the house which we had taken by lease
and was built for our occupancy, we took up our abode at Knox
College. On entering, the Dr. said to Mrs. Willing, ' Now, we
have come to stay a fortnight with you, and then I am going
home.'* On Friday, we remained in the house, several friends
calling. In the morning he was busy in getting two boxes of books
for students opened—they were standing in the hall and caught his
eye as soon as we entered. 'See,' said he, 'they are here before
us.' He wanted to carry up some of the volumes himself, when
two young friends came and assisted. They were put in his own
room, and he began to arrange them. One or two of the students
called and got their copies, (of Cunningham). On Saturday afternoon there was an eclipse of the sun. He came out to the green
and we stood under a tree, and then walked up and down, watching
its progress.

" He then went in and had a long talk with Rev. Mr. Sanson,
Church of England. Other friends also came in.

" Sabbath, 7th August; very fine day; we left early and walked
slowly to church, meeting friends who congratulated the Doctor
on looking so well. He heard with great comfort and satisfaction
a sermon from Rev. Mr. King, from Luke xii. 40 ; ' Be ye also
ready'—subject, ' sudden death,' in connection with a solemn event
in the congregation—death by drowning of two young men, cousins,
of the name of Mackay—they had been in church the Sabbath
before. The Doctor spoke of the excellence and appropriateness
of the discourse.

" He rested till evening, when he preached in Gould street, to
a large audience from 2 Cor. xiv. 15, 16, on the triumphs of the
Gospel, beginning with an account of the progress of God's work
in Scotland—referring to his visits to Ferryden, Perth, &c.
Towards the close of the discourse he dwelt much on the words
' who is sufficient for these things.' Dr. Tempest drove him home,
he was quite lively ; came down stairs ; joined us with Mr.
King at worship.

The last records in his own day-book are very brief :

" Friday, August 6.—Staying at Knox College. Sabbath, 8th,

---

* Precisely that day fortnight he removed to the "house not made with hands."

B B

preached in the evening in Gould street, on 'Now thanks be unto God, which causeth us to triumph in Christ ;' greatly delighted.

"Tuesday, 10th August.—Wrote to Principal Willis and Dr. McVicar, of Montreal," (his last letters).

The letter to Dr. Willis was as follows :—

"KNOX COLLEGE,
"TORONTO, 10th August, 1869.

"MY DEAR DR. WILLIS,—We sailed from Liverpool on the 24th July, by the Cunard steamship *Russia*, and reached New York on Tuesday last, (3rd inst.,) in safety and in health—much mercy. We thought of spending a week at or about the great city of the States, but the hot weather and other considerations changed our plans, and on we came, after one night's comfortable, but fearfully expensive residence at the 'Everett House,' and by the New York Central reached our own city in safety, by 4 o'clock in the afternoon of Thursday. On enquiry, we found that you had gone off to Niagara on the morning of that day, and I hope this will find Mrs. W. and yourself in the healthful enjoyment of recreation for a few weeks. We had much agreeable intercourse in Edinburgh and Glasgow with your relatives, and with many mutual friends. Mr. and Mrs. Jamieson Willis, we had not seen very recently, but, we had frequent meetings—one evening party at their house with a number of esteemed friends, and they were my hearers on Sabbath in the new church at Stockbridge. We saw also, Mrs. Orr Paterson, Mrs. Robert Wodrow, Misses Wingate, &c.

"I preached in about fifty places of worship, and, in the present *dis*-united state of things, by reason of *union* movements, I made no distinctions in my favours—preaching alternately for Dr. C. Brown and Dr. Begg ; Sir Henry Moncrieff and Mr. Moody Stuart, Dr. Candlish and Dr. H. Bonar, Mr. Davidson and Mr. Main.

"I have brought with me a good many books for our library, and something has been done in the way of bursaries, &c.

"I lay my account with giving the opening lecture, on the first Wednesday of October, and of course I will be very busy till then.

"On your return we shall expect a meeting for arrangement of college duties. Mrs. B. joins in all good wishes for Mrs. W. and yourself, and

"I am, Dear Sir,
"Ever truly yours,
"ROB. BURNS."

My mother's journal continues :

"Wednesday, 11th August.—Soon after going to bed complained of chill—got a little better, but kept his bed next day—said to me, 'you had your sickness at sea, I am going to have mine now, and

I shall be the better for it.' A simple remedy seemed to restore him, and he was desirous to fulfil an engagement he had made for the evening. I persuaded him to remain in bed for a rest."

During this day (Thursday, 12th), my wife and I, who had come over from St. Catharines, where we had been spending part of our summer holidays, met with him for the first time since his return. He was remarkably cheerful, chatted freely about his visit to the old country, and seemed as happy and hopeful as we had ever seen him.

The journal resumes :

" He insisted on my going for a little to the house of a friend. When I came in, he was in his own room ; had conducted worship with the household ; conversed with two students, and also with one of our servants about her marriage (she had been waiting for the Doctor's return). He felt weak, but said, as a joke, ' you see how well I have got on !' During the night there was a violent thunder storm, preceded by great darkness, during which I lost my way, in going from one room to another. He slept pretty well. During the noise of the thunder, he repeated the line, ' But the full thunder of His power, what heart can understand.' In the morning he could not be prevailed on to keep his bed—' No, no,' he said, ' I must be *spicy* to-day, Robert saw me in bed yesterday, I must not be there to-day !' I observed his colour very yellow, and told him ; ' Well, but I am better.' He shaved and dressed ; came to his sitting-room and resumed a letter he had been writing to Rev. Mr. Reid,* an account of his visit to Scotland. He wished me to go and see Mr. Blaikie about the house, to enquire about the Mackay family, and to get some little things for him. In the meantime R. and E. came in—and though he spoke cheerfully, his tone of voice was solemn. They had come to say good bye."

We found him looking jaundiced, and strongly advised him to discontinue his writing and to lie down. We had a delightful interview, which an unwillingness to tire him made us abridge. Still, although he looked poorly, there was nothing to excite immediate or serious apprehension.

---

* Our church's invaluable agent, who was ever a faithful friend, for whom my father had a great regard.

The journal continues :

" I was absent for about an hour and-a-half, and by the time I returned he was very ill.   I found his pen in the ink, watch on the table, and no progress made in writing the letter.   He had thrown himself on the bed in the other room, complained of cold, and our little girl of her own accord had run for the Doctor.   She heard him say 'Constantinides.' He came very soon after me, and when he found the Doctor was so ill, said he was glad he was not ten minutes later.   Meantime, kind Mrs. Willing, had applied hot water, &c.   This was the last time he was dressed.   By continued hot applications, stimulants and constant watching, he revived and began to feel comfortable. He slept pretty well, and on Saturday was better. He had two engagements for Sabbath—one West Church, and Mr. Campbell's.   We at once got these filled up, so as to relieve his mind—also gave Mr. Reid the nearly finished letter, that he might have no anxiety about it.   He made enquiries in regard to both, but was satisfied when I told him they were both disposed of.   He said, 'I wished to add two or three sentences to the letter, which I will dictate to you, also to page it.'

" Sabbath, 15th.—He kept his bed, but seemed considerably better.

" Minnie went with Mrs. Willing to church, and the Doctor proposed my going out.   I said, ' no, no, this is your rest day, and it will be mine too—we shall spend it quietly together.'   He slumbered a little, and I read to myself part of the ' Sure and practical use of saving knowledge.' Dr. C. came in about 12, and finding the Doctor better, talked with him for half an hour, and gave him an interesting account of the death of Mrs. Judge R. whom he had attended.   In the course of the day, I read to him part of the   Free Church of Scotland monthly *Record* for August, 1869.   It contained *seven* obituary notices of ministers in Scotland, all of whom he knew more or less intimately—especially Dr. Forrester, of Nova Scotia, and Mr. Buchan, of Hamilton. Of the latter, he had given some interesting reminiscences at a prayer meeting in Hamilton, the day after his funeral sermon was preached, not long before we left Scotland.   He had also written a sketch for his widow, whom he visited. I selected these two, being his most intimate friends—while reading, he was a good deal affected, and said: ' These are to me intensely interesting, read on ;' he also supplied some particulars that were omitted.   Afraid of fatiguing him, I said : 'We had better rest a little, and I will take something else for a change.'   He was sitting up in bed.

" After a little, I brought another book, saying, ' Here is a nice volume of sermons we have had in our bag on our voyage.   I was reading one.' 'O yes, read me one. I picked up that volume in my brother's library, at Corstorphine; my name is on it, I wish that book to be yours. When Dr. Thomson was editor of the *Christian Instructro*, being busy, he sent me that volume to review.   The author is the

Rev. Mr. Cunningham, of Harrow on the Hill, London, an excellent man. You will find the article in such a volume, such a year of the *Christian Instructor*.' I said : 'You must wait until we get our books unpacked again'—(Robert and I found it afterwards, just date and place as he said).

" We had not much more reading, but he continued to sit up, the day was very warm and bright, and he enjoyed the window being open. He said he felt only a little oppression about the chest, for *that* the Doctor prescribed a mustard poultice, which relieved him. As it grew dark, I proposed that for a change, Minnie and I should sing some of her pretty hymns. The hymns were in succession : ' Thy will be done,' ' Jehovah Tsidkenu,' ' Shall we gather at the river,' and his great favourite, ' Nearer my God to thee' (this he always carried in his note book). He said, . ith tears and a tremulous voice, ' that is delightful,' and ' oh dear Minnie, try not only to sing, but to get the spirit of these hymns.'

" I then bid her try one or two more lively, and she sang ' The happy land,' and ' Rest for the weary.' ' That will do, dear, that will do.'

" I then proposed that in case the Doctor should come, if he felt able, we should have worship and prayer first, that he might not be tired or interrupted. He agreed to this and he prayed most solemnly and earnestly, comprehensively asking a blessing on all the services of the day—pleading for all ministers, congregations, &c., as clearly as ever I heard him. This was his last public exercise, and surely it is recorded in Heaven.

" During the night he became worse. Dr. Constantinides brought Dr. Bethune, an old and esteemed friend of the family, for consultation. On Tuesday he was restless—but during that night when Dr. Bethune was watching, he rallied wonderfully."

(So much so, that the countermanding of the telegram sent to me during the day to Chicago, was thought of.)

The journal continues :—

" On Wednesday afternoon, (18th inst.,) Robert and Elizabeth arrived. I think he knew them.

" He tried to look at me, and I believe it was the last of recognition, but utterance had failed.

" After this, he sank into a lethargy from which he never rallied. symptoms of increased prostration, never moving from one position —any liquid rejected.

" The Doctor assured us he was not suffering, but that there would be no rallying. ' He is dying now,' said Dr. C.—who never left, waiting on him as a son, doing any or every thing to alleviate or soothe, so also Dr. Bethune ; to both I will ever be grateful for their unremitting attention. 'Do you think the Doctor is conscious now?' asked my dear friend Mrs. Leslie, (who, thirteen years ago had, along with our early and much valued friend, Mrs. Captain Dick, been my constant helpers during a long illness of the Doctor, an illness then apparently much more severe than the present).

"To Mrs. L.'s enquiry, Dr. C. very beautifully replied, '*No*, the dear Doctor won't be conscious again, till he awake in Heaven!' Heavy breathing now commenced, with intervals of a deep drawn sigh, as if signifying the struggle between the earthly tenement and the spirit seeking to be free. I shall never forget the sound of that sigh, which became less frequent and less intense, as the breathing became gradually fainter and fainter; after twelve hours it ceased, with a gentle flutter—tongue moved a little, and then every muscle was still; and the liberated spirit passed away at twenty minutes past ten, on Thursday morning, 19th August.

"During the night the dying bed was surrounded by ministers and kind Christian friends, every approaching sign of dissolution was anxiously watched—at intervals, fervent prayer was offered, and occasionally a few verses of a psalm or hymn were mournfully sung. As the spirit was departing, the Rev. Mr. King said: Professor Young, will you give thanks? "Praise followed from earth, praise welcomed to heaven."

> " All night we watched the ebbing life,
>   As if its flight to stay,
> Till as the morning hour came on,
>   Our last hope passed away.
>
> " Each flutter of the pulse, we marked,
>   Each quiver of the eye ;
> To the dear lips, our ear we laid,
>   To catch the last long sigh.
>
> " At last the fluttering pulse stood still,
>   The death-frosts through the clay
> Stole slowly, and as morn drew on,
>   Our loved one passed away."

CHAPTER XXI.

MEMORIAL TESTIMONIES.

D R. BURNS died on the morning of Thursday, the 19th of August, 1869, at the age of eighty years and six months. On the afternoon of Saturday, the 21st, he was buried.

On Sabbath, the 22nd, most appropriate sermons were preached in Gould street Church, in the forenoon by the Rev. J. M. King, M.A., pastor of the family, and in the evening by the Rev. M. Willis, D.D., LL.D., Principal of Knox College. Both were subsequently published, and had a wide circulation. From many pulpits in the City and throughout the Province, the event was improved.

It seemed meet that his earthly career should terminate in the College with whose rise and progress he had so much to do.

Friends (principally in Toronto) have erected over his
grave, in the most elevated part of the Toronto Necropolis, of which he was one of the original proje·'tors, a
massive and costly monument of Aberdeen granite, bearing his name and the mottoes of the Burns and Bonar
families, which are singularly appropriate :

> " VERITAS VINCIT "—(Truth conquers).
> " DENIQUE CŒLUM "—(Heaven at last).

Letters of sympathy and regard poured in from all
quarters, representative specimens of which may be inserted.

The Rev. Wm. Fraser, LL.D., of the Free Middle Church,
Paisley, from whom he received very great kindness during
his last visit, thus writes :

"Sept. 27th, 1869.

" I often think of that dear friend whom I so recently met here,
and whose marvellous devotedness and mental energy both surprised and stimulated me. What a life was his ! Ceaseless activity in his Master's cause marked it to its very close. All here loved
him. His last visit was a blessing. No other minister that has
been here has been so loved ; and no wonder, for Dr. Burns had
this characteristic so prominently that all saw it, and acknowledged
it—singular unselfishness. Whatever he did was not for self, but
for his *brother-man* and in his Master's name. You have this assurance, that your beloved companion has entered into a glorious rest."

In another letter, Mr. Fraser writes :

"No minister has ever taken such a deep hold of all this community. All classes and stations revere his memory. I am delighted to hear that there is a probability of a Life of Dr. Burns.
I hope it will be issued early, but one can hardly hope for that with
a life extending over so long a period, and embracing within its due
sphere of action so much that is really *historical* both in Scotland
and in Canada."

Dr. Guthrie, the last to part with him a few brief weeks
previously at the railway station in Edinburgh, and be-

tween whom and himself there existed a strong mutual regard, expresses his sorrowful surprise at the sudden translation :

"EDINBURGH, Sept. 1869.

"Dr. Burns looked so elastic, strong, and hale, that I looked forward to years still of usefulness for him, and was in the habit of saying that of those remaining when he left this country, he was much the most likely to reach the years of the days of his fathers. But God, his God, has seen it meet to ordain otherwise ; and what becomes us so much now but to praise Him, that He spared Dr. Burns so long to you, to us, to America, and to His church, and gave him so much strength to work on to the last. He did indeed die in harness, and after a life of *extraordinary* labours, in which his old age often put both youth and manhood to the blush, he has now entered on rest."

Rev. Dr. C. J. Brown, Moderator of the General Assembly of the Free Church of Scotland for 1872, and an esteemed friend of many years' standing, in a touching and beautiful letter, says :

"EDINBURGH, Sept. 1869.

"How strange it seems to us that dear Dr. Burns, who left us in such vigour and spirit, should scarce have set his foot down again in his adopted country when the voice reached him, 'Come up hither.' And yet, though it must have taken you by surprise, it was scarce surprising either. The real wonder was his previous amazing vigour. What a mercy, and how rare a one, that he should, to such an age, have not only been spared, but enabled to the last to do the work of a young man, with scarce almost weariness. I know, dear Mrs. Burns, that you thankfully feel all this, and are persuaded that without a murmur, amid whatever sorrow, you have been enabled to give him up, even as dear Mrs. Coutts, when, in very early life, she had to part with her admirable husband, and who, sitting on the bed, with her hand under his head, waiting for the last breath, when told by the nurse that he was gone, just withdrew her hand gently and said, 'Is he gone ? then I let go my hold ; my Maker is my husband, the Lord of Hosts is His name.'

"Truly Dr. Burns was taken away like a shock of corn fully ripe, and though we are apt to think of the many things he was still planning, and I suppose engaged with, yet *that* is but our poor thought. His work was done ! The Lord makes no mistakes. We have each our fixed, allotted portion and measure of work, and another comes in to take up what we leave. How blessed to think of that account of the believer's departure : 'Father, I will that

they also whom thou hast given me be with me, where I am, that
they may behold my glory.' You will now exchange your prayers
for Dr. Burns for thanksgivings in connection with his brighter
blessedness ; and you have for yourself and the future in the wilderness, all the promises of leading, strength, consolation, &c., &c.,
until you shall be called to join the innumerable company above.
May the Lord, the wonderful Counsellor, direct you aright !"

The Rev. Alexander Cameron, whom my father often
visited, always with pleasure, in his Canadian as well as
Scottish charges, lets his sympathetic soul overflow :

"ARDERSIER, Sept. 1869.

"MY DEAR MRS. BURNS,—Little did I think when I received
your last kind note from Edinburgh, announcing your intention of
embarking from Liverpool, that the next news from Canada was to
be the death of my dearly beloved friend and father, your honoured
husband.   Yet after all, my dear friend, there is nothing to regret ;
his work was done, and I believe well done in the estimation of the
blessed Master whom he served so long and so faithfully.   Does
any living doubt that he has received the happy welcome, 'Well
done,' &c.? Let us, therefore, not grudge that he has got to his
rest at last, though somewhat sooner, perhaps, than we wished.
He took little rest while here.   If work, and especially work for
Christ, could be said to be any man's meat and drink, it was surely
that of Dr. Burns.   'In labours more abundant.'   He would not
say so, but we will all say it now.   It is long since I knew him first,
slightly, even before he left Paisley ; then in Canada, as my pastor
and professor and friend.   I accompanied him to the backwoods on
preaching tours (no slight privilege).   He licensed me, visited me
at Glengarry again and again. . . . . The more I was with him the
more I loved and esteemed him.   My heart, while I write, is full
to overflowing, my eyes a fountain of tears, yet not tears so much
of sorrow as of thankfulness to God that I ever enjoyed so much of
his society and confidence, and for all that the Lord did in him and
for him.   His last visit to Ardersier with yourself, besides the
gratification it afforded to·myself and dear partner, has left a most
salutary impression upon the people.   The old and godly people
here and in surrounding parishes have never ceased speaking of his
wonderful sermons and addresses.   I believe many congregations
throughout the land will give a similar testimony, while our church
at large was refreshed through his never-to-be-forgotten addresses
to our General Assemblies."

The Rev. Robert Wallace, of Toronto, formerly of Ingersoll, one of the very first students of Knox College,

and the first licensed by my father after his arrival, gives his impressions thus:

"I had the privilege, along with two other students—the first-fruits of the Presbyterian Church of Canada—of being licensed by the good Doctor in 1845, and I have naturally followed his course ever since with deep interest.

"I need scarcely say that he was most indefatigable in his labours. I spent a day with him in this city in 1847, accompanied him in his visits among the people, having an appropriate word of counsel for each, and praying fervently with the sick or the sorrowing. During the evening we visited several public meetings, which he addressed IN SUCCESSION on the subjects which had convened them; and then, at a late hour, reached his own house, apparently as fresh as ever.

"I have met him on his missionary tours, which were frequent, preaching daily, or almost every day.

"He also took great pleasure in aiding and encouraging the young ministers in their various spheres of labour. Several times has that noble worker assisted the writer in administering the sacred feast of the Lord's Supper, at which times his warm sympathy with the Christian people; and his ardent and glowing piety, seemed to get full scope and to be in their proper element. On such occasions he was wont to pour forth, as from a full fountain, the richest exhibitions of divine truth, not merely according to the letter, but with the evident enjoyment of one who felt its power on his own heart—who had an experimental acquaintance with it in its varied applications to human life, and who delighted in the law of the Lord after the inner man, and feasted on the rich repast of which he invited others to partake.

"He delighted to unfold the glory of Christ's work as a Divine Saviour, and the efficacy of his atonement, as well as to set forth the freeness and fulness of the gospel offer as made to all the children of men.

"He was ever ready to defend the faith given to the saints, and to stand up for the peculiar doctrines of our holy religion. Once in the presence of a Unitarian preacher, a friend heard him maintain the doctrine of the divinity of our Lord in a strain of the most fervid and impassioned eloquence, while he deplored, in the most touching manner, the folly and the infatuation that lead men to reject that fundamental doctrine of the Christian faith to their own destruction.

"At the same time, he ever manifested a most catholic spirit, in his readiness to co-operate with all that he believed to be the true followers of Christ, in their works of faith and labours of love.

"He also cheerfully took part in soirées, as giving an opportunity for the people to meet together and cultivate familiar acquaintance with each other ; but he always sought to instruct and edify, as well as interest, the people on such occasions.

"When addressing the congregation of the writer at Ingersoll, he was fond of reminding them that his revered nephew, W. C. Burns, of China, had selected the site of the church when preaching on that beautiful spot, under the trees, in 1846. He had a great regard for his nephew, because of his devoted piety and zeal in the Master's service. His visit to Canada had been like a streak of light. Wherever he went the hearts of ministers and other Christians were quickened, and sinners were greatly if not savingly impressed.

"One thing which greatly contributed to the Doctor's popularity and usefulness was his unselfish, self-denying spirit. In mingling with the people in their homes, even in the newest settlements, he was always content with whatever accommodation and fare they could afford him ; never complained of privations, such as he must have felt ; but on the contrary, he was ever cheerful and happy, and promoted the same spirit among all around him.

"Endowed with a wonderful memory and very ready conversational powers, and having acquired vast stores of knowledge on all subjects, he was the life of any company,—enlivening his conversation by pertinent anecdotes drawn from reminiscences of distinguished personages, from events of former times, from current matters of public interest, and from many sources. It was a treat to listen to him in company, as he poured forth his rich stores of sanctified learning, in a cheerful and pleasant manner.

"Another feature of his character which should not be forgotten was his FERVENT PRAYERFULNESS. Often have I and many others been refreshed by the ardent outpourings of his heart around the family altar, or his earnest pleading in a more private manner, for any brother for whom he sought the blessing of Sion's King. Here was the secret of his power as a worker for Christ."

From one of Dr. Burns' former students, now settled as a minister six or seven hundred miles from Toronto, came the following :

"In this distant part public tributes of respect to the Doctor's memory have been paid. For a week a flag was hoisted at half-mast in front of our Manse, and the pulpit has been draped with black.

"You have often heard him quote the expression 'abundant entrance,' explaining the figure as that of a ship coming into harbour uninjured, with all her canvas spread, her hull unshattered, her masts unbroken, and her rigging not torn. Such an entrance, I doubt not he had."

Another old student, settled at a still greater distance, in the opposite direction, thus acts as the mouthpiece of many :

"Our fathers, where are they? and the prophets, do they live for ever? I cannot realize that he is gone, and to how many will it seem but a myth until the annual gatherings come round, when there will be many a heavy heart and many a bitter tear.

"The event strikes to my own heart as if it were the death of an own father. What a bright record we can all contemplate in your father's life! and how conspicuously does the past place him among the great cloud of witnesses. I cannot give expression to my feelings of reverence for the departed. Such fertility of mind, such unselfishness, such unwearied devotion to the cause of Christ! I cannot look around my study without my eye falling upon some book or manuscript, or manual that is not closely identified with his personal and fatherly counsel and advice. So accessible, so frank, and so painstaking that every moment found him engaged with some one or other of the students in private, helping them out of either personal or educational difficulties.

"How many humble members also on both continents will lift up the prophet's lamentation, ' My father, my father, the chariots of Israel and the horsemen thereof! But we leave him to his rest among the elders who have obtained a good report."

The Rev. Mr. Sanson, Episcopalian Church, Toronto, a very dear old friend, on receiving a memorial from Dr. Burns' library, thus represents the sentiments and feelings of many in other denominations:

"These volumes will ever remind me of one whom I revered and loved, from whom I experienced much genuine kindness, and whose unexpected removal from the church on earth I must continue to deplore. In the circle of my acquaintance I had not another Christian friend like him. His comprehensive sympathy was one of those few things which made this world less dreary and more agreeable. It is seldom that one meets with so much simplicity and godly sincerity—so much hearty love and kindness—so much consideration for others and forgetfulness of self, accompanied by so many rare qualities and valuable attainments besides, as it was my privilege to find in Dr. Burns."

From the Rev. Dr. Hugh McLeod, whose labours in Cape Breton have been so eminently owned of God in connexion with the great revival there, and whom he loved to visit in that interesting field, which was associated with the early efforts of the Colonial Society, we received the following graphic portraiture :

"SYDNEY, C.B., 16th November, 1871.

" My chief acquaintance with your venerable father was formed in the fall of 1845, when, as deputy from the Free Church of Scotland, I visited the British provinces of North America. But from my earliest recollection I was familiar with his appearance, character, and name. I saw him several times in the General Assembly, both before and after the disruption ; often heard him speak, and regarded him as one of the greatest and best men of his day. His voice always commanded the attention and respect of the whole House. Well do I remember how I used to hear him, from time to time, with increased pleasure and admiration.

" His personal appearance was peculiar ; short but stout, indicating great strength. Accordingly his power of endurance was remarkable. He could do the work of two ordinary men. On the Sabbath he usually preached three times, and always with great energy. In addition to his other duties he often preached and travelled long distances on week days. His elocution was distinct and rapid as he advanced, till at length, like a mighty torrent, it swept all before it. Endowed with intellectual faculties of a very high order, and a mind richly stored with various learning, and disciplined by assiduous study, he was always a man of power.

" In his preaching he was argumentative, lucid and impressive. Familiar with the word of God as well as with the windings of the human heart, and possessing a faithful memory, fertile imagination, fluency of expression and teeming thought. His sermons were able, suggestive and eloquent. By his writings, too, he was widely known. In sustaining the periodical literature of his time his pen was ever ready. His contributions, in doctrinal, practical, and polemical discussion, were varied and always to the point. As a controversalist he was acute, searching and convincing. Of the doctrines and principles of the gospel, in all their relations and results, he was the uncompromising champion. The Bible Society, the Society for the Conversion of the Jews, the Anti-Slavery Society, the Colonial Society, the Gaelic School Society, the Cape Breton Mission, and, in short, the various benevolent institutions of the day, had in him a warm friend.

" After his settlement in Canada he frequently visited the maritime provinces—especially Nova Scotia. His visits were always accompanied with happy results, and every one considered it a high privilege to shew him attention. The influence which he excited on such occasions was not confined to members and adherents

of his own church, but embraced a wide circle of Christian association. Wherever he preached, crowds flocked to hear him. To
none, perhaps, does British America owe more than to Dr. Burns,
who may well be called the Apostle of Canada. Not only have
congregations been organised and places of worship built through
his instrumentality, but many souls have been born of the Spirit.
The day when the secrets of all hearts shall be laid bare alone can
tell how many shall rise up to call him blessed, and be to him 'his
hope and joy, and crown of rejoicing in the presence of our Lord
Jesus Christ at His coming.'

"In the summer of 1858 he visited Newfoundland, where he
remained for about a fortnight, and where his labours were very
fruitful. On his return he remained with me two weeks, not to
rest, however, but to work. We were continually going about
visiting the different stations. Although then bordering on seventy
years of age his vigour was remarkable. In all his discourses there
were noble bursts of sanctified eloquence. On every occasion
crowds followed him, embracing persons of all denominations and
ranks, which rendered it necessary for him at times to preach in the
open air. I usually preached in Gaelic what he preached in English.
Mrs. Burns was with him on this occasion, so that his visit was
more domestic than it could otherwise be. She was truly an help-
meet to him, following him in all his travels, ministering to his
comfort, and sympathising with him in all his efforts to do good.
During his stay here he was extremely happy. In all his letters to
me afterwards he referred to the great pleasure which his visit
afforded him. From Sydney we proceeded to Sydney Mines, to
Bras d'Or, to Boularderie, to Baddirk, and to St. Ann's, in all of
which he preached with great power. Thereafter we sailed in a
small boat up the Bras d'Or lake to West Bay, a distance of forty
miles. In the evening he preached, as usual, to a large congregation which gathered to hear him. Next morning I accompanied
him to the Strait of Canso, where he preached, and for ever took
leave of Cape Breton. I returned home. He crossed the Strait to
Nova Scotia, where he remained for some weeks preaching in different localities, and where his name is still so savoury. On his return to Canada he wrote a pamphlet on Cape Breton, giving a
graphic account of its resources, scenery, and religious condition.
He considered it one of the most valuable and desirable portions
of her Majesty's dominions. His estimate is found to have been
correct, and shows how observant he was.

"Some time thereafter I had the pleasure of paying him a visit,
on which occasion I passed several days with him. Some of the
happiest moments of my life were those I spent in his society.
His conversation was always edifying and instructing. His manner was kind, courteous, and gentlemanly. His domestic supplica-
tions were remarkable for their richness and fervour. Without
doubt he was one of the highest ornaments of the church to which

he belonged.   The Lord honoured him above many, and made him instrumental in carrying on His work on earth. He hath taken him home ' to the General Assembly and Church of the First-born, whose names are written in Heaven.'"

The Rev. Dr. Ormiston, formerly of Hamilton, now of New York, was an old and valued friend. They thought alike on many subjects. They worked together in objects of common interest—religious, educational, and benevolent. From the time of their first meeting at Victoria College, in 1844, they drew to one another, and the intimacy remained uninterrupted to the last. His finely-rendered testimony will be acceptable to many :

"NEW YORK,
"December 2nd, 1871.
"REV. R. F. BURNS, D.D.

"MY DEAR SIR,—I very cheerfully comply with your request to send you some brief personal reminiscences of your venerable and venerated father.

"It was my enviable privilege to enjoy his friendship for nearly a quarter of a century, and to share his confidence during a greater part of that period. The intimacy of our fellowship was never interrupted by a single misunderstanding. Its influence at the time, on my mind, was most inspiring and helpful, and its memory now is consoling and grateful. I owe him much. I always found in him a sympathetic and good counsellor, and ever left his presence with higher resolves and nobler purposes to be and to do. The pleasure of our intercourse I have good reason to believe, was mutual, the profit chiefly mine. From the first I entertained a profound respect for his high talents, his resistless energy, his rare readiness, and his eminent and extensive usefulness, and I soon learned to love him for the simplicity of his character, the unselfishness of his disposition, the generosity of his conduct, and the warmth of his affection. Mistaken in judgment, rash in utterance, very resolute in purpose, and decidedly prompt in action, he doubtless sometimes was ; but intentionally unkind, personally selfish, consciously unfair, sullenly implacable, or sternly unforgiving, never. Quick to resent a wrong offered to himself or others, he was equally ready to forgive and forget it.

"I regarded his general attainments as vast, unusually varied and accurate, and specially rich in historic fact, and biographical incident. His memory alike retentive and ready, never seemed to

lose a date or fact, place or person once entrusted to it. His interest in all that affected the welfare of society and the progress of
the province was deep and most intense, and particularly in all
that pertained to the extension of the church, and the training of
young men for the work of the ministry. In all that he did he
was so thoroughly sincere, and so terribly in earnest that he often
seemed impatient of delay, and irritated by hindrances. He had
no sympathy with indolence, slackness or inefficiency, and he had
not only a noble scorn for anything mean, fraudulent or unreal,
but also possessed a rare faculty for detecting falsehood, preten-
sion, insincerity or imposture in others, and when fully satisfied in
his own mind in reference to such matters, no fear of personal inconvenience or public disfavour could deter him from exposing
them. As a friend I ever found him trustworthy, sympathetic and
obliging ; as a brother in the ministry, faithful, affectionate and
true ; able in public ministrations, laborious in the active duties of
the pastorate, prominent and active in all the business of the
church courts, long associated with the management and instruction of the college ; a willing, effective advocate of every good
cause, and an unwearied worker in the field of home evangelization, even to the last. He richly merited the place he long held, as
an acknowledged leader in the Church of God, and a felt power in
the land.

"Though past the meridian of life, ere he entered upon the Canadian field, by his great gifts, his diversified labours, his exhaust-
ing ungrudging efforts for the good of the church, he speedily won
for himself a high place in the esteem of his brethren, even of
those who felt themselves oft constrained to differ from him, and
a warm place in the hearts of the entire people, in whose homes,
lofty or lowly, he was ever a welcome and an honoured guest.
Many a heartfelt simple tribute of honest praise have I heard bestowed on him in every section of the dominion, wherever his eloquent voice had thrilled them from the pulpit, or his rich racy
conversation cheered them at their hearths. No minister in Canada was more widely known, more truly revered, and more personally beloved than Dr. Robert Burns.

"Well do I remember my own first personal interview with him.
It was during a visit he made to Cobourg, when travelling in Canada as a deputy of the Free Church of Scotland. I was at the
time a student at Victoria College. The principal of the college,
Rev. Dr. Ryerson, courteously gave to the celebrated visitor an
invitation to visit the college and address the students. This invitation Dr. Burns accepted, and to me his address was a rich treat.
A small contribution in aid of the then infant Free church was
made by the professors and students, and I was commissioned to
convey it to the deputy. I approached him with great diffidence,
but so hearty and genial was his greeting that the raw inexperienced
student soon felt at his ease with the great gifted visitor. As was

C C

his custom, ere we separated, he spoke directly to my heart, asked my purpose in attending college, and what was my grand object in life, and on ascertaining that I had devoted myself to the ministry of the word, he said much to encourage and stimulate me. He closed, what seemed to me, more like a father's counsel, than a mere casual conversation, very solemnly, while he held my hand in his, saying that the pulpit required a strong, richly-cultured mind, and a sanctified earnestly devoted heart. I never forgot my first interview, or lost the impulse it gave me; and how many other young men he has similarly counselled and cheered, "that day" alone will reveal. He rests from his labours, but his works follow him. It were as delightful as it would be easy for me to narrate many an incident in our common experience, which would strikingly exhibit and exemplify the leading traits of your father's character, and specially mark the ripened mellowness of his later years, but that is not required. The elevated spirituality of his mind, the enlarged charity of his heart, the manifest nearness to God in which he lived, and the purified zeal for the work of the Master, glowing with increasing fervour, which he manifested even amid the infirmities of a good old age, rendered communion with him a great privilege and a great power, too. I rejoice now that it was mine not unfrequently to enjoy the one and feel the other. Among the memories of my heart will ever lie cherished the remembrance of all his kindness to me in my youth, and his valued friendship in my riper years. What a blessing it is that the assured hope of re-union at home mitigates the grief of separation on the way. They are not lost who have only gone before.

"I am, my dear Brother,

"Yours, very faithfully,

"W. ORMISTON."

The College Board and Senate, various Sessions, Presbyteries and Synods of the Church, together with the General Assembly, besides different public institutions, passed highly eulogistic resolutions. Papers and periodicals were warm and hearty in their obituary notices. Extracts from two or three of these will appropriately terminate these memorials.

Some of his earliest literary efforts in Paisley were connected with "The Philosophical Society," an institution than which none in the community has had a more honourable record. During his last visit he revived the intimacy and associations of former times. This testimony is all the more to be esteemed as being a deviation from the ordinary custom:

"PAISLEY, 12th October, 1869.

"The society, having learned with deep regret that the Rev. Dr. Burns had died in Toronto on the 19th of August last, cannot allow the event to pass unnoticed. As the circumstances are special, they in this instance depart from what has been their practice. Dr. Burns was one of the earliest and most active promoters of the objects of this society. Upwards of fifty-three years ago he read papers, and in 1813 was vice-president. For several years he acted as president; and during his long residence here spared no pains to contribute to the efficiency of the institution. On his recent visit from Canada, the land of his adoption, he made himself acquainted with the operations of the society, and took such interest in the proposal to found a reference department in the Free Public Library, that he offered a very handsome donation of valuable works. His address on the occasion was worthy of his natural enthusiasm, and was not only touching in its allusions, but was an eloquent and interesting record of successful work half a century ago. The labours of Dr. Burns in connexion with this society abundantly show that he had that intuitiveness to discover and that power to combine which are the bases of successful investigation, and that if his talents had been consecrated exclusively to scientific or philosophic pursuits, he would have held a foremost place in Britain. He is not the less to be valued because he devoted himself to the welfare of his race through the channels of Christian philanthropy; and the society record with gratitude their sense of the benefits which he conferred by his sympathy and exertions."

From the resolutions of the College Board of Knox College we make the following extract, befittingly embodying the sentiments of those with whom he was most closely associated in the training up of a native ministry:

"The Board, considering that, since their last meeting, God has been pleased to remove by death the Rev. Robert Burns, D.D., Emeritus Professor of Theology and Church History in Knox College, resolve to record, as they hereby do record, their high appreciation of the consistent Christian character of their late venerable father, and of the eminent services which he has rendered to the college and to the church generally. They feel that any statement of theirs can add nothing to the estimation in which he was held, as his ability and zeal and devoted labours in behalf of all benevolent and philanthropic and Christian objects have been universally acknowledged wherever he was known. At the same time they reckon it a privilege as well as a duty to give expression to the sentiments of gratitude which they, in common with all their brethren, entertain, that he was so long spared to take a prominent place in building up and extending the Presbyterian cause in this land, and that, by his disinterested, self-denying, unwearied efforts, he was enabled, through the blessing of God, to contribute so largely to that end.

"Coming to this country with a high reputation as one of the most distinguished ministers of the Free Church of Scotland, he was honoured by divine grace to maintain and extend the same.

"First as pastor of Knox Church, and latterly as one of the theological professors, he gave himself, with all his superior mental and physical powers and spiritual attainments, to the assiduous discharge of the duties devolving on him ; and even when, by reason of advancing age, he felt himself constrained to resign his professorship in the college, he continued as Emeritus Professor to cherish an unabated interest in all that concerned its welfare ; and such was his love of work in the cause of his Master, and such his pleasure in it, that he persevered in conducting classes with his accustomed energy. To him the library of the college stands indebted mainly for its present state of advancement. Even during his last visit to Britain, from which he returned only a fortnight before his death, he was largely occupied in seeking its increase ; and the Board cannot but regard it as worthy of notice that, in the providence of God, he should have been brought back to be summoned away, as he himself could have wished, within the walls of this institution, whose welfare he had so strongly and abidingly in his heart."

The General Assembly, meeting at Toronto in June, 1870 (the first held in Canada), passed a very full and discriminating deliverance, from which we extract the following:

"The Assembly cannot take notice of the death of the late venerable Dr. Burns without recording their sense of his qualities and of the eminent services he was enabled, during a long series of years, to render to the cause of Christ. They are thankful to God for having sent among them one who was so remarkably fitted, in the public circumstances of this country when he came to it, to act as an evangelist, in the best sense of that term. His unwearied labours in preaching the Gospel, in every part of the land, in mission stations as well as in settled congregations, have contributed in a high degree to the prosperity of this church, and have made the name of *Burns* a household word in thousands of families—a name which parents will mention to their children yet unborn, as that of one whom they account it among the privileges of their lives to have seen and heard. His duties as a Professor of Theology were discharged with zeal and fidelity. He had a deep concern both for the spiritual welfare of the young men under his care, and for their progress in their studies. To his exertions mainly the formation of the College Library was due. His preaching tours had much influence in calling forth an increased liberality on the part of the church, in sustaining the college, and his unabated interest in the institution, even after he had become an Emeritus Professor, was shown by some of the latest acts of his life. . . . .

"As a man, Dr. Burns could not be known without being loved. He had a warm heart, and a large and genial nature. A man of great breadth of sympathy, he was notably one who did not look at his own things, but took a lively interest in the things of others. He was generous almost to a fault. His overflowing and manifestly sincere kindliness, his wonderful vitality, his unfailing flow of conversation, and the rich and varied information he was accustomed, in all companies, to pour forth, made him in society the most delightful of companions. . . . .

"His character became in a singular degree mellowed ; alongside of the spirit of power, which was always a predominant feature in it, came out conspicuously the gentler graces of the divine life—eminently among others, meekness and humility ; and no one could converse with him without feeling that, day by day, he was ripening apace for the change which both he himself and those who looked upon his marked and venerable form knew could not be far distant."

The *Record*, the monthly journal of the church, devoted several pages to an admirably-written sketch by the editor, from which we make a few selections :

"Most of our readers will have heard, before these paragraphs meet their eyes, of the death of the venerable Dr. Burns. The event took place on the morning of Thursday, 19th ult., in Knox College, in which, with his family, he was residing for a few days before entering into a house of his own. He had returned from Scotland, on Thursday, 5th, apparently in excellent health and good spirits. He preached on the evening of the following Sabbath in Gould street church, of which he was a member. With his usual zeal for work, especially for preaching, he undertook to preach on Sabbath, 15th, in two of the churches of the city, and also in Knox church, on Sabbath, 22nd. But his working days were coming to an end, and these engagements, so readily entered into, were not to be fulfilled. The evening of Wednesday, 11th, he spent in company with his son, Dr. R. F. Burns, and a few friends, at the house of the Rev. W. Gregg, and was, as usual, genial and pleasant. During the night he was seized with a chill, which returned in an aggravated degree on the forenoon of Friday, 13th. Medical aid was called in, and it was hoped for some days that he would soon recover from what seemed to be simply a bilious disorder. But although he rallied repeatedly, the improvement was only temporary; and, notwithstanding all that medical skill and affectionate attention could do, the disease still kept firm hold of its victim, and, as already stated, he ceased from suffering, and entered into rest, on the morning of the 19th. During the latter part of his illness he was unconscious, and from the first he was happily exempted from bodily pain. His son had left Toronto, and returned to Chicago, but a telegram reached him in time to bring him back to see his loved father in life, although in a state of extreme prostration. It is a very remarkable providence that Dr. Burns should have come back to die in Canada, for whose spiritual advancement he had laboured so zealously, and within the walls of the college, where for several years he was so frequently to be found, and whose interests were ever so dear to him. In another column of the *Record* will be found a communication, evincing the deep interest which he felt, even to the last, in the welfare of Knox College, and of the Canada Presbyterian Church. The communication referred to was begun some days after his arrival in Toronto ; indeed he was engaged in completing it even after the leaden hand of disease had been laid upon him. He still intended to make some additions to it, but was unable to do so ; and we now publish it as it is, believing that it will be read by thousands with peculiar interest, as being the last production of the pen of the venerable writer, the last work of a public kind to which his hand was put, and as showing the very strong hold which the church and her institutions had of his thoughts and affections, even to the end."

The communication referred to above, in the preparation of which that busy hand was arrested, is as follows :

"KNOX COLLEGE, 13th Aug. 1869.

"DEAR MR. EDITOR,—We left Edinburgh for Liverpool on Friday, the 23rd of July ; embarked next day in the fine Cunard steamship *Russia*, and after a fair passage of nine days, reached New York on Tuesday, the 3rd inst. After a day's sojourn in that magnificent city of the 'Empire State,' we left by the Central Railway, on Wednesday afternoon, and reached Toronto in safety.

"It was at one time my earnest wish to have visited the Continent, and in that case I might possibly have seen the celebrated discoverer of the ' Codex Sinaiticus,' and been favoured with the actual inspection of that invaluable monument of an early century in the Christian era. It had been indeed carried by the Professor to St. Petersburg, and there made over to the Czar by purchase, but it had been brought back again to Leipsic for the purpose of a fac-simile transcription. This has been accomplished at the Emperor's expense, and in a style of uncommon elegance. When circumstances put it out of my power to see the original, I was very desirous to see the fac-simile. The University of Edinburgh, I found, had purchased a copy at the price of £34 10s. ; but this was soon superseded by the gift of one directly, as I understand, from the Emperor. The spare one was purchased by Principal Candlish, aided by a few friends, for £25, and presented to the New college library.

" With an inspection of this copy I was favoured by the kindness of my friend, the Rev. John Laing, librarian to the college. It is a magnificent work, in four large folio volumes, on the finest paper, and in the finest style of typography. It embraces the whole of the ' Codex Sinaiticus,' with ample collations from the Cottonian and Vatican MSS., with historical and critical prolegomena, and a variety of miscellaneous illustrations. A German bookseller in Edinburgh, told me that I could have the whole work for about £20 ; but as this was beyond my means, I was obliged to content myself with the Professor's supplementary volume, containing a condensed view of the contents of the larger work, and selected specimens of the Codex. This I purchased for a small trifle, and it is now in the possession of the college library ; and though small, it gives a pretty fair idea of the solid contents of the great work. I should think, that were the managers of the Toronto University or of the McGill College library at Montreal, to apply to the proper quarter, through the Governor-General of the Dominion of Canada, a gift of one copy at least, would be granted by the Emperor, Alexander II.

" With the view of promoting the system of scholarships or bursaries for all the three colleges in the Dominion of Canada, I printed and circulated an ' Appeal on behalf of the Colonies of the West,' my wish being, if possible, to obtain a few 'capitalized endowments' of a permanent character. This was found to be rather up-hill work ; and the only society or body of Christian men who entertained the idea, was the 'Scottish Reformation Society,' who at once made the offer, on certain conditions, of two bursaries of £10 and £5 each, to the three Theological Colleges in the Dominion, and connected with the Presbyterian Church. In each case the conditions have been complied with, and the probability is in favour of their permanence. The subject of competition will be the leading principles of the Protestant controversy ; and the manner of conducting the comparative trial is left to the discretion of the Senate in each of the Seminaries.

" For the first time, the deputies from Canada managed to get a fair hearing in the General Assembly of the Free Church. On all previous occasions they were thrown into the back-ground, and heard at a late hour, and by benches nearly empty.

" We owe it to Dr. Candlish that it was ordered otherwise this time. On the Friday of the 'business week,' and at eight in the evening, a full house listened to us ; and Mr. Cochrane, of Brantford, and I, were cordially complimented and thanked by the moderator, Sir H. Moncrieff, a noble chairman. Three points of importance were pressed on the notice of the Assembly—our mission to British Columbia, our Red River Settlement, and our Gaelic Bursaries. On motion of Dr. Candlish, seconded by Dr. Begg, all these were handed over for consideration to the Colonial Committee, newly appointed, with Dr. Adam, of Glasgow, at its head. On the Wednesday after the close of the Assembly, I was invited to a meeting of committee, when a resolution was cordially passed in favour of a renewed and friendly correspondence with the Foreign Mission Committee of Canada, in regard to the first and second of these subjects ; and as to the third, one bursary for fifty dollars, engaged for during the present year. It is painful to reflect, that the collections for the colonies have always been the smallest of all, and that for years past the operations of the colonial scheme have been sadly crippled for want of means. In addition to the Assembly bursary, one clergyman of ample means, the Rev. Mr. McDougal, late of Dundee, gave me twenty-five dollars for a second bursary, and both of these, I expect, will be renewed from year to year.

" By the liberality of the Rev. Dr. Charles J. Brown and a few other friends I was enabled to arrange with Messrs. Clark, of George Street, for one hundred copies of the two volumes of ' Historical Theology,' by Principal Cunningham, to be sold at a reduced price to the theological students at each of our colleges. The books have arrived safe, and I will be happy to receive orders from such of our young men, from 1867 to the present date, who may not have already been supplied. The Messrs. Clark also presented me with twenty volumes of their choice collection of foreign theological literature ; and these have been equally divided between the Colleges of Toronto and Montreal. I have also brought with me one hundred copies of the Free Church edition of the ' Confession of Faith,' which will be at the service of sessions, and ministers, and students, at the rate of one shilling each. The theological and literary stores of our colleges have also been largely augmented by the presents of books from the libraries of private friends. Some curious articles also, principally Chinese, have been added to our museum.   " R. B."

After giving a sketch of the leading events of Dr. Burns' life, drawn chiefly from a very correct and comprehensive leader of the *Globe*, the article in the *Record* goes on to say :

" Dr. Burns had many qualifications which fitted him for taking a prominent position among his contemporaries, and for being a standard-bearer in the conflicts which the revival of evangelical principles, and the progress of social reforms, brought about in his day. His varied endowments were of a superior order. His reading was varied and extensive ; while a memory singularly retentive and ready enabled him to have at command the results of his reading. His style was clear, manly, and vigorous. His principles were not taken up just to suit the times, but were conscientiously held, and freely and fearlessly expressed. His energy was untiring. As a preacher he was evangelical, impressive, and often powerful. His discourses were full of sound theology, enriched by apt illustrations ; and even to his latest years were delivered with remarkable energy.

" Our revered father held, on most points, too decided opinions, and had too great force of character, not to come occasionally into collision with others, sometimes with those who generally were to be found on the same side with himself. But even those opposed to him respected his thorough integrity of purpose, and his outspoken honesty. There was a heartiness about him which even his opponents could not but like. It is pleasing to add that his last years were full of peace and tranquillity. He had to a considerable extent withdrawn from the arena of public discussion. His character was more and more softened and chastened. Some personal misunderstandings were removed ; and we believe we only state the truth when we say that, before his removal from us, there was not one who did not cherish towards him feelings, not only of high respect, but of warm affection.

" In private life Dr. Burns was genial and loving. His powers of conversation were remarkable. It was impossible to weary of his company, or in it. To the students under his charge he was peculiarly kind and attentive. He manifested a warm interest in their studies, and in everything affecting them ; and of those who were settled in pastoral charges, there were few whom he did not visit and encourage by his presence, his counsels, and his ministerial services. His liberality and unselfishness in regard to money matters were remarkable. One instance of this may be mentioned. A few years ago the Doctor received a handsome sum of money from one of the city congregations of Toronto, for whose benefit his services had been for some time generously given. No sooner had he received this gift than he freely gave it to establish a scholarship in Knox College. Many other instances of this liberality might be given. Indeed we can freely say that we never knew one so utterly unselfish in this respect. . . . . .

" Dr. Burns has gone from us, and we can truly say that a princ

and a great man has fallen in Israel. He has done more for our
Church in Canada than any other man. When few thought of
the spiritual wants of these western provinces, Dr. Burns was instrumental in sending out not a few ministers and missionaries to
gather together the scattered Presbyterians, and organize them into
congregations. When a call was made for one to come and take
the lead here, and assist in organizing a theological institution, he
was ready to give his own services. When books were needed to
form the nucleus of a theological library, he set himself to collect
from his friends, giving at the same time many valuable volumes
from his own library. And so, to the very last, he was willing to
his ability—yea, and beyond his ability—to do whatever was needed
for the supply of ordinances, or for the promotion of the interests
of the Church, and the glory of her great Head. We thank God
for all that he was enabled, through the grace of God, to do ; and
we rejoice in the assured hope that, after such a long, laborious,
and useful life, he now rests from his labours, and his works do
follow him."

In the excellent funeral discourse of the Rev. J. M.
King, M.A., on the "Good Fight," occurs the following
beautifully-drawn portraiture of his character :

"The first feature which attracts attention, in contemplating the
character of the departed, is the extraordinary activity which characterized him, his unceasing application to work, the wonderful enthusiasm and energy which he carried, even in age, into every undertaking.   Sabbath and week day ; morning, noon and night, till
failing sight made it imprudent or impossible for him to read much
in the evening hours ; Scotland and Canada ; our city, where his
form was so well known, and the remote settlements of the Province,
in many of which it was as readily recognized ; the college and his
own residence ; in short, all times and places found that busy mind
employed, working or planning work, preaching, teaching, glancing
through books with dim eye but with quick and sure discernment of
their spirit and worth, writing notices of brethren who had preceded him to the grave, or reviews of works of literature, advising with
students as to their difficulties, arranging the library or taking
means for its enlargement ; never inactive unless when compelled
to cease exertion through sheer exhaustion ; and never satisfied
with any past achievement, but forthwith embarking on new enterprises, laying new plans of work for himself—occasionally too for
others—which looked far ahead. Activity was his delight ; idle-
ness in others—he did not know it in himself—his grief and annoyance.   His very holidays, his periods of relief from his regular duties, were only times of, if possible, more continuous and exhaust-

ing toil ; occasions of long and fatiguing journeys, and of almost daily public services.

"Very closely connected with the preceding, and yet entitled to a separate place in even an imperfect analysis of his character, was the breadth of interest by which as a minister of the word and Professor of Theology in the Canada Presbyterian Church, the deceased was characterized ; the solicitude, which he uniformly evinced for the welfare of the whole church, and for all that could promote its efficiency and honour. He was never the person to be satisfied with the prosperity, however great, of one congregation, or one corner of the field, especially his own ; while other parts of it might be lying waste, given over to neglect and barrenness or something worse. His soul was too large, and his interest in the things of Christ too deep and intelligent, to be contented with so narrow a satisfaction. The whole field, so far as observation or report could make it known to him, was in his eye, and the weakest and neediest parts were just the ones to excite his deepest solicitude, and evoke his heartiest efforts. The Presbyterian Church, since it attained any considerable proportions, has never had a minister who could with equal truth adopt the language of the Apostle of the Gentiles : 'Who is weak and I am not weak ? Who is offended and I burn not ?' 'Now we live, if ye stand fast in the Lord.' This rare but most serviceable quality ; this breadth of view and interest, was in part the cause and in part the consequence of the extensive evangelistic journeys in which he engaged from the first, and in which he persevered to the last.

"Not so apparent, perhaps, to those who knew him only in the distance, as his wide and irrepressible activity, but not less real, as forming part of the man and the Christian, was his great benevolence of heart. All knew him to be abundant in labours ; not all, though many, knew how strong and tender were his attachments, how unexacting he was in the attentions which he claimed from those around him, how prompt and active his sympathies with suffering friends, and within how wide a circle these were exercised, how open his hand to help a good cause or a needy person, how ready to oblige on every occasion, and—what is more difficult—how ready to forgive and forget a personal wrong, with all his pertinacity in adhering to what he believed to be truth and right ; how uniformly kind and cheerful, in these later years at least, his bearing towards young and old. To this feature of his character, to its benevolence still more than to its strength, to the cheerfulness of age in his case, even more than to its extraordinary energy, is the affection due, with which, throughout this Province and far beyond it, his person was regarded. We are safe in saying that for many years he did not enter a house but to make warm friends, if his entrance did not find them already such ; and so his name has become a household word in the land, and the tidings of his death will spread through it to awaken a tender regret in thousands of hearts

" That form, in which was exhibited so singular a union of strength and frailty ; the eye dim, the intellect clear and active ; the limbs supporting with difficulty the still massive frame, the voice ringing out its notes firm and clear ; the step slow and uncertain, the memory running rapidly along an experience of well nigh a century, and able to recall minute incidents at any point ; the hoary wreath of age around the brow, the face lit up with the playfulness of childhood—that form, presenting contrasts so striking, has passed away. It was a sight yesterday which men regarded with wonder not unmixed with more tender emotion. It is only a memory to-day, a memory, however, which many will cherish with sacred respect for long years."

We have already quoted from Principal Willis' admirable funeral sermon. This chapter may appropriately close with one or two additional quotations :

" My attention was drawn to our deceased friend in the comparative youth of my own ministry, and towards the mid-time of his, as one taking a very prominent part in the cause of evangelical religion, and watchfully guarding the rights and interests of the Christian people, at a time when this required no small vigilance and resolution. Men may acquire, on very cheap terms, the reputation of friends of the evangelical interest, when the tide has come to turn in its favour ; but it is due to Dr. Burns to say that he stood against the current when that ran in the contrary way. It is known that a blight had extensively come over churches in Scotland, England, and Ireland, half, or say three quarters of a century ago ; and in the church of Scotland a full exhibition of the truth was, if I may not say the exception rather than the rule, at any rate far less general than happily it came to be in more recent years. Our deceased father and brother took no unimportant share in the work of revival, and reassertion of the true principles of our Scottish Presbyterianism :—and, when I say Presbyterianism, I do not merely think of church government, but of the catechetical and confessional doctrines of our loved native land. I know that in the sphere of his immediate pastorate, (in Paisley) his influence was powerfully felt in the very earliest years of his ministry. I remember—on occasion, I think it was, of my first revisiting Scotland, after my coming to this country—that in a conversation held with me by a worthy minister, now also deceased, who either was of Paisley as his native town, or during his student life had been familiar with that locality, he said that the exertions of Dr. Burns there, in his youth and vigour, told with most observable effect on the community. Not that that Scottish town was without faithful spiritual labourers both in other denominations and in his own ; but in his immediate pastoral sphere, and around, a far livelier interest came to be evinced in religious observances, appliances adapted to the young and to the masses of the population were multiplied, and beyond his more denominational range (so I understood my reverend informer) the example of his energy and public spirit provoked to a praiseworthy emulation."

"During his very latest years, though nominal on the honoured *emeritus* list, he yet was liberal in his exertions, and constant in his solicitude for the good of Knox College. When he prelected less, he conversed as often or more. If we had his autumnal decay, we had also his autumnal ripeness, and the benefit of his large experience. His affectionate interest in studious youth secured to them at all times ready access to his counsels. . . . . . . We shall miss his well-known form, and well-remembered voice, within the walls where he loved to linger, and within which he died. May the spirit of Elijah rest on many of our young Elishas, in the influence of his example of zeal, and laboriousness, and prayerfulness withal! Like other men he had his imperfections; but his excellencies stood out prominent, commanding respect and engaging esteem. Those who differed from him, and contended with him, loved the man. It was not his least praise that by affectionate blandness of manner, united to remarkable powers of conversation, he made himself an ever welcome guest in the humblest Christian abode : while he knew and respected those conventional courtesies of refined society, by attention to which he could command the respect of the highest class. And I can testify to another kindred disposition being conspicuous, one of the best tests of a superior mind, that, on questions affecting the public interests, he was ready to receive light from whatever quarter ; and on matters strictly professional, I have known few who welcomed more cordially the unrestrained interchange of thought with friends or colleagues. Father—patriarch I might say—of Canada's Presbyterian Church—rest in thy bed ! We know who said, ' he is not dead, but sleepeth.' Sleep on a while ; thou shalt stand in thy lot at the end of the days. Mourning relatives may find joy in the thought, that the first morning that has shone on the turf beneath which the departed lies, is that of the day of the Son of Man—of his rising in triumph from the grave, and shedding so blessed a light on its darkness.

"Death, take your part : king of terrors, do your worst. We know the limits of your power. It is not much you can do : it is not long. Each returning Sabbath assures us of the completion, in his people, of the triumph over the grave the Saviour has won in his own person. How consoling the thought —even they who shall never know death, being found alive at Christ's coming, but who shall, in the twinkling of an eye, be changed at the sounding of the last trumpet, even they shall not prevent them who are asleep ! ' The dead in Christ shall rise first ;' not separate, but together shall they ascend to meet their Lord, and enter with like joy on their common inheritance."

APPENDIX.

I. Early History of Knox Church, Toronto.

My venerable friend, the Rev. James Harris, who is enjoying a green old age, has kindly sent me the following "Memoranda of the early history of the first Presbyterian congregation of the town of York, now known as Knox's Church, Toronto:

"The undersigned, a Licentiate of the Presbytery of Monaghan, in connexion with the Secession Church in the north of Ireland, having received the usual testimonials of good standing, as a probationer, sailed from Belfast, for Canada, on the 6th day of June, 1820. He, through the good providence of God, reached Brockville about the 10th day of August, said year. He was cordially received by the Rev. Wm. Smart, then pastor of the Presbyterian Church in that town. He was urged by Mr. Smart to proceed to the town of York, now Toronto, with as little delay as possible, as the few Presbyterians residing therein were anxious to be supplied with the preaching of the Gospel by a minister of their own denomination. He arrived in York on the 28th of August, having conducted religious services at various intermediate places on the way. Having arrived in the town of York, he called on parties to whom he was recommended by Mr. Smart. From said parties he learned that they had not enjoyed, at any time previous, a regular supply of preaching—that they had received occasional visits from the Rev. Mr. Jenkins, at that time supplying the congregations of Richmond Hill and Scarborough; and the prospects, on the whole, were not encouraging.

"There were, at that time, only two churches in the town of York—one Episcopalian, under the pastoral charge of the Rev. Dr. Strachan, late Bishop of Toronto. It was a neat frame building, occupying the site of the present St. James' Cathedral, King Street.

"The other was a Methodist Church, a frame building, situated at King Street West, large and commodious for the time.

"Although, at that time, Presbyterians were pretty numerously scattered throughout most, if not all, the settlements then formed, there were only two Presbyterian ministers as known to the writer of these notes, in the whole region west of Kingston. These were Rev. Robert McDowall ; he came into Canada in 1798, settled at Ernestown, where he was spared to labour in the ministry for many years ; and Rev. Wm. Jenkins, who came to Canada from the United States in 1817. He was originally from Scotland, and belonged to the Antiburgher Church in that land.

"The undersigned conducted public worship the first time, in a large school room, on the first Sabbath of September, 1820. Two diets were held, and God having permitted, we continued to meet for worship in said school-room about a year and six months.

"The congregation considerably increased : entered on Sabbath, the 18th day of February, 1822, a new place of worship then recently completed. The new church was a small brick-building, fronting the hospital, now Richmond Street ; it stood on the present site of Knox Church.

"The new building was erected at the sole charge of Mr. Jesse Ketchum, the cost of pews, pulpit and gallery was assessed on the pews, and paid for by those who became pew-holders. This was the first building erected in York, now Toronto, for a Presbyterian congregation. It continued the only one until about 1827, when St. Andrew's Church was erected.

"The undersigned was ordained pastor of the congregation on the 10th of July, 1823. The Presbytery of Brockville, having, in compliance with a call, moderated in by the Rev. Mr. Jenkins, appointed a committee to visit York, and proceed with the ordination. The committee consisted of the Messrs. Smart and Boyd, ministers. Mr. Boyd not having arrived in due season, Mr. Smart, Mr. Jenkins, and Mr. Scholfield, an elder, who accompanied Mr. Smart, proceeded with the ordination on the day appointed by the Presbytery.

"On the 23rd day of July, said year, a meeting of the recently organized congregation was held for the election of elders. Mr. McIntosh, of the town of York, and Mr. McGlashan, of York Mills, were unanimously chosen. They were set apart to the office of the eldership on the 10th of August following. Mr. McIntosh filled the office about five years, when he was removed by death. Mr. McGlashan died in Nov., 1844, having witnessed the disruption in Scotland in 1843, and in Canada the year following. He was also permitted to witness and take part in the cordial arrangements for a union between those who withdrew from St. Andrew s congregation, in Toronto, and the small congregation of which he had been, for many years a zealous and faithful office-bearer.

"The first communion was dispensed to the first Presbyterian congregation, on the 14th of September, 1823, to twenty-eight members. Mr. Jenkins assisted on the interesting occasion.

" Thus he, who in much weakness, commenced his labours in the town of York in 1820, was permitted, through God's infinite mercy in Christ Jesus, through many infirmities and great shortcomings, to labour in the field allotted him, without interruption, until the summer of 1844. In the early part of said summer, owing to arrangements for a union of the two congregations, into which arrangements the undersigned cordially entered, he demitted his charge to the then recently formed Presbytery of Toronto.

" It is now twenty-five years since the two congregations united, taking the name of " Knox's Church," and the writer of these notes records his decided conviction, that said union has, by God's blessing, tended largely to promote the interests of Presbyterianism, and in connection therewith of vital godliness in the city of Toronto. " JAMES HARRIS.

John Ross, Malcom McLellan, and Edward Henderson were ordained to the eldership in May, 1827. J. H.

II. PRESBYTERIAN PIONEERS.

The Rev. George Bell, .LL.D., of Clifton, has kindly furnished me with the following very interesting statement, with reference to the missionary labours of his father, the Pioneer of Presbyterianism, in the old Bathurst district, which may fitly follow Mr. Harris's narrative:

The settlement at Perth had been formed in 1816, and the Scotch settlers having sent for a minister, Mr. Bell accepted their call, and sailed on the 5th of April, 1817. Fair promises of every comfort had been made by the captain of the ship, which were soon found to be worthless. After they were fairly at sea, the passengers were shamefully treated.

After fifty-seven days of horrors, Quebec was reached, and they escaped from the ship. Mr. Bell was treated with great kindness by the Governor, Sir John Sherbrooke, and promised a free passage to Perth. After waiting some days for the steamer *Malsham*, to be ready to sail, they left Quebec on Saturday evening, 7th June, arriving at Montreal on Monday morning, *horses being employed to help the steamer up the current St. Mary into port !* The passage to

D D

Prescott was made by means of a batteau with four men, the portages at the principal rapids being made by carters, and oxen or horses being used to drag the boat at some of the others. Eight days were spent between Montreal and Prescott, and although the transport was furnished free by Government, the expenses by the way amounted to much more than the whole would cost now. Delayed for days for want of waggons, Mr. Bell went on to Brockville, on the 21st June, where he met with the Rev. W. Smart, of Brockville, and the Rev. Robert McDowall, from Bath, besides Rev. Mr. Easton, of Montreal. The last, together with Mr. Bell, preached at the dedication of Mr Smart's church the following day. The meeting of these pioneers of Presbyterianism in Canada was interesting, and the mind readily passes over the intervening half century, and adores the grace of God for the wondrous progress which has been made in the work so painfully commenced by them and a few others.

From Brockville to Perth was two days' journey, walking most of the way. Perth was reached on the 24th June, twenty-four days from the arrival at Quebec. Next day a house was rented, and the family arrived, suffering severely from the dreadful journey, and almost blinded by travelling a whole day through the forest, swarming with mosquitoes. The house consisted of log walls, a roof, and a floor of split basswood logs loose over a pool of stagnant water. The closeness of the floor may be understood from the fact that one day one of the children fell through, and was with some difficulty rescued from drowning. There were no partitions; no furniture could possibly be procured, and even boards were not to be had, as the saw mill was not in operation. Dr. Thom kindly gave Mr. Bell two boards, from one of which he made a table. But little of Perth was yet cleared; a few log houses had been put up, but many were living in tents or huts of bark. They were thankful even for such accommodation as they had, as some on arriving had to sleep under a tree until they could erect a hut.

The following are extracts about this time :

"Some of the Scotch settlers called to see us, and welcome us to the place. From them I learned that disputes ran high among themselves. I could see that, in discharging my duty here, much patience and caution would be necessary. The people were much in need of instruction, but most of them were careless about it. The moral as well as the natural world seemed to be a wilderness. I took another day's visiting in the Scotch line. There being no road yet opened, I was so fatigued going round swamps, climbing fences, and getting over fallen trees, in the course of my long journey, that at night when I got home, I was ready to drop down. A meeting being held on church affairs—I observed with regret that some came bare-footed, and very poorly clad. The poverty of the people prevented anything being done at this meeting, beyond appointing a committee to manage the affairs of the congregation.

There being no school of any kind in the settlement, I had been requested to open one. I indeed found it necessary for my own children. A log hut was obtained and fitted up, and while the repairs were going on, I opened the school at my own house, with eighteen children. A Sabbath school had been commenced on the second Sabbath spent in Perth, with five children, increased to twelve the next Sabbath, and to fifteen on the next. A man came to be married one day, but that ceremony could not legally be performed, to his deep regret. He said if it could not be done to-day, he would lose the woman, as she was just going to leave the settlement. His simplicity and perplexity were more amusing to me, I fear, than to him.

"The boys and I had commenced clearing upon our park lot, and every morning we got up at four o'clock, and worked at it till breakfast time; but we suffered much from the heat and mosquitoes.

"The upper story of an inn which was as yet unfinished, was rented for a place of worship, and after two-and-a-half months the Lord's Supper was dispensed, Sept. 14th. The number of communicants I had admitted was forty-seven, two of them for the first time. I preached from Rev. i., 5, 'Unto him that loved us,' &c., with much liberty and comfort. We afterwards partook of the Lord's Supper together, and it was to many of us a comfortable and refreshing season of communion with God.

"4th Oct. I set out for the Rideau, where I had promised to preach the next day. On my way I called upon A. Morrison, and prevailed on him to accompany me. It was well I did so, for without a guide, I had never found the way. From his house we had fourteen miles to travel through the forest, with scarcely a track to guide us. We passed the Pike (Tay), and Black rivers, which we had to wade, and two bad swamps. This visit gives a fair sample of Home Mission work at that time. Long journeys on foot, part of the way through pathless forests, wading creeks and swamps, lodging in wretched hovels, sometimes upset from canoes by the unskilfulness of others, to the danger of drowning, and when escaping, having no opportunity of getting wet clothes chang d.

"13th Oct. Set out for Brockville on foot, for at this time there were almost no horses in the settlement, nor anything to feed them. The road was very bad, and it was dark long before I reached Mr. Randall's, where I proposed to pass the night. Thirty miles."

At this time he went to the Quarter Sessions to obtain a certificate to enable him to solemnize marriages, but opposed by high church officials, it was refused on technical grounds, and three months after he had to make another journey of forty-two miles to Brockville, with seven members of his congregation, to get the matter arranged.

At this time (Oct., 1817), Mr. Bell visited Kingston for the purpose of trying to reconcile two parties of Presbyterians—Scotch and American—who were desirous of getting a minister, but who were disputing as to whether he should be obtained from the Church of Scotland or the United States. This journey was made mostly on foot, a small portion of it being by means of a borrowed horse, and a part by a small boat. He regretted to find the two parties irreconcilable.

Perth was a military settlement, and Mr. Bell had much to do with the military officials, both in his own affairs, and on behalf of the poor settlers, many of whom were in a starving condition. He received the utmost civility and even kindness from the Governor-General, and those high in authority, but on coming down the scale there was a great change.

A school-house had been built with money collected at Quebec and other places, on a subscription list " for erecting a school-house at Perth, U.C., for the use of the Rev. William Bell." It had been erected under the direction of the worthy secretary mentioned above, on the public reserve, and by much diligence and sacrifice of time on Mr. Bell's part, a good school had been collected. The house was used for the school on week days, and for public worship on Sabbaths, for more than a year, until the church was ready for use. About that time an Episcopal clergyman came. to the settlement, and Mr. Bell was unceremoniously ordered to give up the school to him. The absurdity of this was so apparent that he resisted for a time, but at length gave it up, observing in his journal " *It is not safe living in Rome and plea-ing with the Pope.*"

At first Sabbath profanation was very common. After the regular observance of public worship was introduced matters improved among those attending. Many, however, were not attending, and to bring an influence to bear on these the following plan was adopted :—" Taking one of my elders with me, I called at every house, shanty and tent, in the village and neighbourhood, spoke of the sin of profaning the Sabbath, and requested the aid of all in preventing it. This had the desired effect, and from this time forward there was a visible reformation." Some years afterwards greater difficulties were encountered. Sabbath breaking became very prevalent, urged on by many who, from their position, ought to have been leaders in giving a good moral tone to society. In opposing vigorously these evils, Mr. Bell aroused a persecution, which for violence of personal abuse, insults and legal prosecutions would scarcely be credible if fully described in our happier days.

In 1829, after a persecuting law suit, in which he was mulcted in damages for his faithfulness in opposing vice, he writes, " Paid £45 15s. 10d., the price of freedom from persecution. O Britain ! how vain is thy boast of freedom."

Mr. Bell had to contend with much ignorance in regard to the administration of church ordinances. A man and woman called one day with a sick child, which they had brought four miles on a dreadfully cold day to be *christened*, lest it should die. The man was known to be a very immoral man, and on inquiry it appeared that neither of the parents was present, and that the persons who had come stated that they were to be godfather and godmother : the father of the child was a drunken and profane man. Mr. Bell stated that he could not baptize the child then, but that if the parents were willing to be instructed in the truths and duties of the gospel, and to follow such instruction, he would do so at a proper time. "The man, on hearing this, became insolent, got up and said he did not care whether I christened the child or not, as he could take it to the priest, who would not object, if he paid him, which he was willing to do. They then left the house, went to the Roman Catholic priest, and had the child christened, paid half a dollar, and went home well pleased. The service was performed in French, of which they did not understand a word."

"The father disapproved of what they had done, when he came to know and wished me to re-baptize the child. This I declined, which so much offended him that he went to a magistrate, and made a complaint, giving a very erroneous account of the whole transaction. On the following Tuesday he was in town, spent the day at the tavern, and blustered a great deal about having me punished for refusing to baptize his child. In the evening he left the village drunk, and next morning, the cold being intense, he was found dead, and frozen stiff among the snow, about half a mile from Perth. When the body was brought in, before the Coroner's inquest, it presented an awful spectacle—the limbs stiff and bent up—the grey hair erect and clotted with snow, and the eyes staring wide open." This was an extreme case, but it illustrates one class of difficulties a minister meets in a new settlement, and among a mixed population.

Numerous cases occurred in which the minister was expected to settle disputes about property, to settle difficulties in families, quarrels among neighbours, &c. The following may serve as a sample :—" Nearly the whole of last Saturday was spent in settling a family quarrel, about the property of a deceased relation. The parties were all Highlanders, named Campbell, and I had much ado to prevent their going to law. With much reluctance on the one side, it was left to arbitration. Dr. Thom and I were chosen, and settled all matters between them. But what violence and talking of Gaelic we had all day !"

Those ministers and elders, who now attend meetings of Presbytery and Synod, have little idea of what labour and suffering were involved in such duties in the early years of the country. Mr. Bell's journals contain records of journeys to Presbytery meetings, requiring from four to six days to reach the place of meeting, perhaps two days being spent in travelling on foot, and the remainder by means of horse-back riding, waggon, small boat or sleigh, as the case might be.

Mr. Bell's field of labour was of wide extent. His congregation proper was very much scattered, and besides attention to them, he made missionary journeys very frequently into all parts of the military settlement, as well as into the older settlements toward the St. Lawrence. In these journeys he had generally to walk, as he had no horse for some years, and the roads were not cleared. In 1820 new settlements were formed in Lanark, Dalhousie, &c. As these contained many Scotch emmigrants, he extended his work among them, which added much to his already severe toil, but he had the happiness of collecting and preparing for settlement, congregations in several places, including Beckwith Lanark, Dalhousie, &c.

" On the afternoon of Sabbath, 17th September (1820) our neighbour, Mr. Brizee, called to tell us that Elder Steven, from Bastard, had just come in from Brockville with a load of settlers' baggage, and was going to preach a sermon at his house, and invited us to attend. We did so, and heard a very odd sermon from Heb. xii. 1. ' Let us lay aside every weight, &c.' He said, as the day was hot, he would follow the advice in the text, and lay aside some of his own *yarn.* Suiting the action to the word, he pulled off his coat, and preached in his shirt sleeves."

Although work was hard, there was much encouragement in the warm-hearted manner in which he was received by those whom he followed in to the wilderness with gospel ordinances, and still more in the manifest tokens of divine favour, giving success for the present and hope for the future. His journals abound in expressions of gratitude to God for deliverances from dangers, and blessings bestowed.

The Rev. George Cheyne, a laborious and faithful Pioneer in the West, sends me these interesting items as to his early labours in Canada :

"I landed at Quebec on the 5th Sept., 1831. After spending a short time with Dr. Harkness, at Quebec, and Mr. Esson, at Montreal, to whom I had letters of introduction from Rev. Mr. Leith, of Rothiemay. Mr. Leith had been some years in America, grammar school-teacher and first Presbyterian minister at Cornwall, and was succeeded by the late Dr. Urquhart in both offices. Mr. Leith, before it was known that he was leaving, had secured from the trustees his appointment as grammar-school teacher to the great disappointment of the authorities of the Church of England, who were then grasping at every thing for themselves. The Church had been organized into a Synod during the summer, and consisted of nineteen ministers. Having been ordained before leaving Scotland to " Amherstburg, or any other place in North America," and as my going to Amherstburg depended on Mr. Gale's

leaving it, I presented my documents to the Presbytery of Toronto.
The Presbytery then consisted of Messrs. Shedd, of Ancaster, Rintoul, of York, MacGill, of Niagara, and Ross, of Aldborough, who,
however, was not present.   I was sent on to take possession of the
congregation at Amherstburg, as there was no inductions in those
days, at least, in remote parts.   Amherstburg had been organized
into a congregation by Mr. Gale, who had gone there as a teacher
without any intervention of Presbytery.   The congregation consisted of about twelve members and thirty hearers ; but a grant
had been given by Government to the church.   Accordingly I went
and took possession, and laboured with some measure of success,
for nearly twelve years.

"An incident, worthy of note, might be mentioned.   In the
autumn of 1832 I went to assist the nearest minister, Mr. Ross, of
Aldborough, about one hundred miles, in administering the communion—the first communion.   As it was a Gaelic congregation as
well as English, it was arranged that I should preach the action
sermon, fence the tables, and serve the first table.   All went on in
the usual way until after the first part of the table service.   After
the pause, and I had just begun to speak, a female at the table, in a
very excited state, clapped her hands, and exclaimed loudly, ' O
Lord Jesus,' again and again.   I stood amazed.   At a glance round the
table I saw that the communicants were all in a very excited state.
I was not then cognizant of the scenes of excitement, noise and
confusion that were prevalent in the country at that time.   A word
from me would have readily put them all into confusion and noise,
but I stood in silence, until Mr. Ross, who was at the table, whispered to one of the elders that I had better proceed.   Instead of
doing so, I remarked ; in the house of God, and especially at his
table, all should be reverence and solemnity, that I was surprised
at what had taken place, &c., and I paused again.   When I saw
that the excitement had subsided I went on, and nothing further
than usual occurred.   It was the first and last scene of the kind
that occurred in the place.   But I was spoken of by Methodists
and Baptists, for the church was crowded to excess, as a bad man,
who had quenched the spirit.   There was at that time no Presbyterian minister at Hamilton, and only one in all the country west
from Ancaster to Amherstburg.

"In the summer of 1834 I visited Sarnia, which had scarcely
been commenced ; made arrangements to preach in the township
of Moore on the Sabbath.   Settlers had just begun to settle in it,
but it appeared to the eye an unbroken forest.   A Mr. Sutherland,
from Edinburgh, had just come, and bought out a Frenchman,
whose farm lay on the banks of the St. Clair.   Seats were erected
in his orchard, made of boards, resting on blocks of wood.   By-
the-by, Mr. Sutherland and family were Scotch Episcopalians, but
they were kind and hospitable.   I always, in visiting the
locality, made my arrangements to spend a night with them, as

there was the place for one or more services. On the Sabbath there was a good congregation, but where they came from I could not see. Being the only Presbyterian minister in that region, I would sometimes go out on a missionary excursion, and spend perhaps six weeks—making appointments as I went, to be fulfilled on my return.

"In 1836 I set out in the beginning of January, preached on Sabbath, in the township of Mersia, and in the course of the week proceeded to Tilbury East, on my way to Chatham, where I had arranged to preach on Sabbath. I arrived at Mr. Graham's about sunset, and announced that I would preach to them next day at ten o'clock a.m., if they could get a congregation. By next day at the hour appointed the house was filled—some from six miles with children to baptize. They had no way of travelling but on ox-sleighs or foot.

"On another occasion, in the autumn, having preached at the front in Moore, I was proceeding back ten miles to Bear Creek, to preach next day at ten o'clock. It commenced to rain when I had gone about three miles—it rained harder and harder as I went on, when I came to a small log-house and clearing; the road was just opened up, but there it terminated. On enquiring how far it was to a certain house at Bear Creek, I was told four miles, and on asking if I could get any one to show me the way, was told no, as it was drawing near night, and they could not find it. I replied, if they could not I was sure I could not, and would have to stay. They very kindly remarked I should be very welcome if I would put up with such accommodation as they had. I alighted from my horse, gave him in charge to the man, and walked into the house. It was about twelve feet square, two men, two women and some children, beside myself. There was a good blazing fire—they were very kind, and made me comfortable. The family was from the North of Ireland—the husband an Episcopalian, the wife and her mother Presbyterians. The brother went with me to church next day, and served as a guide. The houses were, for the most part, in one room, and undivided, but one had just to put up with it as best he could. I enjoyed these missionary tours very much— I was never offered the least thing for my services. I suppose as they were new settlers they had nothing to give, nor did I expect anything. They were delighted to see me and hear the word, and if I was instrumental in fanning the decaying flame of religion I was abundantly rewarded. In most of these places there have been for years flourishing congregations. Tilbury, Wallaceburg, Moore, Bear Creek, Plympton, Sarnia, and in Chatham three large Presbyterian congregations. At an early period, on visiting Chatham, I drew out a petition, and got the people to sign it, praying Government for ten acres of land for church purposes, which was granted. A good portion of the town of Chatham is built upon it, and the Church, in connection with the Establishment of

Scotland, is reaping the benefit of it.   But 'what a friend gets is not lost' you know.

" GEO. CHEYNE."

P.S.—From the great distance I was never able, while at Amherstburg, to attend meetings of Presbytery, except at the meeting of Synod.

III. DR. BURNS' ADDRESSES BEFORE THE GENERAL ASSEMBLY OF THE FREE CHURCH OF SCOTLAND IN 1868 AND 1869.

We have made reference to Dr. Burns' last appearance before the Free Church General Assembly in 1869, when he was greeted with what the *Edinburgh Daily Review* describes as "loud and long continued applause ;" and received what Dr. Guthrie styles a complete "ovation." The Rev. W. Cochrane, of Brantford, then accompanied him. His reception the year previous was not the less cordial, when he appeared in company with the Rev. J. M. King. As a specimen of his addresses on such occasions, we give here almost the whole of the report as it appeared in the *Review:*

Dr. Burns, said :—The field to which I am to allude embraces what is called the British American Possessions, comprehends what is known under the name of the Dominion of Canada, together with some colonies not embraced in that Dominion, Ontario, Quebec, Nova Scotia, New Brunswick, Newfoundland, and Prince Edward Island.   All these colonies have been visited by myself more or less fully, and I am able to tell something of their present condition.   And I hesitate not to say that whatever communications be made to you on this subject, will not fail to cheer and encourage ; for I am decidedly of opinion that there are difficulties everywhere in regard to the great duty of sending the gospel to those afar off and placed in circumstances unfavourable to its progress, still we have had every cause of gratitude to God for the encouragement given in respect to the planting of churches and settlement of ministers, and the diffusion of the gospel generally through these colonies, Twenty-two years ago the number of Presbyterians in Canada was small.   The number of ministers that adhered to the principles of the Free Church in 1844, was only twenty.   Since that time we have got large accessions from young men trained in the country, and by those sent out by yourselves and others, and by the union that has lately been realised between the branch of the United Presbyterian Church in Canada, and the branch of the Free Church planted there; so that we have now 260 ministers—(applause) —13 presbyteries, 2 colleges, one of them—Toronto—in existence for now twenty-two years, and has sent forth about 170 ministers, most of whom are still labouring in the field, though a considerable number have ceased by reason of death.   There are 42,000 members in full communion, and a body of elders in proportion.   We thank God for what has been done in that Province.   Lower Canada, properly speaking, is a very limited portion of the field allotted to us, because you all know that Popery was established in that country nearly a hundred years ago, and when the number of adherents to that system is 900,000 out of a population of little more than a million.   Still, in Montreal we have a large representation of our views in congregations and able ministers; and so also in Quebec. But our principal field is in Canada West, now known as Ontario, and we rejoice in the impression on our minds that God has owned us in this field, and given us cause to hope for greater progress. We have also a considerable number of seminaries, for the preliminary training of young men preparing for the ministry.   In Nova Scotia, we rejoice in the gratifying progress and in the union that has taken place.   The Dalhousie college, founded originally by a highly respected relative of a noble lord, a member of this Assembly, after being kept back from the full exhibition of its blessed results, by circumstances beyond our control, has of late years been placed in circumstances exceedingly favourable for the instruction of all the young men of different denominations, exclusive only of those connected with the High Church Episcopal party.   In connection with Dalhousie College, we have the theological seminary, so long under the charge of Professor King and others; and there is another college for the training of teachers, under the charge of Dr. Forrester.   There are circumstances very favourable to the advancement of religion.   In New Brunswick and Newfoundland we have also cause to thank God and take courage.   Perhaps the most important feature in these churches is the high-toned missionary spirit elicited, particularly in Nova Scotia, including New Brunswick and Eastern and Western Canada.   The maritime provinces have done much in foreign missions, and our Canada church has aided them in that way.   Vancouver's Island and British Columbia have been in a sense committed to our church, and have sent forth devoted ministers, to whom you have been kind enough to give support.   I hope the attention of the Colonial Committee will be more and more directed to this point of the British dominions and the Red River Settlement.   There are not fewer than from 350 to 400 trained in the colleges of Halifax and Canada since their commencement.   We have also had to impart spiritual aid to seven or eight stations in the United States where Scotchmen are settled, and our arrangements with the United States Presbyterian churches about these stations have been of a very agreeable kind. (Applause.) Both in the maritime provinces and in Canada an important union was lately consummated between the Presbyterian churches more immediately in alliance with you and the brethren of the United Presbyterian Church in Canada—(applause)—and the brethren of the church in Nova Scotia not marked exactly by the same designation, but still substantially part and parcel of the same great body.   In regard to both these unions a considerable period has been permitted to elapse before the consummation took place.   Now that that consummation has been completed, the results are advantagous, and one reason is that both in the one country and the other, our impression is that the great principle which for some years had separated the brethren, has been arranged in such a way as was consistent with the leading principles that we, as members of the Free Church entertained, and do entertain. ('Oh, oh,' from Dr. Begg.) The principle on which we set a high value, not higher than it was entitled to, stands with us still.   I am quite aware that there has been a feeling in certain quarters that there has been some ambiguity in the terms employed.   That feeling was cherished by some at the time of the union.   I have always maintained that in both unions the principle is substantially the same. 'Hear, hear,' from Dr. Begg and the left of the chairman.) And we have gone on in the spirit of love.   Many points there are unquestionably of mutual forbearance. (Loud cries of 'Hear, hear.') We agreed together in holding the great principle of the Headship of Christ over the nations—(cheers and counter cheers)—comprehending in that a general and vague idea of certain Christian influences to be diffused over the whole masses.   We have not been satisfied with that. ('Hear, hear,' from the left of the chair.) We have maintained that nations as such, and the rulers of this world in their legislative and executive capacity, are bound to act under the laws of Christ, and to give their influence in helping on the cause of Christ. (Renewed applause from the left of the chair.) At the same time, in regard to the question of the time and circumstances and mode in which financial aid is to be given, we did allow forbearance. (Loud applause from the right of the chair and all parts of the house.) On that subject liberty was given in both Provinces to hold varied opinions. (Renewed applause.) But in regard to the great obligation laid on rulers to own the authority of Christ in all things, and when circumstances in providence call for it, to consecrate their influence and substance—('hear, hear,' from Dr. Begg, and laughter) —that principle we hold—only at the same time we allow a latitude of opinion as to the way in which that principle may be developed.

(Loud cheers from the right and other parts of the house.) This was peculiarly necessary in our case from the difference of opinion that prevailed, and the fact that a great number of us coming out of Scotland felt that we could not accept aid from a State that had virtually rejected evangelical principles. We published our views on that subject twenty years ago, and while we held fast to the principle I have alluded to, we have, at the same time, declared that for us to accept of endowments in circumstances in which we were placed might have the effect of rendering our testimony some-what ambiguous—(laughter)—looking like a change of sentiment from the views of the Free Church, and necessarily interposing an obstacle in the way of a vital and substantial union with other de-nominations. On these grounds we acted on the principle of for-bearance in regard to the specific application of the principle, while we hold that principle in a firm and unambiguous manner. No doubt a number of years elapsed before that. Had there been any disposition to surrender that great principle, the union would have been consummated sooner. But we thank God for what has been done to present a more powerful front to the common enemy, and I believe, by a late computation made, the Presbyterians of all de-nominations, including those, of course, belonging to the Establish-ed church, form the first in point of number of all the Protestant denominations in the whole Dominion of Canada, and even in Prince Edward's Island and Newfoundland, where they have not seen meet to fall into the Confederate track. We wished to live in love ; yet we could not but feel that there were hindrances to the progress of religion and Presbyterianism. We find also that Pres-byterianism is peculiarly adapted to the genius of the people, and recommends itself even to those who do not come under the desig-nation of Presbyterians. But there is every reason to think, if our colleges are well supplied, and able ministers are sent forth, from time to time, standing firm and fast by the standards of the church —there is no question at all that, by the blessing of God, we may expect not only peace and harmony, and progress among ourselves, but the extension of the Gospel in districts beyond those immedia-tely allotted to us. (Much applause.) When we think of the Indian mission, which is now going on most successfully—when we think of the French mission, in connection with which there are six stations —we are encouraged to hope that our Colonial churches will be one of God's instruments of great and growing usefulness in building up the walls of Zion, which are salvation, and setting up its gates, which are praise. I rejoice that it is again permitted me, after having passed my fourscore years, to visit the land of my fathers, and to rejoice with you in the bright prospect set before us."

The following, extracted, in substance, from the same source, gives but an inadequate idea of his last address before the Free Church General Assemby in 1869, which excited a very deep interest :

" Dr. Burns, who was received with loud and prolonged applause, said he rejoiced to have another opportunity given him to say a few words in regard to the great interests of the land of his adoption. He had not been in Canada since he last addressed the General Assembly, though if God spared him, he hoped to return thither soon, considerably restored by his residence in Scotland, and greatly refreshed by what he had seen and heard since he came here. He looked forward to returning to the scene of his labours for the past twenty-four years with something of renewed relish, springing from what he had seen and heard in that Assembly, and also in friendly private intercourse with brethren. But though he had not been in Canada since he last addressed them, he had been in regular correspondence with the official brethren who had charge of matters connected with their church ; and he had been instructed by them to call the attention of the General Assembly of the Free Church to some particulars in regard to the Presbyterian Church in Canada, and the relations in which they had hitherto stood to the mother church. The first point was in regard to the Red River Settlement and the mission of the aborigines connected therewith. The settlement of the Red River now dates back somewhat more than sixty years. Some time after the settlement began, appeals were made to the Established Church for ministers, particularly ministers having Gaelic. No attention was paid to these appeals in any quarter. At the Disruption, instant application was made from the Selkirk settlement in the Hudson's Bay region to be furnished with ministers. The Colonial Committee were unable to meet the call, and transmitted the papers to the Canadian church ; and in three months that church designated and ordained a minister, whom they sent up the Red River colony, a distance of nearly 2,000 miles, and after an absence of eighteen years that brother continues there a faithful servant of Christ in that interesting colony. He has since been followed by two other ministers—forming the legal number to constitute a Presbytery. With these there have also been sent two missionaries to the aborigines, and application has been received for a sixth minister. Now, surely, it is very interesting to find that such a number of congregations, holding by Presbyterian order, and appearing by their representatives in the Synod of the Presbyterian Church in Canada, have been fixed in that colony—a field never touched before. And this has been occupied by the Canadian church without aid in men or money from any other source whatever. And now he was instructed to bring earnestly under the notice of the Free Church Colonial Committee the desire of the Canadian church to have some help in regard to the mission to the aborigines in the Red River Settlement. The second point to which he was instructed to call attention was in regard to British Columbia, including Vancouver's Island and the great Saskatchewan Valley, 1,000 miles long and 300 miles wide, now laid open to set-tlers from all parts of the British empire. It was gratifying to have been able to send out three missionaries to that colony. The obli-gation to do more was greatly increased by the opening up of the great region named, and he had been instructed to call attention to the desirableness of assistance to some extent from the Free Church in this department of mission work. In addition to these fields of mission work, the Canadian church has aided the Presbyterian church in Nova Scotia in sending a mission to the New Hebrides; they have also in times past sent a missionary to India, and have been in corres-pondence, with the view of sending a missionary to China. Perhaps there was a tendency in new churches to go even beyond the line of duty in sending abroad foreign missionaries. There is a fascina-tion about foreign missions—particularly those connected with India and China—that interests the minds of young men, perhaps beyond labour in ordinary fields ; but he desired, in accordance with his instructions, to call attention to the claims of British Columbia on the Free Church of Scotland. The third point to which he had to call attention was, the provision they were accustomed to make on behalf of their Gaelic young men, of whom they had a large num-ber. They had been sending missionaries to colonies of Highland-ers in different parts of the United States ; and recent intelligence from Illinois and other places showed clearly the duty of the Free church to look after the Celtic settlers in these regions, by aiding in sending them missionaries able to preach in the language of their hearts. The Canadian church had been endeavouring to do so to the best of its means. For some years past they had received no help from home, and he was instructed to plead for a renewal of the bursaries the Free Church was frequently wont to furnish, to the amount of £20, on behalf of Gaelic students, and if it were kept in view that the population in whose behalf the plea was made num-bered from 50,000 to 60,000, the validity of the plea would, he thought, he admitted. Dr. Burns, after referring to other matters of interest, concluded his address, amid warm applause, by a touch-ing and eloquent peroration."

THE END.

Canada Presbyterian Church Pulpit.

SECOND SERIES.

Extract from the Preface.

"It contains, not a collection of pulpit discourses, as in the First Series, but a number of treatises, dealing at greater length and in a more complete manner than any sermon could with themes of the deepest religious interest. In regard to these, the leading doctrines and the practice of our Church are stated, illustrated, and defended, yet in such a manner that the themes never fail of earnest personal application."

Book of Prayer for Family Worship.

EDITED BY THE REV. WILLIAM GREGG,

Professor of Apologetics, Knox College.

Same size as the "Pulpit."

PRICE ONE DOLLAR.

The Elder and his Work.

BY DAVID DICKSON, Esq.

Edinburgh.

Toronto : JAMES CAMPBELL & SON.

www.ingramcontent.com/pod-product-compliance
Lightning Source LLC
Chambersburg PA
CBHW030041130726
47901CB00005BA/1260